Surf & Surrender

A Summer Love Novel

RILEY EDGEWOOD

Also by Riley Edgewood
Rock & Release

Copyright © 2015 Riley Edgewood

All rights reserved. No part of this book may be reproduced or transmitted in any form or by any means without permission in writing from the publisher except for the use of brief quotations in a book review.

This is a work of fiction. Any resemblance it bears to reality is entirely coincidental.

Cover designed by Sarah Hansen at Okay Creations

ISBN-10: 1508428379
ISBN-13: 978-1508428374
ISBN (ebook) 9780986213038

To Nelson again,
For everything since

CHAPTER ONE

QUINN

IN THE LONG run, the difference between a bruised heart and a broken heart is huge. But in the short run? It's really freaking hard to tell what that difference is.

I sit high above the sand with the late-day sun beating on my no-longer-pale skin, contemplating heart things while I watch the ocean. Or rather, while I watch the one idiot in the ocean brave enough to take on riptides as strong as they are right now.

If I wasn't working, I'd be out there with him.

A storm's supposed to hit the coast in another couple hours. Though maybe it'll be here sooner than that. Angry-looking clouds are rolling across the sky in the distance, and the ocean's already rough enough to have scared almost everyone off the beach. Huge barrel waves curve along the surf, breaking clean for what seems like miles. My fingers itch for my board, which is currently slung in the back of my Jeep.

Instead, I keep my gaze on the blond-headed kid who's almost too far out in the water for my comfort. Well, not really a kid. A teenager, probably only a handful of years younger than me. Standing there, the water up to his skinny waist, letting brutal wave after wave crash over him. Granted, he gets up every time he's knocked down, but...sloppily.

I lift my shades to get a closer look, and instantly regret it, slipping them right back down. They say blue eyes are the most sensitive to the sun, and, boy is it true. I have to wear sunglasses even when it rains half the time.

Or, the past few weeks, even when I'm indoors.

To hide the signs of crying.

The thing is, I'm a bit of a crier. Always have been. But these past few weeks? It's been waterworks central. And, while every now and then a few tears fall because I'm sad, mostly these days they come because I'm just so damn *mad*.

The blond kid's friends are calling to him now, standing at the foot of the ocean. I can only make out a few words through the choppy pre-storm wind, but I hear "hungry," and "beer," and "Kelly's," the last most likely a reference to a local bar none of them are old enough to drink at. He doesn't turn around; his only response is to flip the bird over his shoulder. The motion is terse, full of attitude. Something tells me this kid's got even more anger swelling in his veins than I do.

But for now he's facing his battles with the water, and his friends are calling for him to meet them later. And I'm stuck here lifeguarding, uncomfortable on the seat of my rickety wooden platform, wishing I had my board.

Wishing the bruises over my heart would just freaking heal already. Because I know from experience how much worse it could be.

Heart Conditions According to Quinn

Bruised Heart
Description: Achy. Heavy.
Cause: Julian Daniels
Diagnosed: Three weeks ago.
Remission? Just about. Hopefully.

Broken Heart
Description: Flayed. From the inside out. Torn in two. No, screw that. Torn in millions.
Cause: Sawyer Carson
Diagnosed: Four years ago.
Remission? Yes. Definitely. I never, ever think of him anymore. Mostly.

* * * * * *

Typical teenagers, the kid's friends leave a pile of trash on the beach when they go.

"Hey," I yell after the last of them, a burly redhead. "Pick up your shit!"

He looks over his shoulder and flashes me a puppy-dog smile and waves, like he didn't hear me. I point to the trash can right beside him at the start of the path to the parking lot. He sticks up his thumb. And then keeps walking right down the trail between the dunes and off of the beach.

"Jerk," I mutter. The wind picks up an empty chip bag; sun glints across the metallic coating as it's tossed around. A sandwich wrapper joins it a second later, and I hop down from my stand to grab everything else before there's a hurricane of litter whirling out to the ocean.

The sand is warm and shifts under my feet, while ropes of my long brown hair whip into my eyes until I force the entire tangled mass of it back into a ponytail. I scoop up an armful of trash and half-eaten food—and plastic cups with a few sips left of beer in them. Oh, crap. These idiots were drinking?

No wonder that kid's acting so sloppy in the ocean.

I glance out to check on him...

And I can't find him anywhere.

Trash dropped, forgotten, I dash toward the shore, scanning the water.

Did he leave with his friends and I just didn't notice?

No.

Shit.

Where is he?

There are waves for miles.

And nothing else.

My radio's still up in the stand—so's my whistle. I can't call this in, and there's nobody close enough to hear me cry for help. I scan the water again, holding my hands above my eyes to help keep my view focused. Panic ricochets back and forth between my ribs.

Wait...

There.

An arm thrown out, fingers extended. He's still here, in the water. He's still conscious.

I'm updrift from him, which is perfect because the undertow will pull me toward him. I run into the water, angling myself with the flow of the current. I don't have my buoy, but it's too late for that. I can't take my eyes off of his hand—and, *yes*, there's the back of his head; it bobs up once, twice, before going under again—because if he gets swept away while my back is turned, the chances of me finding him again are nonexistent.

The ocean greets me with a smack of cool water in my face, half of which I swallow. It's briny and I come up sputtering strands of seaweed, but he's still in sight. Just a few more kicks and I reach him—right as the biggest wave of the day yawns up above us.

I curl around the kid's back to shield him the best I can, trying to clamp down on his thrashing limbs, but I startle him and he goes completely wild in my arms, tangling the two of us together as the wave thunders down on us.

We go under.

Actually, we go *torpedoing*.

Shooting, twisting, whirling through the water until I have no idea which way is up. All I can do is keep my arms around him. And the kid? He slams his head into my face so hard, he's lucky I don't pass out and leave him to drown all alone. But I stay conscious, and I don't let go. At least he might end up having a drowning buddy. How fun.

Salt water rushes up my nose, down my throat, into my eyes.

We spin for hours.

And then my shoulder plows into solid sand and through the shock of pain, I know it's my chance to get us above water. I squeeze him tighter and scramble to find purchase for my feet, finally able to propel both of us up to break the surface.

Air. In my starving lungs. Even half full of water, they suck in so much oxygen they might burst. I scissor kick and do my best to keep both our heads above water. But the ocean is already sucking us back under, and there's nothing I can do to keep us from getting tossed around again.

My sinuses are on fire and I'm coughing underwater and then there's nothing left in my lungs to release. They burn, greedy for another breath. And this damn kid won't stop flailing. No wonder we're always taught to never, ever go in for a rescue without our buoys, because I can't lift him on my own.

He's bringing us down and for the first time in my life, I'm scared I'm going to drown.

Stop struggling! I mentally beg so hard I wonder if it reaches him, because he finally goes limp in my arms, letting me guide us with the water instead of pulling me against it.

A second later I'm able to break the surface again. This time closer to the shore and after a few strong kicks, the kid's body jolts when his feet run into the sand.

He twists away from me, scrambling for the shore and falling to his hands and knees, spewing out seawater.

I manage to make my way to him, rubbing a hand on his back, saying "You'll catch your breath soon. Let it all out," before I'm retching, too.

When I'm done, I don't know whether to kiss this kid—because *oh my God, we're alive!*—or freaking deck him because he almost killed me.

Well, on second thought, I wouldn't kiss him. Not after all the vomiting.

Decking, however, isn't out of the question. But for now, I rub between his shoulders until he's done. When he is, he flips onto his back and squints into the sky.

And I stop breathing all over again.

I know him.

It's been four years, but I recognize him like I would my own reflection.

I just saved Jess Carson.

Sawyer's younger brother.

CHAPTER TWO

QUINN

THIS YEAR WAS the worst year of my life.

Well. That's not exactly true. At the time, I thought I was having the best year of my life. Which was also incorrect. So, *so* incorrect.

And now?

Now I'm staring at the brother of the boy who *did* give me the worst year of my life, almost four years ago.

"Jess?" I can't stop rubbing my eyes, like maybe I'm not seeing him clearly. I pat the top of my head for my sunglasses, but they're long gone, swept away by the ocean. "What...? I mean how...?" I can't come up with the words to ask.

"Yeah, I'm okay, thanks for asking," he snarls at me. *He snarls at me.* The boy I once thought I'd know forever but haven't seen in eons. He shoves up into a seated position, his chest still heaving.

Confusion is a drug and I'm spinning.

He looks like Sawyer. Blond, shaggy hair. Green eyes. Sharp chin.

Even covered in sand and seaweed, bedraggled and out of breath, and glaring at me, he's the spitting image of his brother in my memory.

It takes everything I have not to allow my whirling emotions to spin me straight back into the past with Sawyer. Because the last time I saw him? He looked just like this. Though he never glared at me like he wished I'd curl up and die.

"Take a picture, it'll last longer," Jess snaps. "Get *off* of me." He yanks his shoulder out from under my hand. I hadn't realized I'd reached out to him. Maybe I wanted to see if he was real.

"Is Sawyer here?" The question funnels up from my belly and shoots out of me so fast I don't have time to try to stop it.

I haven't said his name in so long—haven't even allowed myself to think it—my throat tightens as the shape slips out.

Sawyer.

"Fuck you." Jess shoves to his feet, flinging wet sand everywhere. Even into my mouth, which is hanging open.

Because, *whoa*. Just when I thought nothing else could shock me today, he cusses at me.

Jess, who once was twelve and wore braces and blushed whenever I was around and giggled when I tickled him.

Jess, who once was nine and so nervous to go on his first sleepover that he cried. Sawyer teased him, but I told him the story of how I wet the bed at my own first slumber party, which made him laugh. And then he hugged me and I think I started to love him before I even started to love Sawyer.

This, though? This is not that same boy.

I spit out the sand and scramble after him, wincing at the pain that explodes in my shoulder when I push myself up. "Wait."

He stalks away, ignoring me.

"Jess!" Shouting slays my already raw throat. Scraped up from too much salt water. Tense from the lingering tightness over long-buried memories.

He spins. "*What?*"

"I... I have to write a report about the save." Not the line I meant to go with, but the fury across his face has me biting my tongue on anything more personal.

"I was fine. You're the one who almost killed us." He turns

away again—and stumbles to his knees. Stumbling a second time when he tries to get up.

I rush toward him. "You need to get checked out. You could have—" Then the smell hits. Booze rolls off him in waves. "You're *drunk*."

"So?" He stands, unsteadily, and I grab his arm to keep him from walking away.

I do the math. "So you're *sixteen*." Holy shit, Jess is sixteen. How did he get so old? How did the anger in his eyes become so ancient?

"Like you didn't drink when you were sixteen." He pushes me away, a little harder this time. "Leave me alone, Quinn. I'm fine."

Hearing him say my name is almost as shocking as everything else. It's been so long. And his tone, once so adoring, is now annoyed. Worse than annoyed. I dig my toes in the sand, wishing I didn't have to look up at him to make my point. I'm not short, but he *is* tall. Almost as tall as his brother. "You almost drowned."

"No, I didn't." His breath is sour from alcohol and it hurts my heart.

"You drank half the ocean." I rattle off the things he needs to get checked for. ARDS, hypoxia, swelling in his brain—but he shakes his head.

"*I'm fine.*"

I reach out to take his pulse, but he snakes his wrist out of my hand like he's been burned. Which burns me in turn. Right in the heart. "I get that it's been a long time, but…what did I do to deserve this attitude?"

His expression darkens and he looks away, not answering.

"It's okay." I'm dying to reach out again, to squeeze him, because underneath all that anger, he looks so lost. "Talk to me, Jess. What are you doing here?"

Is your brother here, too?

Your dad?

Are you all back? The family I thought I was a part of for so many years?

I don't ask the questions burning through me, but maybe he sees them when he looks at my face because he shakes his head and says, "You don't know me anymore, and I don't owe you anything."

"Maybe that's true." My tone comes out sharper than I intend, probably to combat the way he's hurt me. "But you do have to let me call an ambulance. You do have to get checked out."

"You can't make me stay."

I glance down the beach. There's nobody left in sight and the last of the sun is about to be swallowed by gray. I still haven't called this in. "Even if you're fine—of which I'm not convinced—I could get fired if I let you go without a report."

"Like I give a shit." And he really, really looks like he doesn't. Which would be fine, but I'm pretty sure I could tell him I'd *die* if I let him go and he still wouldn't give a shit.

I wonder how to categorize this kind of heartache. "What is *wrong* with you?"

"Nothing. Just leave. Me. Alone." His eyes are a lighter green than his brother's, and they're flashing with so much steel I take a step back.

I study him for a moment to gather control of my thoughts. Of my emotions.

He's not wheezing and his breathing's back to normal. So that's something, I guess. "You're not driving anywhere, are you?"

"I'm not *that* stupid."

"Well, you *did* go into a super rough ocean while drunk and almost drown."

But he's already walking away. He swipes up a ratty towel—I actually recognize it from years ago—and kicks one of the empty chip bags as he passes the spot where his friends were set up earlier.

"Nice," I call after him. "Glad to see you still care about the environment. Oh—*and you owe me a pair of sunglasses.*"

He doesn't give any indication he's heard me, just wraps that towel around his shoulders, sliding it back and forth a few times before settling it into place. It's the same motion Sawyer used to make before wrapping himself in his own beach towels. In fact, with that very one.

Like a complete dope, I watch Jess's back all the way until he's out of sight. Imagining he's Sawyer.

Wondering what Sawyer looks like now.

I watch the spot where he disappeared for a long time. Until the first dollops of rain splash down.

I make it back to the lifeguard stand just in time to hear an order over the radio to fly the red warning flags along the beach and head home. My shift would've ended in fifteen minutes anyway, so the storm won't cost me more than a few bucks.

Past the dunes, at my Jeep, I can't help but look for Jess. He's not anywhere nearby, though.

And I'm not sure it's really him my eyes are searching for so hungrily, anyway.

No. I'm greedy for a glimpse of Sawyer and I hate myself for it.

I open the door to my Jeep and slide inside right as the rest of the sky opens up. Windshield wipers on. Blinker to turn onto the street. I almost reach for the radio, but tuck my hand into my lap instead. Music—lyrics—of any kind aren't a good idea right now.

Driving. Thinking. Breathing. Everything feels very fragile, very on the surface. Like I'm made of glass, but I'm stretched so thin that one errant thought could be enough to shatter me.

Enough to grind me down into the past.

But I draw in a deep breath and keep my head high.

I can't get lost in the past. I don't have time to wallow.

I have a date to get ready for.

CHAPTER THREE

SAWYER

"DON'T DO IT," I warn my brother. "The results won't be pretty."

He swings his fist. Slow and sluggish and I don't have to move my face an inch because he misses by a mile. His body follows his fist and I catch him, wrapping an arm around his neck, before he lands face-first against the wall of Kelly's Tavern. I drag him like this, in a headlock, toward the door. One of his dumbass friends calls after us, some linebacker-looking kid, telling me to chill, but I look over my shoulder and he sits his ass right back down when he sees my expression. Smart kid.

As we pass the bartender, I apologize to him for the scene, but he shrugs like it's not a big deal. Which probably has more to do with the fact that Jess is underage than actually not giving a shit about the three broken glasses smashed on the ground—and whatever else Jess destroyed before I got here.

I shove him out the door and into my car. "You throw up in here, I'll rub your face in it."

He flicks me off.

"Right back at you."

Damn it. I thought coming home might do him good, but

he's falling harder here than ever.

The road back to his place is bumpy and the way he clutches his stomach over every pothole worries me—a lot. I'm not in the mood to clean up vomit.

"Don't tell Dad." His head rolls back, thunking into the seat's headrest.

"Little too late to think about the consequences." I stare back with a steady face when he scowls at me. Let him worry awhile. I won't tell Dad, though. Guy's got enough on his mind these days; he shouldn't have to deal with his shithead son. Guess that description could go for either one of us, but Jess is the one he's still responsible for.

"You're such a—" He doesn't get a chance to finish because we hit another hole and the little shit leans forward and throws up in my car.

I swerve into a beach parking offshoot and slam on the brakes. Reaching over his back, I throw the door open and shove his shoulder to adjust his aim outside the car. The seat belt gets in the way and then hits him in the chin when I rip it off of him. But finally he's puking on the ground instead of my floor mat.

The irritation zipping under my skin jacks into something harsher. I jump out my side and dash around the car, but by the time I'm there, he's slipped out into a ball on the ground. He looks damn pathetic, but no way does he get off this easy. I grab the back of his neck, lifting him until his head's over the puddle of puke on the floor of my car. "What'd I tell you?"

"*Lay off me.*" He fights my grip, but I've got two inches and thirty pounds on him. Plus, I'm sober. And pissed.

I push his face closer to the stuff that's already permeating through my entire car. "What did I fucking tell you?"

He's really grappling against me now. And I'm really not budging.

"Let me go and I'll tell you about Quinn."

This—the shock jolting my system—loosens my grip more than anything else could. "What?"

He turns his face sideways to look up at me. I give him that much leeway. Because I'm still not sure I heard him right. Then he says, "I saw Quinn."

Fragments of memories barrel through my mind so fast I almost lose my breath.

Long, slender fingers tracing hearts against my callused palms. A white daisy tucked into hair that's brown like autumn and windblown and trailing down her back for miles.

The somehow both sweet and rough scents of salt water and sand. Laughter like sea glass wind chimes spinning in the breeze.

I want to ask where. How. When.

I want to crack his skull open and climb into his memory to see her again.

I rub my face with my free hand to wipe it all away. "Goddamn it, Jess. She's the *one* person I told you we couldn't see if we came back."

"Two," he slurs, squirming on his knees. "Two people."

It's true. But she's the only one who matters. The only one who ever has.

Quinn.

Jesus. Just her name in my brain is enough to make my gut jump.

So I let go of Jess's neck.

He face-plants into his own puke and comes up spitting, swearing. I shrug and try not to laugh at the horror in his expression. It's hard. Which means I'm out of the grip of the past. "You wanted me to let you go, so I did."

"You're such a dick."

I can't deny it. Instead, I grab a beach towel from the backseat and let him use it to wipe off his face—and then my car. He gags the entire time, and nothing could bring me more pleasure.

"How'd she look?" I ask a few minutes and miles later. I don't expect an answer. The kid's eyes are closed so hard they look swollen.

"Skinny," he slurs. "Stupid."

"You sure you weren't just looking in a mirror?"

He mumbles something I'm pretty sure is, "Fuck you," but I let it slide because I'm remembering in more than just splinters of snapshots. More than a hand or a laugh. Quinn.

Skinny? Maybe. She's always been slight.

Stupid? Not a chance in hell.

One of us would've run into her sooner or later. The Outer Banks is a big area, but the spots locals prefer are few. I'm surprised it's taken the two months it has.

Thing is, though, if it happened to Jess, then statistically my chances seem smaller now. "*Goddamn it, Jess.*"

But he's snoring. And I shouldn't be asking about her anyhow.

I spend the rest of the ride trying to figure out how to get the smell out of my car—and quick, because I have a fucking date tonight.

CHAPTER FOUR

QUINN

"PUT ON SOME blush," my mother commands, smoothing a hand over my hair, fixing, I'm sure, some tiny errant flyaway. "Somehow you manage to look pale through your tan. Are you coming down with something? And grab a cardigan before Chase gets here, or change your dress. It's not appropriate as it is."

"I don't need a sweater." I breathe in the waxy scent of her lipstick mixed with her sharp perfume. It's actually not a horrible combination, but I step out of her reach and fight the urge to roll my eyes. I should've stayed up in my old bedroom until the last minute. I don't know why I came down to let my mother preen me.

I don't know why I agreed to get ready at my parents' house in the first place.

It probably has something to do with the fact that my mother's the one who arranged the date. *This* I know why I agreed to do, though. To get Julian out of my head. I'll do whatever it takes, even if that means succumbing to my mother's meddlesome ways and allowing one of her ritzy friend's sons to take me out.

It might, too, have something to do with not wanting this

guy, this *Chase*—who's sure to be completely stuck up—to judge my tiny, ramshackle apartment. When he picks me up here, he'll see a huge, pillared front porch rising into the first of two decks of a pristinely kept house. Way more the style he's used to, I'm sure. Fancy houses. Elegant, pedigreed girls, sweet and demure. I can't do much about my ancestry or personality, but at least the first image he gets won't turn him off.

Still, I'm not grabbing a cardigan. Letting him make assumptions about the house is one thing, but if this guy can't handle spaghetti straps? Well, basically, he's out.

"I'm perfectly happy with the dress I have on," I say. "But thanks, as always, for your unsolicited opinion."

"Sarcasm is below you, Quinn." She sniffs, lifting her chin a notch.

"And your pretension is something I'll never understand," I shoot back.

"A dignified demeanor isn't pretense." Her blue eyes flash. "People of a certain stature are expected to behave with a level of class I wish you'd adhere to."

Please. You've held contempt for people below that certain stature before we were even close to crossing above the line, is what I want to say. But we've been down this road so many times I have no traction left in my soles. Instead, I stare at her hairline. "Your gray is growing in again. Wow—it's so much thicker than it used to be."

Now she smooths her own hair, the panic on her face almost laughable. "I have an appointment next week. Maybe I should call Stefan and tell him I need him sooner."

I shrug, raising my eyebrows. "Do you really want to be around when Chase gets here...?"

"I don't want to be rude, but..." She pauses, and I actually see the weight of pros and cons swimming in her mind. If we didn't have nearly identical features, I'd swear I was adopted.

"It's not rude—he'll be here to pick *me* up, not you."

My response is the push she needs and, after reminding me about our standing brunch date tomorrow (we have two a week every summer, though I've been trying to push for just one forever), she finally leaves me alone in the sitting room, the clip of her heels down the hall growing lighter and lighter. When she's well away in a different part of the house, I check my reflection in the monstrous, gilded mirror in our—*their*—entryway. And then I sigh, because she's right about the blush.

I'm not coming down with anything. It's the shock from seeing Jess, from thinking of Sawyer, still written across my under-colored cheeks. In the slight wildness of my eyes. In the jitters jumping and biting like fleas in my stomach.

And suddenly Sawyer's face is swimming in front of me. Smirking. *"The Quinn I knew would've laughed in her mother's face before letting her pick out her date."*

I push through the mirage, brushing it away while wishing at the same time I could stare at his face forever, answering in my thoughts. *Yeah, well, you walked away from the Quinn you knew.*

Chase better be amazing.

Because it's not one person I need to use him to forget now. It's two.

As if on cue, the doorbell rings.

So much for the blush.

I open the door and take my time studying the guy on the other side. Brown hair, brown eyes, freckles smattering his nose. A friendly expression that makes me want to like him immediately... Even if he *is* wearing pressed khakis and a starched, stiff-looking button-down.

"Hello, I'm Chase," he says, his words shaped fully and all polite. "You must be Quinn?"

I stick my hand out to shake his, right as he shoves a triplet of red roses at me.

"Oh. Thanks." I smile at him. Points for bringing me flowers—and for not going overboard. Detractions for the boring choice. Still...I already have something specific in mind for them. "Do you want to come in while I find a vase?"

I leave him in the sitting room and only remember I should've offered him a drink when I'm already in a storage closet half the house away. Oh well. And *perfect*—my supplies are still here, tucked away. I grab an old shoebox from the stack and fill it about an inch up with a mixture of Borax and cornmeal. I dig out space for the rose heads and then, after clipping the stems short enough to fit in the box, I cover the buds with more of the mixture. They're fresh and fragrant even through the mix. Hopefully they won't blacken too much in the drying process.

But even if they do, I'll find a use for them.

"I meant to tell you, you look beautiful," he says, standing when I reenter the sitting room.

"We're even. I meant to ask if you wanted a drink." A few seconds later I cringe. "I also meant to say thank you for the compliment."

He laughs. "Should we go?"

We step out to the porch and, through the almost chilly humidity left over from the storm, a waft of cigarette smoke hits me. A creak on the deck above us tells me my father's sneaking another one. I don't blame him—I bet my mom's been up to preen him, too. And he doesn't even have any place to go. I wonder if he yearns for the days when jeans and a T-shirt were just fine to wear around the house... Not that my mother ever liked it, but she let it slide. Sometimes, at least.

Chase's car is sleek and silver, low-to-the-ground and expensive-looking. Especially next to my beat-up Jeep. He opens the door for me, and when I drop into the car, it smells like leather. And a hint of the roses he brought with him.

It's a promising aroma.

And, when he slides in opposite me, flashing a friendly, not-at-all-stuck-up grin, I think this could be a promising date.

CHAPTER FIVE

QUINN

NOPE. NOT A promising date.

It's lovely, don't get me wrong. Surf and turf to my belly's content, romantic lighting, thriving conversation. But...

I don't feel it.

Chase is cracking jokes, left and right, and I'm laughing—because they're actually *funny*. He's attractive. He even smells good, which is sometimes hard to find in a beach-based boy.

But there's zero spark.

Not the way there was the first time I saw Julian.

And don't even get me started on Sawyer.

Damn it.

I wonder if we'd have a spark if I hadn't seen Jess earlier today. If my mind wasn't so filled with stupid Sawyer. But if I'm honest with myself, probably not. Which makes me a freaking idiot.

"What's spinning in that mind of yours?" He catches me, lost in thought.

"That I had the wrong idea about you," I admit.

He checks with me and then shakes his head when our waiter stops by to ask if we need anything. "The wrong idea, huh?"

I was hoping there could be something between us. But, before that: "I figured you'd be a typical rich jackass."

He takes a sip of wine. "Ouch."

"My point is that you *aren't* those things. I mean, yeah, you're rich, obviously—" Obviously? God, what am I even saying? "—but you're not typical. You're not a jackass."

He grins. "Well, I misjudged you, too, so I guess it's fair."

"Oh yeah?" Intrigued, I swallow my own sip of wine. "How so?"

"I've always heard that Jack and Lillian's daughter was sort of a wild child. Out to do her own thing, devil-may-care what the rest of polite society thinks." He cuts off a piece of steak, popping it in his mouth and swallowing before continuing. "Yet, here you are. Respectable and polite."

Is it wrong that my reputation among the uppity parental crowd gives me a secret thrill?

"I don't know about all that," I say. "You haven't seen what comes *after* dinner."

I mean to joke, to make him laugh, but it comes out flirtier than I intend, and he reaches across the table to grab my hand, his smile stretching wider. "Color me intrigued."

Great. So now I either look like a jerk if I move my hand, or like I'm interested if I don't.

Feeling like a total chump bucket, I slide my hand out and awkwardly knock my knuckles on the back of his hand. Twice. "What I was talking about was... I mean..." I clear my throat. "There's this secret bonfire I know about tonight, if you want to go."

Maybe I shouldn't extend the date—I don't want to give Chase the wrong idea. But...I also think he's fun and funny and maybe I can get him to see me as friendship material instead of writing me off completely when I tell him this won't be the next great American romance.

His expression dims, and he discreetly pulls his arm back. But he's a trooper, and doesn't shut down completely. Just gives me an appraising look. "You're on the circuit?"

Well, color *me* amused. "You know about the circuit?"

"I've even done a round or two," he says. "Back in the day. When I was a *teenager*."

"Maybe we've met before."

"Nah, I'd remember you."

Oh, jeez. I should probably blush here, but I just feel anxious. I fiddle with the leftover asparagus on my plate. "If you're thinking it's still a teenager thing, don't. It grew up as we did. Very different atmosphere these days."

The circuit is a weekly summer bonfire, the location kept secret until the last minute to avoid cops or outsiders getting the scoop. A text chain is initiated when the first person sends out the location. The location decider changes week to week, the current secretly picking the next.

"Last time I was there, three or four years ago, I saw a huge fire, people drinking till they puked, and some really bad—but really fun—decisions being made. I kind of remember making one or two of my own, actually."

Now I laugh. "Okay. Maybe it hasn't changed *that* much. But we're older now. So it's cooler. Obviously."

"How do you know where it is?"

"My best friend texted me a few hours ago." With explicit instructions to show up or else. She meant it because she misses me. But there actually is an *or else* if I don't go tonight. I haven't been to a circuit fire yet this summer, and if you miss too many you get culled from the invitation list.

"And who'd you text after?"

But I just cock an eyebrow and shake my head. "You know I can't tell you that."

"Where is it?"

"Oh, come on. You *know* the same goes."

"Then how am I supposed to drive us there?"

"So you want to come?" And, when he nods: "I'll give you directions along the way."

He rolls his eyes at me when I offer to help pay after he signals for the bill. I roll my eyes right back. "Sexist."

"Just polite," he corrects me. "I have a very strong-willed, very pro-women's rights sister. Not a chance in the world she'd allow me to end up a chauvinist, believe me. But I am paying for your dinner. I chose the spot. You can pay on our next date. Deal?"

I sigh like I'm giving in instead of using the opening to tell him there won't actually be another date. Because I'm a total chickenshit. "Anyway, tell me more about your sister. She sounds awesome."

CHAPTER SIX

SAWYER

I'M TIRED.

I'M tired from working all day, and my back complains so loudly I can't wait to get horizontal.

I'm tired from the earlier encounter with my dumbass brother.

And I'm really, really tired of this date.

Morgan. Came into the shop and flirted until I asked her out. Brown hair, blue eyes. How could I resist? But she's a poor man's substitute for the only girl I've ever wanted. They always are.

Against my better judgment (hell, against anybody's better judgment), I let her talk me into coming to the bonfire all the way at the base of Nags Head. Now she's sitting here, shivering next to me on this damp log way back from the flames, and I don't have a jacket to offer her. It's June at the Outer Banks. It shouldn't be chilly. She scoots a little closer, squeezing her bare thigh against my jeans, practically begging me to put my arm around her. Which isn't going to happen. I'm an asshole for taking her out in the first place; I'm not going to lead her on further.

A random-looking assortment of people stand around the fire, sparks flickering high into the sky, the spice of burned wood lingering in the night. The occasional bottle makes its way into the flames, shattering, the leftover alcohol creating miniature blue and white and yellow fireworks. Someone's truck is pulled onto the beach, bumping bass through wood-smoked air; more people gather there, standing around, laughing, sitting on the opened bed, legs swinging. I can't make anyone out from where I sit, which is fine by me. I've already seen one person I know, and she was more than enough.

Gianna Marcel. Quinn's best friend. I almost panicked when I saw her, certain Quinn would be near. She wasn't. And now I'm sitting here with Morgan, hiding on the outskirts of the party because if Gianna sees me—if she's still friends with Quinn and if she's the same girl I knew those years ago—I won't be leaving here until she's got my still-bleeding balls hanging around her neck.

Thankfully, it's dark. Clouds from the earlier storm are blocking the moon, and I'm obscured from view back here in the shadows. Morgan probably thinks I'm looking for a little action. I'm not, but I'm pretty sure she is, sliding the side of her body against the side of mine.

I should look at her, let her see on my face that it isn't going to happen, but I can't pull my gaze from the circle around the bonfire. My eyes refuse to stop searching for the girl I already know isn't here.

I can't believe the circuit's still around. I can't believe I agreed to come. Actually, that's bullshit. I don't lie to myself. Ever. I agreed to come the instant Morgan suggested it, even though I'd been about to take her home, and I know exactly why I did.

I agreed because of my idiot baby brother. He saw Quinn today. I wanted to pummel him with jealousy, and it unraveled the control I spent years assembling. One mention of her erased it all.

I agreed to come because I thought I might catch a glimpse of her.

The last time I came to one of these, it was with Quinn. Exactly one week before I never saw her again.

Of course she isn't here. All the good times we had on the circuit are probably her worst memories now.

"I'm cold," Morgan purrs, squirming against my side.

"Wish I had a jacket for you," I say, honestly.

"Aw, you're a sweetie, Sawyer." She traces a heart on my thigh. Another poor man's substitute, and this one turns my stomach sour.

"Maybe I should take you home—we can turn on the heat in the car."

"I could think of a few other ways to get warm, you know." She tiptoes her fingers a little higher, presses against me a little harder.

I'm not unaffected. *I* don't want her, but my body's not so choosy. We should leave before I make a mistake. "I have to work early. We should go."

"I don't want to go yet. Let's have a beer first. Just one," she pleads, pointing in the direction of the keg. "A little buzz will keep the chill away."

I stand, her hand trailing slowly down my leg in the process, and squint toward the people gathered there. Gianna's not among them. Guess it's safe. Safer than sitting here with Morgan and her short skirt and her exploring fingers, anyway.

The sand is wet and cold under my feet, and halfway to the keg I'm almost sidelined by the even colder, wetter shoulder—body, really—of someone rushing up from the ocean. Instantly, I'm tense, ready to go.

"Watch it, bro," he shoots over his shoulder, and even though I didn't see his face, I recognize the gravelly voice. Danny Simmons. We played Little League together growing up. A girl's laugh chases after him, right before she scampers by me, too. Blonde. Not Quinn. They're both shivering, sharing a towel, a few yards past the keg when I get there a second later.

I force myself to relax. I'm not the guy I was four years ago. And I'm not the even worse guy I was three years ago. Or two. I don't fight for no reason anymore and I'm not going to start shit with Danny just because he ran into me and was a dick about it. Not worth it. Even if the thought of hitting someone—or something—right now has my blood singing, begging for that release.

Instead, I reach around the keg, grabbing a plastic cup for Morgan and taking the tap from another guy when he's finished with it. I watch Danny while I pump beer, but he's too busy sticking his tongue down the blonde's throat to notice.

"*Gross.*"

I glance over my shoulder, and *shit*, Gianna's standing there. But she's not speaking to me. She's glaring daggers toward Danny. A second later, though, that glare shifts to me. It cycles around to shock, to confusion, and then centers right back into an even more pissed off glare. "Sawyer?"

"Hey, Gianna." I try to smile while mentally preparing to protect the fellas in my pants. I gesture toward her hair the best I can with the tap still in my hand. "Like the pink."

Her hand automatically smooths the thick, bright stripe of hair jutting across her forehead, but the compliment doesn't faze her.

"'Hey, Gianna'? You disappear for four years, and you think you can just up and 'Hey, Gianna' me?"

She doesn't shove a finger in my chest to drive her point home, but she might as well have.

"Gi—"

"No. I don't know what you're doing here, but if you so much as look at Quinn, I swear to God you'll be crawling home instead of walking."

"Still the same, sweet Gianna, I see." Then my brain catches up to her words. "Quinn?"

"Don't even say her…" But whatever else Gianna's saying falls on deafened ears. Even the music dulls to a hum.

Because behind her, I see Quinn.

Walking toward the bonfire. Wearing a jacket two sizes too big for her, next to the dude I'm sure it belongs to. But I barely process him.

Quinn.

She's taller. Still sexy as hell. Her hair's wild and blowing in the wind. Just like I've imagined every time I've pictured her the past four years. Same straight nose. Same delicate neck. Same jaunty smile. Punches me in the gut that it's not directed at me.

She doesn't see me yet, and Gianna shoves me back toward the shadows, toward the log where Morgan's waiting. "Get out of here. She doesn't need to see you."

When I don't move, she shoves me again, pinching a bit of flesh before swiping her hand away, and in the back of my mind I realize I could be in for some pain if I don't do what she says and she chooses to bring her knee into the equation. But I no longer care about the well-being of my balls. I have no room left for anything other than the fact that I'm sharing the same air as Quinn for the first time in four years. For the first time in one thousand, four hundred and sixty-one days. If she turns her head, just a little, I'll be able to look into her eyes. *Jesus. Turn your head, Quinn.*

"Sawyer," Gianna hisses. "You shattered her. Do you really want to break the very few pieces she actually managed to put back together? It took her *years*." She doesn't touch me, but her words slice through my stomach so fast and so effortlessly, my guts hit the ground before I feel the pain.

I step back without another word.

I shouldn't have come. I don't have the right to want to share

Quinn's air anymore.

So before she has the chance to look our direction, I slip back into the shadows, far from the light of the fire.

I hand Morgan her beer and drop down on the log a foot away from her. We need to leave, but I need to figure out an exit strategy that doesn't involve Quinn seeing us first.

"Where's yours?" Morgan asks.

"I'm driving." I stare at the fire, not moving when she shifts closer to me. "Morgan, we need to—"

"Here," she shoves the cup at me, "a few sips won't hurt anything."

I turn my attention to the drink in her hand. It's tempting, but if I take it, I'll down it. If I take it, the monster under my skin will end up doing something I regret. "I'm good, thanks."

"You okay, sweet Sawyer? You look tired." Her tone is kinder than I deserve, especially as I can't remember the last time I actually looked at her face. Still can't bring myself to do it. She's nothing like Quinn, but I asked her out because something about her sparked a vague reminder. I don't want to see it now.

"A little. It's been a long day," I say. But the truth is...it wouldn't matter if I hadn't slept in weeks.

Quinn is here, somewhere across the flames.

I'm wide awake.

CHAPTER SEVEN

QUINN

MENTALLY, BY THE time we reach the bonfire, I'm both kicking myself for not being into Chase and running through lists of girls who might be good for him instead. He's too funny, too sweet, too *not what I expected him to be* to be single.

Gianna came to mind, but she lasted there less than a second. She's beautiful—dark brown skin, eyes like amber, body like a sexy, sexy hourglass—and she's the smartest person I've ever known. But she's also cynical as hell. She'd eat him alive.

Not that you'd know it by the smile lighting her face as she rushes up to us and wraps me in a quick hug, spinning me in half a circle. "Quinn, baby. Where've you been?" She turns her head to check out Chase, and her next words come out silkily. "Oh, never mind. I see."

"Your hair!" I ignore her tone and tug at her now-pink bangs. Her long, natural, grown-for-*years* hair is gone. Replaced with a pixie cut—and neon streaked bangs. I can't help cracking up because they truly, truly suit her. "You're literally my spunky little pixie girl now."

"My mom's going to freak," she admits, rolling her eyes. "But even if I live with her while home from school, I'm twenty-one years old and can make my own damn decisions. Plus, tonight aside, it's already hot as fuck for the summer. Long hair is for the birds—and, of course, for you, Q." She sticks her hand out to Chase, who takes it, looking a little apprehensive. "Hello, I'm Gianna. You're adorable."

"Gianna of the text messages?" he asks.

She skillfully raises a brow. "Gianna of the please, please go grab us a couple drinks, you mean?"

"Gianna of the extremely subtle, anyway," he says, laughing. Then he glances at me. "Beer?"

"Please." And when he's gone: "Gianna—Jesus." But I'm laughing as I say it.

"He's cute," she says. "Like, *why'd you even bring him here* cute? Turn straight back around and get after it."

"Chase is great," I admit. "But…no spark, unfortunately."

"Really?" Disbelief narrows her eyes as she stares over my shoulder, watching him for a minute. "That boy's made of sparks. Just pick one. Or two."

Hmm. Maybe Gianna's an option after all. "He's great, Gi. Even his family sounds cool. His sister? Carleigh? I want to be best friends with the girl. Pre-law, determined to someday defend people who can't do it themselves. She's actually spending the summer in DC at Georgetown early to avoid a cop she used to date—because *she egged his car to break up with him.*"

"That's kinda ballsy."

"Yeah, well, apparently he made an overly aggressive arrest of a person whose only crime was that they were Hispanic…"

"It sounds like you've got sparks with her, at least."

"Maybe I do." Now I raise a brow with almost as much skill as she did, smiling—until I notice Danny Simmons standing to our side, nodding. I level him with a glare. "What?"

"Made it through all the dudes in the area, movin' on to the chicks, now?" His full lips curve into a sneer. "I'd pay good money to see that. Even more if you'd let me join in."

I loathe this guy in way too many ways to list. Gianna's silent by my side and I hate him more for her than I do for myself. "Fuck off, Danny."

"I told you, doll. I'm going to ruin you." Sneer's still there, but his brown eyes are empty of emotion.

"And I told you good luck with that," I say, my voice strong. This guy…this virginity-taking, cheating-on-my-best-friend, heart-breaking dickwad… There's not a single thing he can do that will affect me in any way. Not anymore.

I wish I could say the same about Gianna. But she's still quiet in the most heart-wrenching way. I brush a fleck of sand away from the top of my hand like I don't have a care in the world. "Listen," I say, my tone also careless, "I get it. Gianna's impossible to get over—even though you're the one who fucked it up—I get it. But you've got to stop finding reasons to trail after her like a pathetic little puppy. It's sad, hon, and completely transparent. *Move on.*"

"That's funny coming from you, my little slut puppy—are you so anxious to find a doggy friend? Wag your tail a little and I'll let you know if I'm interested."

"Seriously, fuck off, Danny." Gianna finds her voice and steps forward, and though he doesn't back away, he definitely flinches. I laugh. There she is, my ferocious little pixie, and she's not done yet. "Where's your latest victim? That poor blonde you were suffocating with your tongue a minute ago?"

"Don't be jealous, Gi," he says. "There's plenty here to go around—as you *both* know."

And with impeccable timing, Chase returns with three red cups full of beer.

I'm not sure how much he's overheard, but I'm assuming at least some, because there's not a trace of his smile when he nods toward Danny. He hands me a cup, then Gianna, holding on to his own. "What's up, man? I'm Chase."

Danny doesn't bother nodding back. "You with Quinn?"

"Yeah. Y'all are friends?" Chase slides closer to me, knowing, I'm pretty sure, the answer already. I both love and hate his closeness.

"We go way back," Danny says. "*All the way* back, you could say."

"Nobody would say that." I sigh, and fight a small wave of embarrassment. "Get lost, Danny. Go make some other girl miserable." Then I glance at Gianna, nervous my words were insensitive. But she's rocking her fierce little glare and I'm glad for it. Maybe she's finally moving forward.

Danny shrugs, not a care in the world, addressing Chase instead of me. "Not trying to infringe here, bro. I just wanted to say hi to little miss orgasmic—oh, *sorry*, I meant organic. Though with all the dudes she plows through, both titles fit."

"Wow. A play on my parents' business. You're *so* clever." I fight the urge to kick sand at his face. His words are harsh, but considering the source, I shouldn't let them get to me. I slide out of my flip-flops and twist the tips of my toes into the damp sand anyway.

Chase looks studiously at Danny, as though he's judging him and finding him lacking. "Are those the manners your mother raised you with?"

His reaction's a little mild for my tastes, but that's only because I'm itching for a fight. Because, Jesus, enough is enough with this guy. "Plus, Danny, let's be real. Like you'd know a single thing about making *anyone* orgasmic."

"Gianna never complained."

"Not to *you*." She scoffs. "But believe me, it happened."

Finally, something hits its mark and Danny's jaw clenches. "Bitch."

"Yep. That's me. *Queen B* of the puppies. And you? You're not a part of the pack. You're just a prick." She transfers her cup to one hand and holds up her pinky finger, wiggling it in the air. "And not a very impressive one, either. Know what I mean?"

I bust out laughing, the sound traveling over every other echo of conversation around the bonfire, and clutch her arm. I love her so much right now. Then I notice that under my hand, she's trembling. I really hope it's from the coolness in the air, or even from rage, but I think it's probably more from heart pain.

"Ouch, man," Chase says, laughter in his tone. "I can't figure out why you're still standing here after that."

Whatever Danny's response was, it's drowned out by the sound of glass shattering and a loud shriek. We all turn toward the bonfire as a girl with long brown hair sprints in our direction, laughing as she passes us.

And behind her?

Sawyer Carson.

Shock is an iron collar tightening around my neck.

No. It's Novocain, making my face completely numb.

I recognize his stance before my gaze even gets to his face, and the sudden understanding of his shape is an electric cannonball slamming into my chest, where it sits still for a moment, ticking, ticking... The enormity of it is too heavy to leave room for breath.

Then we catch eyes, and the damn thing explodes in my veins.

The entirety of me buzzes. Under my skin. Vibrations. Jolts. They hurt.

They burn.

They *thrill*.

3 Things More Shocking Than Seeing Sawyer Again

1. A strike of lightning.
2. A live electrical appliance dropped in water.
3. Nothing. Sawyer's face in front of me is the third most shocking thing there is. It even wins over a defibrillator.

Though if my heart doesn't start beating again soon, I may need one.

* * * * * *

He's changed. Where he used to be lanky, he's toned. His skin looks like honey in the backlit glow of the fire, and his eyes are such a bright green, I can see their color even in the dark.

There's a tension in his posture, some dark thing coiled under his skin, barely kept in check. And whatever it is, it's all about me. He still hasn't looked away.

He's sexy as hell.

But I can't just stand here studying him. I need to move. To act. To do something.

For instance, breathe. I need to breathe.

So I do, the air sizzling in my lungs.

A few years back in lifeguard training, I learned the best treatment for electrical shock is prevention. A little too late for that now, but maybe I can save myself from complete electrocution. In my mind, I sheath myself in a Sawyer-shock-repelling layer of rubber.

Now, at least, I can shape my lips into the form of a smile. And when I speak, my voice comes out so steadily it's almost smug. "Sawyer. Hello."

CHAPTER EIGHT

SAWYER

TINY AS SHE is, I'm not surprised Morgan's drunk after one beer. Or maybe it's just her personality that has her making such a spectacle; guess I haven't given her much of an opportunity to show it this evening. But somehow she gets a hold of two empty liquor bottles and tosses them in the fire. And it turns out they're not completely empty, and flames shoot sky-high. As if that wasn't enough to grab the attention of everyone around, she dashes straight toward Quinn, laughing as she passes.

And now here we're standing, Quinn and I, less than ten feet apart. I cross the sand to her. I have no choice. Maybe if she hadn't seen me, it'd be different. Maybe if she hadn't said my name. But she did, and I'm pulled without a single say in where my feet take me. Then I'm here in front of her and there's panic in her expression.

The moment goes quiet around us, and I drink her in the way I've needed to all these years.

Her mouth is shaped like a heart. Perfect, even more so than I've imagined over time. Her cheeks are sharp, and her eyes are huge and black in the night, though I know they're actually blue like the ocean before a storm.

She is so familiar. I remember exactly how our bodies fit together. And, yet, somehow she's also a stranger. Well. Not somehow. I know exactly how.

There was a time I could reach for her and ease the anxiety in her eyes with a kiss. A hug. Any sort of contact. But that time's over, and I feel it harder in my gut now than ever. Instead, words come stiffly out of my mouth. "Quinn. It's good to see you."

Understatement of the year. Of my life. Seeing her is like the first inhale of oxygen after almost drowning. Saying her name to her face is like losing something, but also gaining the world.

"You, too." Her words are just as rigid.

I lean in to hug her and she lets me. She doesn't return it—in fact, she holds her beer cup between our bodies—but she leans toward me, and she doesn't shove me off. For a minute, I can't breathe. For a minute, I have her in my arms and I'm *happy*.

Then I realize she's being polite. The girl who loved me would've given me a black eye and a bloody nose by now. And all my arms are touching is another guy's jacket.

When I pull back her eyes are blank, not panicked at all. Guess I imagined it. Wished for it. For something, some reaction. I was worried she avoided the bonfires because of the memories that might plague her. It's laughable now, that thought.

"*Sawyer Carson?*"

For the first time, I take my eyes from Quinn's face and glance around. Danny, smirking. Gianna, frigidly furious. Quinn's jacket-less dude, a little baffled. It's Danny who's spoken, so I address him first. "Danny Simmons. Long time."

"Damn, dude, you back from the dead? What's it been? Two years?"

"Four." Quinn's stepping back, away from me. Her eyes still blank. But her movements are stiff and I think maybe she is reacting after all.

"Not quite," I say, clenching my jaw when Jacket-less puts a hand on her shoulder, like he thinks she needs a steadying presence. The girl I knew never had trouble standing on her own two feet.

"We used to fucking throw down, dude!" Danny pushes out a fist for me to bump, but I don't have it in me. A moment ago, it was clear he and Quinn were getting into it. I'm not about to tap fists with him—or anyone—after that.

"That was a long time ago," I say, instead.

After a second, he drops his fist, shrugging. "Sure."

"Yep. It's like we're strangers now," Gianna says. "So maybe we should all go our separate ways." She moves forward to grab Quinn's hand, glaring at me. "I think Morgan's waiting for you."

As if on cue, Morgan calls to me from down the sand a ways. "Sweet Sawyer! I thought you were taking me home?"

Quinn sucks in a deep breath, and the briefest flash of pain angles across her face, the first true sign of emotion I've been allowed to see. It's gone so quickly if I'd blinked, I'd have missed it. I want to explain, to say *something* to make it better, but before I can, Gianna speaks again. "You're *such* a class act, Sawyer."

"I'm taking her home to her own house," I say. I hold up a hand, telling Morgan to wait.

"Good for you," Quinn says. Her expression slays me with its impassivity. "Disappear for four years and come back to date an eighteen-year-old. Same age as you when you left, *funny*, isn't it?"

"Speaking of leaving," the guy with his hand on her shoulder says, "maybe we—"

"She's nineteen," I say, wanting to kick myself and still not able to shut up. "A year older than when I left."

Why the hell am I defending myself? I'm at fault. I hurt her. But seeing her again, putting a face to the guy she's dating—it's not like I thought she was waiting around for me, but seeing his face? It makes me feel raw. On edge. Like I want to fucking pummel someone.

"Maybe we should head out," her guy finishes his sentence.

"It's fine," she says. Her eyes are level on mine. "I'm fine."

"Yeah, well, these things were a lot cooler when I was younger. Let's go find something better." He's fighting for her attention, this guy, but at the moment Quinn and I are the only two people in the world.

"I'm sorry," I say.

Now she drops her gaze, shaking her head. And I guess I was wrong about our singular moment because she turns away from me, and it's him she responds to. "You're right. The circuit's seen better days. Let's go."

She doesn't look back, and when Morgan decides to half-stumble, half-dance her way back to me, Quinn doesn't move from her course. They pass side to side, insignificant to each other. I'm not sure why it stings, but it does.

The guy, whose name I never did catch, slings a familiar arm across Quinn's shoulders, and I swear to God something inside me busts wide open.

"Told you," Gianna says, stony irritation crossing her features when I look at her. "Told you, you needed to leave."

"Who needs to leave?" Morgan asks, planting herself to my side. Her tone is clueless and too bubbly for the moment. "I thought we were leaving, but do you want to stay, Sawyer?"

I gently extrapolate my hand from hers when she grabs it. "No. Let's go."

"This got so awkward so fast," Danny says. "Wait. I'm remembering something..."

"Don't go there, Danny." Gianna fixes her stare on him. I'd probably feel a little less tense without it directed at me anymore—because her glares have always been really fucking severe—but whatever Danny's getting at is starting to bug me.

"What are you remembering?" Morgan leans into me, but points to Danny.

"*Oh yeah*," Danny says, ignoring her, his focus on my face. "You used to hit that, didn't you?"

"Talk about Quinn as a *that* ever again and I'm gonna rearrange your face." It's instant, the fury pounding through me. Needing release. Begging to launch itself in the form of a fist straight into this guy's mouth. Even when he looks away.

Instead, I stare up at the sky, letting the brightness of the stars against the blackness sear into my vision.

"Who? That girl from before?" Morgan asks. I feel her gaze on my face, but I can't look away from the sky. Not until I'm a little calmer. Damn if it isn't going to take hours at this point. Everything's boiling in me.

"Oh, that's right," Danny says. "Never mind, you never got between those long, long legs."

My eyes snap back to his face and I let a little of my fury slip into my expression. "It's time for you to walk away."

But he doesn't. "I know you never did because—how embarrassing, somehow I forgot *I'm* the one who took that sweet little v-card when you left town. You missed out, bro."

His casual confession steals the air from my lungs.

Somehow the crackling sparks of the bonfire are instantly louder, roaring in my ears, completely covering any of the outside conversations going on around us. The salty ocean air feels heavier, damper than before. The sand under my feet is gritty, crumbling. He stands here, watching me, waiting for my reaction. For the first time I can remember, I don't know how to have one. His words hit an inner pause button I didn't know I had, and I'm stuck.

"Too far, Danny. You always take things too far. You're such an asshole." Gianna's voice sounds far away, because right now my focus is tunneled completely into this guy. All I see is his face. The smug pride across his mouth and in his eyes. The careless stance, as though he has nothing to lose.

"Didn't stop you from jumpin' on this ride, doll." He pumps his hips toward her. "Don't worry, you have more bedroom talent in spades. Granted I was Quinn's first, so all she did was lie there. I'm sure by now she's picked up more than a few tricks."

Beside me, Morgan slaps a hand over her mouth, but I only notice from the farthest corner of my consciousness. She slides away from me and toward Gianna, maybe to show solidarity. Maybe because she was close enough to feel the chainsaws start up in my veins, slicing right through to my fists, demolishing that pause button from a second ago.

But I'm not going to swing them. I'm not going back to being that guy. Words are just words. And Quinn's body is her own. Even if I feel sick over the thought of Danny in the same room as her, much less the same bed. But he's about two sentences away from making me change my mind. So I offer a final warning. "You need to shut the fuck up."

He holds up his hands, as if to make peace. Then he says, "Quinn's fucked pretty much everyone along a hundred miles of the beach coast *at least*. So if you want a turn, try just knocking on her door. It's basically a guarantee."

Yeah. That same thing that busted wide open inside of me at seeing Quinn? It rears back and completely fucking explodes.

So I do rearrange his face.

My fist slams into his mouth, harder than I've ever hit anything in my life, with the most satisfying *crack*. His teeth cut through my skin.

And, Jesus, it feels good.

CHAPTER NINE

QUINN

"SO THAT GUY was a douche," Chase says, glancing at me from the driver's seat. "Are you okay?"

I nod even though I'm not sure if he's referring to Danny or Sawyer. No. Must be Danny because Sawyer wasn't awful. He was just *there*.

And maybe I need to adjust my list. Maybe Sawyer's more electrifying than lightning. Because this rubber suit I've wrapped myself in?

Yeah. It hasn't done shit.

He struck, hard, and I'm fried.

No. Not fried. I'm humming, buzzing, wired.

Jittery as fuck.

God. And he brought *Morgan*? She's friends with Gianna's little brother. I feel sick. How deluded have I been, thinking I was over him?

"Are you sure you're okay?" Chase slides his hand off his gear stick, lets it hover above my leg, then thinks better of it. "It's okay if you aren't. If you want to talk about it...or, I don't know. We could go get ice cream or find a bar. Get drunk. I'll hire a cab to take us home."

I should respond, but I can't work my mouth at the

moment. I stare straight ahead, watching streetlights pass us by. The brightness of the neon lights have nothing on the glare under my skin. Because *Sawyer.*

I just had to go and remind him it'd been four years. Like I've been counting every day.

Which I haven't been.

Mostly.

And then I just had to give him a hard time about dating Morgan. Like I'm jealous.

Jesus.

I'm still so freaking charged. Everywhere. Fingers to feet. Up the back of my neck. Between my stupid, traitorous thighs. The song on Chase's sound system pulses through me. Low and deep, with enough bass to make me squeeze my legs a little tighter.

Why does Sawyer still affect me this way?

And suddenly—*finally*—I'm pissed.

Disappear without a damn trace and then come back and set off fireworks inside of me? No. Fuck that. He doesn't deserve this reaction.

I look at Chase, studying his profile for a moment. It's sweet, really. And honest. The kind of profile I *want* to be attracted to. It's my turn to reach over the gearshift. I put my hand on his thigh. "Hey. Pull over."

He meets my gaze for a second. "What?"

"Pull *over.*" I squeeze my fingers and his leg jerks.

He turns down a random street, idling his car halfway off the road. "What's up?"

I hit him with my most inviting expression, and I inch my hand a little higher. "You can't tell?"

"I have some idea," he says, "but I didn't think—"

"No more talking." I slip over the console between us, straddling him—with only the slightest amount of clumsiness in my maneuvering. But, hey, making it over a stick shift isn't going to be graceful no matter how I approach it.

His eyes are wide and his breath is drawn and I can see that he wants me.

"Quinn." My name shakes a little in his mouth.

Sawyer. "Chase."

When I shift in his lap, his chest expands with an extra intake of breath. His hands creep around my waist. "This is sudden."

"So?" And then I push my mouth to his. Except I close my eyes when I do it, and it's Sawyer's face behind them. His lips parting so eagerly to mine.

Below me, it's Sawyer stiffening through his khakis. The bulge in his zipper pushing into the thin fabric of my panties. And I grind. Grind. Grind against him.

But it's very much Chase a second later who breaks the kiss, gently pushing against my shoulders until our mouths part. The moment I open my eyes regret slams through me. "Shit."

"I can't decide whether or not I mind being used for whatever you're exorcising from your system." He laughs, lightly, a blush across his cheeks evident even in the dim lighting. "Clearly certain parts of me don't mind at all... But I think the important parts do. I think I should take you home."

"I'm so sorry, Chase." Humiliation is a river of boiling water flooding my limbs. My face is so hot, I'm not sure how my skin isn't melting off. "I..." I have nothing to say. I should get off of him, but I can't make myself move.

"It's okay. You don't have to say anything."

"Yes. I do." Damn it. I'm living up to the reputation Danny threw around my shoulders tonight.

Though, in truth, I've been wearing it a lot longer than that.

I slide back along Chase's lap, until the steering wheel pushes against me. "I had an affair with my English professor the whole past year." The confession just falls from my mouth. This isn't what I meant to say. But now that this particular dam's cracked, it all rushes out. "He decided to come clean right before exams that he's married. Because who *wouldn't* think that was a great time wreck someone?"

It's the first time I've thought of Julian without a twinge in my heart. Guess that's one way to cure a bruised heart. Run into the guy who actually broke it. It's a small relief though.

Any residual feelings for Julian, any remaining longings for our fling, have been extinguished. Not the anger, of course. That's still there, burning away at me.

I don't know how my body's coping with every emotion pulling through it. I had enough of a load to carry without Sawyer returning. Now that he has? I'm not sure why I'm not exploding from the pressure of everything I feel.

"That's really rough," Chase says. "Your teacher sounds like a dick."

I shrug. "Yeah, well. I never even thought to ask."

"That doesn't make it your fault." He shifts a little, and I realize this is the weirdest spot I've ever had a conversation. On the lap of a dude I'm not going to get with, hunched over because of the low roof of the car. But I don't want to move yet. This is freeing, letting the story out.

"It does a little. I owed his wife enough to at least inquire."

"Did he wear a wedding ring?"

"No."

"Then why would you have asked?"

I shrug again, wincing a little this time because my shoulder's still sore from earlier, when I saved Jess. It feels like a century ago.

"It's weird, I thought you were jumping me to get that other guy from the bonfire out of your mind. Not the asshole. The shaggy blond one."

Out of my heart, more like. "He's...a different story."

"And so you thought to yourself, hmm, Chase is smoking hot. I know, maybe *he'll* help rewrite the pages of my...stories?"

"Something like that." Half a smile flits across my face. He's a really freaking good guy.

I lean forward again, kiss him again. Slowly this time, trying, *trying* to make something spark. But without Sawyer's face in my mind, nothing happens. I sigh, pulling away.

"Still nothing?" he asks.

"I wish there was. You have no idea how much."

"Maybe someday when you're not working through these other things." But he looks a little relieved.

"Wait," I say, my hands against his chest. "You don't feel it either, do you?"

He thinks for a moment. "I...feel like I *could*, if you were open to it. Does that count?"

I laugh. "I have no clue."

"At least let me have a hug," he says. "Friend to friend. Because I think you could use one."

When I nod, he pulls me back in, tucking me against his chest. And I sit here, against him, and I breathe. And I breathe. And I breathe until tears swell behind my closed eyes and threaten to spill over. Because Sawyer. Jesus. Sawyer. Seeing him again makes me feel like every bone in my body's been replaced with something new. Something sweet and something painful.

I pull back to wipe my eyes, ending the moment. "Thanks. I maybe needed that."

Chase lifts a shoulder. "Anytime."

Just as I unwrap myself from his arms and start to untangle myself from his lap—climbing back into my seat turns out to be a million times more awkward than climbing out—blue and red lights flash behind us. Followed by two short blips of a siren.

I glance back and see a cop car stopped there. "We're not in a no-parking spot or anything, are we?" And when Chase doesn't answer, "You've only had, what, like a drink and a half, right? Wine at dinner and half a beer at the bonfire?"

"Less than half." Chase is strangely terse, staring in his side-view mirror.

"Don't worry," I say as the muffled sound of a car door shutting thumps behind us. "This isn't a big deal."

A moment later, Chase curses. "You know how I told you my sister egged a cop's car?"

"Yeah... Oh. Shit. Is this him?"

"Yep."

CHAPTER TEN

QUINN

"I'M SORRY ABOUT this." Chase rolls his eyes at me before turning to face the policeman standing by his window. "Is there a problem?"

"Looks like it." The officer ducks down for a better view in the car. And I'll admit it. He's hot. I see what Chase's sister saw. Chiseled cheeks. Full lips. Strong brow. But his eyes are kind of mousy, and his expression's even more smug than the one Danny rocks most of the time. His tone is falsely bored. "You two should know better than to conduct yourselves this way in public."

Oooh. He saw me on Chase's lap and assumed...pretty much what anyone else would assume.

"How exactly do you think we were conducting ourselves?" Chase asks.

The cop looks at him as if to say, *please, you know exactly what you were doing*. "Shame you chose to expose yourselves in such a publicly viewable location. Damn shame. Really. I'm going to have to take you in for public indecency."

"Um, what?" I lean forward, catching his eyes. My stomach is a sinking ship. "We didn't...nothing was exposed. I swear, Officer...?"

"Vincent," he answers. "Officer Vincent. Why don't you go ahead and—"

"There was no public indecency," Chase says. "We were just talking."

"Actually, I found you sitting here with your dick in your hands," he says, and then directs his beady gaze my way. "And you, sugar, really should put your shirt back on. Bra, too."

I bite my tongue. Because I'm fully clothed, but I'm pretty sure if I tell him he's a fucking dumbass, we'll get in even more trouble. That drowning ship in my stomach explodes into jagged pieces, like this cop is a freaking iceberg. "Listen, Officer. We're really sorry. It won't happen again."

"That's what I'm about to make sure of. Go ahead and step out of the car, please. Both of you."

"Christ, Peter, this is *illegal*." Chase doesn't move, so I follow his cue. This entire situation just…doesn't feel real.

"Sir, this is a public road. Anyone could've come upon you. Even a child. And then you'd be in even bigger trouble, trust me."

Chase bristles. "Don't *sir* me. I'm sorry Carleigh egged your car. I'm sorry she left you. Maybe if you weren't a racist piece of shit, she would've stayed."

Whoa. He's going all badass all of a sudden, but it's totally the wrong time for it. I put a hand on his leg, trying to calm him a little, whispering, "That's probably not helping."

The cop's expression has gone completely stiff. Furious. "Get the fuck out of the car. Don't make me use force. Or…on second thought, go ahead."

Make my day. At the most inappropriate time, I have the urge to giggle. Because I'm so tempted to complete the quote it almost slips from my tongue. I bite it back, but that damn giggle tumbles out.

"You, too." He points at me. "Out. Now."

Chase looks at me, an apology written all over his face. "I forgot that would affect you, too. Shit. Sorry."

Officer Vincent cracks his knuckles. We scramble the hell out of the car.

Which is how I end up in handcuffs, in the back of a freaking police cruiser. All for a kiss that meant nothing. Well, not nothing. It got me Chase, as a friend...I think. Still. I'm not, per se, a *good* girl. But I'm not a bad one either. I've never been in the back of a cop car. Not that it feels real yet. Maybe there's only so much shock a system can handle at once, and Sawyer's already taken more than I had to give.

"Do you just drive around searching for me endlessly?" Chase asks. "I'll sue you for harassment. I'm sure it isn't the first time. You better believe my family has the best lawyer in the state."

"Chase," I hiss. "Chill." Where's the nice guy who was hugging me just a few minutes ago?

I guess he's not so nice when it comes to someone messing with his sister. Which makes me like him even more.

Officer Vincent stares at us in the rearview mirror for a second. "*Actually*, we got a call about a beach fire a few blocks from here. Finding you on my way was just...very fortuitous." He laughs and I swear if he had a mustache he'd stroke it, evilly.

Chase and I meet eyes. Shit. I hope Gianna is gone already. Wish my phone wasn't in my bag on the floor of Chase's car. But I'm sure it's too late at this point anyway. And I seriously doubt she already left—the circuit usually goes all night... Unless Danny being so awful made her want to leave... Hmm. For the first time, I think maybe him being such a complete ass could be beneficial.

"Listen, sir, Officer Vincent, I mean... We're sorry for this confusion. I don't think it's necessary to take us all the way to the station. The lesson's totally been learned here," I plead in the most respectful tone I can muster. "I'm sorry I laughed before. I do that when I'm nervous—it wasn't at you."

But he doesn't bother responding.

Because this isn't about me laughing. It isn't about the law. It isn't about whether or not Chase and I were actually getting it on. This is all about his personal vendetta against Chase's sister. I thought I had it bad with Danny, but he's just a knucklehead who runs his mouth about ruining me because I caught him with someone else and told Gianna.

This is way worse.

It's finally sinking in. This is real. I'm in handcuffs. And not even for anything kinky. I'm in the back of a freaking cop car being hauled to the station.

Fuuuuck.

There's not a chance in hell this won't reach my mother somehow. I can only imagine what she'll say.

I wish I didn't freaking care.

The station is a weathered red brick building with a gray, rickety shingled roof and a half-empty lot in the front. My palms are sweating so much by the time we park I wonder if I could just slip out of the cuffs and make a run for it. But Officer Vincent took way too much pleasure in making sure these things were good and tight.

When he steps out of the car to get us, Chase whispers, "Don't say anything else from this point forward. It doesn't matter when it's just him because he'll lie regardless. But around other people, keep your mouth shut, okay? Anything you say can get you in trouble for real."

I nod, nerves waking up all along my skin. How is this real life right now?

Officer Vincent walks us through the glass doors and down a hallway where we reach a blonde officer behind a desk. Chase and I stand a few feet behind.

"Chrissy," he says, the flirtatious smile evident in his tone. "See you after your shift?"

She twists her hair up with a pencil, a skill I've, admittedly, never mastered. "I'm off in twenty."

"I'll be out as soon as I'm done booking these bozos."

Booking us? Jesus. This is a disaster.

She bats her eyes, and I come *thisclose* to exaggeratedly gagging. Like he knows, Chase elbows me. I roll my eyes at him and he bites back a smile. Guess we'll always have humor if nothing else.

Then it all stops being funny.

Because guess what happens next?

We get freaking photographed. And fingerprinted.

Like real criminals.

And Officer Vincent shoves us in two seats in this huge booking area and threatens that he'll be right back. Not like we could go anywhere—there are four other cops sitting around in the space.

"We really do have the best lawyer in the state," Chase whispers. "If it comes to that."

"Thanks." But if it comes to that, my parents will throw their own ridiculously priced lawyer at the situation. Man, they are never, ever going to forgive me.

In another section of the room, a large, shabby-looking man belches with an impressive volume. He grins at me. Or at Chase... At least in our direction. Pretty sure he's so drunk he can't really focus. At least I won't feel as bad as this guy will when I wake up tomorrow morning. Probably, anyway.

Officer Vincent comes back a few minutes later, with a sandwich and a coffee. He sits at a table across from us, taking his time unwrapping the cellophane wrapper, rolling it into a ball, holding it over a trash can, dropping it in. He takes a huge bite, chews grossly, with his mouth open. Just watching us. Maybe I don't get what Chase's sister saw in him after all.

I wish I had a water. The air in the station is dry and stale smelling. The inside of my mouth feels sticky. And a second later it parches completely.

Because Chase tips his chin toward the entrance to the room and says, "Guess everyone's getting arrested tonight."

My focus follows his chin. Straight to Danny, who's sneering at me through a shockingly bloodied face and a nose swollen to at least twice its regular size.

Behind him?

Only slightly less bloodied, is Sawyer.

CHAPTER ELEVEN

QUINN

THIS HAS BEEN the most unsettling day.

To put it lightly.

In fact, I feel like this one day has stretched out for years. And I'm ending it in handcuffs, at a police station...and so is Sawyer.

Chase and Danny and other officers and that one drunk-off-his ass dude are here, too, but they're all in the peripheral, and just barely. Because once Sawyer and I lock eyes, he's the only one I see.

There's a shiner forming on his cheek and a dried trickle of blood extending from the corner of his mouth. I hate how much I long to go to him. Like four years haven't passed. Like he didn't break my heart. Like he still deserves for me to care about him. Because all I want to do right now is stroke his face, wipe away the blood. Comfort him. Ask what the hell happened with Danny. Though that's an easy answer. *Danny* happened.

Sawyer's hair is as chaotic as it ever was, though I notice now, it's a darker blond than it used to be, and there's a hint of it peppering down his jawline. Five o'clock shadow, or whatever time it is right now. The boy I used to know is a man now. His face is more angular. His stance more defensive.

His eyes, however, are as bright green as I've remembered. He uses them to stare back at me, and I wonder what he sees. I used to be able to read his expression as easily as looking in a mirror. Not anymore.

Why did you leave me? Where have you been? It hurts, needing to know these things. The fresh round of curiosity picks off a long-closed scab and I'm bleeding uncontrollably, all over the place.

"These the two little shits causing the scene at the beach fire?" Officer Vincent calls across the room to the cop with Sawyer.

The other cop nods. "Yep. Yours from there, too?"

"Nah. Caught this guy giving it to her *real* good in a car. In public."

Sawyer's impassive expression opens straight into disgust. And, funnily enough, it's exactly like looking in a mirror this time. Because his feelings reflect my own. I want to shoot to my feet and head-butt Officer Vincent and call him the liar that he is, but Chase nudges me with his knee and his words are too fresh in my mind: anything I say here can get us in worse trouble. So I hang my head and study the worn blue carpet, digging my toes back and forth across the threadbare material, hating this stupid situation. Hating this stupid cop. Hating my stupid self for getting us—Chase and me, that is—into this mess.

Who cares what Sawyer thinks? It's none of his business what I was, or in this case *wasn't*, doing with Chase in his car. Nobody. Nobody cares.

Except…

I really fucking care.

I look up to him again, hoping to tell him with my expression that what he's just heard isn't true. But he's no longer watching me. He's walking away, following the cop, following Danny. Not a single backward glance in my direction.

Inside, I fall to pieces.

Chase nudges me again. This time I look at him, at the

concern across his features. "It'll work out," he says.

I don't know if he's talking about us being here at the station, or whatever he saw between Sawyer and me, or something completely different, but I cling to his words.

Officer Vincent sits back across from us, taking casual bites of his sandwich, watching us watching him. His thing with Chase was already personal, but he just made it that way with me, too. And I can't even snark about it. Biting my tongue is not my style, but I don't want to make things harder for Chase.

Or, okay, for me, either. I shift in my chair, my ass uncomfortable against the hard plastic seat.

A second later, another cop storms into the room, barking, "Vincent."

Chase's whispered word comes out almost a sigh. "*Yes.*"

"What?" I whisper back.

He smiles, slyly. "I know him."

"Luis. I thought you were off?" Officer Vincent shoots to his feet, wiping his mouth with the back of his hand and standing a little straighter than I've seen so far. He's nervous, which makes me suddenly hopeful.

The other cop strides toward us, crossing his arms when he gets to Officer Vincent. "That's Carleigh's brother."

"*Busted.*" I can't help it. The word just *sings* through my lips. But I wouldn't take it back even if I could.

Neither cop acknowledges me, but within fifteen minutes, Luis is driving us back to Chase's car.

"Sorry about that," he says when he drops us off. "Officer Vincent is having a bit of a rough time."

"Please," I say. "That was total harassment."

Chase looks at me, shrugging. "It's over now."

I can't believe he's being so complacent about this. "Well, I'm not comfortable with my information being in the system now. Fingerprints and picture—like I'm actually a criminal, even though we weren't doing anything."

Luis—or Officer Santiago, as he introduced himself—shakes his head. "Once it's been processed, which happens automatically, only a court order will remove it. I can get you the names of the best lawyers for it, if you'd like."

Ugh. Lawyers. Parents. Law. Just...ugh. "Well, what about Officer Vincent? He doesn't get to get away with this, does he?"

"It's no big deal," Chase says.

And thank God I'm not into him, because any lady boner I had toward this guy would've been wilting so fast right now. "*Yes*, it is."

Officer Santiago shakes his head again. "You can file a complaint, but then lawyers get involved and...if you really want to go down that road, I can take you through the steps. But it doesn't sound like you do."

No. No lawyers. But it doesn't keep me from fuming. Not when he lets us out of his car and not on the silent ride home with Chase.

Finally, I can't take it anymore. "What is your deal?"

"Nothing." He doesn't meet my gaze, just watches out the windshield.

"Chase. That cop's a complete prick, and you just let him get away with walking all over us. We're in the *system* now—and we're *adults*—this could really mess with our lives. Why don't you want to do something about it?"

"We have information in the system, but we aren't connected to any crime. It won't affect anything."

"How about your pride?"

Now, at least, he flinches. "You might not care about your reputation, but I do. My family does. If we get involved with the law, it makes us look bad. My dad's business depends on how he's received."

I'm stung. Because I don't know if he means my reputation in the community as an upstanding citizen ,or my reputation for...having fun. The kind Danny's so quick to flaunt. "You're in the right, though. That won't make anyone look bad. You should seek action."

"It doesn't work like that."

"Yes, it does."

"Oh, really? And what about your dude? That Sawyer guy?

Are you going to take action against whatever it is he did to you—because it's clear he did *something*. And so far it just seems like you're cowering about it."

Stung twice over. "I'm not even going to dignify that with a response. It's not the same thing at all."

I reach for the dashboard and turn on his sound system in time to catch the end of Gold Rush Standard's most recent hit, "My Apology." Lead singer Luca James's voice thrums through the air, and I try to concentrate on it instead of what Chase said.

> *I shouldn't have left you there.*
> *I should have begged forgiveness.*
> *Sometimes nothing means anything and*
> *I forget how to feel*
> *Until you*
>
> *Twisted secrets.*
> *Covered lies.*
>
> *Somehow I let me ruin everything.*
> *Everything.*
> *Why'd you let me*
> *Let me ruin everything?*
>
> *This is my apology.*
> *My apology.*
> *For it all.*
>
> *Can't believe I let me let me*
> *Ruin it all.*

I usually love this song, but I'm too frustrated to enjoy it at the moment.

Now, on top of everything, I'm thinking of apologies. And how Sawyer owes me a pretty freaking huge one.

And how Chase is maybe kind of sort of just a little bit right.

I've been cowering.

Or cowering-ish, anyway.

And screw that. Sawyer left. This is *my* town. I'm not going to slink around, scared—or, more likely, hoping—to run into him just because he's back.

I'm going to find him. And he's going to give me answers, whether or not he wants to. We're going to have this out.

And then... I'm going to move past it.

Chase pulls into my parents' circular driveway, the white stone gravel crunching under his tires. "Quinn, listen. I don't want to just let it go, okay? But I have to look at the bigger picture. I don't want to make things harder for Carleigh, and anything involving Peter will."

I sigh. "Fine. Use your *being a good brother* card to get off the hook. You win."

"Good. I'll take it any way I can get it." He smiles. "I don't want to part on bad terms. I want to see you again."

"Oh..." I thought we'd covered this base... Crap.

"No, I mean as friends," he clarifies.

"I'd like that, too." My smile comes more easily than I thought it could, given the circumstances of the evening. "Next time I'll even tell you where I really live."

I hug him and tell him to stay where he is when he opens his door to come to mine. He waits until I'm in my Jeep and waves as he drives past.

I grab my phone from my bag to call Gianna before I hit the road. I'm assuming she's okay because she didn't get dragged down to the station with Sawyer and Danny, but I'd still like to hear it for myself. My battery's on its last dredges, though, so I start my car and reach for my car charger, but unsurprisingly I've misplaced it somewhere.

I already have a few missed texts from Gi, which I manage to check before my phone dies completely.

Where are you? Call me back.

And then: *I don't know if I should tell you this or not. But I would want to know if the tables were reversed.*

And then, making my heart beat a little faster: *Just know I will never, ever, ever be Team Sawyer, okay? He sucks.*

And: *But Danny was talking his usual shit about you after you left. And Sawyer broke his face for it.*

And finally: *Ugh. Call me back already! So much to talk about!*

My phone dies as the last of her words reach my eyes.

It takes a moment (a minute? An hour? A year?) for it all to sink it.

Sawyer kicked Danny's ass *for me.*

I…don't know what to make of it.

But then, I do. Partially, at least.

I realize he still cares.

On some level, he still cares enough to defend me.

CHAPTER TWELVE

QUINN

SO HERE'S WHAT went down four years ago.

Picture this...

The boy I've loved without bounds for two years. Sawyer.

The girl he's loved without restraint. Me.

A night in early June, a little chilly in the beach breeze. One week after my seventeenth birthday. A tent on the sand under a clear and starry sky.

The tent is lined with strands of white Christmas lights, though I'm confused at first as to where they're plugged in. Then I realize, they aren't. Knowing Sawyer the way I knew him then—and, believe me, I knew every inch of him, inside and out—he found solar-powered ones, or something like that.

Somehow he's made it appear as though the stars in the sky have netted our tent, twinkling and fragile.

Kicking off my flip-flops, I unzip the flap of the door and shove myself through, a little gangly and a lot eager to throw myself at him. A lot eager for the night we've planned. The one we've waited for.

But the tent's empty of Sawyer.

It smells like him though, all faintly sage and citrus spice, mingling with that familiarly musky beach aroma of sand and salt water. Worried, suddenly, that I'll ruin the perfect bouquet of scents, I steal a sniff under my arms. But the vanilla tones of my deodorant are holding strong.

The side of the tent facing the ocean is unzipped, letting the breeze in through a screened window. The shushing sound of the waves calms me, and for a moment, I'm glad I have a second to myself. I stare out at the water, watching the stars and moon dance and flow in their reflections.

The floor's padded with a thick blanket, soft against the bottoms of my feet and, beneath the tent lining, the sand squishes when I move. In the corner, as my eyes adjust to the weird orangish lighting coming through from the stranded lights above me, I make out a weathered wooden crate flipped upside down to support an old-school radio.

I let my smile soar. He remembered.

Must've been at least a year and a half before, I mentioned how much old technology makes me feel nostalgic, and sweet. Maybe, probably, because my parents' organic foods store was developing into a chain at that point, and they were going nuts with every modern thing they could buy. But I had a soft spot for old beater cars (like Sawyer drove back then...wonder if he still does) and rotary phones and rusty metal electronics... And the radio he's left for us tonight? It even has a crooked old antenna—and, because he knew it'd make me grin, he tied a sloppy bow around it with a big red ribbon.

I swear I've never loved him more. Though I wake up pretty much every day feeling the same way.

He's the punctuation to my sentence. I'm the grammar to his lines. We're made for each other. Perfectly.

I've never been more ready to give him everything, never been more ready to take the exact same thing from him.

I wonder where he is. Most likely, he ran out on a last-minute errand to grab something unnecessary, but thoughtful. I wish he'd finally understand the only thing I'll ever need is him.

I sit cross-legged on the blanket to wait.

I should probably feel nervous, but I don't. We may be virgins, but there's barely a spot on either of our bodies that hasn't been seen by the other, and kissed, and caressed... No, I'm not nervous. I'm *ready*.

I run my tongue over my teeth; it's still a pleasant surprise not to find braces there, even two months later. I feel more mature with my new smile. Less like a kid.

And tonight, I'll let Sawyer make me a woman.

The thought makes me giggle. *A woman?* Is that still how girls refer to themselves after losing it?

Who cares? I just can't wait to do it. Can't wait for Sawyer.

I can barely contain myself, slapping my hands in different rhythms along my thighs, hurrying him in my thoughts. I hope he likes the matching bra and underwear I bought yesterday, preparing. My hair is straight down my back—actually cooperating through the beach humidity for once. My nails are freshly trimmed and pink. I doubt he'll notice, but they make me feel feminine. Pretty.

So does he.

Twenty minutes later, I'm still drumming against my thighs. But now I've grown a little nervous. Where is he?

Did he forget? No. He set up the tent. Of course he didn't forget. He texted me where to meet him as soon as we found out the circuit's location for the night. As soon as we knew where it *wouldn't* be, and this cove is so private that if the bonfire isn't here, we knew we'd have total privacy. *Romantic* privacy, with the waves in the distance and the moon overhead...

Maybe he stopped by the bonfire for a beer first? But...that doesn't jive with the boy I love. He's just as excited for tonight as I am. He'll want to be here with a clear mind.

A gust of wind shakes the tent and a bit of sand flies into my face even though I'm mostly protected by the fabric walls around me. I wipe a few grains from my lips. "Come on, Sawyer. Where are you?"

I grab my phone, call him. It goes to voice mail after two rings. Which...usually means someone's cleared the call instead of answering. But Sawyer wouldn't do that.

I bite my nails.

I force myself to stop biting my nails—don't want to ruin the effect of two painful years with braces. Plus, my manicure. *And* plus, there's nothing to be nervous about. He's out there. He's coming to me.

This is our night.

I crawl over to the radio, twisting knobs and dials and working through static until I find a slightly faded country station.

There. Now I'm calm again. Twangy, honeyed love songs. Couldn't set a more perfect tempo for the rest of the night. Sawyer will be here soon. I just know it. I simper a little, anticipating everything we're about to do.

But another twenty minutes later, I call Gianna. When she answers, I can barely hear her over the din of the bonfire. Music, breaking bottles, laughter. But I make out enough of what she says to understand that Sawyer's not there.

I text him.

Twice.

A third time.

When an hour hits, I push out of the tent for the fourth or fifth time, standing on the sand, stretching my legs and looking toward the beach exit, willing him to walk out through the dunes.

Nervousness turns to fear. Has he been in an accident?

No. He's the safest driver I know, and serious accidents here are rare with speed limits as low as they are. Just in case, though, I call his home line. His father.

It rings and rings and rings.

I try Sawyer's friend Danny, but he's at the bonfire, too. And he's drunk. But he swears he hasn't seen Sawyer.

I call Jess, who *just* got his first cell phone. He was so excited to give me his number. The memory has me smiling. But this call goes straight to voice mail, and the smile slides off of my face. The fear inches back up along my spine, but I do my best to shake it off.

Nothing's wrong.

Everything's fine.

I should just wait. Tomorrow we'll laugh about this, me being so nervous for nothing.

When Sawyer gets here, though, I'm gonna let him have it...before I let him have *it*.

I crawl back into the tent, playing with my phone, but distractedly. Really, I just want my phone right in my hands when he calls me...

I play, and I play, and I play.

See, at that point? My world just didn't make sense without Sawyer. It literally didn't cross my mind that he wouldn't ever show.

Poor, stupid, naive girl.

It took me three hours to leave that night.

Three days to realize he was truly gone.

And three years until I met Julian, and a few of the remaining crumpled pieces of tissue and muscle crawled back together between my ribs to form something resembling at least the outline of a heart.

CHAPTER THIRTEEN

SAWYER

ORDINARILY, JIGSAWING THE form of a surfboard out of a roughly shaped sheet of foam is one of the few things in this world that shuts off my mind. The blank is my canvas, and I'm its shaper. There's something pure, soothing about the process. But today, in this small workroom behind the surf shop where I work, all it's doing is making the pounding under the bruise on my cheek harder. I carefully edge out the pointed shape of the shortboard's nose and lift the saw, letting the excess foam fall away and placing the tool on a table against the wall.

I plane the underside, and then the top, only enough to graze the softer white foam beneath the surface. Next, I'll shape the curve of the rails, but damn, I need a break first. A Pepsi and some fucking Advil. It's not just my cheek throbbing. My head, too. And my knuckles. Danny's teeth really did a number on them last night, and I've been working them hard all morning. Trying to erase everything about last night. Uselessly.

I peel the mask off my mouth and nose, letting it hang around my neck, unzip and step out of my dust coveralls, and then push through the door into the surf shop.

It's brighter in here, and my headache has me squinting for a second. Rajesh is behind the counter with a customer.

Actually, not with a customer. Not based on the tilt of his head, the flirtatious smile, the way he reaches out to stroke the guy's shoulder.

Rajesh and his dudes. I bite back a smile, clearing my throat. They both glance over to me, but Rajesh doesn't remove his hand. Guy's got no sense of propriety.

Probably one of the reasons we get along so well.

"Your face," the other guy says. "What happened to you?"

I ignore him, addressing Raj. "Inventory done?"

"Yes." He sighs like he's hurt I'm even asking. "That guy Wyatt called about his fish hybrid," he adds, drolly, "again."

"Tell him his board'll be finished tonight," I say. "The resin's curing for the next couple hours. I just have to drill the hole for the leash, set it, and then re-gloss the board. He'll still have to wait three days to pick it up. As I've already explained. Twice."

"Why do you have to wait that long?" Rajesh's guy asks. I head toward the refrigerator at the side of the counter to swipe a Pepsi, leaving Rajesh to explain about resin and setting times. The guy whispers, "Is he *always* this cranky?"

I know what Raj will say before he says it. "Yep."

I duck under the counter, rooting around for the spare bottle of Advil that's around here somewhere. While I'm digging through the way-too-many piles of random crap on the floor—Rajesh needs to clean this place up—the bell over the shop's front door jangles. Next to me, Raj shoves a hand on my shoulder to keep me in place. "Heartbreaker. Incoming."

A small part of me thinks maybe he's warning me that some gorgeous girl's just entered the store and that I need to get my game face on. Somehow, a much larger part of me knows it's that and so much more. Maybe I've been expecting it. Hoping.

My knees crack when I rise, and there she is. Quinn. Standing in the doorway, glancing around the shop, her hair pulled back in a ponytail that swings opposite the direction of her face. I follow her gaze, trying to see it the way she might. Surfboards on the walls. Swimwear. Shades. Flops. Apparel. Nothing out of the ordinary, though I'm suddenly wishing there was something to make the place spectacular.

Well, actually, there is. And she's standing in the doorway. And she's making my chest tighten like a screw twisted so hard the head strips.

"Quinn." I say her name and her eyes zero in on me.

Rajesh leans across the counter toward his guy, lowering his voice. "Let me show you the snorkeling equipment we just got in. It's in the back."

"It's cool. Stay." I put a hand on his arm, stopping him. Quinn still hasn't moved. Neither of us has looked away yet. Like it's a game, a dare, a promise. "We'll go in the workroom."

She quirks an eyebrow, as if to say, *oh, really?*

I nod toward the door at the side of the shop. *Oh, really.*

She moves first, which irks me for some reason. Like I couldn't find the balls enough to take a step before she did. So I beat her to the door. As if that levels anything. It's like I'm eighteen again, stupid and brutish.

In love.

But that's nothing new, doesn't matter if I'm eighteen or a hundred.

I open the door, holding it for her, trying not to inhale as she walks through, failing. Sweet like honey and salty like the ocean. Same scents. Same Quinn.

I shake my head. Not the same Quinn. I can't afford to think like this.

One more glance back at the shop to make sure Rajesh has it covered. *Okay?* he mouths. I don't answer. I step over the threshold and close the door.

Quinn turns to face me, standing in the middle of the space, between the shaping rack and glassing stand. She's crisp, clean. Beautiful. Out of place against the dusty blue walls and sandy floors, the old broken equipment... She's a stained-glass sculpture, somehow both delicate and strong, standing in a field of ashes.

I don't want to shatter her.

But at the same time, I want to yank her ponytail down, let that long chestnut hair cascade around her shoulders. Peel that dress off her body.

Take what she offered all those years ago.

Take what I've missed all this time.

"Your face is totally fucked up." Her voice finds a way to come out sweet and bitchy all at once.

I shrug against both tones. "How'd you find me?"

"It was hard," she admits. "You don't exist online anywhere, which, let me tell you, is really annoying."

I couldn't risk her finding me these past years. Couldn't risk what it'd do. To both of us. "And?"

"And I searched all your old favorite spots around town." She doesn't say "our" favorite spots and it digs into my gut, like she's cut herself from the memories. Because every one of my favorite spots around here became that way with Quinn by my side. "Then," she continues, "I really thought about it. I figured you'd need a job, and we both know you don't handle waiting tables well."

She hasn't forgotten everything then.

"This is the third surf shop I've tried," she continues. "I knew I'd get to you eventually."

"Guess you figured me out." I take a step down toward her and remember the mask and goggles hanging around my neck. I pull them off, tossing them on a small stand beside the stairs.

"Not even close."

"You still prefer dresses?" Another step. One left until we're on the same level.

Not that we've ever been on the same level.

"I guess." She glances down, pulling at the thin purple fabric that rests so enviably against her frame. When she looks up again, there's nothing fragile about her expression. "In case you're wondering, I came for an explanation."

"What do you have to explain?" I ask, ignoring what she really means. "What you did with that guy last night is none of my business." I've been doing everything I can not to think about it. Because thinking about it, thinking about the girl Quinn is compared to the girl I used to know—and how I haven't been here for any of it—makes me want to punch the wall, break something. I shove my hands in my pockets.

"Don't be an ass." She doesn't hesitate to put me in my place. "I want to know where you went, Sawyer. I want to know why you went. I want to know how you managed to pretend you had a heart for so long before you broke mine like it was nothing."

Maybe I'm made of glass too—though I lack that fragile prettiness she so easily captures—because her words are strong enough to grind me into dust.

There are so many things I could say right now, the most important that her heart's been my everything from the day I first met her, but I shake my head. Because she's not going to get to hear any of them.

CHAPTER FOURTEEN

QUINN

I SAID IT. Exactly like I practiced. I didn't stutter. I didn't stumble.

I'm rather proud of myself.

Then he steals my moment, and my breath, simply saying, "No."

It...doesn't compute at first. "What?"

"No." He takes the last step down to the floor, though even now I have to look up at him. He must've grown at least two inches in the past few years.

Not that I'm noticing. And I definitely don't have the urge to go to him, to lightly run my fingers over the bruise on his cheek. To...do other things involving touch.

Fuck. Okay. Deep breath.

The room smells sharp, like resin and sawdust, and a little toxic. But Sawyer took off his mask, so it's safe; the scents must be residual.

"What do you mean, no?" I wish the shock of seeing him would wear off already. But it hasn't. Not even a little. I recognized the top of his head the moment he started to stand from behind the counter. But I chickened out and looked away. Now we're standing here in this dusty, narrow, mostly empty room, and there's nowhere else to look. "Sawyer?"

He doesn't repeat himself, just stands there with his hands in his pockets, his face impassive.

There was always a stillness in Sawyer, and I'm discovering he never lost it.

But if he thinks he can stand there all calm and nonchalant and I'll give up all easily, he's truly forgotten the girl he once knew.

"Who's the guy behind the counter?" I ask, angling my head toward the door behind him, redirecting the conversation for a second, needing to get my bearings. "I haven't seen him before."

"Rajesh."

"Rajesh," I try the name out, liking it immediately. I love the way it shapes in my mouth, the way it sounds.

"He's gay."

I laugh. "So? I can't like his name?"

"Just so you know he won't go for you."

"Jealous?" I want him to say yes. I want to make him jealous. Even after all these years. I want to affect him the way he affects me. Even though he shouldn't. He shouldn't affect me at all.

"Just trying to keep you informed."

"Funny. I didn't think that was something you cared about."

The gauntlet's thrown.

And his face is back to impassive.

"Sawyer. Come on. I want closure. I want to move on."

"From what I hear, you've had no trouble in that department."

"Fuck you." The words slip out quietly, tight with the pain his own words sliced into me, cutting right though the thrill of wondering if he was jealous, wondering if I still affected him. "You don't get to judge me."

"I'm not judging you, Quinn. Jesus. I know I don't have that right." He runs a hand through his hair, making a thin layer of sawdust rise in the air. "But don't come in here on some moral high ground like I owe you *so much* when you've been having a fine time without me." Something in his expression flickers. Hurt? Anger? I can't read him anymore and I hate it.

I also want to take a bite out of the angle of his strong, strong jaw. I hate that almost as much. My body's betraying me, making my anger—my *years* of anger—seem less and less significant.

"Those two things aren't as connected as you seem to think," I say, letting my face shape itself in an anger anyone could decipher. "I'm allowed to be both devastated by you and out doing my best to forget you." Just like, I hope, I'm allowed to be both hurt and extremely turned on.

"Sounds like they're pretty connected to me." He scratches the corner of his mouth with his pointer finger—finally, it's a tell I recognize. He's wrestling with some internal struggle here, too.

"So either they're connected, which gives me leeway to come in here on some moral ground, or they're disconnected and I'm just a slut who once had her heart broken by you. Whichever way you look at it, you owe me an explanation."

"I'm not going to give you one," he says. "I'm sorry."

I recognize this look in his eyes, too, the solid wall of determination. But I also recognize the smaller signs he's trying not to give. The re-tucking of his hands in his pockets, so forced casual. The heaviness in the way he swallows. He is still affected by me in some way. And...maybe it's a physical thing. We've never been lacking there. Which means I have one trick up my sleeve. I just have to figure out if it's worth the risk...

"Why?"

He shakes his head, not giving me anything to go on.

"I don't understand," I say. "What does it matter to you now? Nothing. You never came back; you never even called. You made it clear it didn't matter to you. But it does to me. Can you just find a small part of yourself that wants to give me something?"

"There are plenty of things I want to give you." His voice is low, threatening in the most deliciously nonthreatening way, and his eyes widen like he didn't mean to say what he did.

If I touch him…

If I let him touch me…

Maybe I'll get my answer.

Maybe I'll tumble down the Sawyer rabbit hole all over again—and maybe I'll relive that pain of the crash landing.

Maybe it'd be worth it.

All these *ifs*. All these *maybes*.

I need something more concrete.

One way or another, I'm not leaving here without getting something I want.

Answers—or a bite of that golden skin.

Or, if I'm lucky, both. And yes, okay, call it a weakness, call it *whatever*, but getting to have my mouth on him just one more time? I'm suddenly desperate for the chance.

I let my gaze drift down his face, over his chin; it lingers on the smooth skin between his jaw and his neck. Even after four years, I know just what he'd taste like if I put my mouth there, if I ran my tongue along the slope.

Heat simmers in my belly, trickling a little lower.

I meet his eyes again, swallowing a sudden excess of saliva. I have to be careful here, need to take my time. Misdirection's worked in the past, though he was eighteen the last time I managed it successfully. "You work here? This place is pretty cool."

He studies me, but I don't think he's got his finger on what I'm doing. Soon, he'll have his fingers elsewhere if I get my way. "Just a standard surf shop."

Like anything could ever be just standard when he's around.

I glance up. There's a blue tarp hanging from the ceiling. "What's that for?"

"Blues out the room. Like the walls. Helps to keep a sharp contrast for the whites of the boards when they're shaped."

"And this?" I flick my toes against a bucket at the base of a wooden stand that extends like a balance beam with padded rods rising at each end. There's an identical bucket attached to the base of the second leg.

"A bucket with cement."

"I can *see* that," I say, dryly. "What's the whole contraption for?"

"It's a shaping stand. The cemented buckets keep it from wobbling."

"So it's pretty sturdy?"

"Yeah." He's still studying me, still trying to figure out the switch in conversation.

I still need to figure out how to get it where I want it. "I should probably know these things."

"Why?"

"Um, because I surf."

He laughs. "Barely."

As though he has any freaking clue about me anymore.

"Sawyer, Sawyer." I keep my tone light, wagging my finger. "I'm not the same little girl you used to know. I've learned a lot about riding..." I pause, watching the effect my words have. Loving the new kind of stillness that falls over him. "...the ocean."

His Adam's apple slides up and down his throat when he swallows. I've thrown another gauntlet—and this one's going to work.

Enjoying the intensity of his gaze on me, I turn and walk to the back of the room, not that far, trailing my finger and leaving a line in the dust along a worktable. I touch one of the white foam boards leaning against the wall. This I actually recognize. It's called a blank, I believe. A canvas that will be shaped into a longboard, and it stands at least two feet taller than I am. Sturdy enough—maybe—to hold the weight of two bodies. Even if one of them is rather tall and Sawyer-shaped. "What's this?"

"It'll be a longboard. Until I shape it, it's a blank."

"And this goes on the shaping stand?" As if I don't know. As if any idiot wouldn't be able to figure it out.

"Yeah." His tone says *no shit, Sherlock*, but his gaze is appraising.

My next breath finds the air crisper, somehow. Blooming with tension and a little sweet, too. "Show me."

"Why?"

"God, Sawyer. I just want to see, okay? Give me *something* here." There's a silent battle of wills, and neither of us looks away. But the moment passes, and I win. Biting back a triumphant smirk, I step aside to let him lift the blank. His arm grazes mine.

He lays the board gently—in a way that makes me yearn to be handled the same exact way—across the stand. When he steps back, I press against it with my hands. Sturdy. "Could I hop up here?"

"No."

I smile at him. And then I push myself up, careful in my balance, flipping to sit on it. "Whoops."

"Get down. You're going to ruin it." He sounds exasperated. And unsure. And like he's starting to get it.

"Maybe you should help me with that." I shift back, making sure the board wiggles a little and gasping like I might fall. But I go too far and the entire thing starts to slide backward. Panic thrills through my stomach, right before he smacks his hands down on either side of me, catching the blank before it tips me backward. Steadying me while unsteadying me at the exact same time.

The thrill in my belly accelerates rather than melting away now that I'm safe from falling. It slides a little lower, too, and I realize maybe I'm not as safe from falling as I think.

He's careful to keep his hands far from my legs, while not so far that his face is forced to come too close to mine.

But really, he's just giving me the perfect amount of space to spread my thighs in front of him. My knees press into his T-shirt, skimming his stomach along the way, and when his abs jolt at the contact, I let a small laugh slip out. I sound bold.

What I am is skittish.

Energized.

Starting to *long*.

Yeah. Being this close to Sawyer is the opposite of safe.

"What are you doing?" His voice is rougher than a moment ago, and I'm pretty sure it's not from the exertion of balancing the board.

"Have you really forgotten my moves, or are you feigning ignorance?"

"Neither." A moment spreads between us... There's hesitation in his eyes.

Then there isn't.

He slides his hands toward me, slowly, along the edge of the board, until his thumbs graze my knees. I close my eyes for a moment to fully enjoy the shocks of pleasure from the contact, and when his calloused palms run up my thighs, his skin scratches my own in the most arousing way.

"This?" he asks, his green eyes dropping to my mouth, lingering, lingering before dragging back up to meet my gaze. "This is what you want?"

I nod, not sure if I can trust my voice to come out without shaking. Because it's all I've ever wanted.

His hands on me. His breath brushing my face. His heart beating so close to mine.

Oh, fuck it. I'm going for this even if he doesn't tell me what I want to know.

I came here armed with nothing but false bravado and empty words. They aren't enough to keep me from falling back down the Sawyer rabbit hole. Spiraling, spiraling, spiraling into needing him.

But...needing him isn't the same as forgiving him, and maybe as long as I hold on to that knowledge, it's okay to give in to how I want him.

Because right now? I want him so badly my body's aching in a way that almost *hurts*.

I shift my hips, slightly, side to side—just enough to have the pads of his fingers digging a little tighter into my skin, just enough to make him swallow again. "Yes," I say. "This. Exactly this."

"What are you *doing*, Quinn?" he repeats, but the answer's in the air between us already, more solid than even the board I'm sitting on.

"What *aren't* you doing, Sawyer?" I reach down between us,

feeling him—already hard, there's the boy I've always loved. Or, the boy I *used* to love, I mean. Ready in an instant. Just as I remember. I wrap my fingers around him the best I can over his pants.

Suddenly, his hands are at my waist and he's pulling me off the board.

But he deposits me on my feet on the floor and he turns away, and my insides start to sink, low. Too quickly, too precariously low. I'm in some real danger here, emotion-wise. He shouldn't still have this much effect on my heart. My body? Maybe. My muscles, my nerves, my *everything* still remember the techniques he used to train them into feeling the best life has to offer.

And they all begin to *sing* when he jerks the worktable away from the wall and shoves things off of it with one sweep of his arm. Papers and clunky tools go flying, crashing, tumbling to the floor.

"So rough," I say, going for droll and ending up with quivery words. "The board could've worked just fine."

He turns back to me, holding out his hand, his voice going coarse. "I don't have your catlike balance, honey. If we're doing this, I want something steadier beneath us. I don't want to have to focus on the force of gravity."

"What do you want to focus on?" But I think I know his answer. And I think it's making me a little weak. And a lot turned on. And a lot...just...*everything*.

His answer's so serious, it's like he's never spoken such truth in one word.

"You."

CHAPTER FIFTEEN

SAWYER

I'VE BEEN READY for this moment for *years*.

I shouldn't be playing along, like everything's fine. Like it's only a physical thing between us. But that's how Quinn's rolling with it, and there's not a person alive who could stop me from following her lead right now.

"This isn't going to be comfortable," I say. The table I've cleared is dusty. Rough. She deserves more than this. She deserves everything I'd planned four years ago, and more. But there's not much else in the room with us—and I'm sure as shit not about to leave for someplace else and break the moment. Even if I should.

"You've made it clear I can't have the comfort I want from you." Her words have bite and they grip their sharp little teeth at the center of my chest, yanking. The sting lessens when she says, "I want something else at the moment, and trust me, Sawyer, if you make it *comfortable*, I'll be disappointed."

I need to hear her say it. "What are you looking for at the moment?"

"You." She throws the word back at me, and I wonder if my expression goes as drunk as hers did when I said it.

I study the table because I can't look at her face, not when I'm pretty sure there are zero guards up across mine. Let her see too much and I'll spook her. Or intrigue her. I don't want the first, won't allow the second.

I also can't put her on this disgusting table. I can't stand the thought of her perfect skin covered in the muck of the workshop. But I can't fathom the thought of not taking what she's offering.

I'm hard as a fucking baseball bat, but this is more than that. Years ago, I found the strength to walk away from her. It feels impossible to do again. Even just to grab something to make her more comfortable…

"Give me a second." My words come out too gruff, giving away more of what I'm feeling than I'd like, and I turn toward the store so she can't see any more of it on my face.

"Where are you going?" Her voice is husky and confused and it takes everything I have not to turn around and slam her on to the table to satisfy the want I hear mixed with everything else.

"Give me a second," I repeat.

Walking with a boner is difficult and kind of painful. But walking into the store with a boner is going to be worse. Fuck.

Quinn's stare drives heat into the back of my neck as I take the steps toward the door. I clear my throat and adjust myself at the same time, hoping she won't catch it, but she giggles and that heat jumps up to my ears. At least my work pants are a looser fit than jeans. Still kind of wish I had on boxers. Because even letting my dick go upright, no longer against the grain, so to speak, boner against material is an uncomfortable sort of tickle at best.

I pull the door open, quiet as I can, but Rajesh must be watching it like a hawk because he sees me immediately. But eye contact's good. When the door shuts behind me, he says, "Haven't heard anything breaking or crashing, so I guess you're still alive."

"Guess I am." I take the three steps necessary to a stack of the beach towels we sell, grabbing a couple. The shop's still empty other than Raj and...I should probably ask this guy's name, but, yeah. Not at this exact moment.

"That's all you're going to tell me?" Rajesh cocks his head to the side, disappointed.

I don't care. "Yep."

I turn back toward the workshop, thinking I've made it without notice. But before the door shuts behind me, Raj's guy whispers something about a pitched tent.

We don't sell camping equipment.

My brief flash of embarrassed irritation falls away, though, when I find Quinn waiting for me, one eyebrow raised in the sexiest little expression. "Thought you might be ditching me in here," she says.

"I was gone like five seconds."

"Felt like eons." She doesn't say anything about the last time I left her, but it's sitting heavy in the air between us anyway.

I hold the towels out. "Just wanted to grab these."

"Why?" She leans back against the table, all forced casual.

"For the table." I clear my throat. Shit. Everything's stilted all of a sudden.

"Wow." Now she looks puzzled.

"What?" I close half the distance between us. Even with the different tension between us now, I want her more than I've ever wanted anything.

"It's...thoughtful," she says, also thoughtfully.

It kills me that she seems surprised I'd think of her. It kills me that she doesn't remember the way my every thought was always for her. Or maybe she's rewritten her memories. I can't blame her for it if she has.

We really shouldn't be doing this. I really should walk away. But the way she's looking at me? Batting those long lashes and licking her lips with little darts of her tongue... It's a wonder I have room left for a single thought in my brain.

Plus, she could be walking away, too, and she isn't. So screw it. I know I'm being selfish. I won't give her the answers she wants, but I'm taking what she's offering anyway.

I walk past her and spread the towels on the table. "Thought a little padding might make it more…comfortable. Don't worry, though, honey. Nothing else will be."

And the words work a little magic, because the rush of heat thrashes back between us. I can tell before I even turn around to find her smiling. She traces a finger along my jaw. "Good."

I almost fucking detonate. Instead, I slide my hands around her waist and lift her, spinning us and shoving her onto the table. Her eyes widen when her ass hits, like the roughness surprises her. Turns her on. I grip her jaw, this time not rough but not too gentle, either. "Good."

Her pupils go wide and there's nothing like it, seeing the way she wants me. Now.

Her dress is hiked up her thighs and I run my hands down them. Her legs are soft and smooth and there's a crescent-shaped scar on her knee that I remember back from when it was still stitched up. Skateboarding lesson gone wrong. Damn did she cuss me out for that one. Enough to scare the shit out of me back then—or, more likely, it was the sight of her in pain that scared me so bad… Now, though, she's adorable in the memory.

But here in front of me? Adorable no longer fits.

She's red-hot sexy.

Quinn.

My Quinn.

My Quinn for the moment, at least. For the here and now.

She licks her lips one more time, and I take her face in my hands and I pull her toward me and I kiss her.

I mean to do it briefly and lightly, to ease us back into the ways our mouths used to know each other, but there's nothing brief about this. Nothing light. It's instant intoxication.

She parts her lips to me and my tongue circles hers and in all the years I've tried to remember the way Quinn's mouth tastes, nothing's ever come close to reality. Sweet and fresh. Warm and soft.

She reaches between us and jerks my pants unbuttoned, smiling against my mouth when she discovers it's all me down there beneath them. She pulls her mouth from mine, her eyes appraising. "Hello, old friend."

"He's rather happy to see you," I manage. Jesus, how does she do this to me so easily? My hands are steady, one wrapped through her hair, the other on the table. But inside I'm fucking shaking, like I need her so much I'll tremble into nothing if she ever stops touching me.

But when she does, it's to drag her hand back up between our bodies and lick her palm, base to fingertips, slowly—twice, without her gaze ever leaving mine—like there's all the time in the world even if everything inside of me is zinging in anticipation. And when she wraps it around me again, every ounce of blood in my body zooms straight for where her hand is.

I pull her face closer to mine, to kiss her again, but she puts a finger against my lips, holding it there between us. "I want to watch your face, Sawyer."

I nip at her finger. "I want to eat your mouth, Quinn. I don't know if I can stand this."

She just sitting there, looking up at me, biting her lower lip...working her hand.

She twists her wrist and she circles her fingers around me, climbing them higher until she's there at my tip, using the heat from her palm to swirl over me, switching directions every time I'm just about to remember to breathe. I jerk in her hand, twitching, twitching, and almost let go altogether.

Think about fucking sports, man. Jesus. Haven't had her hands on me in almost four years. Can't come in the first minute.

Oh God, sports thoughts aren't gonna do jack shit.

I grab her wrist, stilling her hand. "Let's not rush this."

She quirks half a smile, her eyes glinting. "Don't remember you being so quick to...hit that peak."

"It's a slow build, baby. We're just getting started."

Her breath catches, and the sound is the best thing I've heard all day. Week. Year.

"It's my turn," I say, "to refamiliarize myself with a few of my favorite parts of yours." Even if the ones I always loved the most are off-limits. Her heart. Her mind... But I push the last thought away. Today is about the physical, and Jesus does this girl rock that part like a goddess.

I fiddle with the edge of her dress, pushing it higher up her leg. "What's under this?"

"More than what *you've* got on," she says. "Why don't you find out?"

I don't need a second invitation. I shove her dress around her waist and take in the panties I'd *almost* think she wore on purpose to drive me nuts. They're tiny and white and lacy, and I bet I could tear them off in one yank.

"You don't need these." I slide them over her thighs, down her knees, and let them fall to the floor. I push between her legs, keeping those knees nice and wide, and kick her panties behind me. I realize a second too late that she might've wanted to wear them again, after, but now they'll be too dirty. I glance back at them, a tiny bundle on the grimy floor. I almost apologize, but then the thought hits me that she'll have to walk out of here panty-less. As if I wasn't hard enough already, I fucking *swell* at the thought.

And turning my attention full back to her, back to where she sits spread before me, nearly kills me. "Jesus, Quinn."

She's beautiful. Every single part of her.

Sitting there with her legs sprawled out...

I want to let go, to lose control, to shove her back against the table and give her exactly what she's telling me she wants.

I want to bury my face in her. Make her scream my name. Wrap her legs around the back of my head and use every part of my face to spread her, tease her, torture her, fucking devour her.

But first I stand before her, sliding my hands along her thighs, pushing them further apart, letting the air sweep across her most exposed, sensitive spots.

"Sawyer." My name's little more than a sigh through her lips. "*Touch me.* Jesus."

"Still bossy as ever." I push my hands higher, slipping my thumbs along her inner thighs and into the creases between her legs. She's so unbelievably sexy. Lean, toned, tan legs. I don't doubt she's been surfing these past years.

"Still like to take your sweet fucking time." She runs her tongue along her teeth and I want to kiss her, to suck it into my mouth with my own. I refrain. For now. Because there are other things I want to do with my tongue, too.

"Still make you fucking wet, though, don't I?" I gently swipe a thumb across her and feel the truth of my words; she's soaking wet already and we haven't even gotten to the good part. I want to make her wait, torture her just a little longer, but I can't help myself.

I use my thumb again, slowly slipping it over her, feathering it through her, parting her and then, finally, gently, circling into her. Quinn's stomach jumps with her intake of breath, and I draw my gaze up her body. She's leaning back on her hands, her smooth belly taut under the fabric of her dress with the way her back arches. I slide one strap down off of her shoulder. Then the other, pulling at it until her breasts are free. No bra, and I want to fucking cry from the injustice of her ever having to cover these things up. Small and full, creamy skin. Her nipples are pink-tipped and tightened. Perfect as they've always been. Too tempting to resist, especially because I remember just how sensitive they are to even the lightest touch. I lose another fraction of restraint and take one in my mouth, slipping a finger into her at the same time.

"*Oh, God.*" Her two words are a goddamn melody and she tastes like cotton candy-dipped apples and for the life of me I can't remember why I never order dessert. I never want to take my mouth from her skin. I take her nipple between my teeth and tug, gently, hungrily. When she pulses against my hand, around my finger, my entire system sparks.

Taking my time, keeping control? Yeah, that shit's not gonna happen for long. I'm pretty sure I could jumpstart a damn car battery the way I'm jolting. The only thing I want to jumpstart right now is Quinn, and she doesn't even need my help. She's purring like a kitten in soft little sighs, arching harder into my mouth when she tips her head back.

Another finger. Jesus she's warm. Getting wetter by the second. I want to crawl into her, lap her up from the inside out.

I take as long as I can, using my tongue to tease her nipples, my free hand to stroke her legs, her knees, her calves. I work my mouth down the sweet skin of her chest, nibbling with my teeth along the way so she doesn't get too…comfortable. I mean to peel her dress the rest of the way down her body, but once I'm there I can't be bothered to take the time.

I drop to my knees in front of her; they hit the concrete hard enough to scrape through my pants, but I barely feel it. Her head snaps up, and she looks down, meeting my gaze and gnawing on her lip. She starts to close her legs, but I slide my fingers out of her and push her thighs wider apart, my face raised to hold her stare the entire time.

"Sawyer." Her cheeks flush and for a moment we're teenagers again. She's nervous. Uncertain. But she's breathing fast, too, and I know how turned on she is.

"I've seen your body before, Quinn. Now's no time to be shy, honey."

She bites her lip harder, completely unaware of how fucking hot it is. Or, maybe she knows exactly. Makes no difference to me. She just is.

Then I drop my eyes, and my heart rate goes from sixty to infinity. "Not in a million years have I even come close to remembering how goddamn exquisite you are."

Every soft pink curve. Every delicate line.

I turn my face and gently sink my teeth into the skin of her inner thigh, needing to make her nerves jolt the same way mine are and when she whimpers, I know I've succeeded.

I swear to God I planned to take this slow. I swear to God I meant to lick my way up the insides of her legs, tease her with my tongue until she begged. To breathe on her, hot and cool, until her toes curled. To give her a break, let her catch her breath between courses.

But these techniques are the ones we perfected together; they're comfortable; they're what she'll expect. She deserves the unexpected. The thrill.

Plus I can't fucking wait that long.

So I don't give her a chance to breathe. I pull her knees, yanking her toward me, gripping her hips. I take just a few seconds to nuzzle her, to revel in the moment, in her scent, and then desperate for a taste, I thrust my tongue straight into her.

CHAPTER SIXTEEN

QUINN

HOLY FUCK.

I have no idea how Sawyer knew I wasn't in the mood for some slow buildup, but damn did he ever read me.

He's using his fingers and his tongue and even his freaking nose to drive me wild, pushing against me, in me, through me. Air shoots up from my lungs, tunneling through my mouth and out my lips. My fingers grip the towels behind me, twisting through the fabric. *His* fingers are nimble and gentle, teasing me, spreading me so that his tongue has further reach, flicking back and forth... and I've never been this close to coming so quickly.

Oh sweet Jesus.

He's making these circling motions with his tongue that have me shifting my hips, pushing up against his mouth.

"Sawyer. Slow down."

I'm not even sure he hears me. I'm not even sure I actually say the words.

"*Sawyer.*" I twine my fingers through his hair and still he doesn't stop. He does lift his eyes, though, bright green straight up at me. I am transfixed. I am soaring. I can't look away.

He lays his tongue flat against me for a moment—breathing

through his nose and the air hits me, tickling in an almost painful and also yummy way—and then he's just lapping, lapping, *lapping* my skin in long, slow licks. And everything inside me, everything between my legs is about to erupt into something intense and velvety and *hot*.

The room is so quiet, so sharply quiet, the sounds of my breaths, little exhales growing bigger and faster, fill the air like an off-beat song. I couldn't stop it even if I tried.

He grazes me with his teeth and maps me with his fingers and curls his tongue along my skin and into me.

And I lose it. Sensations spark, spark, explode inside of me. My blood is rushing electric through me. Wild. Heat sizzles down my belly, exploding between my legs. My muscles clench and I come undone against his mouth. Bucking through the hardest orgasm I've maybe ever had. Saying-screaming-moaning-whispering-thinking his name as I come.

And I come.

And I come.

Until my blood trembles in my veins.

Until I nearly slide like jelly down the table.

My body is a traitor.

A wonderful, completely satisfied traitor.

I slip the straps of my dress back up my shoulders. And somehow Sawyer's suddenly standing in front of me, saying something. His mouth is moving, but time must be slowing down between his mouth and my ears because all I hear right now are the echoes of my own gasps.

"What?" I ask, eventually, when he's staring down at me with an amused smirk across his annoyingly perfect mouth.

"Are you going to tell me what you're thinking? Because I'd sure like to hear whatever thoughts are making you look the way you do. Like you're ready to eat me alive."

A little embarrassed and somehow already aroused again, I shrug. "Not thinking anything."

Then I wish I'd admitted at least a little to him. About how fucking pleased I am. About how I don't think I'll be able to stand for another few minutes. Nothing emotional. Just physical. Because now that I've had this once, his hands on me, his tongue in me... I want it again. And soon.

Screw emotional anything.

Just for now. Just for...a week. I'll give myself a week to enjoy this.

Why, *oh why* did I purposefully take the condoms out of my bag before coming here? Oh. Wait. To keep myself from doing exactly this.

But screw that decision, too.

"Get a condom." My request has his face tensing, then slacking—and then tensing again. I could laugh if I had room for it in my state. I lift a brow as suggestively as I can. "You pulled this table out like a man with a plan."

"I don't have one." He clears his throat. "A condom, I mean."

"*Please.*" I don't believe him. Sawyer's basically a walking piece of sex on a stick. No way he doesn't stay prepared. But...one quick glance downward shows me he's more than ready to roll. He's not playing hard to get. He's too *hard* for that. Jesus. Now I'm revving even harder than I was a second ago, thinking about *that* in *me*. "I bet Rajesh has one. And also...why the hell is your shirt still on?"

"Do you want me to go ask for a condom or do you want me to take my shirt off? I'm not walking in there without one."

"First one then the other, Einstein." I roll my eyes, but really it's toward myself because, yeah. I just want to see his damn chest. The abs that felt so tight against my knees earlier. The skin I know is browned from the sun. I wonder if he tastes as good as he did years ago. And now I'm making myself uncomfortable at the thought. I cross my thighs, leaning back on my hands...trying not to enjoy the tight sensation between my legs too much. "So go," I tip my chin toward the door behind him, "get a rubber."

He stares at me a moment longer, and I think he's struggling with something, though what I'm not sure. Only when he heads back into the shop do I realize...we're about to finish what we started four years ago.

But this time, we're not virgins anymore.

We know what we're doing.

Still, for the briefest moment I think maybe I should pull back. He walked away from me without a backward glance. He doesn't deserve what I'm offering.

Plus, I came here for answers, and he won't give them to me. Deep down, I remember these things.

It's just that I'm all *achy* between my legs. *Needing.*

It's just that my skin is still zinging from his touch, greedy for more.

If I walk away now to punish him, I think... I'll be punishing myself, too. Which, okay, is probably the most ridiculous logic ever, but I'm clinging to it like a lifeline. So I'm giving in to what I want. Here, in this dusty blue, resin-scented, surfboard-building room. I want Sawyer as much as I ever did. And I'm finally going to have him.

Except he comes back empty-handed, shrugging and not quite meeting my eyes. "Rajesh is fresh out."

"Well that's damn inconvenient."

"Feeling frustrated?" His mouth quirks. "You didn't seem so a moment ago..."

I blink at him, all innocence. "But Sawyer... A moment ago I was having a rather intense orgasm. How can a girl not want for more after that?"

"Lucky for you then, honey, my tongue's not even close to tired."

"Is that so?"

And he shows me exactly how true his words are until my toes are curled and I can't breathe and I'm not sure how I'll ever walk again because my bones have all melted into honey.

CHAPTER SEVENTEEN

QUINN

"TAKE OFF YOUR shirt," I demand at some point, later, when I've come back a little closer to earth. "I can't believe you're making me ask twice."

"You're not exactly asking," he says, a cocky little smile across his mouth. "But if you insist."

"I do." My hands ache to slide his shirt up his chest and over his head, but I tuck them under my legs because something about that feels...too personal.

I mean, not that we haven't spent the last who knows how long getting very personal. Maybe intimate is a better word. There's something intimate about helping him with his shirt, sober, in the daylight. More intimate than I want. So I watch, instead, as he peels it off. And I do my best not to drool because his body's everything I'd imagined. And more.

Skin tanned to a golden hue—which makes me wonder how long he's been back here, at the beach. Unless he came from someplace else that was sunny and warm. But I'm not about to get distracted wondering about all that. Not with what I have in front of me. Perfection in a stomach. Perfection in a chest. Shoulders. Arms. *Everywhere*. He's cut, but not bulky. Lithe and muscled. Pecs just full enough that I want to lick them.

So I do.

I hop off of the table where I've been perched—relieved not to simply sink into a well-sated puddle onto the floor—and I put my mouth to his skin. His nipples are small, brown. They harden under the flicker of my tongue, and I smile against his chest. My hands work a little lower.

A tug of his zipper and his pants slide to the ground, pooling around his ankles. His fingers are pressing into my back, weaving circles across the skin of my shoulders and his breathing's already heavier, like he knows what's coming. He remembers the way I learned his body the same time he learned mine. I know what makes him tick. And he knows I know.

After one slow lick across his chest, I pull back to ask, "Is it safe?"

His brow furrows. "Is what safe?"

"I want to touch you with my mouth, Sawyer." I love the way he swallows at my words. The desire in the quick flare of his nostrils. The way his hands pull at the skin of my back with more force than a moment ago. "I want to wrap my lips around you...but I need to know that it's safe."

"I..." He rubs a hand over his face, and I nearly pout at the loss of contact between my shoulder blades. "Christ, Quinn. You have nothing to worry about there. But if you feel like you have to reciprocate just because I—"

"Gave me multiple orgasms?" I arch a brow. "Sweetie. I never barter with my gifts. We can't...fuck," for some reason, saying this makes me blush, like I'm a teenager all over again around him, "but I want to make you feel at least half as good as you made me feel." I can't remember wanting to please someone as much as I do right now. I want my mouth full of Sawyer. Still, after all this time. "Even if you don't deserve it."

I wonder if he'll have any sort of comeback here, but he only clenches his jaw in the most annoyingly sexy way. Like maybe he wants to tell me his secrets but won't. Yet.

I'm not giving up, but I'm not pressing it, either. Not now.

Not when he licks his lips, slowly, and swallows, even slower than the last time, like he's savoring any remaining taste of me in his mouth. Which makes me so freaking hot I nearly don't give a shit about the lack of a condom and beg him to bend me over the table. Or even... Oh, God. Over the years I've had the biggest fantasy of him taking me from behind against a wall...

With the greatest of restraint, instead, I run my lips across his collarbone. I work my way down his chest and stomach, pausing here and there, balancing myself with my hands along his body, enjoying the salted flavor of his skin. Like sun and sand and ocean. The scents of sage and citrus drift from his pores, as they always have, and begin to bring back memories of years ago. But I shut them from my mind because all I want to focus on is this moment. Sawyer in my hands. Rough concrete under my knees. The muscles of his hamstrings tensing under my palms.

I slip one hand up to grab his exceptional ass and then I tiptoe my fingers around his hip until they're able to circle his erection, sliding up and then down to his base, and guiding him to my lips. The wetness already waiting at his tip hits my mouth in a tangy, masculine flavor. I wrap my tongue around him and pull him further in. When I glance up, his chest heaves in my peripheral vision, and when we catch eyes, he slams a hand out to grab the wall. He looks almost like he's in pain—a pleasured sort of pain. Which tells me I'm doing exactly what I should be.

I know how to curl my tongue around the exact spot to make him shudder—right near the tip. And I do it. And he does shudder. Over, and over, and over. I work my hands along him, and under him, and around to his ass, kneading at his skin.

Licking, licking, sucking.

Until he loses himself.

And then gently sucking just a little bit more.

"Quinn," he moans, the fingers of his free hand tightening through my hair and easing me carefully away from him. "I'm about to fucking fall over."

I wipe my mouth and lick my lower lip for good measure, standing and tracing my fingertips up his legs and stomach and chest. "Satisfied?"

"You've never left me any other way."

"Guess you taught me well, all those years ago. Before you left."

"Quinn..."

"Not pressing it," I say. "Let's just enjoy the moment. For now." But I let my hands fall from his chest, balling them by my sides.

"You were an excellent student back then," he says, smiling as though he didn't notice me slide back a few inches. "But you've picked up a few impressive tricks."

My first instinct is to stiffen, to defend myself. But a closer look at his face tells me he's not judging me for the past few years. Just complimenting my style. He's pleased. With what he just received, not that I've picked up tricks.

So I smile back. "You haven't even seen anything yet."

Then I wish I hadn't said it. I sound like I'm going to give him all the time in the world to discover my talents. And thinking about time... I glance around for a clock, not finding one.

"Got somewhere to be?" he asks.

"Brunch with my mom," I admit, wishing it was any day but Wednesday so I could stay.

But the way he shuts down is shocking, immediate. No trace of his easy grin. No open gaze. No relaxed stance. He just...closes.

"What? You can't tell me you still hold a grudge against my mom."

"Yes. I can." His words are short and even though we're less than a foot apart, there's suddenly an entire world between us.

And it really freaking pisses me off. "You've got nothing to stand on here, buddy. You proved her right."

"That I wasn't good enough for you?"

"Jesus. Always so stuck on that." I yank my hair back into a knot. "No. That you'd hurt me. *Newsflash, asshole.*"

Emotions are fickle, annoying things. Somehow I've gone from completely turned on and wanting his hands all over me, to completely turned on, wanting his hands all over me, *and* wanting to freaking slap him at the same time. I could probably use a good slap, myself. What was I *thinking?*

I shove past him, snatching my purse from the base of the shaping table or whatever the hell it's called, and stalk to the door to the store.

I pause at the handle. Just for a second. Just to breathe.

Don't turn around. Do not turn around. I don't *need one last look.*

Then he says, "Forgot your panties."

I spin around as he's scooping them up from the floor. And of all the damn nerve, he throws them at my face. I catch them, glaring.

And I throw them right back, just as hard, at his face. "Keep 'em. Something to remember me by. Because this? What just happened? It's the last you're getting from me. Ever."

He balls them in his fist. I wish it didn't oddly turn me on. I really freaking wish that. He shakes his head. "Good. It shouldn't have happened anyway. Don't go fucking running to Mommy over it, either. Tell me you've at least grown up that much."

"Fuck you, Sawyer. *She* was there for me when you weren't. *She* stuck around while you were off doing whatever the hell you've been doing." I pause to catch my breath again, which is perilously close to hitching, perilously close to letting tears loose. His expression is still shuttered, but his lips are pressed into a straight line and it's the way he used to look when I'd hurt his feelings. But I don't need to know about his feelings. Not after this. "And you know what? Keep your reasons for leaving, too. I don't give a shit anymore. Not about a single thing that has to do with you or where you've been or anything in your future either."

As far as exit lines go, I'm actually pretty proud of myself. I slam the door open and stride through it.

Too bad I'm too pissed to bother watching where I'm going, because I collide right into the chest of the second to last person I feel like seeing right now.

Sawyer's father.

CHAPTER EIGHTEEN

QUINN

"*MR. CARSON?*" I stare at the man in front of me, too shocked to keep my expression neutral.

His nose is red, almost purple-tinged. He smells like soured liquor. His hair is thin and greasy, more ash than blond, and his eyes—ones that used to rival the brightness of Sawyer's—are faded and bloodshot. And the hands he's using to steady me after I bounced off of him are shaky against my shoulders.

He's blinking as though he's as shocked as I am. "Quinn?"

"Hi." I flash as much of a smile as I can manage. Given that I haven't seen him in almost four years. And, also, given that I have no underwear on under my dress, and I just gave his son a blowie. But mostly for that first reason. Missing Brock—or now, more formally, Mr. Carson, I guess—hurt almost as much as missing Sawyer. And Jess.

If I close my eyes I can see him the way he was four years ago. Vibrant, tanned, smiling. *Hey, girlie*, he used to say after I'd fight with my mom. *How about we go out and get an ice cream?* Or a pizza. Or...watch Jess's Taekwon-Do lesson. Or...anything fun and easy. That's how things were between us then. Not this. Not this unsteady, awful tension stretching between us now.

"It's, um... It's really something else to see you," he says.

Something else, I can't help but note. Not *good*.

"You, too." My system's beginning to right itself again, so I step back and his arms drop to his sides. "But I have to go. I'm late." Which actually might be the truth. But either way, I need to get out of here. Away from him. Away from Sawyer.

Back to real life.

I tap his arm, all awkward, hating how papery his skin feels. How old. "Have a good day."

He nods, lost in thought for a second. Or maybe just drunk and confused.

It hurts, between my ribs and in my belly, to see him like this. He almost always had a beer in hand back when I considered him family, but what I'm seeing now shows that things progressed way beyond casual drinking. This is the remnant of the man I used to know. The one whose arms I cried in when Sawyer and I fought. When we watched a sad movie. Whenever I was upset.

But he's not a part of my life anymore. And he didn't call me once, either. Not an email. Not a card. Nothing. As though I'd never been a part of his family. I shouldn't care what shape he's in.

I shouldn't.

But I do.

My eyes blur as I make my way through a few swimsuit racks toward the exit. But Sawyer's coworker, Rajesh, intercepts me. "Quinn?"

"Yeah?" I raise my brows, wondering how he knows my name, but then remember Sawyer saying it when I first walked in.

Rajesh's brown eyes are friendly, and he leans against a shiny metal rod holding surf brand T-shirts. "Is he alive back there?"

"Brock?" *Barely*. The thought almost kills me.

"No—Sawyer."

"Lucky enough for him, he is. Excuse me." I shove past him and right out of the Surf Spot. I don't care how friendly this guy's eyes are, he doesn't get to ask me about Sawyer. Especially if his concern is for Sawyer instead of me. Not that

I'm having a pity party, but come on.

I've had enough of today already and it's not even noon.

And I really need some underwear.

Unfortunately, my dad's running late to brunch, so for the first twenty minutes it's just me and my mother. Which is basically the worst. At least he's coming. With the way he travels up and down the coast visiting their chain of stores, checking in with branch managers and marketing plans and other business-type things, it's not rare for me to spend Wednesday mornings alone with my mother—and those times are painful.

Like right now. If I have to answer one more question about Chase, I might shoot myself. I mean, Chase is awesome, but the way my mom's eyes glint with that matchmaker glee—only because of who his parents are—makes me beyond irritated. Which, considering how irritated I already was after my...visit with Sawyer, is saying something.

At least I've got eggs Benedict on the way.

"All I'm trying to explain," she goes on, "is that engagements happen faster and faster the older you get."

"I'm not old. I'm not even out of college." God, where the hell is my dad? "And even if I was, I'm not going to marry Chase. I might not even get married at all." I say it mostly to enjoy the shock on her face. But it might be true. Only one person's ever made me think along those lines and, well... *That's* not going to happen.

As if on cue, my dad arrives, greeting us both with quick pecks on the cheeks. He grabs a seat between us. "What'd I miss, girls?"

"Oh, you know. The usual. Mom's trying to marry me off before I'm twenty-five."

My mom sighs. "I ordered you the salmon and asparagus, Jack. I hope your meeting went well?" When he nods she offers him a rare, real smile. He's the only one who ever gets them. I think it's because he's the only person in her life who knew her growing up, so she knows he understands her in a way nobody else ever will. She cut off anyone else who even knew she had a childhood. I've never understood why, and she never speaks of it with more than passing allusions. But it's the tiny moments between them, when she shows genuine affection, that make me love her. Because it's nice to know she's capable of emotion.

Then her attention's back on me. "Don't be so quick to dismiss the possibility, sweetie. He has a good family, and I'm sure they'd be happy to ensure their son settles down faster than that daughter of theirs."

"*That daughter of theirs* is pre-law. And she sounds awesome," I say.

"From what I hear," my mom lowers her voice like she's some co-conspirator, "she's given them quite a few reasons to worry lately."

"Yeah. Horrible things. Like actually caring about what goes on in the world outside the palace she grew up in." I don't know Chase's sister, but I'm not going to sit here and let my mom tear her down.

"Headstrong girls grow into fine young women," my father says, patting my hand like he's giving me a compliment. Which, I guess, he is?

"Isn't gossiping beneath you?" I ask my mom, my tone about as prim and proper as it's ever been. Totally faked, but I guarantee she doesn't realize it. "Really, Mother. Think of the example you're setting. How ever will I grow into a fine young woman?"

And she actually looks embarrassed, like rather than believing she shouldn't gossip because it's mean, she believes it should be below her. I want to shake my head. I want to tell her that I was basically arrested last night—though it'll be more fun to let her hear that from one of her upper-class friends, so I hold back.

I want to tell her I left a pair of panties with Sawyer right before I came here.

I won't though. Because his stupid little barb about running to Mommy really stung. Plus, I don't think I could ever say it in front of my dad. Even if he'd probably just smile blandly and pretend it didn't bother him.

I do wonder if my parents have heard Sawyer's back in town. The Outer Banks is a big area, but they—well, really, *she* manages to find out everything there is to know about anyone who's anyone. Not that she'd consider Sawyer anyone.

Which pisses me off more.

"I heard someone talking about Sawyer the other day," I say, unable to keep from mentioning him. Because I'm itching to pick a fight. Over a guy I don't even like.

Don't even *want* to like, anyway.

My mom looks at my dad and back to me. "Well, there's a name from the past. I can't imagine why he came up."

Really, Mother? He broke my heart—who cares how much time has passed?—yet you find it surprising that he'd ever come up? I come so close to telling her where I just came from. Really, really close.

"He…was only mentioned in passing," I mumble, chickening out. "I didn't really pay attention."

"There's a family to stay away from if there ever was one," she says, pausing to let the waiter disperse our plates as brunch arrives. "Chase's family, however, is much better. They—"

"Please, just stop," I say, silently fuming that she's so quick to toss off the Carsons, silently fuming that I can't blame her because she helped pick up the pieces they left me in. Silently fuming that I still want to defend them regardless of what happened four years ago. Regardless of the fact they don't deserve it.

The thing is, my mom never liked the Carsons, not from the day she discovered I was with Sawyer. Because she's a damn snob. But I won't call her on her pretension because I believe that—in this *one* instance—her heart's in the right place. She really was there for me when Sawyer wasn't. She patted my back while I cried so hard I gave myself a migraine. And again the next week. And in the months after… She saw how devastated I was and even if she wasn't so stuck up, she'd want me to stay away from them now because of how badly they hurt me in the past. However, I can at least say this much: "I'm not going to date Chase. I don't care who his parents are."

My mom studies me, so disappointed. "What exactly is it that you have against people of society?"

"You mean people who are rich? Because I'm pretty sure we're all people of society." I want to scream at her. I keep it in, though. For now. "I have nothing against wealthy people. But I'm not going to date someone just because his parents can wipe their asses with hundred-dollar bills." Damn. I was so close to no snark this time.

"I'm more concerned you'll end up with someone *because* they're poor just to drive me crazy."

"Girls," my father says. "Let's take a—"

"Are you listening to yourself?" I glare at my mom. "I wouldn't date someone to get at you—you're the farthest thing from my mind when I..." I stop myself from saying *when I let someone into my pants*, but just barely. And only for my dad's sake.

"Poor people are lazy." My mom whispers, but she pushes her words through her mouth so sharply they hit me like a yell. "They're bad with money, and they look for easy schemes. The welfare rate is—"

"*You* used to be poor," I shoot back to shut her up because holy hell, if she continues going down the path she is, I may never speak to her again. "We all did."

Her mouth parts. Shuts. Parts again. "And look at us now. I only say those things for their own good."

"For whose own good?" I don't understand—not that I ever follow her logic, but this is...something else. Maybe it's hard to think through how disgusted I am. "Poor people?"

"Lillian," my father says, warning in his tone. He pats her hand this time. "Just because people of...our stature were unkind to you in the past doesn't mean you need to repeat their actions."

My mother rolls her eyes so hard I almost don't notice the way she flips her hand under his so they can twine fingers—just for a moment before she pulls away. Every once in a while these sweet little things slip through and make me reevaluate her. Until she says things like, "You're wrong, Jack. I pushed myself higher, I pushed *us* higher, because of the way we were snubbed. Those people made me stronger. And perhaps my own attitude will give others the drive to better themselves as well."

"*Mom.*" I look to my dad, hoping he'll back me up, but he sits there concentrating on his asparagus, slicing it, studying it, eating it like my mom hasn't just said the most asinine things.

"I know, I know." She waves a hand to brush the words away. "Not appropriate brunch discussion. I apologize."

I want to tell her she needs to look up the definition of *empathy* and maybe try to put it into practice. But I let it drop because it'll have absolutely no impact. It's actually almost refreshing when she steers the conversation back to Chase. Until she stretches it out to the point I'm ready to stab myself with a butter fork. Finally, I say, "Fine. I won't discount him. Unless you say one. More. Thing. About him."

It shuts her up, but giving in irks me. I think maybe that's just how today's set to play out anyway. With me being mad. Giving in to what I wanted to do with Sawyer and leaving without the answers I went there to demand. Running into Brock the way I did. Dealing with my mother for this entire excruciating brunch... Can't *wait* to see what else is in store.

At least it's not long before I have an excuse to book it out of the restaurant because I have to get to work. But I end up late anyway because I get stuck behind an accident. And then I can't find the sunscreen I usually leave in my glove box—and I forget about it between my Jeep and the stand, and by the end of the day I'm burned to a crisp.

Seriously. Screw today.

I'm in bed before the sun's even set. Headphones in, music pushing every other thought out of my brain. Blackout drapes closed, blocking all the light. Eyes shut tight, but even that doesn't stop me from seeing every moment with Sawyer today, over and over again.

I fall asleep imagining him in my mouth again, so it's no surprise I dream it all night long. I wake up with my hand halfway down my pajama pants, desperate to wrap my lips around him all over a second time.

Jesus. I'm ready to go. Like, right now. I push my hand into my underwear and I'm not sure I've ever woken up so wet. So trembly. In so much need of release.

Goddamn it, Sawyer.

I don't want to give him the pleasure of making me come again, even if this time, he's only in my mind.

But the urge to give it to myself is too strong.

I picture him the entire time. His skilled fingers. His demanding tongue. His eyes looking up at me. My hand across my belly is *his* hand splayed there, twisting my skin, pulling at me, sliding up to tease my breasts until I'm gasping. It's *his* other hand in my panties, flicking against my skin, curling into me, twisting until I can't even gasp because I have no more air.

And a few minutes later when my toes are curling so hard my feet ache, and my back is arching toward the ceiling, uncontrollably and even painfully thanks to my sunburn, I moan the exact words I've been thinking since I first woke up. "*Goddamn it, Sawyer.*"

CHAPTER NINETEEN

SAWYER

THE WAVES ARE good and angry today, but the ocean is packed because it's Saturday and Outer Banks natives are out in swarms among the vacationers. Which sucks because I'm in the mood for a long, hard ride.

Some tweenager paddles past me, her board slamming into my shin because I didn't hook my own out of her way fast enough. It barely stings, but I rub it anyway, feeling my irritation grow. Then she looks over her shoulder and apologizes, her braces flashing in the sun, and I feel like an asshole, even though my annoyance isn't with her.

I dragged Jess out of bed this morning, looking for some brother-type bonding because I've been feeling kind of bad about dropping him in his own vomit, but he texted his stupid-ass friends along the drive and invited them. Including my least favorite of the bunch, some freckled bonehead who can't surf for shit, the bruiser-looking one who told me to chill when I found Jess at the bar the other day. At least he leaves after an hour in the water because he has to work. The tools he grumbles about never getting to use make me think he works for an electrical technician. I actually know a few local people in the industry, but I don't care enough to ask if he wants any introductions.

Because he's a little shit. And when he asks my brother if he's got anything planned for later in the week, eyeing me all slyly like I don't know he's trying to goad Jess into another drunken escapade, I want to shove his face under the water until he agrees to get the fuck out of my brother's life. Because Jess's turning out to be just like him. A little shit.

So no, I'm not going to offer to help his friend. It's a lesson I wish could pull into a conversation with Jess. Don't be a dick because people won't go out of their way to make your life easier. But I can already tell how well it'd go over with him. Which is to say, not at all. He's in the selfish years of his life, the ones where he already knows everything, doesn't have to listen to anyone else, and thinks he can get away with anything he wants to.

"Hey, shithead," I shout to him instead, motioning to the decent size of the swell on the horizon. "Get ready."

Rather than responding with his usual know-it-all attitude, he smiles. "Thanks, dude." Then he rides it like a champ and pride funnels through me until I'm smiling, too.

At my place later, he helps himself to a beer from the fridge. It's a strange dichotomy, my desire to avoid being a second father to him, while also doing my best to keep him in check. He sees my hesitation and cracks open the can, chugging before I can tell him not to.

"Watch it," I say, deciding on the spot. "You only get two of those all night, so you probably want to pace yourself. Pizza's not even here yet."

He lowers the can, wiping his mouth and burping loud enough to make a lesser man wince. I shake my head. "Amateur hour."

He strolls by me, crossing from the kitchen to the living room, asking, "Is that a challenge?"

"You tell me." I rip a burp of my own, and it practically vibrates through the house. Jess laughs, so I do it again, catching up to him and blowing the air from my next one in his face. I shove him down onto the couch. "Beat that."

We spend the next twenty minutes trying to outdo each other, and by the time the pizza gets here, I can tell he's feeling a little sick from all the swallowed air.

"If you puke on my couch, you'll be eating it this time," I warn, watching his face filter through queasy when he takes another sip of beer. He rolls his eyes, so I add, "Dude, this is the only nice piece of furniture I own." It is nice, too. Comfortable. Not down to the barest of threads like the one I just got rid of.

"You wouldn't have to worry so much about your precious sofa if your table wasn't covered with all your papers and shit." He gestures to the dining area behind us. "It looks like a miniature jungle." He has a point; my table's my workstation these days, cluttered with papers and variations of different houseplants. "What the hell are you doing with all that anyway?"

"Comparing phyllotactic spirals." And when his expression goes blank, I explain, "Analyzing the different ways plants arrange their leaves for collecting sunlight to copy the design and use it to gather solar power." I could talk about this for hours—it's a refreshing change from the past few years of poring over natural grazing migrations with Rajesh, in school and then after graduation—but Jess's eyes are glazing so hard right now, I refrain.

I really do need to pick up some office furniture for the second bedroom, which currently holds a lot of blank space with a few certificates and credentials on one wall. But whatever. At least I have a nice couch. Plus I like the lighting in the dining area, the way the windows face out to the east so I can get up early with the sun to get work done. It's good for the plants, too. I like how much space the table gives me for laying out multiple design specs.

Maybe I should at least pick up some tray tables or something.

"You want me to clear a place for you at the kiddie table?" I ask. "Or can you drink your beer and eat your pizza like a man on the couch and watch a movie at the same time?"

"Kiddie table? Please. And fuck you, anyway," he says, but not in a shitty way. "I'm not gonna puke over half a beer."

"Oh yeah?" I ask. "What's the count up to these days? What was the limit you passed before you got in my car?"

"Whatever." He shrugs, full of forced nonchalance. "That was a one-off."

"You sure about that?" I study him. He studies the movie. I lean across to his end of the couch, tapping my fist into his arm. "Jess. You said you'd get your shit together if we came back to the Outer Banks. You swore. No more cops. No more getting wasted. No more skipping school." No more scaring the shit out of me every time my dad calls to tell me Jess hasn't been home in three days and isn't answering his phone.

"God, chill." Teenage rage tightens Jess's entire body. "It's fine. I had a rough day that other time. It's the summer so I couldn't even skip school if I wanted to—*which I won't.*" He takes a huge breath, visibly trying to relax. "And I'm not gonna vomit on your stupid couch. My stomach's fine." Like he's trying to prove it, he shovels half a slice of pizza into his mouth.

"Rough because you saw Quinn?" Shit. I wasn't going to ask. Damn it, I have zero control where she's concerned.

Jess glances at me mid-chew, starts scowling, speaks with his mouth full. "I don't want to talk about her."

"Why?"

He shakes his head, swallowing his food with the last of his beer. A part of me wants to press harder. Quinn was like a sister to him. But another part thinks talking about her's a bad idea for me, too. And the biggest part of me doesn't want to rock the mood for the rest of the night. Especially because I'm about to tell him he has to have a soda before his next beer. So I let the Quinn thing go.

Wish I could let her go.

I grab another slice, shoveling more in my mouth than he did with his. It's another contest, and this time we're both feeling pretty ill by the time it's over.

Jess only finishes his second beer for the night to prove he can. I don't even bother. We're both passed out before midnight.

CHAPTER TWENTY

QUINN

"I SAW JESS," Gianna tells me a week after the surf shop incident involving his stupid brother. "That kid's a mess."

I'd smile at her rhyme if I didn't hate the truth it contained so much. "Yeah, he really is, huh?"

She straddles her surfboard, bobbing next to me in the salty water. "He literally stumbled into the shop yesterday, drunk as hell. His friend had to carry him out. I don't even think he recognized me."

"What *happened* to him?" I shake my head, regret lacing my ribs tightly together. "He used to be such a sweet kid."

Gianna shrugs. "So did I."

Now, I laugh. "Gi, you've been many things in your life, but sweet? Let's not get carried away."

"My mother thinks I'm sweet."

"Yeah. She has to." I grin, splashing water at her.

She opens her mouth to respond, but we both feel the change in the water at the same time. The wind kicks up a bit and the water behind us dips backward.

"Take it!" she says—and I'm paddling my arms hard before she's even finished. The water shoves us forward in the biggest surge we've seen all afternoon, wild and frothy. A few more strokes and I pop to my feet with *perfect* timing.

I follow the dropline to the base of the wave—*but so does Gianna*, *that snake.* She drops in, peeling to the right above me and shoving past with a huge smile, spraying me in the face with water.

I shake my head and slice into the barrel of the wave as it breaks, just a few feet behind her. Soon we're surrounded completely by the curved wall of water.

And then she eats shit.

She's fine; I can tell right away it's not a bad fall, and I sweep around her, laughing until I can't breathe. Serves her right, the little barrel thief. I accelerate past her, through a bottom turn, and it propels me to the front side of the wave's lip. I kick my tail out to release my fins—and for a moment I'm airborne.

The wind rushes against my face. Heat from the sun dries the tops of my shoulders. I close my eyes, breathless with it all. When I land back against the wave, my board is steady under my feet and I glide *perfectly* with the water. This rush—there's nothing else like it. Not even the feel of Sawyer's hands against my skin.

Well, okay. Maybe that comes close.

When the ride's over, I paddle back to Gianna. She's waiting for me on her board and waves away whatever she thinks I'm going to say when I get here. "I know, I know. Serves me right."

I push into a sitting position on my surfboard, salt water lapping against my thighs, and nod. "Bet your ass it did."

"I'm fine, thanks for asking."

"Oh thank goodness." I pause to catch my breath. "I was really worried when I saw you here sitting on your board without a care in the world."

This is one of the reasons we love each other so much, I think. She can dish it out—but so can I.

"So while you were off on your joyride without even checking to make sure I didn't drown, I had some time to think."

"Wow. What was that like?"

"I think you should talk to Sawyer." Her suggestion cuts the sarcasm from my sails.

"What?" I squint at her and shade my eyes with a hand, searching her face for a sign that she's joking. "No. I told you. Never bothering with that again."

"Oh, please. You can't even say that without your voice wavering. You're not done with him—even though *you should be*. And I'll kick your scrawny ass if you even think about actually getting back together with him."

"Not even the slightest possibility of that," I say, hoping my words are a lie.

Wait.

I mean, knowing the words are truth.

Ugh.

"I do think you need closure, though. I mean, specifically for your legs when you're around Sawyer—but also with him in general." She wipes a wet strand of pink hair out of her eyes, looking at me with a soft smile so I know she's joking about the legs part. Hell, she's not really wrong, anyway. "But I was mostly talking about Jess."

God, I forgot we'd just been talking about him. I'm such an asshole. "Talking about Sawyer makes my brain all fried. But you're right."

And she is.

The Jess I used to know has to be there somewhere still. But this path he's on... He needs help. Maybe Sawyer doesn't know how bad things are. I splash the water, making miniature waves with my fingers. I wish I knew what their lives had been like the past years. I wish I had a little more insight to anything about them. I should've talked to Sawyer about Jess when I stopped by his shop. Even if he wouldn't give me answers to anything I wanted... Jess is important to us both, whether or not he hates me.

I promised Jess a long time ago that I'd be there for him. And then he disappeared from my life before I could keep my word. But maybe talking to Sawyer about him is a small restitution for what I wasn't able to do while he was gone. Not that Jess'll thank me for it, but it's the best I can do.

A fresh edge of guilt stabs my chest. He's only sixteen, and he's so messed up. I wonder if things would be different if I'd been able to keep my promise. "Shit. This sucks."

"I could tell Sawyer," Gianna offers. "If you really don't want to see him again."

I almost laugh, but the thought of not seeing Sawyer again is *so* not funny. God. Why can't I just be over him? Why are my damn emotions as unpredictable as the ocean these days? I wrap my hair into a sticky, salt water-drenched bun. "No. I'll talk to him."

"Quinn..." She trails off, sucking on her lower lip. It's her tell—albeit a rare one—for holding something in.

"Just say it," I say, even if I know where she's about to go.

"Are you okay about Sawyer? For real? Because...it took you a long time to heal after the first round."

"We're not going another round." I can't even come close to making my words sound genuine. Hell, they may actually be true, but I don't *want* them to be. And Gianna's always been able to see through my bullshit.

"You blew him the second you were alone with him."

"Whoa." I throw a hand up but can't block the sting out of what she says. I fling water at her instead, grabbing my board to steady myself when a swell pushes me up higher than I'm expecting. "Be a little bitchier, why don't you?"

She wipes water from her eyes. "It's the truth."

"That's not *exactly* how it happened."

"I know." She sighs. "But Quinn... I'm really not saying this to be a bitch. I love you. But don't you think maybe you should chill with the physical shit? I can tell by your face when I say his name... *Sawyer*—" She points at my face, though I swear I haven't even blinked. "See, just like that. You're coming apart all over again."

"I'm not," I say. And I think this part actually is true. "I'm still attracted to him, yeah. But I'm not that brokenhearted seventeen-year-old anymore. I'm not going to break again."

"I just want to make sure of it, okay?"

I nod and glance at my watch. "Shit. My shift starts in thirty."

"Take the next one in," she says, all intensity gone from her tone. She said her piece, and things are back to normal between us just like that. "I'll call you later."

"By the way," I say, waiting for the next surfable wave. "Did you borrow my wakeboard?"

"No. Why?"

I shrug. "No big deal. It wasn't in my Jeep the other day... I thought I had it in the back. Maybe someone stole it."

Gianna laughs. "If you need me to go all bruiser on some thief, let me know."

"I'll be sure to keep that in mind." I laugh, too, because as tiny as she is, I know firsthand she can do it. More than likely, I left the board someplace, though. Wouldn't be the first time. Wouldn't even be the third or fourth.

"Hey, text me that Chase boy's number, will you?"

Huh. I *knew* something might work there... "You sure you won't eat him alive? Because he's pretty great, Gi."

"I can't make any promises." She arcs a brow. "You know me."

"I'll send it." I glance behind us and see a roll in the water on the horizon. "But don't make me go all bruiser on *you*."

"Love to see you try." But her mouth quirks and she can't quite swallow her laughter.

When the swell reaches us, I paddle to gain momentum, grabbing my board at the chest line and pushing up to my feet as the unbroken wave peaks into something steeper. I flip her off over my shoulder right before re-angling my board to take the drop and cut across the water.

Then? There's no stopping me. I'm flying. Salt whips my face and the wind whistles into my ears. I can't keep a grin from parting my lips. Carving a wave is just...amazing. Fast like a roller coaster, with just as much stomach-dropping. I slice into the water, fanning a spray of water into the air. Exhilaration streaks through my chest.

The water takes me higher.

Faster.

And faster.

Then... Oh crap.

I. Eat. Foam.

My leash gets tangled, and the wave *completely* has its way with me.

Water floods my nose and my mouth and my eyes, and then spirals me toward the shore so hard I almost bite my tongue off. I'm somersaulted onto the beach in a mixed-up clump of person and surfboard...and sand. Everywhere. In my mouth. In my hair. In my eyes. Down in my swimsuit in places I don't even want to *think* about.

Which is fine because the only thing I can think about is how bad my head hurts. Holy mother of all brain freezes. My sinus cavity screams at me—I think I snorted in at least an eighth of the ocean.

And the beach is crowded. I just provided hours of memory-replay entertainment for at least fifty people.

I wave off a few of the ones heading my direction to, I'm assuming, see if I'm all right. When I stand, waving weakly to Gianna, she wraps her arms around her waist and falls forward onto her board, she's laughing so hard.

What a bitch.

Though maybe I deserve it for laughing when she ate it earlier.

Guess karma's a bitch, too.

CHAPTER TWENTY-ONE

QUINN

"ARE YOU OKAY?" A stocky, sunburned redheaded kid stops me by the beach exit. "I saw that wipeout—you need a doctor or anything?"

I don't know whether I should roll my eyes. I can't tell if he's being sincere, or if there's a hint of condescension—and for someone clearly younger than me, it's annoying if there is. I study him a moment longer, and then... "Where do I know you from?"

He shrugs. "Dunno."

A little kid screams in the distance, and I look over his shoulder to see a toddler squealing when her father tosses her in the air. He's throwing her a little higher than my lifeguarding senses are comfortable with, but whatever. She's fine. I drag my eyes back to the guy in front of me, but when my gaze passes over the trash can a few feet away, I remember. "You're the little shit who littered right in front of me the other week."

"Doesn't ring a bell." Down go his eyebrows, furrowed like he's confused. But there's panic in his eyes. "You must be thinking—"

"Of a different totally built redheaded teenager in the exact same green swim shorts that you have on now?" I ask, smirking. I should let him off the hook, but he's squirming now, and damn if it isn't kinda funny.

Then he says, "You think I'm totally built?" and his cheeks turn even brighter red than his burn. "Because I think you're totally—"

"Oh, God. Go ahead and stop right there." I bite back a smile. "Listen...?"

"Mason?" he fills in the blank, his blush creeping down his neck.

"Mason." I dig my car keys out of my beach bag. "Go hit on a girl your age. Thanks for asking about my wipeout. I'm fine. But I'm late." And starving. I need to grab food and somehow still get to Kitty Hawk in the next twenty minutes. I walk past him, but turn back a second later. "Hey—you know Jess Carson, right?"

He freezes, not even blinking. "No."

Wow. He's definitely lying. Jess was with Mason's group of friends the day I saved him. I wonder if Jess picked a fight with him or something to get this sort of reaction. Though their sizes are so different, Jess wouldn't stand a chance.

Unless he learned from his brother, maybe. Skinny, but scrappy enough to make up for it. Not that Sawyer's very skinny anymore... But I'm not about to start thinking about *that* right now.

Maybe Mason's got a crush on Jess's girlfriend. Or some other high school drama thing. Whatever. If I had more time I'd pick at this until I learned something about Jess, but I drop it because I don't have time—and this guy really doesn't want to talk about Jess. "Well. Have a good day, Mason."

"Yeah." He smirks. "You, too."

I jog to my Jeep because I'm really short on time now, but when I get there, it's my turn to freeze. There's a gift, wrapped with ribbon, leaning against my windshield.

A frame. A breathtakingly gorgeous piece of craftsmanship. Two sheets of thick glass edged together with tarnished iron.

The *perfect* thing for displaying pressed wildflowers. I reach across my hood to grab it, unwrap the bow, and check along the iron edges for a merchant's mark—because I *have* to buy more of these—but there's no stamping, or anything otherwise identifiable, anywhere.

Then... I think of Sawyer. This is something he'd do. So sweet, so thoughtful... But that can't be right, can it? We didn't leave on good terms and I still hate him and it just doesn't make sense.

Who else could it be, though? Not Chase—it's definitely not his style.

Not...ugh. Definitely not Julian.

And other than that I'm stumped.

Damn. I think I want it to be from Sawyer.

Which is stupid because I hate him.

With my mind, at least.

It's just my heart refuses to agree.

As much as it pains me to admit it.

As much as I *swear* I'm not going to do anything about it...

I still think about him for my entire shift. Even more than I think about food. Which, considering I didn't have time to grab anything to eat beforehand, says a freaking lot. It says so much, in fact, that I head home after work instead of to his shop to speak with him about Jess like I'd planned, because I need to get my thoughts in check before I face him again.

Knowing I'll wait to fill the iron frame until I find the perfect flower combination to dry, I place it on the side table beside my couch so it's the first thing I'll see every time I come in. Even though it makes me think of Sawyer.

And, because of it, or maybe just because of how I'm wired, it's almost a week before I think I have my stupid longings under control enough to see him again.

As soon as I walk into his shop, as soon as I see him...I realize I didn't wait long enough.

He's leaning across the counter, a towel wrapped around his waist, shirtless, with his back to me. Even if this was the first time I'd lain eyes on him in years, I'd recognize that flex across those shoulder blades. Those sharp, muscled shoulder blades.

Covered by that smooth, tan skin.

Great. And now I can't stop swallowing.

He's talking with a brunette working behind the counter, and she's snapping her gum and laughing at something he's said and I wonder if they're sleeping together and I hate the way it makes my heart bottom out, I hate that I even care. But let's be real, we've moved way past the part where I try to lie to myself about the things I feel for him anymore.

Because, fuck it. I still burn for him. Yearn for him. Make stupid, cheesy rhymes in my mind for him.

The trick here, I think, is to make sure he doesn't discover any of it. Which might be kind of hard because I want to sprint through the store and jump on his back and lick his neck.

His hair's wet and messier than usual—well, usual as so far as the two times I've seen him this summer—like he's just come in from a rough surf. He shakes his head and a drop of water must fling onto the girl because she wipes her cheek and giggles. The sound is...grating. He laughs, too, and apologizes. Also grating.

I was the girl he used to make laugh. For hours. Days. Weeks. It was me he wanted to tease smiles out of. And now his back is to me and another girl's getting that gift.

Jealousy's a weird emotion. I can't remember the last time I felt it. Maybe back when a girl in my senior class claimed she'd spoken with Sawyer a few months after he'd left town, when I would have given anything and everything to hear his voice. I understood what people meant, then, about seeing red. I wanted to stomp her into the ground. But it turned out she'd been lying just to mess with me because I'd offended her when I didn't go to a party she threw. I've never been so close to punching someone. Even knowing she was full of it, my heart still managed to disintegrate all over again.

And, damn it, here it is again, reacting in a way I wish it wouldn't, hopping all over the place at the mere sight of his stupid shoulder blades.

"Hey, Quinn." Rajesh's voice booms at me from the side, damn my stupid Sawyer-tunnel vision.

My cheeks heat. I'm caught. Sawyer starts to turn and before he catches me, too, I look at Rajesh, smiling through my blush. "I seem to have misplaced my wakeboard. Thought maybe you could help me with that."

"Me?" He tilts his head, his eyes laughing like he knows exactly who I'm here to see. And, he did completely bust me staring at Sawyer. "You thought *I* could help you?"

I clear my throat. "Or anyone who works here, I guess."

I *feel* more than see in my peripheral, Sawyer making his way toward us. He waits until he's close enough to touch me before speaking. "I got this, Raj."

"*I got this, Raj?*" I snap, finally looking at Sawyer. His words totally offend me, even if I can't put my finger on why. "Like...what? I'm something to be handled?"

"And this is where I step away." Rajesh throws his hands up, backing slowly—exaggeratedly—away.

"No," Sawyer says slowly, drawing out his next words. "*I got this, Raj,* as in Rajesh just clocked out so he shouldn't have to worry about helping customers."

"Oh." Well, shit. I drop my gaze to the rack of rash guards hanging beside us, running my fingers over a few of the shoulders. "Sorry." God, it burns, apologizing to him. A small flare of anger makes it easier to look back up into his face.

He's staring at my neck and swallowing. He used to have a fascination with kissing me just above my collarbone. I drag a finger across the skin, fighting a smirk when his eyes follow the motion. I wonder if he's thinking about it now.

I am.

Damn it.

"Guess it's easy to make assumptions about what you might mean, given your track record of being *so forthcoming.*" There. Situation fixed. Now his gaze is heavy on mine, and even a little pissed.

Good. Anger's better than the other thing.

"New wakeboard. That's why you're here, right?" His tone is as pointed as his expression.

"Are you working?" I ask, just as pointedly. "I get that

Rajesh is off. But you've still got sand on your chest." He does. A dusting of brown sand I'm dying to brush away with my fingers. "Kind of unprofessional."

"I walked in from lunch literally five minutes before you got here, Quinn." He unwraps his towel and even though I try so hard not to, I glance down. Board shorts. Obviously he wasn't naked. God. "Is this better?"

"You might want to try putting on a shirt."

"Last time you were all *take off your shirt, Sawyer*, and now it's *put your shirt on, Sawyer*." He smirks. "Hard to tell how to please you these days."

"Pretty sure you know *exactly* how to please me." The sentence just slips out and hangs in the air between us.

"Glad I haven't lost my touch," he finally says. I wish his expression wasn't so smug. I wish I wasn't secretly so pleased that the tension between us is as strong as it was the other day. Stronger, maybe.

I wish he would fucking tell me why he left and where he went and why he didn't ever contact me or even say goodbye.

But I especially wish my heart wasn't searching so hard for reasons to forgive him without even hearing his reasoning. To believe he's still the same kindhearted Sawyer who'd never do something like that without a very good reason.

To believe he's the same Sawyer who once loved me more than life itself.

Or at least I thought he did. Maybe I was wrong. I was probably wrong.

And I still freaking want him so much my skin feels like it's stretching toward him.

And now he's studying my face like he's been able to read this entire stream of thoughts. Fuck. But he only points to a wall lined with wakeboards. "See anything you like?"

Oh, man. Such an easy line here. Look at him. Say, *you*. But I bite it back. "Maybe that black and green one."

"Want a closer look?" He heads toward the wall and I follow, trying so hard not to notice the width of his shoulders. The shape of his ass under his board shorts. How perfect his hair would be to tangle my fingers in right now...

But that last part disappears when he turns and asks how much I weigh.

I stare at him, deadpan. "Not a chance."

"Quinn, like I care about the number. I need it to figure out—"

"I need a board in the 130 to 139 centimeter range, but I like them on the shorter side for less weight." The lighter the board, the easier it is to maneuver in the air when I flip across a wake. "And I want one with an aggressive rocker."

"You like that nice pop into the air, huh?" Sawyer knows exactly what I mean. "Picked up some tricks over the years?"

"Thought we'd already established that."

"Is that the real reason you're here?" His eyes flash, but I can't tell with what. Hope? Annoyance? Repressed desire? (God, please be the first or third option.) "Because I don't think it's a good idea."

"That's not why I'm here." But his stupid rejection stings anyway. Guess I was wrong about the frame. If he thinks it's a bad idea for us to hook up again, he's definitely not about to be making some romantic gesture like leaving a handcrafted frame on the hood of my car. No matter how much I'd hoped it was him... "I actually do need a wakeboard, but... I also wanted to talk to you about Jess."

Now I can read Sawyer's eyes with no problem. Apprehension.

CHAPTER TWENTY-TWO

SAWYER

"WHAT ABOUT MY brother?" Whatever Jess did to bring Quinn here pisses me off.

She should be here because she wants to see me.

Shit. What I mean, what I really need to get through my damn skull, is that she shouldn't be here at all. Especially looking like she does. Another dress. White this time, and crisp against her smooth, tanned skin. It's like she knows exactly what it does to me. Like she wants to torture me.

I'm not saying I don't deserve it.

"Is this..." She glances around the store, her eyes resting on a few of the customers wandering around. "Is this the best place to discuss him?"

"So you're not here to sing his praises, I take it?" I clench my teeth to stem my irritation with him. It doesn't really help. This kid needs to get it together. He's doing his best to throw away everything, but I'd give anything I have to help him get back on track. He needs to open his fucking eyes and see it.

"Can we go back in the workroom for a minute?" Her eyes dart toward the door and back to mine. Every time they hit me it's a blow to my gut.

"No. If we got back in that room, it'll be for more than a

minute and we won't be talking." Fuck. I've lost all control around this girl, and it's killing me. By her quick intake of air, maybe it's killing her, too. I want to shake her. One of us has to have self-control and maybe it should be me, but why the hell isn't it her? Why the hell does she look at me like she has faith I won't hurt her, like she thinks I'm the same boy I was before?

I probably look at her the same way. But in her case, she is the same girl. Yeah, years have changed her, but her heart's right there for me to see, and she's got the same soul she's always had. Mine disappeared along the way, which is why it's torturous for me not to take her back to the workroom and slam her on the table again. And again. And again.

Worse than that, even, is how happy I'd be if I could just take her hand and never let go.

Instead, I say, "Let's grab a table out front. Brandy's fine watching the counter for a while."

"Brandy." Quinn says the name like it's sour in her mouth. "She looks like a Brandy."

"Pretty and nice, you mean?" I ask, kind of enjoying the flare of irritation in her eyes.

"You dating her, too?" Quinn asks. "Like Morgan, I mean. Not that you and I are... You know what? Forget I asked. I don't care."

Yes, she does. I should let her think I'm playing the field that way. Like our backroom hookup didn't mean anything to me. It'd spare us a lot of future pain, probably.

"I'm not dating anyone, Quinn." The truth is worth speaking to see the way she shivers when I say her name. I look away from her, closing my eyes until I find the will to walk toward the store's exit. I push open the door, the bell dinging, and wait to hold it for Quinn. She's still standing where I left her, a disappointed frown across her perfect lips. She straightens them into a line when she notices me staring and breezes past me like it's no problem at all to walk away from the temptation of the table in the back room.

Yeah. Right.

I glance at Brandy. "You got the store for a minute?"

She sighs, and I tell her she owes me. Just a few weeks ago her apartment became the proud new owner of my really old, threadbare couch, and I'm not about to let her forget it.

She blows a bubble. Pops it. "Then I guess it's no prob, boss."

Outside, Quinn is already sitting at one of our two tables. She's got her shades on to face the sun, but I push the table's umbrella up anyway. Her eyes have always been sensitive even with sunglasses.

"Thanks." Her tone is cool. Like in the past ten seconds she's doused the attraction burning the air between us.

"Yep." I sit across from her. It's probably a good thing her eyes are covered, considering how easy it is to get lost in those deep blue depths, but her mouth is hard not to take in, especially when she chews on her lower lip. I'm at half-mast just watching her.

Four years I spent remembering what that mouth felt like wrapped around me. Two weeks ago she showed me how not even close to the truth those memories came. If she doesn't stop chewing on that lip, I'm going to have a problem.

"It's nice out here," she says, tilting her head to the ocean, visible up the street a block away. We can hear the waves from where we sit.

"It is," I agree. "Good views." But right now I'm thinking more about the girl sitting in front of me.

"So, about Jess..." She trails off, waiting for me to tell her to continue. To tell her I want to know what's going on with him.

If she's still hesitating, this might be worse than I'm thinking. Which helps dampen the wood in my shorts, but I'd rather suffer through blue balls than deal with the anchor of dread sinking in my stomach. "Tell me."

"I ran into him a couple weeks ago on the beach." She twists her hair up away from her shoulders. Her neck is long and tempting. It makes me not want to be all the way across the table from her. "He was drunk."

I let out a breath. "That's nothing new, unfortunately."

"No, you don't get it. He was drunk *in the water* when it was about to storm." She swallows heavily and now her lower lip quivers, and it slays me that she still cares so much about my brother. It's so much more than I deserve. Not Jess, though. He deserves someone like Quinn to want him to be okay. She looks out at the ocean in the distance for a moment. "He almost drowned. I had to save him."

"Are you sure he wasn't fooling around?" I pull in air through my nose, slowly. Please let him have been fooling around. "He's an idiot sometimes, but he wouldn't—"

"He nearly killed both of us, Sawyer. He's a mess."

This instantly infuriates me. Rage is hotter than the damn sun and my blood's about to boil over with it. "Jesus, Quinn. I'm sorry. He's a little dickhead."

He never told me. He almost drowned and didn't think it might be information to share with someone who'd care about it. I see him at least twice a week, and he never mentioned it. So much for the day I found him at Kelly's being a one-off.

Why did I believe him? Wishful thinking, maybe. Fuck.

"And last week he showed up wasted at Gianna's ice cream shop. What happened to him, Sawy?" She uses her nickname for me for the first time since we were teenagers, and if I wasn't paralyzed with the terror that comes with imagining my little brother almost dying—and dragging Quinn down to the depths of the ocean with him—it'd probably make me happy.

"Life," I say, my voice rough. I clench my jaw to keep from saying more.

"Where have you guys been this whole time?" She's not asking for herself, not trying to wheedle information out of me like the last time. She wants to connect the dots between the Jess she knew then and the Jess she met two weeks ago.

"Different places," I say. "Jess moved around a lot with my dad."

"I saw Brock, too," she says. "That day in your shop. He..." She looks away again, but her expression is determined when she looks back. "He's a mess, too."

There's no judgment in her voice, but guilt shotguns through me anyway. I should've done a better job holding us together. I failed. "Yeah."

She opens her mouth. Closes it. She gets that I don't want to talk about it. "Where were you while they were moving around?"

"College." I can't stop picturing Jess going under, taking Quinn down with him. Drunk in the ocean before a storm. What is wrong with him? I want to kick the shit out of him. I want to hug him until he cries and just fucking lets me fix things for him.

"But... I looked for you at Duke. I drove up almost every weekend for two months searching for you. Directories. Classes I knew you'd registered for." There's no emotion on her face or in her voice, which must take a lot of control. Again, she slays me. I hate myself. Now I'm picturing the weekends she spent searching for me in a place I was far away from And wondering, though I have no right, at what point she gave up searching.

"I withdrew my acceptance," I tell her. "Took a year off."

"What about your scholarship?"

I shrug, like it doesn't still pain me. "I went...elsewhere."

"Where?"

I shake my head. It's too easy to talk to her. Too easy to slip into old habits. We're dangerously too close to having the conversation there's no way I'm going to have. Not when it will destroy me. Not when it will destroy her.

She shakes her head right back at me, her eyebrows arching above the oversized ovals of her shades. "Come on. You've got at least a year left and now that we're back in each other's lives—I mean, even just for right now, at least—you think I won't find out where you go to school?"

"I'm not going back."

"Well, that's just stupid. Why? You're just going to quit? God, Sawyer, you have all the—"

"I graduated in June," I say.

"You can't waste your..." Finally, she stops talking. "Oh."

"Oh." I let out a small smile. This is kind of fun, watching her do the math, watching her readjust her assumptions.

Almost as fun as it'd be to let her discover the diploma hanging in my otherwise empty guest bedroom. But that'd mean she was in my guest bedroom. And I'd really want to make sure I had a bed in there first. Not that I should be thinking like this. Shit.

She puzzles her brows. "You took a year off, which means... You graduated college in three years?"

I nod.

"But...why? Why push yourself like that?"

I tested out of most of the intro level classes. But that wasn't the real reason I worked as hard as I did. "Someone told me once I'd never amount to anything. That I'd end up like my old man." The memory still burns. Enough to make me want a drink, something stiff, something with a burn to cover the shit I'm remembering now. "Want to go get a drink?"

"I—what?" She offers half a smile, confused. "Aren't you on the clock?"

"Am I?" I gesture to us, to the table, to my bare shoulders. "Not very professional here—might as well take it to a bar."

Half a smile turns into half a laugh. "You really already graduated from college?"

"That's the word on the street."

"What was your major?"

"Engineering."

"Biological?" She remembers.

"Agricultural," I say, nodding.

"Like you always wanted." She throws a real smile at me this time. Brilliant enough to make me look away.

I want to tell her what it was like, what I've done. But all I say is, "Yeah."

"But..." She glances at the shop behind her, biting her lip again when she faces me.

"But why do I work at a surf shop?"

"Yeah."

"I enjoy it, Quinn. I like the work. I like the hours. I like that it lets me stay near the ocean." *And, for now, near you.*

Also, I'm halfway paid off to owning this place. But let her think whatever the hell she wants.

"Did you...did you believe it, when that person told you you wouldn't amount to anything?" she asks, lifting her sunglasses to look at me directly. Bright blue eyes, dipped in an emotion similar to sadness. Similar to understanding. Another glancing blow to my gut.

I shrug. "Doesn't really matter anymore. I know my worth now."

"I hope that's true."

"Why?" I ask. "After...everything." I wave a hand, like I can just wave off the past four years. "Why would you hope that still?"

"I know your core, Sawyer. I know who you are. You're a dick and I hate you for not telling me everything, and you broke my heart and I'll never forgive you for that. But I know you. You're the same you've always been."

I shake my head again, sadly now. "I wish you were right, Quinn. But you aren't. You should stay away from me."

CHAPTER TWENTY-THREE

QUINN

SAWYER TELLING ME to stay away from him is like a challenge. And I don't back down from challenges. Especially because I mean every word I say to him. I do know his core. I see his love for Jess. I see the dedication in his soul—the one that pushed him to graduate college a year early. God.

He *is* a dick.

And he *did* break my heart.

But I see what it does to him, when I look him directly in the eyes. I see the way he tries to keep a straight face, the way he doesn't want to be affected. He is, though.

For the first time in forever, I allow myself to believe that, whatever made him leave me four years ago, he didn't do it to be mean. He didn't walk away laughing, which is something I've had plenty of nightmares about. He had a reason and, whatever it was, it was bigger than how much he loved me. It still is.

"Why?" I ask him. "Why do I have to stay away from you? You're back. I'm here. And there's still something unfinished between us."

"It's not a good idea, Quinn. I can't tell you what you want to know. If there's anything between us, we need to remove it."

If there's anything between us? Please. I almost roll my eyes. And the rest of what he says... Well, his words hurt, but not as much as they would if I truly believed he wanted to remove it.

"Can I take you somewhere?" I ask, the words just popping out. I don't have a destination in mind, but I'm pretty sure he's close to ending this conversation, pretty sure he's retreating back into the shell who won't share himself with me, and I'm not ready for it.

"Where?" His one word answers are annoying.

I shrug. "Just somewhere. We can get lunch. Or a drink, like you wanted. Just somewhere to talk."

"I'm working."

"Are you?" I gesture to us, to the table, to his bare chest. "Not very professional here—might as well take it somewhere else."

He laughs. "Throwing my own arguments against me?"

"No need to create my own material when you've already laid the groundwork." I smirk. "Like a good engineer would."

"Different kind of engineer, Quinn." He stands. "I need to get back in there."

"I promise I won't ask you anything you don't want to answer," I say, not standing. "Just...hang out with me, Sawyer. Give me an hour. We haven't even finished speaking about Jess."

He scratches the corner of his mouth and looks over my shoulder for a moment. He sighs when he looks back. "An hour. I can leave for an hour, but I have a client coming in after that to pick up a board... Don't get any ideas about what we did the last time."

"Okay." But it's like another challenge, and now my mind's flooding with plenty of ideas about what we did last time. Especially because if he really wanted to remove this thing between us, he wouldn't be coming with me.

He goes to grab a shirt and tell Brandy to watch the shop. By the time he's back with me, unfortunately shirted, I've got the most innocent of expressions across my face. "My car or yours?"

"Still got the Jeep?"

I point to it down the street.

"Always loved that ride."

I pull my keys out of my bag. "Then let's go."

The passenger side's all jacked up, has been for over a year, and I have to unlock it from the outside to let him in. "See. I'm such a gentleman," I say, opening his door. He laughs.

When I slide into my seat, he glances at my legs, so I hike my knees up a little—still *so innocently*—so that my dress rises higher along my thighs. God, I love making him swallow as hard as he does right now.

"Where do you want to go?" I ask, driving to the main strip, picking a direction at random.

"Anyplace you feel like," he says. "I'm not eighteen anymore. I can actually afford to go the places you're used to."

"The places I'm used to?" At first, I'm offended, but a second later, it rolls away. What he says isn't about *me*; it's about him. "The only places I've ever wanted to go were the ones where you are."

If he notices my slip into present tense, he doesn't show it. "There were places you deserved to go where I could never take you. Just the way things have always been. People born in the gutters and people born to be better."

There's not a trace of self-pity in his voice, but it hurts my heart that he stills thinks about the world this way. He always has. It was such a struggle for him that his father was a cashier in my parents' store. Like he wasn't good enough for me.

But if his father never worked for my parents, I might never have ever spoken to him. He might not have ended up with a flat tire in the parking lot the same time my tutor was dropping me off to grab dinner with my mom, who was working that night. I wouldn't have been able to offer him my father's Jeep's spare.

And, okay, it totally didn't fit his sedan. But it got us talking.

We talked, and we talked, and we talked, and somewhere right there I started to fall in love.

"Never mind," I say, pulling a U-turn. "I know exactly where we're going."

"Out for lobster?"

I laugh and shake my head. "You have your secrets, now I have mine." I glance at him, and he's already focused on my face. There's nothing like the thrill of his gaze. Intense in every way, every time he's ever looked at me, from that first day we met to right here in my car. My abs tighten involuntarily and saliva gathers beneath my tongue. "To clarify, you think I was born...to eat lobster?"

"I always wanted to take you someplace fancy." He pauses. "And, honey, yes. You were. You've got more class in your pinky finger than anyone I've ever met."

I can't help it. I crack the hell up. "What if I was allergic to shellfish? That would *suck*."

He clenches his teeth, not amused. "That's not what I'm saying."

"I know, but come on. How the fuck do *you* define the word class, Sawy?" I pause to laugh a little more. "Hell, I just said fuck. Twice. And hell. *And* I made sure my dress hiked up higher when I sat down because I knew you were looking. That is not classy, I'm afraid to say."

"I *knew* you did that on purpose." Finally, he laughs, too. "Okay. You're crass. You happy now?"

I nod. "Yes."

"But you were also built for the best life has to offer." He says it so quietly, so sincerely, I sober straight up.

"And you think you weren't?"

"I think..." He shrugs. "I think I don't give a shit what people think I was built for." His hands are fists in his lap; the muscles in his forearms strain with how tightly he's clenching his fingers into his palms. It hurts him to admit this. Or maybe there's more. I'm not sure.

But I am sure, now, that I'm heading in the right direction.

"Did you leave something on my Jeep?" I have to ask, closely watching his expression. Wondering if—*hoping*—he'll smile and confirm the frame was from him.

"What do you mean?" He doesn't blink an eye, and his tone is halfway puzzled. Not forced at all.

"I just...never mind." I stifle a sigh and do my best to ignore the spiral of disappointment in my belly. I knew it wasn't him. I'm still curious about who really left it for me—but right now, all I want to think about, all I have room for, is Sawyer. Sitting next to me, sharing the same air. And it's amazing.

We drive in a quasi-comfortable silence for almost twenty minutes. We've only been here once, years ago. I wonder if he'll recognize it, but he stays quiet as we pull onto the busted-up street. I do my best to avoid broken bottles, but it's difficult.

"Remember this place?" I ask, pulling up in front of a small, crumbling one-story house. One of its windows is boarded.

"I do." He studies the house. "And I get what you're trying to prove. But it's not the same."

"You're right," I say. "It's not the same. Because this is where I grew up—where I spent the first eight years of my life. What your father provided for you and Jess? It looks like the Ritz compared to this. So if you're not meant for the best life has to offer, I'm sure as shit not, either."

"Quinn—"

"No. Listen to me." I wait for him to face me. "It hurts me, Sawyer, that you might consider my worth based on the money my parents have. Which, by the way, they came into when I was eight because my grandmother slipped in a freaking convenience store and sued." I can't remember if I ever told him this. I must have because there was a time when he knew every single thing about me, but maybe he needs the reminder. "Because, you know, wearing flip-flops while it was raining wasn't her fault. *Clearly*, the store was to blame. I mean, if *that's* not trashy, I don't know what is." I swing my door open, slide out. "Yeah, my parents took the money and made it grow—but so would *so* many other people if they were handed a check like that."

"Where are you going?" He leans across the seats to look up at me.

I hold on to the hood and swing myself partially back in. My face ends up closer to his than I intend, and his gaze drops to my mouth so quickly I almost miss it. He swallows again, and I...

Kiss him.

CHAPTER TWENTY-FOUR

QUINN

ONCE. LIGHTLY. A brush of my lips against his.

Again, with a little nip of his bottom lip.

I pull away and deserve a freaking gold medal for resisting a full-on daylight make-out session.

"Quinn," he growls my name and I almost dive back in. "What did I tell you?"

"Don't tempt me like that, then," I say. "Plus, you could've pulled back."

He's fighting a smile. I don't fight mine at all. Finally, he blows air through his lips and lets himself out of my car, too. "What are we doing?"

"It looks empty," I say.

"That doesn't mean you can go in." He walks toward me, halfway around the back of my Jeep. "Where's your spare?"

"Live a little, Sawyer. Wait. What do you mean where's my spare?"

"Pretty easy question, I think."

"Smart-ass." I make my way to him—and discover an empty space where my spare used to hang at the back of my Jeep. "What the hell?"

"You didn't use it? Was it there earlier?"

"No, and...I don't know. I haven't been studying the back

of my car recently." I trail my finger over the hinge where it usually hangs and a trace of unease passes through me. "Someone might be fucking with me. Stuff keeps going missing from my Jeep."

"Have you reported it?"

I shake my head. "Small things. Sunscreen. Phone charger. Shit I could've easily lost on my own. Then my wakeboard...and now my tire."

Who would take my things? And why *those* things? It seems so random. But also not random—*because they're all from my car*. A stronger tremor of unease swims over me this time.

"Maybe someone got a flat and stole it?" he asks.

Right. Okay. That's probably it. My tire's definitely stolen—but everything else? It could've all been me misplacing shit.

So I shake it off. And I smile at Sawyer because a moment ago, my mouth was on his. And because of that, today is a day for smiling. "It's weird. I was just thinking about the first day we met and how I tried to offer you my spare then."

For a moment, he still looks concerned. Then he shrugs, maybe pushing the worries aside the same way I am. Because he knows today's a day for smiling too. "It was your dad's spare back then. You weren't even old enough to drive."

"Whatever. I'd driven like...at *least* ten times behind my parents' backs by then." I roll my eyes, all exaggeratedly. "Anyway, come on."

"What about your tire?"

"I'll get a new one." I shrug, walking toward the house. I refuse to be creeped out about a missing spare tire. Not right now.

Sawyer doesn't follow me at first. "You can't just go inside."

"I'm not, *jeez*." I cut across the yard and wait at the fence to the backyard. "I grew up here. I want to visit memory lane for a minute." Not that I have a ton of amazing memories, or anything. Rich or poor, my parents have never been the type to make big family memories. My dad's always been a bit in the background. My mom's always been...striving for the next best thing.

"Are you aiming to make it two trips to the police station this month?"

"Sounds like a challenge to me." But thinking of Officer Vincent McDickwad does put a damper on my mood. Screw him, though. "You coming or what?"

I reach over the gate and let myself in. The fence is an improvement. We had a chest-high chain link when I lived here—same thing when I stopped by half a decade ago. Now it's wooden and almost as tall as I am.

The grass is trampled and sparse. No change there. But a double swing set sits in the middle of the small yard, and for a second I swallow around a lump in my throat. Good for the people who put it in. That and the fence. Small improvements make a huge difference. Maybe this is why the window's boarded. Maybe they put their savings here, instead.

Or maybe the window broke last week and the family's out buying new panes for it right now.

My imagination would flood the world if I didn't rein it in sometimes.

Sawyer stands beside me. "Memories coming running?"

"Nah." I move forward and drop into a swing. It squeaks under my weight, and I wrap my fingers around the chains.

"It's weird to picture you here. Or your mom." He glances around the yard, taking it all in, before resting his gaze back on my face.

"And what? My dad fits the part?" I try to laugh. Fail. It's hard to keep the conversation light—or flowing at all—when he stares at me the way he does, like he's hungry, starving even, and maybe not for food.

"Want me to push you?" He slides past me, behind me, grabbing the swing chains above my hands.

Maybe it's my imagination again because he's not even standing that close to me, but I swear I can feel the heat from his chest sinking into my back.

I push my feet against the ground until my back really does connect with his stomach.

I slide my hands up until they collide with his and stroke

one of his wrists with my thumb.

I hold my breath.

He does, too. But his heart's beating faster and faster, throwing itself between my shoulders.

I close my eyes. "Sawyer…"

He pulls the swing back and shoves it forward so hard I almost go flying.

My stomach drops on the downswing and I don't open my eyes because the tingles in my belly flood straight down between my legs. He steps out of the way when I swing back, giving enough room so I don't kick him in the face—but he can still reach my back. His fingers sear my skin through my shirt when he pushes me. I swing higher, and higher, and higher. His hands touch me lower, and lower, and lower each time… Behind my shoulders. The base of my ribs. At the small of my back… Until they wrap around my waist, just for a fraction of a second, before releasing me again into the air.

I grin because if he reaches lower this time, the next stop will be my ass, and my back is arching in anticipation.

But the next stop is a literal stop. He grabs the swing instead of me and holds it even with the ground, breaking the seesaw of thrills running through me. "I can't do this."

Yes, he can. But maybe he's the one who needs a push this time.

"When you left, did you go because of me?" I dig my feet into the ground, stilling the swing completely and twisting to look at him. "Can you just tell me that? Did I do something?"

"Jesus, of course not." He doesn't mean to say it, I can tell by the set of his jaw after the words slip out. But it's all I need to hear to know I'm right, that he still cares for me, and once he's said this much, maybe he figures he can share a little more because he continues. "You think my entire family would uproot because of something a seventeen-year-old girl did? *You were a part of us, Quinn.*"

"If I was a part of you, then why didn't any of you ever call me? Write me. Fuck, *anything* to let me know you were okay, so I could be okay." Not that I would've been okay. Not without him.

He sighs. "I couldn't tell you anything then. I still can't."

"Okay."

"Okay?" Half a smirk slides across his face. "What do you mean?"

I slide as much sincerity into my voice as I can. "I'll be okay with it. If I wasn't the reason you left, and if you didn't stop caring for me, I don't need to know anything else. Not if it means I'll lose you again now, too."

"You can't forgive me so easily."

"I don't forgive you," I say. "But I'm not walking away from you, either." I could be setting myself up for disaster. I could be being an idiot girl who refuses to see the obvious. But I don't think I am.

And the thought of walking away now, just because he's keeping something from me—no matter how huge it is—makes me feel physically ill. Literally. My stomach is rising like a roller coaster just considering it.

"We can't be together." He doesn't even bother unclenching his jaw to speak, so the words come out rough. Strained.

He's about to break. Needs only one more push, I think. "Why?"

He shakes his head.

"Fine. You can't tell me. But you're with me, Sawyer, right now. *You're with me.*"

"You need to take me back to the shop."

"What if it's a secret?" I ask, clinging to the gossamer strand of suspicion as it flits by. My mom would kill me for reuniting with him. Gianna, too. Not that I'd ever be ashamed to be with Sawyer, but maybe...maybe he has reasons for needing this to be a secret. Maybe I'll take him any way I can have him—because I see his heart. I know he still wants me the way I want him. "What if nobody else knows about us. What if we just...try?" I've never begged anyone to be with me before. Not once in all the years he's been gone. But nobody else has ever been worth it. "If it doesn't work out, nobody can give us shit for it because nobody will know."

"I can't tell you the things you want to know. You can't forgive me for it. We can't tell anyone we're together. This sounds *really* healthy." His sarcasm is biting. Sour. But he's also not saying no.

"Can you walk away?" I ask. "Again, I mean. Right now, can you walk away from me?"

I push myself out of the swing and spin toward him until we're no more than an inch apart. "Tell me, Sawyer. Tell me you can walk away again and I'll take you back to the shop and—"

"Stop." He shakes his head, his mouth pressed. "You have to stop, Quinn."

And he walks away.

CHAPTER TWENTY-FIVE

SAWYER

KEEP WALKING. JUST keep walking.

I make it to the fence line before she catches up, grabbing my arm and asking, "What the hell?"

Something inside me snaps and I spin to face her. Instead of stopping though, I grab her shoulders and circle us until her back hits the fence. She *grins*. I clench my jaw and slam a hand beside her head against the wood. I want to shove her legs apart. Take her here against the fucking fence. "Don't tell me to walk away and then *touch me*. Jesus."

Her eyes go wide, but not with fear, and her grin turns smug. "I wasn't telling you to walk away. I was asking if you could." She glances slyly to my hand beside her face and back to me. "Guess we've got our answer now, huh?"

"What is wrong with you, Quinn?" I'm this close to breaking—and she's begging me to. "This can't be what you want, can't be what you'll take. Some back room fuck with zero promise of anything else."

"You didn't fuck me in that back room, in case you've forgotten. Unless you count your tongue..." She trails off, considering, remembering. Making me remember, too. "And yeah, I'd definitely count that, actually. But look at you. *Feel* you." She reaches between us, rubbing me with her hand, taking me from semi-stiff to full-on fucking metal rod. "You want me. I want you. Why can't that be enough?"

She pisses me off. "Why the hell would you ever accept it as enough?"

"Because it's better than the alternative," she speaks simply, and my anger peels away, leaving room for all the shame in the world. I broke her four years ago. She was strong enough to suture herself back together, and if I stay I'll pull out all those stitches. Her undoing will be mine as well, again, but I'm not strong enough to take another step.

I rest my forehead against hers. "Nobody can know about this, Quinn, and I won't tell you why. I won't make you any promises." Even if I want to give her the entire damn world.

She closes her eyes and her breathing picks up. "Okay."

"Okay." I close my eyes, too, enjoying the feel of her skin against mine. One word, one small okay, and years of tension drain from my shoulders. I've lived with heavy chains of regret trapped around my ribs and they're loosening now. I haven't breathed this easily in four years. But when I open my eyes again, she's crying.

She gives a gentle shake of her head when I pull back to ask what's wrong and wraps her hands around my back to keep me in place.

"I'm crying because I'm happy." She lets her tears fall, trailing down her cheeks. "I've missed you. For four years, I felt like my soul was made of wet sand. And I know there are no promises from you—and I'm not making any either, okay? Because maybe this won't be enough for me. But for now? God, tell me you feel it too, Sawy."

A tear drips from the side of her jaw and I capture it with my mouth, letting its saltiness linger on my tongue. I catch the next one, too. I trail kisses up her cheek to the line of her lashes and I kiss her nose and kiss down the trail of tears on her other side.

She trembles and smiles when she opens her eyes. "Hello."

"Hello."

"Do you still want to leave?"

I study the house for a moment. It's dark inside, empty. "No."

"What do you want to do?"

"Freeze time."

She blinks, not expecting my answer, and her eyes fill again. "Me, too."

"But we're going to have to do something about all this crying."

Now she grins. "I can think of a few things."

I flash my teeth, lowering my head until our noses are practically touching. "So can I, honey. Believe me. I think I'll start right here, actually."

Her lips part. She thinks I'm going to kiss her, but I think maybe it's actually time to take it slow. As long as I can last, anyway.

I run my fingers along her arms until they find her fingers where they're locked around my back. I tug one of her hands away and pull it up to my mouth.

"I've always loved your hands," I say into her palm, punctuating my words with a small flick of my tongue. She draws in a sharp breath and I sink my teeth lightly into the heel of her palm. "So delicate. Such long fingers." I trail my lips across the tops of each one, ending with her thumb and pulling it into my mouth, swirling my tongue over it. "I thought about your hands a lot the past four years."

She's breathing faster and her pupils dilate, the black centers contrasting even more with the deep blue irises around them. I fucking love that I can turn her on just by giving her hand some attention. I can't wait to work my way along the rest of her. But I will wait. This time, I will take it slow.

She traces lines up and down my back with her free hand and slides it under my shirt, running it along my lower back, sending spikes of adrenaline up my spine.

I press my tongue against the pulse point of her wrist, dragging my teeth against her skin, and her head falls back against the fence. "Sawyer…"

"Such graceful arms," I say, kissing my way up to the inside of her elbow, concentrating here, too, at her pulse, and speaking into her skin. "Like a fucking ballerina. I can't wait to make you spin."

She says my name again, more like a moan this time, and I think maybe her world's already starting to twirl. I work my way up to her shoulder, smiling. "Your skin tastes like candy apples. I never forgot that, and I can't tell you how happy I am it hasn't changed."

She turns her face to look at me. "Really? Weird."

"Tasty," I correct her and lick my way to the side of her neck, nipping. "You have no idea how delicious you are."

She sighs and quivers against the fence, letting her head drop to the side, giving me more access to her smooth, silky skin. I really take my time here, tasting every inch of her long neck, pulling her earlobe into my mouth, teasing it with my teeth until she moans for real.

"I'm about to melt into this fence."

"Go ahead, honey. I'll catch you." I kiss my way from her ear down to the base of her chin, slowly, slowly, memorizing the edge of her jaw with my tongue.

I used to know every single curve of Quinn's body. I knew exactly where to place my mouth if I wanted to tickle her, to make her laugh. Exactly where to place my mouth to make her squeeze her legs tighter together, to make her wet. For however long we have in this…whatever it is we've agreed to…I plan to spend every moment I can refamiliarizing myself with any spot significant to her—and to add meaning to the ones that aren't yet.

"Will you please. Just. Kiss. Me?" she begs, nudging my face with her chin until I meet her eyes. When I do, there's no turning back. I'll have to work on her other arm later because her mouth is parted into a tiny "o" and her tongue is darting out to wet her lips, and fuck self-control. Fuck. It.

I brush my nose against hers and she smiles, loving that I'm giving her what she asks for. I run my tongue across her lips, tasting every inch, corner to corner, before licking the inside of her mouth. She tastes like candy here, too. I scrape my tongue along the ridges of her teeth and she slides her tongue through my lips, tasting me, too.

But I'm not ready to give up control and I grab her wrists, holding them above her head with one hand, trailing my other down the side of her throat, tracing waves across her collarbone, dipping lower to caress the tops of her breasts until she moans into my mouth and pushes herself more firmly into my hand.

I drop her wrists, wanting all ten of my fingers to trace her body, and she wraps her fingers through my hair. Her knees begin to bend and she slides down the fence, pulling me with her, until she's sitting on the ground and I'm kneeling between her legs.

Not once do our mouths part.

Not once do I want them to. Not ever again, if I can help it.

CHAPTER TWENTY-SIX

QUINN

HIS TONGUE FILLS my mouth and explores everything. My teeth. The roof of my mouth. The underside of my tongue.

Every time I try to take control of the kiss, he pushes back, puts me in my place. I smile against his mouth because here, and only here, am I okay with this, with him taking control.

Not for long though. No, this won't last that long at all. Not with the way I need him right now. All of him. Everywhere.

I push forward until he sits back on his heels. I keep my mouth on his and I climb onto his lap, crossing my legs behind his back. He's rock solid under his board shorts, and the only thing separating us on my side are my panties. My thin, *very* forgiving panties.

I rock my hips and he groans into my mouth and I want to eat his damn tongue if that's what it'll take to pull him farther through my lips.

My elbows are hooked around his neck, like holding his face captive against mine will give me the thing I'm craving most. The closeness I've been dying for for four years. Longer than that, really.

A sound like a growl works its way up his throat and it's so fucking sexy, the fluttering between my legs becomes something a little faster. A little stronger.

The sound deepens and he releases it into my mouth and like I weigh nothing, he rocks back onto his heels and stands. Oh, holy hell. My legs are still wrapped around him, but gravity sits me heavier against him, where he's so hard, and I'm about to fucking lose it. I twist my hips and writhe and moan back against his lips and he walks me backward until we hit the fence again, so hard it nearly knocks the air from my lungs.

Still, "Condom. Now," makes it out of my mouth.

He bites my lower lip, shaking his head. "Board shorts. Surfing. Don't have one."

"What the hell," I groan. I could kick myself for not putting one back in my bag after my first visit to Sawyer's shop. "Are you trying to freaking kill me?"

But he shushes me and buries his face in my neck and grabs the top of the fence for leverage. And then I'm hitting the fence, hitting the fence, hitting the fence so hard every time he slams his hips against me I'm going to have bruises between my shoulders—*and* along my inner thighs. Yum.

He's straining against me, thrusting, ramming, *torturing* me and all I want to do is reach between us and free him from his shorts. Push my panties to the side. Screw a rubber. I need him. But I can't because I'm holding on for dear life and he's giving no quarter here. My back is slamming into the fence so hard I'm nervous we'll break it. I'm nervous about splinters, too, somewhere at the far end of my mind, but who the fuck cares about a little bit of pain when the boy you've loved your entire life is pressing himself as far as humanly possible inside of you through thin layers of clothing? I swear to God his tip is *right there* and somehow we're about to have sex for the first time without even taking anything off and I don't give a single fuck because I need him there, to fill me, so bad I'm almost in pain with the way I'm throbbing.

I pull his hair so hard I'm shocked it doesn't come away in my fingers, and he lets a slow, sly laugh escape. "You always liked it a little rough."

"Shut up," I breathe through his lips. "Just shut up and don't fucking stop."

He doesn't fucking stop.

Groans turn to grunts, now, little growls and sharp tugs with his teeth against my lower lip, against my neck. The friction of his erection rubbing, shoving against me, pushes that fluttering between my legs into pulsing and builds to a crest and my orgasm gives barely any warning before it flows through my entire system. From my head to my toes. From the inside of my belly to the wetness I feel flood between my thighs.

Only when he puts a hand against my mouth do I realize how loud I've been moaning. But he's been moaning, too—I can hear it in my memory of the last few seconds. And when he lets go of my mouth to grab the fence again, his hips are at rest except for the occasional reflexive jerk, making his breath come out in shaky little laughs.

It takes a minute, but when my own breathing's slowed enough for me to speak, I bat my lashes all innocently and ask, "You need a new pair of shorts?"

"You need a new pair of panties?" he shoots back, his eyes dancing.

"Proud of yourself?" I raise a brow. "You seem quite smug at the moment."

"Honey, I just made you come and didn't even have to take your clothes off."

I laugh and slowly, gently, unwrap my legs from him, sliding back down the fence. "Pretty sure I did the same to you, *honey*."

"True," he concedes. And for a pause, we stand here, grinning at each other like idiots. I can't remember a moment when I've been this happy.

Somewhere down the street a car alarm blares and we both jump. Sawyer looks around like he's just remembering where we are. In someone else's backyard. Could be busted any moment. "We should go," he says.

"What about your plan to freeze time?" I ask, knowing he's right but still wanting to stall the moment a bit longer.

"I changed my mind," he says. "I don't want to freeze time with you. I want to claim every second as it passes. See what happens next."

I throw my arms back around him and press the side of my face into his chest. "I need you to hold me for at least a few of these precious seconds you speak of."

"Easiest thing I've ever done." He squeezes me against him, his heart picking up speed. Or maybe it's mine, throwing itself against my chest so hard it's the only thing I hear.

A few seconds pass way too quickly and soon he's stepping away, taking my hand, and tugging me toward the gate. I stop before we open it. "This has been an awesome day. No matter what happens when we step out of this backyard. Thank you."

"Best day I've had in four years," he says.

I squeeze his hand and let him lead me back into reality.

Right as the homeowners pull into the stub of a driveway.

"Shit!" I smile and wave, all awkward, as though hanging out in their backyard is a regular, accepted occurrence that they're *just fine* with—and I rush to my car. Sawyer beats me to it, cursing when he can't get the passenger door open. I can't help giggling as I slide into my seat and reach through to push it open for him.

The guy, an older man with salt and pepper hair, jumps out of his car and shakes his fist at us, but I only see him in my rearview because I'm hauling ass to get out of here.

"That was close," Sawyer says, glancing behind us.

"Imagine what they would've found if you'd actually had a condom this time!" I expect him to laugh with me, but he grows quiet instead. "Or...not."

"Maybe we should take it slow," he says. "Where that's concerned."

"Why?" I'm seriously considering stopping off at a gas station to buy condoms and breaking one out in the damn backseat of my car.

"Because, Quinn, it's sex. I want it to mean something to you. When it's with me, I mean."

It takes a moment for his arrow to hit its mark, but it hurts when it does. "Well, ouch."

"I didn't mean it like that."

"Yes, you did." Tears sting my eyes, again. Painful ones this time, so I stare straight out my windshield and refuse to let them fall. "Don't worry, then. Sex between us? Off the table for a while."

"Pretty sure anytime we bring a table into the picture, sex is going to be right back on it."

I don't laugh. It'd be funny and sexy any other time. But not while my pride is sliced in half.

"You left. I waited for you for hours in that tent, ready to give myself to you, and you never showed up. Never spoke to me again." I've never regretted the decisions I've made regarding my body. Until now. "What I've done since then isn't anything you get to comment on."

"You slept with Danny Simmons."

Okay. So there's one thing I've always regretted, one thing I always will. "Yep. I did. I went out and screwed the first person I could when I realized you weren't coming back." I stop at a red light and look at him, but now he's staring straight ahead, a muscle in his jaw clenching, unclenching. "Look at me."

When he does, his eyes are tortured.

"Stop judging me," I say, quietly. "I care about you, Sawyer. I want to be with you, to try this thing even if you can't tell me your secrets. I'll do my damn best to accept it. But if my past, my history, is something you can't get over, you might as well get out of my car right now. Because I can't change anything about it. And I don't want to. I'm sorry if you can't handle it, but the things I've done? They're how I held myself together. Every person I've been with has been another step away from the memory of you. And I'm grateful for them—even when they didn't know that's what they were doing. You almost killed me. I couldn't function. I couldn't *breathe*. I couldn't—"

"Stop, please." His voice is almost as broken as his expression. "I'm sorry. I'm so sorry. I won't ever forgive myself for what I did. I wake up hating myself every fucking morning, okay?"

"No." I shake my head. "It's not okay. I don't want you to hate yourself—especially when I don't feel anything like that toward you. Very much the opposite, in fact. But I need you not to judge me. It's the one thing I can't—"

"I'm not judging you. I—" The car behind us honks and Sawyer pauses. I missed the light going green. I drive forward, hating dragging my eyes away from him. He clears his throat. "I want sex to mean something with us, because it's you and me, Quinn. Our first time. You didn't—"

"Of course it'll mean something. You just said—it's me and you. How could it ever be meaningless?"

"Let me finish." He's looking at me so intensely the side of my face burns. I glance at him as long as I can spare from the road, and nod. He drags a hand through his hair. "You didn't wait for me."

"I already told—"

"I understand why," he says. "I don't blame you. Never will. But the thing is, Quinn, I did. I waited. For you."

CHAPTER TWENTY-SEVEN

QUINN

IT DOESN'T MAKE sense at first, what Sawyer's saying.

He waited for me.

"You...?" I look at him. He watches me. He waited for me. For sex. "I don't... *How?*"

"You need me to explain the mechanics?"

I'd roll my eyes if I wasn't so shocked. But I am shocked. Like, need to pull my Jeep over shocked. "No. I mean..." What do I mean? "Look at you, Sawyer. How the hell did you manage to wait? Did you always know you'd come back? Or were you at college in a monastery? Or..." I shake my head. "I just... How?"

I'm starting to tremble and I don't know why. My heart is aching and I don't know why. I can't meet his eyes all of a sudden and...I do know why. "Sawyer—"

"I wasn't a saint," he says. "But nobody else ever—"

"Ever what?" My voice is raspy, dry. I need water. A gallon of it. A freaking lake and a straw. "Came on to you? Wanted you? Offered to bang you? Because I call bullshit on all that."

"Measured up. Nobody else ever measured up."

"To the memory of a gawky seventeen-year-old?"

"Don't." His tone is sharper now. "Don't act like what we

had wasn't significant because of our ages."

"I've spent the last four years screwing around to try to forget you—clearly, unsuccessfully. I don't think anything about us was insignificant." I don't know why I'm doing this. Being such a bitch. Throwing my past in his face. "I'm sorry. Can I start over?"

"That'd probably be nice," he says, not looking at me.

"I'm not reacting very well, here." Great, now my voice is wobbling. "But did you know you'd come back? Is that why you waited?"

He shakes his head. "I didn't think I'd see you again. And I just told you why I waited."

God. Why is everything hurting my heart right now?

Things That Hurt My Heart This Time

1. He waited for me without knowing he'd ever see me again because nobody else was worth it to him, while I gave everything away because I didn't want him to be worth it.
2. He thought he'd never see me again. He accepted it.
3. He's an amazing, beautiful boy and I don't get to tell anyone else he's all mine. For now.
4. The *for now* tacked on to the end of the last sentence.

* * * * * *

I don't know what to say because he's shared something so unbelievably sweet and special, but I'm so devastated by it all that I can barely breathe. He's waiting for me to get a grip. He's waiting for me. Again.

A full minute passes.

Another.

"I need to get back to work," he says. Guess he had to wait too long.

I nod. And I drive him quietly back to his shop, finally finding my voice the moment he opens his door. "Sawyer, listen. I'm a little blown away, okay?"

He shrugs. "I get it."

"This means something," I manage. "It means...a lot. I have some mental adjustments to make, but you're..."

"Perfect?" He throws a cocky grin like a lifeline, like he knows exactly what I need.

"Let's not get carried away here, buddy." I grin back. "What time do you get off?"

He raises his brows.

"*Of work.*"

He laughs. "I close tonight."

And I've got dinner plans with my parents, which I'm definitely not about to bring up in front of him again. I don't want to fight about my mom a second time. Especially considering that with the *one* exception of how supportive she was when he disappeared, we're pretty much in complete agreement about how awful she is. But admitting that to him feels like a betrayal for the months she spent consoling me. Instead, I say, "My college roommate is coming to town this weekend. Friday. Want to come hang out with us?"

"I'm not sure that's a good id—"

"Oh, right. We're keeping this a secret." Almost forgot in the wake of the bomb of a his confession. "Well, what if you come out with us and we pretend like we're only friends?" I really want him to meet Cassidy. "Her boyfriend, Gage, is performing at Port O' Call. We can even drive separately...though hopefully one of our cars will see a little backseat action before the night's done."

"All right." He sighs. "See what you do to me? Didn't even have to twist my arm."

I slide a hand into his lap. "I could twist something else, if you wanted me to. Gently. And with my mouth."

"You're just full of temptation today."

"Only today?"

"You fishing for compliments?'

"Just pointing out that if you think *this* is tempting—" I squeeze his thigh, making him jump "—you've got no clue what's coming for you."

"You. You'll be coming for me," he says, smirking. "Again

and again and again."

Damn it, if I didn't already need clean panties, I would now. "Wow. Okay. You win the banter award."

"Is it still banter if it's also a promise?"

"Does it stop being just a promise if I straddle you right here?"

"Fuck, Quinn. You're about to send me to my appointment with a boner." Something out my windshield catches his attention. "Shit, there's Wyatt now."

I follow his gaze toward a guy walking into the Surf Spot. "Oops." I slide my hand higher until I'm cupping him. And yeah, he's got the start of a swell. "Hello, there."

He grabs my wrist with a groan. "This guy already hates me." He pries my hand away, lacing his fingers through mine instead. "He's a pain in the ass. Don't make me go in there with wood."

"Keep holding my hand and I'll stop teasing you," I promise. Because I want a moment to let it sink in. Sawyer's holding my hand. He's holding my hand and we're seeing each other and the world feels like an endless possibility for happiness right now.

Then he leans across the console between us and feathers his lips over mine.

I part my lips to let him in, but he pulls away with a regretful little smile, adjusting himself and making me laugh.

"I definitely can't walk in there if I keep kissing you. I might not be able to walk at all if I don't leave now." But he kisses me one more time, anyway. On the cheek, though it doesn't lessen the way his lips sear my skin. And then he's gone. Sliding out of my car and walking away.

"Hey!" I call after him. And when he turns, "Port O' Call's on milepost eight."

"Don't pretend I wasn't the one who introduced you to that place years ago."

I grin, shrugging. "Thought you might've forgotten. Be there at seven thirty."

"Never forgot a single thing where you're concerned."

"If you weren't already out of the Jeep, I'd be jumping you right now."

"You're killing me, Quinn."

"Good." And when I remember the entire reason for stopping by today, I add, "You'll talk to Jess, right?"

"Yeah. That kid's got a wake-the-fuck-up fist heading straight for his face."

I'd laugh again, but damn if he doesn't look completely serious.

I spend the rest of the day sighing dreamily like an idiot and picking flowers to press and frame. I arrive home with a rather gorgeous collection. Clumps of blue-eyed grass flowers with delicately winged petals that will look gorgeous pressed between glass, as will my clusters of pink wood sorrel. Then the twenty or so wood anemones—I'm already drooling over my mental image of the stark white flowers contrasting the deep blue frames I have waiting for me back at school—and a mixture of pinkshell and flame azaleas that won't dry very well, but will look lovely in a vase at the center of my dining table.

Which makes me think maybe I'll have Sawyer over for dinner sometime.

Which makes me sigh wistfully all over again.

Which makes me roll my eyes at myself.

CHAPTER TWENTY-EIGHT

SAWYER

I PLANNED TO spend my day off with Rajesh. Surfing. Studying houseplants and comparing the way their leaves grow to those in the wild. Instead I find myself at my father's apartment first thing in the morning.

I brought him coffee but drank it on the way over to try to push myself into a better mood. It's hard when I barely got any sleep last night. I couldn't stop reliving the way Quinn felt pressed against me yesterday, the way it felt slamming her against the fence, nearly taking her right there. The sounds of her moans. Which are the last things I'd ever complain about—shit, I'd live in that memory all day, every day if I could. But every other thought was spliced through with the image of my stupid-ass younger brother drowning. I couldn't stop picturing what would've happened if Quinn hadn't saved him.

I spent my night turned on while simultaneously alternating between feeling like I was going to throw up and being really pissed off. Now I'm at my dad's door still feeling sick and really pissed off. At least I'm not turned on. Took care of that in the shower. Just have to do my best not to think of Quinn.

Damn it. There she is. In my mind. Her wide blue eyes; her red inviting mouth opening to say... *Condom. Now.*

Fucker.

But she disappears when I let myself through the front door because the first thing I see is my dad, strewn lopsided on the couch, snoring like a damn chainsaw with a half-empty bottle of Jack Daniels tucked next to him. At least it's not completely drained. Guess that's something. I nudge him with my knee, but he doesn't budge, doesn't even hiccup in his snores.

The rest of the apartment is a disaster. Two kitchen cabinets hang wide open. Empty take-out boxes litter the counters. A mountain of laundry is piled on an armchair across from the couch; I can't tell if it's clean or dirty. Fuck it. I scoop it up and shove it all in the washing machine, searching a good ten minutes for detergent. I find it tucked behind some cereal boxes. I can't begin to fathom how it got there.

I tidy up the rest of the place the best I can, quietly at first, but as my irritation grows so does the sort of noise I make. Slamming doors and drawers, stomping through the dining room and living room. Still, my dad doesn't budge. It shouldn't surprise me; I gave up on him ages ago. But he promised, *he swore*, he'd do better by Jess.

Damn it. I cleaned to try to get rid of some of this anger, but all it's done is roar through my mind, through my veins, until it's the only thing I feel. I bang Jess's bedroom door open and find him passed out just like our old man. Hanging halfway off a chair, snoring with a video remote control gripped in one hand. Empty beer cans by his feet.

"Get up." I poke his shoulder, rougher than I probably should, and his eyes snap open right before he hits the floor.

"What the hell, man?" His words are so slurred with tiredness—or maybe drink—I can barely understand him. He flicks me off and tucks into a ball on his side, snoring again an instant later.

I want to kick him. So badly I turn away from him and sweep out my arm, bulldozing everything off the top of his ratty old desk. A few papers; a few more beer cans. Nothing nearly satisfying enough. I slam a fist down on top of it. The pain vibrating up my arm helps a little.

I duck down in front of Jess. "Wake up." Nothing. I push

his shoulder. "Wake up." He waves me off, choking through half a snore.

I shake a few of the beer cans, finding one still half full. I pour it on his face. He comes up spitting—and swinging. "Jesus Christ, Sawyer. Leave me be."

It's easy enough to move out of the swing of his fists. I wait for him to chill and then lock my arms around him, picking him up and tossing him on his unmade bed. He's light. Should he be so light? "Are you eating these days, you skinny little shit?"

He closes his eyes. "Why are you always such a dick?"

Because otherwise I'd break. Otherwise you'd have me on my knees begging you to get yourself together, and we both know that wouldn't work. "Because you're always such a fuck-up. Get your act together and I'll be sweeter. Hell, I'll bring you goddamn flowers."

"Pansy," he slurs, rolling onto his side.

"You want pansies? I'll bring you a bouquet." I probably know more about flowers and bouquets than necessary, but Quinn's always been into them, and it turns out I've always been greedy for information about anything that makes her who she is.

Jess doesn't respond. Snoring. Again. This time I leave him be and pick up his room. Though I hit my limit when I find plates covered in mold under his bed. I toss them in the trash, and I sit on the now laundry-less armchair across from my sleeping-it-off father. I wait.

It's another hour before he cracks open one bloodshot eye. It wanders the room and when it lands on me, he drags a hand across his mouth, and pushes himself up to study me. "Son." His voice cracks with leftover sleep.

"Pop." I'm surprisingly calm. The time spent waiting for him gave me a chance to think. "We need to talk."

"I'm not feeling so hot this morning. Might be coming down with something. Can we reschedule?"

"No."

He yawns and nods, resigned. "Figured as much. Let me grab a coffee."

"There's a fresh pot on in the kitchen."

"Appreciate it."

"Leave some for Jess."

He doesn't respond, and he's still bleary-eyed when he returns to the couch, handing me a fresh cup first.

"Have you seen Jess's room?" I ask as soon as he sits down.

He meets my gaze. "I give him his privacy."

"Guess that's why he doesn't bother hiding all the beer cans."

He flinches, glancing at his cup. "Teens drink."

"Not the way he does. He said he'd straighten up if we came back here, and he isn't doing it."

"We aren't leaving again."

"What if it's what's best for Jess?"

"If I thought it was, we'd be out the door. But I don't believe that."

I want to get on board with him. Hell, especially after yesterday with Quinn. After any day with Quinn. But Jess...before we came back to the beach, he was spiraling so bad his next step was juvie. Or worse. So he's who we have to think about now. "Dad—"

"No. I also came home for this job—and I've managed to keep it." He juts his chin up, like it's something to be proud of. And it is, really, considering it's the first time he's kept a job longer than a few weeks in years. But he continues, "And because I need to be close to where your mother rests, and God help me, I'm not leaving her again."

His eyes go glassy and my own damn throat thickens. I only have bits and flashes of memories of my mother, but I know my dad remembers her like she was here yesterday. A moment goes by before he says, "Jess isn't leaving either."

I lean back in my chair, forcing my posture to remain relaxed. "I will wait this out just a little while longer. But if I'm going to agree, then you need to get some help."

"You think if I could afford to hire someone, Jess would let some nanny tell him what to do? I'd have to hire a damn supermodel to get any sort of reaction from him. Even that might not be enough."

"No—it's time for *you* to get help."

He shakes his head when my words sink in. "I'm functioning just fine. Bills are paid. Your brother's fed. Alive."

A functioning alcoholic. He accepted it years ago. The problem is, I accepted it, too. "Is that what life's worth to you? You can *function*? Your youngest son is *alive*?"

He doesn't answer, but the shock wiping the tiredness from his face tells me maybe I've started too strong. Except I'm starting to realize I should've started even stronger a long time ago.

For years I told myself not to parent my own father. I had my own demons to deal with, and I was in no shape to deal with his at the same time. But it hits me, sitting here, that I can't expect Jess to get his shit together if he doesn't have at least one role model to mirror on a more regular basis. "You need to get clean. Or I'm taking Jess."

"You're not taking Jess." No trace of tiredness in his voice this time. He stares at me, hard, but I don't look away. He clears his throat. "If you're that worried, you could always move—"

"No." I'm not moving in with him. I can't, and we both know why.

The last person I hit before Danny Simmons? My father.

I had quite a bit of practice before him, but my aggression was always leading toward my dad. He was drunk and saying things he shouldn't have been saying, and I was so angry with him for so many reasons. I didn't even try to stop myself. My fist landed right below his eye, and he went down. It was like a bucket of razor-sharp ice, watching him fall. I helped him up and couldn't stop apologizing. I'll never forget the way he looked at me, so broken. I'll regret it for the rest of my life.

But some days I worry I'll have the impulse to do it again. Like right now. Knowing he was so wasted on his own last night he had no clue what Jess was up to.

Keeping distance from my dad keeps the anger in my gut leashed—but I'll never be too far away, not while he's responsible for my brother. After that...time will tell.

"Well, you aren't taking your brother."

"Then you know what you need to do."

"Where is this coming from?" He studies me, looking genuinely bewildered. I can't blame him. I've ignored his shit almost as long as he has. I guess we both figured a drinking addiction was better than a few of the other bad habits so many people have. But not anymore.

"Jess almost died a couple weeks ago," I say, watching the bewilderment slip back into shock. "He was wasted in the ocean on a rough day and he started to drown. That's where this is coming from."

He drags a hand across his face. "I... I didn't know, Sawyer. Shit. If I'd known—"

"It's bad enough that I didn't know," I say, my own composure slipping into something a little darker. "But that you didn't? What sort of father are you?"

"The kind who struggles his entire life to provide for his two ungrateful sons." He's saying this out of hurt, out of anger—same as my own words—but it doesn't stop the burn that comes with them. "Kids get away with things sometimes. Even if I was the best father in the world, he'd be able to slip things by me."

"If you weren't a drunk, he wouldn't be able to get away with half as much," I say. "I know you love him, but what Jess needs right now is more than that."

He's silent for a while and I give him the time he needs to process. When he speaks again, he sounds defeated. "I can't just snap my fingers and stop drinking."

The fact he's thinking about it is a start. One he's made before, but this time I'm not letting him fall backward.

"I have money put aside," I say, not including that it's in a college fund for Jess. "I saved most of my half of what Rajesh and I earned when we sold the designs to our...system." We designed a farmland grazing system to fence and herd livestock along paths similar to those taken by grazing animals found in nature. Natural herds are kept closely contained by their predators and have to relocate after eating, flattening, and shitting all over an area, only coming back once it's regrown. We put together plans that should help ensure the maintenance and restoration of rangeland ecosystems. But my dad usually stops listening as soon as I mention the word grazing, so I refrain from trying to explain it for the millionth time. Especially considering the most important part of this conversation: "I'm going to give you some of my savings, and you're going to use it to check yourself into a clinic to dry out. I'll take Jess while you're gone, and he'll come home when you're back."

"I'm not taking your money. You're my kid." He said the same thing when I offered it to him to help with rent, or groceries, or anything to make things easier. But this time he doesn't get the final say.

"Sometimes the lines between fathers and sons get crossed," I say. "This is one of those times. You can go voluntarily, or I can take Jess away through legal means." It's murder on my heart, saying these things. Until I imagine drowned Jess, bloated on the beach somewhere. Then it gets a whole lot easier. "Take your pick."

He sips his coffee, but his eyes slide to the bottle of whiskey at the end of the couch. "I need some time to think about it."

"I'll give you five minutes." I drink my own coffee, as though I've got all the time in the world.

"Damn it, Sawyer. You can't just spring this on me."

"Spring this on you?" I laugh, though there's no humor in it. "This has been years in the making. Four at least, but if we're honest, it goes back farther than that, too. You swore if we came back here you'd get it together." Jess swore he'd get his shit together, too, if he could come home and reconnect with his old friends. And I swore to myself I'd keep away from Quinn.

Guess none of us keep our promises.

"We came back here because I had a job offer. And I've held it down steady these months. I am together."

"No. You're not."

"Let me try AA first," he says, changing tactics. "It worked last time."

"Not really." I point at the Jack Daniels. "Working for a little while isn't the same thing as working for life."

He sucks in a deep breath when I say *for life,* and I know how hard it must be to consider the rest of your life without one of your driving forces.

Much like I felt when I walked away from Quinn.

"One mistake," I tell him, praying I won't regret giving in. "One drink from here on out, and we do this my way." I push off the chair and swipe his bottle of Jack Daniels, taking it into the kitchen and dumping it down the sink. The fumes burn my eyes and nostrils. Not that I mind whiskey on my own, but it's hard to take this early in the day. For me, anyway. Not so much for my father.

He's still sitting there when I return, staring into space.

I want to stress my point to him again, to make sure it's really hammered through his skull that one more step out of line will land him in rehab no matter what, but I swallow the words. "You didn't mention seeing Quinn."

He glances at me, unsmiling. "Neither did you."

It's true, and she's probably not something we should talk about right now, anyway. I pull my phone from my pocket, doing a quick Internet search. "Grab your stuff."

"Why?"

"I found a meeting that starts in twenty minutes and we're going." Then, after thinking about it, I add, "Wake up Jess, too. He's coming with us."

CHAPTER TWENTY-NINE

QUINN

I HAVEN'T HEARD from Sawyer since I dropped him off on Monday, and I'm a ball of annoyingly nervous energy by the time Friday night comes around.

Cassidy and Gage got a later start than they'd planned, so we're meeting at Port O' Call instead of my place. Which is maybe for the best because they'd probably be irritated with me here. I've changed my outfit at least five times. I curled my hair. I brushed it out and straightened it.

So stupid. I know. But this is my first date—even though it's a secret one—with Sawyer in four years. And not a minute's gone by this entire week when I haven't been remembering how it felt to kiss him again. How it felt to have access to his amazing mouth. To his amazing body.

How it felt to have his hands on me. To feel him *so close* to pressing into me.

God. Maybe I need another shower. A cold one.

But a glance at my phone tells me I don't have time.

I double-check the locks on my Jeep, like I do every time I get to it or leave it now. They're still locked. Nothing's been taken. My new spare tire is still there.

Good. I slide into my seat breathing a little easier.

Cassidy and Gage are already at the restaurant when I arrive. He's checking something out on the stage, all tousle-haired and laid-back rocker styled, and she's relaxing with a beer at a nearby table, all big-boobed and gorgeous. God, sometimes I'd kill for boobs like hers. Though...I do love the way Sawyer's able to palm mine. Hmmm. Going to need to quit thinking about that right now.

Gah.

I love his palms. And I love his fingers and I love imagining and remembering the way they feel lazily trailing up my thighs—and everything that comes after...

Shit. *Get it together, Quinn.*

The bar's half full and the tables visible through the railing of the open second level, the restaurant area, are packed. "It looks like it's going to be a good crowd tonight," I say, after hugging Cassidy and Gage hello.

Cassidy's eyes shine and she turns to Gage, tucking a few blonde strands behind her head. "This is so cool!"

He waves her words off, but his eyes shine right back at her. "I've played places like this plenty of times."

"Yeah, but this time it's with your own songs." She wraps him in a hug and he tries to be discreet when he takes a sniff of her hair, but I totally catch him.

He shrugs. "I like her coconut shampoo."

"You like what it reminds you of." Cassidy untangles herself from his arms, shaking her head, sharing some happy inside memory.

"Oh, God. Gag me," I say, but my tone's light, and joking. Which is a first when it comes to them, I think.

They're so *unbelievably* in love...it used to make me sick, the past year when he'd visit her at school—and when he moved into our apartment building, it was almost too much. Now I think of Sawyer and I don't feel so grossed out anymore.

Cassidy and I have an odd relationship. We're roommates, but we've never been close. It seemed like we could've been, when we first met my freshman year. But the next year we moved in together, and her brother died and she shut me out.

She shut everyone out, basically. But especially me because I was there. All the time. And I tried—I tried to get her to talk to me about it; I tried to get her to hang out for a girls' night, for anything—but a girl can only handle so much exclusion from another person's life before they stop trying, and I discovered my limit with Cassidy.

Last year she came back changed. Happy. In love. And this time she was the one trying to get to know me—but Julian was uncomfortable with anyone finding out about us, so I kept her at arm's length. I figured she'd hit her limit, too, but when she texted that she wanted to come visit this summer, I jumped at the chance to say yes. Because Julian's out of my life, and I want her to be back in it. Especially since she's moving in with Gage next semester, and I don't want to lose touch.

My phone vibrates where it sits in my purse against my hip. It's a text message from Gianna. *We're here.*

We?

I turn, looking for her, just as she comes through the door—with Chase.

She's looking at me, but he's looking at her and something about the moment just…makes sense. I can't keep a smile from spreading. Something tells me Gianna's going to be in trouble.

"I had no clue you were coming," I say to Chase after a round of hugs and introductions. And shit. I still hadn't figured out how to explain Sawyer's arrival to Gianna, much less with Chase in the mix.

He nudges Gi with his elbow. "She leads, I follow."

"Sounds about right, when Gianna's involved." I raise a brow at her. *This isn't weird for you?*

She mirrors my expression. *Nope.* "He might be a keeper," she says, loudly. "But don't tell him I said so. Then he'll get an ego big enough to compete with mine and I'll have to let him go."

Chase sticks his fingers in his ears. "I hear nothing."

"Good boy." She pats his arm. I raise a brow again and she adds, "I'm queen B of all the puppies, remember?"

"All too well." Stupid Danny Simmons. And Chase doesn't

seem to mind being petted, or referred to as a puppy, so... I drop it.

"I think I like you," Cassidy says to Gianna. "Queen B of all the puppies? I don't know what that means, but it already makes me want to follow you."

"I think she and Teagan would get along," Gage says, earning another brilliant Cassidy smile. "Has she called you back yet?"

Cassidy shakes her head, her face falling. "She freaked me out this morning..." She glances at me. "We met Teagan for breakfast today, it went...longer than we thought it would. That's why we got into town so late."

"It's okay," I say. "I'm just happy you're here at all."

Teagan's Cassidy's best friend from her hometown in Virginia. I met her a few times the past school year when she visited, but mostly briefly because I was always on my way out to see Julian or had him hiding in my bedroom. The memory has my face flaming. I can't believe I let myself get swindled that way. What a waste of a year.

But then I see Sawyer at the entrance and the flames in my cheeks slide way, way lower. Who cares about the past when my present looks the way he does? A day or two's worth of stubble along his sharp jaw, perfectly messy hair, and electric green eyes zeroed in on me. White T-shirt, dark denim jeans, and his hands in his pockets. Sexiest beach bum I've ever seen. And, let's not forget the washboard abs beneath that shirt. Or the vee that edges out of them like an arrow straight down to another one of my favorite parts.

"I'll, um, be right back," I say to whoever's listening. "Getting a drink. Or something."

I tilt my head toward the bar and he meets me there.

"Why didn't you give me your number?" he asks, leaning against the bar, all casually even if his tone is way accusatory. "I tried the one you had four years ago, but it's disconnected... Or you could've come back by my shop."

I grin. He's been missing me, too. "Forgot about the number thing. And we had plans for tonight—I didn't want to drop by sooner and push my luck."

"So you thought you'd push me into going mad instead?" he asks. "Don't ever stay away that long again."

"Careful, Sawyer." I slide a stool between us.

"What?"

"You're making me want to kiss you. And that'd blow our cover." I press my hands on the padded seat in front of me. "Now I'm resorting to furniture blockades."

"'Admit it, you always want to kiss me."

"Guilty as charged." I drum my fingers along the seat. "You ready to meet Cassidy?"

"She's important to you, right?"

I nod.

"Then you don't even need to ask."

"God, now I *really* want to kiss you."

"Feeling's mutual, honey." He glances at my mouth, and I lean forward on my hands across the chair...

And then backward.

I don't care if we're a secret, but he does, and I don't want to push him into revealing anything before he's ready.

So mature of me.

Even if stepping back a second time, pushing away from the stool, is really freaking hard to do.

"I've just realized how much I hate being in public with you," he says.

Then don't make us keep this secret. But I simply smile and say, "Come on, I'll introduce you."

CHAPTER THIRTY

QUINN

I DIDN'T TELL anyone Sawyer was coming, but only because I didn't want to have to lie to my friends about him. As we approach the table, I realize it might have been a mistake.

Cassidy greets him with a huge smile and Gage shakes his hand, easy. But...the other half of the group isn't quite so welcoming.

"Sawyer, this is Chase," I say.

Sawyer looks at me and says, stiffly, "I didn't realize you'd be bringing a date."

So much for keeping this thing between us a secret. No way my friends aren't going to notice his jealousy.

But his reaction makes me a little happier than it should. I'm not the biggest fan of jealousy, but knowing Sawyer's affected by me in any way will never, ever get old.

"*My* date," Gianna says. "But thanks for making this awkward since Chase took Quinn out first." Her expression is deadpan, but I recognize the dry sarcasm. Not sure Sawyer does, but he's more relaxed than a moment ago, so maybe it doesn't matter.

"Nice to meet you, man." Sawyer holds his hand out to Chase, who takes it after a moment of hesitation.

Chase slides his gaze to me for a moment before responding to Sawyer. "You two are..."

I say, "Just friends," at the same time Sawyer says, "Ran into each other at the bar..." He trails off and I look away to keep from giggling. We really suck at this.

Gianna, however, is not giggling at all. In fact, if her eyes were skewers, I'd be a shish kebab—the kind that's burned when it falls over the hot coals, at that. I give a tiny shake of my head and plead with her through my own expression to stay chill. As if there was ever a chance of that.

"I need to go to the bathroom," she says. "Which means, via girl code 101, you have to come with me." She stands and walks toward the restrooms without waiting for a response.

"Uh, you want me to come, too?" Cassidy asks.

I should tell her no, that I'll be fine on my own. But what I actually say is, "God, yes. Please. I need a witness, I think."

"You need a bodyguard?" Sawyer asks, his face impassive. Is he offering to come face the fire with me? I lift a brow to ask, but he doesn't give any response. I wish I knew what he was thinking right now. I wish he'd tell me I could be honest with my best freaking friend about us.

Suddenly, I'm mad. Mad at him. Mad at our situation. Mad at myself—because to stay with him, I'll keep his precious silence. His *stupid* silence. And I know I'm overreacting, *considering it was my own damn idea*, but I still don't bother answering him, reaching out instead for Cassidy's hand and leading her to the bathroom.

Gianna's washing her hands, her eyes still blazing in the mirror when they meet mine. "Spill it," she says. "Now."

"Hey," Cassidy says, tone calm, "maybe we should—"

"Nope. Stop right there." Gianna fixes her pink bangs and spins to face us. "Cassidy. I like you. I really do. I want us to be good friends and I especially can't wait to hear your stories about Quinn while y'all are at school together. If you don't tell me, I'll get you drunk and get them out of you anyway. But right now? She and I are going to have this out because I watched her fall to pieces over that guy out there, and I'm not about to do it again."

Cassidy glances at me and back to Gianna. "I...don't know what to say anymore. I think I like you even more than I did a second ago, but I think I'm a little afraid of you now, too. Sorry, Quinn..."

"*Traitor.*" But I smile, letting her off the hook. Then I look at Gianna, long and hard. "It's not what you think."

"Did he tell you why he did what he did?" She glances at Cassidy. "Did she tell you he disappeared four years ago without a word, after they'd been together for years?"

"No," I say. "He didn't tell me. And, no, I hadn't told Cassidy, so thanks."

"Actually," Cassidy says, "you did. The first year we met. But I'm *only* right now putting this all together."

"Oh." I have no recollection of this. I never let myself talk about Sawyer. Unless it's with Gianna—and only very rarely. "When?"

"Sig Ep party. You were drunk."

Well. That makes sense.

"So far it sounds exactly like what I think," Gianna says. "I bet you're sleeping with him, too."

I glance below the row of green bathroom stalls, making sure nobody's listening. No feet. "Nope."

"Liar. You blew him a day after you saw him the first time. *No way* are you not sleeping with him now."

"I swear that's the truth." I sigh because even telling her the truth feels like a lie right now. And because the judgment in her tone stings. "But Gi, he's back in town. And he was a huge part of my life. Can you blame me for wanting to know him again? Maybe this will heal the parts that never set correctly after he left."

"Or maybe they'll end up beyond repair."

"Maybe it's worth the risk."

"Fine." Her expression flattens. "But I won't help you pick up the pieces this time."

"Maybe you won't need to," I say. "But we both know you'll do it if it comes to that. It's why I ever take any chances, Gi. Because I have you. And you have me."

"I feel like I'm going to fucking cry," Cassidy says, throwing an arm around my shoulders and sliding against me. "You girls are so sweet. And…it's possible I've had a little bit too much to drink already."

Gianna keeps her gaze on mine. "I still don't know how you can forgive him."

"I'm not sure I have." Great. More honesty that feels like a lie.

Cassidy squeezes me. "I think sometimes people we love react badly to bad situations. Sometimes they make really stupid decisions. And sometimes you have to let it go; you have to find a way to forgive. Otherwise, what's the point?"

"How is she supposed to be able to forgive him, if she doesn't know why he hurt her?" Gianna fires back.

Cassidy opens her mouth, but I speak first. "I know his heart, Gi."

"You want his heart to be a certain way because you used to love him. You don't see him clearly."

"Maybe," I admit. "But I don't think you do either. Because of how much *you* love *me*. So I can't fault you for it. But I *can* ask you to play nicely, and I think you will for the same reason. Because you love me."

"God. You're annoying." She shoves past me, but stops, holding the door for Cassidy and me to follow. "I *hate* when you play the damn BFF card like that."

"But you'll still be smiling by the time we get back to the table," I say sweetly, breezing past her. And she is. At Chase instead of Sawyer, but at least it's something.

The guys are all sitting around the table with menus.

"I don't go on for another hour and a half," Gage says. "We figured we had time to grab a bite."

"Good." Gianna pulls her chair out, sliding into it next to Chase. "I'm starving."

Cassidy sits next to Gage. He leans over to whisper in her ear and a second later she's giggling. I...sit a chair away from Sawyer. I'm not mad at him anymore, but Gianna's comments hit their marks. He looks at me questioningly, but I study a menu instead.

Chase takes Gianna's face in his hands, checking her over.

"What?" she asks.

"Just making sure there aren't any scrapes or bruises."

"Please, like *I'd* be the one you have to worry about?" She shakes her head, but smiles.

"Excuse me," I say. "Let's not make any assumptions otherwise, either." But they're all canoodley and I don't think they even hear me.

"You okay?" Sawyer murmurs.

"Yep. Thanks, bodyguard." I stare at my menu.

A second later, he switches seats, sliding closer to me. "You don't seem okay."

"Are bodyguards supposed to care about their wards?"

"You don't need a bodyguard, Quinn. You've always been able to take care of yourself. But I'll be whatever you want."

"No, you won't," I say to my menu. "You can't. And I'm trying to hold on to everything that makes it okay with me."

He grabs my hand under the table, weaving his fingers through mine, and just...holding it. It's exactly what I need.

He waited for me. He kisses me like he loves me when we're alone. It's not an act. I can be with him like this or not at all.

"I choose this," I say, running my thumb over the back of his hand.

"Good," he says. "Because I can't walk away again."

My heart freaking *glows*, but I glance at him with a wince. "Oh, this is awkward. I was talking about the spare ribs."

CHAPTER THIRTY-ONE

QUINN

WE MAKE IT through dinner. There's laughing. Drinking. Even Gianna defrosts a little toward Sawyer. She doesn't fall all over him or anything, but she answers when he asks about her parents. About their ice cream parlor. About her brother.

She doesn't want to warm up to him, I can tell. But the thing about Sawyer is that...he's still Sawyer. And being around him for any amount of time reveals it more and more. She's remembering the boy he was instead of the boy she's hated all these years. And every time he runs his fingers discreetly over my knee under the table, I'm remembering that boy too.

We move to the bar when the restaurant staff starts to clear the tables from the dining area in front of the stage, and Gage sets up. By the time he's ready to begin, the place is slammed and my stomach has butterflies for Gage. He, however, seems completely at ease, sitting up on a stool with his guitar in his lap. And Cassidy's standing there at the edge of the stage with the biggest grin I've seen in a long time. Granted, I haven't had any mirrors around when I've been smiling at Sawyer, so she probably has a little competition there.

Gage kicks off his performance with a song he says is called "Popsicle Sticks." But it has nothing to do with Popsicle sticks, which I think is weird at first—and then, I don't care. Because his lyrics are sweet and deep, and Cassidy's eyes are shining with tears, and Gage is really freaking talented.

"He could go places," Chase says to me a few songs into the set when Sawyer's getting a fresh round of drinks and Gianna's off catching up with someone she knows from work.

"He should tour," I agree. "And I bet Cassidy would go with him—she goes out of town every chance she gets for her travel blog, anyway."

He leans a little closer. "Are you okay?"

I know he's asking about Sawyer. I nod. "I think so."

"Good."

"What about you and Gianna?"

"She said you were okay with this?"

"*Yes*. I love you two together. Just be careful because her bite's even worse than her bark."

"It's one of the things I like about her, actually."

I grin at him, and Gianna shows up a moment later to pull him out to the floor to dance. She motions for me to join them, but Sawyer's walking back with another drink, so I wave her off. Because all I really want to do is lean against Sawyer while nobody's watching.

He must want that, too, because the instant Gi and Chase are looking at the stage, he drops our drinks on the bar and wraps a hand around my hip, pulling me back toward him until my shoulder blades hit his chest. He breathes deeply and his heart thumps against my spine; I turn my face so that my cheek is against his shoulder and it's my turn to breathe deeply, letting his Sawyer citrus scent flood into my lungs.

We stay this way for maybe a minute—though it feels like the flash of a second—before he slides out from behind me. I turn toward him and he whispers, his teeth nipping my ear, "Jesus, I can't wait to get you alone later."

I fight a shiver.

And then I fight a frown.

He hands me my drink and studies my face. "I'm sorry about the alone thing."

"Me, too." I keep my tone light, but I know he can still read my disappointment. I should step away. Get it together. "I have to pee."

"Good to know." He smiles, trying to help with the mood. And I appreciate it. But my own face falls the second my back is to him. Maybe it's the second vodka cranberry hitting me. Maybe it's being around two of my happily dating friends. Maybe it's just me. But this is hard.

I wait for the bathroom to clear out, leaning against the wall and scrolling through my phone. When a spot at the sink opens, I wash my hands and scrutinize my reflection in the mirror. I don't *look* like my heart aches. But...I'm also not exactly glowing with happiness, either. Maybe it's a good thing. Maybe it'll help keep the secret.

Then, of all people, Morgan walks in. "Oh, hey!" she says, all smiles. "You're Sawyer's friend, right?"

"Yep." I try to smile at her, but all I manage is to flash my teeth.

She doesn't seem to notice. "Is he here?"

"Yeah, but I think he's with someone." I should try to speak a little nicer. I know I should. But God, I'm sick of pretending to feel one way when it's another emotion running through me altogether.

"Oh, that's good. I am, too! It won't be awkward."

God. She's not competition. I need to loosen up. "Well, have a good night."

"You, too!" She smooths her hair down in the mirror.

I walk out of the bathroom and almost right into Danny. I study his face, checking for any leftover bruising from his fight with Sawyer, but it's all gone. Unfortunately.

"Quinn." His lips curve into a nasty smile. "You look like you're feeling kinda *tired*."

"Nope. Pretty sure that's just the shape of your boring old routine."

"No," he says, shaking his head. "It's you. Tired, tired girl. Up all night with the dude of the week again?"

I step to the side, but he slides in front of me. "Come on, Quinny. Tell me I'm right and I'll let you pass."

"You got me. I'm such a slut-bag. Good one." I'm so close to not feeling any of the shitty things he says to me. I think he knows it, too, because it's like he ups his game every time I see him, so he can get just one more dig in before they become completely ineffectual. I sigh. "But if you're looking to get back in my line, you can take your place right after the last guy on earth."

"Don't flatter yourself. I've got something better lined up," he says, his eyes darting at the door over my shoulder.

Morgan. Of course. "Always going after Sawyer's sloppy seconds."

"So you *admit* you're a sloppy lay."

This time I don't bother trying to step around him. I barrel through him, knocking him back because he's not expecting it, and ignoring the *bitch* he throws at me.

Screw him.

And screw my mood.

I just want to listen to Gage. And share the air with Sawyer. And make it to the end of the show, when I can slip into the back of his car for some persuasive reassurance that this is all worth it.

But through the crowd, I discover Sawyer's no longer alone at the bar.

He's with my mother.

She's taking him in, dragging her eyes down his T-shirt and jeans, the sneer on her face turning my heart to ice and instantly shoving the frigid splinters of a headache behind my eyes. I force my way through people until I'm in front of them.

"*Mom.*" I push myself next to Sawyer, but he takes a huge step away, running into a guy standing beside him near the bar, not looking at me. His hands are in fists by his sides and he's staring at my mom. I massage my temples with my thumbs, glaring at her. "What are you doing here?"

She glances at me, sniffs. "Why is Chase over there with his arms around Gianna? Shouldn't he be with *you*?"

"*What are you doing here?*" And why is it so tense I can barely breathe? "Is Dad here?" I glance around, but don't see him anywhere. But no way would my mom come to a place like this by herself. Well, honestly, I'd never think she'd set foot somewhere like this period.

"Your father's in the restroom." She wrinkles her nose like she's in there with him. "I'm only here because you told me your friends from school were performing. I thought I'd drop by to see."

"I don't remember saying anything about this to you." I try to catch Sawyer's eye, but he's looking at my mom like she's something on the bottom of his shoe he can't scrape off. "If I did, it certainly wasn't an invitation."

"Don't be rude, dear." She's forced to raise her voice because Gage's transitioning to something louder and a little heavier on his guitar. "You mentioned it at dinner."

It's...true. I wanted so badly to talk about Sawyer, I rambled on about everything else I could think of instead. But I didn't *invite* her. I clear my throat, my mind spinning in its search for something to ease the awkwardness of the situation. "Well. I guess you see that Sawyer's back in town…"

"This was a mistake," Sawyer says, suddenly, roughly. "One that won't happen again."

"What are you talking about?" I stretch my hand toward him, but he's already out of reach, elbowing his way through the crowd.

And, a second later, he shoves right out the front door without even a backward glance.

For a moment I stare after him, shocked.

Then? I'm *pissed*. "Mom," I whirl on her. "What the hell?"

"Sweetie, he isn't worth your concern. Let's just enjoy the music." But there's a tight little smile on her mouth, like she's won some round I didn't even know I was a part of. "If, of course, you can actually call this music."

"Yes, he is worth my concern." I turn to follow Sawyer, but she grabs my wrist, tightening her fingers like a vise, pinching my skin. "*You're hurting me.*"

"Do *not* go after him." Her eyes flare and she comes closer than I've ever seen to showing an emotion in public other than placid composure. "He's trash, and he proved it years ago. Don't you remember the way he destroyed you?"

It's *almost* as though she's going for motherly concern with that reminder, but instead of love beneath her words, I hear something else. Fear… But…that wouldn't make sense. "He's *never* been trash. If you're afraid I'll end up with him…" Fuck it. "*Maybe you should be.*"

I've never wanted to hit my own mother, but when she laughs, I come close. "Don't be ridiculous," she says. "Have you met his father? Trash breeds trash."

I'm done. "Have you met yourself? Class is something in your soul, in the way you treat people—not based on how much money you have. You're the perfect example. Loaded, and yet beyond tacky—and, in case you couldn't tell by my tone, *embarrassing.*"

"Lower your voice." She tightens her grip when I pull my arm again. People are looking at us.

So I raise my voice instead. "Trash breeds trash, though, Mother. If you weren't trash maybe you would've raised a better behaved daughter." Okay. Maybe this is taking it a little too far. But she's still holding on to me and she's throwing insults at Sawyer he doesn't deserve and he's not even here to stick up for himself and she is really, really pissing me off.

Her face pales. "I was *there* for you when he broke your heart. *Where was he?*"

Damn it. Now I feel a tiny bit bad. "I will always be thankful you for being there for me then—but right now you have to let me *go.*" I yank free and spin away from her, shoving through the crowd. I fling myself through the doors to the outside, racing into the parking lot.

But Sawyer's gone. God. I don't even know what type of car I should be searching for.

And I still don't have his freaking number.

I might murder my mother for the havoc she just wreaked on my night. I was doing a fine job of sabotaging it all on my own in my head before she appeared and turned it into a complete shit show.

I step back into the bar to tell her off some more and tell her to leave—and to have another drink or sixteen—but instead of heading straight to my mom, I arrive just in time to see a crowd forming on the edge of the dance floor. Right as Danny slams his fist into Chase's face. And then Gianna jumps on Danny's shoulders, driving an elbow into his neck.

Oh, Jesus.

CHAPTER THIRTY-TWO

SAWYER

"*FUCK.*" I SLAM my hand on my steering wheel over and over until my entire arm vibrates with pain.

I put everything at risk, and running into Quinn's mom could've destroyed it all.

Why am I so weak around Quinn?

One smile. One bat of those long lashes. One peek at one of her slender shoulders under a dress strap. And I lose the self-control I've built for years.

"*Goddamn it.*" I blow through the start of a red light. Yeah, because getting pulled over right now will help things.

I yank the volume up as loud as it'll crank, until the heavy beat of screaming rock music is almost enough to make my ears bleed.

I want to punch someone.

Streetlights blur into neon yellow lines in my peripheral vision.

I *need* to punch someone.

Because if I don't, if I don't give in to this pull to destroy something, there's no way I'll be able to keep tricking my mind into thinking it's anger I feel.

Because what it really is, is fear.

I'm on the cusp of losing everything and I'm fucking terrified. I can't walk away from Quinn again, but I don't know how to save the rest of my life if I don't.

"*Fuck.*" I have to leave. There's no question about it. *I have to leave.* Because it's not just my life that will be affected by being discovered back in town. Logically, I understand it. But Quinn has a hold of my heart and it's there, that exact spot, where I don't have any control.

Forcing her from that hold is going to kill me.

CHAPTER THIRTY-THREE

QUINN

I WAKE UP hungover as a mother effer. The entire space from my lips to the back of my throat is so caked with dried-out alcohol-laced saliva, that peeling my tongue off the roof of my mouth is painful.

I crack an eye open, expecting Gianna to be beside me in bed, the way I vaguely, dreamily remember her climbing in last night, but she's not here. I do find, however, a half-empty water bottle on the nightstand on her side of the bed. I really, really need it. But thinking about crossing to reach it feels like running a marathon. With blades sewn into the soles of my feet.

It's definitely too far away.

I close my eyes and drift off again.

At some point later a huge clanging crash sounds from outside my bedroom door and scares the complete shit out of me, and I sit up so fast the world spins. I slide out of bed and tiptoe—because every step causes an earthquake in my brain—out of my room.

Gage looks up from the floor across the living room at the start of my kitchen. "We, um, broke your vase." He sweeps a hand over a pile of red broken clay by his feet.

"I'm so sorry," Cassidy says, walking out from further back in the kitchen. Her cheeks are bright red, her lips a little swollen...like maybe she's been kissing someone. Gage. Against my kitchen counter where the vase just happened to be sitting.

"Oh, *God*," I whisper, squeezing my eyes shut. "I don't care about the vase. I don't even care that you were getting it on in my kitchen. Just. Stop. Shouting."

"We weren't getting it on!" Cassidy faux-whispers.

I open my eyes, staring at her with a lifted brow. Gage stands, laughing. "Yeah, we were."

I throw a hand up toward them—and immediately relocate it to press on the pounding at the crown of my head. "Seriously. Volume control. Please."

"How about coffee?" Gage says, quietly. He pads into the kitchen and bangs around at a much lighter volume, returning with a cup still steaming.

He passes it to Cassidy, who meets me halfway as I stumble toward my dining table and slump into a chair. "Why aren't you guys hungover? And where are Gianna and Chase?"

"Gage never gets hungover," Cassidy says, rolling her eyes in his direction. "And I drove us all back here last night."

"You did?" I have...zero memory of this.

"You might want to buy a new couch," Gage says, his eyes laughing.

"Why?" I ask. He drops his eyes and Cassidy starts to giggle. "Oh, God. Did you guys—"

"Not us," Cassidy says, pointing to a still blown-up air mattress in a corner near my bedroom door. "We were there."

"Right." I have a vague, vague, vague memory of them bickering about forgetting the pump... "Then why—"

"Chase and Gianna, man," Gage says.

I shake my head. "She slept with me."

Didn't she?

"Yeah, well, she came out of your room around four thirty," he says. "I can tell you the time with accuracy because she wasn't exactly quiet—and then—"

"*Neither were they*," Cassidy finishes, still giggling.

And even as hungover as I am, I giggle, too. Because go, Gianna. "Right in front of you guys?"

"Technically the back of the couch was facing us, but, uh, yeah." Cassidy walks into the kitchen and returns with her own cup of coffee. "They gave an impressive vocal performance."

"I can't believe I slept through that."

"I can't believe you're functioning... Hey, cool—does this thing still work?" Gage picks up the handset of the old-school navy blue rotary phone I keep on a stand by the wall. He listens for the dial tone, hangs it up. "It does—that's awesome."

I make a sound that's at least close to resembling a laugh, both because he appreciates the old technology I'm fond of...and because I'm not sure how I'm functioning, either. Then I remember the fight. The memory slams into me so hard I get dizzy. "Shit—*is Chase okay?*"

Quinn nods. "His eye was barely bruised. No doubt that other guy's hating life this morning, though."

Danny. Dick of the century. I almost ask what the fight was about, but I have no doubt Danny ran his mouth to Chase about Gianna. It's what he does. "And Gianna?"

"She winked at me when they snuck out a few hours ago, so I think so."

Guess if they screwed on my couch they weren't in too bad shape. "What..." Oh, God. "What happened to my mom?"

Gage stands. "How about I make some eggs?"

"That bad, huh?"

He winks at me, slipping out of his seat. "I was on stage. I wouldn't know."

"Liar." When he's back in the kitchen again, I turn to Cassidy. "Give it to me straight."

She bites her lower lip, considering. "Okay. Your dad? Total sweetheart."

"Not a single memory of him being there."

"I know how it goes." She reaches across the table to grab the top of my hand, squeezing it before letting go. "Your mom? She's...an experience."

"What'd she do?" And why is my heart beating faster?

"Nothing that bad," Cassidy says, maybe a little too fast. "She might have, uh, yelled at me a little bit."

I'm silent for a moment, staring at her, kind of...not comprehending. And then I do. "*What?*"

"I came over to see if she was okay after the fight, but someone slammed into me and I spilled my drink on her very expensive shoes."

Humiliation is hot and swampy against my hangover. "I'm so sorry."

"Nobody's parents are perfect," Cassidy says, her eyes kind. "Believe me—I stood there, took it, apologized, and then walked away. Your dad took her home right after."

"Where was I during all of this? Please don't tell me I let her get away with that."

"Slamming shots at the bar with a girl named—"

"*Morgan.*" Shit. I hate the fragments my memory's staring to glue together. "She and Sawyer... We were... We were taking shots and talking shit about how stupid Sawyer is." My heart lurches and rips halfway down the middle. "I'm such an asshole."

It's like...it's like I've cheated on him. Like bonding over him with someone else breaks a code we've developed since he came back to town. The one where we might not always understand each other, but we have each other's backs anyway. Like when he defended my honor and punched Danny even though I was on a date with Chase.

Like when I tell him I want to be with him and I'll keep it a secret and not ask about the past because I trust his heart anyway.

Like when he kissed my tears away that day by the fence of my old house. Even though I cried them out of happiness, because of him.

I hate myself.

"You were pretty mad at him." Cassidy swallows some coffee, watching my face. "Wanna talk about it?"

"No." I drag a hand through the tangles of my hair, yanking when my fingers snag, and immediately regretting the resulting boost in headache. "Well, yes." Am I still sworn to secrecy if there's a chance I told people—even freaking Morgan—last night anyway? "I don't know."

"Why did he leave?"

I shake my head, remembering the way he stared at my mom. The way he turned and walked out without looking back...

"He left because my mom showed up. They never got along before, when we were together growing up—but last night was a whole new level." As soon as the words leave my mouth, something tugs at the back of my mind.

Last night *was* a whole new level.

I think... I think Sawyer was *scared* of my mom.

I put my coffee mug down, slowly, on the table. I really don't like the way anxiety's wrapping itself around my heart, squeezing like a damn boa constrictor.

When we were teenagers, my mom didn't like Sawyer, because she's a stuck-up snob. Sawyer didn't like her because, well, she was a bitch to him. But he never backed down. He took what she threw at him, stayed respectful (respectful-*ish*, at least), and stood by my side because he loved me and our being together meant more than his pride about my mom being a shallow snot. Plus, his dad worked for my parents, so I think Sawyer didn't want to rock the boat too much. Maybe my mom didn't either, for the same reason. Because she certainly never held back on my account, but she never actually forbid us from seeing each other. Like that would've worked, anyway.

But last night...

Sawyer left. He didn't even look at me.

It doesn't sit right.

What am I missing? If Sawyer's a puzzle, and let's be honest, he definitely is, it's like the pieces are trying to come together to at least form the edges for me... But the main image is still broken apart in the box. And I freaking suck at puzzles.

"You okay?" Cassidy asks. "Need to go back to bed?"

I lift my eyes to her. "No. I...I'm so sorry, but I have to leave. Will y'all be okay here for a while? The beach is two blocks up the road, just go left out of the parking lot. I'll meet you there—in an hour, tops."

She looks up as Gage comes back with a plate of scrambled eggs. They exchange a glance weighted with something I can't quite read. "Actually," Cassidy says, "I think we're going to head out a day early—don't hate me!"

"Why?" I ask, though, honestly, I'm a little relieved. I'm too distracted to be as fun as I wanted to be for Cassidy. "And of course I won't hate you. Never, ever."

"I just... I think Teagan could use a friend. She's..." Cassidy glances at Gage again.

"Having a meltdown," he finishes for her.

"Go rescue her," I say.

"And you go rescue Sawyer," she says, because she obviously knows he's who I'm going to see. Really, Cassidy's smarter than I sometimes give her credit for. I mean, I always think she's smart—but sometimes she's just on another plane with her intuitiveness.

I hug them—and shovel some of Gage's scrambled eggs into a tortilla for a breakfast burrito on the road. If I don't eat something, I'll pass out before I get halfway to Sawyer's shop. Which, *annoyingly*, is still the only way I know how to get in touch with him. One more hug, and Cassidy promises to lock up, and then I'm on the road.

Getting to the shop takes both years and no time at all. But once I'm there, time stands still completely. My blood—my stomach—is running on undercurrents and I'm...scared. I want to see him, hell—my heart's dancing just knowing how close he is—but there's a nervousness coursing underneath the want and I can't put my finger on why. I think he'll be able to tell me, though—*if he chooses to*. Which makes my anxiety even stronger.

I walk into the shop. Rajesh is behind the counter and Brandy is showing another girl a surfboard. When Rajesh sees me, his face slackens, purposefully expressionless, and it makes me want to throw up.

"Sawyer's gone," he tells me when I walk toward him.

"Gone?" *Gone. Gone.* The word echoes through me. "What do you mean?" *Gone. Gone.*

Just like last time.

Rajesh's eyes fill with empathy. "He's not coming back."

CHAPTER THIRTY-FOUR

QUINN

I DON'T KNOW how long I stare at Rajesh.

A second.

A minute.

An entire year.

Everything's gone to cracked glass inside of me, and one little motion is going to send it all to shards.

"Give me his number." My mouth barely moves to form the words, and even that's enough to send another fissure racing through me.

Rajesh sighs and his expression turns pained. "No."

"No?" I blink. "What do you mean *no*? You guys work together. You have his number."

"*Worked* together," he corrects, and the crumbled glass begins to avalanche through me, making my breath hitch. "I can't give you his number. It's...an invasion of privacy."

"I will come here every single day," I say, trying to push steel into my voice instead of the terror I actually feel. "Every. Single. Day. Until you—or someone—tells me how to get in touch with him."

"I can't."

"Well, what about Brandy?" I glance at her. She's twirling a strand of hair around her finger, hand on her hip, laughing at something her customer's said. "You think she'll be as taciturn as you? Because I don't."

I start to turn toward her, but Rajesh says, "*Wait.*"

I look at him, not saying anything.

And he sighs. "God. I could get in so much trouble for this."

"Thank you." Relief is the smallest bit of sunshine. "I won't tell anyone you gave me his number."

"I'm not," he says. "But... Come back in a couple of days, okay? Give him some time. Let me try to talk some sense into him."

"Wait." Suddenly, the situation becomes a bit clearer. "You're *friends* with Sawyer. Not just coworkers?"

He nods.

"And you know things about...me and him?"

He hesitates. Then says, "He's going to kill me for this."

Never has the thought of anyone getting killed given me hope before. But his remark eases some of the weight in my heart. Sawyer has someone he can talk to. I wish it was me, but God does it feel nice knowing he's not totally alone. Then, I take a chance: "Tell him something for me, because I know you'll call him the second I'm gone. Tell him I know. Tell him I figured it out—that my mom has something to do with his leaving." My words come out more certain than I actually am; I'm really grasping at straws here, but last night...there's something I'm not getting. But it's there, right below the surface.

And when Rajesh's eyes widen, I know I'm on the right track.

And it makes that broken glass crystallize into something more like dried ice, burning through the pit of my stomach. A different kind of pain. "Tell him I'll be dealing with her. Immediately."

Rajesh struggles with what to say, opening his mouth, closing it, looking into the distance... When his eyes meet mine again, he looks resolved. "Good."

It's the last straw needed for grasping. He's confirming my worst fear. She does have something to do with why Sawyer left. This time...and—Oh, God—the first time, too? I grab a pen attached by a chain to a credit card signing pad and snatch a surf lesson flyer from beside the cash register. I scribble my number on it. "Tell him to call me. Tell him I begged." *Tell him we're fucking idiots for not exchanging numbers before this. Jesus.*

"This thing with Sawyer... It goes really deep. There might not be an outcome that makes anyone happy. Just remember that Sawyer's not...he hasn't had it easy. I don't know that this situation is healable." Rajesh gently tugs the flyer out of my hand, his thumb brushing over my fingers. But I can't look at him because I'm fucking losing it. I want to reach across the counter and shake the entire story out of him. His words are crushing the hope that was floating under the fear regarding my mom's involvement. The hope that said maybe if I can get this whole thing cleared up, Sawyer and I can be together for real. Rajesh squeezes my hand before sliding his own away. "If it helps, I'm team Quinn all the way."

"Thanks." I turn without another word because I have to get out to my car before I break down.

By the time I make it to my parents' house, my breakdown is over. I'm composed.

I'm composed, and I'm furious.

My blood is ice cold and so is the expression I greet my mother with. She's in the second-level sitting room, dressed in a pantsuit with freaking pearls. My father's reading a book in a lounger across the room. He glances up when I enter, smiling. "Hey, sugar."

But my eyes are all for my mother. "What is the deal with you and Sawyer?"

She clears her throat, studying her nails before meeting my gaze. "If you aren't here to apologize for your abysmal behavior last night, then perhaps you should simply go."

"Girls, what's going on?" My dad's face is puzzled, and it looks genuine, but...

"Do you know, too?" I demand.

"Know what?" He glances from me to my mother and back again.

"Jack, why don't you go... I don't know. Sneak one of your cigarettes," my mom says, waving a hand toward the door. "Let Quinn and me have some girl time."

Girl time. The phrase sounds gross coming from her. "What she means, Dad," I say, "is that she fucked up and doesn't want you to know about it."

"Language!" She shakes her head.

"Yeah, that's what's upsetting."

"What's upsetting," she says, "is that your father isn't denying his filthy habit."

I look at him, pleading. It's the perfect time for him to grow a backbone. The perfect time to call out my mom on her shit. But he gives me a chagrined look—and then keeps his head down as he shuffles from the room.

Again, if I didn't share her same narrow nose and his sharp chin, I would never believe I came from either of them.

I turn toward my mom, still sitting calm as can be, and change my tactic. I let my eyes dip in concern and keep my tone light, friendly. "Mom. I need you to explain what's going on." I sit slowly down on the lounge my father vacated. "Tell me what happened with Sawyer, please, so I can try to understand."

She taps a finger against her lap, not buying it. I lean forward and add, practically choking on the words, "So I can stop wanting Sawyer in my life. Tell me your side of things."

"I'm to presume he's already given you his?"

"I just... I want to make things right between us. I want us to be on the same side." I'm lying so hard I feel disgusted with myself, but I must be growing more convincing because she leans back, a grateful smile crossing her lips.

"It does make me feel better that you'd come to me before believing anything that boy's told you." She says *that boy* like she's eaten something sour, and for the second time in less than twenty-four hours, I actually want to hit my mom. Not only in defense of Sawyer, but also because she just confirmed she's had a hand in whatever secrets he's keeping.

I take a deep breath. Exhale it slowly. "What happened?"

"I told you, trash breeds trash."

Oh my God, I might strangle her. Another deep breath. "And what pushed you into that belief?"

"Oh, it's a universal fact, sweetie." She closes her mouth, pleased, like she's gotten some life lesson through to me.

"And...?" Not the nicest tone this time, but I'm about to snap.

"I told you he was no good, all those years ago, didn't I?" And, when I give as much of a nod as I can, she says, "His father stole from us."

CHAPTER THIRTY-FIVE

QUINN

BROCK STOLE FROM us.

I blink. "What?"

"We gave that man every advantage—more than he *ever* deserved—and he turned around and stole from the store."

"Like, groceries?" I ask, knowing already that's not it. But my mind's spinning, refusing to catch up with my mother's confession.

"Money. A lot of it."

"He wouldn't do that."

Brock would not do that.

He wouldn't.

But... If that's the case, why don't I detect bullshit in my mom's tone?

"This is why I never told you, sweetie. I knew it would hurt you."

She's not wrong. I'm in pain. My heart. My stomach. My mind. "I don't understand..." Then, maybe, I start to. Slowly. "He...didn't go to jail, did he? I would've heard about that." And I saw him the other day. And Sawyer...not that he would've told me, but I would've *known* if it was something like that.

My mom stays quiet.

"Mom. Tell me what I'm missing."

"No, he didn't go to jail. I told him he had two choices: leave town or I'd press charges." She leans back, her features somewhere between placid and smug.

"You're the reason they left?" Something sharp and hot flames through my veins, but I'm having trouble placing what it is. Anger? Check. Disappointment? Check. But there's something else, something I haven't grasped yet...

"He's lucky for my kindness." Her expression doesn't waver, no sign of remorse whatsoever.

"Your *kindness?*" I gape at her. Part of me knows she's right. The other part...refuses to acknowledge a single thing that would ever place me on her side in any situation.

"He embezzled from us. From *you*. Was I supposed to pat him on the back and tell him it didn't matter? That isn't how life works."

"Um, considering I was in love with his son? Yeah, back patting all around." I hear the words as they leave my mouth; I hear how crazy I sound. What Brock did was... I pause, waiting for it to truly sink in.

What he did was wrong.

God, it was so wrong. He was like family to me. But... I can't find the anger I should maybe feel for him. This is a circumstance of the heart, not of logic, and I can't stomach any of it. I can't make sense of what I'm learning. Not if it places Brock in a negative light and my mother as someone who was wronged. It doesn't add up.

It's like I need Brock's help figuring it out.

Because *Brock* was never too busy to help me with math homework. *Brock* was never too busy to play board games, or card games. Hell, he taught me how to play poker and then tied it into math lessons. *Brock* was never too busy to ask me about the things in life I cared about—like flowers, or art, or ice cream flavors—the way my mother was.

"Really, sweetie," she says, dryly. "You've been apart from the man for longer than you even knew him. What does it still matter now?"

What does it matter now?

I want to tear at my hair. How does she not get this?

"Are you a fucking robot? God, Mom. Years don't erase the fact that you love someone." I swallow against the ball of tears rising in my throat from all the memories. "He was *always* there for me. Brock was more of a parent to me than you've ever been."

"Quinn." She jolts as though I've slapped her and then stares at me, not even blinking, a soured shape returning to her mouth. "He broke the law. He worked his way up the ranks—higher than his lack of education could ever have allowed, which, for the record, I *told* your father was a mistake—and he swindled us for over a hundred thousand dollars."

"You still didn't... Wait. What?" I break off, rocked when what she's said makes its way through my mind. "A hundred *thousand* dollars?"

An image I hate flashes through my mind: Brock standing in a circle of piles and piles of cash. It leaves a biting sort of taste at the back of my throat.

But it doesn't makes sense.

It doesn't sound like something Brock would *ever* do.

"How did you know it was him? Not somebody else?"

She rolls her eyes. "We hired an investigator, obviously. She collected the evidence we needed to send him away for a long time."

"You investigated Brock?" It hurts, a lot, in my stomach for so many reasons. "You couldn't have talked to him about it? Or at least *me*?"

"Business decisions can be tough sometimes—"

"And what? It wasn't personal?" I spit. "That's such a bullshit excuse—it's *always* personal."

She brushes an invisible fleck of nothing from her pant leg, and when she meets my gaze again, her eyes flash. "Actually, it was personal. To me. To your father. To *you*. Brock took our trust and spit on it."

Brock's face plays on a reel in my mind again, this time, the way he was in the surf shop. Drunk, confused...ruined. My mom did this.

Or... Brock did this.

But he must've been desperate. Brock has a kind heart. He'd never steal that much money if he wasn't desperate for it.

"*Why?*" I ask. "Why did he do it? What did he need the money for?" Brock's never led an extravagant lifestyle. I just don't get it.

My mother sniffs, lifting her chin. "I don't know."

"You had him investigated. Of course you do."

"Only on our end. Proof that he took the money. I know how he took it. I know he took it in smaller sums over a six-month period." She pauses, maybe to let it sink in. But I'm not sure that'll ever happen. "However, I never uncovered the path the money took once it was out of our hands, so to speak."

"Right," I say, my tone flat. "Because you just wanted him gone. And, conveniently, Sawyer with him. That's it, isn't it? You let it drop as long as he left. As long as it tore me and Sawyer apart."

"I suppose if you want to look at it that way, yes."

Her lack of denial about pushing Sawyer out of my life falls between us like a wrecking ball dropping straight out of the sky, passing right by us and dragging me down, down, down to a place I may never get up from.

I know it's wrong, what Brock did. But...the way my mother handled it—the way both my parents did because, Jesus, my dad *must've* known, and this realization freaking kills me—what they did was wrong, too.

"As a person, as a *mother*, didn't you care about Brock's sons at all? They'd already lost their own mother to childbirth. Didn't you care that you were uprooting a family that had already been through so much?"

She doesn't even have the decency to look away. "I cared—I still care—about my daughter."

I can't be bothered to respond to her. I'm not even sure she knows what her words actually mean. Instead, I'm wracking my brain because I don't understand why Sawyer wouldn't have told me any of this. Maybe he was embarrassed? But...he still would've said goodbye, even if he didn't tell me about Brock. There's no reason for him not leaving a note, not calling me, not...*something*. What am I missing?

And then... I think I get it.

"Sawyer wasn't allowed to talk to me, was he?" I ask. "You took an already shitty situation and bent it to your advantage. You made it part of the deal."

She hesitates, her expression tightening... And then relaxing. "He was not to speak with you, see you, touch you. Nothing." Her tone is confident, self-righteous. "From that point forward, he was out of your life."

"How?" My voice cracks over the simple word. "How could you do that to me?"

"You have a bleeding heart, Quinn. If he'd said goodbye—what good would it have done, except make it even harder for you to get over him? You would have felt sorry for him, for his father." She shapes her expression into something resembling pity. Like it's pitiable that I'd show compassion to people I loved. "You're stronger for it now. For what you've been through."

"You thought it would be easier to let me break completely?"

"I was there for you. I made sure you healed."

"*You lied to me.*" Here it is. The thing I couldn't place my finger on before. And this realization hurts more than anything else, that the most tender moments I ever received from her were under the guise of a lie. "You knew why Sawyer was gone, you knew why my heart was broken, and you could've made it easier. You could've told me."

"It would have made it worse."

"For you, maybe. No, definitely," I say. "But for me? At least I would've known. I wouldn't have spent *months* losing sleep just wondering why they left. Why *he* left."

"I'm not the villain, Quinn," she says. "What Brock did—"

"Do you know, the only reason I've attempted to maintain a relationship with you, the only thing that's kept me from giving up on you completely, is the kindness you showed me when my heart was broken." My voice cracks and I blink back tears. "But it wasn't kindness. I was in pain—because you caused it."

"*Brock* caused it."

"Brock did something horrible," I admit. "But you did something cruel."

"Another way to look at it might be that I cared too much about you to watch you waste your time with someone who wasn't worthy of it. I still do." Her eyes flash, solid with determination. She will never, ever let me be with Sawyer.

Well, fuck that.

"You don't care about me." I laugh at the absurdity of my realization. "You care about the version of a daughter you aspire to have. Which I'll never, *ever* be."

"You're better than that family, Quinn." She hesitates again. "I've known people like them, from that walk of life. They're...they can be awful."

"I'm not better than that family. I was *in* that family. God. Look at *you*. Money oozing out of your pores and you're the worst kind of awful."

"Don't talk to me about the worst kind of awful. I've protected you from that your entire life."

"You should've protected me from yourself, then. I can't *believe* I thought you genuinely cared about my heartbreak when Sawyer left, when the whole time you *knew*... I'm done with you. Done." There's not a trace of a lie in what I'm saying this time. Her admission cut any tie she had to tether me with.

"Don't be ridiculous."

"*Ridiculous* is letting your daughter sob night after night after night without giving her the sort of closure you could've. Ridiculous is orchestrating things the way you did to ensure my heart broke in the first place. Ridiculous is… You know what? Forget it." I bite back anything else I was going to say. All that matters is that this is over. I'm finished with her, with both my parents.

"Surely we can get past this," she says, sounding unconcerned and making me rage even harder.

"We won't be getting past this now or ever. *That's not how life works.*"

"Don't be so melodramatic." She bounces her foot, a sign of agitation. "What's done is done. Moving forward, we can work something out. What will it take?"

"What will what take?"

"A new car? A house—I'd gladly buy you something better than that shack you live in now since you refuse to live here. Or maybe something better for your last year of college?" Now her eyes are wide and earnest. "What will it take for you to let this go?'

"Let this go?" I stare at her, my jaw hanging practically against my chest. "You're kidding, right?"

"You accepted my apology when I offered you the Jeep a few years ago."

"Yeah. Five years ago. Because I busted you for not sending birthday party invitations to my friends you didn't think deserved them. Also? I was sixteen. What teenager wouldn't take a car for any reason at that point? But this? This doesn't even come close. There's not a single thing money can buy that will ever make me forgive you."

"We threw your sweet sixteen at the club, Quinn. Certain types of people aren't…welcome there."

"Oh my God." I can't—I literally can't—comprehend how we share DNA. "Poor people, you mean. My friends who didn't have Mc-fucking-Mansions."

"Sawyer was there. Gianna, too," she reminds me, like she deserves a prize for it.

"What happened in your past to make you so unbelievably vapid?"

"Vapid? If you only knew the things I've had to..." She trails off, breaking eye contact to study a row of books—just for show, never been read—against the wall. "I want what's best for you. I always have. Your father and I worked extremely hard to get to where we are now, and I'd hope you'd be a little more grateful for what we've provided."

"Grandmother fell and sued to get you where you are," I spit back at her.

"Yes, your father and I took the money she gave us, but we worked hard *every day* for years to build our business." She actually has the audacity to look hurt. And, fine. Deep down I know what she's said is true.

"Well, thank you, for paying for my education and giving me my Jeep. Don't forget Grandma left me an inheritance, too, so I'll pay you back in full—right now, if you'd like."

"Family isn't a business transaction. It's a love transaction."

"What are you? A walking Hallmark card? Do you have a clue what love really is?" I'm so mad I'm literally seeing stars in my vision. "Because you're married to a man who's afraid of you—and your only daughter can't stand the sight of you."

"Quinn—"

"I know what love is. Not because of you—or, sadly, Dad—but because of Sawyer. He had my soul then, and even now it belongs to him."

She scoffs. "Letting someone own you isn't the same thing as love. *Believe me.*"

"Funny, weren't you just trying to buy my love with another car or even, hell, a house? That's just another way of owning someone, isn't it?" I stand, my hands in fists at my sides. "And Sawyer owns my soul the way I own his. They're one and the same and you ensured we were apart for four years—even when you saw how shattered I was. Even when you knew how happy he made me." I turn toward the door, so furious I have to walk away now before I do something I'll regret.

"If you're leaving to go to him, I forbid it."

Just when I think she can't surprise me further—she always finds a way. I glance over my shoulder and laugh. "Forbid me? I'd like to see you try."

But then she says, "I still have the evidence I need to prosecute his father. Take one more step out that door and I'll use it all."

CHAPTER THIRTY-SIX

QUINN

I SPIN BACK toward my mom so fast I nearly fall, the angry stars at the sides of my vision, blurring and momentarily blinding me. "You wouldn't."

"To protect you? You have no idea the depths I'd go to."

"Protect me from who? Brock? Believe me, I've never needed protection from him. From Sawyer? Well...we've never even used protection, so I guess you're too late there."

She blanches and I smile because my misleading words hit the exact spot I was aiming for. Fury pummels through me, swift and loud until what she's saying barely comes through. "...better than this."

I don't know if she's talking about me, herself or someone else—or what I/she/they deserve better than.

"Tell me. What's a hundred thousand dollars to you?" I ask, honestly wondering. "All things considered." I wave to the room we're in. The ceiling's tall enough for three rooms. The bookshelves built into the walls are edged in marble. The furniture is leather—and switched out at least once a year for better models. The chandelier above us is crystal and likely weighs a ton. I could probably sell it and feed a small country.

"A huge sum of money."

"For some people."

"For any person."

"How much was that strand of pearls hanging around your neck?"

She runs the necklace through her fingers. "It was a gift from your father."

"Right. And he probably spent, what? At least a fifth of a hundred thousand dollars on it."

"I understand your point, Quinn. But what I own, what we choose to spend money on—it doesn't excuse what that man did."

Somewhere deep down I get it. She's right. But I don't want to let her win any points here because at the heart of it all she sits before me a shallow, bitter woman who doesn't deserve to be on the right side of anything. And she lied to me without blinking an eye.

"I have almost that much from Grandmother." It's in my savings account, just sitting there. I've worked really hard not to have to touch it. I wanted to use it someday to—actually, it doesn't matter. I'll make my own money. "It's yours. I'll put a check in the mail, and I'll make monthly payments for the last bit of it until the debt is paid off. And starting now, from the moment I set foot out the door, you stay out of my life and you certainly stay out of Brock's and Sawyer's."

"That's not—"

"If you press charges, I'll never speak to you again. I'll smear your name at your precious club. I'll... I'll sleep with the sons of every one of your friends and make sure they all know about it. I'll cover myself in tattoos. I've always wanted one anyway, but I'll go overboard and get all sorts of ink I'll end up regretting, but regret will never be stronger than the pleasure of your horror over my full tatted sleeves. I'll make you *miserable*, and I will hate you for the rest of my life."

"You can't mean that. I know you're upset, but I'm your mother."

I laugh, humorlessly. "There's not a word in the dictionary to describe what I am right now. But I can tell you this much: Upset? It's the understatement of the decade. Century. I'll never trust you again. Ever."

Her face just melts. Slides into sadness.

It's the first real emotion I've seen from her in years.

Maybe I should feel bad. Maybe I should try to see the situation from her point of view.

But screw that.

"Do we have an agreement?" I ask, staring at her until she meets my gaze.

"I don't want your money."

"Well, you know what I don't want? To find out how easily you lied to me. I don't want to be forced to spend four years away from the boy I love. I don't want his sweet and innocent twelve-year-old brother to grow into a miserable and troubled sixteen-year-old. But those things happened. So I guess we don't always get the things we want—or, in this case, what we don't want. You should have the check in a few days."

"I said I don't want your money."

"But what? You want Brock to keep suffering even though you have an opportunity to recoup what you lost?"

"I want him to face the consequence for what he did."

"He's *been* suffering for four years already. He can barely manage to walk through a damn surf shop without stumbling. Believe me. He's suffered. And so has everyone else. God, Mom. Jess is still just a kid and he's so messed up. Your punishment rocked the lives of innocent bystanders—myself included."

"You're far from innocent, as you've made abundantly clear here today."

"Ouch, burn, Mom. Wow. So painful to hear your judgment," I deadpan. "I'm leaving. If you set one foot in the direction of any one of the Carson family, I'll make every single thing I've threatened—and a *whole* lot worse—a reality." She opens her mouth, but I throw a hand up. "Hell. If you even say another word before I'm out of earshot, I'll do it."

The line her lips make when they press together is the most satisfying thing I've seen all day.

I walk away from her, down the stairs, and almost out the

door. Then I remember the roses Chase gave me those weeks ago, and I go back for them first, before leaving the house for good.

I'm done with this family. Who needs them? I'll have my own with Sawyer. And Gianna. And Cassidy.

And I'm starting with Sawyer right now. I'm not leaving his shop again until Rajesh tells me where to find him. I'd hate to have to hurt Rajesh for it, especially since he's a friend of Sawyer's, which means maybe he'll be a part of my new family, too. But if he refuses again, he may end up with a bloodied lip, with the mood I'm in.

I make it just past my own apartment on my way to the shop when I nearly crash into a car braking in front of me, because I almost don't see it.

Turns out those stars in my vision? They weren't there because I was so angry. They were the start, I discover as pain slices through my head so bad I nearly lose my vision, of a migraine.

I manage to get my car to the side of the road.

I manage to call Gianna and beg her to come get me.

I manage (swear to God it feels like a close call) not to die by the time she arrives with Chase.

They manage to get me home, and by the time Gianna's tucking me into bed, I'm shaking from how bad my head hurts.

"Are you sure I shouldn't call an ambulance?" she asks, dropping to a whisper when I wince.

"No," I whisper, too. "Not much they can do for a migraine."

I used to have a prescription, which I'm sure expired a couple years ago, but Gianna promises to call my doctor and get one faxed to the closest pharmacy.

She does it, sending Chase to pick up the pills. I take one, curling into myself in pain and waiting for it to kick in. At some point, I pass out.

And sleep for a day and a half.

CHAPTER THIRTY-SEVEN

QUINN

"A DAY AND a half?" I sit up, throwing off my covers when Gianna tells me how long I've been out for. "I thought I was dozing for, like, a few hours." I stand, shoving my shirt off my head and searching for my towel. I need to shower away the sleep still hanging on to my brain.

But my legs have different ideas. *They* think I should tremble all over and sink back to my bed. "Damn it."

"Q, you haven't eaten more than a few sips of soup the past day. Let's start with baby steps."

"I need to find Sawyer."

"I know." Gianna sits gingerly beside me. "I can't believe it. All this time I've spent hating Sawyer—like wishing I was magic and could plaster his skin with warts and boils and gaping wounds that never scab over and... And the whole time, he was protecting his family."

"While my own family was full of shit."

"Hey." She grabs my hand, waiting for me to slowly turn my head toward her. "I'm your family. And you know I'm not full of shit."

"Most of the time." I smile at her, squeezing her fingers.

"*That*," she says, smiling back, "gets a pass because I've

spent the last day taking care of your pansy ass, and *I know* if you were thinking straight right now you'd never make such a claim. Otherwise you might wake up tomorrow with warts. And boils…"

I laugh, but sober up a moment later, repeating, "I need to find Sawyer."

"You are *really* going to love me in a second."

"Why? Is he sitting out there waiting for me?" I mean, I doubt it—but the way Gi's eyes are dancing, it almost seems like a possibility.

"Do you really want him to see you like this?" she asks, side-eyeing me with a lifted brow.

"Wow. You missed your calling as a life coach."

"Oh, please. You need a shower before you go to Sawyer. He's spending the day surfing in Duck by the pier."

"How do you know?"

She shrugs. "Chase flirted it out of one of his coworkers."

"You didn't mind him flirting with Brandy?" I can't imagine it. Not the *hands off everything I have, including my last damn bite of pizza* Gianna I know. "She's really pretty."

Gi rolls her eyes. "Nah, he flirted with some dude Rajesh."

This I can imagine—and it's both funny and awful. "Oh, God. That's wrong, Gi."

"It worked." Her grin stretches to Cheshire proportions. "So you can either stay on your high horse about flirting for information being morally questionable—even though we both know you've done it a thousand times—or you can thank me for telling you where to find Sawyer."

Pretty sure there's no question about which option I choose here.

"I expect a phone call later," she says before I leave. "Tomorrow, at least, since I'm pretty sure you'll be…busy tonight. But I have some gossip for you, too—the cops busted the circuit again the other night and, get this: they arrested Danny again. I wasn't there, but I heard it was a total scene."

"Really?" I try to sound interested, but I don't care about the circuit right now. And I especially don't care about Danny. I don't care about anything other than finding Sawyer.

"Plus, before that, a bunch of high school kids showed up, apparently. Which is strike two for the bonfires. We need to do some major reorganizing or the circuit's going to fizzle out." She pauses, laughing. "Get it? Fizzle out? Fires?"

I smile at her.

She sighs. "Fine. Whatever. Go get Sawyer back."

This time, my smile is genuine. And then I'm out the door.

When I get to the beach, even though the sun is blinding across the water and the sand is crowded, I find him almost immediately. Out on his board bobbing over waves which, unfortunately for him, aren't very rough. I drop my stuff and strip down to my suit and jog toward the shore, watching him the entire time. He's just sitting on his board though, staring into the distance.

So Rajesh totally lied to me.

I've never been so happy to have been lied to before. Because it means Sawyer didn't leave for good. It means I have a chance to make everything right.

I dive into the water and when I come up for air, he's staring straight at me. My stomach launches itself into my throat and I raise a tentative hand in the air, scissor-kicking my legs underneath me. He hesitates, and then waves back.

I swim toward him, my strokes steadier than I feel and when I reach him, I hang on to his board, squinting up at him. Wish I brought my shades.

"You found me," he says.

"I did." I try to match my tone to his, which is hard to read.

"How?"

"Rajesh."

"Of course."

"Don't be mad at him. Chase pretended he was looking for you…and he might've flirted a little…and Rajesh might've succumbed. And I'm really sorry about that. I'll apologize to Rajesh as soon as I can."

But instead of looking pissed, Sawyer's smirking. "Guarantee you Rajesh milked that flirting for all he could. He's not an idiot."

I start to smile, because I can picture it so clearly. Straight as an arrow Chase—complete with a bruised eye from the fight last night—trying so hard to flirt with Rajesh, probably bright freaking red the whole time. And Rajesh secretly laughing so hard on the inside. But...then Sawyer continues and my smile falls away. "And don't be mad at Rajesh, either. He wasn't lying—I told him to tell you I wasn't coming back. Because I wasn't planning to. Then he called me and told me what you said..."

"Are you still leaving?"

"I'm not sure." He watches me so intensely, I can tell he's dying to ask what I know now. Because I understand, finally, why he can't tell me himself.

And I'm dying to tell him. First, though, "If you didn't mind me knowing where you are now—why did you wait for me to find you, instead of coming to find me?"

"I thought it should be your call if you wanted to see me again, after speaking with your mom." He holds my gaze.

I stare at him. Hard. Harder. Waiting for his words to make sense, but they never do. "Why the hell wouldn't I want to see you, Sawyer? I owe you a huge apology. And a million kisses—if you'll still take them."

His expression's wary. "What exactly do you know?"

"Everything," I say. "About Brock. About my mother's ultimatum. That you couldn't ever talk to me again or she'd press charges against your dad... I get it, Sawyer. God, I get it."

"What my dad did was—"

"Wait," I interrupt him. Because I've been thinking about this from the moment I stepped out of my house. Cassidy said something that stuck with me the other night: sometimes people we love make really stupid decisions, and we have to find ways to forgive them.

And it's easy to try with Brock. Because no matter what he did, he loved me.

And I love him.

So I keep my eyes on Sawyer's, and I say, simply, "What your dad did was forgivable."

Breath shutters out of his mouth, like maybe he's been holding it in for four years. "I can't believe that's the word you'd use."

"Well, believe it. And you know what else? My mom's backing down." I smile and expect one in return, but he disappoints me, frowning instead.

"There's no statute of limitations on embezzlement in North Carolina. She could turn around anytime she wants and destroy him. Destroy my entire family." He drags a hand through his waterlogged hair, sending trails of water down his face. "I love you, Quinn. Always will. But I can't let that keep me from protecting my family. I'm sorry."

I love you, Quinn.

I want to bask in the three words he put in front of my name so much it hurts, but I'm not even sure he's realized he said them. "Listen to me, Sawyer. She's not going to do anything."

"I'll never be good enough for you—and she'll do whatever she can to keep us apart. God, it's half my fault she came down so hard on my dad. She was looking for things because she didn't want us to be together. If I wasn't in your life maybe—"

"Stop thinking like that," I beg. "Sawyer, let it go."

"How? What my dad did was wrong." Sawyer frowns, looking away from me.

I want to ask him if he knows why his father did it. But he won't tell me even if he does. Sawyer's good like that. He's protective of the people he loves. We'll have the conversation someday, probably soon. But for now...for now we get to talk about anything we want. Freely. In the open. And I want to do so much more than that.

I grab his knee (*oh God finally contact finally finally finally*), and I press as much of what I'm feeling as I can through my fingers. Love; so, so much love. "He must've been desperate. Okay? I told you it's forgivable."

"Not for me." When Sawyer looks at me again, his eyes are full of pain. "I can't forgive him. Sometimes I even hate him."

"Sawyer..."

"You said it yourself. He broke the law. He ruined what we had. And Jess? Jesus, Jess has been so fucked up these years. I can barely stomach looking at my dad."

"But you love him."

He nods. "I can't be with you if it puts him at risk."

I grip him tighter. "It doesn't. Not anymore. Now that I know everything? My mom's got her own ultimatum to deal with. Trust me. She won't turn him in. It doesn't matter that we're talking...or doing anything else we feel like doing."

But he's not ready to take the bait I'm trying so hard to entice him with. He's still frowning. "What if she—"

"I told her I'd sleep with every one of the sons of her country club friends if she presses charges." I laugh, but he continues to frown. "*Not* that I'd really do it, but she doesn't know that. I told her I'd never speak to her again. I'd cover myself in tattoos. I'd marry a homeless man. If her point is to keep us apart because she wants to protect me, she now understands what I'll do with that sort of protection. And...the financial aspect is being taken care of."

His expression sharpens. "What does that mean?"

"Just that she'll have the money back and there'll be no more complaining about it."

"Don't bother." He shakes his head. "I offered it to her. A year ago. She turned me down."

"Excuse me?"

"I... Right after graduation, Rajesh and I sold a set of designs for a process we'd been outlining. Made a decent chunk of change." His cheeks redden in the most adorable way. "The first thing I did was try to give it to Lillian. But she told me it'd be making you a prostitute. That if I paid off my father's debt to have a chance to see you, it'd be like you were a whore, bought and paid for."

"She is such a *bitch*." I'm surprised the heat in my blood isn't causing the ocean to boil over right now.

"She wouldn't take it even if I promised never to see you again anyway."

"Because she couldn't ensure it. She couldn't believe you'd keep good on your word. It wasn't ever even about the money. It was about trying to control *my* life. Control who *I* loved." I submerge completely, holding my breath until I feel like I might burst. But when I come back up, I'm smiling.

His frown turns to confusion. "What?"

I smile wider. "I was just remembering a few minutes ago when you... When you said you loved me."

"I do, but—"

I shove a wave of water at his face. "Don't you dare follow up with a but. You know how I feel about that. There shouldn't be a condition on love." Then I smile wider. "You said you *do*. So, basically, that's twice you've told me you love me."

He's fighting a smile now; maybe it's not quite sinking in for him the way it did for me. So I push against his knee—and, in turn, I shove him right off his board into the ocean. He comes up sputtering, reaching for his board. When he grabs it, I duck under it and resurface between his arms, wrapping my legs around his waist. "Come on, Sawyer. Catch up." And then... "Oh, wait. You *are* up." I wink at him and swish my hips back and forth, gently rocking myself against the start of his erection.

"Quinn." He shakes his head. "What are you doing?"

"Sawyer." I can see the hope in his expression, and the way he's trying to fight it. "Don't you get it? What my mom's been holding over your head to keep us apart? It's over. We can be together. And, even better, your dad has nothing to worry about."

CHAPTER THIRTY-EIGHT

SAWYER

"IT'S OVER." I repeat Quinn's words, but they're like a fog covering my thoughts, not sinking all the way in. My body, though, my body's applauding the news so hard it's a wonder I haven't torn through her bikini bottoms yet. And like she knows, she twists against me in the most perfectly painful way, her eyes dancing. Her movements send about a gallon of blood pulsing straight down my gut and riding up to the very tip of where I'm pressed against her. Jesus.

"No more hiding anything," she says, leaning forward to whisper in my ear. "We can have each other. We can be together. No more secrets, Sawyer."

No more secrets, Sawyer. I wait for the tension to drain from my shoulders. I wait for my spine to unclench. But maybe I've been holding myself tight so long I don't know how to relax. "It's hard to trust after all this time that she's going to let it go."

"Because of me, don't you see?" She slides her body against my again, until I'm so stiff it's almost all I can think about. But there's too much on the line right now for my brain to blank out all the way—as much as it wants to. I focus on what she's saying, instead. "*I'm* the reason she's tried so hard to control everything. And she's lost me already, the moment I found out the truth. Now all she has left to cling to is her precious reputation, and if she takes another step in the wrong direction, I'm going to do everything within my means to ruin it."

"That's not a whole lot to cling to," I say. "Maybe she'd rather get revenge. Maybe you knowing the truth will spur her into not giving a shit about her reputation."

Quinn stares at me—and then bursts into laughter. "Have you ever met my mother? She'd run over a little kid in the street if stopping would mean missing a hair appointment."

It's not a funny image. It isn't. But damn if I'm not laughing in a second myself because, yeah, Lillian's exactly that obsessed with appearances, so much so that she'd stop at nothing to make a hair appointment. Maybe the laughing is the first sign of loosening up. Then Quinn puts her mouth to my neck and laps at my skin with her smooth tongue and one vertebrae loosens with a sigh. Her lips find my jaw and another one unclenches. She runs her hands up my body to hook them around my neck, and my shoulders lighten a few pounds. I grip my board a little harder when her teeth find my earlobe, nibbling, nibbling. And when a wave swells beneath us, pushing me harder against her, the rest of my spine unwinds itself into something much, much more fluid.

No more hiding. My dad's not going to end up in jail because I'm holding Quinn right now.

I can hold Quinn.

I can kiss Quinn. In public. Without needing to look over my shoulder after.

We can have each other.

I'm smiling so hard it almost hurts, and the moment Quinn frees her lips from my jaw, I capture them with my own. The inside of her mouth is somehow both sweet and brackish, from the salt water she's licked from my skin. Her tongue circles mine and she moans against my lips and when another swell lifts us I slide one hand down her back, dipping below her bikini, tracing the gentle curve of her ass with my fingertips.

Her skin is chilled from the water and smooth because, well, she's Quinn and she's always been covered in velvety smooth skin. I slide my hand further down, gnawing at her lower lip when her breathing quickens, and when I make my way to the middle of her legs, to play with her and slide one finger into her, her moan turns into a whimper.

God, I love the way she feels. Soft and tender, and when I flatten my palm against her, she's warm, a hidden spot of melted sunlight against the coolness of the ocean. And so unbelievably inviting.

She drags her hands back down my chest, freeing me from my shorts, wrapping her fingers around me and giving a little squeeze that has me groaning. "Pull my suit to the side."

"I don't have a—"

"Doesn't matter. I'm clean, I'm on the pill, and you've never done this before."

My entire system fucking goes hot at that, and I yank the small amount of fabric away—just as she curses and ducks under my arms, resurfacing a few feet away.

"You've never done this before," she repeats, more slowly this time, treading water. "Shit."

I get what she's thinking. "Listen, honey, this is the perfect spot for my first time. Please. Come back. I'm dying here, hanging out by myself."

She giggles. "Nope. No way, Sawyer. The first time we do this, it's going to be without an entire beach-worth of an audience. I need to get this right."

"It'll be with you. It's going to be right no matter what." I glance toward the beach, and yeah, it's crowded. But we're in our own little area of water and the waves are all crumblers right now, so there are only a few stragglers on their boards out as far as we are—but they're not close enough to have any clue what we're about to do. "Get your sexy ass over here."

She splashes water toward me and laughs. "Sorry for the blue balls, babe. But you'll have to wait until tonight."

"Quinn," I groan. "You've got to be kidding me."

"Meet me in the cove when the sun sets. You know the one." She flashes her bright blue eyes at me, blinking like she's innocent, but her wide, sexy-ass grin says otherwise. Then she dips under the water and doesn't reemerge until she's almost at the shore.

Damn it. I'm stuck in the water with my useless surfboard, a grin I can't quit, and a boner the size of a damn city.

CHAPTER THIRTY-NINE

QUINN

I'M AT OUR cove way earlier than I need to be, but I want it to be perfect. And to turn away any random people—not that this place gets a lot of visitors, tucked away the way it is, and surrounded by plenty of other, bigger, busier beach on either side. It's why it's been the perfect spot for the bonfire circuit in the past. It's why it was the perfect spot for us to start this the night we almost did four years ago.

There are a few fishermen out in the distance, but the likelihood that they'll cross back through this small sand embankment is pretty much nonexistent. To my left sits a half-rotted piece of an ancient cottage sticking up in leftover jagged peaks from the ground, and I'm otherwise surrounded by chest-height dunes and beach grasses. Though the dunes have shifted some, not much else has changed over the past four years.

I spent the day crafting with flowers until I was too antsy to be patient with the process. And now, setting up early, thinking about what's about to happen, helps to keep me from fixating on the emotion I don't want anywhere near me tonight. The absolute disgust at the the lies my mother fed me four years ago. I mean, I knew she was awful, but this...the more I think about it, the worse it gets.

God. No. I'm not going to think about her. Not another second. She doesn't get to ruin this, too.

I turn to head back to my car for one last trip, but Sawyer's standing by the beach exit. Way earlier than he needs to be, too. And suddenly my mind has room for nothing other than him.

Okay.

Oh, God.

I thought I had another thirty minutes to figure out how to stop feeling so damn anxious. But nope. Here he is. All sexy as hell and barefooted and just... *Yum.*

Okay.

Play it cool.

Yes. Play it cool.

I point toward the sun, still very much in the sky, and call, drolly, "I said not to come until the sun had set."

"I wanted to watch it set with you," he calls back, and great now I'm basically a melty puddle of goo beneath my skin. "Plus, you're not the boss of me, honey."

And then he's striding oh so purposefully toward me and really just forget the whole playing it cool thing because I'm running at him and I'm throwing myself into his arms and he's wrapping them around me and spinning me in circles and I'm giggling and I'm nervous and excited and feeling like it's about to be *my* first time, too.

Which, in the most important way, it is.

I kiss his mouth, his nose, his cheeks, his chin. I never, ever want to stop kissing him. But eventually he puts an end to it by placing me on the sand and stepping back to study my face. I drink in his, too. The straight slope of his nose. The strong cut of his jaw. The tiny freckle above an eyebrow—nearly hidden by the blond mess of his hair hanging against his forehead... When his gaze meets mine again, his solemn, studious mouth slowly parts into something much more breathtaking. A grin. All for me.

And his eyes, so bright, so deep and vivid green, *they dance.*

And I start to fucking cry because he's looking at me so unguardedly and it's been four years since I've been allowed this sort of access to Sawyer.

I know I already cried over this in my old backyard against the fence, but I don't even care that it's happening a second time when it makes him put his arms around me again. I definitely need to learn how to cry on demand if this is the reaction it inspires. Because this is where I want to live now. I want to take up residence in his arms. He'll be my shelter.

I'll be his.

Behind me, the ocean's roaring out a forced whisper, its tempo both unhurried and chaotic. Much like what I'm feeling right now. As though on one hand, time is molasses between us, sweet and slow—while on the other, everything's whipping around us, between us, through us, with no rhyme, no rhythm. An outer layer of wildness circling the calm, which somehow remains serene.

Which maybe, I think, is also how love works.

I'm happy. I'm happy and I feel secure. Everything here is…just…*right*. Like my soul's breathing for the first time in four years.

"I brought a blanket," he says. "But I guess we don't need it. Is that—"

"The tent you set up for us four years ago?" I finish his question. "Yes."

"Figured you'd burn it."

"I wanted to. So many times." I turn to look at the weathered, blue contraption, leaning against his chest. "But I couldn't ever bring myself to do it. It's been in a box for years."

"You're such a softie." He's teasing me, but his words are tinged with a tenderness that makes my eyes wet all over again.

"I think giving up the tent would've meant the last strand of hope was snapped."

"You held on to it." He wraps his arms around me and we stare at the tent a while longer, taking in what it once almost meant to us—and what it will after tonight. The leftover sun isn't particularly hot anymore, but Sawyer's skin scorches me with a very different sort of heat through our clothes. I shift a little, letting my shoulders enjoy the shapes of his pecs. He pulls me more tightly against him and for a moment I forget to breathe, because we're pressed so closely together now even the seam between us is blurred, and still, it's not enough. Eventually, he says, "I'm actually going to get that blanket. We can sit and watch the sun set."

"Will you grab the cooler from my Jeep?" I tug at the top of my dress. It's strapless and has a tendency to dip down. Not that I think Sawyer would mind... "There's food. And beer."

He ducks through the tent for my keys and goes to grab everything else. When he returns, we spread the blanket, a ratty old yellow thing, big enough to stretch out on and shield us from the sand. I sit between his legs leaning, again, into his chest. But a moment later I twist toward him, because there are things that need to be said and things he needs to hear, and now's the time.

I sit on my knees before him and I take his hands. He lifts a brow. "What's up?"

Deep breath. "I can't believe for even one second I allowed myself to think you'd do anything to purposefully hurt me. That for all these years you *chose* to break my heart and walk away. I should've had more faith. I hate myself a little because I didn't—and I understand if you do, too."

His mouth slants into half a smile. "Not in a million years. Your—"

"Wait. Let me get this out, okay?" I give him a second to nod. "I'm so sorry for what my mom did to your family, and I'm sorry for the role she's played in hurting Jess and in how she twisted the things that were important to you—like family loyalty, something she'll never understand—and made them into things that bound you to her. I'm so happy you're here, that you came, that you're with me now, in spite of everything. You could hate me as much as you hate her, and you don't. And..."

"Is that all?"

"Almost." I glance at our hands, the way our fingers are tangled together, the way they're meant to be. "And I want you to know that tonight, what we're about to do? It means everything to me. Everything."

He's very, very still for a second, studying me, that same half smile still across his mouth. "You know what means everything to me?" he asks. "You. You do, Quinn. It's not tonight I've waited for all these years. It's you. And before this sun sets? I want you to tell me every single thing I've missed the past four years. I haven't asked before now because I..." He clears his throat. "I didn't think I could endure knowing you more deeply if I had to leave again."

God, he's sweet enough to make my limbs go all melty. And I'm an asshole, because I can't keep my filthy mouth from saying, "Well, you're about to—"

"If you're going to say something about how *deeply* I'm going to know you before the night's out, I'm way ahead of you." His grin goes full tilt and mine joins it. "Can't stop thinking about it, actually."

"See, you already know me *deeply* enough to know where my mind was headed."

"But I want to know everything," he says. "Because I love you, Quinn. You already know it, but four years away from you was torture. I wanted you to forget me so you weren't feeling the same pain I was, while at the same time I hated myself because I wanted you to love me still, too."

I lean forward, gripping his face. "I loved you then. I love you now."

He rises onto his knees and then he presses his mouth to mine. For a moment, it's the only thing I know, this feeling of his lips against my own. This feeling of his hand wrapping around the back of my neck. This feeling of his fingers winding up through my hair...

And then he pulls away.

"That's it?" I ask, raising a brow.

"I told you. I want to know you."

I place my mouth so close to his that my lips brush his when I speak. "I'm an English major. Art minor. I want to open an arts center when I graduate. Bring in the best of the best to teach week-long workshops and charge ridiculously high admission fees for those who can afford it. And then use all their money to provide scholarships for kids who can't rub two nickels together." I caress his cheek with my thumb, loving the way the focus in his gaze tightens. "And that, sir, is all the information you'll be getting from me without...working for it."

I pull his face to mine, opening my mouth to him, and he retaliates by yanking me down on top of him. It's a fluid, easy transition and I find myself straddling him and he finds himself with an erection. Or maybe he's had it for a while, but it's the first chance I've had to notice and now it's the only thing I'm thinking about. A very, very large part of me wants to simply slip out of my panties and allow that very, very large part of him to slide into me...

But I want his first time—our first time—to be more than a quick fuck.

I mean, a quick fuck with Sawyer could be hot. Will be hot, maybe on the next go round. And probably a ton of other times in the near future. But tonight? Right now? I'm going to take my time.

And apparently he feels the same way because in another fluid move, he rolls us until I'm on my back and he's pressed up on his forearms above me. "Favorite color still green?"

"The exact shade of your eyes," I say. "Always has been."

He pays for the information with his lips on my neck, running them along my skin until my head arches back and my nipples tighten, going completely hard, dying for his attention. As if on cue, he rubs his thumb over one, a little roughly... A lot perfect. I bridge my back, pressing into him.

"No bra tonight, honey?" he asks against my skin.

"Didn't see much need for one," I manage.

"You drive me fucking crazy." He uses his teeth now, to tug at the tender skin along my jaw, and his hand tugs down the top of my dress until it's bunched at my waist. "Always have."

"Nothing makes me happier." My words come out breathy. "Except, maybe, when you kiss me."

"Oh, honey, I'm going to kiss you. Thoroughly. There won't be an inch of your body left unexplored by my lips." He lifts his head to watch my face, and then his eyes lower to my chest and he wets his mouth. "By my tongue."

And like he needs to prove his point, he leans down to lick my lips, dipping his tongue through them, his eyes wide and on mine the entire time. His fingers pull at my nipples, teasing me and traveling lower. Down my stomach, across the bottom of my dress, along the tops of my thighs.

"Tell me a secret," he rasps against my mouth, his fingers inching higher, dancing up under my dress.

There's only one that comes to mind.

"I didn't just love you then and love you again now. I never stopped loving you," I rasp back against him, my hips starting to rock, shifting back and forth and reshaping the sand below the blanket. "And I never. Ever. *Ever* stopped wanting you."

He groans. "Likewise, Quinn. On both accounts. You have no idea." But I do. I do have an idea. He never stopped loving me, wanting me, and the knowledge blooms flowers in the spots I thought would never heal in my heart.

"Tell me another one."

I glance to the side, where his forearm is straining against my face. His other hand is at the spot where fabric meets skin between my legs, and I'm about to go fucking crazy with the way I'm beginning to throb. "I've been fantasizing about tasting you again, ever since I had you in my mouth in that backroom."

He shudders, grazing my shoulder with his teeth. "Funny, I was just thinking about how badly I want to taste you again, too."

Like he wants to prove it, he curves one finger under my panties, whispering something hot about how wet I am—I'm sure I'd hear him more clearly if his touch alone wasn't enough to make my senses slip away—and then he brings his hand to his mouth, to suck me off of his finger, and something about watching him enjoy my flavor makes me so fucking turned on I hook a leg around him and, like some kung-fu master, flip us over so that I'm straddling him again. This time *I'm* in control.

He's staring up at me with a wicked little expression, like he's allowing me to think I'm in control. Like it's cute if I think I'm calling the shots.

Well. Game on.

He's about to see just how much control I have.

CHAPTER FORTY

SAWYER

SHE WANTS CONTROL, but so do I.

This is going to be an interesting little game.

Maybe I should give her the lead, as she has a slight advantage in experience, but I'm not a damn saint so that advantage is very, very slight. I doubt I'll be able to let her keep the lead. It's always been one of the things that makes us work so well together, this constant battle for leadership along the more intimate lines.

The sun's falling through the sky, lighting Quinn from behind so a halo wavers around her shape. Christ, she's beautiful. The wind flings a few strands of hair into her face; they stick to her mouth and after she peels them away, slowly like she's trying—successfully—to tease me, she licks her lips. Her lashes shutter halfway down, half hiding her bright, bright blue eyes.

"Jesus, you're sexy," I say, reaching for her waist, needing to bring her down on top of me. Wanting her body pressed to mine. Needing to taste her mouth again.

She grabs my hands, pressing our palms together and pushing them over my head. I get what I want, but she gives it to me her way. We both know I could swing my hands down, but we both know I won't. Yet.

Plus, the way she's leaning over me to hold my wrists places her perfect, perky breasts directly in line with my face. I lift my head to capture one pink nipple in my mouth. She stills above me, but when I circle it with my teeth and lap against it with my tongue, a purr slides creamily up her throat and her hips begin to rock.

Pressing her hands against my arms, she crawls back along my forearms, her breast slipping sadly out of reach, until we're nose to nose—and she's seated right on top of where I'm dying to feel her the most. She slides her cheek against mine and whispers so close to my ear it almost tickles. "I thought we'd make tonight all about pleasing you, Sawyer."

She's pressing down harder with her hips, making these tiny circles, and I think if she gets to keep control I'll last maybe another thirty seconds, and we aren't even out of our clothes yet.

"Don't you remember?" I grab her wrist and flip her onto her back so fast she gasps. "The thing that pleases me most is driving *you* wild."

Her expression filters through pouting to excitement to demanding and back again so fast I grin and claim her mouth with my own before she can decide which one to settle on. My tongue slips through her lips easily, finding hers and circling, teasing, tasting. Jesus, she's sweet. I want to make good on my promise. I won't leave one inch of skin unexplored.

She sighs, disappointed when I break the kiss, but when I drag my mouth across her cheek, the corner of her mouth twitches and she turns her face to give me access to her neck. I take my time getting there, sliding my lips around her jaw and across to her tasty little earlobe, pausing here to enjoy it while my hand explores her chest, her breasts, her nipples so tight I can't keep myself from pinching one—and then the other after her entire body jerks against me, and she pushes herself past my fingers into the center of my hand. Her breasts are small and firm and perfect for my palms.

She's perfect. I slide my hand lower down under the bunch

of her dress. A whimper echoes faintly in her throat, quiet, but it vibrates against my chin so I give in to what she wants, dragging my tongue down the side of her neck. I shove her dress below her waist, and that sweet whimper builds into a moan.

She's so temptingly warm under my palm, and I steal a glance at the golden glow of her skin between her ribs, and down her smooth belly. Her stomach rises and falls under my touch, faster and more ragged with each breath. I catch a glimpse of fabric, small and red. "Christ, Quinn, what's with all the lace panties? You trying to kill me?"

She shifts her hips up, little tease. "I noticed what you liked the last time."

"You can wear a paper bag and you'll still be sexy as fuck. But damn do I love you in tiny pieces of lace." Dying to dive down beneath that lace, instead I crawl over her, focusing on that soft, sweet center of her throat. She tastes like salt and sand and every time she swallows my mouth rides the motion like a wave.

When I'm satisfied with my exploration of her graceful neck, I move lower, tasting the skin across her chest. Quinn grips my hair, pulling roughly. "Sawyer."

I don't lift my mouth to respond, but if she wants something rough, the blood roaring through my veins makes me more than happy to comply. I shove my knee between her thighs, forcing them apart and sliding it further up until I connect with the thin fabric of her panties. She moans and arches her back, letting the motion ripple through her body until she's writhing against my knee and I'm about to stop what I'm doing and fuck taking it slow, fuck all this exploration, all I want is to be inside her. The blanket is bunched between us, lifting her hips slightly higher, just into that perfect positioning...

But this is our first time and I want it to last.

"We have all night," she says, reading my mind. "We can do this more than once."

I lift my head and slide my chest up her body until our faces are even. She blinks up at me, and again I almost toss aside every scrap of control I'm barely hanging on to as it is.

"More than twice," I say, kissing her. Hard. She bites my tongue in response and I pull it from her mouth with a grin. "Or more than three times, if I get my way." I slide a hand between my knee and twist the scrap of lace to the side. She's so wet I'm instantly harder than before, throbbing, thundering, rock solid.

"That's all?" she asks, lifting one perfect brow, reaching between us to free me from my pants. "Only more than three times?" Warm air hits me and her fingers squeeze and I clench my jaw to keep from exploding right here, right now.

"Honey, I plan to spend tonight making you so sore you won't be able to handle a fourth round."

"I'll never not want another round with you." She slips her hands under my shirt, pulling it up and over my head. I lift onto my knees to help, and quick as a cat she slips onto her knees, too. She tosses my shirt into the sand and pauses before me. Our bodies are so close they're almost touching. She takes one deep breath and her nipples graze vertical lines up and down my chest. She edges the tip of her fingernail across my lower abs and when I jerk at the contact, my cock slides up the soft skin of her belly. I'm wet at the tip and I notice her noticing—and when she licks her lips another surge slams through me. Even harder the next time, when she drags her finger across it and pushes that same finger into her mouth, like a fucking lollipop.

Jesus.

"I love the way you taste, Sawyer."

"I love watching you taste me." I should probably say something sweeter here, but she's swirling her tongue around her finger and I want it to be around me so bad I can barely think.

The sun's falling lower in the sky behind us, and it casts her in the most beautiful glow. She uses her still wet finger to trace a line across my collarbone and dances her hand down my chest, over my heart, which is beating hard enough that I know she feels it, past my stomach, lower and lower, pushing my pants down to my knees and kissing my neck and gripping me again—and again I almost fucking rupture.

I close my eyes, hold my breath, and wait for some semblance of control to make its way back to me. She...doesn't help, wrapping her hands along me, twisting, tugging, pulling, ducking her head down to kiss my chest.

Two can play this way, though. When she leans back to look up at me, I hold her face still between my hands. She tilts her chin toward me, expecting a kiss, but instead I drag my hands down her chest, cupping her breasts, teasing her nipples with my thumbs, watching the way her eyes lose focus. Her grip tightens and I groan. I glance down and the image of her thin fingers weaving around me, gliding along me, is so fucking hot I jerk in her hands. She laughs. It's a sexy laugh, a throaty one, like she's heady with the power she has over me.

I dip my hands lower, slowly trailing my thumbs down her ribs and the sides of her belly until they're hooked in the waist of her panties. Slowly, so slowly, I roll them down her hips, her thighs. She lifts a knee, letting me pull one leg through, and when she puts it back on the ground she's spread wider on her knees than before.

Everything in me stills for a second while I take her in.
Her face. Her body.
Her heart.
I can almost hear its beat from here. And it's all for me.
Every goddamn thing about this girl is gorgeous.
Her face. Her body.
Her heart.

"Want to know one of my biggest fantasies?" I ask, the stillness suddenly replaced with the pound of excitement jumping through my veins.

"Aren't we about to fulfill it?" she asks, slyly. I reach between her legs, dipping a finger into her—holy Jesus, she's so wet, so warm—and I press my thumb against her, lightly and then harder, until that sly expression slips into something sharper.

"Yes, we are," I say, my voice rough. "But there's something else before that..." I let the words trail off, watching puzzlement cross her face and flow into something more like excitement.

"What?" She works her hands, works her hands, works her hands and if she doesn't stop I'm really not going to be able to.

"You. On your knees, just as you are. Except over my face."

"Oh." Her blush is immediate and almost as beautiful as she is. So is the way she bites her lip. She's imagining it now, too. And her hands pause for the moment, thank God.

Mine haven't, though. I slip another finger into her, twisting it with the first, my thumb making tiny circles and pressing harder until she's breathing so fast I think she might come before I have the chance to eat her—and I'm too thirsty for her taste to let that happen.

So I slow down. A little. "What do you think?"

"I think I'll do whatever you ask me to right now, Sawyer. You want me on your face? Have me. You want to skip that part and *slam into me*"—she slows these last three words down until they're stretchy like pine sap, and I clench my damn jaw so hard it almost breaks—"we can do that, too."

I'm breathing heavy like I just ran a homer and without another word I scoop her up, reaching behind her, right under her ass, and pulling her on top of me as I fall to my back. Her panties hang around her ankle and I reach past her to loop them off of her foot and bring them behind her back, resting just above her ass. She's straddling my neck, watching me, and I can see she's nervous.

But she's turned on, too. The truth is soaking my Adam's apple.

I hook both hands through the legs of her lace underwear and stretch it across her back, using it to pull her forward until—after one last moment of hesitation on her part when she sets the brakes with her hips, giving in just a second later—she's finally resting over my face.

"God, you're perfect, Quinn." I want to say more, to really make sure she understands the truth of my words, but I can't. I need to feel her. Taste her. Eat her. I bury my nose against her, inhaling her sweet scent and nuzzling her until she's moaning and tensing her thighs against my cheeks. I look up to find her staring back at me, her face flushed, her expression focused, and the skin of her belly tightening, quivering.

I lick her, slowly, enjoying every second of tasting her, and using my chin to nudge the tender skin just past where I plan to bury my tongue. And then I do.

I grab her ass and hold her against my face, pushing my tongue into her, circling it until I find the spot that makes her gasp.

And gasp.

And gasp.

Her head falls back and the heels of her hands press against my forehead and she takes the reins, riding my tongue, pressing herself against my mouth and moaning sweet little moans and all I can see is the delicious view of her peaked nipples rising and falling every time she breathes, every time she bucks, and if there were a word for being harder than rock solid, that's exactly what I am right now.

When she comes I lick her harder than I've ever done before, tasting her, swallowing her until she collapses above me, her stomach rounding over my face, and slides to her side, panting, trembling.

Grinning. "Holy fuck, Sawyer."

She's out of breath and I lose the battle with a smug smile. "A first for you?"

She hesitates and I immediately wish I hadn't asked. I don't want her to be uncomfortable, and it makes no difference to me what she's done before. All that matters is right now—and every day of the future.

"A definite first," she says, and thank God for it because with the pleasure that runs through me with her words, maybe it did matter to me. Then she says, "You were my first—now I'll be yours."

And I'm thanking God a second time because if she's not riding me within the next moment, I actually might split down the middle—I'm so hard there's no place else for the pressure to go. I start to sit up, but she pushes me back.

She straddles me, without touching me, but she's close enough that barely a hair could pass between us and I feel her warmth and it takes every last shred of restraint for me not to buck my hips and take her. I grab her waist, holding her steady. Maybe I'm holding myself steady. Who the fuck knows anything right now other than the need jackhammering through me.

She rests her palms against my chest, letting a small, smug smile flit across her mouth. "You ready for this?"

"I'm ready for you," I say, aching so bad, needing to feel her around me so bad, the words barely make it out. "All of you."

She reaches up to tug her red lace panties out of my hand—I'd somehow forgotten I was holding them—and tosses them toward the tent. "Always ruining my undies, Sawyer."

I shrug, pushing sand up toward my ear. "I'll get you a new pair."

"Or maybe I'll pull a *Sawyer* and stop wearing them all together."

The thought of that... "Jesus, you make me swell any harder than this, honey, and I might actually fucking die."

"Just one more thing," she whispers. "Got to do something about your pants."

My pants, I realize a second behind the times. Tucked around my ankles. I want to tell her I don't care, they won't hinder a damn thing—but she turns around and straddles my thighs, facing away and reaching, reaching, holy Christ reaching down to my ankles to push my jeans all the way off and every. Single. Inch. Of her beautiful body is there for me to memorize. Pink and perfect and wet and holy shit I'm about to resort to preteen-style premature explosion any second now.

She looks over a shoulder, wiggling her hips. "You doing okay?"

"You going to make me beg?" Because I'm half a second away from doing just that. Half a second away from grabbing her hips and slamming her down onto me before she's even turned around.

"Nope." She spins back toward me, straddling me again, and oh my fucking God she lowers onto me.

Slowly.

Inch by inch by inch, keeping her eyes on mine, a little smile across her beautiful mouth, until I'm all the way inside of her, and I've never known anything like this sort of pleasure.

Until she starts to roll her hips.

"Hold on," I beg. "Hold on, hold on."

But she laughs and refuses to stay still and I'm not going to last much longer and I'm going to make the best of it while I can. I reach up to grab her breasts, but she catches my hands, lacing her fingers with mine and falling over me, so that our hands are by my head and she's smiling against my mouth. "You have no idea how long I've wanted this," she whispers, biting my lip.

"Pretty sure I do," I somehow manage.

She shakes her head, rubbing her mouth over mine and then straightening, rolling her hips harder and harder. She arches back, holding my thighs, and I grab her hips, my fingers tightening hard enough to make her gasp again, but not to hurt her. I just need to hold on because I look down between us and oh fuck I'm watching myself sink into her and slide out, slick with her wetness, and...

Fuck.

I can't hold it anymore.

I come.

Hard.

CHAPTER FORTY-ONE

QUINN

WE LIE TOGETHER, breathing for a few minutes or hours or years, grinning at each other. Eventually, I start to slide off of Sawyer, but he grabs my hips. Rough. Keeping me in place.

"Give me a second, honey," he says, his voice dry as sandpaper. "That was only the beginning."

And just like that I'm quivering.

And just like that I feel him shift inside of me, beginning to spring back to life, so to speak.

And just like that I'm rocking my hips and he's getting harder and harder and his fingers are digging into my skin and *oh my God* he feels so good inside of me.

I feel him everywhere.

Everywhere.

I lean forward to kiss him and, okay, maybe in not the smoothest maneuver he's ever managed, he flips me onto my back with a few disjointed adjustments and holds my hands above my head, palm to palm with his. The sand is smooth against the backs of my hands and the blanket stops somewhere around the middle of my shoulders, so I know my hair's going to be tangled with sand—and I've never cared about something less than this. And when he's pushing into me hard and fast and furious again, it turns out I love the sensation and the way the grains shift under my head each time it's jerked with the motion of our bodies.

"Tables have turned, huh?" he asks between kisses, biting my lower lip. It may be bleeding before the day's over if he keeps working it the way he has been.

"For a newbie, you've cut straight through the learning curve," I say, my words coming out uneven between choppy breaths. But every time he thrusts, my breasts are shoved against his chest and my nipples are aching and thrilling and my legs wrap around his waist and my hips are rising so he has even deeper access. And he takes it, pausing for the briefest moment to angle higher on his knees...

"I've imagined this exact moment with you so many times, Quinn, it's almost been choreographed for years. Plus...I've watched a few...um...tutorials."

"Porn, you mean?" I laugh, and then he's slamming into me—and I mean *slamming*, like so hard I'm going to have the best bruises ever tomorrow—and I'm moaning and making noises I didn't know I was capable of, but I'm tightening around him and my stomach is closing in on itself, unable to handle the fireworks racing through me, down me, all the way to my feet. I wrap my legs around him and buck my hips harder and harder, needing that force, that friction between us and I think I stop breathing for a second because oh holy hell there's just too much to *feel* right now to remember something so trivial.

He pauses again, and my heart's beating so fast I wonder if it's going to punch straight through my chest. But while I appreciate the moment to breathe, which I do, pulling in huge bursts of air, I'm already impatient and *aching* for that same sweet roughness. I rock my hips and he pushes back, holding me still with his weight, laughing a little. "One second, honey."

He frees one of my hands and licks his fingers—and then his palm—simply saying, "Getting rid of the sand," when I raise a questioning brow. And then I get it because he's reaching between us to slide his now-sand-free fingers over me, through me, spreading me and pulling my skin in a way that's somewhere between painful and a tickle with an entire continent of silky sweetness in between.

He shifts his hips again, sliding slowly halfway into me and then back out, slowly halfway into me and then back out—and just as I'm about to beg for more, he thrusts hard and fast and all the way in, rocking me so hard *I fly*.

This time he doesn't stop.

Even when I beg him to slow down because the shape of the orgasm forming under my skin is almost frightening in its intensity. I never knew what this could be like, doing it with someone I love. And now I never want it any other way.

Despite my begging, he grins a wicked little grin and keeps driving into me, pulsing his fingers against me, biting my neck, my chest, my everywhere, and when I come this time I scream so loud he covers my mouth a second before jerking rigidly into me one final time of his own.

Thrills ripple through me from the center of my belly to the center of my legs, skipping like stones down my thighs and out my arms and up my neck, and there's not a spot on my body that isn't quivering and spent and deliriously, deliciously happy.

I think, maybe, as I lie beneath him, holding him, panting, that I've just experienced an orgasm four years in the making. My body's been waiting for this. To feel him, to be with him, to have him completely inside of me. To let him complete me the way he just has. To know I've done the same for him… It's beautiful. And perfect. And like nothing I've ever imagined possible.

Sawyer collapses on top of me, his weight almost too heavy for me to breathe—but when he tries to slide off, I tighten my legs around his back and wrap my arms across his shoulders to hold him in place anyway.

Because I love this.

Our hearts hammering furiously against each other. His forehead pressed against mine, sweaty—not sure which one of us, probably both—and he's breathing as hard as I am and when I shift my hips a little to let him slip out of me, he does so with a shaky giggle. I instantly pull his mouth to mine again because after all the rough, hot sex, that giggle was the smallest sign of his innocence, and I love him so much right now I feel it *everywhere*. Running through my veins. Beating in my heart. Tingling in my palms and in my stomach.

We missed the pinks and golds of the sunset, but now the sky above us is a swollen bruised purple and over Sawyer's shoulder, the first few stars are beginning to shimmer and I wouldn't change a single thing.

"This is the night we should've had four years ago," he says, his breath washing over my face.

"This is the night we should have every night from now on," I say.

"Maybe we should take it to the tent," he says.

"That requires moving."

"True."

So we lie here for a while longer. Eventually I roll out from under him, though, needing at least one full breath. He watches me and when I tilt my head, questioning his expression, he says, "I could lie here and watch you for the rest of my life."

"You'd probably get hungry."

"Yeah," he agrees. "And it'll be too dark to make you out in a few more minutes."

"Speaking of getting hungry," I say, pointing to the cooler he retrieved earlier. "How's a PB&J sound?"

"Almost as good as having you one more time."

I raise both brows this time. "Already?"

He glances down and I follow his gaze. Semi-hard. Wow.

Even more surprising is the light pulsing, spiraling down my stomach and resting between my legs. *Already.*

"But we can eat first," he says, grinning. He rolls to his side and I admire his perfectly shaped, albeit pale, ass before he sits up.

By the time he turns around again, though, I'm already in the ocean. Rinsing off.

He drops the sandwiches and jogs out to join me. "You

know," he says, splashing in to me. "Sharks come out at night."

"They do," I say. "But I needed to rinse off. I managed to get some sand, it turns out, in a few...un-sand-welcoming places."

He dips under and rises again dripping wet, pushing his hair away from his face, and he's so unbelievably sexy I can't do anything other than stand here, the water lapping at my waist, and stare. Ocean droplets slide lazily down his chest and trim stomach. Water clings to his lashes and shimmers in front of his eyes. Eyes, I notice, that are studying me as intensely as I'm studying him.

I wade toward him, needing to touch him, to lean into his chest, to have all of him against all of me. He wraps his arms around me and I listen to the thumping of his heart. "Want to know what my fantasy is?"

"Tell me and we'll do it."

"Ah, we need a wall for it, unfortunately. The tent just isn't sturdy enough."

"You have to tell me now." His voice is husky

I grin into the space between his ribs. "Over the years I...I always had this fantasy of you...taking me from behind, me pressed against the wall."

"Jesus. Let's get out of here and find some place with a wall."

I laugh.

"Sorry about the, um, awkward flipping you to your back earlier," he says. "I'll get the hang of this with a bit more practice. I'm a quick learner." It's sweet that he's feeling vulnerable about this.

"Sawyer, you started my night off letting me ride your face and ended it slamming into me to build a second orgasm. I'd say you've got nothing to worry about."

"What do you mean ended it?" He smirks down at me, jutting his hips against me so I'll feel his now full erection.

I smile up at him. "I love you, Sawyer. And I'd like to help you out here... It's just that right now? I might be willing to leave you for a PB&J."

"Too bad there won't be any left." He scoops me up, tosses me out farther into the water, and by the time I resurface and swim to the shore, he's already scarfed down an entire sandwich, wrapped himself in a towel—and is waiting for me, holding out one of each.

I grab the towel first, wrapping it around my chest, and then the sandwich. Which is gone in about three bites. So I go for a second, and so does he. We eat in silence, smiling at each other, the only sounds coming from the shushing of the waves and the squelching of the sticky bits of peanut butter when we peel our tongues from the roofs of our mouths.

I pull a beer from the cooler and toss him one, too. He tugs me onto the blanket with him, sitting down and settling me between his legs. He sweeps hair away from the side of my neck and presses his lips gently against me, murmuring, "I love you."

I press the side of my face into his chest, looking up at him. "I love you, too."

He kisses me and we clink our beer bottles and we sit and watch the ocean and the stars.

CHAPTER FORTY-TWO

QUINN

AFTER A WHILE, I remember what else I've planned for the night. I push myself up, off the blanket. Sawyer reaches out for me, but I say, "I'll be right back—gimme a sec," and walk to the back of the tent, pressing the button at the end of a cord hanging there.

The twinkle lights I've hung across the top shimmer to life. Just like the ones he left for me four years ago. He watches me, without smiling, but his eyes soften in the corners and I know it means as much to him as it does to me. "These aren't the same ones you had, so it's not exactly the same this time, but I figure it's close enough?"

"You're pretty fucking cute, you know that?" He stands to meet me, pulling me against his chest. "Why don't you show me what's inside that tent now? Or let me show you how good I plan on making my word for another round. And another after that, if you're still game."

"No question I will be," I say, scraping my teeth against his chest. "I already am. And as for inside, there isn't much. Just an old radio with a ratty red bow."

His grip around me tightens. "I can't believe you set it up the exact same way."

He leads me toward the tent, and I say, "We'll have to be

careful because of all the sand...it could get *really* uncomfortable."

"Maybe I'll clean you with my tongue, first," he says, his voice a little gruff like he's imagining doing just that.

And so I let him.

And so, in turn, he lets me.

At some point we find a faded country music station on the radio—the same one, I imagine, I found four years ago—and we spend the rest of the night exploring each other's mostly sand-free bodies with twinkle lights flickering above us.

It turns out he was right. By the time we could go in for a fourth round, I'm too sore. I'm too tired. I'm too...sated. So I tell him we can save it for the morning. And I fall asleep against his chest while he runs his fingers through my hair.

Except in the morning, I wake with dried saliva halfway down my chin, feeling about as sexy as a pile of crumbled dirt, and Sawyer's not even beside me anymore.

I find him drifting in the ocean, eyes closed, chest up toward the sun. The gentle swell of waves lifts him more fully from the water, and I could stare at his body all day. He seems so...relaxed. Different from that stillness in his soul, it's like...he's let go of a stress long carried. And I grin because I have too.

We found each other again and we don't have to hide anything, and I am his and he is mine.

And together? It turns out? We are freaking starving.

"I'll take you for breakfast," he says, drying off while I slip into the extra dress I brought. Skipping the underwear and twirling them around my finger before tossing them at him. He holds them out delicately, studying them and licking his lips. "Then, I'll take you to my house. To my bedroom. Hell, to the stairwell if we can make it that far."

"Maybe just to your car," I say, smiling. "After we eat, of course. You're taking me to Stack'em High, I'm assuming?"

He steps into his jeans and pulls on his shirt from last night after shaking out the sand. "Like I'd ever take you anywhere else."

"I don't know. Someday I might get sick of pancakes." I hand him one of the throwaway toothbrushes I packed and use the second one for myself.

"Yeah, the day the ocean freezes over."

It's true.

I follow him to the restaurant because I'm guarding in Kitty Hawk later today, which is where we're eating. I'll leave my car here and he can drop me off later...after his house...or stairwell. Oh, God. Maybe I don't need pancakes. Maybe I'll just take a bite of Sawyer. And let him take one of me. And another. And another...

But when we slide into a booth next to each other and my order comes, I'm forced to reconsider. I wonder if I'd be able to realistically choose Sawyer over pancakes if I could ever only have one of them again. I mean, I probably could. It's just... Fluffy pancakes. Butter. Real maple syrup. There's no better combination in the world.

Then Sawyer slips a hand up my leg, under my dress—like *all the way up my leg and then between them both*—and, yep, I could walk away from pancakes on the spot.

"I'm starving," he says, with a wicked grin.

I point to his plate. "Your omelet awaits."

"That's not what I want." He slides his hand away from me and he licks his freaking fingers and I swear to God I squirm in my seat because I'm instantly throbbing for him.

"Jesus, Sawyer," I hiss, grinning. "Stop doing that!"

"What?" He shrugs, his eyes twinkling. "We have a lot of time to make up for and," he licks his finger again, "you're tastier than anything they offer on the menu."

I lift a hand, catching our waiter's eye. "Check, please!"

But then I catch someone else's eye. Erika Covington. Perfectly coifed (faux) blonde chignon, pink blazer, poised as always, sitting with her grandchildren, and staring at me with disdain. I have no doubt my mother will be the first person she calls as soon as she's left the restaurant.

Which means I have to call my mom first. With a not-so-gentle reminder that she's not allowed to get upset when I'm spotted with Sawyer.

"I'll be right back," I say, sliding over Sawyer's lap and out of the booth. "I left something in my car." Not a lie. My phone. It slid off my console when I braked a little too hard on the way here, and I forgot to grab it.

I find it on the floor tucked under my surfboard and I almost hit the call button, but then screw it. I don't feel like speaking with her, so I text her instead. *Out with Sawyer, saw your friend, Erika. Sure she'll call you to gossip, but if you so much as breathe a word of the things you're not allowed to say, I swear to God I'll carry out every single threat I promised.*

Not that my mother would ever mention Brock to Erika. Erika comes from super old money, and discussing anything about finances would s*imply shock her, oh, the drama*—excuse me while I roll my eyes so hard they almost fall out—but I don't want the image of me sitting with Sawyer to spur my mother into going to the authorities like she threatened for so many years.

And...now that I have my phone in hand, maybe it's time I get Sawyer's phone number. I smile to myself and hop out of my Jeep and discover Jess standing on the sidewalk in front of me, skateboard in hand. He's scowling. I wave.

"I know you're here with my brother." He shoves his skater cap lower across his forehead.

"Actually, I'm on the sidewalk with you." I try to smile, but he sneers harder. Guess cheesy jokes aren't going to work on him like they did four years ago. "Jess...I'm sorry. Can we talk? I've missed you. A lot."

"Screw you." He swings open the door to the restaurant and slams it behind him, leaving me gaping on the sidewalk. And I watch him search for Sawyer—and then storm to our table, and sweep our plates onto the floor shouting something so loud the entire restaurant turns to watch.

Oh, shit. Is it awful that I kind of want to slink back into my Jeep?

But I can't make Sawyer stick it out alone. Not when Jess is so furious. I dart into the restaurant and grab his elbow when his arm cocks back—to do who knows what, as Sawyer's too far away for him to hit.

"Get off of me," Jess rounds on me, his eyes furious. "You don't get to ruin my family a second time. Go away, Quinn. You're such a *bitch*."

I blink, frozen to the floor. His words are like razors scraping through my stomach. He glares at me. "You think I don't know what you're up to? Now that we're back and getting settled and you're just going to fucking have your fun and toss—"

"That's about enough out of you." Sawyer doesn't raise his voice, but it's sharp enough to slice through whatever else Jess was about to say, through whatever I was about to respond with. He throws a wad of cash on the table, pushes himself out of the booth, and grabs his brother around the back of his neck, squeezing so tight, Jess winces.

"Sawyer—" I start, but he cuts me off with a look.

He shoves Jess through the restaurant and out the door. I…tiptoe behind them, casting apologetic glances around the room, my face flaming. Erika Covington's watching me blandly, without even raising an eyebrow. My mom's going to get such an earful… But I'm more concerned with Jess at the moment. With why he's so angry.

And with the way Sawyer seems furious enough to kick his ass into next Tuesday.

CHAPTER FORTY-THREE

QUINN

SAWYER SHOVES JESS through the crowded parking lot and onto a patch of grass before letting him go. Jess's hands are balled into fists by his side, and I wonder where his skateboard is. I turn and find it discarded by the exit of the pancake house. I run back to grab it, but by the time I'm back to the patch of grass, Sawyer's face is directly in front of Jess's and I can't make out what he's saying because he's speaking so low. But his jaw is set and his expression is menacing—and Jess, the little dummy, isn't backing down. And then he shoves a fist into Sawyer's stomach.

Sawyer doesn't budge, doesn't even back up a step. Doesn't drop his gaze. And his jaw flexes and I can tell he's so mad he might be about to do something he'll regret. I sprint up to the grass, shoving my way between them. "What is *wrong* with you, Jess?"

"According to Sawyer, everything," he spits at me. "But he's the one fucking it all up."

Sawyer puts a hand on my shoulder and Jess stiffens at the sight, yelling that he's a traitor.

I step away from Sawyer—no need to piss Jess off more

than he already is. Sawyer says, "Tone it down."

"You tone it down. You think I don't know you've been with her for weeks? I saw you at the bonfire. I saw you." Jess's voice cracks, and so does my heart. "You're such a fucking hypocrite. Telling me I couldn't talk to her and then doing it anyway."

"Things have changed." Sawyer glances at me, but the tension is back behind his eyes. The same tension I thought was gone for good.

"I went looking for him, Jess," I say. "Not the other way around. And I've wanted to see you too—you have no idea how badly."

"Too bad I don't want to see you," he says. "*You ruined my life.*"

"I said that's enough." Sawyer steps toward Jess—and Jess shoves him. Hard. Right as a cop car passes on the road. And a second later the lights flash and beep and the officer pulls into the parking lot.

"Jesus Christ, Jess." Sawyer shakes his head. "You know we can't afford this." He looks at me. "Quinn. You should leave. I'm sorry. Call me later."

"But I still don't have your number," I say, lightly, hoping to make him smile, because my words are ridiculous considering everything we did last night. It's kind of funny, or at least I think it is. But his expression doesn't change. Neither does Jess's. "I'm not just going to leave you guys here, anyway."

And then I regret saying it because the cop who steps out of the car is freaking Officer Vincent. The one with the vendetta against Chase's family. The one who takes pleasure in being a supreme dickhead.

"What's going on here?" he asks. His face is turned toward Sawyer, but his eyes are hidden behind mirrored shades. I slide a little farther away, hopefully not too noticeably. Because my presence here isn't going to do Jess any favors.

"Just a friendly family discussion," Sawyer says.

Jess scoffs.

I take a deep breath.

Officer Vincent cocks his head. "Do I know you?"

I shake my head and drop my eyes, almost expecting to see my stomach there on the ground with how fast it falls.

"I do. I do know you."

Well, shit. Maybe if I'm a brat here, he'll forget about Jess and Sawyer.

I sigh and lift my face—but he's not looking at me, he's looking at Jess. "You're the little smart-ass who mouthed off to me when I busted up that beach fire last week."

"He's had some issues," Sawyer says, stepping to stand just slightly in front of Jess. "But he's cleaning up his act, sir. I promise. I'm sorry for any trouble he may have caused at the beach fire. Really." His voice is so sincere it's almost hypnotic.

"Yeah, well, he's on my radar now," Officer Vincent says. He lifts his shades to look directly at Jess. "You'd best be staying off of it from here on out."

Jess stares at him, sneering. God. I want to reach over and pinch him. But I also don't want to get noticed myself.

Too late, though. Officer Vincent glances at me, smirking. "Great company you seem to keep these days, doll."

He's still shaking his head when he gets back in his car. He frowns at us before driving away.

I turn to Jess with a shaky smile. "Well, if a run-in with the law doesn't bond us, I don't know what will."

"Fuck you."

"Jess. Chill." Sawyer wraps an arm around his neck, holding him steady, but Jess shoves away from him, his eyes hot on mine.

"It's your fault we left," he says, quietly. I think I'd rather he yelled, because my heart is starting to crumble. "And you acted like family—you had my number, my email, my everything, and you never once called. So fuck you, Quinn. You ruined my life. You ruined my dad's life. You should've seen Sawyer. Drunk all day every day, crying like a fucking pussy." His own eyes are bright red now, though. "You didn't even care. You ruined us and you didn't even care."

"You have it backward," Sawyer says, jerking his arm.

"Listen to me. It wasn't—"

"Sawyer, don't." I say, also quietly. If Jess doesn't know about his father, he shouldn't find out now. Or ever, if it can be helped. I can't stand my mother for who she is, but it's easier knowing she's not a good person. Brock is a decent man, and Jess shouldn't know him any other way.

"I heard you and Dad," Jess says. "Saying it was all that Westwood bitch's fault. Don't deny it."

"I would never say that," Sawyer looks at me, pleading. But he doesn't need to. I know he wouldn't.

"Dad did. And you agreed."

"Jess," I say. "I'm sorry. I...I didn't understand why you'd all left, and I was really upset. I shut down, okay? And I couldn't get in touch with you later. Your number was disconnected. And you didn't have a Facebook profile that I could find, nothing. I missed you *so much*, though. Can we start over?"

"No. You broke your promise and you acted like I never even existed." He snaps his mouth shut, like he didn't mean to admit as much.

"My promise?" I can't believe it didn't dawn on me that he'd remember what I'd said.

Pain flashes across his face and I hate myself for causing it. "Of course you don't remember. You're so fake it makes me sick."

"I never forgot that promise, Jess—I just wasn't given an opportunity to keep it."

"What promise?" Sawyer asks, looking between us.

I open my mouth, but Jess beats me to answering. "None of your business." And he shoots me a look of half fury, half panic. He doesn't want me to say anything in front of Sawyer. So I press my lips together even though I'm dying to prove to him that I do remember. He was bullied. He trusted me enough to tell me, and I promised I'd look out for him.

And a week later, he was gone.

"It doesn't matter, anyway," Jess continues. "I hate you, Quinn. I don't give a shit about some stupid promise anyway."

"*Enough.*" Sawyer's word comes out in a growl, and he

moves toward Jess.

I'd step between them, but I can't. Can't move. Can't breathe.

I'm in too much pain.

I hate you, Quinn.

Jess pulls something from his pocket, flings it at Sawyer. It flashes and bounces off of his chest onto the grass. Neither of them look down.

Still practically crippled with pain, I slowly, slowly, lean over to grab it. A silver coin, with a triangle in the middle and "To Thine Own Self Be True" and "Twenty-four Hours Recovery." I think it's a sobriety coin for AA.

"You're getting sober?" I ask, trying to infuse my tone with warmth, no matter how broken I'm feeling. "That's great, Jess."

But he doesn't even look at me, just keeps his gaze even with Sawyer's. "I don't know—*am I?* Because the only way I'll be able to *handle* you being with her, is with a drink in my hand."

And just like that my heart closes in on itself. "Jess..."

"This is a family matter, and *you* aren't a part of it anymore." He still doesn't look at me.

Neither does Sawyer.

Oh, God.

"You guys remember when Sawyer tried to teach me to skateboard?" Now I begin to ramble, desperation to make some connection cutting through the pain that froze me. I hold up Jess's board. "Should we try again? See if I can get a matching scar on my other knee?"

Finally, Sawyer looks at me. "I need to handle this. Just call me later, okay?"

I hate how unemotional his tone is. I hate everything about this entire moment. I hate the way my voice shakes when I repeat myself. "I...still don't have your number."

He reaches for the phone I still clutch in the hand opposite the skateboard. I hand it to him and he adds his number. And I say goodbye and don't even have a chance to kiss him, and my heart hurts because I'm afraid I won't get to do it ever again.

This feels that huge.

I place Jess's skateboard on the grass beside him. I try to catch his eye, but he refuses to look at me and I refuse to cry, so I turn and I walk away, trying really, really hard to figure out what just happened and how the world's shifted. Trying really, really hard to keep my balance.

When I reach my Jeep, I turn back, but Sawyer's looking at Jess, and Jess's shoulders are heaving like he's breaking down, and I want to crumble to the pavement and have a breakdown of my own because it's not just my heart in pain. I hurt everywhere. Somehow I started the day in complete bliss and it's turned into a complete nightmare.

I close my eyes and when I open them again, I focus on Sawyer a second time. Faith. I need to have faith in Sawyer. He'll work this out with Jess. Everything's going to be fine.

And until then, I'll surf. I'll hit the waves and clear my head until my shift this afternoon. And by tonight everything will be fine.

...

Okay, that's total bullshit and I can't even come close to making myself believe it. I'm off balance, and I'm pissed, and I want to roar. And a good rough surf will help get it out.

When I open my door to grab my board, it's gone.

"Mother *fucker*." I glance around, but other than a family with three kids getting out of a minivan, there's nobody else in the parking lot.

Then it hits me. "*Jess*."

But...

My board was in my Jeep when I went to find my phone to text my mom—and I ran into Jess right there. And have been with him ever since.

Not Jess. As much as it would make sense for it to be him.

Fuck.

So in broad daylight and in a matter of, like, *minutes*, someone stole my surfboard from my locked Jeep. Regardless of the daylight, I get the chills, suddenly feeling insecure in the town where I've never felt anything other than safe.

Which is really the last thing I need right now, on top of everything else.

I tick off the count on my fingers. Surfboard. Spare tire. Wakeboard. Sunscreen. Car charger... What else?

There's a hundred-dollar bill in my glove box for emergencies—and it's still there when I slide in to check. So either this thief is a moron or they're trying to make me paranoid. In which case, mission freaking accomplished.

I glance in my rearview mirror. Sawyer and Jess are still arguing. I can't go running to Sawyer for comfort, not when the last look I saw pass through his eyes was defeat. Jess looks my direction and I start my Jeep, backing up right away. I've already taken too long to leave, and I don't want them to think I've been sitting here watching them. But as I pull out of the parking lot, I can't decide where to go.

Police station? Ugh. The thought of returning there after my first experience... I'd almost rather leave my doors unlocked with a sign for the thief to take whatever the hell he wants next time. And after a second round with Officer Asshole just a second ago? Forget it.

Home? So I can pace aimlessly before I have to work? No.

My parents' house? Don't make me laugh.

And then I know. Gianna's working today.

As soon as I walk into her shop, as soon as she smiles at me and I feel the coil of tension unwind in my stomach, I know I made the right decision. This is where I should be.

"Excuse me, miss, but we don't open for another hour," she says.

I try to smile. Fail.

"Oh, shit." She crosses to me from behind the counter immediately, pushing me into a metal chair at one of the small round tables filling the front of the shop. "What's wrong?"

She slides into the chair across the table from me, expectantly, but I don't have the words yet. Instead, I reach into my bag and pull out the Mason jar I brought in from my car. "Here, I made this for you."

She drops her attention from me to the jar and I watch her

take it in. The burlap fabric covering the bottom quarter. The few circles of lace wrapped haphazardly (yet, in reality, oh-so-painstakingly) around the glass. The three dried red-turned-burgundy roses, angled and gorgeous, trapped permanently beneath the metal lid.

"I can't believe you made this—I mean I *can*—but God. I just remember when you were learning how to dry flowers and they always crumbled..." She rolls the jar gently in her hand. "But this is so delicate. It's gorgeous. It's going on my nightstand. No. Wait. On our entryway table so everyone can see it."

"Cool." The word comes out flat. I sniffle and try to pull myself together, try to put more emotion in my next sentence. "They're the flowers Chase brought to me the first time I met him."

She's quiet for a moment, looking from the flowers to me and back again. "That seems...weird."

"I thought so too, at first," I admit. "But if he hadn't taken me out, you guys never would've met. So it's like...our date was really fate's way of bringing you two together."

She lifts a brow, considering. Lowers it, accepting. "I'll buy that. This is too pretty to feel weird about." She places the jar gently on the table between us, studying it a few seconds longer. Then she meets my eyes and asks a second time, "What's wrong?"

"Well, someone stole my surfboard." I'm able to keep my tone light, almost bored like it's no big deal. "And I think they've been stealing shit from my Jeep all summer."

"Holy shit." Her eyes widen—and then narrow. "You wouldn't be this pale over a stolen board. What else is wrong?"

"I'm pretty sure it's over with Sawyer, Gi." And this time my voice breaks. I'm so scared it's the truth. There was something in Sawyer's face. In the set of his shoulders. In the fury of Jess's expression. I tell her everything, the words flooding out of me so fast and so broken, it's a wonder she understands me at all.

But she does. "No way," she says. "There's just no way you could've finally waded through all the bullshit keeping you apart, just to have one night together before losing each other again. I refuse to believe it. And so should you."

I shake my head, but she stays on me until I promise not to give up hope.

Then she brings over a tub of ice cream, and we both dig in.

"You want me to come stand guard outside your car tonight?" she asks through a mouthful of mint chocolate chip.

"No. But I love that you really would if I asked."

* My Forever Family *

1. ~~My parents.~~ No. Just no.
2. ~~Sawyer.~~ Pretty sure he's out now, too; no matter how positive Gi's trying to be, my gut tells me I'm losing him.
3. ~~Brock and Jess.~~
4. Gianna.

* * * * * *

I might not have Sawyer. I might not want my parents. But I have Gi. She's my family. She always will be.

CHAPTER FORTY-FOUR

SAWYER

QUINN'S TEXTED ME four times. Once each day since we last saw each other. I've texted her back once each day in response. That's it. I should give her more; she doesn't deserve this after everything. But if I give her more than this, the dam I have in place will bust and I'll give her everything. Which will leave nothing for Jess.

How are you? Working on Jess.
Any better? No.
I love you. I love you.
This is really painful.

I don't know how to respond to her most recent message because I'm not sure a word exists to describe how I feel. I want to break something. Or someone. Which is why I'm cleaning dishes in the kitchen of my dad's place instead of watching baseball in the living room with him and Jess.

Jess, who's been attached to my damn side for four days. Certain I'm slipping off to see Quinn every time I try to go somewhere without him. He isn't wrong.

The easy solution here is to tie him up, toss him on his bed, and do what I want to do. But I can't take the easy solution when it comes to Jess. He's a disaster. My dad's a disaster. But they're trying, for me. My dad made us scrambled eggs for dinner last night, but his hands shook the entire time because they don't remember how to be steady without a drink. I can't slip out and leave them on their own now. Jess will find a way to drink to rebel and, like a two-person domino set, my dad will tumble down the exact same way. *Fuck.*

I slam my fist on the counter and they both turn to stare at me. I level Jess with a look and jerk my head for him to join me. He rolls his eyes, but when I very slowly put down the plate I'm holding and turn as if I'm coming to him, he hops off the couch and heads my direction.

My dad lifts his eyebrows, but goes back to watching the game when I motion for him to stay where he is.

"It wasn't Quinn's fault we moved away," I say quietly, for the hundredth time. "How long is this going to last, Jess? You're punishing the wrong person."

He shrugs. "As soon as you stop caring if I drink or not."

What he's really saying is as soon as I stop caring about him. He's sixteen and a mess and acting like a little shit, but I get it. I just don't get why he's blaming Quinn for this. "What promise do you think she broke?"

He shrugs again. "It doesn't matter. That's not why I hate her."

"You were twelve the last time you saw her, Jess. Memories can play tricks on us. You missed her, you even cried."

"No, I didn't."

"Well, now I know there's something wrong with your memory." I try to smile. "What I'm trying to say is, maybe it hurt too much to miss her and you let yourself hate her instead."

"No. *I actually hate her.*" He sets his jaw, for the hundredth time.

I fucking lose it. I shove his shoulders, walking him back until he slams into the refrigerator. "Why, Jess? Tell me. Now.

Before I dropkick it out of you."

He stares at me, jaw still jutting out, defiant because he knows I'm full of shit. My dad clears his throat from the living room, but I ignore him because he also knows I'd never actually hurt Jess.

It's unspoken, but there, between Jess and me not to mention anything about the situation with Quinn to my dad. I can't bring myself to tell him because if he confessed what he did to Jess, confessed that it's his fault we had to leave, I don't know what Jess will do. He's already on such a bad path himself. And if I tell my dad about Quinn and he doesn't try to help by telling Jess it's actually his fault? I won't be able to forgive him. So instead Jess gets to never forgive Quinn.

"Okay," I say, resigned, a chainsaw of regret tearing through my gut. "You win."

"She *sucks*, Sawyer." He sounds so whiny, so snotty, so goddamn sure of himself, I have to push myself away from the fridge and turn from him because I actually am tempted to dropkick his scrawny ass.

When I look at him again, though, he's picking at a pimple on his cheek and the fact that he's sixteen hits me in a new light. He's young. When I was sixteen, I met Quinn. I had a stable home. My father wasn't a drunk—not like he's been the past years anyway. Jess has...well, he has me, and he has a father doing his best to get sober. A father he can still respect because, aside from all the drinking, he has no clue the sort of man he's been in the past.

"If it means that much to you, I won't see her." My voice comes out strangled, hoarse, like I've been screaming at the ball game on TV with my dad. "But I need to be decent about it. I need to tell her goodbye. I can't just walk away without another word. And I hope you'll be the kind of man who can't do that in the future either."

My father strolls into the kitchen, whistling under his breath. He reaches around Jess to open the fridge and pulls out a bottle of water. It takes every ounce of my self-control not to cuss at him. If he hadn't done what he did, if he hadn't stolen from

Quinn's family, if he hadn't fucked up our lives, I never would've left Quinn. I never would've had to walk away again now.

But then it fucking murders me when his grip isn't strong enough to twist off the cap of the water bottle on his first few tries. All three of us pretend not to notice, and it takes another few seconds for him to get it, giving the anger in my veins time to cool off a little.

"Whatever." Jess's tone is bland, like he's suddenly chill because he's getting his way. "Do what you have to do."

"Don't let him go anywhere," I say to my dad, still a little gruffer than I mean to. "I'll be back in an hour."

"Like I can't make my own decisions," Jess scoffs.

My dad cuffs him on the shoulder. "We'll be right here, don't worry."

I trust him only because I have to.

So the text I send Quinn today is to ask for her address. When she sends it, I drive to her and cuss the entire time because it takes me almost half an hour to drive three miles. Saturday beach traffic makes me want to set fire to the world.

Finally, I'm there. Finally, I'm in front of her door. Finally, I'm knocking.

She opens the door a few seconds later and she takes one look at me and her face falls and I know she knows.

She smiles sadly. "At least you're saying goodbye this time."

CHAPTER FORTY-FIVE

QUINN

I'VE BEEN BRACING myself for this. But one look at Sawyer's face, the destruction across his expression, almost undoes me. The only thing holding me together as I let him into my apartment is the fact that he's as upset as I am—and that he's doing this, he's ending this, for Jess. I can't come between that. Even if every inch of me is dying to scream that Jess is a kid and emotions are fickle and maybe it will pass. Sawyer won't take that risk, though, and I shouldn't either.

So I'll be strong.

Or I'll try my fucking hardest.

I walk through my tiny living space, pointing to the kitchen, pointing to the dining area. "Not much to see, really. It's just my place for the summer."

He doesn't say anything, and when I glance back at him, he's studying the metal frame I found in my car that day that feels like forever ago.

"Oh." My voice comes out toneless. "I meant to ask if you made that for me."

He looks at me, his brows furrowed, and doesn't say anything.

"I found it on the hood of my car one day. Made me think

of you. Wishful thinking, I guess." I shake my head. "Maybe I have a stalker. Someone stealing shit from my car and trying to pay for it with one tiny frame." It should maybe freak me out a little more, but I don't have room for the pressure of panic like that at the moment. Not with the lead-filled heart already sitting so heavy between my ribs.

"You never figured out what happened to your spare?" he asks.

"Nope."

"Did you report it?" His brow dips, like he's worried about the theft.

"Nope." I realize he doesn't know about my surfboard. Guess there's no reason to tell him now. Not when he's here to break things off. Not when my life doesn't get to matter to him anymore.

But that's not fair. I shouldn't be so bitchy.

I know my life matters to him—and I need to hold on to that knowledge if I want to get through any of this and come out at least partially whole on the other side.

It's just that the saying's true and life's a cruel little bitch and shit doesn't always work out the way you want it to. The way you know in your gut it *should*.

"When do you go back to school?" he asks, letting the spare tire thing go.

"A month and a half," I say, trying really hard not to picture the rest of the summer without him in it. "What about you? I mean, will you guys stick around town this time?"

He shrugs. "Depends on Jess. If he keeps his shit together, yeah. But I'm not sure about some of his friends. And it depends on my dad, too. If he can stay sober enough to keep his job this time." Another shrug. "My shop goes to half days after October 16th. Might take my board out to the Bahamas for a month after that."

"Oh. Fun." I don't want him to tell me these things. I don't want to know what he'll be doing if I'm not a part of it.

I also want to know everything.

But I bite my tongue to keep from asking anything else.

"I'm sorry, Quinn." He holds my gaze. "Jess—"

"Hates me."

He looks like he might deny it, but only drops his gaze. "Before we came back he was so close to just completely...unhinging. He got arrested. He hung around with druggies. He was a wreck—way worse than what you've seen here." He laughs, but it's sour. "Trust me, this is an improvement."

"I'm sorry," I say, my heart breaking for Jess now, too. "I hate that for him. For all of you."

"But it's not enough of an improvement. He needs a better role model than my dad. He needs to know that what he wants matters, that he's important. And for some stupid fucking reason he's fixated on..."

"Hating me." I get it. Or...maybe I don't. "I love Jess, Sawy. But he's sixteen. And confused about a lot of shit... Maybe giving him everything he demands is more enabling than helpful." I'm not sure where this is coming from, if it's me trying to think of what's best for Jess, or what's best for me. It's too confusing. I'm too...defeated.

"I don't know. Maybe you're right," Sawyer says. "But we've tried everything, and I think in this case—"

"You're going to give him what he wants."

He doesn't answer, just watches my face. He doesn't have to say anything, though. I've known it from the moment Jess melted down. Sawyer's family's everything to him.

Oh, God. This is it, then. It's over.

But I can't bring myself to be the one to say it.

Neither, apparently, can he, and after a few minutes of silence the air is so heavy with the tension of those unspoken words that I feel like I'm drowning.

I think about telling Sawyer what I'd promised Jess, to take care of him—and the reason for it. But I can't bring myself to break Jess's confidence when it was so clear he didn't want me to say anything. And...he's got Sawyer to take care of him now anyway.

I think about suggesting that *I* speak to Jess, that I try to explain harder to him that I didn't break my promise. But I'm sure Sawyer already thought of that, and if he thought it was a good idea he'd say so. And Jess will think I'm saying whatever it takes to be with Sawyer.

He wouldn't be right. But he also wouldn't be wrong.

Why didn't I think to speak to Jess about all of this earlier? Like...the first time I saw him? Or any time after?

God. Because I was wrapped up in Sawyer—the thought of him, the sight of him, the taste of him...

Because I'm *so self-centered.*

Sawyer slides his hands into his pockets, shifting on his feet a little. We stare at each other, neither opening our mouths to speak. Until the drowning sensation is too much to handle.

"That's the bathroom." I point. "In case you need to use it." *Before you go*, I can't make myself say.

He offers a whisper of a smile. "I'm good."

I open my bedroom door. "And this is where I sleep."

"Still have your Hop?" he asks.

"Poor Hop got lost in the college transition. I still miss her sometimes." My stuffed bunny. Had her from the day I came home from the hospital. I really do still miss her sometimes. In fact, I could use a good cry into her fur right about now. Not that she had any fur by the time I left for school, but that's beside the point.

The point is that Sawyer's walking out of my life again.

The point is I can't blame him for it.

The point is I'm halfway to breaking down right before him.

He strides past me into the bedroom and I follow, looking around as though through his eyes. Green walls. Lilac comforter on the bed. Dried flowers in frames along my dresser and hung around the room.

"Suits you," he says. "Simple and pretty."

"You calling me simple?" I ask, trying to infuse humor into my question.

He turns to face me. "Not in a million years."

Silence stretches before us. Seconds into minutes into eons.

"Can you hold me, maybe, for a minute before you go?" My

voice sounds small, weak even, but I don't care. It's a shared vulnerability between us, and I don't need to hear him speak to know he's feeling as hopeless as I am.

He crosses the room in three steps and folds me into his arms. I want to cry, my chest aches to let it go, but I won't. He nudges my chin up toward him, and when I lift my head I see my sadness reflected in his expression, and all I want to do is erase it completely. I want the Sawyer from yesterday and the night before. The one who floated in the ocean, hands behind his head, relaxed and finally free from the weight of the world.

I rise on my tiptoes to brush his lips with my own, soft at first and then harder, more demanding, and I give my freaking all, trying to kiss away anything sad between us, even if only for a moment. Because I know now it's all we have left.

We kiss and we kiss and we kiss until my mouth is numb and my lips are swollen and my throat is raw from breathing in his exhaled air. My fingers are so tangled in his hair, I'm not sure I'll be able to extract them. Maybe I should laugh and make a joke about it being my master plan so he can never leave me.

But it just isn't funny.

His palms are sweaty against my lower back because he's been holding me so tightly. He slides them higher now, pausing at the strap of my bra, tapping lightly at the latch, questioningly.

I look at him. "Yes."

If I can have him one more time, there's nothing in the world that's going to stop me. He must feel the same way, because he has me naked practically before I get the word out—and I don't take much longer than that to undress him, too.

But...then we stand here, quietly taking each other in. Like it's the last time.

Because it is.

Maybe it'd be easier if he did what he did last time and left without a word.

But the thought launches vertigo through me. Not getting to say goodbye again would kill me.

At least this time I can study him. Make sure to take in every single detail.

So I do. And I think he does, too. We stare at each other until the silence is so heavy I might crumble from the weight of it.

"Sawyer." My voice breaks. But I won't cry. I won't. And I won't beg him to reconsider.

"Turn around," he says, his voice gruff. "Hold on to the wall."

It takes a second for me to understand.

He's trying to give me my fantasy.

A parting gift.

But sadness sits so heavily in my stomach I don't think I'll be able to enjoy it. "Kiss me again."

He wraps his hands around my jaw and he stares into my eyes and he holds my face like it's the most fragile thing in the world. His head dips toward me, and then he feathers his lips over mine the same way he's holding me. Gently. Sweetly.

One small sob escapes from my mouth into his and I can't do this anymore. I cut off the kiss and spin, grabbing the wall with my arms spread away from my face, my elbows bent.

He places his hands on my shoulders and runs them lightly up my arms to cover my own hands, and then he pushes them up along the wall until my elbows are straight and the side of my face is against the wall. He leans against me, pressing his chest against my back, resting here for a breath, then two, then three...

His hands roam back down my arms and shoulders and back, circling around to my breasts, and sad as I am, my nipples still tighten under his touch, my breath still quickens. I try to memorize the feeling and maybe he does too, because he rests his forehead at the base of my neck and pauses again, the sounds of our breathing the only noises in the room for a moment.

Then his mouth is at the side of my neck and he's kissing me and murmuring that he loves me, and I try to say it back but can't get the words around the broken bits of my heart stuck my throat. His fingers trace circles down my ribs and across my belly and between my legs, where he gently parts me and plays with me until, yet again, he manages to push my sadness to the side, and almost immediately I'm slick with the way I want him.

While my soul's been aching for his from the moment I opened my door to him—from the first moment I met him, really—my body aches for him now, almost excruciatingly, in a much more physical sense.

One hand comes around my hip to cup my ass, sliding down along the curve all the way to the middle of my legs where his middle finger dips into me, curling in a *come hither* motion, once, twice, again and again until my breath hitches. He adds another finger, a little less gently this time, and his teeth sink into the skin of my shoulder. He pushes his fingers deep, deep, deep into me until his palm is flattened between my legs and the fingers of his other hand are spreading me, playing me like an instrument, shaping me and pressing against me harder and harder until I'm pulsing, tightening around his hand and my knees are quivering like slowly melted butter.

My stomach begins to flutter, the feeling growing lighter and lighter, flowing lower and lower and he's teasing every single spot between my legs and I can't stop moaning, can't keep my eyes from shutting to fully sink into the sensations, can't keep from lowering one arm to cup my own breasts, needing the pressure, the extra touch.

He trails a hand up my stomach, leaving a path of moisture along my skin, and up my neck and over my chin. He hooks his fingers in my mouth between my teeth so that the saltiness of my own body mingles along my tongue and at the exact same moment he shoves a third finger into me below, rough and demanding, and I come against his hand immediately with a moan bordering on a yell.

With a shove of his hand he spreads my legs farther apart, pulling his finger from my mouth to grab my waist, and he slams his hips against me so that his erection flattens between my legs. It's enough to have me coming even harder against him, rocking my hips and sliding along the length of him. He pulls back, tightening his fingers into my skin, repositioning himself and then pulling me down onto him, filling me to the hilt at the peak of my orgasm and I drop my head back against his shoulder, crying out.

Then he's ruthless. Shoving, slamming, hammering into me so hard my arms shake from the pressure to keep from banging my face into the wall. He's biting my neck, my shoulders, and grabbing my hands, pushing them tight against the wall while his hips are bucking, bucking, bucking so tight against me there is zero space between us and I'm rocking back to take him in deeper and squeezing myself around him.

His knees bend into the backs of mine every time he thrusts; he's grunting against my skin, and I'm gasping every time he pushes further into me. My entire body tightens, and hot sensations rush between my legs and up my belly and down my thighs. He's pushing me flat against the wall with a rumble coming from his chest; it's vibrates against my back, and it rips up his throat and out of his mouth in a groan in my ear.

I swear to God if he wasn't holding me up, I'd slide right down the wall into a puddle of... I don't even know what, and I don't have time to think of anything because everything's going really, really, really hot—*white hot*—and another orgasm bucks through me so hard I lose the ability to breathe or see or anything at all.

He comes a split second after me, shoving himself so hard into me I'm literally lifted onto my tiptoes, and the side of my face is pressed so flat against the wall I wonder if it'll leave a mark, and I've never been so full of someone before and I never want to feel anything else and my orgasm crests through me and circles around him, pulsing, pulsing, pulsing, pulling us together until we're spent, breathing hard and good for nothing, letting the wall hold us up because without it we'd be fucking toast.

Burnt toast.

Buttered toast.

Crumbled toast, sticky with jam.

I almost laugh at the ridiculous direction of my thoughts.

But the moment I gain the ability to find something funny, I also gain the ability to remember that this was my last time with Sawyer. I suddenly hate my body for feeling the pleasure still riding through it when the rest of the world seems so bleak.

"This sucks." I lean my forehead against the wall, closing my eyes.

"I'm sorry."

"I am, too."

"Quinn."

I don't respond.

"Quinn."

I can't.

"Look at me," he says, his voice a complete mess. "Quinn, turn around."

"No." I open my eyes to stare at the wall; I painted it green at the start of the summer in an effort to match his eyes without even realizing it. The color doesn't come close by a long shot, but I think I'm going to have to paint over it the second he's out the door. "If I turn around I'm going to attach myself to you and never, ever let go. So you need to leave. Okay? Thank you for this. For..." I shrug, not sure of where I'm going.

"*Thank you?*" He laughs without humor, and his breath hits the back of my neck, hot. He pushes at my shoulders, but I don't budge. I am a statue and if I move an inch I will crumble.

"Turn around. I want to kiss you." His voice cracks. "I need to kiss you."

I bite my lip so hard I taste blood and I focus on the wall and I don't turn around. Not when he slides out of me, trailing wetness down the inside of my thigh. Not while he dresses with the clanging of his belt filling the room like the saddest bell in the world.

Not when he tells me he loves me.

And not when the door shuts behind him.

CHAPTER FORTY-SIX

QUINN

IT'S BEEN A week.

It's been a week and I'm still standing.

So damn if I haven't grown a little in maturity, because around this same time four years ago, I couldn't even get out of bed.

Hell, I'm such a grown-up, I mailed a check for *eighty-two thousand dollars* to my mother.

I'm such a grown-up, I had my landlord install a deadbolt on my apartment door. And I have an appointment to have an alarm installed on my Jeep next week.

Plus, my apartment is spotless. My fridge is stocked. So is my wine rack. Well, it's missing a few bottles after last night, but I'll replace them tomorrow. I have an order in for a new surfboard—not, obviously, at Sawyer's shop. It stings going to a competitor, but I know he'd prefer it.

I deleted his number from my phone. It's almost laughable, how short a time it spent in there.

I mean, not really. Nothing's really laughable right now.

But it will be.

I think, anyway.

Someday.

Like, for instance, I'm going out with Gianna tonight. I told her to bring Chase—see? *More* evolving—but she told him to stay home, said we'd have a girls' night. Which sounds pretty perfect. As long as there's a lot of alcohol.

Except when we've just made it into Kelly's, haven't even ordered our first rounds yet, and Gianna nudges me. "Uh, do you know her?"

She points across the bar. There's a woman walking toward us with purpose and staring straight at me.

"No?" I stare back. She's got long brown hair, freckles across her nose, and huge eyes. I've never seen her before in my life. But she certainly appears to know me. When she's within hearing distance—which is to say, close, because the DJ's playing at a glaring level—I smile, tentatively. "Hi."

She rears back and slaps me so hard the sound rings out louder than the music. And it stings like a fucking army of bees.

"God, that felt good," she says, massaging her palm with her thumb.

Something inside of me snaps.

Because, seriously, that hurt. And also? What the hell?

"Seriously. What. The. *Hell?*" I slap her back just as hard.

She rubs her face. I rub mine. Gianna looks like she's ready to freaking rumble and I'm inclined to feel the same way.

"Who the hell are you?" I ask, my breath heaving. "And what the hell was that for."

"Allison Daniels." She sneers at me and when I don't react, she repeats, "*Daniels.*"

Oh. God.

"Um..." I stammer. I stammer and I come up with nothing to fill the void. Because she's Julian's wife.

"Yeah." She stares me down so hard it's a wonder I don't sink into the floor.

"I didn't know he was married. I'm sorry. I'm beyond sorry." I don't know why she's here, or how, or anything, really. But guilt is a brick slamming straight into my gut and I will never, ever forgive myself.

"Bullshit."

"I swear. And...if you want to slap me again, go ahead. I won't hit you back this time. I just...didn't know who you were." I feel like such a wuss for saying it, for standing here with my cheek out, but I slept with her husband and I'm not sure there's much worse you can do to a person.

She rears back again and I brace myself—but Gianna snakes out a hand to grab her wrist. "Try it, I dare you."

Allison keeps her hand in the air a second longer, but when Gianna holds her gaze, she slowly lets it fall. Gianna might be small, but she's got some serious spark with her snap. I'd smile under any other circumstances, but I nudge Gianna now, instead. "Chill, Gi. She's the one who's been wronged."

"I get it," she says to me, but keeps her eyes on Allison. "She's the teacher's wife, the dude you screwed?"

Hearing it makes me feel sick.

"Exactly," Allison says. "*I'm* the one who's been wronged."

"Look, it sucks your husband's a scumbag, okay? But he didn't tell Quinn about you. No, wait." She shakes her head when Allison starts to speak. "And maybe Quinn should've asked—maybe Quinn's partially to blame—" she glances at me, mouthing *sorry*, but there's no need because I agree with her "—but if you hit my friend again, while she might stand there and take it, I won't."

"Whatever. I didn't come here to cause a scene anyway. I just needed to look you in the eye," she says to me, her mouth quivering in a way that makes me want to slap my own face. "I wanted you to see the woman you made a fool of."

Then she walks away.

I tell Gianna to wait for me, and I go after Allison, because I can't stand it. I can't stand that I did so much damage.

"Hold on." I grab the door before it swings shut in my face.

She doesn't turn around, but it suddenly doesn't matter as much because Julian is standing outside waiting for her and I'm frozen in place.

"I'll be in the car," she tells him. "You have thirty seconds to join me or I'm leaving without you."

"Allison," I say. She glances over a shoulder, not bothering to face me fully. "I know I already said it, but I *am* really sorry, and I wish there was something I could say to make it better. For what it's worth...when he told me about you, he cried because he thought he'd lose you."

A tear escapes and trails down her cheek before she looks away. I loathe myself.

Almost as much as I loathe Julian.

I study him, all prim and structured, and I'm so fucking angry I could spit. What the hell did I ever see in this guy? Yeah, he's got a hot face, all angles and jaunty, but God, look at him. He's standing as straight as if someone shoved a ruler up his ass—and it's not just because he's uncomfortable. He's always stood this way.

"You brought your wife here?" I cross my arms over my chest to keep from slapping him, too. "What is wrong with you?"

"I'm sorry." He pleads with the most pathetic look on his face. "I confessed everything. I couldn't stand the guilt. And she wanted to see you."

Incredulous is not a strong enough word for what I feel. "And you said what? *Sure, babe. Let's take a little road trip to the Outer Banks and stalk the student I fucked all year without mentioning I was married?*"

"Something like that." He doesn't drop his gaze. At least he has the balls to face me head-on.

"How did you know where I was?"

"We went to your apartment first, but you were getting in your Jeep when I drove up. She made me follow you."

"How'd you get my address?" My mother's address is listed on school records... "Wait—have you been stealing my shit all summer?"

"What?" The confusion on his face seems genuine, but I know what a snake this guy is. "I would never steal from you."

"Would *she?*" I honestly don't blame her if so. I think actually I might feel better if it's been Allison.

"Quinn," he says my name with such familiarity I want to gag, "we've been in Raleigh all summer. She didn't know about you until last night."

Well, shit.

"This must be the douche," Gianna says, coming to stand beside me.

I nod. "This is definitely the douche."

Julian has the grace to look chastised.

"I think your thirty seconds are up," I tell him, just as Allison lays on the horn from a few cars away. "I hope it works out for you guys... But if it doesn't? I hope she finds someone a million times better than you."

"I'm sorry," he says, standing there lamely.

"God. *Doesn't anyone ever get sick of apologizing?*" I'm sick of it. I'm sick of him. I'm sick of everyone. Well. Everyone except Gianna. I turn to her, saying, "I'm going home. I'd apologize for leaving you here, but..."

"You're sick of apologizing." She gets me, and I give her a grateful smile.

And I head toward my car across the lot. She says something to Julian as I walk away, but I don't hear what it is. I don't care, anyway. Let her tear him to bits if she wants.

The problem ends up being that as I'm heading toward my Jeep, Danny Simmons is in my path, heading toward the bar. I fully plan to ignore him, but it's like he knows how fantastic my night's been so far, and he jogs to me to make it even better.

"Hey, princess." He slurs the greeting, clearly drunk.

"If you're here to tell me how tired I look again, it's because I am tired." I cut to the chase. Because I just don't feel like dealing with him.

And then...I think about how he stressed the word *tired* the last time.

And how, coincidentally, one of the things I'm missing is a tire.

And whatever snapped inside of me when Allison slapped me roars back full force. I shove him so hard he stumbles into a parked car, slamming his elbow into it. "*You've* been stealing shit from my Jeep."

CHAPTER FORTY-SEVEN

QUINN

"YOU HAVE NOTHING I want," Danny says, rubbing his elbow and running his eyes over my body. "Why are you acting like such a psycho?"

"Please," I snarl. "You've been messing with me all summer and I'm sick of it."

Add Danny to the list of things I'm sick of. Put him right up there at the very top.

He laughs. "Man, what crawled up your ass?"

"I'm not sorry I told Gianna about you. Never will be. So get. The fuck. Over it. I know you have my spare tire—which, considering you drive a Civic, is just stupid—and I want my surfboard back. Now."

"I have no idea what you're talking about," he says. "But you do look tense. I'd be happy to help you relax, honey..."

He calls me honey and I think of Sawyer and I want to cry.

"Your mom must be sorry she had you." It's the meanest thing I can think to say. And, somehow, it works.

His mouth snaps shut and when he opens it again, he speaks low and forceful. "You know nothing about my mom, Quinn. Don't you ever mention her again."

He storms off and I think maybe there's a deeper story

there, and maybe I even feel a little bad, but only a little. Mostly I'm just glad he's leaving me alone. And even more than that, I'm pissed he didn't immediately give me my stupid surfboard.

Then he turns, flips me the bird with both hands and tells me to go fuck myself.

I don't feel bad anymore.

And I do what I probably should've done weeks ago. I report all my missing things at the police station.

"So, to be clear, you're filing a report for missing sunscreen?" Officer Santiago—the nice cop who drove Chase and me back to Chase's car at the beginning of the summer—asks, smiling.

"Yep." I smile back. "Okay, no, but it was the first thing I noticed missing. No—wait, it was my cell phone charger."

"And it escalated in types of things until now it's your surfboard?"

I nod.

"And you think you know who it is?"

I nod again.

"But you don't want to give me the name?"

It's tempting. *So* tempting. "I'm not fully certain and I..."

"I get it. But you have to understand, Quinn, there's not much to go on. Nine times out of ten, nothing's recovered in cases like this."

"I know, but...I just needed to do something." Though now it feels kind of silly.

"Well, I'll make note of it and if anything comes of your report, I'll let you know, okay?"

"Does it help to know I always lock my Jeep?" I ask. "So whoever's doing this might have a criminal background if they can bust into locked cars—and without breaking windows or anything?"

"Not really. But it's in the report, okay?"

I feel a little like a jackass walking out of the station. But my surfboard was expensive. And I needed to do something to expel some of the rage boiling through me. Because it was either this or lose control completely and sleep outside Sawyer's shop and beg him to reconsider as soon as he shows up for work in the morning.

Because at the base of everything else I'm feeling, I just miss him.

Officer Vincent passes me on my way out, smirking, but I ignore him.

"What was that all about?" I hear him ask, all annoyingly smug, as the door shuts. I don't care. Let Officer Santiago tell him everything. If it puts Vincent on the case—and, in turn, on Danny's ass—all the better.

On the case. That's a weird phrase when applied to anything in my life. So official. It's weird, someone's stealing stuff from me. It's weird I haven't been very weirded out before this. My life in general feels weird right now. My ex-boyfriend's current wife slapped me across the face. The boy I love lives in my town and he loves me back and we can't be together. My parents also live in my town, and I want nothing to do with them anymore. Actually, screw the word *weird*. It's all shitty. Really shitty.

I hear the downward spiral in my thoughts, I do. *I'm* getting weird. But it's all a bit much to take in and I think my soul's turning out to be a fragile flower, not strong enough to withstand so many different things going on at once. I want to sleep for a month straight.

When I get home, I find another frame, this time on my porch. This one's made from a rose gold-tinted metal and it's hexagonal rather than rectangular and boxed out a little bit with space for dried, still-full flowers rather than pressed and I want so, so badly for it to be from Sawyer, but I know it isn't.

I glance around to make sure I'm alone, just in case this is actually from the thief... But Danny wouldn't ever do something like this and...this doesn't feel creepy. It doesn't feel connected to my random missing things. The frame is beautiful and I want to keep it. So I take it inside and I set it next to the other one. And then I go to bed, reliving that slap from Allison over and over and over again.

When my cell phone wakes me in the morning, I answer

saying Sawyer's name. I must've been dreaming of him. But it's my mother whose voice reaches me. Like a cold shower. "I've decided if you want to see that boy, I won't do anything about it. Now, your father and I would like you to come to brunch at ten, like usual."

I hang up.

And then, on second thought, I sit up, kicking off my covers because at some point the AC turned off last night and I'm sweating, and I call her back. Because who cares that she's *so graciously* changed her mind about Sawyer when it's too late now, anyway. And she still really sucks and she still needs to hear it.

"Did we get disconnected?" she asks when she answers.

"I hung up."

"Well, really. Was that necessary?"

"Yes, but then I realized I have something to say to you."

"If it's about brunch, I'd like to hear it. If it's about that other thing, I think we've said all we need to say to each other."

"*That other thing?*" I take a deep breath. "The thing where you lied straight to my face for years? That thing where you allowed your daughter to feel the worst pain of her life?"

Silence.

"Do you know how old Sawyer's little brother is now?"

More silence.

"Come on, Mom. I even mentioned it the other day."

A sigh.

"Sixteen," I say. "He's sixteen and he's a wreck because you forced his family to move out of town. I just need to make sure you really understand what you did. That's all I wanted to say. You destroyed more than just my relationship with Sawyer. You took away a stable childhood, and I don't know how you live with yourself."

A long pause, and then, "I wanted to tell you I ripped up the check you sent us. Not that the bank would've accepted such a large amount like that anyway."

I want to scream at the phone. "Are you listening to me *at all?*"

"Are you coming to brunch?"

I roll my eyes and hang up again. Then I turn my phone off and roll back over, deciding to go back to sleep until I have to leave for work.

But I wake up much sooner than that because, suddenly, I realize I've been so consumed with my own devastation, I haven't been thinking clearly.

I do need to speak with Jess.

He's so angry with me. He's so angry with the world.

I have to apologize.

Not to try to soothe him into forgiving me so I can be with Sawyer. I couldn't see it clearly before, how I could speak to him without any sort of ulterior motive, but I can now. Because he's Jess. And he's hurting. And I owe him an apology for not keeping my promise to him, an explanation for why I haven't been there for him when he's needed me.

And if I hadn't been such a chickenshit about my history with Sawyer, I would've done this the first day I saw Jess. I should've. No wonder he hates me so much.

I don't bother with a shower, just throw my guard stuff on and head out the door to find him.

Except when I get to the parking lot, my Jeep isn't where I left it.

It's gone.

Stolen.

CHAPTER FORTY-EIGHT

QUINN

"WELL, ON THE plus side, this will move up the priority of your case," Officer Santiago tells me.

I kind of want to hang up on him. The plus side? There is no plus side. My Jeep was stolen. I feel sick. Gross. Dirty, somehow.

Gianna offers to chauffeur me to work and I tell her to pick me up early. Because I have a feeling I know where my car is and if I'm right, I'm going to sit right there and call the cops and wait for them to show up and arrest Danny's stupid ass. But when we arrive at his neighborhood, there are only two cars parked in his driveway. His Civic and a silver SUV.

"That doesn't mean he didn't stash it somewhere," Gianna says, parking along the street. "Plus, I want to know whose SUV that is."

She doesn't have to convince me. I don't care about the SUV, but I want to watch his face for signs of weakness when I ask him where my Jeep is.

"If some slag opens his door, I'm going to be so pissed," she says, walking up the sidewalk.

I elbow her as we walk in stride onto his doorstep. "I thought you were happy with Chase?"

"I am," she says, ringing the bell. Aggressively, three times. "But that doesn't mean I want Danny to be *happy*. Or getting laid."

"Okay." I get it. Kind of.

The person who answers the door, though, is definitely not some girl Danny's banging. She's way too old for one thing, with more gray than brown in her hair. And the entire right side of her face is mottled with a bruise.

"Mrs. Simmons?" Gianna's sounds as horrified as I feel.

Danny's mom throws a hand to her face. "Gianna. I thought... I was expecting my sister."

"Are you okay?" Gianna asks. "What happened to your face?"

"*Gi*." I elbow her again.

"I'm fine, hon." Mrs. Simmons says. "Just going to stay with my sister for a while."

"Ma?" Danny's voice travels down the entrance hallway before he does. The minute he sees us, his expression drops from concerned to pissed. "What the hell do you want?"

But I can't just demand to know where he stashed my stolen Jeep in front of his mom, especially with her face as broken as it is. "To speak with you in private."

He sighs. "I don't have your stupid spare tire, or your surfboard. Quit wasting my time with this shit."

"Language," his mom says, shaking her head and then glancing at me. "I'm sorry. I raised him to treat girls with more respect than this."

I say, "It's okay," right when Danny says, "Believe me, Mom. If you knew the way she gets around, you wouldn't care how I treated her."

Gianna sucks in her breath, but Mrs. Simmons beats her to whatever she's going to say. "Danny. You sound like... You sound like your father."

And she starts to cry. Nothing dramatic, but big fat tears roll down her cheeks and she glances at me and Gi, excusing herself.

"Happy now?" Danny asks.

"Are *you*?" But I drop my eyes to study my feet, shame washing through me. Even though he's still a prick, he's a prick with some pretty hardcore baggage, and...I don't want to go easy on him, but shit. How can I not?

"Is she leaving him?" Gianna asks.

"Who knows," he says. "She says the same thing every time."

Then he shuts the door in our faces.

It's a silent ride for a while on the way to Kitty Hawk. Finally, I turn off her stereo. "You knew about his parents?"

She nods.

"I had no idea."

"I don't think it's something he shares with many people."

"But he did with you."

Another nod.

"You guys... You guys were closer than I thought."

"We were pretty close. Then he showed his true colors." Now a shrug—and even though I know she can feel my gaze on her, she stares out the windshield. "I don't think he has any clue your Jeep's missing."

I sigh and turn my gaze out my window, watching the buildings go by. "I think you're right."

Damn it.

Danny didn't steal my Jeep. Probably.

I glance at Gianna again. There are so many things I want to ask her about Danny now, but nothing I say will change the fact that he cheated on her, so I let it drop. Plus, she's happy with Chase. So all I ask is, "Can I borrow your car tomorrow?"

And she's so lost in thought, all I get in return is a third nod.

She's back to herself the next morning, though, picking me up with a bouncy smile.

Chase is riding shotgun, so I'm pretty sure he has something to do with it.

"Hear you have some car trouble," he says.

"Hear you're up for the role of Captain Obvious," I say.

Gianna laughs, and when we get back to her parents' place,

where I'm leaving them, she says, "Pick me up from work at eight. Chase's sister's in town so *he* can't collect me this time."

"I would if you'd just agree to meet my family," he says, sliding out of the car.

Gianna shoots me a look I can't quite read. She doesn't respond to Chase until we've switched places and she's walking up her driveway with him.

They'll work it out, I'm sure, especially considering the way he so easily drapes his arm around her shoulders. And for now, I've got my own plan to worry about.

I let the car idle on the street for a minute and I call Rajesh. When he answers, I say, "Everything still good?"

"You're in the clear."

I assume since he's not more specific that Sawyer must be with him. Which is perfect, just as we discussed when I called him at the shop last night. Now, all I need is for Jess to be home. I double-check the address with Rajesh before we hang up, earning a, "Yep," from him. So he's almost definitely with Sawyer, and it makes me want to scrap everything I'm about to do and find them instead.

But I don't.

I can't.

I drive, instead, to Brock's apartment to find Jess.

There's a thick hook of nervousness yanking through my stomach when I park. Brock will be at work, so I won't have to see him, but according to Rajesh, Sawyer's basically keeping Jess on house arrest these days. So he should be here. I just... I hope he'll answer the door. I hope he'll give me a chance to explain. Not that I even know how I'll explain. But I have to do something.

I take a deep breath—at least my tenth since I've parked—and I knock on the door.

But Jess doesn't answer. Brock does.

Shit.

CHAPTER FORTY-NINE

QUINN

BROCK STARES AT me, and, throat gone dry, I stare back. I wonder what it must be like to see me, someone who looks so much like the woman who ruined his life. No wonder he wasn't exactly friendly when I saw him at the surf shop.

He clears his throat. "Quinn."

"Mr. Carson." I clear mine a second later.

And we stare some more.

He still looks like hell. But now instead of soured liquor, the mingled scents of coffee and soap waft off of him. His hair is still thin, but it's not greasy anymore. His eyes remain bloodshot, but they're not so confused and the green isn't quite as faded.

He looks so much more like the man I remember.

The one who took me to the ER for stitches my sophomore year, when Sawyer tried to teach me to skateboard and I busted my knee. And during my junior year, when I was so sick with the flu it felt like the plague, and my own parents avoided my part of the house like it actually *was* the damn plague, this is the man who made a spot for me at his place. *He's* the one who made me soup and brought me cool rags for my forehead.

"Um—" he starts to say, but doesn't get a chance to finish.

Because I throw my arms around him. Hugging him as tightly as a person can.

Because he's more family to me than my own mother, and I haven't really spoken with him in four years.

Because he's Brock. And I love him.

He stiffens, awkwardly pats my shoulders—and, when I don't let go, finally relaxes into the hug, returning it. "Hey, girlie."

"Hey," I say into his shoulder.

"Sawyer's not here."

"I know."

He stiffens again, for a very short moment. "I expect you're here for an explanation, and I suppose it's long overdue. Come on in."

He pulls away, motioning for me to enter, but I don't cross the threshold. I peek over his shoulder, looking for Jess, but I don't see him. "I was hoping to speak with Jess," I say. "Too, I mean." Because now that I'm facing Brock, I need to speak with him, also. There's too much unsaid, too many things I don't understand.

"He's still snoring. Come in, I'll start some coffee. The scent'll lure him out eventually, and we can speak in the meantime." He's slipped into a more comfortable, familiar tone, even if it's resigned.

"Okay." I hesitate a second longer and then step through the doorway, past him, and take the short trip to the living area.

"Have a seat. Let me get the pot started."

I take a seat in an old armchair, taking in the apartment while he bangs around in the kitchen. It's small, sparse. But also somehow homey, and clean. The air smells faintly of a lemon-based cleaner, like maybe the apartment's been scrubbed recently. For a moment, I panic because maybe they're getting ready to move again.

But I do my best to quell it, because maybe it'd be better if I didn't have to share the town with Sawyer.

Yeah.

Right.

God. Why won't my insides stop sliding like melted ice? Why won't my heart stop hurting so damn much?

When Brock comes back, handing me a tall cup of coffee, I've almost gnawed my lower lip off. I think he thinks it's about him, because he takes a deep breath, forcing it out of his mouth and sitting on the couch opposite me. His words come out shaky. "I'm sorry, girlie. For what I did. I won't blame you for hating me."

"I..." I think about how to say this. "I only just found out and I would never, ever hate you." I want to stop here, just leave it at that. I study my hands for a moment, trying to keep the rest of it inside. But I look up, meeting his eyes before I speak again, because of course, I am going to speak again. "I don't understand, Brock... Why did you do it?"

He takes a deep breath and, with an unsteady hand, places his coffee on the small table in front of him. "On the rare occasions he chooses to use it, Sawyer's blessed with a mathematical intelligence not many come by."

I...don't make the connection immediately, so of course my imagination runs wild. This is because of Sawyer? Brock took the money for Sawyer, and it has something to do with math? Maybe Sawyer's scholarship to Duke was a lie somehow, and Brock needed the money to pay for his education. But does that mean Brock forged the scholarship letter? Does that mean—

I pause mid-thought when I realize Brock is staring at me, waiting for a response. So I nod, hoping he'll go on.

"His mother was an English teacher. And while she could manage our financials down to an exact penny, that's about as far as her abilities went in the math department." He pauses again, as though I should be interjecting here. But I'm at a loss. I still can't make the connection. Eventually, he continues. "What I'm saying is that Sawyer got his math abilities from me. Not that I've ever been good for much else in the brains department, but I'm good with numbers."

"Yeah, I know," I say, drawing the words out. "You used to help me with my homework."

"I'm good with numbers, and I'm good with cards, and I'm bad with money."

And in an instant, it all makes sense.

"Poker?" I ask. "You were gambling? Like...beyond the games you used to play with us... For real money?"

"I thought I'd found a shortcut to an easy cash flow. For a while, I really had." His eyes are twinkling a little more than they should be while he tells me these things. And maybe he realizes it because he drops his gaze and the next time he looks up, his expression is sober. "But you throw in a predisposition for some nasty drink habits, and things got out of control in ways I'd wake up the next day and not even remember. But I kept going back. I couldn't stop."

"But you didn't... I mean, I never—"

"Suspected any of this?" he asks. "You'd be surprised, girlie, how easy it is to keep things from people who aren't looking for them. Especially when I'd been able to keep up a good face for my sons their entire lives." He breaks off, looking distant for a moment. "Not as much anymore."

"So you took the money to gamble," I say, and for the first time I'm actually, truly stung with disappointment. It seems so...trivial. Like maybe it didn't matter to him that I was in his life, that he was hurting my family.

Then he says, "No. I took the money to pay back the debt I accrued, because the people I owed threatened to take it out on my sons."

I sit back, needing the chair to steady me. Because holy shit. "Jesus, Brock."

"I know." His face falls; he looks so ashamed. "I fucked up. Bad. But it didn't give me the right to break your parents' trust. To break your trust."

I don't know what to say. I can't process how I feel. Sick. Sad. Relieved all three of them are okay. Or, alive, anyway.

Then I look at Brock and he's grabbed his coffee and is chugging so quickly there's no way he's not wishing it was something harder. Suddenly, I know exactly what I feel.

Crushed for him.

And I know what to say. "It was four years ago, and it doesn't change a thing regarding how I feel about you."

He lowers the mug, slowly. "Girlie, I'm just so sorry." His voice breaks, and it almost kills me.

It's easy to forgive him when it's so clear he's never forgiven himself. "Thank you, Brock, for apologizing. But I don't care about any of it. I'm sorry you found yourself in such a horrible position. And I'm sorry my mom's *such* a bitch and forced you out of town."

I expect his face to relax, but he levels me with a stern gaze—one he used so sparingly back in the day, when I'd done something to make him mad. "I appreciate the sentiment, but I think you need to take a long hard look at the facts."

"I don't care about the facts. You're—"

"You say I *found* myself in that position? Quinn, I *put* myself there. I could be in jail right now, and the only reason I'm not is because your mother didn't press charges when she could have. I owe her. More than just money."

He doesn't get it, though. I lean forward, toward him. "The only reason she didn't press charges was to keep me and Sawyer apart. It wasn't out of any sort of benevolence, trust me."

"No. You trust me. She called me just yesterday to tell me she knew I was back in town, and we worked out a payment plan that's much more flexible than I deserve."

My jaw snaps open so wide it nearly lands in my lap. "What?"

"She's not my biggest fan, and she made it quite clear—not that I blame her. But I came back to town knowing full well she could press charges if she found out. But she isn't. So give your mama a little more credit."

"I'm not..." I trail off because I don't even know what I'm trying to say. "I'm not...sure I can. I'm having trouble wrapping my head around this."

"Wrap your head around *this*, then. What I did was wrong. These past four years have been hard, but still much more pleasant than I deserved. I don't care what your mom's motives were. I just care that I've not spent all this time where I rightly should have been—behind bars."

"But Jess..." More trailing off. I take a sip of coffee to cover up the fact that I'm starting to sound like an idiot. "Jess is such a..."

"Bonehead?" Brock finishes for me.

"No offense, but yeah." *At least that*, I almost say.

"Imagine what he'd be like if his daddy was in jail."

I can't believe that thought hasn't crossed my mind before now. "I don't want to imagine Jess that way. You either."

"You don't want to imagine me what way?"

I spin in the chair. Jess is behind me, looking tired. And pissed.

CHAPTER FIFTY

QUINN

"DAD," JESS SAYS. "Whatever she's saying, it's not—"

"Jess," I say. "I'm not saying anything you need to worry about."

He glances at me, suspicion—and more than a little fear—passing across his features. "Then what are you doing here?"

He's nervous I'll tell Brock about his drunken almost-drowning experience. But I told Sawyer, and Sawyer's already taking care of it. That's enough. I'm not here to get him in more trouble. "I'm here to speak with you."

"*Why?*" If attitudes could punch, his would be giving me a black eye.

I glance at Brock and then back at Jess. "Maybe we can go into your room?"

Then I cringe because it sounds weird, me asking a sixteen-year-old boy to hang out in his room.

But Brock says, "Go ahead. You want some coffee, Jess?" His tone is light, easy, as though the conversation we've just been having doesn't weigh at least a ton.

"No." Another scowl. This time directed at Brock instead of me, but Brock ignores it, just grabs a remote and turns on the news. "We'll talk more whenever you'd like, girlie," he says, winking at me. Like he has the same old faith in me he always did. Like he thinks I'll be able to get through to his funny little knucklehead son.

Like maybe he doesn't know Jess's issues go so much deeper than that.

I wonder if he has any idea how scared Jess used to be that he killed his own mother. How certain he probably still is that he did so. I study Jess a second longer, a second harder. He's tense, coiled, and so angry. At me. At life. Probably a combination. And suddenly I'm a little mad at Brock—for someone who has so much insight to his own mistakes, he doesn't seem to have much when it comes to Jess. And I'm a little mad at Sawyer, because he should've worked harder to make Jess feel...I don't know. Important, maybe.

And I'm a little mad at myself.

More than a little.

Jess was twelve and depending on me and I let him down.

Now he's sixteen and clomping back to his room, and I follow him, noting the stark difference between it and the rest of the apartment. Pigsty is too clean a word. There's trash everywhere and a faint rank odor. He drops onto his bed, which is rumpled and covered with halfway folded T-shirts, facing me with a stony and still-tired expression.

"Did you sleep under all of those?" The question just slips out.

"I know why you're here, so just get it over with."

"Um... Okay." The only other place to sit is a chair piled with crumpled fast-food wrappers and tissues that look...a little stiffer than maybe they would if they were filled with snot. He scoffs at whatever he sees in my expression. Then his eyes slide to his closet and the sneer falls from his face, his cheeks turning red.

Gross.

Gross, *gross*. I bet he's got dirty magazines in there.

Oh, gross. I do not want to think about Jess and dirty magazines and dirty tissues and just... Ew.

I also don't want to touch anything that would require

clearing the chair. So I stand and lean against his closed door. "Jess—"

"It wasn't my idea. Just so you know." His sneer's back.

"What?" Was I ever this confusing as a teenager? Probably. Actually, definitely. Especially after Sawyer left. I probably didn't make sense for at least half a year. "What wasn't your idea?"

He blinks. Looks away. Looks back. "To move here again."

"I'm not upset you're back, Jess. I'm happy to see you."

"That's bullshit."

"It's not. But I know why you must think that. I—"

"You wouldn't even look at me that day on the beach."

Now I blink, processing. "The day you almost drowned…? I didn't have any clue you were there until you were in the ocean—and your back was to me there. I would've said something. I would've hugged you. I would've—"

"You didn't know I was there? Some lifeguard you are."

He…has a point. I should've known he was there, on the beach, before he got in the water. "You're right."

"I *know*." So much attitude. So much teenager.

So much hurting. On both our parts. "Well, I'm looking at you now."

"Maybe. But you don't *see* me. You don't know anything about me."

"I used to." I cross the room, sitting at the opposite edge of his bed. "And I'm so sorry I let you down."

He shoots off his bed, stomping to where I was standing a moment ago. "You don't even remember what—"

"What I did to let you down?" I stay seated, not pressing any sort of closeness. "Yes, I do. I never forgot about my promise. And I'm the biggest asshole in the world for not keeping it."

His brows raise when I cuss, and for some reason the innocent surprise throws me back four years into the past.

Jess. Twelve years old. Crying.

A boy he'd gone to school with had taunted him on the beach, telling Jess he'd killed his mother by being born, and Jess was wrecked over it.

He wouldn't tell Sawyer what was wrong, but he told me. And I promised to take care of him. I promised him that he'd be okay because his mom loved him all the way from Heaven—and that he hadn't killed her, but that she'd stayed alive long enough to let him live, a gift she was happy to give him—and until he saw her again, a long, long time from then, *I'd* take care of him.

A week later, Brock took the family and left town.

And I was so devastated by the loss of Sawyer, so brokenhearted, it was ages before I even thought about the promise I was forced to break to Jess. At the back of my mind, I realize there might not have been anything I could do to keep the promise—but to a twelve-year-old boy? That wouldn't matter. To this sixteen-year-old? I don't think it does, either.

Now he won't look at me when I tell him what I never forgot. "Will you let me be here for you now?"

"You're only saying that because you want to screw Sawyer."

"I...don't know how to address that, but you're wrong. Even if you don't change your mind about whether or not Sawyer and I can see each other." *God, please change your mind about that, kid.* "I love *you* outside of the way I love him, okay?"

"Whatever. I don't even need you anymore anyway." But he looks at me now and instead of anger across his face, there's determination. Desperation, even.

"Maybe I need *you*," I say, keeping my tone light. "I don't have a brother of my own, but I always considered you the closest thing to it. I've missed you for four years."

"I haven't missed you at all." His eyes flash and that determination sinks right back into animosity. "Get out of my room."

I open my mouth, but eat my words when I notice his lips are trembling. He's in pain. Because of me. Still. And my being here is making it worse.

So, mechanically, I do let myself out of his room. I mumble another apology and walk out of the door he's thrown open. Behind me, the sound of something hitting the wall, shattering, fills the air.

I don't see Brock. Maybe it's for the best.
I let myself out.
I go to work.
Jess hates me. Brock...made some good points about my mother that I really don't want to consider. Sawyer's out of my life, and I probably just pounded the final nail in with my attempt to speak with Jess.

And as bright as the sun is, as scorching as its light is, all I feel is darkness.

I survive the next week. I even get used to the stupid hatchback my insurance company rents me. I even go out with Gianna and Chase for a few drinks one night.

I'm still standing.

Yeah, and okay, I'm counting down the days until I head back to school, but whatever.

And I'm seriously considering never coming back to the stupid Outer Banks, but whatever.

I'm standing. I'm working. I'm surfing. (On my new surfboard that's just not the same as my old one, but whatever.) I'm avoiding any place I might run into Sawyer. Which is annoying because this is my town, too—but it's also necessary because my heart isn't strong enough to see him again.

Then Officer Santiago calls to tell me my Jeep's been found, abandoned in a handicap spot in the Kitty Hawk Walmart parking lot.

And finally, finally, a sliver of sunlight breaks through the darkness of my monotonous emotions.

Bitch has been keyed into the side of my poor car, but I don't care. I have it back and I'll paint over it. Or not. Maybe I'll just consider it an extra bit of character to the side of the car that barely opens without force anyway.

I don't have to drive something rented that smells like cigarettes anymore. My Jeep smells like sunscreen and pineapples and, okay, a little bit like weed—which, yet again, makes me think Danny's the one who took it for a weeklong joyride. That, plus the *bitch* thing. But *God* I love driving it again.

I know it's just a car. But it's mine. And I needed a win.

So I work my shift later and I reschedule my appointment to install an alarm and I smile at least some of the time. Because things are getting better. Not great. My heart's still in pieces. I'm still creeped out that someone's messing with me... But at least my Jeep is back.

Then a week later, Officer Santiago calls to let me know they caught the guys who stole it.

"*Guys*, plural?" I ask.

"Yep. You want to come down to the station?"

"Yeah, I do. I *really* do." Before I hang up, I have to ask, "Is one of them named Danny?"

Oddly enough, the answer is no.

Then I get there and after the woman at the front desk waves me into the booking area, the first person I see is Sawyer.

CHAPTER FIFTY-ONE

QUINN

SAWYER'S NOT IN cuffs, but Jess is. His eyes are swollen from crying and he's trying—and failing—to wipe his nose with the shoulder of his shirt. Officer Vincent's next to them, his expression so leeringly pleased it's clown-like.

I look at Sawyer again, trying to ignore the jolt of longing that strikes my belly, cutting through my confusion. "I don't get it."

I can't believe we're both back in this blue-carpeted, dingy room.

I can't believe Jess is in handcuffs.

I can't believe how...not shocked I am. Not that I expected it to be Jess—especially because he was with me when my surfboard was stolen. But because...I don't know. I feel a little like I'm dreaming.

Sawyer doesn't quite meet my eyes, but jerks his chin toward the wall and when I follow the motion, I see the red-headed kid I've encountered a few times at the beach, Mason. He's not crying like Jess, but he's in cuffs and standing next to a woman who's clearly his mother. Same red hair. Same stocky build. She's not crying, either, but she's staring at me, worry digging a divot between her eyebrows.

Then I notice he's wearing a polo shirt with "Pop-Your-Lock" stitched into the chest and things start to click into place. No pun intended.

"That's how you broke in," I say. "You work for a locksmith. And you took..." I almost say *my surfboard*, but I glance at Jess and change my mind at the last second.

"He only works the front desk," his mom says, her tone pleading. "Mason's a good boy."

A good boy who broke into my car. Several times. I feel like I should be angry. Or, again, at least shocked.

All I am is longing for Sawyer to *look* at me. But he's studying the shabby desks, the two police officers in a back corner sharing some joke, the wall clock tick tick ticking through the air...

"Where's your dad?" I ask.

"On his way." He finally meets my eyes, but only briefly.

"These idiots didn't bother checking whether or not the Walmart parking lot had surveillance cameras. Spoiler alert: *it does*." Officer Vincent nudges Jess with his elbow more roughly than necessary. Sawyer stiffens, clenching his jaw. Still not meeting my eyes. But I don't need his gaze on me to understand how bad he wants to hit the officer beside him.

If desires were reality, though, he'd have to step in line. Because Jess is cringing in pain and I already freaking hate Officer Vincent. A lot.

"Quinn." Officer Santiago comes through a side door, greeting me with a smile.

I'd smile back...

But my mom's with him.

"It's just so shocking that a *Carson* boy would pull something like this," she says, looking straight at Sawyer.

His hands go to fists at his sides and he shakes his head. And if we're forming lines to hit people, maybe my mom can stand in front of Officer Vincent.

"Why are you here?" I ask her, shooting daggers the best I can with my eyes.

"My name's still on the car's registration," she says.

"Dad told me that was all taken care of years ago." God. Why did I ever let them give me that stupid car? Okay, I love my car, but still. I should've paid them for it as soon as I had access to my inheritance. Or, even better, I should've been saving up to pay them back for it with my own earned money. I hate feeling obligated to them in any way.

I hate how ungrateful my thoughts sound.

She waves a hand to wipe my words away. "Apparently we have to let the DMV know, officially. Just as well I'm here, though."

"*Why?*"

If she says anything about turning Brock in I really will hit her.

"You didn't bother to tell me about your car troubles, sweetie. But now that I know, I can hold your hand through the whole process." Why is she speaking to me like we're old chums?

"What whole process?"

"Pressing charges," she says. Oh my God, of course that's what she's here to do. Reap the punishment of the father onto the son. I can't believe I let her little games—letting Brock pay her back, giving me her blessing about Sawyer—trick me into thinking she was a better person than she is.

"Pressing charges?" Mason's mom sucks in her breath, and the rest of the room comes back into focus.

I look from Jess to Sawyer and back to Jess. Jess's eyes are closed and Sawyer's studying my mom. "No," I tell them all. "I'm not pressing charges."

My mom looks at me, her gaze shrewd.

But she doesn't say anything.

"Quinn," Officer Santiago starts. "That's generally how this whole thing works."

"I forgot..." I clear my throat. "I forgot I told Jess he could borrow my car."

"Oh, come on." Officer Vincent rolls his eyes, grabbing Jess's arm and jerking him back toward him. "That's bullshit and you know it."

Sawyer finally looks at me and when we catch eyes, he holds my gaze and it's like the rest of the world falls away. I want to say something to him, or I want him to say something to me, but I don't know what. I just know I never want to look away. But, of course, I have to. Especially when I feel the pressure in the air telling me Officer Santiago's waiting for my attention.

When I give it to him, he asks, "You sure?"

There's no hesitation in my answer. "Yes."

My mom...still doesn't open her mouth. She's not fighting me on this.

"You know we can get you for falsifying a report," Officer Vincent says. "It's you or these morons. Don't be as dumb as they are."

But Officer Santiago's already walking to uncuff Mason. And then Jess, who rubs his wrists and glares at Officer Vincent. Until the officer snaps his teeth at him. Then Jess shrinks back against Sawyer.

"Thank you," Mason's mom says. She steps toward me, her arms out, but thinks better of it. She pulls her son out of the station. We can hear her yelling as soon as they're through the doors into the lobby. I mean, really screaming. I'd feel bad for him, but, you know, he stole my car.

And speaking of car thieves. I step toward Jess. "Are you okay?"

He opens his mouth, but Sawyer speaks first.

"You won't ever have to deal with my family again," he says. "We'll be out of town before the summer's out."

"Sawyer." My heart shatters. "Didn't you hear me? I don't want to press charges. I don't care about my car. Jess is a kid. He made a mistake, who cares?"

"I care." He shakes his head. "My family can't keep doing this to yours."

He glances at my mom—and then he walks out of the station without giving me a chance to say anything else, dragging Jess by the scruff of his neck.

Jess wriggles out of Sawyer's grasp for a split second to turn and look at me. "I didn't write bitch. I swear."

The door closes behind them before I can reiterate that *I don't care.*

Officer Santiago offers me a kind pat on the shoulder—and Officer Vincent laughs. Snidely. I scratch my chin with my middle finger. He rolls his eyes.

Then they're walking away, too, and I'm sinking into a chair by the wall. God. This shouldn't skewer me the way it does. It's not like I thought I'd have Sawyer back. I've been working my ass off to get rid of that dream.

But seeing him again.

Seeing him again and watching him leave. Again.

It's excruciating.

My mom comes to stand beside me and lays a hand on my shoulder. "It's better this way."

"Anything you think is better is generally the worst." But I let her hold my shoulder, because I haven't forgotten what Brock said. Especially now, when she didn't push me to press charges when I didn't want to. "Why did you decide it was okay for me to be with Sawyer—*not* that I need your permission—and why did you call Brock to work it out?" I glance up at her, and her expression is haughty. Stuffy. I don't know why I expected to see a little remorse, or tenderness.

"Because," she says, sniffing. Also haughtily. "I do love you, you know. And I realized..." She pauses, her mouth puckering like her next words taste unpleasant. "You were going to do it anyway, so I might as well give my blessing. Those threats you made—which we will *never* mention again... Well, I'm fairly certain they gave me an ulcer." Her fingers tighten on my shoulder, as though she's using me to steady herself against the memory.

I feel like maybe I should tell her I'm sorry. Maybe I shouldn't have been quite so nasty about it all. But when I open my mouth, the words won't come. I can't apologize because she still hasn't. And right now all I can see is the disdainful purse to her lips; right now all I can remember is that her decision in the past is a huge part of why Sawyer and I can't be together now.

And, at the base of it all, all I can think about is the way she lied straight to my face. It hurts, a raw sort of pain. I'm not how long it'll take to get over it.

So I need more time before I can apologize to her. Because to make the words sincere at all, I have a feeling I have to forgive her first. And that is going be a process—one that might be more than I have to give, because I know she won't make it easy.

But we'll see.

Then she says, "Obviously, you aren't associating with him anymore. And, truly, sweetie, it's better this way. Erika Covington told me about the scene those boys caused at the pancake house. I told you about trash in families. It sticks."

I stand, shoving her hand away from me. "Don't say another word. If you ever want to have any kind of relationship with me—which even now is going to take a long time to form—I'm begging you. Just stop."

Before she can say anything else, I walk away. Out of the station, to my Jeep, and I blast Gold Rush Standard all the way home.

I call out from work and I turn my AC down to frigid, and I change into ratty old sweats and a way too big for me T-shirt. I sit on my couch with a half-empty pint of ice cream, a salad server spoon, and a beer. And I dig in until the ice cream headache is strong enough to reprieve my heartache for a minute.

Then I repeat.

Repeat.

Repeat.

CHAPTER FIFTY-TWO

SAWYER

HALFWAY BACK TO my father's place, I almost turn the car around and go back for Quinn.

I can't believe I left her. Again.

Because of my family. Again.

Other than to tell him to call our father and let him know to come home instead of to the station, I can't bring myself to say a word to Jess. I'm so fucking mad I'm pretty sure I'll say something I'll regret.

My dad beats us there, and I shove Jess through the front door, growling, "Tell him."

The damn kid breaks down crying again. I don't know what the hell to do with his tears; I'm too used to his shitty little attitude. I pat his back a few times, and push him further into the room until he drops into the armchair across from our dad. He's still crying, but he's not getting off the hook. I stay standing, crossing my arms. "Now."

He takes a shaky breath and stares at me instead of my dad. "I stole Quinn's car."

"*That's* why they took you to the station?" My dad's on his feet now, looking between the two of us.

"My friend—this other guy, stole it, I mean. I was just there for a ride." He picks at a few of the threads sticking up from an arm of the chair.

"Goddamn it, Jess. You know what? I'm done," I say, speaking before the thought's finished crossing my mind. But it's the truth. Between my dad looking so shocked that Jess could've done something like this, when it's not even the first time he's been called by the cops because of my brother, and Jess trying to pass the blame off on his stupid friend, I'm really fucking finished. "I can't keep putting you both first if you won't do it for yourselves."

"What are you talking about?" my dad asks, still looking confused.

"Quinn," Jess says, bitterly, rubbing his eyes. "He's talking about Quinn."

I move to him, leaning down to grab the chair's arms, and put my face an inch from his. "Listen, kid, I'm still going to be on you to get your shit together, and if this incident—*that you fucking lucked out on*—didn't scare some sense into you, just wait until you see what I have in store." I stare at him until he swallows, making sure my point sinks in. "But I'm not staying away from her anymore."

He takes a shaky breath. "I don't even care, okay? She came over and tried to talk to me, but I already took her car so it was too late and I couldn't tell her it was okay. But I don't even care."

"She came over?" I straighten, dragging my eyes from my brother to my father, who's very pointedly not looking my way. "When?"

"Couple weeks ago." Jess shrugs, trying to appear nonchalant, but his face is tense and his eyes are still red. "Tell her I'm sorry, okay? Tell her I'm really, really sorry."

"Why didn't you tell me?"

Neither of them has an answer.

"Wait." Jess jumps up as I'm about to leave and dashes to his room. I hear the squeaking slide and the thud of his closet door forced open, and a second later he returns with a surfboard. "Give this to Quinn."

I take it and the moment my fingers wrap around the board, the meaning of what he's giving me sinks in. "You stole her surfboard?"

"It's not as bad as her car." He drops his gaze to his feet, ashamed. "We were just...messing with her. I'll get her wakeboard back, too."

"You stole all those things? Not just her car, but before that. Her spare tire?" I wait for him to look up, but he doesn't. And everything sinks in even further. "Jesus Christ, Jess. That's why you were such a little shit about me being with her, isn't it? You were ashamed. You didn't want to get caught stealing her stuff?"

He lifts a shoulder, lets it drop.

"You made her feel like shit. You broke her heart, kid, and you made me do the same damn thing. You made me walk away from her. You—" I cut myself off because I'm afraid of what will come through my mouth, and the kid has enough to deal with as it is.

So I leave. Before the door closes behind me, though, I hear my dad tell Jess that he's grounded. That it's time they had a come to Jesus discussion about reality. And I hear the start of my brother beginning to sob.

It helps to dull the sharp edge of fury running through me as I drive to Quinn's, knowing that maybe he's finally, finally breaking down. It's been a long time needed. By the time I get to her apartment, I've calmed considerably. Where my brother's concerned, anyway.

I raise my fist to knock, but Quinn opens the door before I have a chance. Her eyes are red and she's clutching an ice cream container. The air blasting from her place is frosty.

"Sawyer?" She tugs at her oversized T-shirt. It's so big on her it falls from one shoulder, and my mouth goes dry. Which it has no right to do, considering how much begging she deserves from me before I even come close to noticing that soft, lickable shoulder.

"Quinn." Shit. What do I say? How do I make up for all I've put her through, including everything today?

How do I keep myself together when all I can think about is sliding those hole-riddled sweatpants down her hips?

How do I find the words to explain to her that I love her so goddamn much, all I want to do for the rest of my life is breathe in the same air she does.

"I...was just going out for more ice cream," she says, blinking. And then, "That's my surfboard."

"Jess had it."

"Oh. Yeah. I figured." Her shoulders droop. "That's why you're here, then. To give it back. Thanks."

I lean the board carefully against the wall outside her door. Then, praying she'll forgive me for acting before explaining, I take her face in my hands. Her chin feels so delicate against my palms. I run a thumb over her cheek, and I watch her eyes widen, her pupils swell. I hear her intake of breath and I take one of my own, inhaling her salty, ocean-water scent.

I kiss her.

CHAPTER FIFTY-THREE

QUINN

SAWYER IS KISSING me. Softly. Skimming his lips over mine, dipping his tongue gently through my mouth. There's a delirious happiness struggling to force its way through my veins.

But I can't let it in.

Because I don't know why he's here. I mean, I do. To give me my surfboard.

But why is he kissing me?

I should stop. I should ask. I should...do something.

What I end up doing is dancing my tongue with his and pressing my mouth harder against him.

Because Sawyer.

Sawyer.

His name is a breeze through my mind, silky and sweet, and I don't care why he's kissing me, just that he is.

I drop the empty ice cream tub, and it splatters cold leftover chocolate on my feet.

He nudges me backward and, without breaking the kiss, we walk into my apartment. He reaches behind him to shut the door, and when it closes with a click it's like a gunshot jerking me away from him, backing me up until I hit the arm of my couch. "What are you doing?"

"I'm done," he says, stepping toward me. "I'm done walking away from you."

A teeny, tiny bit of that crazy happiness slips into my bloodstream, making my breath come a little faster.

But still, I'm skittish. Nervous. Because my heart can't take this if it's not real. Not that Sawyer's lying, but things happen. Things that take him from me that are out of his control. And I can't do it again. "What about Jess?"

"What about *you*?" he says. "Why can't I just think about you?"

"Because it's not who you are. Because half your soul belongs to your family—as it should."

"My entire soul belongs to you, actually." He takes another step, his eyes bright and steady on mine. "If you'll have it, I mean. After all the shit I've put you through."

It's like my brain's on a spin cycle and I can't make sense of anything enough to hold onto. But when I try to slow it down, it just freezes completely. So I still can't make sense of anything. "But Jess… And you're leaving town…and—"

"Jess is a bonehead. Jess stole your damn car. Jess is probably in the middle of a complete breakdown with my dad right now, which I actually think is a good thing. But Jess doesn't get to dictate my life anymore." Another step. "And I'm not going anywhere. Unless it's with you."

I look at his mouth on accident. And his tongue slides through his lips to wet them. And I gnaw on my own lower lip because it's starting to throb to connect with his. I meet his gaze again. "What about the Bahamas?"

"You'll come with me."

"I'll be in school in October."

He shrugs, unconcerned. "We'll go over Christmas. Through the New Year. Or we won't go at all. I don't care what I'm doing or where I'm going unless, like I said, it's with you."

Spending Christmas with Sawyer.

Suddenly, there's a lump in my throat.

I'm imagining a future with him. One that includes holidays. For the first time in four years.

It's too much.

My heart thumps against my rib cage so frantically it almost hurts. "Are you serious, Sawyer? Like, for real serious? Because... I'm not doing this if you're not all in—no matter what else life throws at you, at either of us."

"Honey." Another step and now he's close enough that I could reach out and touch his chest. My fingers start to itch to do exactly that. "I'm all in."

Another, more substantial dose of happiness slides through me. I try to smile, to show him, but the problem with being this close to Sawyer, close enough to breathe in that never-forgotten musky sage scent, is that lust comes rushing right behind the happiness, combining to overpower it until I can't tell one from the other and all I'm left with is a beautiful sort of longing. The need to feel his hands on my skin.

"Do you trust me?" he asks, sober.

I nod.

"Will you let me touch you?"

I swallow.

And I nod. "If you don't do it soon, Sawyer, I might beg."

He cups my face and I breathe very, very deeply. He watches me, his eyes focused on mine.

He shapes his hands down my neck, running them over my shoulders and then back to the center of my collarbone.

All the oxygen's replaced with a sweet, tangy tension and I can't find my breath. Can't look away. Can't stop swallowing.

The warmth of his palms seeps through my shirt and into my skin. And when he slowly, slowly drags them down over my breasts, using his thumbs to circle my nipples, the breath I was missing only a moment ago comes flying out in waves. Rough, rough, jagged and choppy waves.

Then his hands are under my shirt and against my skin and my belly's jumping under his touch. The hopping in my blood slides lower, lower when he hooks his thumbs through the waistband of my sweats and slides them over my thighs until they're puddled on the floor around my feet.

"Is this real?" I ask. "I have you now? For real?"

"For as long as you'll have me," he says. And then he kisses me again and my soul begins to sing.

Softly, sweetly, beautifully.

He grabs my hips and lifts me so I'm sitting on the arm of the couch. I wrap my legs around him, pulling him closer until his erection, so rigid through his pants, is pressing against me in the most delicious way, and I drag his shirt over his head.

"I love your chest," I say, sliding my fingers across it. Dipping my head to trail kisses across the same path.

"I love you," he says simply, his voice husky. "So much it might be all I need to live anymore. Fuck food. Fuck water. You're all I've ever wanted. All I'll ever need."

"I love you, Sawyer." God, it thrills me to say it. To watch the smile quirk across his mouth, the gladness in his eyes. "And if you're in this for as long as I'll have you, you can count on forever."

"Good," he says. "Add a couple days to that. A week, a year, a decade."

The pleasure running through me at his words is enough to keep me smiling for...well, forever.

Plus some.

"But..." I run one hand up his neck to hold his face, and the other down his chest and stomach, tracing the ridges of his stomach muscles and pushing under the waist of his pants to wrap my fingers around him, squeezing lightly until he moans. "If you're going to be fucking all those things... Maybe you should start with me."

He has my shirt peeled off and my panties flung across the room before I can blink. And then he's on his knees in front of me and he's sliding my feet over his shoulders and telling me to hold on.

So I do. One hand on the couch and the other weaving through his hair. At first, he doesn't move an inch, just watches my face. Then he slides his hands up my inner thighs, pushing them farther apart and tracing lines along the creases with his thumbs.

And he blows air over me, softly, coolly, until my back begins to arch.

I want him so bad, need to feel him inside me so much, I nearly beg him just to stand and skip this part and *for God's sake, freaking have me already*. But before I can, he leans in and he licks me.

In one slow, slow motion.

Leading with his nose and following with his tongue.

Slowly.

Slowly.

Oh, Jesus.

Parting me.

Curling through me, around me.

Still.

So.

Slowly.

Up to my most sensitive spots.

Folding around me.

Sucking.

Gently biting.

And then he does it again. Dipping his tongue into me, deeper this time. More thoroughly.

And again. And again.

Until my toes are curling hard behind his back and I can't keep from pressing myself more strongly against his mouth.

Until I'm pulling so hard through his hair that he slides his teeth across me, tugging at me, and he growls against me.

That guttural vibration of his voice, thrumming across me, through me... It does me in.

Lightly, at first, my belly flutters and then explodes into fireworks of thrills; they throb and burn through me, sizzling lower, lower, lower, until I'm pulsing around his tongue and he's using his fingers to intensify every. Single. Feeling. Pressing against me. Rolling me side to side. I have to release his hair to push his hands away, because in a moment it's too much for me to bear. Who knew tingling could feel so...deliciously violent?

I'm breathing like I've never had oxygen and when the sensations finally begin to wane, he trails his tongue up my stomach, over one nipple and across to the other, up my neck, over my chin, and finally, finally to my mouth.

When he stands, his pants stay on the floor and he pulls me to him, lifting me from the couch, his erection pressing flat between my legs. I slide my hips so slightly back and forth, back and forth. His own hips jerk, involuntarily by his sharp inhale, and then he very, very purposefully tips into me in one piercing thrust.

I say his name.

I think I do.

I think I say it.

But I don't know because his mouth's still on mine, his tongue's still twisting through my lips and I'm still quivering all over, inside my skin and out.

And in one fluid motion I'm on my back on the couch and he's driving into me and one of us moans or maybe both of us and I've never, ever felt so complete.

I grip the sleek, tight skin of his back and I tug with my fingernails, lightly—but the harder he slams into me, the deeper I dig.

He slows the rhythm, but I know what he's doing and I wrap my legs more tightly around him, pulling him deeper into me, rocking my hips faster and faster.

"Fuck," he hisses into my ear. "I'm not... I can't hold it much longer."

And I smile because he's still so new to this and I love the way I make him lose control.

So I whisper naughty little things to him, words like "fuck me harder, Sawyer," and "can't wait to feel you come," until he's bucking his hips so furiously against me I feel my skin flush from the pounding and soon he's rubbing me raw.

He comes before I do this time, but when his own trembling subsides a bit, he slides a hand between us and uses his fingers again to drive me to the edge of an orgasm, capturing my mouth with his when I tip over, swallowing my long, breathy moan.

Later, he slides out of me, rolling to the side, and pulling me with him against the back of the couch. "Next time," he says, his heart hammering under my hands, placed against his chest. "Next time, I'll have better control."

"We'll see about that," I say, a grin in my voice.

"Oh, that's how you want to play it?" he asks, nuzzling my neck. "Because we both know you like a challenge, but honey, this is one I'm going to win."

"You sure?" I reach down between us, finding him still halfway hard and pressing against my thigh. I run my fingers lightly over him until his abs tighten and he lets out a short, forced laugh.

"I'm very, very sure." He unwraps his arm from around my back and slides his hand over my arm, along my skin until he reaches my breasts, dragging his palm across them and tugging at my nipples until they're tightening into his fingers.

And I'm turned on all over again, but I release my grip around him and push myself out of his grasp, laughing, because I need a freaking break or my body's going to rebel.

I slide off the couch, standing and turning to face him. "Want some water?"

He rolls onto his back, his eyes trailing my body and his erection forming completely. He shakes his head. "Christ, Quinn. If we have forever, I'm pretty sure we'll be spending at least half of it naked, because I need all the time in the world to make up for what we missed the past four years."

"Only half?" I ask, a pout playing across my mouth, making him laugh. "Well, I need about half an hour, Sawy, because you pretty much just slayed me and I'm not sure I could handle you touching me again right now."

He sits up to watch me walk around to the kitchen. "I have something for you."

"Yeah?"

When he stands and drags his pants on and heads toward my door, I try to suppress the sudden panic at the base of my belly. I still can't help but ask, "You're leaving?"

I try to keep my tone light, calm. He pauses. "I don't even have my shirt on—promise, I'll be back before you can count to ten."

Still, my heart tightens when my apartment door closes behind him. Because it's getting too used to this, I think. Him leaving.

But he's back a minute later, holding something behind him, and when he sees the tension across my face he crosses to me, where I've draped myself in a blanket on the couch, dropping to his knees before me. "I swear to you, Quinn. I won't ever walk away from you again."

I close my eyes, breathing deeply, letting the truth I hear in his words wash over me.

Then I say, "But what about when you have to go to the bathroom?"

He smiles. "I won't ever leave you with any sort of permanence, I mean."

"But what if you have to take a really big—"

"Here." He interrupts me, laughing. And he pulls his free hand from behind his back and hands me a frame. Silver, this time, and circular.

I stare at it for a long, hard second before I take it, and I blink back sudden tears. "It *was* you leaving these for me."

He nods.

"Why didn't you tell me?"

"Because I didn't want you to smash them into pieces if you knew they were from me. Because if you kept them, something of me would always be with you even if I couldn't."

"Sawyer, I'd never smash something you made. No matter where you were." I lean down to kiss him, lightly. "Even before I understood why you disappeared, I never got rid of anything that was ever yours."

"Are you saying you still have my garage sale Guns 'n Roses T-shirt circa the mid-90s?" The hope in his eyes is adorable.

I nod. "I slept in it occasionally over the years, when I missed you the most. You want it back?"

He thinks about it, and for a moment I think he's going to say yes and I'm going to have to take back my offer, because no way am I actually going to return it to him. Then he shakes his head. "Makes me hot thinking about you wearing it. Probably barely covers your ass anymore, does it?"

I lift a brow. "Wanna see?"

"Hell yeah."

I find it and put it on, and...he has it off of me in less than a minute. And I end up not getting the half hour break I thought I needed, because I really, really didn't need it after all. We spend the rest of the day and night in nothing but our skin.

Places We Spend Our Time in Nothing But Our Skin

1. Under my covers
2. Over my covers
3. Against the wall
4. Back to my couch

* * * * * *

Looking at that list, it might seem like I'd be the most sore in one very particular area the next morning. But the place I actually ache the most?

My cheekbones.

From all the grinning.

CHAPTER FIFTY-FOUR

QUINN

WE HIT THE circuit a few days later, when the bonfire's in Kitty Hawk for the night.

When we've managed to leave his place.

After multiple rounds of...making up for lost time.

We kick off our flip-flops and he grabs my hand, smiling down at me as we walk through the sand toward the party.

Gianna finds us, first, pulling Chase along and handing us two cups of beer.

"Perfect timing," she says. "Fresh beers all around."

We take them. We drink. We stand around the fire, mingling with people until the heat's too much to take in the already muggy July night air.

"Let's go down by the water," Sawyer says. "It'll be cooler."

He's right. There's a breeze flowing by the water's edge. I enjoy it, watching the moon's reflection as it bobs and weaves over the dark waves; it's a little mesmerizing.

"Did you guys know Sawyer *owns* half of the Surf Spot?" I ask, splashing my toes through the lazy layer of foam rolling at my feet, unable to keep pride from my voice. Not even trying, really.

"That's awesome, man," Chase says.

"Gonna sell it to Rajesh, someday." Sawyer lifts a shoulder, lets it drop. He told me Rajesh is discovering how much he enjoys working the shop and surfing and wants a break from anything engineering-related. Sawyer, though, doesn't want a break at all.

He's got big plans. He's tried to explain them to me, about designing new solar power source renewal systems with plant leaves, which you'd think I'd better understand, given my love of flowers—but the part I've been able to grasp the best so far is the part where he told me he can work on them from almost anywhere. He wants to go back to school eventually, but we'll decide that location together when that day comes—and until then, he'll go wherever I want to when I graduate, even if it's not here at the beach. He says he'll find work wherever I decide to build my arts center, and thinking about it makes my heart swell so much it might break a rib.

I grab his hand, squeezing. He squeezes right back.

"I guess if I'm going to be part of this group, I'll need to learn how to surf," Chase says.

"How did you grow up here without learning?" I ask. "How did I not know that?"

"*Told* you you need to learn," Gianna says to him. "Plus, I'll teach you, baby."

And I start to laugh because, "Chase, you'll have better luck learning from sharks."

"Hey." Gianna mock-glares at me, but I shake my head.

"Please. You have zero patience for people who don't pick up on things immediately." I watch her, smugly, over the rim of my cup as I drink. "Remember teaching me how to play beer pong? You dumped an entire cup of beer on me because I couldn't make a single shot. On my first time playing." I act like I'm going to toss mine on her in a long-due retaliation, and she ducks away from me.

"Um, we were sixteen. I'm not that same girl." Then, when I laugh even harder, she laughs, too. "Fine. I am."

"You're not a very nice learner, either," Sawyer says. "Remember when I tried to teach you to drive stick?"

"No." But clearly she does because she's fighting another laugh.

"I almost lost an eye when you jabbed me with the keys." He looks like he's going to say more, a huge grin across his mouth, but instead he waves over her shoulder, calling for Rajesh to join us.

Rajesh walks over holding hands with a shirtless guy whose abs actually come close to rivaling Sawyer's. He notices me noticing, cocking an eyebrow and holding out his free hand. "I'm Shane."

I drop Sawyer's hand to take Shane's and shake it. "Shane and Rajesh... Your names flow really nicely together."

He grins, but Rajesh shoots me a look that tells me maybe I should shut the hell up. Whoops. But I don't feel too bad because Rajesh is holding his hand, and from what Sawyer's told me, that's the equivalent of a regular commitment-phobe actually to proposing to their boyfriend. Rajesh is that antsy about relationships. Which doesn't make sense to me, considering how much he wanted me and Sawyer to work out.

"By the way," he says to Chase, his tone dry, cutting through my thoughts. "You weren't fooling anyone that day in the shop."

"Shit." Chase shakes his head. "Sorry, man."

Rajesh shrugs and opens his mouth to say something, but the sound of glass breaking and a shriek behind us has us all turning toward the fire.

Where Morgan is laughing and the fire's sparking way higher than it was a moment ago and Danny's picking her up, spinning her around and kissing her.

That idiot's still with Danny. Poor girl.

And maybe he hears my thoughts because he opens his eyes and looks over her shoulder at me, raising a fist in the air to flip me off.

Some things never change.

Even if, at the same time, they are forever changed. Because I know he's had it at least a little rough. His mom's had it a lot rough. So he's a dick, but...that animosity I usually have toward him has disappeared.

Maybe that's the key. Maybe if we just took the time to understand each other's lives, the messier parts wouldn't seem quite as messy. Because we're all a little fucked up.

Danny's still holding his finger out, glaring at me. So I glare at him and flip him off right back.

Yeah. Some things never change.

Sawyer grabs my hand from the air, pulling it down, twining his fingers through mine, and I don't care even a little bit about Danny Simmons anymore.

"That guy's the worst," Chase says.

"Let's not even waste any time on that little bit of truth," Gianna says, bumping him with her shoulder and looking at me. "Back to your place? Group slumber party?"

"I call the couch," Chase says, sliding his eyes slyly to Gianna with a grin he thinks is sneaky.

"That thing's seeing a lot of action these days," I say, laughing when his cheeks turn red enough to be seen even in the dark of night. "But yeah. My fridge is even stocked with beer."

"*We* are going to get food first," Shane says. "Rajesh promised to feed me at some point tonight."

Rajesh sighs. "Fine. But it's gonna be fast-food drive-through or nothing at all, because I'm not taking you anywhere that requires you to wear a shirt."

I laugh, and not caring if it pisses off Rajesh, I say, "You two are adorable."

They're too busy smiling at each other, though, for me to see if Rajesh is mad.

"You know," Sawyer says. "We burned a bunch of calories earlier, and I'm fucking starving. You have beer, but we both know the only food you have is ice cream." He waits for me to concede his point. "Why don't I go with them and grab some burgers for all of us. Meet you back at your apartment?"

I frown, not wanting to separate. But then I remember.

He's mine for a week past forever.

So I smile. And I kiss him, deeply enough to make Gianna snark. And I send him on his way.

Because this time—and every time for the rest of always—he's coming back to me.

ACKNOWLEDGEMENTS

YET ANOTHER MILLION thank yous to everyone who made this book possible, especially:

Katy Upperman. For your texts, emails, insights, and just general awesomeness. You kept me going so often when I wanted to slack off. Thank you for calling this a "Katy" book; you have no idea how much that means to me!

Liz Briggs. Don't even know where to start. Thanks for your always stellar and no-holds-barred feedback. Thanks for cheering me on. Thanks for promising to never ever leave me. #Holdingyoutoit And, also, cheers to our super secret projects. ;)

Elodie Nowodazkij. For inspiring me and for loving my books and for just being so sweet in all aspects. Your S&S feedback was on point—and that email chain with Katy and you gave me the confidence boosts I needed while drafting!

Alison Miller. Your notes were awesome, as always. By the way, I am so ready for The Arsenal. And so is the rest of the world so get on that asap, my love.

Cindy Thomas. Your constant friendliness and the way you look out for me and for your early read of S&S. I am so, so glad to have met you.

Lola Sharp. For reading what you did and for your constant support. I'm ridiculously excited for your current project and I can't wait till the rest of the world gets to hear about it!

Cristin Terrill. For helping me make those first few chapters shine. Even if you refused to make all my copy edit changes at the retreat…

Spreadsheet crew girls: Jessica, Tracey, Ghenet, Alison, Liz, Lola, Katy, & Elodie. For giving me so. Much. Motivation.

Liz Fegley. For the early title brainstorming and plot discussion!

To all the readers and bloggers who were so enthusiastic about *Rock & Release*! Especially huge appreciation going out to Trish from Bedroom Bookworms, and Cindy Thomas (yes, a second mention because you rock). Thank you girls for loving *Rock & Release* the way you did. You made my debut feel like a smashing success and I'll never forget it.

Stephanie Parent. More amazing copy editing. Thank you!

Sarah Hansen of Okay Creations. For another amazing cover.

Cait Greer. Preemptive thank you for your genius formatting abilities!

Nelson. For helping keep me sane—and staying sane yourself—while I was heavy into drafting this story. (Okay, fine. For helping me stay *mostly* sane, at least.)

Baby girl. For giving up precious mama-daughter time while I wrote this. For being absolutely wonderful and making my life so much fuller, so much happier.

ABOUT THE AUTHOR

RILEY lives in the DC area and spends most of her time with her characters, playing with her toddler and husband, and pretending she knows how to be an adult. Former dancer. Current writer. Lifelong lover of accessories, books, and the beach. And cats. Can't forget the kitties, of which she has two.

Visit RileyEdgewood.com to contact Riley!
She loves hearing from her readers!

@Rileyedgewood
Facebook.com/rileyedgewoodauthor

Made in the USA
Lexington, KY
19 March 2016

BREEDING

EVIL

THE AGE OF JEZEBEL

REBECCA MAY

DEDICATION
For my daughter

TABLE OF CONTENTS

DEDICATION··iii
MAP OF ISRAEL···vii
AUTHOR'S NOTE··viii
ACKNOWLEDGEMENTS··ix
THE NIGHT GODDESS··1
THE TENTH PLAGUE···6
THE SEED OF GODS··10
THE HEALING OINTMENT··15
THE SNAIL TALE··21
THE KING'S PARADE···25
THE ROAD TO SAMARIA··30
THE NEW CAPITAL···34
THE KING'S SON··38
THE HEART'S MIND··43
THE HIDDEN MISSION···47
THE PSALM KEEPER···53
THE TREASURE OF SOLOMON··57
THE GATEWAY TO GOLD···62
THE SPIRIT OF ASHERAH···68
THE PROPHECY GAME··72
THE CONVERTS···76
THE PLACE OF FEAR···80
THE ANGEL SEER···85

THE NIGHT VISION················90
THE HUMAN SACRIFICE················95
THE SERVANT'S REWARD················104
THE KING'S ADVICE················111
THE ASKING PRICE················117
THE TWO PROPHECIES················122
THE PHOENIX CAPTAIN················128
THE HARD TRUTH················135
THE ASSYRIAN HERO················141
THE DEPTHS OF EVIL················152
THE BEGINNING OF THE END················162
THE PATH TO PEACE················170
THE WELL-STOCKED WAGON················173
THE LOVE OF THREE LOVES················179
THE CURSED MOUNTAIN················184
THE HEART'S HOME················194
THE NEW NEIGHBOR NEWS················200
THE DROUGHT················210
THE PROPHET AND THE PROPHETS················216
THE NEXT PSALTER················220
THE VICTORY AT KISHON················228
THE TROUBLER OF ISRAEL················236
THE CHALLENGE AT CARMEL················246
THE BATTLE AND THE WAR················253

THE TREASURE OF ELIAH	261
THE GIFT OF ADONIS	268
THE TIME TO GO	272
THE WAY OF THE SEA	278
THE GREAT ESCAPE	286
THE JEWELS OF THE ISLE	293
EPILOGUE	299
AFTERWARD	301
ABOUT THE AUTHOR	302
INDEX OF NAMES	303
BIBLE REFERENCES	306

MAP OF ISRAEL

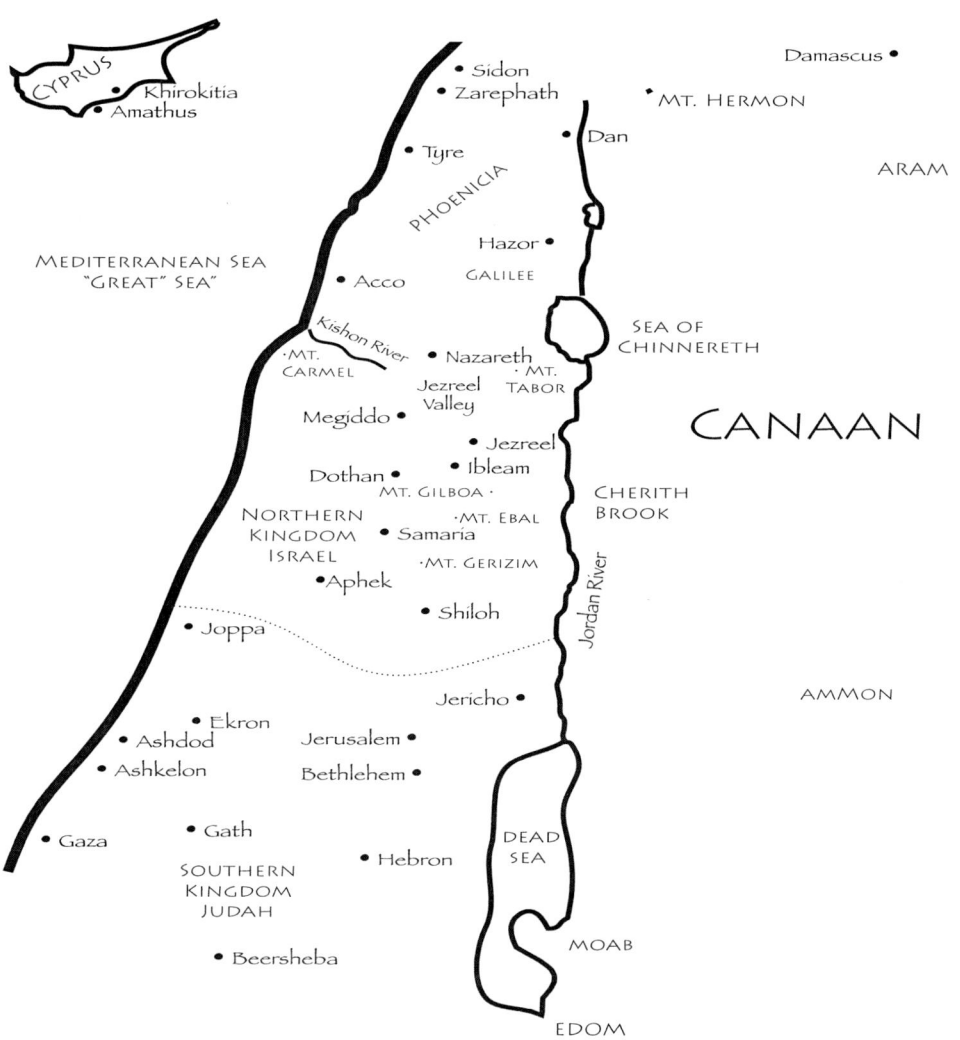

AUTHOR'S NOTE

While *Breeding Evil* is fiction, its underlying stories can be found in the Bible. Whenever one of these stories arise in this book, please know that it was my goal to maintain a faithful commitment to the biblical text. It is the Word of God and as such cannot be changed and should never be altered or manipulated to serve any other purpose greater than itself. If there are cultural, historical, or geographical inaccuracies in my work I offer my sincere apologies. It is my hope that the reader finds my efforts to harmonize with the Bible rigorous, compelling, and sincere. As far as further discrepancies are concerned, it is important I reinforce that unlike the Bible, this is a volume of fiction.

ACKNOWLEDGEMENTS

Several people were vital to the completion of this work.

Ann and Duane Bainbridge, my dear friends and very first investors. Pam Dykstra, Bob and Sherry Sprotte, Tim and Nancy Albers. The Tubergen Foundation, Mike and Vicki Worley, Pat Deaner, Ali and Rachel Asudegi, Jim and Kay Geib, and Dave and Ellen DeWitt. I am forever grateful for your support.

My Study Group. Thirty years together in the Word is no joke. Pam, KK, Nancy, Ann, Sherry, Marcy, Pat, Ami, Judy. You are a force to be reckoned with. Always in my corner. Always an inspiration. Always in prayer.

The board of Outlaw Ministries. There is an inexpressible peace having strong women by my side. Vicki Worley, Tara Kreuze, Heather Kuzma, Debbie DeLine, from the bottom of my heart, Thank You. To my husband, Chuck May. Thank you for handling all the financial details and legal concerns that come with launching and managing a non-profit.

Lara Helmling, my full-time editor and part-time counselor. Encouragement and expertise integrated into one sweet soul. Unfailing patience and persistence. Beyond crossing my t's and dotting my i's, thank you for your companionship as we ran this race.

Dragonfly Consulting. My courage and my sanctuary.

My writing instructor. Paula Doctor

My graphic designer. Michelle Dewey

My cover model. Emily May

My first reader. Ellen DeWitt

CHAPTER 1

THE NIGHT GODDESS

Obadyah left the gate house, hurrying to the princess's chambers. It was the evening before her thirteenth birthday, and the king was expecting him.

Obadiah moved swiftly across the inner courtyard, passing a young maiden drawing water. She paused and bowed her head. He tensed. As governor of the king's eunuchs, Obadyah's presence demanded respect. But, in his mind, he could not escape the truth. He was a slave. And as a slave, Obadyah performed any duty demanded of him, no matter how frivolous or demeaning. Tonight his task was simple: he would accompany the king to his daughter's chambers.

As it happened, Obadyah shared the princess's birthday though he was three years older. It was for this reason he remembered the day of his birth. Tomorrow all of Phoenicia would celebrate in her what, in him, would go unnoticed.

He opened the princess's door.

Jezebel was leaning against the rail of her terrace gazing at the stars. Obadyah silently took his position in the shadows of the portico. The king arrived moments later, quieting his steps when he discovered his daughter transfixed by the night sky.

"Good evening, My Lady," Ethbaal said, startling the princess.

Jezebel spun around and ran into her father's arms. "Today I am a woman!" she announced.

"You mean tomorrow you are a woman," Ethbaal replied.

Prior to his appointment as the king's eunuch, Obadyah was educated in the king's ascension to the throne. Ethbaal represented a new dynasty of Phoenician rulers. Having secured dominion by his position as Priest of Asherah: the mother of seventy gods, he gained respect by the spread of the Phoenician alphabet—a derivative of Egyptian hieroglyphics. The all consonant lettering system gave Ethbaal access to Egypt, Greece, and Rome. With political power and social status to rival Solomon in all his glory, Obadyah knew, Ethbaal was not to be trifled with.

"The midnight bell is imminent, Father. Keep your promise!" Jezebel demanded. "Tell me of my mother!"

"Very well," the King submitted. "I was walking on the shore of the Great Sea one warm summer night." Father and daughter moved to the window, gazing out at the water that stretched unending before them. "The god of the sky, pleased with my presence, illuminated the waters. I could see by the moon's glow all that was mine as king of our majestic land. Shall I describe these gifts to you, my Celestial Prize?"

"No, Father, I beg you, speak of my glory!" the princess said, reaching for her father's hand.

"Very well," Ethbaal conceded. "Now, where was I?"

"Father! You were on the god's sands at midnight!"

"Ah, yes, indeed I was, for I had determined to pause for a moment where the witching hour waves lay calm. It was then, when the moon reached its highest point in the sky, the goddess appeared."

Jezebel squeezed her father's hand. "What did you see, father? Was she alluring? Was she beautiful?"

Jezebel's face flushed with optimism and hope. Simply adorned in her ivory nightgown, Jezebel's cheeks glistened with gold dust, her skin untouched by man or sun. Her rare, sapphire eyes glowed within the frame of her auburn hair. That she was chosen was clear to everyone, especially Jezebel.

"Was your mother beautiful?" Ethbaal replied. "Be silent, My Treasure, and I will speak of her beauty, for her face was as soft as lamb's wool, her skin as creamy as butter, her breasts as faultless as an idol. And her legs. I could speak till morning's dawn of her legs. For they were as sleek and powerful as the palace stallions."

"And what of her hair, Father?"

"I quiver to speak of her hair," the King whispered. "For the black veil that flowed past her hips descended even past her feet. She circled me in silence," the king said as he slowly crept around his daughter. "Her hair wrapped around my legs. Then," Ethbaal came to a quick stop. "As suddenly as she appeared, she began to retreat. When her hair slowly pulled away. I looked down."

Jezebel followed her father's eyes to the floor.

"There you were, lying at my feet. The offspring of god and king."

The young heiress smiled as the evening breeze met her face. "Tell me about Asherah! Tell me of her reign!"

"It is a story to be told, My Priceless Princess," King Ethbaal replied. "For her majesty is as the sun, her companionship the waves of the sea. Her dominion amid cypress and cedar."

"But Father, she hides with the sun's night, she retreats with the waves. And the trees, are they not removed at our pleasure?"

"Is not her divine image carved from the very trees that submit to our tools?" Ethbaal said. "Does not the sun descend but for a time and then reappear with her permission? And the waves you speak of, My Morning Song, do they not retreat so that she might empower their return to our shore?"

"But I watch your warriors do battle. I visit the arena where males display their strength." Jezebel glanced at the eunuch. "I am not a warrior. I am not even a queen," the young heiress sulked.

"You are the daughter of the king, the descendant of a god! And do not forget, you are also a woman. Let go of your fears and know this, I reign not by might but by decree."

"My mother empowers you?"

"Your mother lures me. See you not, my Favored One, how the goddess mocks us with our strength? We prevail in battle by destroying one another. By our own swords, our numbers are reduced. And consider," Ethbaal continued, "our treasures of war. Do they not come home to the joy of the breasts which await us? Tell me, My Beloved, how is it that the two legs which carry me to battle and the two arms which crusade, measure not to the leverage of two delicate breasts? Never forget, My Darling, power is not the ability to destroy but the ability to move strength as it pleases you. We, your male consorts, are shifted about as pawns, plucked like leaves, led like sheep by nothing more than the decorated eyes of our deepest desire. Do you not have jurisdiction over my thoughts? Do you not beckon and I appear? Do you not have mastery over us males from your first wink to your last?"

"The aliens of Canaan speak of one they call 'The Mighty One,'" Jezebel said. "Tell me, Father, does there exist a deity above all deities?"

"Whether Baal suffers at the hand of this so-called Mighty One, this Yahweh, we must await Asherah's reckoning. Deities will always fight for her praise. But know this, My Blessed, a man's soul must journey from his heart to his seed. The woman's desire has no distance to travel. Each beat of her spirit perpetually at her will, her soul sheltered between her breasts. Asherah has conceived you with this protected valley, My Enchanted. Now go! Paint your eyes and adorn your head. Tonight we visit the Festival of the Cakes among the Hebrews."

Ethbaal turned and Obadyah took his place before the king. When he opened the door, Jezebel's attendants brushed by him, hurrying to the princess's side. Obadyah was careful never to let his eyes wander. Still, he could not help but notice there was a new Athena.

Each of the harem, the choicest of Canaanite women, was selected for her unique beauty. To be appointed to the royal harem was the greatest desire of Phoenician women, even though the position came with great personal risk. Each girl was chosen for a specific role, based on the feature of their appearance that fancied the king. The girl whose face most charmed the king was named for Athena, goddess of wisdom. The girl whose body satisfied the king was Adonis, lotus of love. The girl whose hair soothed the king was named Aphka, delight of the earth. The roles were assigned at the whim of the king. And removed at the whim of the princess. When a girl was rejected, the palace hosted public auditions so those of exceptional beauty could take their place.

During the spring festival the previous year, Aphka was released when the braided hair of a voluptuous redhead caught the King's attention. To the relief of the serving Aphka, she was returned to her family to dispose of as they saw fit. One past Aphka did not fare as well. Having encouraged the princess that her hair would become thicker when she entered womanhood, she sealed her own fate. The implication of Jezebel's imperfection doomed Aphka. Jezebel had ordered the girl's head be shaved and that she be forced to eat her hair. Obadyah was forced to carry out the order. His stomach turned and bile rose to his tongue as he recalled her strangled screams as he forced hair into her mouth.

At twelve Jezebel was already devious, well-versed in scheming and manipulation. Masking the insecurities that came with youth, she had an exceptionally creative mind and she possessed a strong sense of self. She knew what she wanted and how to get it. Suggestions were perceived as challenges and came at a great cost to those she viewed as getting in her way. Not long ago, the harem's first Athena painted Jezebel's nails in the likeness of her eyes. The princess, ecstatic, showered her Athena with gifts. But when Jezebel took a stroll on the beach later that day a wave splashed up. The color on her nails bled onto her skin turning her fingers a warm shade of violet. Jezebel responded by ordering Athena's nails ripped out before returning her to the village from which she came.

Obadyah shuddered to think what Jezebel would be like once she gained the authority of a queen. It was only a matter of time.

Each of the royal harem attended to Jezebel's needs, pampering the princess as they competed for her favor and the attention of the King. When Ethbaal's appetite beckoned, his eunuch was charged with the unenviable task of accompanying the young girl of his choosing into his chambers. What brought Obadyah to tears brought Ethbaal no shame. The painted faces of the royal harem added years to their appearance. But when their clothing was removed, their delicate undeveloped bodies revealed, the truth could not be hidden. They were children.

CHAPTER 2

THE TENTH PLAGUE

Jezebel and her ladies made their way through the streets of Sidon, accompanied by the king's eunuchs. As the head of the guard, Obadyah took the lead. Beside him was a boy performing his first duty since his change. Obadyah tensed as he recalled the day he was bound and brought before the king.

Ethbaal ordered a dozen young boys, handpicked by the king, to be castrated each spring. While the boys made for safe servants, their emasculated bodies did not induce fear. For this reason, the king also selected older boys, impressive in frame, boys who had already become men. By cinching their testicles with mane hair, Ethbaal destroyed their ability to produce offspring, robbing them of their dignity and purpose. Sometimes even their lives were taken from them as infection overwhelmed many. The king found these older boys doubly valuable. Although these young men could never father a child, they retained an intimidating stature. Furthermore, once they could not preserve a family line, their only value was in their service to the crown.

Obadyah was the greatest amid the eunuch's of the past season, but that was not why he was taken. While his path to the throne was different, the emasculation that accompanied it was the same.

The streets of Sidon that night were a banquet for the senses. Gentle lyre strings melded with the echo of the shepherd's pipe summoning the girls. The uneven stones underfoot were a welcome indication of freedom from the safe and predictable palace environment.

Roasted grains ruled the streets. When the sweet aroma found Jezebel, she turned towards a small stand of cakes. Spelled out in stones on the ground was: 'Manna of Heaven.' The throng of people parted as Obadyah pushed his way through the crowd, making way for the princess and her maidens to reach the stand and the shopkeep.

"Tell me, alien of Canaan," Jezebel commanded, "which god blesses these cakes?"

"In truth," the Hebrew replied, "no blessing surpasses the gift of your presence, My Princess."

Jezebel nodded, acknowledging her approval of the man's greeting.

"Humbly, do I submit," the peddler bowed, "and tell you of Yahweh's provision. My people who dwell in your midst do so by the hand of our God."

Jezebel, who loved a good story, especially about the gods, was listening intently.

"As you very well know, Sidon's Sunrise, my people, the family of Abraham, were held in slavery by Egypt's pharaoh. For 400 years we toiled under his ruthless hand. It was a princess, a graceful heroine such as yourself, who drew Moses, our deliverer, out of the Nile. And in doing so, drew us out of slavery."

"Was it not Baal who freed you?" Jezebel interrupted.

"Your insight intrigues me," the man replied, "for whether by Baal or Yahweh, O Reigning Flower, Asherah be praised in our delivery to this land."

Jezebel smiled, pleased to see her influence had reached a follower of Yahweh.

"Tell me more of his magic," she ordered, "for I have heard of Moses's incantations."

"Indeed, Cherished Lady. By the approval of Asherah, Moses rained down ten earthly terrors on the Egyptians. His curses began with the sacred river…" the story-teller paused, drawing in ears, "when he turned the Nile into blood!" The gasps of the crowd brought a smile to Jezebel's face. The Hebrew continued, "This was the first of Yahweh's plagues."

"Tis the water and the blood of childbirth!" Jezebel replied at the nods of the women gathered. "This surely is Asherah's seal on these so-called plagues. Continue," Jezebel demanded.

"There were gruesome tests by grucsome creatures as Moses summoned frogs, lice, locusts, and wild animals into the midst of Egypt."

Jezebel's attendants squealed, debating which of the creatures would cause the most misery.

"What followed, My Lady, was a curse of such severity, even the great Thutmose, could not endure. Two attacks against life," the baker said, holding up two fingers. "First, disease among the livestock. Second, boils on the skin of the people."

Jezebel's ladies winced.

"Open, oozing, festering, seeping putrefying boils," the vendor continued, raising his voice to the pleasure of all who'd gathered. "There is no relief, My Lady, no soothing balm, no cool stream, nor even the repose of a single night's sleep amid such agony." The Hebrew leaned in as if revealing a secret intended solely for the ears of the princess. "There also came an attack, not against the flesh, but against the earth itself, Moses issuing two more plagues of suffering," the man held up two fingers once more. "Hail rained down on the people of Egypt, followed by three days of darkness."

"Hail destroys," Jezebel agreed, "but what pain comes with darkness?"

"If I may comment concerning your discernment," the Hebrew replied. "It is said a torment of mind far outweighs any affliction of the flesh. Is that not why we sleep when it is dark? Night sorrow, I submit, would deliver a far greater fear."

Obadyah could see that the story was provoking Jezebel. And he knew why. Jezebel had been told that her birth at midnight christened that hour above all hours. This couldn't end well.

"I count only nine plagues, Hebrew." Jezebel said. "What is the tenth curse?"

"The tenth?" the man replied. "I'm afraid the tenth is far too dreadful to reveal."

"Reveal it! You must! You must!" Jezebel's attendants begged.

The Hebrew addressed Jezebel. "Is it your desire, My Lady, that I speak the tenth plague?"

Jezebel nodded.

"So be it. If I must, I will reveal to you the final plague–the plague of all plagues." The Hebrew paused and drew all ears to him. "Death," he uttered.

"Death?" Jezebel huffed. "Death would mean the end of their suffering! This tenth curse is a reward!"

"Dear Princess, you speak with such wisdom, for indeed death would mean an end to suffering. But it was not Pharoah who bore the curse. Nor was it his servants or the bounty of his countless offspring. It was his firstborn son. Pharaoh was not released from pain by death, he was left to live in the pain brought by the death of his beloved child—a pain, if I might be so bold, far greater than all the previous plagues combined."

Rumblings swept over those gathered. For they knew, each one, what sorrow the sting of death brings for those who remain when a firstborn is taken.

Obadyah scanned the crowd for trouble.

"The words of Yahweh concerning the tenth curse have been protected for us, Pride of Sidon," the man said. "They have been handed down to me from generation upon generation. With your blessing might I share with you this priceless treasure our forefathers bestowed upon us?"

"Permit him! Permit him!" the people begged.

Jezebel smiled, holding the power of the crowd's pleading. She allowed their chanting to wear on. At last, she gave in. "Very well," Jezebel granted. "Reveal to us the words your god has preserved."

"As you wish, Asherah's Chosen," the man bowed. "Hear the word of the Lord," the Hebrew announced as if reading a decree of the King. "Thus says Yahweh: At midnight I am going to the land of Egypt, and all the firstborn shall die, from the firstborn of the Pharaoh who sits on his throne, even to the firstborn slave behind the millstone; all the firstborn cattle as well. Moreover, there shall be a great cry in all the land of Egypt, such as has not been before and shall never be again."

Obadyah cringed. He knew Jezebel would not miss the baker's reference to midnight. What Ethbaal earlier that night glorified as a sacred hour, this Hebrew labeled a curse.

The man rolled up the scroll of the words of Yahweh and tucked it under his belt. As he bowed his head, he reached for a warm loaf and extended it towards the princess. Jezebel's eyes narrowed. Obadyah quickly retrieved the bread. He tore off a piece placing it in his mouth. Having tasted nothing bitter, he held out the loaf to the princess. Jezebel knocked the bread out of Obadyah's hand. It hit the ground to the sound of gasps coming from the crowd. Jezebel turned and walked away.

CHAPTER 3

THE SEED OF GODS

Summer twilight swept the cobblestone streets as the evening torches welcomed dusk. Jezebel continued through Sidon, parading past the locals, oblivious to the glares of those who witnessed her disrespect of the Hebrew baker. As curses were uttered she carried on, laughing with her maidens. Obadyah directed the eunuchs to tighten their perimeter around the princess as he sensed tension building with the Hebrews.

Jezebel paused to look at scarves a vendor was offering. A scuffle could be felt amid the crowd, pushing in on the back of the eunuchs.

"I like this one, My Lady," Athena said.

Hearing the new Athena's voice for the first time, Obadyah paused. He could not stop his eyes from finding her. She smiled at Jezebel. It was effortless, pure. She did not wear her expressions like a garment, as did the rest of Ethbaal's harem. He allowed his eyes to linger, taking in her features with a single breath. Her gentle eyes glowed with the vibrance of azure gems. Her smile captivated him, stirring him in ways that he had denied since his emasculation.

Unaware his responsibilities had slipped from his mind, Obadyah fell a step behind. His attention was ripped back to his duty when in the corner of his eye he caught sight of a man lunging towards the princess. Obadyah's cohort grabbed the Hebrew. Obadyah moved swiftly to subdue the attacker. When the new eunuch put a knife to the man's throat, Obadyah grabbed his hand. Without a word, he shook his head, staying the Hebrew's execution.

As commanded, the young eunuch released his grip.

The Hebrew disappeared into the crowd. He was fortunate to have escaped with his life, and he ran as if he knew it.

Obadyah clinched his teeth, one more second and there would have been bloodshed. How could I be so careless! Then his eyes sought the new Athena once more.

Athena held up the fabric to the princess's face. "Your eyes sparkle with its hue."

Jezebel swelled with pride as she preened with the beautiful cloth, unmoved by the cloud of hostility.

"Begging your mercy, Dear Princess," the shopkeeper interrupted, "May I speak in your hearing?"

Jezebel nodded.

"I have a shawl of such brilliance, tis fit only for royalty."

Jezebel's eyes widened as the boy, who looked the same age as the princess, walked over to a draped table. Lifting a covering, he revealed a hidden box. The Hebrew youth slid the container out and pulled it towards the princess. He removed the lid and set it aside. His eyes brightened as his fingers made contact with the treasure he was seeking. Jezebel leaned in over the table. With careful movement, the boy drew out a violet shawl.

"I dare not tell you of the value of this single piece of cloth," the young merchant said, displaying it before Jezebel.

"And should I demand it of you?"

"Forgive me, Gracious Divine," the boy submitted. "This satin wrap is a gift of the Great Sea. This one shawl, my Goddess, holds the lifeblood of a thousand snails."

"What amount of silver do you ask for this?" Jezebel demanded.

"What silver could I require for Sidon's Jewel to adorn my wares?"

"Would you insult my father? Is there a price the king cannot afford to pay?"

"I should cut off my arm before a single breath insults my king! The garment is as you are, my Lady, priceless!"

"Very well, boy," Jezebel replied, "the silver of 10,000 rock snails will be brought to you by morning's dawn."

The villager bowed. He reached out with the shawl. As he did, his hand grazed the princess.

Obadyah grabbed the boy's arm. The boy released the cloth, pain driving him to his knees. Athena lunged forward, securing the precious veil before it hit the ground.

"You senseless beast!" Jezebel scolded. She swung her hand towards Obadyah, heedless that his action was his sworn duty. The ring adorning Jezebel's finger sliced open Obadyah's face. He released the boy. Athena's eyes found Obadyah as blood ran down his cheek in a steady flow onto his chest.

"My Lady," Athena quickly interjected, "find peace in your beauty," she said, draping the exquisite scarf across Jezebel's shoulders. "Let the fabric comfort you," Athena continued, "for this precious shawl has found its precious home."

Jezebel's anger melted from her countenance. Soothed by the caressing of her mistress of wisdom, the princess floated along, the eyes of every Phoenician reaching for her.

"Is thy destiny known to thee?" A voice moaned from somewhere in the crowd.

Jezebel stopped.

Obadyah searched his surroundings, anxious to locate the source of the voice.

"Who speaks?" Jezebel demanded.

"So," the cracked voice replied, "you are curious about your destiny."

Parting the crowd an old woman appeared inching slowly in Jezebel's direction. The worn cloak which draped her head came down below her eyebrows, her eyes barely visible in the shadows of her hood. She walked with a pronounced limp, her back leg dragging behind her like a dog carrying an oversized stick. Obadyah stepped in front of the witch when she was close enough to touch the princess. The old woman stepped around him, Obadyah's presence merely an inconvenience.

"My future is sure," Jezebel replied. "How dare you speak of my destiny!"

Undeterred by the menacing tone of the princess, the mystic continued. "Surely, the princess does not have full knowledge of all that awaits her."

"Would you risk a prophecy concerning King Ethbaal's prize?"

"Tis not my risk, Violet Queen, which worries me," the old woman creaked, "but rather that which Asherah has shared in my hearing."

"And what acquaintance have you with the gods?" Jezebel demanded.

"Know this, offspring of Ethbaal, as surely as you stand before me now, the goddess of Phoenicia stood before me this morning."

Jezebel took a step towards the hunched diviner.

"Come, child of the gods," the mysterious figure gestured, "enter the tent of enlightenment and hear the wisdom of Yahweh's lover."

Jezebel motioned for her eunuch. Obadyah entered the canopy to survey its security. When he nodded, Jezebel and her harem followed. An embellished rug lay beneath a circle of burning candles. The elderly seer sat down inside the ring of fire, crossing her legs.

"Come," she said, inviting Jezebel to join her.

Jezebel stepped inside the ring. Crossing her legs she sat down across from the Hebrew diviner.

"Do you know of your mother?" she asked, her eyes closed.

"I know the story told to me by my father."

"Would you hear more?"

"Yes! I long to hear of my mother's majesty."

"I will share with you now what the goddess shared with me. What the Mesopotamians call Ishtar, and the Greeks call Astarte is Asherah. Her presence is strong in the crescent moon."

"Yes!" Jezebel replied, "for midnight is blessed!"

"All tales told from your birth onward," the gypsy replied, "will find its magic in that hour of darkness."

"Tell me, enchanter, has Asherah received the seed of Baal or Yahweh?"

Obadyah cringed at the mention of Yahweh. The God of his mother, the God of his people spoken of with brazen disrespect welled up tears inside of him. He swallowed them. What could he do? Chastise the princess for her irreverence towards the living God? Obadyah was helpless, impotent, unable to defend himself let alone the God of his youth.

"You do well to discover the seed of your birth," the old sage replied.

"How might I draw my mother to my presence?" Jezebel asked.

"By that which draws us all, My Lady."

"Love?"

"Love is mighty, indeed. But there is a more powerful devotion."

"What is mightier than love?" Jezebel asked.

"That which contains both affection and allegiance," the crone paused.

"Speak woman!" Jezebel demanded.

"Worship. Nothing soars higher than worship." Reaching into a pouch on the front of her robe, the gypsy withdrew a small idol. "I made this after your mother left me."

Jezebel fixed her gaze on the carved image resting in the witch's palm. The forehead was adorned with small jewels on a string that formed a decorative crown. The figure's eyes were protruding, too large for the size of the deity's face. The skin was smooth clay. Her undersized chin was drawn in towards her neck. The right hand of the idol was clinched into a fist and tucked under her right breast. The left hand was open, the fingers of the goddess extended holding up her left breast.

There were two openings where the idol's arms turned in at the elbows through which the seer slid her finger and thumb. The hips of the goddess began her hourglass shape. It was there the idol ended, the womb the pedestal on which the miniature Asherah stood. Jezebel's eyes widened as she reached for the figure.

"Know this Mediterranean Princess, your mother will extend your reign beyond Tyre and Sidon. But your commitment to Asherah will be tested, your faithfulness challenged."

Jezebel's eyes left the idol resting in her palm. "Who would dare challenge Asherah's anointed?"

The elderly seer held the princess with her silence. Jezebel, trapped between sovereignty and submission, said, "And what will it cost me to purchase my future? Or should you be content to trade your information for your life."

"Contentment is a pearl of youth," the witch replied. "I seek only the pleasure of this day. Observe the creases on my face, for death came calling long before you did."

Jezebel, her threat extinguished, nodded to Athena who reached into the pouch hanging from her shoulder. She tossed a few silver pieces onto the rug. The seer gathered them up quickly and returned her attention to the princess.

"The blood of Jezebel will reign in the Northern Kingdom of Israel, only with the flow of the blood of the prophets of Yahweh." the old woman croaked.

Obadyah maintained his composure though inside he was boiling. The ignorance and arrogance pouring from the mouth of the witch stiffened his back and sent his heart racing. But he could not have prepared himself for what he heard next.

"This is not the end of the goddess's prophecy," the witch pledged. "For should you endure, should you be the impetus of Yahweh's submission, your offspring, daughter of Asherah, will rule all of Canaan!"

CHAPTER 4

THE HEALING OINTMENT

Jezebel stormed out of the mystic's tent without a word. Obadyah followed closely behind, his head swinging back and forth between the princess and her harem who were trying desperately to keep up. Obadyah could not discern what had gotten Jezebel so agitated. She had seemed pleased with the mystics's prophecy and appeared content when the idol had come to rest in her hand.

Jezebel's ladies finally caught up with her and followed in silence. It was clear to all that the princess was on a mission. Obadyah's eyes narrowed as Jezebel stopped in front of the cake stand where their night began. She pushed her way past the few Hebrews waiting for their turn to buy bread. When the peddler caught a glimpse of her out of the corner of his eye he turned to face her. Without a word he offered her the loaf already in his hand. Jezebel reached past the bread and took the scroll he had tucked under his belt for safekeeping. A few of the Hebrews pressing in around her smiled at the sight of their princess giving her attention to the precious words of Yahweh.

She walked a few paces away from the stand and turned. With her eye on the peddler, Jezebel held the words of Yahweh up to the street lantern. The dry parchment sparked with flame. When the vendor stepped towards Jezebel, reaching for the scroll, Obadyah stepped in front of him, blocking his path to the princess. A helpless cry escaped the Hebrew's lips. Obadyah watched the blood drain from the Hebrew's face.

More than anything, he wished he could let the Hebrew save the scroll, but he had a job to do. His heart tore in two when he heard the scroll ignite.

The crowd of Hebrews gasped in horror. Reluctantly, Obadyah turned around. He knew he must watch this crowd for hints of retaliation. Jezebel's vile act was surely eliciting more hate than fear.

Jezebel held the scroll between her thumb and first finger, patient as the flames consumed the last of it. She released the desiccated parchment. Ashes floated to the ground.

Returning from the Hebrew festival, Jezebel marched into the castle courtyard. As the lock on the gate slid into place Athena called out to her princess, "My Lady."

Jezebel turned to Athena whose gaze led the princess's eyes to Obadyah. "Clean up this eunuch!" Jezebel barked, "I don't want his dirty blood marking my father's palace!"

Athena bowed and proceeded back out of the gate they had just entered. Obadyah followed.

When Athena missed the trail to the Mediterranean, Obadyah stopped. Expecting the princess's mistress to lead him to the shore, he paused waiting for Athena's instructions. Sensing his absence, she turned.

"Well?" she said.

Obadyah looked towards the water and then back to Athena. Athena proceeded away from the shore without another word.

Obadyah followed.

The servant pair moved hastily down the street. Polished marble turned to cracked mud as royalty gave way to poverty. About ten minutes east of the castle, Athena turned south on a narrow path that led to a small village. The Phoenicians built circular stone huts. As the outer perimeter rose towards the sky, it narrowed, each row supporting the next. This particular home was easily recognizable as it was the only one in the village with a door. Standing before the haphazardly tethered bamboo, Athena knocked.

"Who's there?" A crusty voice spoke behind the hollow door.

"Uncle Kalbu, Aunt Donatiya, it's me. It's Zoë."

The door creaked as a worn-faced man wrestled it open.

"Zoë! Tis you, my girl!"

Athena embraced her uncle while Obadyah stood at a distance.

"Move over, you old fool," a short, sturdy woman said. Securing her cloak she pushed herself between her husband and Athena.

"Come in, my dear. What has you out at this hour of the night?" the woman asked.

"Aunt Donatiya, I need your help with the king's guard."

"The king's guard? Where?" Athena's uncle walked outside of the hut past Obadyah who stood frozen and silent as he passed. "I don't see anyone!" the loud man said.

"That's because you're blind, you old mule!" Athena's aunt scolded.

Obadyah glanced at Athena.

Athena shook her head.

The small woman proceeded out of the hut and made her way to Obadyah's side. "Forgive him," she said, taking Obadyah's arm. "The clouds that cover his eyes have long concealed the world," she said, "but he seems, each day, to be shocked by that." As she led Obadyah towards the hut, she addressed her husband. "Welcome the king's guard, you old stump!" the fiery lady demanded.

"Forgive me, Sir, please come in," Athena's uncle said, staring in the opposite direction of the eunuch.

"I don't know why you're asking his forgiveness," Aunt Donatiya said, "You ought to be seeking mine!"

"Woman, you have reached your limit on forgiveness," the man barked, "You know you only get five apologies a day!"

"Please ignore him." Donatiya said, as she escorted the oversized eunuch into their undersized home.

"Aunt Donatiya, Papa Kalbu, this is…" Athena paused and looked at Obadyah. Donatiya and Kalbu did the same.

The family of three stared at him, their silence urging him to speak. When he offered no reply, they offered no encouragement.

When the quiet became unbearable, Obadyah finally spoke. "I…am… the king's eunuch," he said.

"Yes son." Donatiya laughed. "That much is clear. But what is your name?"

Obadyah paused once again, making eye contact with Athena and Donatiya, while Kalbu continued to stare at the door.

"I…am…Obadyah."

"Obadyah? I don't know that name," Donatiya replied.

"Aunt," Athena interjected, "we just need..."

"Well, don't leave us in suspense, dear boy," Kalbu interrupted, "out with it! Are you Philistine? Canaanite?"

Obadyah's eyes bounced back and forth between the three Phoenicians now huddled around him as though appraising an unearthed treasure. "I am..I…am…Hebrew and Canaanite."

At that, Kalbu elbowed his wife as if to say, 'I told you so,' only he had not told her anything.

Obadyah could not remember the last time he had heard his own voice spoken out loud. It felt as though he were listening to the words of a stranger.

"Papa," Athena said, "do you have some of your sealing ointment to repair the…to repair Obadyah's wound?"

"I sure do," Kalbu replied. Reaching for the outer wall, Kalbu followed it around to a large wicker basket on the far side of the room. "It's in here somewhere," Kalbu said as he rummaged through his collection of items. Unable to locate what he was after, Donatiya hurried to her husband's side. Muttering a few curses about his ineptness, she began helping him empty the basket.

Left alone, Obadyah spoke to Athena, "Why did you not call me eunuch?"

"Because eunuch is not who you are."

"But it is who I am. I am a eunuch."

"Eunuch is the condition forced upon you; it is not who you are any more than blind is who my uncle is."

"But," Obadyah said, leaning in and lowering his voice, "he is blind."

"No, he is my sweet uncle. It just happens that he cannot see."

"And what more am I than the castrated servant of the king?"

"You are a son, a son of man and gods. A son who cannot…" Athena paused. Her attempt to encourage Obadyah drawing light to the very thing he longed to forget.

When their eyes stumbled upon one another, Athena quickly turned and retrieved a cloth. Sitting down with a basin of water, she began wiping Obadyah's face. With gentle strokes, Athena removed the blood that continued to run from his cheek down his neck and onto his chest.

"Your thoughtfulness must be a welcome gift to the princess," Obadyah remarked.

"I have privileges granted me by the princess. I am not, however, favored by the king."

Obadyah smiled, surprised at Athena's honesty, and fully aware of what being favored by the king meant.

"Thank you, Zoë," Obadyah said.

"Do you not like my palace title?"

"Your given name suits you."

"It is an honor to have been granted the name of a goddess."

"It is no more an honor to bear the name of an idol than to bear the scars which label me: Property of the King."

Obadyah's strong words silenced Athena. As she continued quietly working, Obadyah realized his emotions were getting the better of him.

"We are slaves," he whispered, "both of us. Altered for the crown's pleasure." Frustration swept over Obadyah's face as he feared what might fall from his lips next.

"Are we not distinguished as royal servants?" Athena calmly replied.

"Jezebel is using you, Zoë," Obadyah whispered, "for stolen glory, the cravings of a wicked dynasty." Obadyah's voice was stern, his words reckless.

"Which god?" Athena asked.

Obadyah, caught off guard, did not reply.

Athena asked again. "Whose glory is stolen by our roles in the palace?"

"Yahweh," Obadyah replied, "the God of Abraham, Isaac, and Jacob."

"The God of the scroll? The one destroyed by Jezebel?"

Obadyah nodded. What Athena meant to only clarify her confusion was a dagger to Obadyah's conscience. He had done nothing. Worse, he had protected Jezebel while she destroyed that which is most precious to the Hebrews, the words of Yahweh.

When Obadyah offered nothing more, Athena continued, "Surely, the god of the Hebrews will enable you to serve in the position in which he has placed you. Is he not the god of Asherah's choosing?"

"Yahweh? A consort of Asherah?" Obadyah laughed. "Yahweh is no more a consort than I am!"

"But your people carry the Asherah. They have festivals in her honor. They celebrate her diviners."

"Yes, I know," Obadyah said, his eyes falling to the floor. "My people are stubborn. They do not remember Yahweh's mercy and his wondrous deeds which he performed among them. They would turn back to slavery before they would return to God. Yahweh pleads. But my people stiffen their necks and do not listen."

Obadyah cursed himself. He knew his faith must sound strange. Athena's people celebrated their culture with pride, pointing their anger and frustrations towards the gods. Obadyah, however, was ashamed of his people. It was unthinkable to bear any bitterness towards a God who is gracious and compassionate, slow to anger and abounding in lovingkindness.

"King Ethbaal would see you bound and plunged into the sea for this faith you boast," she said.

"Perhaps that is my fate," Obadyah replied, dropping his head.

"Here it is!" Kalbu exclaimed. With cream in hand, Athena's uncle beamed as though he'd discovered gold. Stepping with haste towards

Obadyah and Athena he lost his footing.

Obadyah lunged, catching Kalbu just before his head made contact with the earthen floor. Obadyah carefully guided Kalbu to a stool.

"Thank you, son," Kalbu said, out of breath.

"Yes, thank you," Donatiya added with obvious relief. "You old sack of bones," she said with a tear in her eye, "how many times must I remind you? Hurrying is for seeing people, not for blind old bats."

Obadyah and Athena gave each other a quick smile.

Kalbu grinned as he opened up his hand, proud of himself that he had not dropped his homemade cream. Sticking his finger deep down into the ointment, he pulled up a glob ready to apply it to Obadyah's wound.

"What do you think you're doing?" Donatiya asked.

"I think I'm helping this nice young man," Kalbu replied.

"With your help, the boy will end up with cream in his eyes, his mouth, and in his nose before you'd find his wound!"

Athena and Obadyah found one another once more with a simple smile. In that brief moment of repose, Obadyah felt free from the contrasts of cultures and the bonds of vassalage.

CHAPTER 5

THE SNAIL TALE

Athena led Obadyah back to the palace. As she walked, Athena's heart stirred. She found him intriguing. How had Obadyah ended up in the King's service? Does he have a family he left behind? Will I ever hear the sound of his voice again?

It brought joy to Athena's heart to think back on the moment Obadyah grabbed the village boy's arm. His subsequent loss of blood marked the beginning of their journey to her aunt and uncle's house. The brisk night walk, the sweet peace of home, the fury of Obadyah's strange faith boiling inside him, all made for the most pleasant hours she had ever experienced.

As the pair entered the courtyard of the castle, Jezebel appeared. Athena's steps came to an abrupt halt, Obadyah nearly colliding with her.

"What keeps you so long from my presence?" Jezebel roared.

"My apologies, Goddess of Sidon," Athena bowed, "I was tending to your servant's wounds and…"

"So it is my fault you return to me at this late hour?"

"No, My Lady," Obadyah interrupted.

"Silence!" Jezebel yelled, raising her hand and striking Obadyah in the face.

Athena had no sooner stopped his bleeding and Obadyah bled once more. Obadyah remained silent and went to his knees before the princess, bowing at her feet.

Jezebel calmed, her anger atoned for by the pleasure of her imminent judgment. "Lead me to my quarters, Athena, while this eunuch faces his chastening."

Athena walked away, fighting the desire to look back. Obadyah had come to her defense. And for that Jezebel would punish him. Not with the whip, nor with fists. Obadyah had endured both in the past, and Jezebel never punished the same way twice. She prided herself on her creativity and the fear she instilled in her victims.

Athena dipped a sponge into the warm water of the copper tub where Jezebel lay soaking. She recalled the contentment she felt nursing the injured Hebrew. Jezebel opened her eyes, catching a glimpse of Athena.

"What brings you such pleasure, Athena?" Jezebel questioned.

"Your presence, My Reigning Delight," Athena replied.

Jezebel appeared dubious. She inquired further. "Where did you take the eunuch when you left the palace?"

Athena did not hesitate. "I led him to the water's edge," she replied, "to scrub him and to search for snail excretions to stop his bleeding."

"So, there are snails on the beach tonight?" Jezebel pressed.

"Yes, My Lady."

"Then, I suppose I will send slaves to retrieve them since they will likely need more to tend to the eunuch's new wounds."

"Yes, My Lady," Athena replied. Jezebel had rendered her powerless. She could neither help Obadyah nor express an ounce of sorrow for his suffering. Athena was quickly learning that anything beyond her callous submission would only further stir Jezebel's wrath.

Leaving the princess's chambers, Athena moved swiftly down the hall. As she made her way to the servant's quarters, a thought came to her. Having learned of Obadyah's god, Athena took a chance and called on Yahweh for help.

"God of Abraham, Isaac, and Jacob," she whispered. "I petition you for a snail, a single snail that might appease the princess's anger and become a source of protection for your servant Obadyah."

Athena crawled between her blankets next to the other servant girls. Laying on her back, she stared up at the blackness above her. *What was I thinking attempting to speak to this new deity? Why would Obadyah's God listen to me?* Athena fell asleep, the conflict inside her submitting to the stress of the day's events.

"Athena, Athena, arise!"

"What is it, Adonis?"

"The princess summons all servants to the courtyard!"

Athena, Adonis, and Aphka hurried to join the other servants gathered at the King's garden. Athena's eyes wandered, eager to find Obadyah. Her focus changed when Jezebel appeared next to her father on the balcony above the courtyard.

"My Prize has informed me of Asherah's blessing upon this house," the King announced. "Asherah has come forth from the heart of the sea, bringing with her a deity's reaping of rock snails." The King paused, welcoming the gasps of his attendants. "This," the King continued, "will ensure our eminence from Lebanon to Egypt. We will lead the world in the manufacture of crimson dye!" The courtyard erupted. "Asherah has spoken! Go!" the King demanded, "gather her treasure."

"Athena!" Jezebel said, "come." The hundreds who served at the feet of the King bowed their heads as Jezebel called Athena to the rooftop. "Look!" Jezebel pointed. Athena's eyes crested the edge of the palace wall. Her mouth fell open. Spiny snails covered the shore like a blanket of snow.

Adonis and Aphka joined Athena in Jezebel's bedroom.

"My seamstress," Jezebel announced. A motherly figure entered her chambers. "Measure Athena and assemble a dress," Jezebel directed. She then turned her attention to Athena. "Asherah has chosen to bless me, Athena. I will praise her by lavishing you. Perhaps, the goddess will be pleased to use you as her messenger once more."

Jezebel turned and left the room. Adonis and Aphka proceeded to undress Athena. Her proportions measured, the girls' bathed Athena in fragrances and goat milk.

What is happening? Athena wondered as the events of the previous day replayed in her mind. *I stood in the home of my birth; I befriended a Hebrew. I prayed to his god. Has he answered me? I asked for a single snail. Yahweh fills the beach as far as my eyes can see. I said one. He brought forth thousands.*

Adonis and Aphka brushed Athena's long chestnut hair until it was dry. Her friends pinned her braids up in loops while Athena sat puzzled. *Is Yahweh indeed Asherah's chosen?* Athena remembered the look on Obadyah's face when she suggested the union of Yahweh and Asherah. *But if Obadyah is right, then why was Yahweh not credited with this miracle? What god allows other gods to receive praise for his actions?*

The girls continued to lace Athena's hair with flowers and strings of pomegranate seeds. *Who is this god?* Athena wondered, *who hears the prayer of a captive and stands by while his follower suffers?*

Any other slave would be elated by the grooming and attention, but Athena was in misery. While she was adorned, Obadyah suffered. As she was pampered, she knew he bled.

CHAPTER 6

THE KING'S PARADE

It took Ethbaal's slaves a week to clear the beach of snails. Jezebel allowed her harem to view the gathering and the beginning of the process of extracting the precious dye. Athena watched. But she also watched for Obadyah. Not finding him, day after day, her fears rose as did her confusion with the Hebrew's god. She could think of only one thing to do.

That night, when all the other girls in her chamber were asleep, Athena slipped out from under her covering and knelt on the cold stone floor. "God of the Hebrews," Athena whispered, "I appeal to you once more. You have chosen to protect my aunt and uncle, though they worship Baal. You have chosen to protect me, though I bear the name of your rival. I beg you now, Yahweh, bring forth Obadyah."

"Athena, Athena, arise!"

"What is it this time, Adonis? Surely there are no shells left in the sea!"

"The princess summons us. A royal caravan has just departed. Make haste, Athena!"

Athena arose fueled by the same adrenaline which had moved her the last time she petitioned the god of the Hebrews. *Has Yahweh heard me once more?*

The girls locked arms and made their way outside. The King appeared. The courtyard of peasants and servants knelt before Ethbaal. "Arise, all who honor the king," came an unseen voice from amid the crowd.

"Hail Ethbaal Sovereign of Sidon," the people recited.

"Go. Prepare your cakes," the King announced. "Assemble your wares and decorate the streets for Majesty and Glory proceed tomorrow's twilight to Samaria. At the invitation of Omri, King of Israel, we celebrate a treaty of peace!"

The assembly roared.

Hopeful that Yahweh moved people with the ease at which he moved sea creatures, Athena scanned the crowd.

"Athena!" Jezebel interrupted. "Is there something more compelling than our journey to Israel's new capital?"

"No indeed, Breath of Asherah, I could not be more pleased." Athena, knowing she was still in the princess's good graces, risked speaking of herself. "It is just that my stomach aches this morning."

"Go, adjourn to your chambers." Jezebel replied. "I will send my father's physician. You must be fit by tomorrow's dawn to help in the decoration of my carriage."

Athena bowed and proceeded to the basement of the palace. She gazed in frustration at the floor next to her bed, where she had knelt the previous night. *What a fool I have become, that I should fall before a foreign deity and care for the wellbeing of a eunuch!*

The excitement the following day was immeasurable, the town displaying the bustle of a harvest celebration. Jezebel set her litter in the center of the courtyard. Servants ran at the bidding of the King's harem. Sprigs of lavender draped the base of the sedan chair on which would reside the pride of Ethbaal. Attendants strung Nile lilies using mane hair along the poles fastened to either side of the sella. The contrasting yellow and pink honeysuckle exploded in sight and scent as Athena, Adonis, and Aphka danced about in celebration of the court's procession to Israel.

As evening approached, the crowds grew. Spirits were high in anticipation of the appearance of the King and his daughter. Musicians lined the palace entrance. Lyre and flute sounded in continuous melody. The royal procession, thirty carriages, were loaded with food, tents, and supplies, everything needed for the week-long journey from Sidon to Samaria.

When the moment of departure finally arrived, a hush fell over the crowd. Jezebel emerged in a milky gown that flowed to the floor in a cascading waterfall of lace. The scarf acquired at the cake festival draped upon her shoulders. Her royal headdress shone in solid gold, trimmed with Arabian jasmine pedals. Aphka and Adonis were glowing, Athena too felt a sense of pride to be a part of something so magnificent.

All heads bowed in preparation for the entrance of the King. No one dared lift their eyes as Ethbaal moved through the courtyard. Stepping up on his carriage throne, his strongest four eunuchs took their positions. All eyes rose and rested upon the King as the poles came to rest upon the shoulders of the King's slaves, one of whom was Obadyah.

Athena's soul sparked. She stared in the direction of the King, rejoicing in the unchained emotion, her feelings masked by the excitement of the crowd. Then Athena remembered the Hebrew god. Who am I that this god would care for my wishes? Of what value is the desire of my heart?

Athena was sure Obadyah had not seen her, his eyes fixed forward in full attention to his role of transporting the King. Twenty eunuchs per day would bear the King, moving his caravan safely from one palace to the next.

Three hours after leaving the city of Sidon, the caravan stopped. As the long process of making camp began, Athena moved amid the chaos in silent search of Obadyah. She knew she would not be able to speak with him. Should their eyes meet it would expose him to further punishment. Still, Athena continued to search.

As night fell on the camp, Athena returned to her tent.

"Where have you been, Athena?" Aphka demanded. "The king has summoned Adonis!"

"I'm sorry, Aphka! Please, do not alert the princess of my absence."

"I will not speak to her," Aphka said, "but you must do something for me."

"Anything. Please. Say your bidding."

"Go in my stead. Prepare Adonis and allow me to retire."

"Rest, my friend," Athena said, "I will tend to Adonis as well as the princess."

Athena found her way to the King's tent. Adonis lay waiting, unclothed atop Ethbaal's bed. As Athena poured scented oil into her hands, the king appeared. She could see him out of the corner of her eye, watching as she anointed Adonis's body. With each slight movement of her hands, Athena could sense his appetite growing. When Adonis's body glistened with jasmine oil the king succumbed to his desire. Athena departed. She made her way from the King's bed to the boiling pots where fires were glowing.

"Shall I retrieve more water, My Lady?" One of the slave girls asked Athena.

"Tend the fire. I will go," Athena replied. Lifting the empty pottery onto her head, Athena found a stream a short distance from camp. She lowered her pot to the surface of the water and slowly submerged the rim. As she pulled on the spout, a hand came to rest on her shoulder. Startled, Athena dropped her pot and spun around.

"Obadyah!"

"Shh," Obadyah whispered. "Forgive me for startling you, I had hoped my presence would bring you peace."

"Then be encouraged, for peace has found me."

Athena and Obadyah smiled, both eager to speak, both fearful of saying too much.

"You must not continue to look for me, Zoë."

"What happened to you, Obadyah?"

"What happened to me is for me to endure."

"You may quiet my voice, but you cannot dissolve my fear."

"Quiet you? I suspect there is nothing which may quiet you." Obadyah said with a smile.

Unmoved by Obadyah's attempt at distraction, Athena continued, "You spared me the pain of punishment. Must you spare me the knowledge of your punishment as well?"

"Pain is a price, nothing more. I beg you, Zoë, let go of this desire."

Athena paused, startled to hear her birth name rolling so effortlessly off the tongue of this Hebrew.

"Should I let go of my desire for your god as well?" Athena asked, knowing she would win his attention by raising the subject which drew the most passion out of him.

"Oh, how you know temptation, daughter of Eve."

"Do you view my concern for your god insincere?"

"I view your concern shares with it the purpose of keeping me in your presence."

"Do you not wish to be in my presence?"

"What I wish is to not see you suffer because we are determined to share words."

"Then tell me, Obadyah! Tell me what she did to you, and I will release you of the restraining power of my words."

"The price is of no consequence. I shudder only at what drove the price. Your princess did not punish me for our delay, Zoë, but for the depth of my fear."

"What fear?" Athena asked.

"The fear I now carry inside me. The fear of your harm."

Dazed, Athena steadied herself. "Jezebel punished you for protecting me?" she whispered.

"You serve a princess who is cunning and perceptive. I paid the price for what she saw in my eyes, a price I would gladly pay again."

"Perhaps you would choose such a fate. But I will not help you display this courage."

"You think only of my flesh and not of my heart, for I would endure the rape of ten barbarians in trade for the sound of ten words falling from your lips."

Athena's head dropped. She closed her eyes. She reached for her chest as it cinched up with pain. Jezebel had triumphed, taking not just a piece of Obadyah's flesh but another piece of his dignity. Athena succumbed to sadness and fear. But it was the weakness she felt that reminded her, Jezebel always got precisely what she was after.

When Athena finally found the strength to look up, Obadyah was gone.

CHAPTER 7

THE ROAD TO SAMARIA

Energy filled the first morning of the king's journey. Excitement among the people had been growing with each step towards the treaty between Ethbaal and the Hebrew king. Peace was possible for the first time in generations. The marching and resting routine went on for days as the caravan made its way south.

Athena could not keep her eyes from Obadyah. When his rotation came and went, she fought to mask her gaze. Obadyah's glances brushed by her, not pausing for even a moment. He was focused on his duty, as she should be.

When the procession was within a day's journey of the new capital, Jezebel motioned for Athena to join her. Obadyah commanded the lowering of the sella. Athena stepped up and took her place at Jezebel's feet.

"Mistress of wisdom," Jezebel said, "tell me of this Canaanite region."

"Samaria is located in the heart of Israel, My Lady. After reigning for six years in Tirzah, Omri has chosen this watchtower from which to rule his kingdom."

"And what of this king?"

"As you know, My Lady, the famed Hebrew of old, King David, named his son Solomon to the throne. But Solomon was not able to follow his father's example. The Hebrew nation divided after Solomon's death—Judah in the south, Israel in the north. Omri is the sixth king of the Northern Kingdom of Israel."

"How did he win power?"

"As commander of the army of Israel under his predecessor, Omri won many battles, but, more importantly, he won the loyalty of his men.

When the troops heard of the former king's murder, Omri's men rushed to crown him. However, the captain of chariots, a man called Zimri, also had aspirations of ruling Israel, and named himself successor."

"How did Omri vanquish Zimri?"

"Tis quite a story, My Grace. Having received word of Omri's men marching towards Tirzah, Zimi set fire to his palace. He died just seven days after he bid himself king."

"He chose death…by fire?"

"So it seems, My Glory. Burning flesh was preferred to death at Omri's pleasure."

"Omri reigns through fear."

"Yes, My Lady. He has had his share of successful battles. After Zimri's death, a man named Tibni opposed Omri. Though Tibni had loyal followers, Omri would not relinquish the throne. Omri battled with Tibni for four years. It was only at the end of that time that Omri became sole ruler."

"And what of their gods?"

"There are some in Israel who revere Baalshamin."

"The Lord of the Sky?"

"Yes, My Lady, for their images bear the eagle as well as the bolt of lightning."

"And what of Yahweh? Does Omri hold him in high regard?"

"Yahweh maintains status as part of the culture of Omri's people. It is the Southern Kingdom of Judah, however, under King Asa, who continues to pay Him homage. His worship, amid the Northern Kingdom royals, is all but forgotten."

"As to her preferred consort," Jezebel added, "whether Baal or Yahweh, I'm certain Asherah will make her choice."

Athena nodded as she recalled the witch who had prophesied Jezebel's reign in Israel. It was no surprise that Ethbaal would credit Asherah with Jezebel's inception, but Athena could not fathom how Yahweh could factor into Jezebel's future. Israel, a patriarchal people, would find little solace amid the fiercely matriarchal Phoenicians.

Athena gazed up at her mistress. All other sights were considered unworthy distractions, so Athena trained her eyes to focus on the object of her reverence. Each frustration, every emotion, all subtle gestures were to be recognized and celebrated by her vassal of wisdom.

Jezebel glowed, her eyes wide in anticipation of their arrival to Samaria.

Then the caravan lurched to a stop.

Athena's heart jumped.

Jezebel's smile fell. "What is it, slave?" Jezebel barked. "Why do you delay?"

The slave below her said nothing.

"Slave! Face me!" Jezebel demanded.

Still, he did not obey. As quickly as her temper flared, it succumbed to fear. Cresting the hill before them was a Syrian bear. Startled by the approaching footfalls, the carnivore advanced on the caravan. With a roar, it lunged, taking swipes at those who were slow in retreat. The King's Guard grabbed their spears in hopes of downing the beast before it reached the princess. Athena could hear Obadyah speaking to the other men on whose shoulders rested Jezebel and Athena.

"Stand tall!" Obadyah commanded, as the platform shook. The bear clawed its way through Ethbaal's men. Jezebel reached for Athena. The king's warriors arrived just as the last man standing before the princess was tossed aside. The bear reared up on its hind legs. With one final lash, its claw ripped through the air in the direction of Jezebel's litter. The King's guards collapsed on the animal, driving more than a dozen spears into its belly. It roared one last time as its head made contact with the dirt road. The King's attendants ran to the carriage carrying Jezebel and Athena. As they lowered the sella, the girls stepped down. Athena looked in Obadyah's direction. *Why will he not turn?*

"Eunuch! Turn!" Jezebel demanded when she noticed Athena starring in Obadyah's direction.

Obadyah turned. His legs quivered. He grabbed his stomach. Blood poured out from between his fingers.

Athena grabbed her stomach. The bear's final swipe had not found air but flesh.

When the king appeared, his men knelt before him with bloodied spears still in hand.

"Are you well, My Glory?" Ethbaal asked, reaching for his daughter.

"I'm fine, Father."

"Praise Baal," the king said, drawing his daughter into his arms. "We shall make camp here and tend to the wounded," the king said. "Build a perimeter!" Ethbaal commanded. "Surround the camp with torch bearers! And find that bear's cubs!"

Athena swallowed her tears as soldiers led Obadyah away. Athena's fear moved through her like venom. She turned, hoping for a safe place to express the emotions welling up inside her.

When her eyes opened, Athena noticed the bear laying on the ground on her back. She had been nursing, her belly swollen with milk, her nipples pink from her cubs recent suckling. The mother bear was fading but continued to draw small breaths through her nose. Athena walked over and knelt down. She reached out and stroked her head. The straw-colored hair covering her body was thick and coarse. But the fur around her eyes and on her ears was silky. The peaceful moments of imminent death calmed Athena. She mourned for the animal who had only behaved according to her nature. All the care she longed to give Obadyah, she poured out on the creature that may have taken him from her forever. Does Yahweh indeed have power over creation? What is his purpose in driving this mother from her cubs? Why send her out, knowing full well it sealed her fate? And why? Why bring forth Obadyah, only to destroy him again?

Athena allowed her anger to fuel her frustration until she noticed the mother bear's claws, each one longer than the breadth of Athena's palms. They bore the stain of Obadyah's blood. As the bear exhaled for the last time, Athena arose with one determination: never to speak to the Hebrew god again.

CHAPTER 8

THE NEW CAPITAL

Athena found only a few hours of sleep the night of the bear attack. She awoke anxious, unsettled, trapped between worry for Obadyah and bitterness towards Yahweh. Athena guided her feet to the ground, forcing them forward. She felt a weight she could not shed, a burden she knew she would have to set down before she appeared in Jezebel's presence.

As the king's slaves prepared for the final day on the road to Samaria, Jezebel's servants tended to their princess. Aphka painted Jezebel's face, braided her hair, and adorned her ears and eyes with jewels. Athena had just begun praising Jezebel's appearance when Adonis broke through the tent opening, out of breath.

"The cubs have been found!"

Athena's shoulders dropped, her demeanor countering her friend's joy in the destruction of the baby bears.

"The pelts will adorn the palace, Athena," Jezebel said. Her cold gaze fell on Athena. "Though it seems this does not please you."

"Forgive me, My Princess. From the depth of the sea, I beg you. Sleep has escaped me."

"Has discernment escaped you as well? How is it that my servant, gifted in wisdom, has no joy for Asherah's gift?"

"Asherah be praised!" Athena replied, "as she surely has spoken in bringing forth these pelts!"

Athena's words seemed to dampen the flame of Jezebel's anger. She must be more careful. Now soberly alert, Athena could feel her emotions were winning the battle inside her.

The day of their arrival to Samaria, the king's caravan met Omri's soldiers to escort the Phoenician convoy into the city. As the cavalcade began its final ascent to the summit of Samaria, pillars came into view. Cresting the hill of the capital, they passed a stone inscription which read: House of Omri.

The road to Samaria paid homage to the arts—a veneration of Hebrew culture. Lyre and lute bathed in a backdrop of fragrances: jasmine, amber, and musk. Men carried torches, the symbolic pillar-of-fire by night. Women wore white, representing Yahweh's presence in the cloud by day.

All eyes were up, eager for seduction. Though Athena's thoughts hung like a millstone around her neck. But she dared not look down.

Samarian townspeople cheered as the Phoenicians paraded before the palace. A central square tower, four windows in height, was crested with battlements. Each stone cut-out was manned with archers, ready to defend the king of the Northern Kingdom.

A crenel-topped arena faced east. Towards the west, the king's residence. Fifteen stone pillars supported the castle keeps, each ornately carved to match those which lined the city's entrance. Athena was in awe. While the simple unsophisticated charm of her aunt and uncle's home appealed to her, the majesty of the king's palace was captivating.

Athena, Adonis, and Aphka stood behind the princess as the King of Phoenicia presented an ivory treasure chest to the King of Israel. No one missed the camaraderie emerging between the neighboring royals. Athena took it all in, and yet she could not help but remember her uncle's warning: 'Corruption follows opulence like a dog on the scent of a rock badger.'

When she woke the following day, Jezebel summoned her harem. Adonis, Aphka, and Athena skipped into the princess's quarters.

"You glow, My Lady."

"Does she not always shine, Adonis?" Aphka snipped.

"Surely you do, Heaven's Gift," Adonis announced, "and more so this morning with news of the prince."

"Well, Athena?" Jezebel said, "might you enlighten me concerning the Prince of Israel?"

Truth, Athena discovered, was a perplexing thing. It cannot be swallowed whole. Like feeding bread to a child, it must be broken off into small pieces. Truth is sometimes hard to swallow. But if you can get it down, it will sustain you. Lies, on the other hand, are poison. Like a viper bite, lies sting. But it is later, when the viper is gone, that the venom does its damage. Still, Athena knew, there were occasions in this life which demanded venom.

"Aphka speaks the truth, My Morning Song," Athena said. "For I too have heard a word of his intentions."

Adonis and Aphka jumped up and twirled about the room.

"You know this with certainty?" Jezebel asked.

"My ears are open in your service alone, My Lady."

"So your ears would not hear news of the Hebrew slave?" Jezebel asked.

"The Hebrew, My Queen?" Athena replied, steadying her voice.

"Surely you have not forgotten about my eunuch."

"No, My Lady, I mean yes, My Lady." Athena replied. And with that, the game was up. Jezebel needed only one stumble to strike.

"And what of my counselor of wisdom, Aphka, that she cannot find words concerning the slave torn by my father's fur rug?"

Athena's greatest fear, that her emotions would betray Obadyah, was happening before her eyes. Jezebel knew the truth. Obadyah had been protecting Athena. Jezebel had also learned of Obadyah's ethnicity, which meant she asked about him without going through Athena. As the bearer of wisdom, Athena's position with the princess, and her life, were now in peril. She had pledged to ignore Obadyah's god, but thoughts of him remained. She knew the risk of calling on him. She knew he had already let her down. But she could not stop the words from coming. *Yahweh, help me!*

The painful silence was broken suddenly by Adonis. "The bravery of your eunuch before the bear was inspiring, My Lady."

"Yes," Aphka added, "I have never seen such a devotion of a slave to his master."

Adonis and Aphka could not remove Jezebel's suspicions, but they gave Athena the few seconds she needed to think.

"My Lady, do you not have a tale of Hebrew courage with which to tempt the prince at this evening's banquet?"

The tension fed by Jezebel's suspicions lost a bit of its potency. Athena proved herself useful. *Has Obadyah's god come to my aid once again?* Athena felt a moment of appreciation. But as the night wore on, her skepticism grew. Confused and wary, Athena concluded Yahweh's actions to be arbitrary, *unless…unless there is something he wants. But what could she possibly have the Hebrew god would desire?*

Obadyah awoke to a young Hebrew girl tending to his wounds. Obadyah surmised that she had already been speaking for quite some time as he seemed to regain consciousness when she was mid-sentence.

"You must lay still," the small stranger said.

"You must not…" Obadyah paused to grit his teeth. "…give so many commands," he said, wincing in pain.

"Forgive me, Sir," she said, "but I expected a man of your stature to be a bit more, you know, rugged."

"Well, I expected a girl of your stature to be a bit more…" Obadyah paused, holding his breath as ointment ran down his stomach burning his raw flesh.

"Well, I'm waiting," she replied.

"… a bit more mute," Obadyah replied.

"Be strong and courageous, do not tremble or be dismayed for Yahweh is with you," the young girl replied.

"I should need His strength if I am to survive in your care."

"What you need is better judgment."

"If I am going to be expected to endure all these valuable lessons, perhaps you might grant me your name," Obadyah said.

"I am Eliah, daughter of Benjamin, keeper of the palace stables."

"And how is it that I came to be so…" Obadyah paused once more, gnashing his teeth. "…so blessed by the stablekeep's daughter?"

"I'm very good at healing gashes, lacerations, and puncture wounds."

"Wounds on a horse?"

"Of course the wounds of a horse. I am the daughter of Benjamin, keeper of the palace stables."

"Yes, you mentioned that."

"I'm sorry, Sir. You just seem…a little…well, slow."

"I am not a lord. I am just Obadyah."

"Greetings, Obadyah! I am Eliah, daughter of…"

"Daughter of Benjamin, keeper of the palace stables."

"That's correct! Well done," Eliah replied, "I do believe you are going to live."

"I suppose that is good news."

"Good news? It is wonderful news! It was no small task closing your skin. After my father stitched these flaps of skin together with mane hair, I laid across your stomach."

"When did you lay on my stomach?" Obadyah asked.

"Through the night," Eliah replied. "The warmth of my body kept your flesh soft while my weight helped stop the bleeding. My father, Benjamin, keeper of the stables, is quite smart."

"That is something, daughter of Benjamin, on which we can agree."

CHAPTER 9

THE KING'S SON

With no sign of Obadyah, Athena feared the worst. Jezebel did not mention Obadyah's death. It was customary to announce such a significant event among the royal guard, yet Jezebel had said nothing. Was she delaying the announcement only for the joy of revealing his death to the Hebrew prince? That certainly would make for a dramatic ending to her tale were Jezebel's slave to lose his life in the protection of his prized princess.

King Omri's dining table stretched the length of the banquet room. It was an exquisite piece, planed olive wood wrapped with ornate carvings of grapes, figs, and honeycomb. Stone-carved statues rose from the table's base. The statue's icon was revealed in the scale-covered headdress and tassel-adorned copulatory organ. The Canaanite fertility god. Both the head and the feet were removed from the idol so that his torso alone served as pedestals.

As Jezebel and her ladies were led in, Jezebel leaned back and whispered in Athena's ear. "Why is that deity missing his head and feet?"

"I have heard this tale, My Lady, concerning the Levantine god Dagon," Athena whispered, "The Hebrews entered our land with an enchantment box."

"A coffer?"

"A treasury, my Lady, of the law given by Moses, the Egyptian. When they brought the box before the temple in Ashdod, Dagon fell. It is said the deity's head and feet broke off in submission to Yahweh."

"The god of the Hebrews is vying for Asherah's hand."

"As the prince of the Hebrews is vying for yours, My Lady." Athena's dread eased as contentment glistened her mistress's face.

Jezebel and her harem circled the room. Led to the center of the table, they remained standing for the arrival of the ally kings. A pageant of royalty ensued as King Ethbaal and King Omri paraded around the banquet, harps and cymbals lauding their procession.

Arriving at the bolsters located at either end of the table, Omri spoke. "For the peace of reigning kings," he said, raising his goblet toward the King of Sidon.

The king's advisors and cabinet nodded in approval.

"For the gods who ensure our favor," the king continued, spreading his arms wide. "For the beauty both prevalent and prevailing," he continued motioning towards Jezebel.

Jezebel held her head a bit higher, her expression one of practiced serenity and arrogance.

"And lastly, for my son, Ahab, the glory of Israel."

Everyone raised their goblets.

Ahab entered with fanfare from the royal musicians. The richness of his princely attire added several years to Ahab's youthful face. Sated by the warmth of honor, the young sovereign found his seat across from the princess. His eyes ticked up and found Jezebel's.

The dining guests settled into conversations. An awkward silence ensued between Jezebel and Ahab.

Jezebel, the more poised of the pair, was the first to engage her counterpart. "Does your culture frown upon women speaking?" Jezebel asked as she leaned back.

"It depends on the woman's words," Ahab replied.

Jezebel nodded, allowing a bit of silence to initiate a contest of confidence.

Ahab yielded. "Were she to adorn a prince with poetic praises, her words would be as welcome as the sunrise."

"And what if her words spoke of her own glory?"

"What words could soar higher than her beauty?"

"Beauty moves bed linens. Words move hearts."

"Then, I shall choose my words carefully, my enchanted guest, for the woman moved by words sits before a man inspired by beauty."

Even as the other guests engaged in their separate conversations, they did not miss the exchange between the two young royals. It was clear to all in attendance that what began as the uniting of kings would end in the uniting of nations.

Jezebel turned to exchange words with her harem.

"When will you reveal your tale, My Lady? My heart aches in anticipation," Adonis said.

"My heart as well," Aphka added. "Please, My Lady, put an end to our suffering."

"You will have your heart's desire. But the prince must first plead for the words he claims he does not need."

"But how, My Lady?" Aphka asked.

"Athena, tell me," Jezebel commanded, "how shall I lure the prince?"

"The prince has yielded to you, My Lady. Your beauty has captured him."

"I care not whether he permits my words!" Jezebel scolded. "He must crave them, lust for them, beg to hear my voice!"

"My Lady," Athena said, "the carvings on the table's edge depict the enchanted box of Yahweh. Ask him of its power, and you will lead him to seek your tale."

Jezebel cast her eyes on the prince. "Tell me, wise prince, of this enchanted box which adorns your father's table."

"You are attentive to the relics of my people."

"I am attentive to elegance," Jezebel replied.

Ahab nodded, raising his glass to Jezebel. "What do you know of Israel's history?"

"I know of the reputation of the Hebrew source of power," Jezebel replied.

"What you speak of we call the Ark of God. Yahweh's Ark delivered us to this land of promise."

"Some say a golden calf led you."

"Indeed," Ahab replied. "My predecessor, Jeroboam, the first King of the Northern Kingdom, determined that we place a golden calf in Bethel and Dan."

"Do your people not consider these false gods?" Jezebel inquired.

"I honor the gods who honor me. I extend my worship to he who expands my kingdom."

"Or perhaps she who expands your kingdom?"

Ahab smiled, sipped his wine, and then continued, "A woman once led my people. She came to rule by the power of her wisdom."

"I'm impressed," Jezebel replied. "Your heroes and heroines are intriguing."

"Reveal your curiosities, My Lady, for I am well-versed in the antiquity of my people."

"You are acquainted, then, with the tale of the Hebrew and the Lavender Princess," Jezebel said.

Ahab's face betrayed his ignorance. "Neither father nor sage has informed me of this parable."

"I cannot imagine since it concerns the princess sitting before you."

"I must entreat you for this hidden story of my people."

"Perhaps, dear prince, when you visit Sidon," Jezebel lured, "I may reward you at your journey's end."

The prince grinned.

Athena pitied him. He had taken Jezebel's bait, as many before him also had. Jezebel even allowed him to recognize the trap so that he would feel empowered, while she maintained control of his desires. But his confidence was an illusion.

"Surely the sound of my voice is sufficient to earn the rights to this story," Ahab replied.

"Your voice compels me, yet it comes and it goes as the passing winds."

"Surely my face, then. Are these features not worthy of your words?"

"Your face is sweet as honey but easily consumed in a moment."

"Surely, the power in my arms and legs demonstrate my worthiness."

"Worthiness is not the key to unlocking the tale."

"Very well," Ahab submitted, "I bow in defeat. For to live another moment without your words may cost me my sanity and, without any doubt, my heart. With the words you crave, I beg thee, share your story that I might find peace."

Just like the walls of Jericho, Ahab fell. His connection to who he was before Jezebel now forever lost. A sadness overwhelmed Athena that she had not anticipated.

"There once was a Hebrew boy," Jezebel began, "whose beauty turned heads. So handsome was this son of Jacob that his features threatened royalty. He came, by Asherah's providence, under his King's rule. The prized youth was sterilized at the king's command and gifted to his beloved daughter. Having proven his strength of mind and body, the Hebrew was granted a position on the princess's litter."

Ahab listened. At each of Jezebel's breaths, he drew closer.

"This princess journeyed to a neighboring king's land," she continued. "Merely a day from their destination, the Hebrew slave, of whom I speak, came to a sudden stop. It was not the marching of feet that caught his ears, nor was it the sound of clashing swords that halted the king's eunuch. It was the howl of a beast, thundering like the rushing headwaters of the Jordan. Without warning, a towering frame of gray fur crested the hill before them. Slicing her way through the line of servants, a massive bear, taller than any man, came within striking distance of the Sidonian princess. The fearless Hebrew did not flinch in the face of death, commanding his fellow porters to stand their ground."

"This slave chose his words well." Ahab winked.

"Indeed. But by more than words did this eunuch prevail."

"He could not have fought the beast!" Ahab replied.

"As David stood before Goliath, so my slave stood, unmoved, even as the creature tore through his flesh. Opening his abdomen with a single swipe of its claw, the eunuch's blood ran. But he did not."

"An epic tale of a beauty and a beast," Ahab remarked, raising his glass.

"One life given, one life taken, one life spared," Jezebel said, motioning to her father's servant standing behind Ahab. When Ahab turned, Obadyah entered the room and made his way towards them. With his head down, he took a knee before the prince of Israel.

"The Hebrew who faced the marauding bear on the road to Samaria," Jezebel announced.

"What is your name, brother?" Ahab asked.

"Slave of Ethbaal: Ruler of the Sidon, King of the Great Sea."

"It is a distinguished title. But what did your Hebrew family call you?"

"Obadyah, My Lord."

"Obadyah? Servant of Yahweh?"

"As you say, My Lord."

"And now you have been chosen to protect the princess."

"Call upon me in the day of trouble," Obadyah said, "and I shall rescue you."

"You speak with courage," Ahab replied.

"I speak the words of King David." Obadyah bowed, stretching out his hand towards the prince of Israel.

Ahab's eyes found Obadyah's palm.

"A gift for your invitation," Jezebel said.

Ahab reached for a leather cord curled up in the center of Obadyah's hand.

"A claw of the bear!" Ahab said. He dangled the bear's nail before his eyes. "The dried blood of her strike remains!" Ahab said.

Jezebel beamed.

CHAPTER 10

THE HEART'S MIND

Athena cherished the sisterhood that naturally developed between the girls of the king's harem, but too often thoughts of the others saddened her. Removed from their homes at an early age, the three female slaves to the royal court had only one another. And yet, it was not long before jealousy surfaced as Jezebel routinely elevated one servant above the others. Fanning the flame of rivalry, Jezebel would beckon one girl away to gain information on the other two. In so doing, she remained secure that the girls' commitment to each other would never surpass their loyalty to her. Working the reigns of her harem was one of Jezebel's favorite games.

Though Adonis spent many nights in the King's chamber, she was the most innocent of the princess's harem. Removed from her family on her tenth birthday, Adonis was the King's favorite from her first day in court. One night, before the girls fell asleep, Adonis told the story of the day Ethbaal chose her.

Family and friends had made a trip to the shores of the Great Sea. As children ran in and out of the tumbling waves, Adonis sat alone. Engaged in the details of her sand castle, Adonis missed the announcement of the passing procession.

As Ethbaal approached, the King caught sight of Adonis. While the rest of the beach bowed, Adonis continued to work. Ethbaal paused, transfixed by the thoughtful and dutiful way Adonis attended to her design. With each movement of her hand through the sand, Ethbaal's desire rose, his eyes no longer looking but longing. It was not until one of the King's guards stepped into her moat that Adonis even paused. When she finally looked up she was gazing into the face of the Phoenician King.

"What are you building?" Ethbaal asked.

"A castle." Adonis replied, "This is the tower, and these are the gates, and this is, well, this was the moat," Adonis scowled.

"Apologize to this beautiful young lady for damaging her moat!" the King demanded.

"My deepest regret," the soldier bowed, "please forgive me."

Ignoring the man's apology, Adonis turned her attention back to her sand castle. "This one is just sand," she said, "But one day, I will live in a real castle."

"Is that so?" Ethbaal replied, "And were I to grant you your heart's desire, would you give such notice and regard to the needs of your king?"

"Oh yes, My Lord!"

"Well, then, I am pleased to grant you your wish."

Adonis abandoned her sand castle and ran towards her parents.

"Be faithful to your king, My Dear," her father said, giving his daughter his parting instructions.

"The gods have smiled on us this day," Adonis's mother said, "granting you, granting us all, our greatest desire. Go now. Go to the pleasure and prosperity of your king!"

As Adonis's mother released her daughter's hand, she waved one last time and then ran to join the King's caravan. Taking Adonis by the hand, Ethbaal strode away with the satisfaction of a great hunter.

Adonis was easy to like. She had not an ounce of ego. Blissfully ignorant, Adonis appeared unaware of Aphka's jealousy or Jezebel's mocking. What Adonis lacked in sophistication, however, she made up for in simple joy. There were days Aphka hated her, the way all females hate each other when one gains the attention of a handsome or powerful male. At other times, Aphka seemed to pity Adonis. And while she portrayed a disgust with Adonis's role as the King's mistress, she craved it all the same.

Being more astute, Aphka was less trustworthy. She would not share with her counterparts the story of her ascent to the castle. Instead, she maintained a cool defensiveness, never overtly unkind but not outwardly charitable either. Where Adonis couldn't think fast enough to manipulate circumstances in her favor, everything with Aphka was a negotiation ending with her vying for own best interests.

Athena's heart often suffered for Adonis. Everyone knew it was a privilege to be petitioned by the King. Athena recalled the sweet fragrance of the oil when she had adorned Adonis for her night with Ethbaal. But it seemed to her less like the arrangement of a bouquet and more like the preparation of a meal. She often felt as though she were flavoring and tenderizing meat—a menu of flesh for him to gorge himself on and then discard—the evidence of his gluttony removed from his sight.

Though Athena was gifted with knowledge, she had no understanding of this desire for flesh. She could see the allure of feeding momentary cravings. As a path towards claiming privilege or manipulating and controlling, that part of desire was clear. She saw the same in the behavior of the gods—power used to fulfill one's desires regardless of the cost to others.

Upon their return to the castle at Sidon, Jezebel called for Athena. "What new insight have you found concerning the young prince of the Northern Kingdom?"

Athena, longing to be outside the castle gates, saw an opportunity and took a chance. "Permit me, I petition thee," Athena replied, "to acquire new information from beyond these walls."

"Is this castle estate too isolated for you, Athena?"

"The same walls that protect us from harm, My Grace, protect us from certain truths as well. Should you be fulfilled with the knowledge bound by walls, I surely possess all that you need. I do wonder, My Sovereign, if a more unbridled word might better meet your desire."

Jezebel, always hungry for gossip, conceded. "Very well, Athena, journey beyond our walls for that which alludes you concerning the house of Omri."

"I shall not disappoint you, Favored One," Athena promised.

As Athena bowed in retreat, Jezebel grabbed her arm. "Of course, you must take my eunuch with you for your protection."

Athena met Jezebel's eyes. "I will be content to travel alone, My Lady," she said, her voice dim.

"A servant of Phoenician royalty? Alone outside the palace walls? You will leave these gates alone," Jezebel said, "the day I bid you farewell."

Athena bowed, "Your wisdom surely exceeds mine, My Grace."

"Heed this warning," Jezebel said, "should daylight fall before your return, my gates will be to you forever closed!"

"As they should, My Lady." Athena nodded.

The following morning Athena stood inside the castle gates, waiting for her escort. She closed her eyes. Not in prayer, of course. And surely not to petition Yahweh, but only to cope with her inner turmoil. Please, don't let it be Obadyah. Jezebel had already shown signs of anger and worse jealousy.

Please don't let it be Obadyah. I'm not ready to see him. What would I say? She told herself not to wish for his presence. But when she listened, her heart was clear. Oh, to hear his voice, to be within his reach.

"Are you ready to proceed, My Lady?" It was the voice Athena longed for and feared.

"Good morning, Obadyah."

"Good morning, Zoë."

Athena stirred at the sound of her real name. It was a name she had set down, that she had walked away from. It was the name she had associated with poverty, yet now, somehow, it felt valuable.

"We have been allotted from now until the sun's retreat to secure new information for the princess."

"Where you lead, I will follow," Obadyah replied.

Zoë sighed. The weight of her fear was heavier than the castle doors. What I would give if these gates could be forever closed, Jezebel on one side, me on the other.

CHAPTER 11

THE HIDDEN MISSION

"Papa Kalbu! Papa Kalbu!" Athena said, rapping on her aunt and uncle's door.

Obadyah, a protective yet respectful distance away, watched as the door, such as it was, gave way. Far from sturdy nor the least bit protective from intruders, the door swung at an odd angle when it was opened. Barely clinging to the structure of the house, it displayed all the signs of being assembled by a blind man.

"It's Zoë!" Kalbu said, moistening his wife's face with his announcement.

Donatiya grimaced and wiped her husband's spittle off her face with the back of her hand. "Yes, I know, you lumpy old toad, I'm the one who can see, remember."

"Oh, yes," Kalbu replied, turning his attention towards his niece. "Come in, come in," Kalbu said, pulling on the door just as Obadyah attempted to follow Athena inside.

"Donatiya!" Kalbu yelled, "the door is stuck!"

"No, it's not, you crusty dry bread, you are closing the door on Obadyah!"

"Many pardons, my friend," Kalbu said, reaching for Obadyah. "Please, come in."

Obadyah had just made contact with the stool offered to him when Kalbu grabbed Obadyah's face in both hands. Obadyah pulled away instinctively, but Kalbu's grasp was surprisingly strong. Kalbu worked him over like a lump of clay.

"How are you healing up, lad?" Donatiya asked.

"Well, thank you," Obadyah mumbled through Kalbu's fingers.

"Papa," Athena interrupted, "A bear attacked Obadyah on our journey to Samaria."

"A Syrian bear?" Kalbu asked.

"Well, it surely wasn't a Hebrew bear!" Donatiya interjected.

Unphased by the relationship drama of her beloved aunt and uncle, Athena continued. "The bear tore through the skin of his stomach."

Kalbu moved his hands from Obadyah's face to his belly.

"Lean back, my boy, let me get a look at your scars."

Obadyah obeyed without hesitation. Catching a glimpse of Athena's smile, Obadyah shrugged, unwilling and unable to resist Kalbu's endearing attention.

"What are you doing here?" Donatiya asked. "The princess hasn't dismissed you, has she?"

"Dismissed us for just this day. We are here on a mission for the crown."

At that, Donatiya jabbed her husband in the arm, pulling his attention away from Obadyah's injuries.

"What mission, dear?"

"As you know, we've just returned from the capital of Israel. Prince Ahab of the Northern Kingdom will ask Jezebel for her hand. Ethbaal will give her to him as he seeks Israel both as a military ally and trade partner. Jezebel seems agreeable to their union, yet she fears losing the power she currently possesses. Is there anything you can tell me which might please the princess? Anything which might entice her?"

"You know more than we do about the Hebrew immigrants," Donatiya replied. "What does the princess seek beyond your wisdom?"

"She seeks something scandalous!" Kalbu said, raising his eyebrows in rhythm with his smile.

"Your uncle's mind is dirtier than the earth beneath his feet," Donatiya said. "Well, go ahead," she continued, "ask him. His eyes have gone out, but his ears work fine."

"What have you heard, Papa?"

"If Ahab wants Jezebel, he will have her," Kalbu began. "It is said he cries and moans, even feigns illness, to move his father's hand in fulfillment of his desires. He may look like a growing young man, but he is quite an infant."

Obadyah laughed, turning all eyes in his direction.

"Obadyah," Donatiya said, "is not your mother Hebrew?"

"Indeed, as am I, though I claim no pride towards my mother's people."

The captivated threesome stared in silence at the half-Hebrew slave in their midst.

"If you have no allegiance to your people, why worship their god?" Athena asked, allowing her curiosity to push its way past the task at hand.

"I am Hebrew not because my mother has chosen Yahweh, but because Yahweh has chosen her." The Phoenecian family continued to stare in unison at their guest. Obadyah met each of their eyes and then continued. "Aunt Donatiya?" Obadyah replied, "why did you bring out honey cakes when we entered your home?"

"They are Zoë's favorites."

"And why present her with her favorites?"

Donatiya smiled as her eyes fell onto the girl she'd raised. "Because she is dear to us," Donatiya replied.

"It is for that very reason we offer Yahweh our obedience. The Law is not a pledge. It is a privilege. We do that which pleases Yahweh, not to manipulate circumstances in our favor, but as a token of our love."

"He called me 'Aunt!'" Donatiya whispered in Athena's ear.

"Why do Sidonians pay tribute to Asherah?" Obadyah asked.

"To receive her blessing!" Kalbu shouted as though the right answer might win him a prize.

"So she is like an employer who pays her workers for their service?" Obadyah asked.

"I suppose so," Athena replied, "however, what pleases her one day may not gain her favor the next."

"Well, she is a woman," Kalbu added, attempting, and failing, to direct his grin towards his wife.

"So the gods behave less like landlords and more like embittered lovers," Obadyah replied.

"The gods are emotional and unpredictable. That is how we know it is Asherah who reigns over Baal," Kalbu added, bracing himself for his wife's jab.

"Does Yahweh not desire his people's worship?" Athena asked.

"Of course He does. But I do not worship Him to gain His favor. I worship Yahweh to give my love. Tell me," Obadyah continued, "should the Canaanites reject Baal, what would you expect to be Baal's response?"

"Baal blesses those who please him, and he curses those who anger him," Athena replied.

"Yahweh is faithful to the covenant he made with my forefathers regardless of our faithfulness to Him."

"Yahweh has bound Himself to a people who reject Him?" Athena asked.

"Perhaps this seems curious. But this I know, it is far more foolish to honor a god who is bitter and selfish than to honor the God who keeps His word."

"I have heard the Hebrew God speaks through his diviners whom you call prophets," Athena said. "Is your mother a prophetess?"

"She is an engraver of psalms. She does not speak the words of Yahweh. She preserves them. She has fifteen precious scrolls."

"She is a musician?" Kalbu asked.

"No," Obadyah laughed. "My mother descends from Ethan the Ezrahite. He was a wiseman who served in Solomon's court."

"Like Zoë!" Kalbu replied.

"Yes," Obadyah smiled, and turned to Zoë. "Just like Zoë."

"You say, 'we' about your worship," Athena said, "but I do not think the Hebrews see Yahweh as you do."

"Indeed, most do not. Hebrews treat Yahweh the same way the Phoenicians view Baal."

"I know how Jezebel will find security in her union with Ahab!" Kalbu interrupted. "Come with me, Son. You must help me load my wagon." Obadyah obeyed, having no clue what Zoë's papa was planning. When the boys were out of sight, Donatiya grabbed Zoë's hand.

"How keen are Jezebel's eyes towards yours?"

"Keen?" Athena asked, knowing deep down that attempting to veil her confusion with Donatiya was pointless. She could no more deceive her aunt than she could deceive herself. If there was one thing Athena had learned growing up, the best thing to do is to confess—and the sooner, the better. "She is quite keen, I'm afraid."

"Have you considered the possibility she has had you followed?" Athena felt a burn in her chest. She lowered her head, knowing she could not undo her actions. "I'm sorry."

"Sorry?"

"I'm sorry for my selfishness. I came here for help and, and, I'm so sorry, I'm just not thinking clearly."

"We will always open our door when you knock, no matter the cost. Well, we will try to open it, anyway." Donatiya smirked.

The lightheartedness of her aunt brought a smile to Athena's face even while the weight of her guilt remained.

"I was heading out this afternoon to sell my pots," Kalbu said, entering the room.

"And...?" Donatiya replied to her husband.

"And…I can hide Athena and Obadyah in my wagon and bring them to Obadyah's mother."

"It is an interesting idea," Obadyah said.

"Papa," Athena replied, "you cannot pull my weight, let alone me and Obadyah."

"I know, I know," Kalbu replied, "but we have made some improvements around here since you left."

"What improvements?" Athena asked.

"Yes, what improvements?" Donatiya added.

Kalbu leaned his head out of the hut window and whistled. Athena and Obadyah saw nothing. He whistled again. And again, nothing appeared.

"Just wait, my girl, just wait," Donatiya said. When she realized her husband's plan, she hurried to their cupboard and began pulling pottery off the shelf.

"Where does your mother live, son?" Kalbu asked.

"Her house is on the northwest side of town. Across the spring halfway up the hill that faces the sea."

"Papa, that's too far," Athena said.

"It would be too much for me," Kalbu admitted, "but your auntie can handle it!"

Athena's and Obadyah's heads swung to Donatiya.

"Your uncle thinks himself a jester," Donatiya replied.

"The best blind jester in town!" Kalbu added.

"I must remain," Donatiya said, "to give the illusion you are still here visiting me. Papa will walk you to Obadyah's mother's home. He will be fine with the help of his new friend." Just then, they heard a knock. "You had better let her in," Donatiya said, "or she's going to kick the door down again."

"There she is," Kalbu said as a creature resembling a donkey poked her nose through the newly expanded front door. "This will be easy work for Palmsquat!"

Kalbu waited for his patchy friend to squeeze through the doorway. The dusty animal with oversized ears and undersized legs hobbled past the dining table. Kalbu reached for the creature's tail as it passed. Grabbing a hold, the animal led him through the kitchen and out the back.

Growing up on the coast of the Mediterranean, Obadyah knew there was a difference between life in the village and life on the bluff. But now, he realized, he could not have imagined how different.

"Go," Donatiya said, motioning for Obadyah and Athena to follow

Palmsquat behind the hut.

Donatiya sat next to the front window pretending to be in the midst of conversation as Athena and Obadyah climbed into Kalbu's wagon. He threw a tarpaulin over them and placed several pieces of pottery on top. As Kalbu led his donkey and buggy around the house past the front window, Donatiya yelled out to him.

"Don't forget to bring back some fresh fish for our guests."

Kalbu walked alongside Palmsquat, leading him up the street as was their habit. He kept his head down, listening for what might be a follower's footsteps.

Athena and Obadyah lay motionless under the covering on Kalbu's supply wagon. They were careful not to speak. But Obadyah's mind raced with questions, things he did not know that he did not know. Questions of culture, customs and heredity. Twenty minutes into their ride, Obadyah could no longer keep quiet. "What in the world is a Palmsquat?"

CHAPTER 12

THE PSALM KEEPER

Obadyah's mother lived north of the village on the highest plateau of the tallest hill facing the Mediterranean. Obadyah had been attentive on their journey to not brush against Athena though they lay only inches apart. When Palmsquat's pace slowed as she met her last ascent, Obadyah reached for Athena, "We are almost there," he said, allowing his hand to linger on hers.

As cart and donkey came to a halt, Athena and Obadyah could hear Kalbu yelling. "I have a delivery for the lady of the house."

Moments later, they heard a man's voice. "Wait here, please."

"Tell her I have psalm pots!" Kalbu yelled.

After a few minutes, Obadyah could hear the voice of his mother. "To what do you refer with these 'psalm pots'?"

"Good afternoon, My Lady. My name is Kalbu. I am a resident of the village of Zarephath. A servant of the King has informed me this day of your interest in storage containers for your Hebrew script." The woman moved her head to the side to get a look at the wagon behind Kalbu.

"Bring your goods around to the back," she replied.

Kalbu kept one hand on Palmsquat as they made their way behind the house. Kalbu paused just before they rounded the corner. His face caught the wind. His mind still craved what his eyes could not see—the cool, salty breeze which linked his senses to his memories of the shore.

The wagon fit behind the house with little room to spare as the hill continued its ascent, rising sharply beyond the residence.

"You are safe," Obadyah's mother said.

As Obadyah sat up, the thick wool covering fell off, revealing himself and a female stowaway.

"Son."

"Mother," Obadyah replied, pushing pieces of pottery aside. "Mother, this is Zoë. And this is her uncle, Kalbu."

"And this is Palmsquat," Kalbu added, the animal's ears perking up at the mention of his name.

"Welcome to my home. I am Samara. And this is my servant Nimshi. Kalbu, Zoë, please allow Nimshi to show you inside. He will bring you wine and dates and will help remove the dust from your journey."

Obadyah extended his hand to Athena, helping her down from the wagon. Nimshi motioned towards the rear entryway of Samara's home. Athena took her uncle's arm, and they followed Nimshi inside.

Obadyah sat down on the back edge of the wagon.

"Please tell me you have not abandoned the king," Samara said.

"I have not abandoned the king," Obadyah replied.

"I am listening."

"Zoë is Athena."

"Oh, Son," Samara said, her head falling under the weight of her son's admission. "You tread on treacherous ground," she continued, finding the strength to meet her son's eyes.

"I know, Mother." Obadyah admitted, his voice soft. Though the head of the king's security in his daily life, now, in the presence of his mother he felt as if he were still a small boy, sitting at her knee, looking for her approval. No longer a dominating presence, simply a baby bird longing for his mother's protective wings.

"You know? And yet I find you concealed with the King's harem in this poor man's wagon."

"We have come on a mission for the princess."

"It is not the princess's mission which has you hidden with her lady."

"We suspected Jezebel ordered us followed."

"That much is clear. What is unclear is why the princess would have you followed on a mission she has ordained. Surely it is not for security purposes as I assume that is your role."

"It is…but…it's complicated."

"Complicated? You mean reckless."

"It was Zoë's idea to…"

"No, Son," Samara interrupted. "It was Athena's idea."

Obadyah broke his mother's gaze. He could not look in her eyes. He was still her son. He needed her to understand, to feel with him the things he could not help but feel. But how could he make her understand what he didn't understand? "Things are happening here even your wisdom cannot discern."

"Perhaps, but what concerns me are the things I am discerning."

Obadyah jumped down from the carriage and began pacing. "Where is Father?"

"You know where he is."

Obadyah raked his fingers through his hair and began rubbing the back of his neck. He turned to face his mother. He had seen her in the distance when out with the king. But he had not looked into her eyes since his castration. "My fate is sealed."

"Only death seals fate."

"Is that meant to inspire me? A life of being used by gods and kings?"

"Gods? Does idolatry appeal to you now?"

"Nothing appeals to me, Mother."

"Your emotions are crippling your reason, Son."

"Must you do that?" Obadyah said, raising his voice. "Must you always philosophize your way to victory? Could I not have one peaceful conversation with my mother?"

"He who loves Yahweh's law has great peace, and nothing causes them to stumble."

"And do you think I have forgotten the truth? I wake to the truth. I walk in the truth. I close my eyes to the truth of who I am every night!"

"And who are you? Are you not my son? Are you not a follower of Yahweh?"

Obadyah dropped his hands to his sides, "How can I be a man of God if I am not even a man?"

"Obadyah, your heart has not been stolen from you. Do you not feel the pulse of it surging through your body?"

"A heart is made for more than the pumping of blood," Obadyah whispered.

"I know, my son, for it is your heart which has brought you here today."

Obadyah stood quiet as he often was before his mother. Though he longed for her encouragement, he knew too well she would never allow motherly love to prevail over sound wisdom.

"You know better than to sneak around Phoenicia with Jezebel's maiden," she said. "Only a heart fully alive can overcome reason."

"My heart still beats in my chest, but for what reason, I do not know."

"Yahweh knows."

"Perhaps, but when will Yahweh tell me?"

"Believe in your purpose, Son. It will give you hope. Discover your purpose as each day unfolds. Allow the mystery of Yahweh's will to sustain you."

Obadyah turned his back to his mother. Samara placed her hand on his shoulder, turning her son back towards her.

"Speaking of mystery," Samara said, "what exactly is a Palmsquat?"

"I think it's a donkey," Obadyah replied. A smile crept onto his face.

Obadyah watched as his mother gave the beast a good look over. As the question of Palmsquat's heredity lingered, the donkey-type creature suddenly sat, dropping her rear to the ground like a weathered dog. Obadyah and Samara laughed.

"Let us go inside," Samara said, "and speak with our guests."

CHAPTER 13

THE TREASURE OF SOLOMON

"This place is grand!" Kalbu said, running his fingers over walls and furniture.

"Thank you, kind sir," Samara nodded. She turned her attention to Athena. "My son tells me you require information."

"Yes, My Lady, we've come to you for your insight into the reigning dynasty of Israel."

"So the princess of Sidon will become the queen of Israel."

"Yes, it seems so," Athena replied.

"Two kingdoms and two kings bending their will to Jezebel's desires."

"Yes, it seems so."

"She has positioned herself well," Samara said. "What more does she seek?"

"More is precisely what she seeks, as contentment eludes those whose every wish is granted."

"Well said, young Athena."

Athena bowed. "Obadyah calls you a keeper of Psalms."

Samara stiffened.

"Of what psalms does he speak?" Athena asked.

"Nimshi," Samara said, "take Kalbu to the kitchen and help him prepare a meal for his…for his…companion."

"Palmsquat," Kalbu interjected.

"Yes, his Palmsquat," Samara replied.

Nimshi nodded, taking Kalbu by the arm.

Samara returned her attention to Athena. "I am a keeper of the psalms of David."

"The giant slayer?" Athena asked, recalling the tale often told by the Hebrew immigrants. Like all the gods' tales, a battle was won, a king was favored, and a competing god humiliated. As thrilling as the story was, it seemed to Athena no different than other god lore repeated for generations.

"You know Hebrew history," Samara said.

"My aunt and uncle sent me to a school where I was trained in the arts, deistic legend, and language. The seers told me David's son received the queen of Sheba."

"Solomon. Yes. My forefather served King Solomon."

"There is a rumor that Solomon's wisdom surpassed all of those who dwell beyond the Red Sea."

"Would you like to hear the testimony of the Arabian queen?"

Athena's eyes brightened.

"Son," Samara beckoned, "retrieve the scroll in the vase by the front entrance."

Obadyah did as requested.

When he returned Obadyah opened the scroll and read, "Blessed be Yahweh your God who delighted in you to set you on the throne of Israel; because Yahweh loved Israel forever, therefore he made you king, to do justice and righteousness."

"If Yahweh requires his kings to be just," Athena said, "I'm afraid… well what I'm trying to say is…it seems as though Omri…" Athena paused, not wanting to offend her host on whom she depended for information.

"Omri's reign is not as Solomon's," Samara said, finishing Athena's thought for her.

"Yes, My Lady," Athena replied.

"Omri is concerned with enforcing his sovereignty and expanding his kingdom," Samara added.

"This is Ethbaal's objective as well," Athena added.

"This is the goal of all earthly kings," Samara said. "But Yahweh has given us a greater purpose—to do justice and to love mercy and to walk humbly with our God."

Athena recognized the conflict inside Samara. It was the same wrestling she saw in Obadyah. They watch their god be defeated and continue to trust Him. Athena could not fathom worshiping a god who would not force kings to do His will.

Kalbu returned with Nimshi in tow. Athena glanced up just in time to see him brush past a vase and knock it from its pedestal.

Athena gasped as did Nimshi.

Samara turned to see what the commotion was about.

By some miracle, Kalbu caught the vase. He held it up, as if he had meant to examine it. Running his fingers over it he said, "This is a really nice piece of pottery."

Athena found Obadyah's gaze. She rolled her eyes, suppressing a giggle.

"I earn a living in the pottery trade," Samara replied.

"Me too!" Kalbu smiled, "but I only sell in the market down by the docks."

"I saw your pieces in your wagon. You are quite skilled."

"Not too bad for a half-blind old man," Kalbu grinned.

"Not bad at all," Samara agreed. "I was wondering if I might order a few pots."

Kalbu sputtered. "Oh…well…my pots are for common use, my Lady. With my failing eyes I… ."

"Wonderful!" Samara interrupted. "I need such useful vessels to be included in my shipments to Egypt."

"My uncle is very creative. He has made an ointment that seals wounds," Athena said, motioning towards Obadyah's scars.

"Have you used this sealing cream on earthen jars?" Samara asked, giving no attention to her son's wounds.

"No, My Lady," Kalbu said, looking confused.

"Do you think it might repel water?"

Kalbu smiled. "I don't know why it wouldn't."

"Interesting," Samara replied.

"Pottery and ointments aside," Obadyah interrupted, "we do still have a mission before us. And the sun has turned towards the horizon."

"Ah, yes, Jezebel," Samara said. "I have a story which may please your princess. It is a tale of hidden treasure told me by my father."

All eyes rested on Samara.

"It is well known," Samara began, "that the king of Israel possessed such treasures as the Ark of Yahweh and the Vestment of the High Priest. The king also had musical instruments made of gold and a great throne of ivory overlaid with gold. But few know of his trophies of war. Spoils that Solomon had hidden. Trophies lost to the annals of time. Items that would be most enticing to the appetite of Jezebel. The one I speak of was written in the scrolls my father passed onto me." Samara paused. "A lost treasure of 300 solid gold shields."

Silence filled the room. Samara's secrets were captivating, even to Obadyah.

"The scrolls speak in detail of Solomon's great wealth, and of these shields, but most Hebrews know only of that which has been preserved in Jerusalem. Solomon commissioned the construction of 300 shields, using three minas of gold on each shield! He hid the shields in a secret location away from the castle, at a place my father called, The Gateway to Solomon's Gold. However, to this day, the scroll has not been found. But this fact I can tell you," Samara said, "King Solomon built a fleet of ships near Eloth on the shore of the Red Sea, in the land of Edom. The famed sailor, Hiram the Phoenician, sent his slaves, along with Solomon's servants, to the king's storehouse. Where they anchored has remained a mystery."

"Until now!" Kalbu jumped in, proud to have beaten the others to the story's end.

"Indeed," Samara smiled. "For I know, by my father's testimony, the crew went ashore at the port of Ophir."

"Thank you, My Lady," Athena replied, "Your words will be my salvation."

"We must head back if we are to make it to the palace gates before sundown," Obadyah said. He took Kalbu's arm and led him to the back courtyard.

Nimshi followed, leaving Athena alone with Samara.

"I cannot find the words to thank you," Athena said, embracing Samara.

"I am pleased to have been of service to you," Samara replied.

Samara and Athena returned to the courtyard. The men were all staring at Palmsquat, napping belly up in the afternoon sun.

Nimshi said, "It appears she has retired for the day."

Obadyah, Nimshi, and Kalbu went to work attempting to prod the bloated donkey to her feet. After considerable effort, the men were victorious and turned to receive the ladies' applause.

Obadyah approached his mother.

"Goodbye, Son," Samara said.

"Goodbye, Mother."

After Nimshi secured the woven tarp over the king's servants, Palmsquat began her descent. She had not cleared the first turn around the house when Athena spoke. "The queen in your mother's story, the queen of Sheba?"

"Yes," Obadyah replied.

"She said Yahweh was 'delighted' in Solomon's reign. I do not know this Hebrew word. Is it something like amusement or enchantment?" Athena asked.

"It is neither," Obadyah replied, "for amusements fade and enchantments deceive. Delight is effortless and pure. It is the simple joy felt in being in another's presence."

Athena savored this new education in Hebrew customs and language. And yet she knew in her heart, it was not the Hebrews but this Hebrew who was leading her out of the dark. But to what? She was determined to find out.

CHAPTER 14

THE GATEWAY TO GOLD

Donatiya welcomed her husband and his castaways with open arms.

"Look at this urn!" Kalbu said, pushing a clay pot into his wife's face.

"I'd rather see it than eat it," Donatiya replied, distancing her eyes to observe the piece. "What is this symbol?" she asked.

"The bird of the sun, a phoenix!" Kalbu replied. "It is the mark of Samara's trade."

"It's beautiful."

"It is, isn't it?"

"Well, that's what I said, you raggedy old tunic!"

Athena poured some water for her papa and Obadyah. Just as she set down the cups, they rattled atop the table. A simultaneous moan and rumble drew everyone's attention to the back window.

"Is she ill?" Athena asked, staring at Palmsquat, who was now belly up.

Donatiya sighed in exasperation. "She's just lazy. And now she's fat."

"If we are to make our new deliveries on time," Kalbu said to his wife, "we will have to feed Palmsquat a few less biscuits."

Obadyah stepped out on Jezebel's balcony and swept the beach with his eyes. The king's guards were in position on shore and the bay was secure. He took his place in the corner of the balcony and nodded for Jezebel to approach. With Adonis, Aphka, and Athena at her side, the princess and her maidens leaned over the edge hoping to catch a glimpse of Theophanes. There was no person in court, man or woman, enslaved or enthroned. whose head did not turn when the Phoenix dropped anchor.

As a young boy, Obadayah often sat at his mother's feet as she spoke of the magnificent Phoenician vessels. Expert boat builders and accomplished seamen, this small coastal region dominated sea trade. With a vastly superior design, Sidonian ships were not only sound, they were also fast. Whereas competing civilizations built one ship for trade and another for battle, the Phoenicians doubled their fleet, engineering payload boats that were capable of war.

Ethbaal spared no expense importing specialty wood for his fleet design. Fir planking from Mount Hermon. Mast cedar from Lebanon. Decking of boxwood from the coast lands of Cyprus. Oars from the dense oaks of Bashan in Galilee.

Obadyah and Jezebel's maidens watched Theophanes disembark. When the captain set foot on the shore, the girls shrieked with glee. Obadyah gritted his teeth to control the shudder that rose within him.

"Oh that I could disappear beneath the swell of his muscles," Adonis whispered.

Obadyah resisted raising a brow at her comment. That Adonis fancied Theophanes was a source of irritation for the king. But it seemed, as long as Theophanes gave Ethbaal more than he took from him, Adonis's fawning would be tolerated.

Theophanes himself pretended to be oblivious to the adoration when it suited him. It seemed that now was one of those times. Theophanes stole a quick glance up to the balcony where the girls stood then drew up his thick muscular frame and sun-scorched skin. He turned his head so his hair caught the breeze, moving with the wind and drawing the attention of both court beauties and castaways. Though Obadyah hated to admit it, there was none more suited for the role of sea captain.

Theophanes turned and ordered the offloading of a trunk of spoils. It seemed Theophanes was finished strutting about the beach like a preening peacock.

When the trunk came to rest on the beach, Jezebel strode from the balcony. Athena, Adonis, and Aphka continued whispering as Jezebel led her ladies down to the courtyard. Obadyah followed. His eyes obeyed him, his nod finding the guard who would inform the king of the captain's arrival. But his ears would not submit, as they reached for Athena's voice amid the praises of Theophanes's admirers.

Theophanes took a knee when Jezebel approached, bowing effortlessly before the princess. When the king appeared at the top of the stairs, he welcomed the captain giving his approval for Theophanes to speak.

"Your bounty, My King," Theophanes said, opening his arms towards the trunk of valuables on display before them.

"Welcome Theophanes!" the king bellowed, heading down the stairs towards his trusted captain. At the king's approach, Theophanes rose. The king smiled, his eyes locked on the trunk sitting open at Theophanes' side. King and captain walked towards the palace halls, moving in unison, attentive only to one another and the spoils which had brought them together once again.

With the men engrossed in conversation, Jezebel led her ladies away to her chambers to prepare her for the evening banquet.

Obadyah had not known Jezebel to miss a meal set in honor of Theophanes. The stories of his adventures at sea and his battles with the gods captivated her. That Theophanes could hold her in a way no one else could surprised Obadyah. It seemed to him a source of weakness in her. And yet, knowing Jezebel as he did, Obadyah now wondered, who was holding whom.

"Tell me, My King," Theophanes said, "How was your trip to Samaria? How does the ruler of the Northern Kingdom fare?"

"Omri has secured his reign and is eager to live out his days in his newly christened city."

Theophanes smiled. "That will mean increased trade with Tyre and Sidon."

Ethbaal nodded. "Omri is currently in need of bronze, ivory, linen, and slaves."

"Are the sapphire and indigo fabrics from the last harvest of snails ready for shipment?" Theophanes asked.

"They are. Deliver half to Jaffa and half to Egypt."

"Consider it done. I will set sail next week for Rhodes, and there I will trade for ivory. I have an acquaintance in Turkey who can provide us with all the bronze Omri desires."

"And what of my slaves, Theophanes?"

Obadyah's ears perked though his face remained an emotionless mask. Theophanes prided himself in pleasing kings, yet now he seemed visibly uncomfortable. Obadyah had known him in his previous role as palace physician. Altering virile boys to create eunuchs, once routine for Theophanes, now seemed too much for him to bear.

Obadyah's stomach clenched as his mind returned, unbidden, to the time he stood uncloaked before the now popular captain. What was once simple compliance for Theophanes was now unthinkable? Obadyah could not help but wonder how his life would have been different had the captain found his conviction just one day earlier.

Anger and betrayal cast a deep shadow into Obadyah's heart when it came to Theophanes. Watching him squirm before the king, he couldn't help but relish the weighty pressure that the king's question placed on the captain.

"You will force me to send a separate ship to acquire slaves?"

"I will cross the Pillars of Hercules for the glory of your throne; however, begging My King's mercy, I cannot deal in human merchandise."

"You test my patience, Theophanes. A time may come, captain, when your convictions cost you your privileged position."

"I beg the gods that day is not today, My King."

"Today you have pleased me."

"May Baal favor you this day and always, My Lord," Theophanes said, raising his cup to his King.

"There is something else I must mention," Ethbaal said.

"You have my attention, Lord King."

"All hearts on Asherah's shore have broken as my daughter has received a proposal from Ahab, the prince of Israel."

"And is this prince worthy of the fairest of all earthly crowns?" Theophanes replied in timing with Jezebel's entrance into the banquet hall.

"Greetings, Theophanes," Jezebel said.

"Greetings, O Fairest Of All Earthly Crowns," Theophanes said, coming to his feet and then taking a knee before the princess and her maidens. "I have just been informed of the proposition made by the heir of Israel."

"He is a boy with boyish looks and boyish dreams," Jezebel said, drawing her father's laughter.

"Boys do eventually become men, My Lady," Theophanes replied.

"And how many sunsets must I wait for this miracle of the gods to occur?" Jezebel asked.

"My princess," Theophanes said, "may I make a suggestion?"

"Speak." Jezebel replied, "I do crave your insight."

"If this boy prince is not yet a man, does this not create for you an opportunity to mold him into a man, the kind of man who will please you?" Jezebel's eyes revealed a mind at work. The prospect of leading Ahab brought a smile to her face.

Ethbaal smiled also. "There is no male equal to your worth!"

Theophanes continued, "You must create for yourself a king worthy of you. He needs only to desire you, My Lady. You can make him desirable."

Ethbaal raised his glass in approval of his captain's advice.

Jezebel's eyes widened, basking in the possibilities igniting her imagination.

Theophanes smiled. "So, My Lady, what story shall I impart for your pleasure? Shall I tell you of the storm we survived on our last voyage? Shall I tell you of the pirates who battled with the mighty Phoenix?"

"Tell me of the Gateway of Solomon's Gold," Jezebel said.

The king's head swung towards his daughter. Obadyah had seen the king wear many emotions before Jezebel, but this was the first time he saw suspicion. Ethbaal's face now bore the same chill of Jezebel's voice.

"Well, there are many legends," Theophanes began, "and myths surrounding the treasure of the King of Israel."

"And which of these stories appeal to you, Theophanes?" Jezebel pressed.

The captain of the Phoenix paused. Always quick to respond, Theophanes never appeared rattled, until now. Jezebel had succeeded where the king had always failed. She had caught Theophanes off guard. His eyes ran to the king when he could not match the intensity of Jezebel's stare.

"There are many stories, but without a map, I'm afraid they are meritless…"

"Better still, what if one knew the location of the port?" Jezebel interrupted. "Should that be discovered, would that lead me to Solomon's gold?"

"Do you have some information you would like to share with your king, My Sweet?" Ethbaal said.

"No, Father. I am merely intrigued as the testimony of Sheba's queen has been revealed to me."

A chill ran up Obadyah's spine. That Jezebel would choose to conceal the site from her father revealed this simple truth: Jezebel had no fear of gods or men. Her lust for power surpassed any desire she had once had to please her father.

Theophanes continued. "The report of the queen of Sheba has brought many from Arabia in search of the priceless shields. To this day, there has been no treasure unearthed."

"Shields?" Jezebel replied. "I had not mentioned they were shields."

"Oh. Well. Is that not common knowledge among treasure hunters?" Theophanes quickly replied.

Theophanes seemed to have recovered. And Jezebel seemed to accept his reply. Having found the rhythm of his words, Theophanes changed the subject. "With no doubt in my mind, your union with Israel's prince will inspire his devotion to seek all treasures for your pleasure, My Queen. I bid you Asherah's blessing on your marriage to Ahab."

As was his habit, Ethbaal offered his prized captain the services of a woman for the evening. As was his habit, Theophanes declined.

"We share a taste for adventure, Theophanes," the king said, "at sea and in our bed chambers. I pledge you this, should you find this treasure of Solomon's gold, I will give you Adonis. It is then you will not refuse me."

"You shower me with many pleasures, My Lord. I will taste the meat of your table," Theophanes said, reaching for a morsel, "but that shall be the only flesh I take from you."

Ethbaal laughed, helping himself to a morsel as well.

"You must not spoil me, My King," Theophanes continued, moving his bite from one side of his mouth to the other, "lest my head grow larger than the bow of the Phoenix."

"Very well," the King surrendered, "Take your leave. Go and enjoy the woman who has anchored your heart to hers."

CHAPTER 15

THE SPIRIT OF ASHERAH

Several months had passed since Athena and Obadyah's ride to Samara's house. Athena longed for another encounter with Obadyah, but she pushed her heart away from where it pulled. The two servants, occupied by their palace roles, caught glimpses of one another as their duties happened to bring them within eyesight. Always careful to mask their expressions, guarding their emotions became second nature.

A few days had passed since word had come to the palace that King Omri of Israel had taken ill. Ethbaal announced his journey to Samaria to pass along his well wishes for the recovery of his ally. Jezebel would accompany him. The princess's harem gathered by the courtyard fountain, awaiting her summons.

"Do you not tire of these entreaties from the king?" Aphka said to Adonis.

"Would you tire of adoration?" Adonis replied.

Aphka shrugged. "What about you, Athena? Do you seek the pleasure of adoration?"

"Yes, tell us Athena," Adonis added, "what is your heart's deepest desire?"

"To feed a man's appetite with my breasts is certainly not the desire of my heart," Athena replied.

"But should his feasting follow his worship of your body, you would know the adoration of which I speak."

"Perhaps," Athena conceded, "but I crave the fellowship of hearts, not feasting of flesh."

"Bodies can fellowship as well as hearts, Athena," Adonis replied.

"I must bow to your wisdom, Adonis, as…there she is!" Athena said, jumping up and hurrying towards the outer wall of the courtyard.

Athena had several informants, both inside and outside of the castle. One of these, a young Sidoneon Athena had met at the street fair, now leaned in towards a crack in the gate. "Servant of the King," she said, "I have received word from Samaria. Israel mourns, My Lady, as Omri, the king, has died."

"Thank you, friend," Athena replied as she stepped away from the wall.

"My Lady, My Lady!" the young informant continued.

"Speak quickly." Athena returned, leaning towards the girl's voice.

"Your uncle, My Lady."

Athena froze. She studied the girl's expression, desperate to ease her fear. "What of my uncle?" Athena asked, pressing her face closer to the gate.

"He has fallen in a fire. He is severely burned."

Athena's breath caught in her lungs. Her heart momentarily stopped beating in her chest. "Does he…is he…will he live?" Athena asked.

"He clings to life. But he does not move from his bed."

Athena returned to Adonis and Aphka. Fighting for her composure, she did everything she could to hide the grief and anguish crawling up her face. Before she could announce the news to the other girls, Jezebel appeared.

"Greetings, Asherah's Chosen," Aphka said. The princess's ladies bowed in unison before their mistress.

"What word do you hear from Samaria, Athena?" Jezebel demanded.

"News of great sorrow, My Glory. The gods have claimed the soul of Israel's king." Stretched once more between what she felt and what she was allowed to feel, Athena hid behind appropriate words of grief at the passing of an allied royal. Her heart raced for she knew the moment would not last, and she feared that her grief would give her away soon enough.

Aphka and Adonis looked at one another and then back at the princess.

Jezebel's eyes narrowed. A smile crept up her face.

"You will be queen!" Adonis squealed.

"Quiet!" Jezebel commanded. "My father must learn of Omri's death from his own sources."

"Why do males behave so, My Lady?" Adonis asked. "Do they not worship our every word in bed? How is it that their ears are closed to the speaking of a woman once our clothes return to our backs?"

"Come," Jezebel replied, "I will disclose to you the secrets of my future with the prince of Israel."

The girls followed the princess through her portico out onto the terrace.

"Gaze from my balcony," Jezebel said, "for it was from this very spot my father first told me of my destiny. Born of the sea, offspring of the goddess, I had only to await Asherah's anointing."

Jezebel was right about one thing, Athena thought. Her father had ventured down to the beach one evening some fifteen years ago. The truth of Jezebel's conception was whispered in the villages behind closed doors. But no one would ever admit to it as even listening to such a tale would amount to treason. When Kalbu first shared the story with Athena, she thought it was nothing more than a myth, a tale of the taverns. That her aunt and uncle swore to its authenticity had not swayed her. But now she knows. Jezebel's birth was no gift of the gods. The seed of doubt she had allowed to lay dormant inside her was taking root. Watered by Obadyah's insight, Athena's fear of the House of Ethbaal was growing into something terrifying.

As Donatiya explained, Ethbaal had gone out for an evening stroll. He was not visited by Asherah that night but came upon an unsuspecting young couple enjoying a night swim. A Phoenician bride stood in the midst of the water. Each step she strode towards shore unveiled more of her young flesh. Her body was slowly revealed. As the final drops of water ran off her skin, the king's gaze quickened his steps.

When the newlyweds realized they were being watched, they seized their cloaks. But Ethbaal's eyes had locked onto his prize. The young husband reached for his wife but the king's guards wrestled the boy to his knees. The last thing he would see was Ethbaal conceiving an heir with his new bride.

Each time the boy turned away, he received a blow to the head. Powerless to protect his beloved, he closed his eyes. But with every retreat came another strike. When the final blow took his life, Ethbaal commanded the lids of his eyes held open. Should there be even a spark of life left in him, this commoner's last act would be to witness his king's sovereignty.

The young girl who lay under the king recognized what was inevitable. She did not struggle nor did she utter a sound. Unable to bear the sorrow of her husband's face, she looked to the stars. She would not let an ounce of her anger be released. She held it all in directing it to her womb. As Ethbaal drove her into the sand, she cursed him by the heaven's god.

With each thrust of his body, she damned the life which would emerge from her violation. Arrogance, she thought as Ethbaal forced himself inside of her. Anger, she thought with his next advance. Bitterness, jealousy, rage. He continued. So did she. Conceit, insecurity, vanity, haughtiness, snobbery. As Ethbaal's violation was complete he removed himself, but not before the innocent new bride uttered her final curse–evil.

According to the story, Ethbaal had the husband's body disposed of offshore. The young widow was then taken to the castle and held in isolation, the King visiting her from time to time to ensure a conception. Once it was clear that she was with child, the king ordered her dressed in a sheer white gown and allowed brief moments outside of her chamber at night. The ghost-like sightings of the veiled girl by the palace staff substantiated the king's story that his child was brought to him by the spirit of Asherah. When the young mother disappeared the day of Jezebel's birth, it was said she had returned to the sea.

Ethbaal's pride swelled as he gloried in having brought forth a deified offspring. The king, however, made one fatal mistake, Donatiya had said. By disposing of the young mother into the sea, Ethbaal led the stolen bride back to her groom. The couple who had been ripped apart by Ethbaal's lust, met again in death, just under the surface of the sea. As the gods of the earth did not see fit to protect them, the gods of the sea would grant them safety until their deaths were avenged.

"You have been waiting for the goddess's word about whom you should marry?" Adonis asked her princess.

Adonis's sly question brought Athena out of her reverie.

"Asherah has spoken concerning Ahab!" Jezebel scolded. "It is Asherah's consort I have longed to discover."

"And has she chosen?" Aphka inquired.

"The morning fog has spoken her wishes," Jezebel replied.

"The fog spoke, My Lady?" Adonis said.

"Should the skies be clear the morning of Omri's death, I would know Asherah's preference is Yahweh. But should the fog descend on our beach, it is Baal Asherah has chosen."

"All praise to Baal!" Aphka replied as she gazed over the palace wall down to the shores of the Great Sea.

"But the Hebrews revere Yahweh," Adonis interjected. "How will you convince the prince it is Baal who reigns?"

"Convince the prince? I promise you this, the future king of Israel will submit to my body and my will, '' Jezebel replied.

CHAPTER 16

THE PROPHECY GAME

Athena longed to see her uncle. With each passing day, the pain in her heart grew. But she could not devise any way to leave the castle.

Aphka had been sent into town for perfumes and spices. Adonis was otherwise occupied with the King. Athena was left to attend to Jezebel. She feared that the strain of worry lay open in her expression, especially now that she was alone with the princess. Though she had refined the art of hiding her true feelings, this heartache for her uncle could be her undoing.

After lunch, Athena followed Jezebel to her chambers. She sat down on a rug on the balcony as Jezebel stretched out on her daybed. Jezebel closed her eyes and leaned back between the two carved dragons which adorned the Egyptian settee.

"Tell me a story," Jezebel demanded.

Athena stared at the mythical beast which framed Jezebel's head. Believed to inspire dreams, the carved dragon narrowed towards the bottom of the chair, turning gradually into a snake.

"Athena!" Jezebel barked. "Did you not hear me?"

"My sincere apologies, My Lady, the warm sun captured my thoughts."

Athena, now alert, began to tell Jezebel another story of reigning gods and goddesses. As she spoke the tireless words of deities conquering and being conquered, Jezebel dozed off. Athena continued her bland tale, the murmur of her voice lulling the princess. Alone with her thoughts, Athena plotted even while she spun her story. *I must find a way to see my sweet papa.*

"I'm bored with these tales," Jezebel suddenly said. "Tell me a story of Ahab's people."

Athena searched her mind for any details she could recall from Obadyah's stories.

"The Hebrews believe this land was pledged to them by their god." Athena said. "They call it The Promised Land."

"All of Canaan?" Jezebel simpered. "The whole of it? Gifted to the Hebrews?"

"Yes, My Lady, from Dan to Beersheba."

Jezebel laughed. "Does it escape their notice that Canaanites continue to live and prosper in their land?"

"Because of the covenants the Hebrews made with the land's inhabitants and the homage they pay to our gods, Yahweh does not drive out their enemies."

"Yahweh would surrender to Baal in His land just to make a point?"

Athena had considered this very thought. Still, she was slowly growing accustomed to Yahweh's strange behavior. And she remembered what Obadyah had said. "Yahweh is sovereign. He has no need to compete with false gods."

"It seems so, My Lady."

"This Hebrew god is mad!" Jezebel declared.

"His actions certainly are perplexing, Asherah's Heiress."

Athena began to dwell on Yahweh once again. She was well aware of the attention he had given to her previous wishes. And yet Athena suspected, He had His own agenda as well. Still, the life of her uncle was at stake. Was it worth the risk of involving Yahweh once more?

"To what is your mind so attentive, Athena?" Jezebel inquired.

"My apologies, Asherah's Glory, I am simply trying to recall more tales of the Hebrews."

"And what has your memory retrieved, having taken its precious time?"

"There was a woman, My Lady, a Hebrew who once ruled Ahab's people."

"I know of no woman who held the throne in Israel."

"You are correct as always, Sidon's Elegance. This woman reigned not by crown but by wisdom."

"Wisdom may serve one who reigns but you cannot gain power by wisdom," Jezebel declared. "Was not Solomon's wisdom but one of many jewels in his crown?"

"Indeed My Lady, it is said Solomon was gifted wisdom by Yahweh."

"Gifted wisdom only after he wore the crown."

"You utter the truth, My Lady."

"Who is this wise woman of whom you speak?"

"Her name was Deborah."

"If this tale be true, if this Deborah did in fact judge Israel, it was not by her wisdom she won the hearts of men but by her cunning."

"It is as you say, My Princess," Athena nodded.

"You have said Yahweh is angry with His people for making peace with the inhabitants of the land and not driving us out."

"It is precisely that which I have heard," Athena replied.

"What is Yahweh prepared to do since He will witness His king uniting himself with a Phoenician who reigns in His land?"

"I know not," Athena said, "but I have received word of a prophet in Israel who is gaining power amid the Hebrew's. The prophet speaks of Yahweh's displeasure with His people and their king. He speaks of bringing punishment on the Kingdom of Israel."

"What threat could be posed by a single prophet of Yahweh?" Jezebel boasted. "Should Yahweh raise up 100 prophets, I shall bring forth 200 prophets of Baal!"

"It is as you say, My Lady. Perhaps Yahweh is not as powerful as the Hebrews claim."

"Perhaps? Most certainly! Yahweh has lost Asherah's hand!" Jezebel declared. "I suspect He will respond as all males do. He will battle and then He will beg."

Athena could not say that she understood what Yahweh was doing and why. But He had put His sovereignty on display time and time again. Jezebel would never see beyond her own appetite and selfish desires. And Yahweh would threaten that.

"Beg, My Lady?"

"Yahweh will fight with Baal and then will plead with Asherah for mercy. As Asherah has ordained, Yahweh is powerless to stop my union and the uniting of Israel and Phoenicia. Ahab will act as the kings before him. He will do what is in the best interest of his throne and his queen, irrespective of Yahweh's preference."

Jezebel's words were as effective as the fishmonger's cleaver. She spoke her will as he swung his knife, with just the right amount of force to sink a blade and send a fish head flying. But there was something new Athena detected in her voice, something peaceful. Athena bristled, wondering what evil the princess was conjuring now.

"I'm glad we find ourselves alone," Jezebel purred.

Athena held her breath as her thoughts tumbled, her mind reeling. What has Jezebel discovered? What is feeding her stone-hearted contentment? Was the moment she had feared was upon her? Did Jezebel no longer need her? Would she be disposed of as every Athena before her? Athena cursed her own pride. How naive to think that she was different, that she could hold the princess's ears indefinitely. That she could do what no other Athena before her had done—sustain Jezebel by the lure of knowledge. Jezebel did not need to be informed, she needed to be empowered. It was never about enlightening her, but engorging her. And now it seems, even that is not enough. Athena panicked. Yahweh! Help me!

"Have no fear Athena, for should you possess the wisdom of Asherah, you shall live and be gifted passage to serve me in Samaria. Should our goddess abandon you, however, I shall be inspired to abandon you as well."

"As you say, so it shall be, My Lady."

"I set this challenge before you," Jezebel said. "Bring me two seers of your choosing, prophets of good reputation, one of Yahweh and one of Baal. Alongside these two prophets, you will stand before me. At dusk you will reveal to me the meaning of my dream. Whoever's interpretation proves true will live. The remaining two will die at tomorrow's sunrise."

Athena's heart raced. She said nothing nor did she look up to make eye contact with the princess.

"Go, for I will order you escorted by your favored eunuch," Jezebel commanded. "And make no mistake, Athena, should you cease to please me in this task, I will proceed to Samaria alone and you will proceed alone to the bottom of the Sea."

Athena stood, bowed, and left the princess's chambers. She knew very well the risk of petitioning Yahweh. He had repeatedly made this one truth known to her; He was available but not predictable. She saw this in the life of Obadyah. And now in her own life. Obadyah was an unexpected gift. And while she knew she longed for him, she also knew Obadyah was not hers. He belonged to Yahweh as much his as the snails which blanketed the beach when she first called out to Him. The awe Yahweh inspired did not come without fear. For He could be stirred, but He could not be controlled.

As Athena made her way down the palace halls, she took a deep breath. Though she shuddered at the thought of the test before her, she was leaving the castle. Soon she would be home with her dear papa.

CHAPTER 17

THE CONVERTS

Obadyah was waiting at the courtyard gate when Athena approached. Her heart leapt as the space between them disappeared. The fear that her feelings for Obadyah might be discovered meant nothing now as Jezebel's test overshadowed her.

"My Lady," Obadyah said with a bow.

"Good afternoon, Obadyah."

"It certainly is," Obadyah replied, his soft smile stealing a moment.

Once they were beyond the ears of the gate's guard, Obadyah spoke freely. "How have you been these past months?"

"Bored," Athena replied.

"Well then today marks the end of your weariness."

"Indeed it does as I will be home."

"Your aunt and uncle are a certain cure for boredom," Obadyah reassured. "However, perhaps these next few steps taken with a friend will bring you joy as well."

"It will indeed. I did not mean to overlook the time granted us. I have wished for it. However, my uncle…Kalbu, was injured, and my mind is consumed with worry."

"Let us pick up our pace," Obadyah replied, "as my heart knows no desire beyond being in Kalbu's presence."

Athena and Obadyah pushed on in silence, each one aching in fear of what they would find.

"Aunt Donatiya!" Athena said, bursting through the door.

"Zoë!" Donatiya replied, jumping up from her stool. They ran into one another's arms.

"How's papa? What happened? Will he live?"

"Slow down girl," Donatiya replied. "Come. Sit by your papa." Donatiya led Athena to her uncle's bedside.

"Move over Palmsquat!" Athena said, giving Kalbu's pet a good nudge. As Kalbu's donkey reluctantly submitted, Athena took her place beside her uncle. The small room that once had felt as though it were closing in around her, now held all that mattered to her. Squeezing herself between her uncle and his beloved animal, Athena welcomed the embrace of the thin flimsy walls of a poor village hut. She placed her uncle's hand in hers.

"Papa. It's me. It's Zoë. I'm here, Papa. Please, open your eyes. Please, Papa."

"He has stirred only a few times since…," Donatiya said.

"What happened?"

"My Kalbu was brought here by your mother's servant," Donatiya said, looking towards Obadyah. "He had gone out to meet Nimshi to deliver the pots Samara had requested."

"And?" Athena said.

"And your papa went to the stone alley where he and Nimshi would make their exchange. Kalbu and Palmsquat were proceeding past a Canaanite ritual just as the priest was chanting incantations over a newborn who had been surrendered by his mother. As the flames were stoked the baby cried and the priest called out to his god. It was then that Kalbu suddenly stopped."

"And?" Athena replied.

"And, well, your papa jumped into the fire to save the child."

Athena closed her eyes and lowered her head. The thought of her sweet uncle rushing into the flames broke her.

"If Nimshi had not been there to pull him from the fire…"

"But papa is blind. How did he…"

"He could smell it," Donatiya interrupted. "He could smell, for the very first time, the hair on the newborn being singed."

"You spoke to him?"

"He was quite alert when Nimshi carried him through the door. In fact, he would not be silenced. He went on and on about being a champion for Yahweh, having stolen the sacrifice to Baal. His face looked like burnt bread, yet he could not contain his smile as he placed the tiny life in my arms."

"But, but, I don't understand." Athena replied. "The Canaanites have always sacrificed children to Baal. They have been doing this for as long as I can remember." Athena's frustration began to conquer her sadness. "We have walked past this countless times! Why? Why? What was it about this ceremony that made papa react the way he did?"

"There was nothing different about the ceremony," Donatiya replied, reaching for Athena's shoulder. "It is your papa who is different."

Athena turned her eyes from Kalbu and looked into her aunt's eyes.

Donatiya continued. "For these past months we have been making deliveries to Samara's home. She has told us of Yahweh, of His love and compassion, His justice and His great mercy towards those who seek Him."

Guilt squeezed Athena as she knew it was by Yahweh's mercy she was granted this time with her papa. Still, the shock was too great to contain. "So…so you worship the Hebrew God now?" Athena asked.

"Blessed be Yahweh who has heard my prayer," Kalbu whispered.

"Papa!" Athena said, reaching for her uncle.

Kalbu winced in pain, his charred skin peeling away at her touch.

"Papa. I love you, Papa. Please don't die. I love you," Athena repeated through tears.

"My… life… for another," Kalbu said.

"See?" Donatiya jumped in. "He fancies himself a soldier of Yahweh. My crusty old warrior," Donatiya said, stroking her husband's hair.

Athena rose to her feet. "It is your god who did this to him!" she said, facing Obadyah.

"My God. Kalbu's God. And your God as well, Zoë," Obadyah calmly replied.

"So you do not deny it!" Athena replied, "Yahweh is responsible for this!"

"Zoë," Kalbu strained.

"Yes, Papa. What is it? I'm here."

"Yahweh has deemed me worthy."

"Worthy? To suffer?" Athena longed to comfort her papa, but even she could hear the frustration, the anger in her voice.

"Worthy to…worthy to…to serve Him."

Kalbu quickly faded out again.

Athena knelt down by her papa. She laid her head on his arm and wept. Neither Donatiya nor Obadyah attempted to comfort her, for they knew nothing would ease her pain. As the tears ran from her face they landed on Palmsquat. "You miss your friend, don't you?" Athena said, stroking the donkey's limp ears. "Aunt Donatiya?" Athena said, turning away from her uncle.

"Yes dear."

"I need your help."

"I am here," Donatiya whispered.

Athena stood with strength in her legs. "I need to know which priest of Baal placed the child in the fire."

Donatiya hesitated a moment before answering. "It was…it was Mattan."

Athena's head fell. Mattan. They had grown up together. Studied together. He was slated for a royal appointment; she was lucky to be at the academy. When their fates met opposite destinies, Mattan never recovered. The day Athena left for the castle, she spoke words of consolation to Mattan. But when she rested her hand on his arm he pulled away and stormed out of the room.

"What do you intend to do?" Donatiya asked.

"I intend to invite him to the castle."

Donatiya looked to Obadyah. The confusion on their faces mirrored one another.

"Jezebel has set a challenge before me," Athena said. "I will stand beside two seers tonight, one of Yahweh, one of Baal. My place in the palace, my future with the future queen, and…and my life now rests on my ability to interpret Jezebel's dream."

"But Zoë," Donatiya said, "how will you know the meaning of her dream?"

"I won't. But neither will the seers who stand beside me. This is not about finding the truth. It's about finding the interpretation which brings Jezebel the most pleasure."

Athena took a step towards the door.

As she did, Obadyah took a knee next to Kalbu's bed. He prayed. "Hear my prayer, O Yahweh, give ear to my cry." He rose, turned to Donatiya, and kissed the back of her hand.

"Thank you, Obadyah."

Athena made her way towards the door. She stopped abruptly and turned. "Where is the baby papa saved?" she asked.

"Rachel is nursing him for us."

"For us?"

"The boy is a gift from my God and my love. He will be our son."

CHAPTER 18

THE PLACE OF FEAR

"Obadyah," Athena said, the servant pair standing together just outside her aunt's and uncle's hut. "I need your help to find a prophet of Yahweh."

"I am here, Zoë."

"Is there a prophet of Yahweh who deceives?"

"Yes, of course. There are many false prophets."

"How might we convince one to appear before Jezebel tonight?"

"We need only put word out on the streets and the most greedy of the deceivers will run to the castle gates."

Athena turned with a spring in her step. Though death was knocking, she borrowed her uncle's strength.

Athena followed Obadyah away from her aunt and uncle's home into the heart of Zarephath. He seemed to know where he was going, like the streets were his own backyard. They breezed by the merchants whose goods lay side-by-side atop overturned crates. They stopped at the last vendor whose place marked the end of the market and the beginning of the fishing district. Obadyah nodded towards the shopkeeper who abandoned his task and moved quickly to Obadyah's side. As Obadyah spoke to the man, Athena noticed a woman behind him pressing out dough atop a moon-shaped pottery being warmed by a fire. Athena smiled at the woman who briefly met her gaze. Returning her eyes to her task, the woman seemed neither fearful nor impressed with the palace inhabitants in her presence. Jezebel's maidens were occasionally seen outside the castle but never this close to the port where men who had been for months at sea did their own kind of shopping.

As quickly as they arrived, they were moving again, Obadyah proceeding into the crowd. He pushed his way past drunken sailors who grumbled in protest but were quickly silenced when their eyes caught sight of Obadyah. Athena matched his steps, never letting herself get more than an arm's length away. When the swarm of people was behind them, Obadyah turned towards the sea. On the north side of the port they found a group of boys fishing off the remnants of a broken abandoned dock.

"Jashar," Obadyah yelled, his eyes finding the boy who occasionally ran errands for Samara.

The group of boys spun their heads towards shore. When Jashar recognized who was calling his name he dropped his net and made his way across the cracked bulkhead. Obadyah placed a hand on the boy's shoulder as he spoke.

"We need your help," he said.

Obadyah's petition brought an eager smile to Jashar's face who swelled with pride as Obadyah gave the boy his instructions.

"Find the chief-seaters among the Hebrews," he said, "and instruct them to appear at the castle gates at dusk."

The moment Obadyah finished speaking, Jashar ran towards the market leaving his fishing net and his friends behind.

"Is it safe to assume a false prophet will appear?" Athena asked.

"Once news of Jezebel's reward gets out, those who seek her praise will not be able to resist."

Athena nodded.

Obadyah looked up towards the sky, his face soaking up the sun like a prisoner who'd at long last been freed. "We have some time before we must return to the castle," he said. "May I show you something?"

Athena smiled, eager for what might be one last adventure with her friend. Breezing through the streets of Zarephath, they walked past the market into the fishing district. Athena laughed as Obadyah's eyes began to water, the smell of raw fish too much for him to bear. Her smile lingered as she recalled having asked her papa why Palmsquat smelled so bad. 'She reclines in fish guts,' Kalbu had said, as if that was a normal thing for a donkey to do. Stinky, ugly, lazy, there could not possibly be a more worthless creature than Palmsquat. Athena's heart tugged. And there was none more valuable.

Obadyah led Athena to a descent that ended at a rocky passage to the water's edge. They both nearly lost their footing more than once. Athena was glad the path was short.

The beach was narrow where they emerged from the trail, and the tide was rising. They scrambled over boulders to avoid being soaked by the crashing waves.

Obadyah moved at a swift pace. Athena struggled to stay close. When they came to a boulder too large to climb, Obadyah jammed his fingers into a narrow crack and pulled himself up. Safely atop the rock, Obadyah laid on his stomach, lowering both of his hands to Athena.

She grabbed hold of him. She felt as weightless as a baby bird as he pulled her up in one swift movement. Moving to the far side of the boulder, he took her hands in his and lowered her to the smaller rocks below. At each touch of his hand, her heart stirred. Yet Obadyah seemed oblivious. He seemed focused on the mission of reaching his destination.

Obadyah jumped down. He raised his eyebrows without saying a word, pointing to an outcropping which hung out over the sea.

They hugged the shore, Athena's fear melting with each step. In no time they arrived at Obadyah's hiding place. Squeezing themselves under a stone overhang, Obadyah led Athena to a spot where a rock had fallen and lay flat just above the breaking waves. He lifted her to the top of the rock and then hopped up beside her. They gazed in silence at the water, listening to the echo of the waves crashing into the shore just beneath their dangling feet.

"It looks as though the rocks above us could collapse at any moment," Athena said, directing Obadyah's eyes with hers.

"Yes, I suppose they could," he replied.

Athena saw where the stone they were resting on had pulled itself away from the rocks above.

"It's dangerous being here," Athena said, her eyes finding the waves.

"It is," Obadyah replied.

"At any moment our world could come crashing down."

"And yet you remain."

"This place…it's peaceful even while I sit in fear."

"Life is both peace and fear, Zoë."

"I long for a life without fear," Athena confessed.

"No, you don't," Obadyah said, turning towards her. Athena's brow revealed her confusion. "Did you not fear for your uncle's life? Did you not fear the pain his loss would bring you?"

"That fear remains," Athena said, turning her attention back to the sea.

"As it should!" Obadyah replied, grabbing her shoulders turning her towards him, "as it will…for you love him." Obadyah removed his hands, and they both returned their gaze to the Sea.

Athena watched as the drips of water, one after the other, merged with the water from which they came—each drop distinguishable for only a second. A brief moment of life and then gone, no longer recognizable, something that only was.

"A life of peace and fear," Athena said. "This is what it means to have a relationship with your God?"

"Yes," Obadyah said.

"It seems my aunt and uncle have made peace with Yahweh."

"And what of you, Zoë?"

At the sound of her real name, her heart skipped. She thought by now she would have been accustomed to hearing him say her name, but it still surprised her. "With Yahweh, I have more fear than peace."

"The fear of Yahweh is the beginning of wisdom."

Athena laughed.

"Why do you laugh?"

"I was reminded of my conversation with Jezebel concerning wisdom. She believes its value can only be measured in its ability to coerce power."

"Are you scared to stand before her tonight?"

"I was. But now, having seen my uncle, and…you…I am eager to hear what will come forth from my lips."

"Do you know what you will say?"

"I have a plan. I plan to ask your god to give me the right words."

"Ask. And believe."

"Yahweh brought forth the sea snails. Twice Yahweh spared your life. He led me to my uncle's bedside. He has also angered me, frustrated me, and saddened me. But he has given me no reason to not trust him. Yahweh will give me the right words."

"You believe."

"I have confidence."

"You believe."

"I have doubts."

"You are wrestling with Yahweh. He enjoys a good fight."

Athena nodded, a lot less surprised than she used to be about the character of Obadyah's god.

"Zoë?"

"Yes."

"Can I sit with you again?"

"I would be thankful to see you again, Obadyah, but you know as well as I do, our fate is determined."

"Only death seals fate," Obadyah replied.

"We sit in the shadow of death."

"But should you not die, should Yahweh grant me my request and you proceed with the princess to Samaria, would you sit with me again, speak with me again, if I were to find you?"

Thinking on Obadyah's words, Athena looked down at the abiding waves. There were so many things wrong with his request. It was illogical, for whoever heard of a eunuch pursuing a girl. It was illegal. As slaves of the king, they were married to the crown. And it was dangerous as it certainly would cost them both their lives were they to be discovered. Despite all this, Athena knew there was only one answer.

"Yes, Obadyah, I will see you again."

She heard Obadyah exhale, and it occurred to her that she hadn't heard his breath in as many beats. He reached over to Athena and placed his hand on hers.

CHAPTER 19

THE ANGEL SEER

Obadyah and Athena approached the gates where several men were gathered. Athena looked dazed, at a loss as to which Hebrew false prophet to choose. Then her eyes found Mattan.

Before she said a word, Obadyah spoke up. "You," he said, pointing to Mattan. "And you," he said, pointing at one of the self-proclaimed prophets of Yahweh.

Obadyah signaled the gatekeeper who slid a large pole aside. With Obadyah pulling from the outside and Ethbaal's guards pushing from the inside, Obadyah and Athena squeezed through the narrow opening. Obadyah helped the gatekeeper return the pin to its latch. Athena slipped down a corridor and turned the corner, but not before watching Obadyah. She saw the faintest slump of his shoulders, and a lump formed in her throat. With a deep breath, she steeled herself for what was to come and proceeded to find Jezebel.

The word on the street was effective in producing many false prophets, and, unsurprisingly, a large crowd. What began as a personal challenge from the princess was turning into a public spectacle. Athena approached Jezebel with caution, as if balancing on the break wall of the sea. Before she uttered a word, Athena reminded herself, *proceed with confidence! You know this princess!*

"Athena! Is this your doing?" Jezebel barked.

"Indeed My Lady, I am to blame. Is it not fitting that your subjects recognize your blessing by Asherah?"

Jezebel paused. Her anger atoned for. "Adonis. Aphka. Prepare Athena for this evening's test."

Jezebel was not one to pass up an opportunity for applause and adoration. Athena had been counting on that. Indeed, she knew this princess. She bowed before her mistress.

"And Athena."

"Yes, My Lady."

"Petition Asherah to speak to you tonight. It would be a pity were this to be the last time you serve me."

Adonis was shaking as she combed Athena's hair. "How are you so calm, Athena?"

"I fear not the outcome."

"Have you no fear of death?" Aphka asked.

"I have fears," Athena replied, "but I have peace as well."

"But how? From where does this confidence come from?" Aphka pressed.

"From her mind, Aphka!" Adonis snipped. "Stop badgering her! Athena will find the right words."

"Words…" Athena said. "We cannot see them nor touch them. And yet one word can bear the weight of a thousand millstones. Words cut, but they also cure," she said resting her hand on Adonis's. "And they can be powerful enough to sustain us…." Athena turned her eyes to Aphka. "Or escort our destruction."

The room was so quiet Athena could hear Adonis's tears as they dripped onto her lap. Athena attempted to change the subject. "I am grateful my testing will come with words," she said, "and not with the satisfaction of the king!"

Adonis grinned, "I would prefer my testing to be under a bed canopy rather than before the eyes of a whole village!"

The girls laughed, relieved to be lighthearted even if only for a moment.

"There are some priests and a few prophets who have gathered and are curious," Athena said, "but it will not be before the whole village I will stand."

"It seems you have not looked at the gates in the last hour," Aphka stated, "people have filled the courtyard!"

"By the gods, Athena, you have gotten yourself into quite a mess," Adonis said.

"Must she be reminded of that, Adonis?" Aphka scolded.

"There is no reason to ignore it either," Athena replied. "This will be the toughest challenge I have had to face in this life."

"Asherah will guide you. Praise her and bless her and be open to her leading," Aphka said.

"I will leave the praise of Asherah to Jezebel," Athena replied.

Athena's counterparts stepped back and took one last look at her. A simple dove white dress flowed from her shoulders to the floor. Golden rings which had encircled the posts of Jezebel's bed now adorned Athena's arms. The tassels which had held back the curtains encircled Athena's waist. The tiny flower accents in the hallway vase were strung together in a band. They now rested on Athena's head.

"You look…you are…beautiful," Aphka said. "Do you not agree, Adonis?"

Adonis stood silent. Staring. "Something is missing," Adonis said.

Athena looked down, attempting to discern what was lacking. "You have made me up like a princess, Adonis, what could possibly be missing?"

Adonis ran out of the room.

"Do you know where she's going?" Athena asked.

Aphka shrugged.

Adonis returned with a small wooden box. She leaped up onto the bed. Athena and Aphka followed and huddled around her. "This was given to me by the king," she said.

The three girls bumped heads as their eyes reached for what was hidden in the box. Adonis slowly lifted the lid. Before them lay a pear-shaped amethyst encircled in diamonds, inlaid in gold. Athena gazed at the precious stone as tears filled her eyes. Adonis reached for the chain while Aphka reached for Athena's hair. She held it back out of the way, but Adonis did not put the pendant around Athena's neck. She placed it gently atop her head, the purple amethyst coming to rest between Athena's bright azure blue eyes.

"Now you look beautiful!" Adonis smiled.

Adonis and Aphka said their good-byes and went to attend to Jezebel.

Left alone in the room, Athena knelt. As the cool floor found her senses, something occurred to her. She had only ever come to Yahweh in petition. She had only ever asked Him to give her what she wanted, what she thought she needed. She had begged Him and tested Him. She had resented Him and had run from Him. And yet He remained. He was there every time she called on Him. Yahweh longed for her to trust Him, and even when she didn't, Yahweh was faithful to her. Every time she cried out to Him. She knew in her heart, now would be no different. But she was different. No longer the girl consumed with her own life, she could not bear the thought of seeking anything more for herself. Even now, when her life depended on it, she would ask nothing of her God. No matter the outcome, tonight, Athena would die. The name she was given in honor of an idolatrous goddess was no longer her and would no longer be hers.

"Yahweh, God of my salvation," Zoë said, "I call on you this night. Not in petition do I call out, but in praise. Thank you for opening the castle doors so that I might see my sweet uncle one last time."

The courtyard was as full as it was the day of the journey to Samaria. The three stone benches which encircled the fountain became the platforms from which each seer would give their testimony. The priest of Baal who had attempted to sacrifice the baby boy redeemed by Kalbu stood atop his stage. A prophet of Yahweh, enkindled by Jashar, stood ready to report. One bench remained open.

A hush fell over the crowd as Zoë was led out of the castle, escorted by four of the king's eunuchs. For the first time that day, Zoë felt fear. She watched as the beads of sweat rolled down the back of Obadyah's neck. Jezebel would not miss a single opportunity to sink the blade of her jealousy. Every muscle in Obadyah's arms clinched, his veins strained to contain the blood his heart was forcing through his body. As Jezebel had scripted, there was nothing Zoë could do to ease Obadyah's pain.

When they arrived at the bench on which Zoë would stand, Obadyah turned. Zoë drew in a deep breath. She had not anticipated the struggle of seeing Obadyah's face. He let his eyes find hers, taking in every detail of the cherub standing before him.

All three seers in place, the king rose from his throne, silencing the people who'd knelt before him.

"My fellow Phoenicians," the king began, "we gather this night in honor of my daughter—goddess of the night, treasure of the Great Sea, Princess of Sidon, Queen of Israel!" The crowd jumped to their feet and roared in applause. The king took his seat. Jezebel rose before the people.

"Citizens of the dominion of Asherah, I bid thee good evening. Tonight we will witness a contest. A battle of wits. A battle of honor. A battle...of the gods!" The people yelled and stomped their feet. They began to chant, "Jez–e–bel...Jez-e-bel...Jez–e–bel."

The princess allowed the uproar to continue, only hushing her admirers when their energy began to drop. "The gods have spoken," Jezebel said, "bringing a vision as I slept. This divinely enchanted dream is marked by mystery. Through whom will the gods speak tonight?" Jezebel motioned to the three seers perched atop the courtyard benches.

The crowd began yelling the names of the candidate they were rooting for.

Jezebel raised her hand, quieting the people. "Enjoy this night, for I pledge to you this: at tomorrow's dawn, the three lives standing before you will face three separate fates. One will accompany me to Samaria. One will be offered to Asherah, cast out for her pleasure into the Great Sea. The final life will be offered to the god of the victorious in his or her preferred manner. Should Yahweh prevail, the loser will be stoned. Should Baal prevail, the losing prophet will be consumed by fire. Should Athena prevail, her will be done. Athena," Jezebel said, "what is your desire, should you prevail?"

Zoë fixed her gaze on Mattan and said, "Emasculation."

CHAPTER 20

THE NIGHT VISION

"I saw a woman coming out of the sea," Jezebel said, recounting her dream to the assembly and the three seers standing below her. "The woman was sitting on a scarlet beast. She was clothed in purple, gilded with precious stones. In her hand was a golden cup and on her forehead was written a name." Jezebel paused as whispers began floating through the crowd. "Speak, prophet of Yahweh," Jezebel demanded. "Who is this woman? What does she drink? Tell us the name which adorns her brow."

The man whom Obadyah had identified as a false prophet of Yahweh bowed his head. "Who else could this be but you, my Glorified Princess? For there is none who is so finely dressed and whose beast, were she to have a beast," the false prophet paused as laughter rolled through the crowd, "would be equally adorned."

"And the cup?"

"The cup, My Lady, is the choicest wine, preserved at the bottom of the sea, raised up in your honor at the rising of your name across this land. The cup is the celebration of your union with the king of the Jews."

"And what of the name, seer of Yahweh?"

"What other name could possibly be given, My Lady, but the name of wisdom: Asherah. By this vision, she has pledged you to our people and our god."

The gathering clapped in approval of the interpretation given by the prophet of Yahweh. Quieting the crowd, Jezebel called out to her servant. "Athena, what do you say concerning the interpretation of the prophet of Yahweh?"

"A fool does not delight in understanding, but only in revealing his own mind," Zoë replied.

The people erupted in laughter as Jezebel turned her attention towards the priest of Baal. "Baal has led you here to reveal his will before our people," Jezebel announced. "How does he speak concerning the meaning of my vision?"

"My Princess, My King, my fellow worshippers, I bring forth this evening the word of Baal. This prophet of Yahweh," Mattan raised his hand towards his competition, "he speaks but one truth. For the woman coming forth from the sea is indeed you, my Reigning Beauty. He fails, however, to recognize the beast. For the scarlet creature on which you ride can only be the phallus of Baal."

The crowd roared in approval.

As the cheers subsided, the prophet of Baal continued. "The gold adorning you and your beast," the priest continued, "speaks to your enduring beauty. The precious stones, the likeness of your immeasurable value as the offspring of Asherah."

Intrigued by the priest's interpretation, Jezebel allowed the rumbling of the crowd to linger. Her curiosity building, Jezebel silenced the people once more.

"And what of the cup?" she asked.

"Ah yes, the golden cup," the cleric repeated. "The cup is the key to your vision, My Princess."

The crowd hushed. The people quieted their breaths as anticipation blew through the crowd like a morning fog. Baal's cleric waited patiently until the air was thick with silence.

"The cup, My Sovereign, contains nothing more than the spark of deity. For the cup contains the life sustaining milk of Baal's stimulation." Playing to the crowd, Mattan let his eyes wander across the sea of people. He stopped when his eyes met Zoë's. He winked.

The crowd roared, the priest of Baal had won over the people.

"And the name?" The princess asked, leaning forward in her throne, "Can you see the name which was written upon my head?"

Mattan closed his eyes in concentration. His head moved slightly from side-to-side as if straining to see the details of Jezebel's vision. Suddenly, his eyes opened, bringing an instant hush over the crowd.

"It is not your name," Mattan replied. "It is your city."

"Samaria?" Jezebel replied.

"Neither Samaria, nor Sidon, My Glory. Jezreel!"

"Jezreel?" Jezebel replied, "The Hebrew village by the valley?"

"Jezreel means 'God sows,'" Mattan replied. "Baal has sanctified Jezreel as the place where his seed must take root."

Jezebel nodded and turned to Zoë. "Tell us, Athena, servant of the crown, what reply do you give the priest of Baal?"

The crowd stilled themselves, eager to hear Zoë's response. Her eyes fell to Obadyah. He clenched his fists. His body spoke his heart. And its message was clear. Zoë steeled herself and locked her eyes on Mattan. "A fool's mouth is his ruin," she said, "and his lips are the snare of his soul."

Laughter broke out once more, as Zoë stood tall, undaunted by her opponent's seething.

"I have granted you your opinion, Athena," Jezebel replied, "but now you must share your interpretation."

Without delay Zoë began to speak. "I too see a woman coming out of the sea. She rides no decorated beast of prey as Yahweh's prophet inferred. And she certainly is not saddled upon a phallus, for she is upheld by no man regardless of the size of his…his manhood." Zoë paused, allowing the crowd to support her rebuttal.

"Neither love nor hatred sway her." Zoë continued, "her royal heritage gifted by the Sea, she carries her pride inland, away from our shores."

"This we know, Athena!" Jezebel interrupted, "you reveal no mystery in stating my reign for the proposal of the King of Israel has been made known to all!"

"You speak of your reign in the Northern Kingdom, in Israel, My Queen. But I speak of the queen of the Southern Kingdom, the queen of Judah."

A hush fell over the crowd, no one knowing what to make of Athena's revelation. That Jezebel would rule with Ahab there was no doubt, but how her reign might extend from the Northern Kingdom of Israel to the Southern Kingdom of Judah, no one could fathom.

Intrigued, Jezebel conceded the stage to Zoë once more. "You may continue."

"The golden chalice which you held in your hand, My Lady, contains neither wine nor excreta but blood." Murmuring sifted through the crowd. "The golden cup and its contents, the blood of the prophets of Yahweh, is a gift from a reigning mother to a royal offspring."

"Asherah will present me with the blood of the prophets?" Jezebel asked.

"No, My Lady. You will not receive the cup. You will give the cup. The blood of the servants of Yahweh is your gift to your daughter."

Gasps resounded as Jezebel leaned back against her throne. Zoë searched for Jezebel's pleasure, desperate to see the lust in her eyes. That burning look Jezebel wore, that piercing face Zoë had so often dreaded, was now her greatest desire. *Have I captured her? Have I won my place? Have I redeemed my life?* The silence of Jezebel's stare revealed a new level of her depravity. And Zoë could think of only one word to describe it—contentment.

The king stood and looked at his daughter. But Jezebel did not respond. Raising his right hand, the crowd became silent once more. "You have heard the testimony of these seers," Ethbaal said. "It is now up to you to decide their fate."

Zoë's heart dropped. She had expected that Jezebel would decide the victor. Finding the vulnerability of the woman she knew was much different than playing to the whims of a crowd.

"What say you of Jezebel's counselor, Athena?" the king inquired.

The people cheered, whistled, and applauded.

"What say you of the prophet of Yahweh?" Some cheers were heard in addition to a few hisses and boos.

"And what say you of the prophet of Baal?"

The courtyard erupted.

The deafening sound carried from the castle to the village. Kalbu, lying asleep in his bed, was startled awake.

"The ground quakes with the reveling of idolatry," Donatiya said to her husband.

Straining, he reached for his wife. "Praise Yahweh, we are no longer counted among the foolish of this world."

Donatiya nodded, her tears falling to the floor. "Go now, you old burnt toast. Go and stand with the house of David." Donatiya, helpless to save her love from the searing pain, wished him to go.

And so he did.

Kalbu gave up his fight just as the chanting began again, "Jez – e – bel! Jez – e – bel! Jez – e – bel!"

Still on his feet before the courtyard crowd, the king raised his hand.

"Very well," Ethbaal said. "As you have spoken, so it shall be! Baal's honorable prophet will accompany the queen to Samaria." Applause rang out as the king nodded, christening his daughter's rise to the throne in Israel. "At dawn," the king continued, "this prophet of Yahweh will stand before the altar of Baal. And you, Athena," the king pointed, drawing every eye to

Zoë, "you shall be delivered to the depths of the Great Sea!"

CHAPTER 21

THE HUMAN SACRIFICE

"Why are you downcast, Athena?" Jezebel asked. "You served me well your few days on this earth."

Zoë raised her head to see Jezebel standing with her two remaining servants.

"Asherah will bless you in the world to come," Aphka said, her tone veiled, mysterious.

"Take comfort in Aphka's words, Athena," Jezebel said, "for I have taken comfort in hers."

Zoë's eyes reached for Aphka's but they were not to be found. The question regarding the source of Jezebel's information was now answered.

"Do not be distraught, Athena," Jezebel jeered, "Asherah will bless us both, me in this world, you in the world to come." Jezebel's mockery was felt, every word scalding and unmerciful. "In fact," she continued, "you should rejoice for I have chosen to forgive you for hiding with my eunuch under the hanging rocks."

Zoë saw Aphka but Aphka would not see her. Aphka had given herself to Jezebel. Her shame was all that was left of her.

Zoë now knew the secret of her time alone with Obadyah was an illusion. There was nowhere to hide, no escape, no life apart from Jezebel.

"I do wonder," Jezebel said, "whether to pity you more for your foul affection for the impotent or your faith in a blind man. Honestly Athena, what tarp could possibly conceal such retching alliances." Unrelenting, Jezebel continued. "Do not fear for your love," she taunted, "he will be consoled by Adonis upon his return."

Zoë's head shot up.

"Oh, have I not mentioned it? Since you persist in leaving this castle with my eunuch, it is only right that he be chosen to cast you into the Sea."

The stones which Zoë feared might crack were crumbling around her. I have led evil to the hearts I cherish most. Zoë ached for each precious soul she had exposed to Jezebel. All she could do now was swallow her tears. Though Jezebel had taken everything, Zoë would not give her the pleasure of her pain and the bitter truth they both now knew. Jezebel had won. That Jezebel was to be feared, that much had always been known, but Zoë had failed to anticipate the depths of her cunning. Having named Obadyah her executioner, it was clear, Jezebel did not simply hate, she was enkindled by hatred.

"You were not entirely worthless to me," Jezebel scoffed. "I do have you to thank for the information concerning Solomon's treasure." Zoë stood motionless, unresponsive to the princess's goading. "You know that young informant you're so fond of?" Jezebel asked, her tone light, casual, as though they were just two friends chatting in the park. "The one you met at the courtyard gates?" Jezebel looked past Zoë as she spoke.

Zoë's throat clenched. It shouldn't have shocked her that Jezebel had known all along. Yet it did. Zoë did her best to hide her surprise, but she could feel her shell cracking.

Jezebel offered a sly smile. "Her name is Rachel. But I suppose you knew that. Anyway, she came to the gates tonight with a message for you." Jezebel's eyes which had flitted about the room became fixed on Zoë.

Zoë held her breath.

"Your uncle is dead," Jezebel said, a grin creeping up the side of her mouth. Jezebel reached for Zoë's reaction. Zoë felt every muscle in her body tighten. Jezebel seemed to be savoring the emptiness that filled the air. She continued to wait. Zoë marveled at Jezebel's patience for her news to have its desired effect.

Zoë remained silent. She kept her eyes locked on the princess but gave her only an empty stare. After a minute of cold silence, Jezebel swept past Zoë moving quickly towards the door. Aphka followed. Adonis remained, her head swinging back and forth between Zoë and Jezebel. Zoë found her friend's eyes. Tears began to roll down Adonis's cheeks.

"Adonis!" Jezebel barked.

Adonis jumped and followed Aphka and Jezebel out of the room. As they proceeded down the hall, the midnight bell rang in time with each of Jezebel's steps. When the final gong was struck, the words of the witch at the street fair returned to Zoë. The curse of midnight had found her. Alone,

Zoë collapsed onto the floor.

It was still dark when the door to Zoë's cell swung open the next morning. Zoë rolled herself off of the stone slab which served as her bed for her final night in the king's palace. My back is going to ache for a week, she thought, taking her first few steps towards her fate. Then it occurred to her that her sore back would only factor into the next few hours, her final hours of this life.

"By mercy of the king," the guard stated, "you have been granted a hearing with the priest of Baal prior to your appointment to the Sea."

Zoë looked up and found herself standing face-to-face with Mattan.

"I cannot imagine the level of displeasure you have caused our princess," Mattan said, "mine being the last face you see before your…departure."

Zoë was silent as she proceeded past Mattan down the candle-ensconced hallway.

"It was a dreadful sight watching your uncle's flesh burn," he said, following closely behind.

Unwilling to engage him, Zoë climbed the stairs which led out of the dungeon towards the path to the Great Sea.

Mattan continued, "You must be so relieved that your dear uncle is blind. At least he could not see his own skin peeling away."

Mattan would revel in every second of the reversal of their fortunes. While he glowed with satisfaction, Zoë's face remained an expressionless mask though Mattan's words salted her fresh wound.

"Still," he continued, "I'm sure he was able to smell it, his burning flesh, that is. The scent of charred flesh would not have escaped him," Mattan sneered.

Ignoring him, Zoë pressed on, her senses beginning to numb in response to what lay ahead.

"Very well then," Mattan said, sounding bored, "since you do not want my blessing, and I would prefer to not give it, I will leave you here. May Baal be roused as your flesh feeds the creatures of the dark waters."

Having had his fill of mockery, Mattan turned. Without another word, he disappeared into the shadows of the pre-dawn morn.

The stone path which led Zoë away from the castle came to an end. As her feet left solid ground and sank into the cool sand, Zoë fell to her knees. Filling her hands, she looked from one palm to the next. Tiny granules ran out from between her fingers. Her life, so fleeting, in her grasp one second, slipping away the next.

The king's guards pulled Zoë to her feet. Bearing her own weight once more, she looked up. Her heart caught in her throat. Obadyah.

Standing by a small row boat where the waves met the shore, his eyes found hers. He dropped the line he was holding and walked towards her. Zoë quickened her steps. She did not take her eyes off of him. He did not break his gaze. The space between them was consumed in a matter of seconds. She reached for him. He wrapped her tightly in his arms. Lifting her up, he turned her away from the guards, stealing her for the last few moments they would share.

"Enough!" the guard shouted. "Release her!"

Obadyah lowered Zoë to the ground. She struggled to gain her footing.

The king's sentry grabbed Obadyah's shoulder to pull him away from Zoë. Obadyah turned. He threw the guard onto his back, clinching his hand tightly on the man's throat. He squeezed. Jezebel's guard thrashed.

Zoë's breath quickened at the rage in Obadyah. The numb reality of her fate gave way to panic. What would Jezebel do to Obadyah in the face of this rebellion? She longed to cry out to stop him, but she did not want to draw any more attention to the scene.

Two soldiers assigned to the skiff caught sight of the tussle and rushed to the aid of their companion. Before they arrived, Zoë placed her hand on Obadyah's back.

"Obadyah," she said.

He looked up. Seeing the concern in Zoë's eyes, Obadyah came to himself. His anger subsided. He released the man who coughed and fought for air.

The guards began yelling at Obadyah the second they arrived. But Zoë's heart pounded loudly in her ears and she could not make out a single word of what they said.

Obadyah took Zoë's hand. He pulled her towards the water so quickly that she struggled to keep up. He lifted her over the edge of the rowboat. Ethbaal's guards hurried to the skiff. When the soldiers were aboard, Obadyah pushed the bow towards the rolling waves. Throwing his legs over the side, he took the seat facing Zoë.

Obadyah pulled on the oars. Meeting the crest of a gentle morning tide, he rowed them out to sea. The peace of a tranquil morning clashed with the horror of what lay ahead, the contrast so fierce, Zoë fought back the urge to vomit.

Arriving at the ship, the captain of the Lynx ordered the embarkation ladder dropped.

Obadyah looked at Zoë, silently gesturing toward the ship.

Zoë climbed the first few rungs and stopped. Nausea overtook her and she vomited violently into the sea. Though her stomach emptied almost immediately, she continued to retch. She heard the men at the top shouting. Still, she could not make out what they said. She felt a steadying hand on her back. She knew the presence behind her. Obadyah had climbed up, pressing his body into hers.

He whispered, "Yahweh will protect you."

Somehow, his words calmed her despite her fate unfolding around her. She continued up the ladder.

Obadyah followed.

As soon as his feet hit the ship's deck Obadyah began giving orders. "Pull the anchor! Command the rowers!"

The captain approached Obadyah. He looked Zoë up and down as she shivered uncontrollably in the cool morning air. "We were instructed to release her at dawn. The sun has not met the horizon."

"She is not to be cast out at dawn, you fool," Obadyah scolded. "She is to reach the ocean's floor by dawn. It is Jezebel's pleasure that the goddess awaken to her offering!"

The men scrambled to comply with Obadyah's new orders. Several pulled up anchor while others coiled the line. The master of the galley gave the command. The rowers moved as one as the captain steered the ship in the direction of the open sea.

Zoë wondered at Obadyah's urgency. *Surely he has a plan. Surely he will save me. Surely he will not throw me into the sea.*

Zoë leaned against the ship's rail, gazing out at the waves. She had always loved this time of day at the edge of the Mediterranean. The lingering night air, cooled by the salty water, lifted off the surface and rushed up the side of the Lynx, the gentle breeze blowing past her face. She recalled the many days she had sought the peace of such mornings. The irony that this was the time and place she might die was not lost on her.

She thought of Obadyah. Each of their few inopportune moments soothed her. He filled the empty space in her heart with a peace she had not known before. She was thankful for the short time they were given and confessed to herself she would rather die this day, having known Obadyah, than to have lived a long life in his absence.

She thought of Samara, Obadyah's intriguing mother. There was a longing Zoë felt to be close to her—a confident, contented woman. Zoë sighed, there would not be another afternoon tea with Samara. She thought of her papa. She wondered if she might find him in the next world. She thought of her aunt and all the sweet moments they shared. She felt no loss in having never known her real parents. The love given by Kalbu and Donatiya was more than she could have hoped for. She could not stop the tears which came at the thought of her dear aunt who would suffer greatly in the days to come. She even thought about Palmsquat and the simple joy the ratty animal had brought to her uncle. Thank you, Yahweh, for Palmsquat, she thought as the rowers halted off shore.

Obadyah led Zoë to an opening in the bulwark. She panicked. Was he not going to save her? "Obadyah, I just thanked Yahweh for Palmsquat!" she said, her mind racing with frantic thoughts.

Obadyah said nothing.

Unbidden tears rolled down her cheeks. "Did you hear me, Obadyah? These were my final thoughts, a prayer about a donkey. Isn't that funny, Obadyah?" Zoë's voice rattled, her arms and legs shuddering.

The sailors watched at a distance, none dared to get close to the cursed woman. Zoë's speech slurred. She continued speaking to Obadyah, but her words became frantic, indiscernible.

"Look at me!" Obadyah interrupted, turning Zoë around so that he might bind her hands and her feet.

Their eyes locked. His were hard as steel. Hers begged him to stop.

Obadyah wrapped her wrists. He knelt down. The breadth of his shoulders blocked any view the sailors may have gotten of her legs. Obadyah looped the rope loosely around her ankles. He stood up and looked at her.

A warm wind began to blow as the sun crept towards the horizon. The morning tide lapped softly against the side of the ship. All was as it should be. They were together.

Then, suddenly, Obadyah tore Zoë's dress from her body. The force of his hand stunned her. Her mind reeled. Obadyah's behavior was so out of character of the boy she had come to love. The crew of the Lynx jeered as Obadyah spun Zoë around, pointing her towards the sea. He pressed his body into hers. Using his own legs to force hers forward he moved her towards the waves one step at a time.

When her toes found the edge of the freeing port Obadyah whispered into Zoë's ear. "If you can hear me, if you have ever heard me, please, Zoë, hear me now. The ropes are loosely tied. When you hit the water, break yourself free."

"But Obadyah..." Zoë began.

"Listen to me! I beg you!" Obadyah interrupted, "Keep your arms and your legs moving. Keep your head above the water. Stay…" Obadyah paused to steady his voice. "Stay alive!"

Zoë opened her mouth to speak, but there were no words.

"Look," Obadyah whispered, "you can see the Phoenix on the horizon. She is scheduled to anchor at dawn. Theophanes will pass by here. He is but minutes away. He will have mercy on you. May Yahweh have mercy on us both."

Obadyah pushed Zoë into the sea.

The last thing she heard before she went under water was Obadyah's voice as he instructed the crew of the Lynx, "Head for shore!"

Obadyah did not look back. The sailors hurried to their positions and the ship came about. As the Lynx gained speed, he felt the breeze of the same air Zoë breathed. He closed his eyes and begged Yahweh to spare the life of his beloved.

As they neared the shore, weakness overcame him. The heartache which had consumed him for his own life now seemed childish. The fear he held for what he could not do for Zoë evaporated in comparison to what he was capable of doing to her. Was Yahweh testing him? Was he punishing him for his self pity? Obadyah had spent his life looking at himself. And now all he saw was his greed for justification.

The Lynx threw anchor off Sidon's shore and the servants of the king rowed out. Obadyah lowered himself to the smaller vessel and returned to the beach where he found Jezebel waiting.

"Is this how you thank me?" Jezebel barked. "A cold scowl?"

"Forgive me, My Lady," Obadyah replied, "I do not have a taste for execution though I acknowledge your mercy."

"I suppose I shall forgive you, eunuch, as I do not have time today for even a single irritation. The Phoenix is arriving this morning." Jezebel said, directing her eyes towards the approaching vessel.

"Yes, My Lady," Obadyah bowed. "I too am eager for Theophanes to return."

"Are you?"

"Indeed, My Lady. I covet the tales of his adventures, as do all who serve at your pleasure."

"Was he not the man who cut you?" Jezebel asked.

Obadyah drew a deep breath, unprepared for Jezebel's confrontation. "Speak eunuch! Is Theophanes not the one who fitted you for the crown's service?"

"Yes, My Lady, it was he who…who… ."

"Is that not the way of a slave?" Jezebel laughed. "Like a beaten dog you tuck your tail and return to your master."

Obadyah, dazed, murmured. "It is as you say, My Lady."

"Very well," Jezebel conceded, "as I am a woman of my word, you shall receive your reward for completing your task."

Obadyah, impervious, bowed in submission.

"But, first, there is one thing I must know."

"Yes, My Lady."

"Tell me, do you feel passion?"

"My heart beats, My Lady."

"Do you somehow believe, eunuch, that it is safe to test my patience!" Jezebel howled. "You know that is not what I mean!"

Obadyah did know what she meant. Yet he stood there, silent, as though telling her were giving a part of himself to her. Giving away a part of him he wished to save, to keep, to protect until he could share it with his beloved.

"Well?" she said. "Speak eunuch!" Jezebel demanded, spit flying from her lips. "Does what is left of your manhood respond to the touch of a woman?"

Exhausted from the events of the morning, Obadyah had no fight left in him. Denying Jezebel the pleasure of forcing pleasure upon him when his heart was broken would merely enkindle her. There was only one way to be free of Jezebel. Give her what she wants. Empty, aching, and out of options, Obadyah lowered his eyes. "Yes, My Lady."

Having freed herself from her binding, Zoë fought to keep her head above water. Her pulse slowed as the sea cooled her blood. She could see the Phoenix approaching. She reached for what she feared was unreachable.

After several minutes of continuous treading, the invading cold began its work on her muscles and her mind. As her body rose and fell with the rolling current, she felt beneath her the watery graves which fed the underworld. How many more waves could she survive? Three, no four, maybe five. Exhausted, she looked one last time at the Phoenix. It was there and then it was gone, her salvation as transient as a lightning strike.

Zoë turned towards shore. She thought about all she had experienced with Obadyah since the Sidonian street fair. She recalled Obadyah's gentle expression as she wiped the blood from his face. She remembered the desperation in his eyes at the creek the night of their trip to Samaria. She thought of his courage, standing tall when the bear attacked. She smiled at the image of his love for her aunt and uncle. She could feel the warmth of his hand on hers at the hanging rocks.

Of all her memories, nothing compared to the security of his presence. How could she ask for more in this life? Zoë smiled, content to let go and be free. She filled her lungs with air one last time. Relaxing her arms and her legs, she released her last breath and drifted beneath the surface of the water.

CHAPTER 22

THE SERVANT'S REWARD

Obadyah gazed out at the ocean from the balcony of the palace guest chamber. The rising sun cast a shadow of the castle onto the shore as it found its place in the eastern sky. Several of the king's eunuchs entered and undressed Obadyah.

Obadyah did not move his eyes away from the sea, his last moments with Zoë circling over and over in his mind. A few minutes later the door opened. The unmistakable fragrance of the king's mistress filled the room. Adonis.

Obadyah could hear Jezebel's attendants removing her dress. When they were finished, the rustling of footsteps faded. The door clicked shut. Obadyah heard the lock slide into place. And then there was silence.

Distraught by the task before him, Obadyah could not bring himself to face Adonis. The sorrow which held him resurfaced. Could she sense his despair? Though he had never spoken to Adonis, he wondered if she knew that there was something special between him and Zoë, an energy they shared, one that he felt the way the wind moved the hairs on his arms.

"The princess has commanded me to seduce you." Adonis said.

Obadyah remained silent, unsure of Adonis's loyalties to Jezebel.

"I do not desire to obey her," she said.

While this brought some amount of peace to Obadyah, he knew that not wanting to please Jezebel and not pleasing her were two separate things.

"I consider myself a faithful servant of the crown," Adonis said, leaving no doubt as to her loyalties. "But," she paused.

Obadyah waited.

He heard Adonis's feet make contact with the floor. She was walking towards him. When he felt her breath on the back of his neck Obadyah began to shake. He wanted to face her, but he could not make himself turn. Then, he felt her touch as she gently draped a bed linen over his shoulders.

"I do not wish to lay with my friend's beloved while she lay on the ocean floor," Adonis said.

Obadyah turned.

As they stood there, face to face, unclothed, Adonis said, "I am at your mercy, My Lord."

Obadyah saw the fear in her eyes. Then it hit him. It was not until he turned that he had considered her feelings, her struggle. He felt ashamed. Obadyah removed the sheet from his shoulders and wrapped it around Adonis. He picked her up, cradled her, and carried her to the bed. "Do not be afraid," he said, gently laying her down. Obadyah sat down on the floor next to the bed.

"Women weep when the pains of life become too much to bear," Adonis continued.

Obadyah sensed safety in the tone of her voice.

"Men, I'm afraid, are resistant to weeping," Obadyah replied as he leaned back against the wall.

"Men are not soothed by releasing tears but by releasing their seed," Adonis said.

Obadyah gave Adonis his attention as he could not fathom what might be appropriate to reply.

"Do you remember the night the king's son was killed?"

Obadyah nodded. He remembered it well. A messenger had brought word that the king's son had drowned, having been thrown overboard when an exchange with some Egyptian pirates went wrong. The messenger left in haste terrified to deliver the news to the king. It was Obadyah who led Ethbaal to the body of his boy that lay lifeless on the beach. But what did any of that have to do with Adonis?

"What began as a calm caressing by the king that night, ended with the tearing of my flesh."

Obadyah's head dropped, weakened by the thought of what Adonis must have endured and horrified at what a man is capable of doing to a woman.

"I had desired to comfort my king," she whispered. "But comfort meant something different to Ethbaal."

Obadyah remained silent. What could he possibly say? Any words seemed weak, insufficient.

"There was something enchanted about her, about Athena," Adonis said, changing the subject. "I think that is why Jezebel feared her so. She was wise, yes, but she was also serene. To be honest," Adonis said, "I knew she was doomed the moment she appeared at court."

"I too saw Jezebel's jealousy," Obadyah suddenly replied.

"Jezebel would never allow someone to best her in charm and beauty," Adonis added.

"How is it, then, that you have survived?" Obadyah asked.

Adonis smiled.

Obadyah smiled back, knowing she sensed his softness towards her.

"What will become of you," Obadyah asked, "when Jezebel leaves for Samaria?"

"Ethbaal will reject me now. He will not have me in his court or in his bed. He will say I am…"

"Soiled," Obadyah whispered, finally realizing the full extent of Adonis's predicament. She was trapped. If she did not lay with him, Jezebel would have her head. If she did, she rendered herself abhorrent to the king.

"Yes." Adonis replied. "Perhaps Athena's destiny awaits me as well."

Obadyah could offer Adonis no assurance, his own destiny as elusive as hers. He knew that Yahweh had a plan for both of them, but he also knew Yahweh was not one to accommodate Obadyah's desires. He was a God of sovereignty, but not divination.

"You are free to take me," Adonis suddenly said.

Obadyah's head shot up. He was moved and suspected Adonis was just being kind, looking to comfort Obadyah in her own way. But he had to be sure.

"Is it your wish that I take you?" Obadyah asked, still wary about how Adonis might report to Jezebel.

"It is not. But I will not resist you."

At that Obadyah reached up, extending his hand towards Adonis. When she placed her hand in his, a tear rolled down Obadyah's cheek.

"So you did love her," Adonis said, leaning forward, looking into his eyes.

"I am guilty of that which you accuse me of."

"Love is not a crime, Obadyah."

"And yet it was unlawful for me to love her."

"It was unlawful for you to pursue her. The law has no jurisdiction over your heart."

Obadyah's face betrayed his surprise.

"Does my knowledge of love shock you?" she asked. "Can not a woman accustomed to pleasing a man also have a heart?"

Obadyah felt the weight of guilt as he realized his thoughts had exposed him.

"I didn't mean to …"

"Only a man would think it is no burden to be forced into bed!"

"I'm sorry, I…"

"Every time I am compelled to accept the king's gift," Adonis interrupted, "I must carry that with me. Men thrust themselves upon us and simply walk away!"

"I am a fool," Obadyah replied. "Please forgive me."

Adonis sighed, her frustration evaporating as quickly as it arose. "You are no fool to have loved her," she replied.

"May I ask you something?"

"You may."

"Can we ever rid ourselves of our emotions?"

Adonis smiled.

"My turmoil amuses you?"

"You are hungry," Adonis replied, "so you eat. You are tired so you sleep. You feel emotion so you…"

"So…I what?"

"So you look for a way to quench your feelings the same way you quench your thirst."

"Yes. Precisely. How can I quench these feelings?"

"You cannot!" Adonis answered.

Obadyah's shoulders dropped.

"Love is not of the flesh, so no feeding of the flesh will satisfy it."

"Who is able to survive such torment?" Obadyah asked. He paused for a moment then spoke up when his own thoughts interrupted him, "What is your name?"

"You know my name."

"Not the name Jezebel calls you. What did your mother and father call you?"

"Ares."

"Ares is a beautiful name. A beautiful name for a beautiful soul. I will pray for Yahweh's mercy on you, Ares."

"Thank you, Obadyah but Jezebel will not permit Yahweh's blessings here."

Obadyah laughed.

"You laugh. Yet you know this to be true."

"Jezebel's gods submit to her because they are the product of her imagination. My God does not seek man's permission nor his approval. The Lord of heaven and earth acts according to His own will."

"If your god is not compelled to act on your behalf, why do you call on him?" Adonis asked.

"When you were a child," Obadyah replied, "who did you call on for your needs?"

"My parents, of course."

"And they did for you what seemed best because they loved you."

"Your god gives you no tool with which to bargain?"

"With what did you bargain with your parents?"

"Charm, mostly." Adonis smiled.

"And did your parents grant you your wishes because you were charming?"

"I used to think I could oblige them simply by my smile. But, of course, now I realize they were only amused by my efforts. They were not compelled by such simple things."

"So it was not what you did," Obadyah replied, "but who you were that moved them to meet your needs."

"Your god hears you and grants you your wishes simply because you are His?"

"He does not grant me my every wish. He does as your parents did, that which He thinks is best."

"Was it for your best that Athena die?"

Obadyah's head fell. His voice followed. "Her casting out is a painful reminder, my best is not always what I desire nor what I reason is best."

"But how can you trust your god after He has done this to you?"

"For the same reason you continued to trust your parents when their decisions disappointed you."

Adonis leaned back against the canopy headboard.

After a few moments passed Obadyah said, "May I tell you a story?"

Adonis nodded and smiled. She appeared almost childlike as she pulled the bed covering up towards her neck and leaned forward as one would reach for the warmth of a fire on a cold night.

"My mother told me this tale when I was a child. When my people returned to this land after the Exodus from Egypt, we were governed by leaders called judges. It was during this time that the Midianites oppressed Israel. Repeatedly raiding towns and villages, they destroyed both fields and flocks. One young Hebrew named Gideon, a valiant warrior, encountered a messenger of Yahweh. Before this messenger Gideon cried out saying, "Oh, my Lord, why has this happened to us? Where are Yahweh's miracles which our fathers told us about, saying, 'Did not Yahweh bring us up from Egypt?' But now he has abandoned us and given us into the hand of Midian."

"If Yahweh loves his people as you have said, surely he did not abandon them," Adonis replied.

Obadyah nodded and continued. "That very night Yahweh spoke to Gideon and said, 'Take your father's bulls and pull down the altar of Baal which belongs to your father, and cut down the Asherah that is beside it.'"

Adonis shook her head. "Was Gideon not terrified to obey this command?"

"Indeed. But he was also faithful to Yahweh. So he decided to act that night. After pulling down the Baal, Gideon used the wood of the Asherah pole to make a fire. He then constructed an altar to Yahweh and offered to Him one of the bulls he had used to destroy the idols."

"Surely he was put to death the following day," Adonis exclaimed, "sacrificed to Baal on the very altar he raised up to Yahweh!"

"Nothing happened next, that is the end of the tale."

"What? This is a terrible story!" Adonis exclaimed.

Obadyah shrugged his shoulders, but his smile gave him away.

"Very funny, Obadyah," Adonis grinned. "Now tell me, please, what happened to Gideon?"

"As you wish, My Lady," Obadyah replied. "When the men of the city arose early the next morning, they noticed immediately their altar to Baal had been torn down. The men said to one another, 'Who did this thing?'"

"Did someone see Gideon?"

"Indeed, they knew it was Gideon who was guilty."

"What did they do to him?"

"The men of the city went to Joash, Gideon's father, and said, 'Bring out your son, that he may die, for he has destroyed the altar of Baal, and burnt the Asherah which was beside it.'"

"I cannot even imagine their fury for he not only destroyed their god, he insulted them by replacing the idol with an altar to Yahweh."

Obadyah nodded, "Gideon not only disrespected them, his actions bore a tone of mockery."

"And what of his father? Were not the gods and bulls his? He, of all the people, had a right to condemn his son."

"The idols were indeed his father's," Obadyah said, "but it seems that Joash had a change of heart. Instead of handing over his son, he said to the townspeople, 'Will you contend for Baal? If he is a god, let him contend for himself, because someone has torn down his altar.'"

"So now we know where Gideon got his flare for mockery," Adonis said.

Obadyah smiled. "Gideon's message was clear. There are many gods, but there is only one God—a message that reached his father as well."

"Whether Yahweh alone reigns, I know not, but this I know," Adonis exclaimed, "Hebrews have much better stories than Canaanites."

Obadyah smiled once more.

"So it is trust which moves the hand of your god?" Adonis asked.

"It is trust which moves the eyes of my God. For this I also learned from my mother: 'The eyes of Yahweh move to and fro throughout the earth that He may support those whose heart is His.'"

"Not even faith moves the hand of your god?"

"Yahweh is neither threatened nor manipulated. Not bullied nor coerced. Those are the behaviors of men. And when our gods begin to act like men, it is safe to conclude they are the product of men."

"Your god sees. Does he also listen?" Adonis asked.

"Of course. Is that not our most consuming desire, to be heard? My ancestors have repeatedly turned to blind and deaf gods. Yahweh, having watched his children give their hearts to Asherah and Baal, has replied to Israel saying, 'Go and cry out to the gods which you have chosen; let them deliver you in the time of your distress.'"

"I believe Athena caught Yahweh's eyes," Adonis said, "for it seems that when she called out to Him, He listened."

"I believe He did."

CHAPTER 23

THE KING'S ADVICE

Theophanes caught sight of Athena as she began to stir on the deck of the Phoenix. He had not known who she was when he dove into the Sea to rescue her. But it was clear now, this was one of Jezebel's harem.

"How much?" a woman spoke, drawing his attention away.

"Ten pieces of silver, one for each of my men," a man replied.

"And for you?" she asked, "what is your price?"

"I want what I have always wanted."

"Are you mad? She is not worth half of that!"

"She is young and beautiful. She would fetch double what I am asking at the slave market."

"Perhaps, but we are not at the slave market, we are at sea. And she looks more like a drowned rat than some exorbitant slave."

"You have my price," Theophanes replied. "What do you say?"

The woman, standing on the deck of the Phoenix, stared at Zoë as she considered the captain's offer.

"Very well," she agreed. Reaching into her pocket, she pulled out ten silver coins and a ring. She placed them in Theophanes's hand.

The men on the ship jabbed one another as the sale meant a night of celebration once the Phoenix dropped anchor.

Theophanes watched as his men lowered Samara by rope to the skiff moored to the Phoenix. Zoë was next. Once the job was done, Theophanes's men moved to other tasks. The moment they were out of sight, Samara changed from a harsh slave owner to a loving matron. She wrapped a thick wool blanket around Zoë's shoulders and guided her to the beam of the rowboat.

Grabbing the oars, Samara's eyes found the captain of the Phoenix. "She may not survive," Samara said. "Her body temperature is dangerously low."

Theophanes nodded. From the corner of his eye, he saw Zoë stiffen. Then her gaze rose to the sky. He looked up. In the bright morning sky, the silhouette of a raptor hovering in the heavens had grabbed her attention. The eagle circled, un-tethered, soaring effortlessly above the Sea. His wings were steady accommodating the updrafts, the tips of his feathers making tiny adjustments as his head turned from side to side.

Theophanes dropped anchor off shore at Sidon. His men rowed him to the beach. As he made his way up the sand path he noticed a pair of eyes following him from the water's edge to the castle. When he entered the courtyard, Jezebel was waiting.

"Why must you do that, My Lady?" Theophanes asked.

"Do what?" Jezebel replied.

"Why must you shine brighter than the rising sun?"

"Do you insist on flirting with me, Theophanes?"

"I am a brave man, My Princess, but I have more sense than to flirt with the future queen of Israel."

"Am I not worth the risk?"

"Indeed you are. But if I am to lose my life in your adoration, who will adore you as I do when I am gone?"

Jezebel glowed. Locking arms with Theophanes, she led him inside. "Come," she said, "sit with me at my father's table. I am in such high spirits this morning."

"Theophanes, my friend, you are late," Ethbaal said as he entered the room.

"Am I, My Lord?" Theophanes replied. "Perhaps I spent too much time in your courtyard this morning."

"You were delayed in my courtyard?"

"Yes indeed, My King. As it should happen, an angel appeared before me," Theophanes said, winking in Jezebel's direction, "and this heavenly creature captured all my senses."

"You surely do not lack for words, Theophanes."

"Welcome words, I hope."

"Undoubtedly," the king replied. "Come. Sit."

"So, tell me, My Lavish Lady," Theophanes continued, "what gives you your special glow this morning? Am I right to assume it is my presence which delights you so?"

"Your presence is a treat, as always," Jezebel replied, "but I shine at the success of last night's event."

"Last night's event? Do you celebrate in my absence, My Lord?" Theophanes asked.

"My daughter has proven her readiness to rule," Ethbaal replied, "by gathering my people before her seers and clerics."

"And whose prophecy prevailed?" Theophanes inquired.

"The prophet of Baal succeeded in winning the crowd and earning a role as my daughter's counsel in Samaria."

"It seems Asherah is content with this victory as well," Theophanes added, "as we sailed on calm waters this morning."

"It is clear," the king replied, "Asherah is pleased with our princess. But enough with the past. Tell me, what treasures have you secured?"

"Perhaps, My King, my gift should be postponed as I dare not rival the victory of our enchanted princess," Theophanes teased.

"You may honor my father, Theophanes," Jezebel permitted.

"Should I be a fly buzzing about my own table?" Ethbaal replied, "that my captain and my daughter grant me permission?"

Jezebel and Theophanes looked towards one another with devious grins.

"Very well then," Ethbaal submitted, "ask My Glory if I should be worthy to receive your treasure."

Theophanes grinned and played his role looking to Jezebel for her approval. "Well, what say you, Lady Imminence, will it please you that I should bestow fortune upon your father?"

"Her father and her king!" Ethbaal added.

"I permit you," Jezebel nodded.

At Jezebel's bidding, Theophanes rose. He bowed to the princess and then turned towards Ethbaal. Taking a knee before his King, Theophanes extended his arm and opened his hand. Jezebel rose quickly and moved to her father's side as Ethbaal reached for the prize presented to him by the captain of the Phoenix.

"Is it…? Is this…?" Ethbaal said, stunned by what lay before him.

"Saul's Signet, My Lord," Theophanes said.

The king reached for the ring. Ethbaal was silent, his eyes aglow as he examined the details of the gold seal. A polished band ascended to a raised bezel on which rested a hexagram, the royal symbol adopted by the Davidic monarchy.

"Where did you…?" The king paused, speechless by what he held.

"What is so special about this ring?" Jezebel asked.

"If I may, My Lord?" Theophanes interjected.

The king nodded.

"The Legend of the Seal of Saul, My Lady, is the gift of sorcery to the one who adorns it."

"It grants the wearer the power of curses and spells?" Jezebel asked.

"Not curses and spells, My Princess, but visions. However," Theophanes paused, "I must admit, your Athena can recite this tale better than I, My Lady."

Jezebel smirked and looked at Ethbaal. Her father, captivated by the ring, failed to acknowledge her. She scowled and turned back to Theophanes. "Athena is…unavailable."

Theophanes raised a brow.

"I wish to hear the account from your lips, Theophanes," Jezebel demanded.

"Your wish is my wish, My Crown," Theophanes bowed.

"There are some who say the amulet was given to Saul, the first king of the Jews, the night he visited the witch at Endor. Though he himself had declared witchcraft illegal, Saul proceeded to the house of a sorceress. And under cover of night he entered. His demand? Call up the spirit of Yahweh's prophet."

"And was she successful? Did the prophet's ghost appear?"

"Indeed he did but he did not bring good news."

"This witch of Endor was a fool!" Jezebel exclaimed. "Sidonian witches bring forth only good prophecies."

"Through the prophet Samuel," Theophanes continued, "it was revealed that Saul's army would see defeat and he and his son would be killed."

"So the ring grants the power to speak with the dead?"

"The ring is a connection to the next world, My Grace, bestowing the power of spirits, both good and evil."

"It should be noted as well that Saul's Signet rested upon the finger of the richest king in Canaan," Ethbaal added, sliding the ring onto his finger.

"I thought David was the most powerful king of Israel," Jezebel inquired.

"David was a mighty warrior," Ethbaal replied, "but it was his son Solomon who amassed great wealth adorning his palace and his temple with the gold and jewels of the Hebrew god's blessings."

Jezebel's face soured at the reference to Yahweh.

"Do your loyalties lie with Yahweh now?" Jezebel snapped.

"I bid you watch your tongue, my young princess," Ethbaal replied, "for your reign is sure, but it is surely not here. Bark out your commands to your husband, but do not forget, when you sit at my table, I am your king!"

Jezebel, without apology, returned to her seat.

The king continued. "My loyalties, my daughter, lie with any deity who blesses me. Should Yahweh see fit, at the wearing of this ring, to bestow on me the favor of Solomon, I will not refuse Him. You have made your alliance with Asherah through Baal. I do not fault you for such devotion. But hear this, gods rise and fall as the seasons. Should you choose to remain faithful when Asherah fails, let me forewarn you, my girl, it may prove to have dire consequences."

With one conversation, the palace had become too small for both Ethbaal and Jezebel. As the king paused, staring at the ring adorning his finger, Jezebel's eyes narrowed. Theophanes, accustomed to the behavior of royals, could read the tension in the room. Jezebel's affections had gone from desiring her father's attention to craving his power. And that was the one thing Ethbaal would never give away, even to his own daughter. Greed oozed from Jezebel's eyes. Clear to everyone present, was this one fact: it was time for Jezebel to leave Sidon.

"Worship that which serves your immediate purposes," Ethbaal continued.

"I will never turn my heart from Asherah!" Jezebel barked.

"Is that so?"

"It was she who delivered the lavender snails. She protected me from the bear who attacked on the road to Samaria. She turned Ahab's heart so that it is not devoted to Yahweh, his God. And last night she spoke through the prophet of Baal ensuring my enemy be sacrificed to the sea. Asherah has chosen me to rule Canaan. I will choose her over Yahweh all my days!"

"Your devotion is compelling, but it is also naïve. Answer me this, my daughter. Should it be right that I honor Theophanes?"

"He has been faithful to you."

"Indeed. And I will continue to invoke the gods favor on his behalf in return for his devotion. Is it right, however, that I honor him if he betrays me?"

Jezebel remained silent.

Theophanes too did not utter a sound, recognizing the trap Ethbaal had set. With one sentence, the king had successfully warned both his daughter and his captain. The king, enjoying the wisdom of the ring, waited patiently for Jezebel's reply.

"Theophanes will never betray you." Jezebel declared.

"Perhaps. But perhaps in a moment of weakness his heart will turn."

Jezebel looked at Theophanes.

"It is true now," the king continued, "that Theophanes is committed to his king. However, he is also committed to his lover. Should she turn his heart in the same way the wives of Solomon turned his heart, how must I respond? By rewarding his duplicity with my praise?"

Jezebel looked dazed, knowing full well what her father had suggested was true.

"Your father speaks the truth, My Lady." Theophanes replied. "His wisdom surpasses us both. I bid you heed your father's advice, for his judgment is sound and I have taken it to heart."

Jezebel rose from the table, her eyes finding Theophanes.

"It seems you have no option," Jezebel said, "but to agree with my father. I ask you only this, Theophanes, is your submission evidence of your wisdom or your weakness?" Jezebel stormed out, having lost the battle but won the last word.

CHAPTER 24

THE ASKING PRICE

Zoë opened her eyes. She felt her body rattling. She could hear wheels turning, squeaking beneath her. It was dark. *Am I dreaming?* She shook violently before losing consciousness again.

Zoë awoke to singing. A calm soft sound like the voice of an angel. *Am I dead?* It was dark. Her heart was pulsing. She tried to move her arms, but they were too heavy.
"Don't move, Zoë," Samara whispered.
As the banging intensified Zoë became more alert. She was in a wagon just as she had been with Obadyah when they'd gone to visit his mother. Zoë drew in a deep breath coughing as she attempted to fill her lungs to capacity. "What is that smell?" she said, her consciousness slipping away once again.

Zoë squinted when the sun caused an unbearable pounding in her head.
"Rest easy, My Lady." Nimshi said as he lifted Zoë from the wagon. Nimshi limped, struggling as he carried Zoë into Samara's house.
"Is that Palmsquat?" Zoë asked, catching a glimpse of her uncle's donkey just before they stepped under the portico.
"It is indeed," Nimshi replied.
Nimshi winced as he laid Zoë down on Samara's bed.
"Where is Samara?" Zoë asked.
"She is here, My Lady. She is heating tea as we speak," Nimshi replied, covering Zoë with blankets.

When Zoë awoke, she felt wet. Had she dreamt of Samara, Palmsquat and Nimshi? Am I back in the ocean? She forced her eyes open. She was in a small bath basin. Somehow, this place looked familiar. It even smelled familiar. But she couldn't recall where she was.

"Thank you, my friend." Zoë heard Samara say. Nimshi appeared in the doorway with a pot. Samara retrieved the warm water from Nimshi and slowly poured it into the bath where Zoë rested. Her eyes met Zoë's. She smiled. "Well, hello there."

The memories, the sights and sounds all collided in her mind. She couldn't make sense of any of it. "Where am I?"

"You are in my home," Samara replied.

Zoë looked around, reassuring her mind of what her eyes were seeing. She was saved, spared death, freed from Jezebel's chains.

"We thought we had lost you when you did not awaken," Samara said. "I had Nimshi move you from my bed to my basin an hour ago. We are slowly bringing the water temperature up."

"I dreamt of Palmsquat," Zoë said.

"No, my girl. I'm afraid you didn't."

"But I saw her clearly in my mind."

"She was not in your mind. She is in my garden."

Zoë's eyes widened. The mysteries of this place were now answered: the familiar surroundings and the smell, which could only be Palmsquat. She was curious to know how she and Palmsquat had both ended up at Samara's home.

"I suppose you are curious to know how you and Palmsquat ended up at my home."

Zoë raised her brows. "Yes, My Lady. That is precisely what I was wondering," Zoë said, just before submitting to another fit of coughing.

"I will be happy to tell you of my adventures this morning if you would be so kind as to tell me how you found yourself floating in the middle of the sea."

"Jezebel sentenced me to die at sea…" Zoë coughed and gagged once more, "a prize for her pride and for her god."

"Well, it's a good thing her god resides in her imagination or we might have had to contend with Asherah, having robbed her of her sacrifice."

Zoë smiled, relieved to be alive and in the care of Obadyah's mother.

"Obadyah!" Zoë exclaimed, her final moments with him catching up with her.

"What about Obadyah, my dear?"

"It was he who cast me out."

"My son carried out Jezebel's decree?"

"She was punishing him for the time we spent together outside of the castle walls."

"Ahh, yes," Samara replied, "I warned him." Samara took another pot of water from Nimshi and poured it into the basin. "Thank you, Nimshi, that will be all."

Nimshi nodded and reached for the empty pot.

"You knew this would happen?" Zoë asked.

"Jezebel's hatred takes aim when she feels threatened."

"How did I threaten her?"

"By having more contentment serving her than she had being served."

"I watched as Jezebel turned on me day-by-day," Zoë said. "Like a cloud in the distance that grew into an intense storm. Her anger stretched over me. And I was powerless to appease it. It was then I knew she would destroy me."

"If there is a lesson to learn from an encounter with Jezebel it is this—she is only soothed by vengeance."

"I didn't belong there," Zoë continued, "I was ready to go, even if it meant going to the bottom of the Sea."

"Why did Jezebel choose the Mediterranean as your place of death?"

"She believes Asherah came forth from the Sea at her inception."

"That is true," Samara agreed. "However, I doubt that is why you were abandoned at sea."

Zoë waited for Samara to explain.

"Jezebel longed for your death, that much is true. But what brought her the most pleasure, I assure you, was that she bid you die alone."

"But I was not alone," Zoë said. "Yahweh was with me." Hearing her own words, Zoë realized she was finally awake. Zoë's mistake was thinking Yahweh wanted what the Phoenecian gods wanted, to use her to secure more power. What was once so mystifying was now perfectly clear. All Yahweh ever wanted was the only thing she ever had to give. Her heart.

"Jezebel can manipulate her surroundings and dispense her hatred," Samara said. "She can trample your dignity, steal your courage, and mock your faith. But she is powerless, utterly useless to control, the thing she wants most in this world—sovereignty over Yahweh."

Samara held Zoë's hands, helping her to her feet as she crawled out of the basin. Wrapping her up, Samara walked Zoë to her bed.

Another fit of coughing overcame her. "I can't stop shaking."

Samara pulled the blankets back and helped Zoë lay down. "It will be some time before your body will calm from the trauma of this morning."

As Zoë slowly relaxed, she wondered about her rescue. "How did you find me?"

"I didn't find you. Theophanes found you. He spotted you through his monocular as he made his final push to shore."

"I saw him raise his sail."

"He commanded his rowers as well," Samara added, "though he did not think he would reach you in time."

"I have no memory of him pulling me from the water."

"Theophanes dove from the ship's rail, not long after your head had gone under. When he surfaced, his shipmates pulled you aboard. After Theophanes cleared the water from your lungs, he breathed life back into you. Then he contacted me."

"How did he manage that?"

"We are trade partners. On every trip to Sidon, Theophanes signals me. Using a reflecting glass, he is able to shine a light directly into my house. I knew Theophanes was scheduled to return to port this morning so I was awaiting his signal. He purchased some of your uncle's pottery and I purchased you."

Zoë's eyes dropped.

"What is it, my dear?"

"It's my papa. Kalbu. He died."

"I know," Samara replied. "I'm sorry."

Zoë kept her eyes down, her tears falling, one after another as she clinched her blanket with both fists.

"I was with him and your aunt when he died," Samara said.

"You were?" Zoë looked up. "How? Why?"

"Palmsquat led me to their home. I have been using your uncle's pots to store my scrolls. The vases I sold to Theophanes this morning were the last ones your uncle made before he was burned."

"How is my aunt? How is Donatiya?"

"She is bereaved. But she is also at peace. Her beloved gave his life in love for another. She knows he could not have done differently. And she would not have wanted him to."

Zoë nodded, thankful to know her aunt was not alone when her uncle died.

Nimshi handed Zoë some hot tea. She wrapped both hands tightly around the cup allowing the warm mist to rise up around her face. She breathed in the sweet honeysuckle which mixed with the scent of Kalbu's beloved pet. Through her tears she said, "I knew I smelled Palmsquat."

CHAPTER 25

THE TWO PROPHECIES

Ethbaal turned to Theophanes. "I have a task which requires your immediate attention."

"I am at your service, My King," Theophanes nodded.

"One of my companions from Bethlehem, a man by the name of Hiel, has set about rebuilding the city of Jericho. He is in need of supplies."

"Very well, My King, I will deliver the cypress we have harvested at Tyre."

"You must depart without delay."

"Yes, My Lord. However, begging the king's mercy, may I make a request of my king?" The king nodded. "I am short one man on my crew…"

"Fever? Disease?" Ethbaal interrupted with panic in his voice. Ethbaal, like all royals, was terrified of any illness. With unlimited power, might, and wealth at his fingertips, his health was the one thing he could not control. Most visitors to the palace were kept at a respectable and often absurd distance. Never was there physical contact between the throne and his subjects. One thing Theophanes knew, the day he brought sickness before the throne would be his last day in Sidon.

"No, no, My Lord, I merely dismissed an indolent sailor. I could fill the post with a Sidonian civilian, however, I would prefer, for this critical mission, a man who has served you well and is loyal to the crown." Theophanes said, gesturing towards Obadyah.

"I suppose I must agree with you, Theophanes," the king admitted. "Eunuch!" Ethbaal pointed in Obadyah's direction. Obadyah hurried to the king's side, taking a knee before Ethbaal. "I have gifted this one to Ahab. He can aid you on this shipment of goods. Then you will deliver him to the King of Israel."

"I understand, My King. However …" Theophanes paused.

"However, what? I pray to the gods you are not attempting to delay your departure."

"No, My Lord. I pause merely to remind the king of the prophecy against Jericho."

"Prophecy?"

"There is a story whispered among the Hebrews that Jericho is cursed." Ethbaal's eyes narrowed.

"As my Lord knows," Theophanes continued, "Jericho was the first city conquered by the Hebrews upon their return to the land of Canaan."

"I know the story of the destruction of Jericho and the earthquake which toppled its walls."

"Joshua, the leader who succeeded Moses, said, 'Cursed before Yahweh is the man who rises up and rebuilds Jericho.'"

"Am I to bear the weight of this prophecy?" The king said, rising quickly from his throne. "Does not Yahweh contend with his own people?" The king threw his hands in the air. "Furthermore," Ethbaal continued, "surely it is the builder who is condemned, not the supplier."

"Indeed, you speak the truth, My Lord. But your companion, Hiel, is Hebrew, a Bethlehemite, and the cost of Yahweh's disregard, I am told, is high."

"What is the price should he defy his god?"

"The one who builds, who does not heed the word of Yahweh, he will do so with the loss of his firstborn son. Tradition states he will die when the workers lay Jericho's foundation. And with the loss of his youngest son he shall set up its gates." A few moments of silence passed as Ethbaal considered the prophecy. "Shall I warn your companion, My Lord?"

"Deliver the goods," Ethbaal commanded. Should Hiel anger his god, and the curse of Yahweh find him, that is his problem and not my concern. And Theophanes… ."

"Yes, My Lord."

"Retain our price before one piece of timber is removed from your ship. Once we are in possession of his silver, you may inform him of this curse. Should Yahweh's word come to pass, we will be found innocent and Hiel will have only himself to blame."

"I am at your service, My King," Theophanes bowed as the king departed. Theophanes rose and pointed at Jezebel's eunuch.

Obadyah left his post and the palace of his king and followed Theophanes to the Phoenix.

Zoë appeared in the garden behind Samara's house.

"Good morning," Samara said, smiling as she continued to prune her flowering shrubs.

"Good morning, My Lady," Zoë returned.

"Samara," Samara corrected.

"My Lady?" Zoë asked.

"Good morning, Samara," Samara repeated.

"Good morning, Samara." Zoë grinned.

"How do you feel? Are you well rested?"

"Yes, My…I mean, yes, Samara, I feel much better."

"Let's return to the house for breakfast."

"I'm not hungry."

"I did not ask if you were," Samara said, sounding very much like a mother.

"Where's Nimshi?" Zoë asked, following Samara across her patio.

"He has gone into town to fetch supplies. He and Palmsquat should be returning within the hour."

"Does it pain him to walk?" Zoë asked as she pulled out a stool.

"It does. But he refuses to rest."

"I do not know of any crippled servants."

"Nor do I," Samara grinned, shaking her head as she set a cup of tea on the table.

"How did he come to be in your service?"

"He was attempting to steady a load of timbers being delivered to the palace. When the horse lost its footing, the load toppled over, crushing Nimshi's legs. They have been bent ever since. Ethbaal had ordered him executed, as one would destroy a lame animal. Theophanes happened to be in the king's company that day. He was able to convince the king to release him into his service."

"But what service could Nimshi offer a sea captain?"

"None, I suspect. Theophanes had not thought that far ahead when he spoke up on Nimshi's behalf. Signaling to me the next morning, he asked if I might use him as an inscriber."

"Surely his price was less than the silver I cost you." Zoë smiled.

Samara laughed and set before Zoë a bowl of plantains. "Nimshi cost me nothing, and in fact, Theophanes pays me to care for him. He has been working for me since that day. He serves me faithfully, grateful to have been granted his life and given a purpose."

Saddened, Zoë's eyes dropped.

"There is no cause for sadness," Samara replied, "Nimshi is quite content."

"It's not that. For I see his heart, he serves you with joy. I am sad, for it has just occurred to me that you and I rode in the wagon up the hill from the shore, forcing Nimshi to walk with Palmsquat. I have caused you so much inconvenience and Nimshi so much pain."

"Be at peace," Samara encouraged. "Having been gifted that smelly beast by your uncle, Palmsquat is Nimshi's only possession in this life. He loves her with a loyalty I would liken to my son's devotion to you."

Zoë blushed.

"I am the boy's mother, dear. I can see his care for you as clearly as you see me now. As for Nimshi," Samara continued, "I can tell you this. He suffers gladly. For his life was spared just as your life was spared. It is true, he walks with pain, but he has discovered the balm that soothes every ache—gratitude."

"Obadyah knew Theophanes would show me mercy," Zoë said. "He would not have cast me out if he doubted the compassion of the captain."

"Obadyah has a lot of anger towards Theophanes, and yet I believe he trusts him."

"Why is he angry with Theophanes?"

"Did you not know Theophanes served as the palace physician prior to his appointment to captain the Phoenix?"

Zoë's eyes revealed her surprise.

"One of his tasks was to prepare the young men who had been selected to serve the king."

Zoë turned away, the weight of that truth overcoming her.

"Theophanes is a good man," Samara continued. "He took no pride in doing what he did."

"I know," Zoë replied. "He had no choice, he could not have defied the king."

"As you may have heard, Theophanes will not transport slaves."

"It is clear he tests the king's patience," Zoë said. "I suppose the treasure he bestows upon Ethbaal outweighs the frustration he bestows on him as well."

"Theophanes carries the guilt of marking the bodies of those boys. Having stolen a piece of their humanity, he now can take no more of man's flesh."

Nimshi's voice rose from the direction of the road. "My Lady! My Lady!"

Samara and Zoë leaped up from their stools and hurried to the front entrance where Nimshi, out of breath, hobbled towards the house.

"What is it, my friend?" Samara inquired, rushing to his side.

"It is the king of Israel, My Lady!"

"Ahab?"

"He has… He has…" Nimshi paused, struggling for air.

"Nimshi, be calm," Samara urged. "Catch your breath."

"My Lady, I cannot be calm," Nimshi said, leaning over, resting his hands on his crooked knees.

"Come inside and sit down," Samara instructed. As she turned to lead her servant into her home, Nimshi grabbed her arm. Samara paused. Her expression revealed her shock and concern.

Zoë's heart caught in her throat. Nimshi's news must be dire.

When Nimshi looked up, his eyes glistened with looming tears. "Ahab has erected an altar to Baal in Samaria. And, My Lady, this he has also done. He raised a pole of Asherah."

Zoë felt relieved. Surely this wasn't such bad news as Nimshi thought. She expected Samara to tell him as much.

"This is the work of Jezebel," Samara remarked. "Stay here, Nimshi. I will bring you some water."

"Please. Allow me!" Zoë said. Not waiting for Samara's approval, Zoë hurried into the house, leaving Samara with her servant.

Zoë returned in haste, descending the front porch stairs just as Samara lowered Nimshi to the ground. She must hear what is so terrible about this news that even Samara would be distraught.

"My Lady, there is more." Nimshi continued, having finished the cup of water delivered by Zoë.

"Yes?" Samara replied.

"The idol masons had no sooner completed their task, and the new king and queen appeared. All of Samaria was present when Ahab and Jezebel entered the temple of Baal to pay homage to the work of their hands. When they exited the temple a man approached. Parting the crowd, he stood before the young king and queen, prophesying before them and before the people of Israel. The prophet said, 'As Yahweh, the God of Israel lives, before whom I stand, surely there shall be neither dew nor rain these years, except by my word.'"

"Do you know the man who spoke those words?" Zoë asked Nimshi.

"He called himself Elijah the Tishbite," Nimshi replied.

"Elijah." Samara's eyes dropped. "Very well, my friend, we must prepare. Come." Samara turned towards the house.

"Should it please My Lady, I will wait for Palmsquat," Nimshi said, gesturing down the hill where his plump companion meandered up the trail.

Samara nodded and remained with Nimshi.

"Who is Elijah?" Zoë asked.

"I know not," Samara replied. "This is the first time I have heard his name uttered."

"Why are you downcast, Samara? There are many prophecies given which do not come to pass."

"Indeed, there are countless seers in the land of Canaan," Samara replied. "However, there are some striking differences between those diviners and Elijah from Gilead."

Zoë listened intently.

"He has made his prediction publicly before the king and the people of Israel—there can be no confusion concerning the words which came forth from his mouth. Also, he states his homeland, putting his family at risk. And then there is his name."

"His name?"

"His name bears the purpose of his message, for Elijah means 'Yahweh is God.' Notice," Samara continued, "the content of his prophecy is destructive. It is not the mild and tasteless slaver of a chief-seater, looking to win the praise and favor of his king."

Nimshi snorted in laughter.

Zoë turned to him in surprise.

"Chief-seaters are those who love the place of honor at the king's table," Nimshi added.

Zoë thought back on all the guests of the king who were granted the place of honor. She had never understood the king's recognition as a bad thing. And yet, there was something distasteful in their appearance—something she had never attempted to interpret, something she looked back on now with queasiness.

"Do you know of any seer who would endanger himself as this prophet has done?" Zoë inquired.

Samara shook her head. "No, indeed, for by his words, his destiny is sure. He is now the enemy of the crown. We must prepare with the expectation that Elijah's words will come to pass. For if the word of Yahweh has found him, this I assure you, drought is imminent."

CHAPTER 26

THE PHOENIX CAPTAIN

Obadyah took his place in line with the mariners. He reached for a box of supplies and mindlessly handed it to the sailor next to him. When all the provisions were aboard, they pulled anchor. The Phoenix and her crew were on their way to Antioch. With his tasks completed, Obadyah stood on the deck, fixing his gaze on the sea. *Has it already been a week since we left Sidon?*

As the Phoenix picked up pace, the ripple of the wake sent him back to the moment he pushed Zoë into the cold deep waters. He watched as the waves rolled away from the hull, each one becoming weaker and weaker until they all disappeared, swallowed up by an unquenchable sea. *Oh Yahweh, what have I done?* Obadyah pleaded with his God once again for the life of the Phoenician girl who lay hold of his heart. Surely, Theophanes would have seen her enter the water. An experienced captain always knew what was happening in the sea around him. But did he respond with mercy? Or indifference?

Obadyah had not spoken a word to Theophanes about that morning, too afraid of the answer. And, if he was honest with himself, too afraid of the captain. If he could just catch Theophanes alone, Obadyah thought, he would ask him. But, Obadyah knew, he had already used that excuse. He had long been out of excuses. Still, he wondered, *Am I strong enough to face the truth?*

The Phoenix entered the open waters of the Great Sea. Obadyah could feel his frustration rising with the pace of the ship. He could not stop the memories of that day from circling in his mind. He was the last person to touch her, his voice the last one she heard. How could he go on with news of her death? A death that came at his hands.

The man who knew the fate of his beloved stood only steps away but Obadyah's confidence in the mercy of the captain had begun to wane. Sensing Thophanes's presence behind him, Obadyah said. "Will you hand me over to my enemy?"

"You are the property of the king," Theophanes replied. "He has declared you a slave of Ahab."

"You have defied kings before," Obadyah replied.

"There is a time to defy and a time to submit. I bid you remember that when you serve your new master."

"Remember?" Obadyah said, turning to face Theophanes. "You have made it impossible for me to forget."

"Are you grumbling?" Theophanes said. "Is this the respect you show your host?"

"It is the respect I show the man who marked me: Property of the King."

"Was it not your wish to serve your king?"

"I was a child. I...." Obadyah could feel himself shrinking before the Captain.

"And now you whine as a child."

Obadyah straightened his back and clenched his fists.

"And what do you plan to do with your indignation?" Theophanes asked. "Think carefully before you decide. Certainly there are situations that demand a fight. But fists cannot be raised with every rise of anger inside of you."

Obadyah looked past Theophanes. Seeing his men who stood ready to defend their captain, Obadayah's fingers loosened. He took a breath releasing the tension of his muscles.

"You've made a wise decision," Theophanes said.

"Do you imagine I am concerned with your opinion?"

"Was it not your eyes spying on me as I approached the king's courtyard? If my opinion does not interest you," Theophanes said, "why take note of my presence at the castle?"

"I care neither for your presence nor your opinions but only for the information you possess."

"Very well," Theophanes replied. "Let us bargain for the information that I possess and you seek."

"Release your men to their tasks," Obadyah said, "that we may converse in private."

"You disrespect me and now you command me? You forget, eunuch, that you are the one in need!"

Obadyah could feel his blood rising, pulsing with thorns, tearing him up from within. When the venom coursing through him found his temples, Obadyah locked his gaze on the captain. "You are right, O. My. Captain. There is an occasion to fight!" Obadyah gnashed his teeth and lunged at Theophanes. His chest collided with the captain's, upending him with the force of a tree toppled by a storm. As Theophanes's back slammed onto the deck, his men rushed to the aid of their commander, each one grabbing for a piece of Obadyah who was quickly subdued. But not before his fist flew. Theophanes would certainly make him pay. But whatever the cost, whatever more Theophanes would take from him, he could not steal Obadyah's satisfaction of watching blood run down the captain's chin.

Theophanes swiftly returned to his feet, his crew having restrained Obadyah. Wiping the blood from his mouth, Theophanes said, "Hang him over the side."

Two sailors held Obadyah as another ran to fetch a line. Securing a rope to Obadyah's ankles, the crew tossed him head first into the Sea.

Theophanes looked over the side. "Lower the line until his head finds the water," Theophanes commanded. The men obeyed and Obadyah sank further. He began to fight for each breath, his head rising and falling beneath the surface as the ship rolled over waves.

Blood rushed to his face and Obadyah's head began to pound. Then his thoughts returned to Zoë and her battle with the Sea. She had trusted him, offering not a bit of resistance as he led her to the ship's edge. In her most vulnerable moments, she gave herself to him. Then, he remembered, he had told Zoë to fight. Tightening his stomach, he raised his head out of the water and reached for the rope. He began pulling himself up, grabbing the line, first with his right hand and then his left.

Theophanes smiled. Several of his men rushed to the side of the ship. As Obadyah appeared to be making progress, Theophanes signaled to one of his deckhands.

"Byblos, if the boy reaches the rail, strike him in the mouth," Theophanes said, wiping the blood from his lip once more. The eager sailor nodded and removed his tunic. When Obadyah's nose crested the edge, Byblos gave him his best shot. Obadyah fell. The rope around his ankles held fast, throwing his body up against the hull of the Phoenix. The men cheered as his head dropped below the surface of the water.

Dazed, Obadyah closed his eyes. Sobering himself he began again. He reached for the rope and pulled himself up towards the ship's deck.

Theophanes nodded. "Maybe the boy has some fight in him after all," Theophanes said.

"Now what, My Lord?" Byblos asked. "Shall I strike him again?"

"No," Theophanes replied, "you have had your fun. However, I dare not deprive the rest of my crew. Theophanes, facing his men, said, "Each of you may strike him once. If he makes it back up after that, allow him to come aboard."

Theophanes's men smiled, eager to obey their captain. Each time Obadyah's face met the ship's rail another man struck him–first on the mouth, then on the cheek, then on his temple. Blow after blow, Obadyah fought his way back to the top. When the final fist made contact, his body was tossed, once more, back into the sea.

Battered, but undeterred, Obadyah gathered himself and reached for the rope one last time. Dragging his body up and over the ship's rail, he fell in a heap onto the deck. With his left eye swollen shut and his lip split in three places, Obadyah lay at the feet of Theophanes panting like an overworked dog. A steady stream of blood and saliva stretched from his mouth onto the surface of the Phoenix.

"You are soiling my vessel," Theophanes said, throwing a cloth in the direction of Obadyah's face.

Without looking up Obadyah accepted the rag and began wiping up the mess made by his wounds.

"Bring the boy some water," Theophanes said.

Byblos returned quickly and handed a jug to Obadyah.

"Thank you," Obadyah said, making eye contact with Byblos.

"So, it seems you are capable of learning a lesson," Theophanes said. "Although I have to say, you could have saved yourself quite a beating had you learned it an hour ago.

At that Obadyah looked up, glaring at the captain of the Phoenix.

"Careful," Theophanes warned, "your emotions have not served you well thus far."

Obadyah paused, searching for the breath and courage to utter his next word.

"You are strong, I'll give you that," Theophanes continued. "But you are also impetuous. And it seems you are a fool as well."

"What joy do you gain by casting your insults upon me?" Obadyah asked, while he worked to loosen the line that had embedded in his ankles.

"Forgive me," Theophanes said, "have I hurt your feelings?"

"I suppose the mighty captain is without feelings," Obadyah replied, his voice straining as he peeled away the bloodied rope.

"Though I maintain a certain resemblance to the gods," Theophanes boasted, "I must admit, I am human. I too have emotions. But I am not deceived by them. You, on the other hand, do not wish to be a slave and yet you enslave yourself to your emotions."

Obadyah made no reply.

"Do not lie to yourself," Theophanes continued, "You attacked me for one reason, your love for yourself. And you survived your punishment for the very opposite reason, your love for another. Tell me, which of these motivations cost you and which one saved you?"

Obadyah sat in silence, knowing full well that Theophanes spoke the truth. Obadyah's consuming desire was Zoë. But now he could see, there were other desires inside him, ones that could distract him, even control him. Impulses he would have to overcome if somehow, someday, he might be worthy of her.

"Do you still cling to your pride?" Theophanes said.

Obadyah shook his head. Was the notoriously conceited captain really accusing him of pride?

"I must say, there are far more noble motivations...a girl, for example."

Obadyah's head shot up.

"Ahh, I see I have your attention now. Are you going to tell me about the maiden who gave your heart its courage?"

Obadyah returned his eyes to the deck.

"I dare say," the captain continued, "a eunuch in love..."

"Cease!" Obadyah yelled, water and blood spraying from his mouth.

"Cease? Cease, you say? Have you learned nothing in my presence?"

"I understand fully! Your words are meant to mock me!"

"You understand nothing. For my words are meant to instruct you."

Obadyah looked away from the captain. He closed his eyes, his heart pounding in his head. He told himself to slow his breathing. It was something his mother had taught him to do. "Breathe with me," she had said when he was ten and had witnessed his friend mauled by a lion. "One, two, three" she had counted as she pressed her hand against his chest. Obadyah took a deep breath and counted. He could hear his mother's voice, confident and calm. He swallowed his anger. He would no longer give Theophanes the pleasure of distracting him. He let out a long slow breath, one...two...three.... And then, for the first time since he boarded the Phoenix, Obadyah took control of his emotions. "Captain," he said, "may I...may I inquire of you?"

"Perhaps," Theophanes replied. "What do you offer in trade for the information you seek?"

"I offer my submission," Obadyah replied.

"Your submission?" Theophanes laughed. "You offer me something I can get on my own."

Obadyah felt a spark of anger ignite inside him. But he closed his eyes once more. And when he did, he saw Zoë. Theophanes was right. It was Zoë who had rescued him, not from his circumstances, but from a far more destructive enemy, his fear.

Obadyah searched for words. Words that might overcome the barrier of one man's ego. "I vow to you my services as well while aboard your vessel." It wasn't enough, Obadyah knew it the second the words fell from his mouth. Obadyah could sense Theophanes looking through him. He was still holding onto a piece of his pride. It was at that moment he knew, he must give up everything to get the one thing he desires most. "And," Obadyah continued pulling himself onto his feet, "I pledge to you my respect, Captain, for the remainder of our voyage."

"I accept your terms," Theophanes replied. "Pose your question."

"Last week you approached Sidon's shore at sunrise," Obadyah said, squaring his shoulders towards the captain, "and…"

"And the young lady who has captured your heart descended below the surface of the water just as we arrived."

Obadyah's heart dropped to his stomach. His mouth fell open. But he held his eyes up. He would keep his promise. More importantly, he would maintain his dignity, even in his submission to this man.

"She was fortunate," Theophanes continued, "to have been rescued by an experienced captain who happens to also be a skilled physician."

Obadyah filled his lungs with air, new air that surged through him like the calm the morning after a storm.

"Take this truth to heart," Theophanes said, "for there is an important lesson here. The physician whom you despise. The physician who marred your flesh and punished your ignorance is the very physician who now delivers hope to your soul."

Theophanes's arrogance, normally provoking Obadyah, fell on deaf ears.

"She lives?" Obadyah said. He did not doubt Theophanes's honesty, and yet, at the same time, he could not believe what he was hearing.

"Her body temperature had dropped so I cannot promise you she has survived, but, you have my word, she was alive when I saw her last."

"You did not…?"

"Inform Jezebel?" Theophanes interrupted. "No," he said, offering no further information.

Obadyah suspected Theophanes was testing his patience. But with news of Zoë's well being before him, he could not remain silent. "Forgive me, my Lord," Obadyah said, "I humbly inquire about the girl's destiny. Should she have survived, please Captain, where might I find her?"

"I sold her to your mother."

CHAPTER 27

THE HARD TRUTH

Zoë's heart soured when she heard the news that Jezebel had left for Israel. She pleaded with Samara. "I must visit my aunt to comfort her, tell her I live and am well." Samara was busy in her garden preparing for the coming drought. She listened to Zoë as she chipped away some of the dry earth with a sharp stone. Samara then placed flat rocks around the root base of each plant hoping the perimeter of rock might hold in the precious water and limit run off.

"Nimshi can speak of your well-being to her," Samara replied.

"Yes, but…"

"You stood before the residents of Sidon," Samara interrupted. "Your face is the rendering of Jezebel's pride, something Ethbaal will surely continue to protect."

Longing to feel the comfort of her aunt's arms, Zoë searched for a crack in Samara's reasoning. "Surely the village of Zarephath is a safe distance from the palace."

"Your appearance anywhere near Sidon will certainly accomplish the end Jezebel desired for you. And should you be forced to pay that price, I can assure you, you will not merely be cast out to sea."

Zoë conceded. She would not see her aunt—not now. She feared not ever again.

"You have given your heart to Yahweh," Samara said. "You must abandon your will as well. Trust that He will care for your aunt just as He sustained you in the sea."

"But how do you know Yahweh will protect her?"

"I don't know Yahweh will protect her."

Zoë was stunned. Samara always had an answer, yet this time, to this most important question, she had none.

"If I knew what Yahweh was going to do," she continued, "there would be no reason to trust. Yahweh gives us glimpses of His character, but He does not reveal to us all of His plans. In knowing what we know, we have good cause to believe. In not knowing what we do not know, we are afforded an opportunity to trust."

Zoë listened.

"Yahweh has given you many reasons to believe. Now you must believe in what you have come to believe." Samara paused. "Can I ask you something?"

Zoë hesitated then nodded.

"Tell me," Samara inquired, "does my son love you?"

Zoë looked away. "He…he has not said as much."

Samara nodded, as a teacher does when she is encouraging a student whose answer was partially correct. "Let me ask you this," she continued. "Did your papa love your aunt?"

"Oh yes, very much."

"How do you know? Did he speak of his love often?"

"Well, no," Zoë confessed. "In fact, I don't know if I have ever heard him say those words, except, of course, to Palmsquat."

"Your uncle did not tell your aunt he loved her? But he told his donkey he loved her?"

Zoë laughed.

"Did he utter his affections for the animal in the presence of your aunt?"

"Yes, quite often," Zoë said, enjoying the memory Samara had stirred up.

"Clearly, you have no reason to doubt Kalbu's love for his beast. But why do you not question his love for Donatiya?"

"His love was always there, always displayed, but not by words, by…by something greater than words."

"Describe it to me, this wordless love."

Zoë drew in a deep breath and looked to her thoughts as she leaned back on Samara's couch. "My uncle was attentive," she began, "perhaps to a maddening degree." Zoë paused, taking a moment to swallow her tears. "You know those sea birds," she continued, "the ones that land on the beach in the spring?"

Samara gave a comprehending smile.

"The males extend their wings, lowering them towards the sand. When their favored female approaches, they flop and dance about. And when their prancing fails, the crazy loons pursue their chosen companion, though the objects of their desire seem to want nothing more than a morsel to eat."

Samara smiled again, "I am familiar with this approach."

"That was my uncle," Zoë said. "He was sustained by his love's recognition of his existence—the calm assurance of her eyes meeting his. And he wouldn't stop until got what he was after, as my aunt was forced to experience each day. Papa was also kind," Zoë continued, "but not how most people understand kindness. Zoë paused to make eye contact with Samara. "You know the priests of Baal who linger outside the temple?"

Samara nodded.

"There are those who run to them the moment they appear. They place coins in the hem of their tunics, but only after the crowds have arrived. They receive praise from their companions who pat them on the back, approving of their very visible good deed. A futile hope their god will repay their kindness. Kalbu was different. He gave—to me, to Donatiya, to his neighbors and even to strangers, neither for recognition nor reputation, but only for the joy of giving." Zoë paused, tired, having drawn each memory from a well deep inside her. Lowering the bucket once more, she pulled up her final thought, and with it, tears. "My uncle was…" her voice strained, "he was the night sky."

Samara smiled and closed her eyes.

"Obadyah told me the God of all creation authored the moon's glow. 'It is Yahweh who has also given the moon to depend on the night,' Obadyah said, 'by Yahweh's decree the moon and the night belong together.'

"He has the heart of a psalmist," Samara replied.

"Many stars shine in the presence of the night sky," Zoë recalled, "but nothing outshines the moon. The darkness surrenders to that one light that outshines all lights."

"You have answered your own question, my dear," she said, opening her eyes. Reaching with her gaze, Samara brought them together as a line that connects two ships. "Remember your own words, Zoë, for by them you know that love is not sentiment. It is confidence."

Zoë wondered if Samara was speaking of Obadyah or Yahweh. "I believe," Zoë replied, "but I am afraid."

"Of course you are afraid. I too am afraid," Samara admitted. "Great is our fear. But great is our confidence as well. Trust my son. Trust your God. Both have given you reasons to hope. And hope, my girl, does not disappoint."

Zoë followed Samara's example and gave herself to trust in Yahweh's upholding of her aunt. The two women of faith proceeded in faith, not having any clue what Yahweh had in store for them or for the ones they loved.

Sailing peacefully with Theophanes from Antioch to Tarsus, Obadyah was quick to respond when beckoned. Completing his duties, with diligence and deference, Obadyah kept his word, fulfilling the promise he made in exchange for word of Zoë.

While Theophanes was ashore his crew remained, preparing the ship for the following morning's departure. Obadyah sensed his efforts to help only disrupted the rhythm the sailors had perfected. Instead, he looked to land. Theophanes had business with a man named Uriah, a relative of a soldier by the same name who had served as one of King David's mighty men. Theophanes welcomed his companion by placing a hand on each of Uriah's shoulders, a greeting typically reserved for family. The nature of Theophanes's meeting with the Hittite made Obadyah curious. He turned to Byblos. "Who is Uriah to Theophanes?"

Byblos shrugged his shoulders and spoke without looking up from his work. "It would be wise not to ask."

The following morning both ship and crew headed south towards Cyprus. Obadyah found himself back on deck. There was little else for him to do. He leaned over the rail and watched the water crash against the side of the hull. When the Phoenix entered the open sea, Obadyah noticed a dolphin breach the surface. He had only ever seen the illusive mammal, the one the Greeks called the sacred fish, at a distance. Now, he could almost reach down and touch it.

Obadyah marveled as the elegant sea swimmer adjusted its speed to keep pace with the ship's rowers. Like a child in a meadow, challenging a friend to a foot race, the dolphin seemed to beckon the boat to carry on. Obadyah pondered its sleek effortless movements. Whereas the Phoenix conquered the sea by might, forcing the water to submit, the dolphin found its way forward peacefully, water and creature moving in agreement, companions, not master and slave, friends.

The cliffs along the Cyprus coastline were the first to become visible as the

Phoenix continued its voyage south along the eastern coast of the island. Still an hour from landing, Theophanes approached Obadyah.

"We will dock at Amathus," he said.

Obadyah nodded respectfully, but said nothing.

"The goddess Astarte resides here."

Obadyah was quick to recognize Theophanes's approach, having overheard his mother arguing with him during one of their business deals. During one conversation concerning the nature and existence of the gods, Theophanes said, "Why choose one? Is it not more logical to either believe in all deities or to believe in none of them? It seems to me preferable to keep them all in one bucket labeled: gods. That makes for easy reference and easy disposal."

Obadyah was beginning to weary of Theophanes' boasting. Still, Theophanes had no love for the pantheon. On that point, he and Obadyah were in agreement.

"I suppose it is more accurate to say Astarte is worshiped here," Theophanes corrected.

"What is your interest in man's gods?" Obadyah asked. "Since clearly, you do not believe."

"Faith is good business," Theophanes replied. "Demand for goddesses is on the rise. The Hittites to the north," he motioned with an outstretched arm, "the Israelites to the east and the Egyptians to the south, they all revere them."

"Revere who?" Obadyah asked.

"Any idol with breasts," Theophanes replied.

Obadyah laughed. "Thankfully your well endowed deities are mobile commodities."

"They are seasonal as well," Theophanes replied, joining in the mockery of the cyclical trends of idol worship. "They migrate like birds, taking advantage of favorable conditions." Theophanes seemed to be enjoying the moment of camaraderie, this place where he and Obadyah could exist together.

"Idols follow fools." Obadyah replied.

"Or perhaps it is the other way around." Theophanes added, smiling as he walked away.

Obadyah turned back towards the shore, the coastal cliffs of Cyprus coming into view. Unsheathed layers long hidden beneath the surface of the ocean emerged before him. He studied the exposed rock—the earth sliced like a cake. The stone walls stood against the perpetual forces of wind and wave. Powerful and imposing, the coastal barrier bled streaks of green and blue, giving away its secret—copper woven amid the strata throughout the island.

As the Phoenix neared the harbor at Amathus, Obadyah could see where the colliding elements had carved out small caves at its base, a deal struck between earth and water. Suddenly, he was back with Zoë when they had escaped inside a similar cave, free from their assigned destinies, but only for the sake of a memory. How could something so full be so fleeting? Life the great jester, the foremost of bullies, forever stealing cherished minutes, moving them from present to past.

CHAPTER 28

THE ASSYRIAN HERO

At port, Theophanes left Byblos in charge of the crew. Following the captain, Obadyah crossed the gangplank connecting the Phoenix to the pier at Amathus. Obadyah had discovered he was not suited for sea travel. Even on solid ground, his body continued to move with the rhythm of swells. It was a normal sensation for sailors, but it was one he did not relish.

"You will adjust within the hour," Theophanes said, snickering as he watched Obadyah steady himself. The two men pushed their way through a scurry of people.

"Where are we headed?" Obadyah yelled over the bustling crowd.

"South," Theophanes replied, arriving at a single-axle carriage. Obadyah paused, unsure if the cart was meant for two. As his eyes swung from side to side taking in the details, Theophanes spoke up, "Well, what are you waiting for?"

Obadyah stepped aboard. Leaning over the side he continued to appraise the chariot.

"It is masterfully designed, is it not?" Theophanes said.

"I have never seen a war chariot drawn by a single horse."

"I modified the yoke," Theophanes replied. "And by moving the footboard back over the center of the wheelbase, a single stallion is able to pull two men."

"Is this construction Celtic?" Obadyah asked, noting the bronze shield adorning the side.

"It is Etruscan," Theophanes replied, "I purchased it in Civita."

Theophanes whistled and the horse nosed her way into the congestion.

"Do you know of Civita?" Theophanes continued, "It is one of the most prosperous cities in the world."

"I have heard of its beauty. A respite for the gods, they say."

"Its charm is mythical, and its culture is, well, look about you," Theophanes said, gesturing with his head. "Cyprus grows in the likeness of Civita."

Obadyah took note of his surroundings, absorbing the sights and sounds. The street, lined with trade stands, resembled the ones he had experienced at the Sidonian fair. But where Sidon produced a handful of idol makers, bakers, and mystics, Amathus boasted a diversity of vendors. Painters, scribes, metal smiths, weavers, musicians, one after the other bordered the street which ran parallel to the shore. Moving slowly through the congestion, Obadyah's eyes jumped from one shop to the next. Egyptian jewelry, Phoenician pottery, Assyrian weaponry all on display, side-by-side in a cultural stew of commerce.

"What is that?" Obadyah asked, gesturing with his head towards a stand of mushroom-shaped fabrics.

"It's called a parasol," Theophanes replied. "Fabric is stretched over bowed reeds and attached to bamboo shoots."

"What is its purpose?" Obadyah inquired.

"To provide shade from the sun."

Obadyah's eyes widened. "How would one hold it while maintaining his reins?" he asked.

Theophanes directed Obadyah's line of sight to a chariot similar to theirs. On it were two men, one holding the reins, the other holding a parasol over the chariot driver.

"I hope you don't expect me to do that!"

Theophanes laughed.

"Look there," Theophanes gestured.

Obadyah did look. What he beheld soothed the ache of uncertainty his heart carried for Zoë. Kalbu's pots!

"Your mother's ceramics," Theophanes said.

Passing by the pottery stand, they entered the black tent passage where women were displaying their bodies with the same enthusiasm as the parasol dealer. Obadyah had heard of such women, Ethbaal's court officials reciting tales of their exploits. It was as if their flesh was something separate from themselves, something easily sold and easily parted with. No one's treasure, the harlot is left with that one satisfaction, the moment when he submits to her beckoning, and her price.

Obadyah hurt for the women who seemed unaware of the difference between flattery and communion. His eyes found each girl as they passed. Some were children, the flicker of light having already gone out from their eyes. The older women, like winter trees, bore little evidence of a previous life, hope having long ago blown away.

"The Phoenicians have shared their crafts and their cults with the people of this island," Obadyah observed.

"Not only Phoenicia," Theophanes replied, "Mesopotamia, Canaan, and Egypt as well." Theophanes spoke with pride, as if he had a vital role in orchestrating the scene before them. "Do you not see it?" he exclaimed. "It is not the preeminence of gods, nor the might of military force, but trade which will one day dominate the world!"

Obadyah could not help but think of his mother living alone on the side of a mountain, content with her garden, her scrolls, and her care for Nimshi. She and Theophanes could not be more different. He, energized by the bustle of a city crowd. She, at peace with the rising and setting of each day's sun.

Obadyah was relieved when the congestion and noise of the port of Amathus was behind them. As their chariot moved from stone to clay, Obadyah drew in the clean salt air.

The two men traveled in silence, their horse climbing a series of gradual hills that eventually led them to the top of a cliff overlooking the Sea.

Theophanes tugged on the reigns and the chariot came to a halt. "We shall let the mare rest a bit," he said.

Obadyah jumped off of the platform eager to feel the earth beneath his feet. He could hear water trickling in the distance. "Is that a spring?"

Theophanes nodded. "Follow the trail around that outcropping," he said pointing.

Obadyah removed his sandals and sank his feet into the cool stream meandering down the hill towards the sea. After a few minutes' rest, Obadyah made his way towards the cliff's edge. He paused to take in the view.

"The top of the cliffs offer a majestic sight," Theophanes observed.

Obadyah stood in silence.

Theophanes, clearly not accustomed to being ignored, continued, "Looking up at the sheer rock face from the water can make a man feel small," he said. "But standing here, atop the mighty crags of Cyprus, we are giants."

"The height changes only our view, not our stature," Obadyah replied. "From the bottom we are small next to the towering rocks. From the top we are small before the expanse of the Sea."

Theophanes scoffed.

"Lie on your back," Obadyah continued, "if I have failed to convince you. Measure yourself against the sky."

"Why is it you long to be small?" Theophanes asked.

"Why do you try to convince yourself you are big?"

"Boy!" Theophanes said, "you sure don't think like a man!"

"Perhaps that is because I am not a man."

"Perhaps you are not! Remind me to buy you a parasol on our way back to the ship!" Theophanes said, returning to the chariot. Obadyah reluctantly followed.

As they traveled on, the terrain changed, gradually ascending a mountain. They had left the Phoenix more than an hour before. Not knowing where they were going, much less how far it would be, Obadyah began to wonder about this journey. Theophanes suddenly stopped the chariot in the middle of Obadyah's silent reverie.

"We're here," he said.

Obadyah looked around curious as to where 'here' was. Before him was a cluster of boulders each the size of a ship. The thorns and thistles which had lined their path crept up a shallow incline. Wrapping around the tops of the exposed mountain stone, the blonde brush framed the edge of each rock.

"Follow me," Theophanes said.

Obadyah obeyed. As they climbed the ascent before them, the ocean slowly came into view. Reaching down, Theophanes placed his palm on the crest of one of the boulders. Swinging his legs over the edge, he landed on a flat surface below. When Obadyah followed, his feet froze where they stood, silenced by the beauty his eyes beheld—a home hewn from the face of the stones assembled atop Cyprus's highest cliff.

Theophanes proceeded down a curved stairway. Obadyah followed. When they reached a marble patio below, the two men turned. Before them lay four carved cave chambers. Each one framed by pillars which set one room apart from the next.

Obadyah stumbled as he stepped back so that his eyes could take in the whole of the majestic structure.

"Well? What do you think?" Theophanes asked.

"It's…it's stunning," Obadyah replied.

"It is, isn't it."

Obadyah nodded, speechless at the beauty of what stood before him. As his eyes swept from one side of the dwelling to the other, an elderly man appeared.

"Captain!" the old man exclaimed, moving slowly towards Theophanes.

Theophanes approached the man and extended his arms. "My dear friend, how do you fare?" He asked, placing a hand on each of the man's shoulders.

"Well, Sir, very well." the old man replied, his eyes locked onto the captain.

"And where is that adventurous grandson of yours?" Theophanes inquired.

"You mean that mischievous grandson of mine?" the old man replied. "Ashur!" He yelled, directing his voice back towards the rooms.

"Yes, Papa," a boy said, his head appearing from behind the rocks which lay above the rooms.

"Come here, boy! Make haste! The captain has arrived."

"My Lord!" the boy exclaimed, jumping from the roof down to the ground level patio where the three men awaited him.

"Use the stairs, son! Is that not why we have made them?"

"Sorry, Papa." the boy said, running to greet Theophanes.

"You would think my name was 'Sorry Papa' with how many times this child must apologize each day."

Theophanes smiled. "This is my dear friend, Tukulti," Theophanes said, presenting the old man to Obadyah. "And this is his grandson, Ashur." he added, placing his hand on the boy's head.

"Hello, My Lord. Welcome," Ashur said, nodding before Obadyah.

Tukulti waited, allowing his grandson to greet their guests properly, in the manner he was taught.

"Tukulti," Theophanes said, "may I present to you my son, Obadyah."

Tukulti's eyes widened, his gaze locking onto Obadyah like he was a net overflowing with fish.

Obadyah, shocked, attempted to keep his face neutral and indifferent as he directed his attention towards Tukulti. Obadyah was not ready for his father's admission. He had expected to be introduced as the king's slave or perhaps one of the crew of the Phoenix. He could not remember the last time his father had called him his son.

Tukulti grabbed Theophanes's shoulder and began congratulating him as if he had become a new father at that very moment.

"Your son?" Tukulti repeated, his gaze on Obadyah unbroken.

"Yes, my son," Thophanes repeated. The four men stood together in silence, none knowing what to make of the revelation or how to proceed.

"Well?" Theophanes finally said, "Are you going to welcome him or must he be content with Ashur's greeting?"

"Forgive me, My Lord," Tukulti replied, moving towards Obadyah. "It is an honor to meet you, Sir."

Theophanes laughed as Tukulti continued his inspection of Obadyah.

"He is not for sale, Tukulti." Theophanes smiled.

"No! Of course not!" Tukulti replied. "He is magnificent!"

"He is, isn't he." Theophanes agreed.

Obadyah opened his mouth to greet Tukulti but the words caught in his throat. That Theophanes would claim him so freely, so effortlessly, almost with pride as though it were something he said every day, shook him. Still unable to speak, Obadyah offered his greeting to Tukulti in the form of a respectful bow.

Tukulti turned to Theophanes. "Sir, please rest and allow me to prepare a meal for you and your son."

"I have longed to hear those words since we docked." Theophanes said, making his way to one of the rooms off the patio.

"And you as well, My Lord." Tukulti said, gesturing to Obadyah, "please retire for a spell while I prepare your supper."

Obadyah, still reflecting on the past few moments, could not have slept if he tried. "I shall remain outside, if it pleases you."

"Yes, indeed. Tis' your residence, sir. Proceed at your will," Tukulti said, bowing towards Obadyah.

As Tukulti entered one of the center chambers, Obadyah looked at Ashur who had not stopped looking at him.

"I did not know the captain had a son," the boy said.

"I did not know the captain had a home," Obadyah replied.

"Have you been sailing long with your father?"

"I do not sail with Theophanes. I am a servant of the king."

"Which king?" Ashur asked.

"I was commissioned by Ethbaal, King of Sidon. However, I have recently been pledged to Ahab, King of Israel."

"I was named after a king." Ashur said. "My name is short for Ashurnasirpal, King of Assyria. My grandfather was named after Ashurnasipal's father, Tukulti-Ninurta."

"How is it that you have come to Cyprus from Assyria?" Obadyah inquired.

"My family was killed by the king." Ashur paused as if looking for permission to continue. It had been years since Obadyah had conversed with a child, their honesty and frankness something Obadyah was no longer accustomed to. He had to remind himself that Ashur was not angling for a particular response, just eager to share and hoping for a friend.

"How were you able to survive?"

"My papa," he said, pointing to his grandfather who was busily moving about in the lower level kitchen. "He saved me."

Ashur, his responses as short as his stature, waited for Obadyah to provide the next question.

"Your papa brought you here?"

"When my papa returned home and found that his family was killed, he cried for a whole day. He cried until he had no more tears. So he went to our well to replenish his supply of tears. When he raised the bucket, what came out was not water but me," Ashur said, placing his hand on his chest. "It was then my papa knew he had to escape. So he headed west towards Canaan."

"You bear the name of the man who killed your family?" Obadyah replied.

"I bear the name my mother and father gave me." Ashur said, his back straight, his voice steeled.

Obadyah cursed his thoughtlessness. The boy's name was all that remained of the family that loved him. It was clear he would take pride in that until the day he died.

Not waiting for an apology, Ashur turned and ran back towards the kitchen. "Papa," he shouted. "I'm going to show Obadyah Aphrodite's tears."

"Okay, son. But return at sunset," Tukulti replied.

Ashur, already half-way back to Obadyah, shouted into the air. "Yes, Papa!"

Ashur led Obadyah from the lower level courtyard towards the cliff's edge. He ran across a ridge paralleling the shore, jumping from stone to stone with the pace and grace of a gazelle. Obadyah struggled to keep up even while the span of his own strides were double Ashur's. As a few trees and shrubs began to appear on the landscape, the rock path gave way to a patch of moss tucked up under the shade of a leaning boulder. Ashur stopped in the middle of the spongy moss, and began to jump.

"You try it!" he said.

Obadyah moved towards Ashur.

"Take off your shoes!" Ashur directed.

Obadyah obeyed. Setting his shoes aside, he stepped onto the soft bare ground. He pushed up on his toes, feeling the tender moss rise and fall beneath his feet. A strange subtle silky anomaly in a land of immovable stone. Obadyah marveled at the distinct patch of earth, a presence so delicate even the rocks revered it.

Seemingly convinced his new friend had sufficiently enjoyed the moment, Ashur continued on. Soaring over obstacles, he knew his way by heart, his bare feet finding each flat landing.

Obadyah scrambled to put his sandals back on, eyeing Ashur as he got further away. He ran to catch him, surprised that he could be as nimble as the young boy on the uneven surfaces.

With one final jump, Ashur landed on a rock bridge which crept out away from the shore. His hands in front of him, he crawled like a mountain lion to the center of the rainbow shaped formation hovering above the Sea. Swinging his legs over the edge, he took a seat.

"The water has cut a hole through the rock, see?" Ashur said, pointing to what was impossible to miss.

"I see that," Obadyah replied, crediting his new friend with the arch rock discovery.

"Look. You can see the coral below the water's surface," Ashur pointed. "And look there." He pointed up towards the shear surface before them. "Do you see it?"

"See what?" Obadyah replied.

"Aphrodite's tears." Ashur said, pointing to the face of the cliff where the water had pushed its way through two round holes. The copper infused ground water ran down to the shore in streaks of blue and green. Obadyah stared at the natural wonder and then turned to Ashur.

"Why is she crying?"

Ashur shrugged his shoulders. "Papa says females cry sometimes for no reason."

"Perhaps she cries because she is trapped inside the stone,"

Ashur laughed.

"May I tell you a story?" Obadyah asked.

"Were you saved, too? Was your life spared as mine was?" Ashur asked. "Is Theophanes your champion?"

Obadyah sighed. The thought of his father as his champion had never entered his mind.

"My mother is my champion," Obadyah said.

"But mother's do not carry a sword."

"Not all champions triumph by steel."

Ashur nodded, not entirely understanding but entirely trusting of his new friend.

"Once upon a time," Obadyah began, "my people, the Hebrews, were enslaved in Egypt. After 400 years of harsh treatment, my ancestors begged Yahweh to deliver them from the abuse of the reigning Pharaoh."

"Who is Yahweh?"

"Yahweh is the living God." Obadyah thought of how to explain Yahweh to this young boy who likely only knew of a plurality of finite deities. "All other gods will bow to Him," Obadyah said.

"If He is so powerful, why did Yahweh leave the Hebrews in slavery?"

"It was not the right time."

"My papa says gods are fickle."

"Yahweh is not fickle, He is patient. He had a plan for His people. He knew the perfect time to deliver them from evil."

Ashur nodded. "King Ashurnasirpal is cruel. What did Pharaoh do to your people?" Ashur asked.

"He appointed taskmasters over them to afflict them as he burdened them with heavy labor. Day and night they slaved under Egyptian whips. But the more he abused my people, the more the descendants of Israel grew."

"Did your people revolt and escape?" Ashur asked.

"Shall I skip to the end," Obadyah teased, "or would you prefer to hear the whole story?"

"The whole story! Please!"

Obadyah smiled and continued, "So, with the rising population of Hebrews, Pharaoh worried they might soon outnumber the Egyptians. Fearful, he passed a law which he was convinced would bring the Hebrew expansion to a halt."

Ashur turned his attention away from the water and stared into Obadyah's eyes, "What was his decree?"

"Every newborn Hebrew boy would be thrown into the Nile."

Obadyah watched as Ashur's eyes swung to the sea.

"It just so happened, at that time," Obadyah continued, "a young Levite couple had a son. Their baby was beautiful and they loved him and they refused to cast him out."

"What did they do? How did they hide him? Wouldn't they be discovered once the boy grew?"

"If you can pause for a moment I will tell you what happened."

Ashur put his hand on his mouth permitting Obadyah to continue.

"After hiding their little boy for three months, they realized their secret would soon be uncovered. But the baby's mother had an idea, a way she might possibly save the life of her son."

Ashur appeared thoughtful. "What was her name?"

"Who?"

"The baby's mother!" Ashur gave Obadyah a reproachful look.

"Oh. Her name was Jochebed."

"What could she possibly do, this slave mother? They had no power to save anyone, especially a baby!"

"You are right, Ashur, for only by Pharaoh's pardon could the baby be spared."

"But how? How could Jochebed be granted a hearing before the king?"

"The Levite couple knew they could not appeal for the life of the boy. So Jochebed devised a plan. She took a woven basket and covered it over with pitch. She then put her son into the basket and set it afloat among the reeds on the bank of the Nile. Jochebed returned home. But, Miriam, Jochebed's daughter remained. She hid herself on the shore observing the basket at a distance. It was not long before the daughter of Pharaoh came down to the Nile for her regular time to bathe. Upon seeing the small basket tucked among the reeds, she sent one of her maidens to retrieve it. The princess looked inside and saw the beautiful baby. When he started crying she had pity on him and said, 'This is one of the Hebrew children.' It was then that Miriam appeared before the Egyptian princess and said, 'Shall I go and call a nurse for you from among the Hebrew women so that she may nurse the child for you?' Pharaoh's daughter said 'go.' So Miriam went and retrieved Jochebed."

"The baby boy was saved and he was returned to his mother?" Ashur replied.

"Indeed he was. But this is not the end of the tale. For when Jochebed appeared before the princess, the princess said, 'Take this child away and nurse him for me, and I will give you wages.'"

"So Jochebed got him back and she was paid to care for her own son?!" Ashur's face lit up. He grinned, looked at Obadyah, scrambled to his feet and jumped off the cliff.

Obadyah rose with a start, looking down just in time to see Ashur enter the water. Without a second thought he followed, pushing himself off the rock platform. The speed of his fall caused him to shout with a youthful joy he had long forgotten. His plunge into the water shocked his senses further. When he reached the surface he spun in a circle and looked for Ashur. Seeing him a few fathoms away, he swam towards the boy.

Ashur smiled, splashing Obadyah when he was close enough.

The two new friends laughed as they tread together in Aphrodite's tears.

"I awoke this morning as I have every morning," Ashur said. "I thought this day would be like every other day. But today is different."

"Yes," Obadyah agreed, "today was different."

They made their way to the shore and climbed up on one of the rocks below the stone arch they had just thrown themselves off of.

"Shall I tell you the end of the story?"

"There is more?"

"There is more. Will you remain until the end this time?"

"I'm sorry," Ashur replied. "I had to celebrate."

"There was cause for celebration!" Obadyah said. "The baby's life was spared, just as your life was spared. Just like the Hebrew mother, your mother found a way to hide her boy so that you might be saved."

"What was the name of the Hebrew baby?" Ashur asked.

"He was called Moses, which means, to draw out."

"Moses," Ashur repeated out loud.

"In my culture," Obadyah said, "it is common for people to change their name to represent their character or their calling."

"So Moses could be my Hebrew name! I was drawn out of the well just as Moses was drawn out of the Nile!"

"Indeed you were."

CHAPTER 29

THE DEPTHS OF EVIL

Obadyah and Ashur, still dripping from their venture into the Mediterranean, stepped off the cliff trail onto the stone patio of Theophanes's home.

"Looks like you boys need to dry off," Tukulti said, reaching for more wood to place on the fire. The boys stretched out their hands towards the flames. "You did not ask Obadyah to jump, did you, son?"

Ashur's eyes swung from the fire to the face of his new friend. "Well, I…"

Obadyah winked at Ashur and quickly spoke up. "He did not need to ask," Obadyah replied, placing his hand on Ashur's shoulder.

"What do you think of Aphrodite's tears?" Theophanes asked, appearing behind them.

"I say leave her in the rocks and keep her crying," Obadyah replied.

Ashur's hearty laughter echoed against the backdrop of the cave room from which Theophanes had emerged. Obadyah smiled, pleased to have brought joy to his new companion.

The fire was warm and welcoming, the patio having settled under the shade of the setting sun.

Tukulti turned to Ashur. "Son, fetch some wine for our guests."

Ashur hurried towards the kitchen.

"The boy has grown since my last visit," Theophanes said. "Yes, indeed," Tukultli replied, "but only in stature, not in discernment."

"His heart is pure," Theophanes said, "discernment will find him in due time."

"Your optimism exceeds mine," Tukulti said with a smile.

"As does my wisdom," Theophanes replied, "so you best listen to me."

Tukulti laughed, nodding enthusiastically. Before Tukulti could muster a response Ahur appeared holding a jug in one arm and four cups in the other. He distributed a cup to each of them. But when Tukulti reached for his cup, he spoke up.

"We are in need of only three cups, son," Tukulti said. Ashur's shoulders fell but he quietly submitted to his grandfather and turned back towards the house with his cup in hand.

"Come, Tukulti," Theophanes pressed, "grant the boy a man's drink in celebration of our evening."

Ashur spun around, his gaze locked onto his grandfather.

Tukulti found the hopeful eyes of his grandson and nodded.

Ashur straightened his back and quickly returned to the fire taking a seat with the other men.

As they ate, Obadyah watched his father interact with Tukulti and Ashur. Theophanes and Tukulti spoke effortlessly, sharing stories of the island and adventures on the sea. Ashur remained quiet, consuming the gift of company and camaraderie as easily as he did his wine. While Theophanes's tales were familiar to Obadyah his tone was not. The same adventures woven for Ethbaal were repeated for Tukulti and yet somehow they sounded entirely different. A candle flickered in Obadyah's mind when he realized why. Something changes when stories are told for the benefit of the listener rather than the renown of the teller.

When the conversation came around to the advancement of reigning kings, Tukulti interrupted Theophanes.

"Captain. If you wouldn't mind pausing for a moment while Ashur bids us good evening."

Theophanes nodded and turned to Ashur who locked his eyes on his grandfather.

"But I'm not tired, Papa."

"Tired or not, I am still your papa."

Obadyah marveled at the interaction between Ashur and his grandfather. Where he and his father trip and stagger their way through every conversation, Tukulti and Ashur seemed to get along even when they weren't getting along.

"Yes sir," the boy replied. Tipping his cup up above his head, the three men watched as the final drop of wine Ashur had saved splash onto his tongue.

"Good night, Papa. Good night, Captain. Good night, Obadyah."

"Good night, Moses," Obadyah replied, nodding towards Ashur as he made his way to his room.

Obadyah saw Tukulti and Theophanes give one another a strange look, but Obadyah offered no explanation. And the two older men knew not to ask for one.

With Ashur a safe distance from their conversation, Theophanes spoke up. "Tell me, Tukulti, does the king of Assyria push west?"

"West, north, and south, my friend. His army grows, his conquests grow, his spoils grow. This is not your typical dynasty, My Lord."

"Nonsense," Theophanes replied. "I shall find his weakness and buy his favor just as I have with Ethbaal and Ahab."

"My Lord, I urge you, do not approach this king. He reasons not as a man but as a god."

"He may think himself divine, but he is just a man. And I know how men think. Has there ever been a king I have not won?"

Tukulti sat in silence, his look grim. Obadyah could see that Tukulti was wrestling with something. It was obvious he had something to say. And eventually Theophanes noticed it as well.

"Is it the size of his army you fear?" Theophanes asked, "For whether he boasts thousands or tens of thousands, armies move by the word of their king."

"It is not that, My Lord, it is…"

"Is it his progress in weaponry? For I have heard he has abandoned bronze for iron."

"It is not that either, it is…"

"Is it the structuring of his forces? For that too has reached my ears—Ashurnasirpal training divisions of lancers and charioteers, bowmen and cavalry. All of these tactics may make for a powerful ruler, but none make him invincible."

"I will speak now, My Lord, and you will listen." Tukulti said with an authority he did not have and a tone he had yet to take.

Obadyah felt a prickling sensation move up his spine when Theophanes quieted and gave his attention to his friend. What was forthcoming could only be dire, Tukulti's eyes now fixed and sober.

"Ashurnasirpal is neither solidifying his reign nor is he fortifying his kingdom. He is building an empire. He is methodical and efficient, but that is not what makes him more dangerous than the others. It is his cruelty and his pleasure in cruelty. A man? Yes. But a man empowered by an evil not of this world!"

Theophanes remained silent as the voice of his old friend rattled.

"I have not told you what happened to my family."

"I know your family was killed by Ashurnasirpal," Theophanes replied, "there is no need for you to relive the account."

"But there is a need! A great need, My Lord! For I am not speaking of the fact of their deaths, I am speaking of the manner in which they died."

Obadyah did little to brace himself for Tukulti's story. Having lived in the wake of Jezebel's depravity and witnessed her evil firsthand, he had thick skin where treachery was concerned. Little did Obadyah know, nothing could have conditioned him for what he was about to hear.

"When storms are upon us," Tukulti began, "we fear. But the calm, the lull before the storm, is heaven's warning, preparing us for what we are about to endure." Tukulti sighed. "Nature is merciful that way. But there was no warning when my children were slaughtered, no dark cloud in the distance. No thunder announcing lightning's strike."

Tukulti grabbed a stick and began poking at the logs on the fire. "I had been to the city, a day's journey, to purchase figs and spices for the cake my wife would prepare in celebration of our grandson's birth. I whistled on the way home," Tukilti said, shaking his head. "It is the one thing sad people cannot do. Did you know that, My Lord? When you are overcome with sadness you can still do many things. You can walk and talk. You can even eat. But you cannot whistle."

Tukulti dropped the stick he was holding and covered his face with his hands. "My son…" he paused, his voice shaking. "I saw my son first," Tulkuti said. "As I approached from the road…I could see that he had been speared…through his stomach. Like a piece of meat on the end of a butcher's knife, they hoisted him up into the air, and…and left him to bleed out…to suffer a slow death. Suspended above the ground, my son would have been conscious of the rape of his daughters. Their bodies were laid at the base of my son's execution stake. The girls…" Tukulti swallowed. "The girls were covered with blood, their small delicate bodies displaying the evidence of their abuse."

Obadyah lowered his head. His hands were gripping his thighs as he struggled to bear the words spoken by Tukulti.

"I suppose rape and torture are common fates to be suffered at the displeasure of a sadistic king. But this ruler…this ruler, My Lord," Tukulti said looking up at Theophanes, "he is not common. For this was just the beginning of what he had done to my family."

Tukulti stood up and moved slowly across the stone patio towards a stack of logs. One at a time he loaded his arms and strolled back to the fire.

Tossing each log in, Tukulti found his place and lowered himself to his bench. Theophanes and Obadyah remained silent, patient for Tukulti to find his next words.

"As my granddaughters were brought to their father, left to die within his sight and sound, my grandsons were brought to their mother. Their chests were split open. The space where their hearts should be visible lay empty, nothing left inside them but a hollow cavern of blood and bone. Do you know," Tukulti said, his eyes catching Theophanes, "I spent a day in search of them, their hearts. They were not to be found." Tukulti's voice dropped with his eyes back to the fire before him. "They were stolen," he continued. "Ashurnasirpal afforded me nothing, not even the dignity of a burial for the souls of my boys. But that was not the end of my suffering." Tukulti stopped to wipe a tear that ran down his cheek. "My grandsons were flayed. The skin of their backs fastened to their mother's face. She died by suffocation, by her own son's flesh as…"

Obadyah sprang to his feet. His actions were so sudden, so unconscious, he surprised even himself. His body was making demands his mind could not process, his heart pumping blood faster than his veins could move it. He turned away from Tukulti, unable to bear another word. Shame overwhelmed him as he realized he could not even endure a picture, while Tukulti was forced to endure the reality.

"Obadyah!" Theophanes yelled.

Obadyah knew his behavior embarrassed his father, but he could not face him. He wanted to have the strength to endure with Tukulti as he relived the horrific tale. He wasn't angry with his father for yelling at him. Were he strong enough, he would have done the same. Obadyah looked down at his hands. They trembled. He told himself to stop shaking. His body would not obey him.

Tukulti continued, stearing each word towards Theophanes. "This man as you call him," Tukulti said, "he follows no rules of war, nor is he mindful of the laws of nature. Even wild beasts do not behave as he does and attack unprovoked." Tukulti said.

"Obadyah!" Theophanes said, demanding his son's attention.

Obadyah turned.

"Sit down and listen to Tukulti."

"Listen?" Obadyah roared, "You would have me listen? I am not the one who should listen! It is you who will not hear!" he said. Obadyah stormed past his father towards the room closest to the fire. Just before he crossed the threshold, Obadyah turned. "If you make a deal with this Assyrian king," he said, "you will not hear the sound of my voice again!" Lying down on a mat in the room just off the patio, Obadyah could hear Tukulti and his father continue their discussion.

"I'm sorry," Theophanes said.

"Do not be sorry, my friend. Would you prefer to have a son who is able to endure such a tale?"

"I suppose not," Theophanes replied, "but Obadyah is so emotional—too emotional to survive in this cold-blooded earth."

"Two sons driven by the heart," Tukulti said.

"And now all I have is Obadyah, and he is angry with me."

"Have you not told him what happened to his brother?"

Obadyah sat up, his ears reaching for his father's next words.

"No," Theophanes replied.

Obadyah strained for the words that he had hoped might fall from his father's lips. As well as the one's he hoped wouldn't.

"I had thought....Maybe.... It's just, well, Obadyah and I, we're not close."

"If you were honest with him," Tukulti suggested, "perhaps then, you could be close."

"Perhaps. But I have business to tend to. And Obadyah is set to serve Ahab." Obadyah fell back onto his cot. His hopes for his freedom falling at his father's next words.

"Obadyah's future is with Israel."

"It seems your son is right, My Lord," Tukulti said. "You listen but you do not hear. You, me, Obadyah, even Ahab…everyone's destiny is tied to Assyria. This ruler will sharpen his appetite until he has control of the world. Remember, he is cruel not for the reputation gained by cruelty, but because he craves it."

Theophanes rose to his feet and began pacing.

"Do you not see?" Tukulti continued. "Ashurnasirpal prowls like a roaring lion, seeking someone to devour. Your only hope, my friend, is to never cross his path."

"Tukulti?" Theophanes said, pausing a short distance away.

"Yes, My Lord."

"What happened to your wife?"

"Her fate and the anguish which accompanies it surpasses all my pain."

Obadyah told himself to not listen. He covered his ears so he would not be able to hear. But when Tukulti began to speak he lowered his hands. He would not compound his shame in having walked away by granting himself mercy. He did not deserve to spare himself the rest of Tukulti's heartache.

"As hard as it was to see my family destroyed before my eyes, at least with them I knew their fate. I know not what happened to my wife, and not knowing is worse than death."

Theophanes awoke to the smell of baking bread. He swung his feet off his bed and slid them into his sandals. Stretching as he walked, he made his way from his room to the kitchen.

Tukulti greeted his friend as he prepared their morning meal.

"Did you sleep well, My Lord?" Tukulti asked.

"I did indeed." Theophanes replied. "You have done beautiful work here," he said as he grabbed a piece of fruit from the bowl on the counter. "Comfortable quarters, delicious food, amazing views," the captain continued. "It is more than I expected." Theophanes threw a segment of orange into his mouth.

"Do you not expect excellence from me?"

"Yes, of course. Forgive me," Theophanes bowed, "I stand in the presence of an artist."

Tukulti smiled as he continued to work.

"Have you seen Obadyah this morning?" Theophanes asked, while pouring hot water over a cup of dried leaves.

"He retired late last night. He and Ashur left early this morning to chase the sea turtles."

Theophanes nodded as he sipped his tea.

"I warned them not to linger," Tukulti continued. "as I expect you will be moving on today."

"The boys enjoy one another's company."

"They do indeed, My Lord."

"How are our supplies?" Theophanes asked, finally getting down to the business of his visit.

"Secure. I have developed a strong bond with the autochthonous. The Cyprus natives faithfully maintain the perimeters of our caves."

"Might they be coaxed to report our…goods?"

"They know nothing of the cave's contents. They are born of the soil of Amathus. They have no loyalty to immigrants."

"Have you forgotten, Tukulti, we are immigrants."

"I have not forgotten, My Lord. And they have not forgotten your faithfulness to them either."

"I made a simple purchase, nothing more," Theophanes replied.

"You rescued their tribesmen from the Damascus slave market."

"It was for my own purposes that I retained them."

"Do not underestimate the power of mercy, My Lord. That you would redeem those who were condemned, that we might receive them as sons. There is, my friend, no greater debt."

"Do not think too highly of me, Tukulti, their redemption has served me well."

"And me and my grandson. And, by the way," Tukulti added, "you may dictate to me my tasks for I serve at your pleasure. But my thoughts, they shall be mine."

"You are a very stubborn old man."

"Yes, I know," Tukulti replied. "I have perfected this trait from observing My Lord."

"Must you go so soon?" Ashur moaned, his crestfallen eyes reaching for the Captain's sympathies.

"Must you ask me the same question every time I leave?" Theophanes replied, placing his hand on the boy's shoulder.

Tukulti handed Obadyah the sack of food he had prepared for their return to the Phoenix. Their eyes met in a moment of camaraderie, no words were needed to convey.

"I have a new question, My Lord," Ashur said, reaching for anything that might keep their guests a few moments longer in his presence.

"Very well, you are permitted one new question," Theophanes said, "but only one, so think carefully."

Ashur did not think for even a second but blurted out, "Will you allow Obadyah to stay with us?"

Obadyah could not subdue the smile which crept up his face. Ashur wanted him to stay. If only he could. If only there was a way. If only this life were a place where boys could have wishes and somehow find what their hearts desired.

"Obadyah has important tasks ahead of him," Tulkulti reminded his grandson.

"I'm not so sure about that," Obadyah replied, smiling at his new friends.

"Farewell," Theophanes said, simple and unemotional. He mounted his chariot and awaited Obadyah.

Ashur approached Obadyah and motioned for him to give him his ear.

Obadyah bent down giving Ashur his full attention.

"We will swim again, one day, in Aphrodite's tears." Ashur whispered, his declaration containing no hint of uncertainty.

"You keep her crying," Obadyah replied, "and I will find my way back."

After an hour of silence they approached their final descent to Amathus. Father and son stepped down giving the horse a lighter load to navigate the loose stone of the downgrade.

As the port city came into view Obadyah thought back on the past twenty-four hours. It occurred to him that this was his first taste of a life of freedom. Ashur's spontaneous spirit brought back memories of adventures he had had with his own brother. Obadyah prayed as he walked, asking Yahweh to grant him another meeting with the boy. And the old Assyrian, Obadyah thought, was priceless. Skilled beyond description. Committed to his work and his grandson. Brave in ways Obadyah never dreamt possible. In stature, half the size of Theophanes, but his heart, Obadyah thought, twice that of his father's.

While he was grateful, Obadyah would trade it all for one more ride under the tarp of Palmsquat's cart. Sunsets, warm fires, peaceful moments with new friends, all easily surrendered for one minute with his beloved. He knew he should wean himself of his thoughts of Zoë. The ache and worry he felt for her was debilitating and he had to prepare himself for what he would face in Samaria. But despite all his reasoning with himself, he could not suppress the desire overpowering him, the desire to bring Zoë to Cyprus—a place whose beauty suited hers. But then the reality of his future confronted him. Jezebel. How will he stand in her presence let alone serve her?

"Do you know the difference between you and me?" Theophanes asked, breaking their silence.

Obadyah waited, not knowing where to start.

"You listen to your heart," Theophanes said, "I tell my heart."

Obadyah did not respond, doubtful his father's insight would amount to much.

"You pace when you hurt," he continued, "and shout when you are angry. And when you are frustrated, you kick rocks."

Obadyah looked down as the stones he had not even realized he had kicked rolled down the hill before them. "Maybe listening to your heart is better than talking to it," Obadyah replied. "Maybe you would be a more pleasant person if you kicked rocks sometimes."

"Would you have Tukulti respond to his circumstances as you do?"

"As I do? You mean feeling heartache in the midst of heartbreak?"

"There is no emotional response suitable to Tukulti's experience," Theophanes replied. "Should he shout, cry, or kick all the rocks on this island, the reality he faces remains. His heart is well because he has told his heart to be well. Should he awake without that determination, how could he survive having seen what he has seen?"

Theophanes paused.

Obadyah knew Theophanes wanted him to respond, but he wasn't willing to dignify his father's lecture.

When Theophanes's patience ran out he continued, "Stop waiting, son! Stop moaning about how you want things to be. Decide to be content."

Obadyah's ears perked to his father's plea. Theophanes had never addressed him as his son. While his tone still carried an edge of disappointment, Obadyah could not help but wonder if his father's words had something else behind them. Not love, of course. That was too big a step, a gap so great even the great Theophanes could not traverse. But there was a hint, if only a whisper, of compassion.

Theophanes continued. "It was when Tukulti was determined to overcome, when he quit listening to his broken heart and began directing it that he was able to live, to survive, to serve and be father to the only family he had left in this godforsaken world."

Whether Theophanes was right about Tukulti, Obadyah did not know. But he was right about one thing. Sometimes all you can do is fight to survive. Whether Jezebel leaves him any family to serve, that would rest solely in the hands of Yahweh.

CHAPTER 30

THE BEGINNING OF THE END

"Welcome Theophanes," Ahab said.

Theophanes and Obadyah approached the King of Israel and knelt before him.

"Arise. My bride will be pleased to see you."

"I come bearing gifts," Theophanes said.

"So, I have heard." Ahab grinned. "A captain, a physician, and a treasure hunter. Fear not, for I will allow you to buy my affections."

"Theophanes!" Jezebel squealed as she entered the room, her ladies in tow.

"My Fair Queen," Theophanes replied, taking a knee.

Jezebel reached for Theophanes.

Theophanes stood and took her hands in his.

"I am here to deliver your eunuch, My Lady," Theophanes announced. "Compliments of your father."

Ignoring Obadyah, Jezebel kept her attention on the captain. "Come," Jezebel motioned. "You have arrived just in time to see my archers perform."

"I regret that I have been unable to witness the advances of your army, My Sovereignness."

"Allow me to enlighten you."

Obadyah followed the royals and their attendants as they proceeded through the castle towards the courtyard behind the king and queen's residence.

"I am eager to hear of your recent adventures," Ahab said.

"I am eager to report, My Lord. But I am certain my tales will be far more to your liking with a jug of wine."

Ahab laughed and waved at an attendant.

As the wine was poured, the king and queen took their seats.

"Come," Jezebel said, beckoning Theophanes to her side. She pointed to one of her archers who approached. He lowered his eyes and extended his hand. A royal arrow. "The cock feathers were imported from Gaul," Jezebel boasted.

Obadyah locked eyes with the archer as he raised his head. The pride that had adorned his expression faded when he caught a glimpse of Obadyah's disgust.

Ahab beamed. "My bride has spared no expense, importing Egyptian craftsmen as well."

Theophanes raised his glass to the royal couple as the bowmen loaded their arrows. Jezebel nodded to the captain of the guard who motioned for his archers to identify their nocking point. A man in chains was escorted out onto the grass and tied to an Asherah pole. The men readied their aim.

Obadyah's heart seized. He clenched his jaw. Jezebel gave the order. Three archers released their bowstring, each arrow finding its target. The man buckled, his legs giving way beneath him. His escort brought him to his feet and raised his hands above his head to expand his lungs so that he might expire quickly. Jezebel spoke up.

"Leave him," she commanded. The slave obeyed, dropping the man's hands to his side and then tightening the belt which secured the man upright to the Asherah pole.

If you leave the arrows in place," Jezebel said, "his life remains, for three, sometimes even four shots."

Theophanes nodded in recognition of Jezebel's discovery.

"These prophets of Yahweh are particularly stubborn," Jezebel continued. "But their feeble determination only provides more practice to my archers."

Obadyah's eyes found the gaze of Jezebel's victim. The two men reached for one another in silent agony, Obadyah wondering whose fate was worse. Tears tumbled down Obadyah's face as Jezebel commanded the second strike. The archers fired, filling the man's chest with arrows. His head dropped, his weight supported solely by the ropes holding him to Asherah's homage. As Obadyah watched the man's chest rise and fall with his final breaths, Jezebel commanded her archers again. The prophet found the strength to raise his head one last time, facing his executioner while the final round of arrows opened his flesh.

Obadyah turned his gaze to his father, gauging his reaction.

Theophanes turned to Jezebel. "Power suits you, My Lady."

Obadyah burned with anger. While his pulse quickened with each breath, his father casually conversed, seemingly unmoved by Jezebel's malevolence.

Ahab smiled at his new wife.

"It is a role I was born to play," Jezebel replied.

"While I long to indulge in the queen's praise," Ahab interrupted, "might we get down to the captain's business?"

"Should you cherish my wishes," Jezebel declared, "present your queen with the heads of all the prophets of Yahweh."

"I have granted the consecration of 450 prophets of Baal!" Ahab replied.

"Tell me," Jezebel inquired, "is the King of Israel unfit or unwilling to dispose of a few worthless seers?"

Theophanes gave Jezebel an approving nod, celebrating her sovereignty over her new husband.

"In the midst of a drought," Ahab replied, "you would have the palace attend to the destruction of prophets over the storing of grain?"

"Only if it pleases you, My King," Jezebel replied.

Eager to prove there was no demand which could not be met by the crown, Ahab submitted. "I will grant you your desire, my darling, in trade for…" Ahab paused, "for the services of the slave of your father."

All eyes swung to Obadyah. He drew in a quick breath as he felt the weight of their gaze. Having glorified Obadyah's bravery on their first trip to Samaria, Jezebel would now be forced to choose. What would give her more joy, Obadyah wondered, his presence, a reminder of her victory over Zoë, or the heads of the prophets of Yahweh? Obadyah did not know Jezebel to admit defeat. He swallowed bracing himself for her reply.

"I suspect my slave will serve you well," Jezebel said, her gaze locked on Obadyah. "As he was faithful in carrying out my judgment on Athena."

"Congratulations, my King," Theophanes said, raising his glass. "And to you as well, my Queen," Theophanes added.

Ahab grabbed his chalice in celebration with Theophanes but Jezebel did not secure her glass.

"This slave has served you and your father well, My Lovely Queen," Theophanes continued, "and now, by the power of your word, he will serve your husband." Theophanes had managed to find the words to smother Jezebel's anger.

"Very well," Jezebel agreed, "the slave is yours."

Jezebel rose suddenly. Theophanes and Ahab hurried to their feet in respect of the queen, but Jezebel was already too far away to notice. Marching towards the palace she barked at the soldier securing the door, "Fetch me the commander of the King's army! Today marks the beginning of the end of the worship of Yahweh!"

"You are blessed, indeed, My King," Theophanes said, once Jezebel was out of sight.

"Am I?" Ahab replied, the two men trading the look that men exchange when not in the presence of a woman.

"You were wise to bargain for the slave," Theophanes said. "By the gods I pledge, he will serve you well."

"So you trust him?" Ahab replied, the men discussing Obadyah as if he was not standing in their midst.

"With my life, My Lord, for it is by this slave's hands I appear before you this day."

Ahab looked over at Obadyah who made no eye contact with the king. "I have heard the story of this slave remaining before a charging bear. It is because of his courage that my queen lives. With what other heroism do you credit him?"

"Perhaps you remember, My Lord," Theophanes began, "how the winds stirred up the sea, a fortnight back, capsizing an Egyptian vessel."

"Yes, of course. But surely Phoenician craftsmanship endured such tests of nature," Ahab replied.

"My ship is sound, My King. As the sea churned, the Phoenix danced. It was the security of my vessel which angered the gods. The wind began to assault us from different directions. Under this tension, the fore stay broke free. Without command this slave hoisted himself up the mast and secured the line with his bare hands."

Obadyah listened as his father wove a yarn of heroism for Ahab. Theophanes spared no details in a tale that was wholly the product of his own imagination. Obadyah could not deny his father's gift, a parent spoon feeding an infant.

"I myself cannot fathom the pain he endured," Theophanes continued, "as the rigging tore through his palms. His flesh burned, My Lord, in defiance of the gods."

"Slave. Come," Ahab demanded. "Show me your hands."

Obadyah obeyed. The scabs which had formed after having dangled overboard the Phoenix cracked as he attempted to stretch out his fingers. His palms, still pink and swollen from his father's discipline, bore a resemblance to raw meat.

"It is this kind of strength I seek," Ahab replied, content with his newest acquisition. "I must appoint an overseer. It is imperative he be both strong and loyal."

"You have chosen wisely, My King," Theophanes said. "And I would be a fool to remain when the King's business is pressing." The king stood, permitting Theophanes to stand. "Please, my Lord, accept with pleasure these humble treasures I have assembled in honor of your new dynasty."

Ahab received Theophanes's gifts and bid the captain farewell.

Obadyah, alone with his new master, awaited his instructions.

"Ethbaal trusted you," Ahab began. "Theophanes trusts you. I would like to trust you as well. But trust comes with time and tasks. Therefore, I bid you your first duty. Oversee the construction of a retreat for my queen in Jezreel."

Obadyah left the presence of the king and wandered the streets of Samaria. When his eyes were open, he took in his surroundings. When they were closed he saw the prophet of Yahweh hanging from the points of Jezebel's arrows.

Obadyah rubbed his shoulder. It ached from the king's branding, the tattoo mark which would allow him to access what he needed to complete his first task for Ahab. The burn was a nice distraction.

Obadyah's new position in the Northern Kingdom of Israel was a vast improvement from his service in Sidon. If for no other reason than that he was not confined to the palace residence. Still, this first task was far greater than anything ever before demanded of him. And while he served the king of Israel, he knew his success or failure would be measured, not by Ahab, but Jezebel.

Proceeding down the street in Samaria, Obadyah passed a tavern. He paused when a chariot parked outside caught his attention. Adorning the side of the chariot was an Atruscan shield similar, if not identical, to the one he had seen on his father's chariot. His eye's left the shield and drifted to the opening of the tavern.

Commissioned at the age of twelve, Obadyah often wondered how free men lived. Having listened to endless tavern tales of those who sat at the king's table, his curiosity got the better of him. He stepped inside.

Caves were common throughout Canaan. The soft porous limestone of the region made for viable carving and provided shelter, storage, tombs, and in this case, a lounge for city workers.

Obadyah made his way through the hewn opening to a counter displaying a variety of fermented juices. With each step the room grew darker. Oil lamps lit the far wall where a handful of locals were gathered. As Obadyah approached, the circle bellowed out laughter, the kind not heard from sober men. When his presence was felt, a man turned. A commotion made its way through the group. The circle of men began to part.

What were they all looking at? Obadyah wondered. Is it obvious that this is my first visit to a tavern?

"Obadyah!" Theophanes shouted, "Welcome to Melqart."

"Melqart?" Obadyah replied.

The men broke out in laughter once more.

"Melqart is the tutelary deity of Tyre, the Lord of the City," Theophanes said, raising his glass.

"Yes, I know who Baal-melqart is. I just hadn't received notice of his relocation to Samaria."

The men's laughter filled the room again.

"The god remains in Tyre," Theophanes explained, "but his spirit resides…"

"At the bottom of your cup?" Obadyah interrupted, laughter consuming the crowd once more.

"Who is your friend, Captain?" the bar-keep asked.

"This is the King's new overseer," Theophanes replied.

At that the room went quiet.

"Is it true, My Lord?" one man asked.

"Of course it's true," Theophanes exclaimed. "Turn boy, let the men see your branding."

Obadyah turned to the left revealing the symbol burned onto the back of his right shoulder. A sphinx with an ankh held between its paws. Inscribed above it, the Hebrew letters: Yod, Zawin, Bet, Lamed. YZBL.

"Welcome, My Lord," the bartender said, sliding a cup across the counter. "What shall I pour you?"

"Tea, please," Obadyah replied, prompting more laughter from the tavern regulars.

"That's enough," Theophanes said. "You have had your enjoyment at the boy's expense. Disperse so that we may talk for I have business with the crown."

The men scattered, turning their attention away from Obadyah and Theophanes.

"They obey you as though you own the place."

"I do own the place," Theophanes replied.

At that Obadyah took another look around, surprised once again of the world in which his father lived, a world he did not know.

"Congratulations," Theophanes said.

"Congratulations? For which are you congratulating me, for witnessing the execution of Yahweh's prophet or for remaining a slave?"

"You are not just a slave. You are the leader of all slaves belonging to the king."

"The highest slave and the lowest slave have one striking similarity," Obadyah replied.

Theophanes shook his head and then tried a different approach with his son. "In my recent travels," he began, "to the far reaches of the sea I have witnessed a new kind of creature. It is sleek, its skin similar to that of a dolphin. But it is much darker, almost black. And where the dolphin's covering is pulled taught, this creature has a cluster of wrinkles around its neck. It has a rear fin with which to propel itself through the water. However it uses its front two fins to pull itself up onto rocks. Once ashore this creature drags its lower half on its belly across the sand like a drunken sailor. Its eyes are big and its jaw full of whiskers. And its nose is stubby as if someone gave him a blow square in the snout."

"Is there a name for this creature?" Obadyah asked.

"I know not its name, but the men on the Phoenix call it a 'squeal,' because of the whining which perpetually comes out of its mouth."

Theophanes's story found its target.

Obadyah smirked at his father's dig.

"Very good, son. You have matured since our voyage together. So, tell me," Theophanes inquired, "what task has Ahab assigned you?"

"He desires a residence in Jezreel."

"This is great news! This job suits you."

"I am no builder."

"You need only to oversee the construction. You can hire an architect, a stone mason, a carpenter, and laborers."

"I don't even know where to begin. It will take years to complete."

"I have a friend who dwells on the hill facing the Jezreel Valley. His name is Naboth. He is a trusted companion. He will help you find the men you will need to complete your task."

Obadyah looked down as he turned his cup of tea around in his hand.

"With your determination, Naboth's help, and the king's resources at your disposal, you have everything you need." Theophanes rose from his stool. "I must depart. I have Ethbaal's tasks to tend to. I will be making a delivery to the river at the arrowhead point of the Jezreel valley this time next year. I will bring you cedar, ivory, and linens." Theophanes paused and then put his hand on Obadyah's shoulder. "I did not know it was you who carried out Jezebel's orders, casting out the girl."

"Zoë," Obadyah replied.

"Yes, Zoë. Well, I want to tell you I'm sorry." Theophanes removed his hand and turned towards the street.

Obadyah felt something creep up inside him as he watched his father walk away. He couldn't quite identify the feeling. It was subtle but it was there. He could not deny it. He felt alone. Suddenly he said, "I will meet you at the western window to the Jezreel valley this time next year."

Theophanes stopped and turned back towards his son.

Obadyah said, "If it does not cause you too much trouble, My Lord, might you bring word of the girl's well-being?"

"Zoë," Theophanes said.

"Yes. Zoë."

Theophanes nodded and then was gone.

Obadyah had no sooner allowed himself a bit of optimism where his father was concerned, and his thoughts gave way to his suspicions. Surely Theophanes was only promising news of Zoë in order to ensure his appearance at their rendezvous point. And yet, Theophanes had easily gone years without seeing him when he was a child. Why show interest in him now? Obadyah forced those thoughts from his mind, grabbing hold of this one hope. In one year he would get news of Zoë. In one year he will know whether his beloved still lived. *I will proceed to Jezreel and busy myself with the construction of the king's residence. And then perhaps Ahab will free me and I will find her.*

"What do I owe you for the tea?" Obadyah asked.

The barkeep looked confused. He paused then replied. "Nothing, My Lord, the king's overseer eats and drinks anywhere he pleases."

CHAPTER 31

THE PATH TO PEACE

Zoë could hear talking coming from the next room. She sat up and rubbed her eyes, straining to recognize the voice. She couldn't place it so she rose and grabbed her cloak. When she came around the corner she could see Jashar standing in the entryway.

"He was present at the execution of Yahweh's prophet," Jashar said.

"Who was present? What execution?" Zoë asked.

"Obadyah," Samara replied. "It seems Theophanes has delivered Obadyah to Ahab. And he no sooner arrived at his new palace and he was forced to witness Jezebel entertaining the captain by slaying a prophet of Yahweh."

Zoë's heart fell. Obadyah continued to suffer at the pleasure of Jezebel. While Zoë was comforted and cared for by Obadyah's mother, he was an arm's length from evil.

"The murder was brutal, My Lady," Jashar said, "the prophet…"

"That will be enough Jashar," Samara interrupted.

"Yes, My Lady."

"What more must he endure?" Zoë said softly.

"Yahweh has not forgotten about Obadyah," Samara said. "He is strengthening him for His use and a greater purpose."

"How can witnessing butchery possibly strengthen a person?"

"Pain is a powerful impetus. It overwhelms the senses. It will not be ignored. Whatever Yahweh is planning for Obadyah, He has his attention."

"Is there ever an end to His lessons?" Zoë said. Her tone, she knew, betrayed her. It was not a question. Though she was learning how to be true to herself and she was coming to trust Samara more each day, she continued to doubt. Especially concerning Yahweh.

"No," Samara said. "There is no end to His lessons."

Zoë did not respond. Samara's answer was unsatisfying, but not unexpected. Samara never apologized for Yahweh. Nor did she make excuses for His actions. Even when those actions affected the ones she loves.

Samara continued. "Do you know why?"

Zoë shook her head.

"Because Yahweh knows what is best for those He loves."

Zoë had heard the same from Obadyah. It was no easier hearing it now than it was then. But Zoë was committed to being honest with Samara. "Why are we never good enough the way we are?"

"You tell me," Samara replied. "For you know as well as I do that Yahweh is not the only one who longs for our growth. Have you not, from your youth, striven for maturity, even excellence?"

Zoë fell silent, thinking on Samara's words.

"Are these noble pursuits when you wish them for yourself, but an imposition, an offense, when Yahweh wishes them for you?"

"I suppose not, but…" Zoë did not know what to say next. "It's just that…" She paused again, searching for the right words.

Samara did not help but waited patiently for Zoë to find what she was looking for.

Finally Zoë said, "Is there ever peace with Yahweh?"

"Ahh, peace." Samara replied. "Well, I suppose it depends on what you mean by peace."

Zoë chafed at Samara's response. "I mean what everyone means! Does Yahweh have His own definition of words that we are not privy to?"

Samara smiled, thoroughly confusing Zoë. "Let me tell you a story."

"May I stay, My Lady?" Jashar suddenly said.

Zoë's head whipped around. She had forgotten that he was still in the room.

"Yes Jashar, you may stay."

Jashar smiled and settled himself onto the couch next to Zoë.

Despite her frustration, Zoë could not help but give Jashar a quick smile. His own struggle with Yahweh certainly lay before him, but right now he was just a boy who longed for a story.

"Obadyah used to wrestle with his brother," Samara began. "The boys spent so much time tossing one another about that I often had to send them outside to finish their disputes. Obadyah didn't like to fight. But his brother did. So Obadyah conceded to a daily battle but then also conceded the victory. It simply wasn't in his nature to fight nor was it important to him to win. One day, Theophanes happened to be here during one of the boy's skirmishes. He jumped in, surmising that Obadyah needed help. But Theopanes did not help by rescuing him from the fight. Instead, he showed him how to gain the upper hand and defeat his brother.

"It is you who values winning. Not me!" Obadyah had said.

"Maybe someday you too will need to win," Theophanes replied.

"No I won't!" Obadyah yelled. He tried to stomp off, but Theophanes grabbed him.

"Despite Obadyah's pleading," Samara said, "Theophanes spent the day teaching Obadyah, not just how to fight but how to overcome. How to dominate. Even how to kill."

Jashar's eyes were as big as dates, his attention locked on Samara.

"Obadyah, more than once, voiced his objection. He even said, 'Why can you not just let me be!' You see," Samara said, "Obadyah wanted Theophanes to leave him in peace."

"And why didn't he?" Zoë asked. "You yourself said, it is not in him to fight."

"It was no more in him to fight when he wrestled with his brother than it was after he learned how to fight from Theophanes. And it was not in him when we watched his brother get beaten at the docks. Still, he ran home that day and begged Theophanes for more fighting lessons."

"I want fighting lessons," Jashar said.

Zoë and Samara smiled.

"I do not blame my son for not wanting to fight. In fact, I'm proud of him. But, sometimes," Samara said, "it's better to get better, even if it's something that goes against our desires and even our nature. Theophanes knew more about what Obadyah needed than Obadyah did."

Zoë realized how much she didn't know about Obadyah. There was so much yet to discover. When she considered all that had happened to him. All he has already seen and experienced, she marveled at his strength and endurance.

"Sometimes," Samara said, "it is not about what's inside the person we love but what's in the world the person we love must live in."

CHAPTER 32

THE WELL-STOCKED WAGON

Leaving the Malqart tavern, Obadyah made his way to the palace stables looking to outfit a wagon for his trip north. When he arrived he found the stablekeep tending a stall. As he approached he heard the man whistling while he completed his chores. Obadyah recognized the tune but could not place it. The stablekeep, a smaller man, perhaps twenty years Obadyah's senior, was fully engaged in mending a gate which seemed to have come loose from its hinges. "Excuse me, Sir. I come on behalf of the king."

The man abrubtly turned. His eyes widened as Obadyah revealed Ahab's newly seared brand on his shoulder. "Yes, my Lord!" the stableman said. "I am at your service."

"I require transportation and supplies for a journey to Jezreel."

"Indeed, My Lord, allow me to stock my best wagon." The man motioned towards his best wagon.

"When might I return?"

"With My Lord's permission, it will take the remainder of the daylight hours to acquire the provisions. Would it please My Lord to return at dusk?"

Obadyah nodded and reached out to thank him.

The man paused, hesitant to make contact with Ahab's overseer.

"Fear not, Sir, my name is Obadyah. I walk in the light of Yahweh."

Obadyah knew there were few Hebrews left in Israel who revered Yahweh. And perhaps he was taking a risk. But he felt emboldened by his new position and the stablekeep had a peaceful voice, one that felt familiar. It was then he placed the tune the man had been whistling.

"You sing the songs of David," Obadyah said.

The man smiled, took Obadyah's arm and placed his other hand on

Obadyah's shoulder. "I am Benjamin."

"Benjamin?" Obadyah asked. "Father of Eliah?"

Benjamin nodded.

"I am in your debt for my healing," Obadyah said, "young Eliah nursed me following an unfortunate encounter with a bear," Obdayah said, placing his hand on his stomach.

"We are in Yahweh's debt, each one of us, for his great mercy, My Lord," Benjamin replied.

Wandering the streets of Samaria, Obadyah felt untethered, free. Yet he knew this was an illusion. As long as Jezebel was controlling the king, she would continue to control him. When Obadyah made it to the outskirts of the city, he found a gathering place at the bottom of the road. He sat down. Exhaustion overwhelmed him. Leaning up against the trunk of an olive tree, he nodded off and fell into a dream.

"It's your turn, Dyah."

Obadyah reached down and chose a stone. He lined up his target, stepped back, and let the stone fly. It struck the hive hanging from the limb above them. The two boys started running–a quick turn around some trees, a sprint down the road, and then up onto the boulder resting on the shore. Side-by-side the brothers jumped into the warm water of the Great Sea. Obadyah surfaced. Laughing as he drew in a breath, Obadyah spun around. He was alone. His brother could not be found.

Obadyah was stirred awake by the sound of a crying baby. Searching for the source, he saw a young mother and father walking past him on their way into the city. The father nodded in Obadyah's direction. The mother smiled. Obadyah returned a pleasant greeting and rose to his feet. Stretching his back, he gazed up at the sun. He had been asleep for longer than he had planned. He followed the family of three into town and found the Hebrew who was manning the stables.

"Thank you, Benjamin, for your urgency in seeing to my request."

Benjamin bowed. "May Yahweh's cherubs who protect His mercy seat watch over you as you journey to Jezreel."

"May the peace of Yahweh find you always, brother," Obadyah replied.

"And you as well." Benjamin bowed again.

Obadyah set out, eager to get a few hours down the road before he made camp for the night. The wagon was full, but a manageable load for the mule. The beast plodded along, keeping pace with Obadyah.

An hour after his departure Obadyah intersected the path of the northbound trail. The congestion of the main road fell behind him. The beat of his steps, the turning of the wagon wheels, and the hooping of the hoopoe bird, now the only sounds accompanying him. There was something soothing about the quiet. Then it struck him. He was alone. It was the first time in his life he had ever been alone. Before he had a moment to think on that further, the mule paused to eject the meal he was fed prior to their departure.

Obadyah sighed and sat on the side of the road to wait for the beast to finish his business. "I believe I know a friend of yours," he said. "Perhaps you know her. You would remember if you had met her," Obadyah said, removing his sandals. "What does she look like? Interesting you should ask. She looks very much like yourself only her legs are shorter, her belly plumper, her fur spottier and her…her deposits stinkier." Obadyah rubbed his feet as the last steamy plop hit the ground. "Okay, maybe yours are equally stinky. In fact, maybe you two are related."

The mule wandered a few feet from the path to gnaw on a clump of weeds.

"What? No comment?" He crossed the leather laces around his calves. "Yes, well, I suppose I would not admit it either. No worries, my friend," Obadyah said as he stood, "I will not hold it against you." He grabbed the reins and led the mule back to the path. "We cannot choose our family. This much I know."

As the wagon started rolling again, Obadyah continued his conversation with the donkey, the beast occasionally turning his head as if he were listening. "How much longer can you walk?" Obadyah inquired to no reply. "Perhaps you have another hour in you now that you have…you know, lightened your load."

Obadyah made camp in the Samarian hill country, six miles north of Israel's capital. He had hoped to get further, but night was upon him. He freed the beast from the wagon and tethered him to an acacia tree a few paces off the road. Collecting some tumble brush, he made a fire and hung his lentil pot. He fed and watered his travel companion then returned to the wagon. Retrieving a wool blanket Benjamin had included with his supplies, Obadyah found a flat piece of ground and laid down next to the fire.

He gazed up at the night sky, the darkness unending. He closed his eyes to find a smaller place to begin to deal with what felt overwhelming.

His thoughts swung between all that he was thankful for and all that still haunted him. Joy for the memories of Zoë. Sorrow for the suffering he had caused her. Gratitude towards his father for pulling Zoë from the sea, and anger for all Theophanes had done to him. Peace for the moment, a night away from the watchful eyes of the queen. But fear, always fear, for no one within Jezebel's reach could ever rest easy.

"Yahweh," Obadyah spoke aloud, staring up at the night sky. "How majestic is Your name in all the earth, having displayed Your splendor above the heavens. When I consider Your heavens, the work of Your fingers, the moon and the stars which You have ordained; What is man that You take thought of him, and the son of man that You care for him?" Obadyah prayed. And, though he could neither understand it nor explain it, for the first time in his life, Obadyah prayed for his father.

Obadyah awoke the next morning to the sound of rustling inside the wagon. He listened intently hoping to identify the animal. Hyrax was common to those parts. Being social creatures, they never hunted alone. If there was one in the wagon, there would be six nearby waiting for their scavenger brother to return. Obadyah had heard the jackals howling throughout the night. Perhaps one of them made their way into his wagon? If so, an arduous fight awaited him. He glanced at the mule to see if he was reacting to the noise. He had his backend to Obadyah, scratching his muzzle on the bark of the acacia tree. Noting this, Obadyah concluded it was not a jackal.

As the wagon covering continued to shift, Obadyah continued to deduce his challenger. A sand fox? No, probably mongoose, a solitary creature, one of the most annoying of the rodents of Canaan.

Obadyah crept towards the wagon. He picked up his prodding stick and readied himself to strike. With one quick motion he ripped off the tarp. He yelled, hoping to startle the creature. To his surprise, it was no creature at all, but a young girl.

"What are you doing here?!" Obadyah bellowed.

"Please do not strike me!" Eliah begged, her arms raised protecting her head.

Obadyah lowered his stick. "Why are you…? How did you…?"

"Please do not strike me!" Eliah replied.

"Lower your hands. I'm not going to strike you!"

"Do you promise? Do you promise you won't strike me?"

"Yes, yes, I promise, now lower your hands."

Eliah obeyed but remained still, tucked amid the dried beans and wine at the front of the wagon.

"Why are you here?" Obadyah asked.

"I'm hiding in your wagon."

"Yes, yes, I know you are hiding!"

"Are you angry? Have you decided to strike me?"

"No! I told you! I am not going to strike you!"

"But you work for Jezebel and she strikes anyone who upsets her."

"Actually, I work for Ahab."

"Well Ahab married Jezebel so he is just as mean as she is!"

"Yes, perhaps. The point is I want to know why you are in my wagon."

"I belong to you," Eliah replied.

"We are getting nowhere," Obadyah murmured.

"Of course we are getting nowhere," Eliah interjected, "you have not yet hitched the wagon."

"Please stop talking," Obadyah begged. "And tell me why you are here."

"Well, which is it?" Eliah asked.

"Which is what?" Obadyah replied.

"Do you wish for me to stop talking or do you wish for me to tell you why I am here?"

"What I wish and what I need are two different things," Obadyah grumbled.

"Sounds to me like you are indecisive. A man should not be indecisive. My father is not indecisive."

Obadyah, seeing his window at last, spoke up. "Does your father know you are here?"

"Yes, of course he knows. He filled your wagon yesterday when you ordered supplies."

"I remember your father, and I remember ordering supplies, but I do not remember ordering a little girl."

"Well, you did not get a little girl, you got a young lady. And you know what? Sometimes things just appear when you least expect it."

"Yes, things like a sour stomach or an Egyptian mongoose. But not a little…"

"Oh, mongooses are so very cute," Eliah squealed. "Can we get one?"

"We? We are turning this wagon around and heading back to Samaria."

"But you can't," Eliah said, jumping to her feet.

"And why not?"

"Because of Jezebel."

Obadyah caught his breath. He lowered his head and turned away from Eliah. In all his concern for himself and his new task, he had forgotten about Jezebel's decree: Death To Every Prophet of Yahweh. He kicked the stones at his feet. Benjamin, so desperate to spare his daughter from the sight of Jezebel's slaughter, risked sending her away with a slave of Ahab.

"My father told me never to return to Samaria. My father told me you were kind and you would care for me."

Obadyah turned back to face Eliah. He began rubbing his neck.

"Well?" she continued. "Was my father right? Are you kind?"

"I am…I am kind. But I am no father."

"I already have a father. What I am in need of is a friend."

Obadyah closed his eyes long enough to take three deep breaths. When he opened them, he was looking upon the face of his new friend. "Okay," he said, "I will take you as far as Dothan and I will help you find a family there."

"Dothan is awfully close to Samaria. Jezreel is fifteen hours from here. We better start looking for a new family when we get to Jezreel. Do you have any breakfast?"

Obadyah, desperate to avoid another argument with the young lady, decided not to object. He was also quite certain, however, he would not make it all the way to Jezreel. He wondered, in fact, how he would survive the day.

CHAPTER 33

THE LOVE OF THREE LOVES

"Tell me about your donkey." Eliah said, skipping along next to Obadyah.

"My donkey is right here," Obadyah replied.

"No, not Buckets. Tell me about the donkey with the short legs, the plump belly, and the patchy fur."

Obadyah sighed as he realized Eliah had listened to every word he had uttered since they departed Samaria. "The donkey I spoke of is not mine."

"You sure know a lot about her. What is her name?"

"Palmsquat."

"Palmsquat?"

"Yes. Palmsquat."

"Palmsquat and Buckets." Eliah said, "their names go together."

"How do you figure?"

"They are both named after things they like."

"Your father's donkey likes buckets?"

"He likes fetching buckets. I would say to Buckets, 'Buckets, want to go to the well with me?' And then Buckets would fetch our bucket. And then we would go together to fetch some water."

"Palmsquat liked fish guts," Obadyah said.

"Is she dead?"

"No! She's not dead!"

"Well, you said 'liked' not 'likes.'"

"I know what I said! She is not dead. She likes fish guts."

"Well, then I agree with you," Eliah replied.

"You agree that Palmsquat is not dead, or you agree that she likes fish guts?"

"I agree that fish guts make stinkier plop."

"Oh good. I'm so relieved we agreed."

Obadyah, unsure what to do next, put his head down and continued walking. He had hoped for a few minutes of quiet, but Eliah's mind moved at twice the pace of their steps.

"Why do you like Palmsquat so much?" she pressed.

"I did not say I like her."

"Yes, you did!"

"No, I didn't!"

"Yes, you did. I heard it in your voice when you spoke of her."

"From under the tarp? Amid the bread and beans? You heard what my voice sounded like?"

"Yes, of course! It's not like I had anything else to do while my butt was warming your beans!"

Were all little girls like this one? Obadyah wondered. A storehouse of words? While Obadyah had to scour his mind for each word he spoke, Eliah's words fell like a rainstorm.

"Speaking of your…bottom," Obadyah said, "you did not go…you know, in the wagon?"

"What? No!"

"Well, surely you have had to go since we left Samaria!"

"Of course I had to go. I was just sneaking back into the wagon after I went this morning. You know, when you found me."

Obadyah nodded.

"So," Eliah continued, "why do you like Palmsquat so much? She sounds like a pretty worthless beast to me."

Obadyah, desperate for a break from the endless questions, said, "Choose a rock from the trail before us, any rock, and hold it tightly in your hand."

Eliah smiled, eager to play Obadyah's game, whatever it was. She surveyed the road for a moment and then reached down and chose a stone. Having squeezed it as Obadyah directed, she awaited his next instructions.

"Open your hand. Look at your rock and describe it to me."

"It is the color of the earth."

"Yes, and?"

"It is the size of my hand. It feels smooth like butter."

"Turn it over. What else?"

Eliah used the finger of her right hand to tip the stone resting in the palm of her left hand.

"There is an indent here," she said pointing to the stone. "Look. My thumb fits in it perfectly." Eliah rested her right thumb in the impression.

"Now look at all the rocks on the road before us."

Eliah watched as they passed by stone after stone after stone, treading on each one as they moved down the trail.

"Do you see how similar they are?"

Eliah nodded as she continued to stare at the stones, some stepped on, some kicked aside, most ignored.

"It is from among these you have chosen the one in your hand. Seeing all these other stones you may have some doubts about the one you've chosen. But you need only to remind yourself of the details you have observed, features that belong only to your rock and your doubts will fade."

Eliah's eyes moved back and forth from her stone and the countless stones before them.

"Perhaps," he continued, "you may look down and notice a new rock." Obadyah reached down and picked up a stone. "This new stone seems to have everything your stone doesn't have. Where your rock is smooth, this rock has ridges. Where your rock bears an indent, this one appears flawless. You might wonder, should I toss my rock aside in favor of this new more beautiful stone?" Obadyah held out his closed fist in Eliah's direction. "But then you look at the rock in your hand."

Eliah looked at the rock in her hand.

"And you realize, this is my rock. You do not love it for its beauty nor do you hate it for its flaws. You cherish it simply because it is yours. In fact, the things which you had thought were imperfections, you now realize are the very things that make it special."

Eliah closed her hand around her rock and made a fist just as Obadyah was doing.

"I may show you my rock," he said, opening his hand. "And you might be confused as to why I love it so much. The reason you are confused is because you are looking at it the way everyone looks at it. To you it is no different than the stones beneath your feet. I may describe to you why I find it appealing. You would not see that beauty. Indeed you could not see it for you have not chosen it, I have."

"But, Obadyah, Eliah said, "it's just a rock."

"Is it?" Obadyah replied. "Then toss it aside."

Eliah looked at the stones on the ground and then stared at the stone in her hand.

"You heard me," he continued, "return your stone to the earth where it can disappear with all the other stones. Throw it back, for it is only a stone."

Eliah did not obey. Her eyes wandered back and forth from her stone to the ground before her.

"Go on," Obadyah continued. "Relieve yourself of the burden of carrying it and the worry of caring for it."

Eliah continued to hold her stone.

"It is doing nothing but weighing you down," Obadyah added. "Who would choose to make one's journey harder? Be free of your concern for such a thing!"

Eliah curled her fingers around her stone and dropped it into the pocket of her dress. Obadyah smiled and then placed his stone into the fold of his belt. They continued north, Obadyah having earned himself a few moments of silence.

"Who is Zoë?" Eliah asked.

Obadyah stopped in his tracks and turned to Eliah. "I did not mention Zoë. I know I didn't."

"Not as you walked, no. You said her name in your sleep."

Unable to deny it and terrified to discuss it, Obadyah tried a new tactic. "How about you allow me to ask you a question. Surely I have earned the right to one question."

"Hmm. Yes. I suppose I will permit you one question."

"Thank you, My Lady," Obadyah said as he bowed before Eliah. "Do you have a mother?"

"Doesn't everyone have a mother?"

"That is not what I meant. I…"

Eliah laughed. "You have not been around many girls, have you?" Eliah asked.

"I had a brother."

"Where is he?"

"He died?"

"How did he die?"

"I don't know," Obadyah replied, "nor do I know how I ended up on the receiving end of your questions once again."

Ignoring Obadyah's complaint, Eliah continued. "How is it that you do not know how your own brother died? Does anyone know how he died?"

"My father knows."

"Why have you not asked him?"

Obadyah said nothing. He did not know why he had not asked his father about his brother. Perhaps he didn't want to know the truth. Perhaps Theophanes was responsible for his brother's death just as he was responsible for Obadyah's chains. Perhaps he still feared his father. Or perhaps he simply did not want to give himself one more reason to hate him.

"My mother died when I was born," Eliah said. "Some father's cannot raise a child, you know, the one who caused the mother to die—especially if the baby is a girl. But my father was not like that. He loved me with the love he had for me and all the love he had for my mother. And he even loved me with the love my mother would have shown me. Some babies have no love. I had the love of three loves."

"Eliah?" Obadyah said.

"Yes."

"What was it that you heard in my voice? When I spoke as I slept?"

"Something soft. Something that made me feel safe, like the blanket my mother made for me before I was born. My father, Benjamin, heard it in your voice, too. When you spoke to him at the stables yesterday. What he heard in your voice, my father called it chesed, lovingkindness."

CHAPTER 34

THE CURSED MOUNTAIN

After a day on the northbound trail and after many conversations about Palmsquat and Buckets, Obadyah and Eliah met the final ascent to the town of Dothan.

"Once we find a stable for Buckets, we can look for an inn to stay for the night," Obadyah said.

"Might we buy bread cakes? There is a merchant in town who makes the most wonderful loaves with toasted grains and dates. My mouth is just…"

"Your mouth is just wearisome," Obadyah interrupted.

"My mouth is just craving fresh bread," Eliah corrected.

"You are the one who did not finish your butt beans at lunch."

"I have no taste for butt beans," Eliah replied. "Besides, you wear the king's mark. We can get anything we want!"

"How is it you know so much about Dothan?" Obadyah asked.

"My father brought me to the Well here."

"That is a long walk for a drink of water."

"We did not come here for water. We came to see the Dreamer's Well."

"The Dreamer's Well?"

"You do not know of the Dreamer's Well? Are you sure you are Hebrew?"

"Yes! I am Hebrew!"

Eliah shrugged. "I had to check. All the Hebrews in Samaria know about the Dreamer's Well."

"I am from Phoenicia."

"Phoenicia? Yuck. That is the home of Baal."

"Yes. I know." Obadyah sighed.

"I'm glad you at least know that!"

"Are you going to tell me about the Well or not?"

"I will tell you, and I will show you," Eliah announced. "After my belly is full, of course."

"Yes, of course."

Obadyah listened as Eliah reassured Buckets he would be content at the Dothan stable. He then made his way into town with Eliah in tow. As the smell of honey intensified, Eliah quickened her steps, eventually taking the lead. It was not long before Obadyah struggled to keep up. He wondered how such a small creature could move so fast.

Eliah would get a few steps ahead of Obadyah and then turn and scowl at him. After her third silent reprimand, she put her hands on her hips. "When I stop and look at you, it is meant to coax you into a faster pace."

When Obadyah maintained his stride, Eliah took matters into her own hands. She returned to his side and grabbed his arm, dragging him ahead. Her arm stretched out between them as she pulled him along like a reluctant sheep.

"There!" she squealed. Eliah pointed at a small storefront a few paces ahead of them. Releasing Obadyah, she ran into the bakery.

Obadyah entered the shop just as the man behind the counter turned.

"Eliah? Is that you?" The baker greeted as she approached the counter. The baker, a soft and jolly man, appeared in the disheveled state of a diligent worker.

"Yes, sir, it's me. We are here for a honey loaf."

"Yes, My Lady. Coming right up!"

The baker reached over the counter and handed Eliah the warm bread. "Who's your friend, Eliah?"

"This is Obadyah. He's my new brother."

To his surprise, Obadyah found himself grinning. But when he looked up he noticed the baker did not share his expression.

Obadyah stepped past Eliah and extended his arm to the baker who did not extend his in return.

"Forgive me, Sir," the baker replied, "if I do not greet you properly. My hands wear the dust of my trade." The baker held up his floured fingers.

Obadyah nodded and looked at Eliah. "Shall we go?"

As they turned to walk away, Obadayah caught sight of the baker whose demeanor changed when the only eyes left on him were Obadyah's.

"So," Obadyah said, nudging Eliah as they walked through town, "I'm your brother now?"

"Well, yes. What else would you be? I mean you are fairly good looking,"

She paused to chew. "But I doubt the town folks would believe I am your wife. And besides," she said, throwing another bit of bread into her mouth, "you are too grumpy for me. I need a man who…"

"Who is patient," Obadyah interrupted.

"Who is decisive," Eliah countered.

"Well, you better find a man who has lived with many loud sisters, because talking to you is like trying to stand before a wave in a storm surge."

"We are here!" Eliah announced. Shoving the loaf into Obadyah's chest, she ran down the hill on the outer perimeter of Dothan.

"This is the Dreamer's Well?" Obadyah asked, tearing off a pinch of bread.

"This is it!"

"So, what kind of dreams come from this well?" Obadyah mumbled through a mouth full of bread.

"No, no, Obadyah." Eliah said, grabbing the loaf from his hand. "This isn't a well of dreams, it is The Dreamer's Well."

"Who is The Dreamer?"

"Joseph, of course. Do you know the story of Joseph?"

"Joseph has a well?"

"He was in this well, just before his brothers sold him to the Midianites."

Obadyah's brow gave away his confusion as he grabbed the loaf back from Eliah.

"Shall I tell you the story?"

"If you must."

"Okay, brother. I'll help you out," Eliah said, reaching for the warm sweet bread.

"I do know the story of Joseph, I just don't know this detail."

"The details are the story, brother."

"Very well, sister, will you please share with your brother the details of the story?"

"With pleasure," Eliah replied. "So Joseph had this dream where he saw his brothers bowing down to him. And that made his brothers mad."

"Weren't his brothers mad because of the colored tunic their father had given to Joseph?"

"Yes, that's right."

"That seems like an important detail," Obadyah insisted.

"As I was saying," Eliah continued, "Jacob liked Joseph best, probably because he was the son of Rachel. She died giving birth to Joseph's brother just like my mother died giving birth to me. I don't blame Jacob for having extra love for Joseph. I bet he was really sad about losing his wife. But all that extra love sure made a mess of things."

"Love has a tendency to do that."

"What do you mean?"

"Nothing," Obadyah replied. "So, I know Jacob loved Joseph, and I know he was sold as a slave to the Ishmaelites. But what does that have to do with this well?"

"My father told me that Joseph's brothers argued about what to do with him. Some wanted to kill him and bring his bloodied tunic to their father. They couldn't come to a decision so they tossed Joseph down into a well… this well."

Eliah and Obadyah leaned over the edge of the circular rocks and gazed down into the darkness. "When Joseph's brothers noticed a caravan approaching," Eliah said, her voice echoing, "they hoisted him up, and… well, you know how the story ends."

"Joseph's brothers and his father end up in Egypt," Obadyah said, "where Joseph had become a ruler. In the end, his brothers bowed down to him just as his dream had foretold."

"That's right."

"It was Judah who convinced his brothers to sell Joseph rather than kill him," Eliah said. "Judah saved Joseph just like you saved me."

"I did not save you. Your father saved you."

"Obadyah?"

"Yes."

"Thank you for…for…"

"For having patience with you?"

"For letting me have the bed at the inn!" Eliah said, snatching the bread from Obadyah's hand and racing towards town. Obadyah followed after Eliah, catching her just as the trail met the street into town.

"The sun is setting," Eliah exclaimed, "what shall we do?"

"We shall go to sleep," Obadyah replied. "I have three days of walking ahead of me."

"We have three days ahead of us," Eliah corrected, hopping along, waving at the locals who were milling about. Obadyah smiled as he observed Eliah, the glimpses of the life of a child brushing past him in quick evaporating moments.

Arriving at the inn, the innkeeper led them to their room. A side table with a lit oil lamp illuminated a small bed against the wall. Eliah hopped onto the bed while Obadyah spread out the blanket from the wagon and laid down on the floor.

"But Obadyah," Eliah whispered, "are you not going to sing me a song?"

"You can go to sleep this one night without a song."

"No, I cannot!"

"Very well. Sing your song, but make it short."

"But you must sing with me."

"I'm not going to sing. I don't know any songs."

"You don't know any songs? Not even one song?"

"I know one song. But I'm not going to sing it."

"Don't be scared, brother, I will sing it with you."

"I'm not scared! And I'm not singing with you."

"How about humming it? Can you hum it?"

"You are impossible."

"Actually, I am irresistible."

"Is that so?" Obadyah said, rolling over and pulling his blanket up over his head.

"So is that 'no'?" Eliah asked.

Obadyah did not reply.

"It sounds like it's a 'no,' but I just want to make sure."

Obadyah did not say a word.

"I mean, I don't want to leave you out."

The room remained quiet.

"Okay, so 'no' on the song, then."

A few more moments of silence passed, and Eliah began to sing:

> In the shadow of his wings
> In the shadow of his wings
>   There I sweetly rest
>   There I sweetly rest
> In the shadow of his wings
> In the shadow of his wings
> My soul is sweetly blessed
> My soul is sweetly blessed

After repeating her song a few times, Eliah's voice trailed off. Obadyah waited to make sure she was asleep. Then, he took a deep breath and closed his eyes.

"Shh. Do not fight or I will open your throat."

Obadyah tried to sit up. He couldn't move. He tried to fill his lungs. There was a heavy weight on his chest. His eyes popped open and he surveyed his surroundings. There were two men holding him down. A third man had a knife to his throat, while his other hand covered Obadyah's mouth. Instinctively, Obadyah began to struggle.

"Quiet!" the man said as the other two men attempted to keep Obadyah still. Obadyah, now alert, gathered himself and made eye contact with his assailant. "We have business with you," the man whispered. "We can take care of it here next to the little girl or we can step outside."

Obadyah quit struggling.

"I am going to remove my hand," the stranger said, "and you are going to keep silent, yes?"

Obadyah nodded.

The man removed his hand from Obadyah's mouth. Slowly, he pulled his blade away from Obadyah's throat. The two men holding Obadyah down released the tension of their grip.

The three men rose to their feet. Obadyah did as well, all of them careful to not make a sound. Obadyah looked over at Eliah who appeared to be sound asleep, completely unaware of what had just taken place right next to her.

The two men who had been holding him down crept out of the room. Obadyah followed. The man with the knife quietly shut the door behind them. He pushed Obadyah on as the men in front led him outside around a dark corner behind the inn. The two men in front who seemed to just be following orders, suddenly stopped. Obadyah turned to face his abductor.

"Do you remember me?" The man asked, pointing his knife in Obadyah's direction.

"You are the baker who gave Eliah bread."

"I am," he said, tightening his grip on his knife. The two men who had taken the lead each grabbed one of Obadyah's arms. They threw him back against the wall. "Now tell me, who are you?"

"I am Obadyah."

"Do you think this is a joke?" the baker replied. "We are prepared to take your life! Fail to answer me and you will not see the dawn!"

"You know who I am. Is that not why I am here? I am Ahab's overseer. I have been commissioned to…"

"To destroy the prophets of Yahweh!" one of the assailants interrupted.

"No!" Obadyah replied.

"You deny it?" the baker said.

"I do not deny there is a decree, but..."

"But what? You have changed your mind now that you have a knife to your throat?" the other man said.

"No! Please. Let me explain."

"Yes. Please explain how you have disposed of Benjamin and have stolen his daughter!"

"Steal Eliah? Now you are the one making the jokes."

A shuffle of footsteps in the distance caught everyone's attention. They all waited in silence until the sound of footfalls evaporated. "Let's finish this and get out of here," one of the men whispered.

Then the other man spoke up, "When this overseer fails to report, the king will send another. We have only a day or two. We need to move!"

"Please," Obadyah begged. "allow me one minute to explain."

"You heard the man, we do not have any spare minutes," the baker replied.

"Just answer me this," Obadyah replied. "Was Eliah scared today?"

"What are you talking about?"

"You said I killed Eliah's father and stole her. You saw her. Was she sad or frightened of me?"

"Are you saying she does not know her father is dead?"

"Benjamin is not dead! At least he was not dead when I left him."

"Very well, Overseer. You have earned yourself one minute. Speak."

"As I said, my name is Obadyah. I walk in the light of Yahweh. I have been ordered to manage the construction of the King's residence in Jezreel."

The baker lowered his knife. His demeanor changed. Whatever else Obadyah might reveal, it was clear, the baker no longer perceived him as a threat.

"What do you know of the King's decree against the prophet's of Yahweh? We have only heard rumors."

"I stood in the presence of the king and queen when the proclamation went forth. Jezebel...she...she bartered for the lives of the prophets of Yahweh. It is by her word they stand condemned."

"Bartered? The lives of the prophets have been condemned in trade? For what?"

"For...for...me."

At that the men restored their grip upon Obadyah.

"Finish him!" One of them said, "You heard him. He is the reason our people will suffer. We must find a way to warn the prophets."

"He is not the reason," the baker said. "He is just the prize. Release him."

"But he will…"

"You heard me! Release him!"

The men holding Obadyah loosened their grip.

Obadyah shook them off. "I am no one's prize."

The baker began to pace. "Well, son. I hate to be the bearer of bad news, but that is precisely what you are. Now go in peace, for I do not condemn you for Jezebel's wickedness."

"I cannot go in peace! There will be not an hour of peace as long as the lives of Yahweh's servants are threatened."

The baker stopped pacing and faced Obadyah. "It is not simply the lives of the prophets that are threatened. It is the life of the nation that is in peril! We cherish Yahweh's chosen, because we cherish Yahweh. We preserve his prophets to preserve His word. Jezebel would see the blood of prophets run, but, do you not see? It is the sustaining power of His word she drains!"

Obadyah said nothing. The vision of Jezebel burning the scroll containing the words of Yahweh during the Hebrew festival returned to him.

"You are under orders," the baker continued. "I'm afraid there is nothing you can do. Besides, you must care for little Eliah. Benjamin must be in great fear if he has left his daughter in the hands of a servant of Ahab."

"He did not leave her in my care," Obadyah replied. "He left her in yours."

The baker's head shot up.

"Eliah told me that she was instructed to sneak out of my wagon when I stopped in Dothan for the night. She was supposed to find you."

"How did you discover her?"

"It seems she could not get herself comfortable amid my pots of beans. When I saw the tarp move, I thought she was an animal. Of course now that I know her, I am inclined to favor my initial assessment."

The baker chuckled. "She is a spirited child. Certain to be something you are not accustomed to, yet you are her only hope of protection. For we will be traveling to warn the prophets. I'm assuming you warned Benjamin when you saw him?"

"Warned him?"

"Of this decree. Benjamin is not safe."

The hair stood up on the back of Obadyah's neck. "Why?"

"Did you not know? Benjamin is a prophet."

Obadyah's head fell. He could not find the strength to make eye contact with the baker. Staring at the ground, Obdadyah said the first words that came into his mind. "Please. Please allow me to help you."

"How can you help us? You work for the woman who seeks to destroy us."

Obadyah's head shot up when an idea came to him. "You will need provisions," he said to the baker, "and a safe place to hide."

The baker swallowed hard. "We have not even had time yet to plan for this."

"Ahab trusts me," Obadyah said, "I will complete my assigned task. As I do, I will ration the king's supplies. I will sustain you by Ahab's own table."

The three men looked to one another in silent consideration of Obadyah's plan.

"You just focus on bringing word of Jezebel's decree to the other prophets."

"I can do as you say," the baker replied, "but we must do more than merely warn them. We must protect them. Where shall we go? There is no place in Israel free of the eyes of Jezebel."

"I know a place," Obadyah replied.

The three men who were ready to take the life of Ahab's overseer listened eagerly for his next words, their lives now resting in his hands.

"Proceed north to the valley, follow the ridge east to Gilboa. Circle the mountain on the north side."

"You send us to the place of Saul's death?"

"Ahab fears the curse of Gilboa."

"He and the rest of Israel."

"But you are not like the rest of Israel," Obadyah said. "Now listen. For you will find two caves with hidden entrances, each one able to house fifty men."

The baker began to pace as he considered Obadyah's plan.

"I will proceed to Jezreel," he said, "and put men in place to complete the construction of the king's residence."

"But with the drought? And…"

"And?" Obadyah replied.

"And, well, son, you are sincere. And I believe you when you say you want to help. But, I fear, you are just a boy and perhaps you do not know fully what Jezebel is capable of."

Obadyah smirked. If he only had time, he could describe for the baker in grotesque detail how well he knew the queen of Israel. But now, he must rely on the strength of his plan. "While Ahab executes his wife's decree," Obadyah said, "I will have the authority to use his goods as I see fit. I will sustain the servants of Yahweh. The prophets must be gathered without word or discussion of the location of the caves. Their families must believe they have been abducted by Jezebel. It is the only way the location will be kept secret from the king's men. As I receive rations, I will deliver a portion of them to you myself. Such few provisions will not be missed. We cannot save all of the prophets. But once Jezebel is satisfied with the blood she has shed, we can return each servant of Yahweh to their family, quietly, one-by-one."

"What about Eliah?"

"You are correct. I must keep her with me. I will continue with her to Jezreel and find a safe place where she can await Benjamin's return. Proceed to Samaria. Find Benjamin! Each day that passes will mean more lives sacrificed by Jezebel. Now go!"

The baker turned to walk away. And then stopped. He turned.

"Amos," he said, placing his palm on his chest.

"Amos," Obadyah nodded. "Tell the men guarding the caves that the Captain has sent you to replace them. Tell them: The Phoenix is rising."

Amos walked back to Obadyah, he sheathed his knife and put his hands on Obadyah's shoulders.

"Thank you, brother."

"Do not thank me. Just find Benjamin."

Amos nodded. He and his men disappeared into the night.

CHAPTER 35

THE HEART'S HOME

"Eliah…Eliah…wake up."

"Papa?"

"Eliah it's me, Obadyah. We must leave."

"Obadyah? Where are we?"

"We are at the inn, in Dothan, remember?"

Eliah stirred and rubbed her eyes.

"I want to get an early start this morning. Come, you can sleep in the wagon." Obadyah helped Eliah to her feet. He grabbed their blanket and wrapped it around her shoulders. They crept out of the inn and made their way towards the city stables.

"Smell that?" Eliah said, "The baker is up! Can we stop for bread?"

Obadyah was about to say 'no' when he noticed a pouch on the ground just ahead of them. The steam from the freshly baked bread filled the darkness. When they reached the bakery, Obadyah looked down. 'For Eliah.' Eliah recognized her name scribbled into the dust. Knowing now, she is the daughter of a prophet, her ability to read did not surprise Obadyah.

Eliah smiled and grabbed up her gift. Obadyah drug his sandal through the dirt to erase the message and they proceeded down the street. Having harnessed Buckets to the wagon, Obadyah helped Eliah into the back. He pushed the supplies aside so she had a space to lie down. He took the round warm loaf from her hands, placed it under her head, then tucked the blanket around her. Eliah closed her eyes, asleep before Obadyah could cover her.

Obadyah moved swiftly out of the city. The trail descended as he traveled north. When they entered the Dothan Valley, the rising sun woke Eliah. She poked her head up above the side of the cart to see Obadyah walking beside

Buckets. When Buckets stopped for his morning routine, Obadyah smiled at Eliah.

"Good morning, My Lady."

Eliah jumped from the wagon bed. Without a word, she proceeded behind a boulder on the east side of the trail. Obadyah moved to the back of the wagon to tear off a piece of bread. When Eliah returned, he offered her a bit. She threw it into her mouth and climbed back up on the wagon, still without a word. Her behavior confused Obadyah. Not knowing what to say, he left her alone and grabbed Bucket's lead.

After an hour on the trail, Obadyah began to hear Eliah sniffling. When he listened more intently he could tell she was crying. He panicked. He had heard his mother cry once. And when his father attempted to console her she began beating on his chest until he gave up and left. Tukulti had told Ashur that girls sometimes cry for no reason. Is this one of those times? Should I stop and check on her? Does she want to be left alone?

"You know you could stop and check on me," Eliah whimpered.

Obadyah stopped and turned towards the back of the wagon.

Before he could ask her what was wrong, she said, "Girls don't just cry for no reason."

"Oh, I know." Obadyah replied. "What is the reason for your tears?"

"No. Obadyah!" Eliah corrected. "You don't say it like that! You are supposed to say, 'Are you well?'"

"Are you well?"

"Of course I'm not well. Is anyone ever well when they are crying?"

Obadyah raked his hand through his hair. He had never been so uncomfortable in all his life.

"Well, don't just stand there staring at me, give me a hug!"

Obadyah obeyed. Walking towards the back of the wagon, he reached out for Eliah. She leaned into his chest.

"You need to squeeze me a little harder," she instructed. "Good hugs always hurt a little. That's how you know the difference between the real ones and the empty ones."

Obadyah kept squeezing Eliah until she quit squeezing him.

When she pulled herself away, he said, "Can we go now?"

"No, no, Obadyah," she corrected. "You should say something like, 'Do you need anything?' or 'Is there anything I can do for you?'"

"But you needed a hug and I gave you a hug."

"Yes, but you need to check if there is anything more you can do."

"What more can I do?"

"I will let you know, once you ask."

"Eliah," Obadyah said, "Do you need anything or is there anything more I can do for you?"

"No, I'm fine. I just needed to cry this morning, that's all."

Obadyah stood in silence unsure what to do next. When further instructions were not forthcoming, he proceeded slowly back to Bucket's lead.

Eliah followed, and they continued their journey north.

"So," Eliah said, "who's Zoë? Is she your beloved?"

"She is my friend."

"Yes. But you love her?"

Obadyah, weary, confessed. "Yes. I love her."

"I knew you loved her by the way you talked about her in your sleep."

"What did I say?"

"Hmm. I don't think I'm ready to reveal that."

"Eliah! What did I say?"

"I'm just going to keep that to myself for now."

Obadyah conceded, shaking his head.

"Tell me about her," Eliah commanded. "Is she beautiful?"

"Yes, she is beautiful."

"How beautiful?"

"Very beautiful."

"You are not going to say it like that, are you?"

"Well, I…"

"No, no, no! Eliah interrupted, "You can't just say, 'you are very beautiful.'"

"Why not? It's true."

"My father tells me I am beautiful. You don't want her to look at you like that do you?"

"How is it you know so much about women?"

"Because I am a woman."

"You mean a girl?"

"I mean a lady."

"Agreed. Continue."

"So, you do not just tell her that she is beautiful. You tell her how she is beautiful."

Obadyah nodded, adjusting to his role as a perceptive student.

"Let's practice," Eliah continued, "Tell me something about Zoë."

Obadyah thought for a minute and then blurted out, "Her eyes are as big as the moon."

"I've got quite a job ahead of me," Eliah remarked under her breath.

"But they are!"

"So when you think of her you think of the moon?"

"No. When I think of her eyes I think of the light of the night. For a world without her would mean darkness for me."

"Perfect. Tell her that."

Obadyah smiled.

"What else?" Eliah asked.

"Her skin is as soft as the underside of a snail."

"Just as a general rule, we ladies don't like any part of us compared to slugs or snails."

"How about a lamb?" Obadyah replied. "We had a lamb when I was your age. Its ears were so silky, my brother and I had just about rubbed the fur off of the poor thing. Zoë's skin is like that, soft and silky as a baby lamb."

Eliah nodded. "Very good. What else?"

"I know!" Obadyah said, starting to show some confidence. "Her touch is like a bolt of lightning."

"But, Obadyah, lightning can kill people. Is there something a little less scary than lightning?"

Obadyah began thinking out loud, "Hmm, something that is powerful and unstoppable? A waterfall!"

"Like the one at Engedi!" Eliah said.

"When I was young," Obadyah recalled, "my mother took me to the falls at Mivzar Dan. I had never seen anything so pure, so constant, so powerful."

Eliah smiled. "You are ready to speak of her beauty."

Obadyah and Eliah made camp just outside of the village of Ibleam.

"Tomorrow we enter the Jezreel Valley," Obadyah said, tucking Eliah's blanket around her in the back of the wagon. "Get some rest. We still have several days of walking ahead of us."

As Obadyah made himself comfortable on the ground next to the fire, Eliah hummed herself to sleep.

Obadyah and Eliah spent three days in the Jezreel Valley. The valley, the heart of beauty and productivity, was now waning in the face of an impending drought. The green which characterized the region was losing its vibrancy. The gray which usually kept to the hills was gaining ground in the valley.

Obadyah pointed towards the horizon. "There it is," he said, "Jezreel."

"But we have seen many settlements," Eliah replied, "are you sure this is the right one?"

Obadyah stopped and knelt down on the trail before them. "Come. Look," he said, grabbing a stone. Obadyah drew a curve on the ground in the shape of a J. "The Great Sea Coast is here. On the eastern side of the Mediterranean, just off the north western point is Galilee." Obadyah drew a circle in the dust representing the Sea of Chinnereth. "Below the Sea, down here," Obadyah drew an oval south of Galilee that stretched north to south, "this is the Dead Sea."

"And the Jordan river lies between the Sea of Chinnereth and the Dead Sea!" Eliah said, using her finger to draw a squiggly line connecting the two seas.

"That's right." Obadyah smiled. "The land of Canaan is here." He pointed to the land which rested between the Jordan river and the edge of the Sea. "Now, about half way down the Jordan river valley, there is a valley that runs west away from the Jordan River. Obadyah drew the shape of an arrow head on the ground. The point touched the shore of the Great Sea. The two blades fanned out away from the Sea, the barbs of the blades reaching towards the Jordan River. "Here," Obadyah said, pointing with his rock. "We are here." He circled the stem of the arrow where it connected to the shaft.

"Jezreel is the connecting point!"

"Exactly." Obadiah replied. "And do you know what the arrow points to?"

"Mount Carmel?"

Obadyah smiled. "You know the land."

"My father taught me. He is a prophet of Yahweh."

"Yes," Obadyah smiled, "I remember."

"Where are you from, Obadyah? Where is your home?"

Obadyah looked at the map on the ground. He followed the western coast of the Sea north of Galilee.

"Tyre and Sidon are here. They are the prominent settlements of Phoenicia. Samaria is here," Obadyah continued, pointing to a central area on his map south of the Jezreel Valley. "And, Jezreel is here," Obadyah said.

"You can't have three homes."

"Who says?"

"I say. You have only one heart, so you have only one home," Eliah declared.

Obadyah looked down at his map and thought about each of the places he had identified. He then took his stone and drew an island in the Mediterranean Sea.

CHAPTER 36

THE NEW NEIGHBOR NEWS

Obadyah and Eliah could see the outline of a structure ahead of them.

"Each stone is meticulously placed to accommodate the gentle downward grade of the earth, see?" Obadyah said.

"Does that mean they will have a good bread oven inside?" Eliah asked.

"You must learn to appreciate a few things other than warm bread," Obadyah suggested.

"Why?" Eliah asked.

Obadyah said nothing, unsure himself if structures were more important than bread.

Still several steps away, they could see a covered patio on the rooftop.

"Are you sure that is it?" Eliah asked.

Obadyah nodded. The home was precisely as Theophanes described it. They picked up their pace for the last few steps of their journey. When they arrived, Obadyah strung Bucket's lead over a hitching post while Eliah continued to the opening of the home.

"Hello?" she said.

Obadyah approached. He and Eliah leaned in together. "Anyone home?" Eliah cried. There was no answer. "Perhaps he is in the vineyard," she said. "Let's look for the trail."

"Let's stay here and wait," Obadyah suggested.

Eliah ran past Obadyah as though he had not said a word. Obadyah spun around, following the dust kicking up off the heels of Eliah's sandals.

"Look," she said, pointing to a boulder situated above the valley. When Eliah arrived next to the giant stone she jumped, reaching for the flat surface atop the boulder. She grunted as she pushed herself up on the tip of her toes.

"Having some trouble?" Obadyah asked.

"Help me, Obadyah!" Eliah pleaded.

Ignoring her, Obadyah locked his fingers on the upper rim of the boulder and pulled himself up. He looked out across the winding rows of vines.

"Beautiful," he said. "Glorious," he added.

The perch was high enough to provide a clear vantage point from the house to the vineyard, and down to the valley floor. Row after row of grapes wove back and forth in well groomed tiers. The green leaves of the wine plants jumped off of the canvas of rocky soil beneath them. Men and women fifteen, twenty, maybe thirty were busy tending to the plants, some harvesting, some tilling, some restringing support lines for the creeping vines.

Eliah started to whine. "Obadyah! Down here! Remember me?"

Obadyah continued to gaze out across the vineyard, enjoying both the view and Eliah's frustration.

"Now you are just being rude," Eliah said, folding her arms across her chest.

Obadyah, satisfied, knelt down. He extended his hand to Eliah and pulled her up.

Eliah looked down the hill. "Beautiful!"

"Is that not what I said?" Obadyah replied.

About halfway down towards the valley, a man in a white tunic stood up. The worker who had gotten the man's attention pointed in the direction of Obadyah and Eliah. The man in the cloak dusted himself off and proceeded up the hill towards them.

Obadyah jumped down in anticipation of greeting the master of the estate. Eliah took a seat atop the stone, her feet dangling over the edge.

"Shalom," said the man in white as he drew near.

"Shalom," Obadyah replied, nodding in respect of the land owner. "My name is Obadyah. This young lady is Eliah." Obadyah reached for Eliah and lowered her to the ground.

"Obadyah is not my husband," Eliah announced.

The man laughed and then placed his hand on his heart. "Allow me to introduce myself. My name is Naboth."

"I greet you in the name of Theophanes," Obadyah said, "captain of…"

"Captain of the Phoenix!" Naboth interrupted. Moving quickly to Obadyah's side, Naboth placed his hand on Obadyah's shoulder. "Are you his shipmate?"

"No, My Lord. I am his son."

Naboth's eyes widened. He reached for Obadyah again. Now with one hand on each of his shoulders he said, "Then I welcome you as my son."

Obadyah nodded, unsure how to reply.

"You must be tired from your journey. Please, accompany me to my home. Grant us the privilege of tending to your needs."

Eliah took Obadyah's hand and began pulling him up the hill after Naboth. Arriving at the entrance, Naboth reached for a ram's horn strung on a leather cord hanging from a notch on the doorframe. "Allow me to notify my workers," Naboth said. Taking the horn in his hand he blew it in the direction of the vineyard—two short bursts followed by one long burst.

"Please," Naboth said. Opening his hand towards his home, he welcomed them in.

Eliah hurried inside, Obadyah followed.

To their left as they entered, five vertical poles supported a large wooden cross beam framing an open air gathering space. To the right an indoor stable with feeding troughs for baby animals, sheep, goats, and fowl.

"Look!" Eliah said, pointing to a lamb resting on a straw bed.

Obadyah smiled and then urged Eliah on.

Naboth directed them to a ladder at the end of the hall.

Eliah climbed up, Obadyah followed close behind. They stepped off onto a rooftop terrace that overlooked the vineyard stretched out below them. As Obadyah took in the expanse of the valley, he found himself holding his breath.

Eliah tugged on his tunic returning his gaze to the terrace. "Sit here," she said.

Obadyah complied, taking a seat next to Eliah. Above them, a canopy of woven material draped over a vine that broke up the sun's rays while allowing the wind to pass through. The cool breeze that rushed up the side of the valley found its way across the roof terrace and welcomed them.

"This is grand!" Eliah announced. Obadyah leaned over and whispered, "You better not just tell Lord Naboth that his home is grand. You better tell him how his home is grand."

"Good advice," Eliah nodded.

When Naboth stepped off of the ladder onto the rooftop, Eliah was ready. "Your home is the cleanest, brightest home I have ever seen," she said.

"Thank you, My Lady," Naboth replied. "I have sent for tea and dates. Would you prefer wine?"

"Tea and dates sound…"

"Wonderful!" Eliah said, interrupting Obadyah. "Your house smells good, too."

Naboth laughed, "Well, thank you again, My Lady," he said, nodding towards Eliah. Turning his attention to Obadyah. "So, the son of the captain," Naboth began, taking a seat facing his guests.

Naboth's graying beard shone off the darkened skin of his sun beaten face. His aging eyes fell in the direction of a broad smile which wrapped his face in an unmistakable contentment.

"Yes, My Lord," Obadyah replied.

Naboth continued. "You look like your father."

"I am afraid so. But my heart I received from my mother," Obadyah replied, immediately regretting his criticism of his father.

"Then you are truly blessed, my friend, as Theophanes speaks faithfully of your mother's heart."

Obadyah forced a smile, as though that were something he heard often.

"And how is it you have been granted the blessing of your beautiful young travel companion?"

"Jezebel wants to kill my father," Eliah announced. "His name is Benjamin. He is the stablekeep at the palace in Samaria. He is a prophet of Yahweh."

Naboth flinched. His eyes fell to the floor. He appeared nervous all of the sudden and made no reply to Eliah. He turned his attention to Obadyah. "Forgive me, Obadyah," Naboth said, then paused. "But…your marking… are you not Ahab's…"

"Before we discuss my business," Obadyah interrupted, "may I make a request of you?"

"I am at your service, servant of the King."

"I believe Eliah would like to sit in the company of your new lamb."

Naboth looked to Eliah. Her face brightened.

"Please, Eliah," Naboth replied, "proceed as you wish."

Eliah jumped from her seat, and hurried down the ladder.

"She is a dear girl," Naboth said.

"She is," Obadyah replied. "She has a few trying qualities as well."

Naboth and Obadyah shared a brief smile before Obadyah spoke up. "As you have discerned, I am Ahab's overseer. How the son of the captain of the Phoenix has come to serve the king of Israel is a story for another time. What you must know today is that Ahab has tasked me with the construction of a new residence in Jezreel."

Naboth closed his eyes and drew in a deep breath. When he opened them, he narrowed in on his guest. "Forgive me, Obadyah, but perhaps you can help me understand. You claim an allegiance with your father, you state your commitment to Yahweh. And yet the seal of Jezebel freshly burned into your skin."

"I share your confusion, Lord Naboth." Obadyah paused and gathered himself. "I too often wonder who I truly am. The circumstances of my life have been…" Obadyah stopped. What exactly was he ready to confess? That his life had been difficult? Whose has not? He remembered his father's words as they left Cyprus. He needed to let go of the past and be present today, take ownership of what he could control in this moment. Obadyah leaned forward and said, "I am the son of Theophanes." It wasn't just an observation. His voice was determined, stern. It was said with pride. He was leaning on his father's reputation and friendship with Naboth. And, Obadyah knew, he was also leaning on Theophanes.

Obadyah held onto the strength in his voice, "And, while I am also branded by evil, I give you my word, before all else, I am a son David, worshiper of the Lord of hosts, who sits enthroned above the cherubim."

"I believe you, son of Theophanes. And so, I will waste no time in entrusting you with this. Benjamin is dead."

Obadyah's mouth fell open. "What…? When…?

"Word is moving swiftly through the land. Jezebel has destroyed every prophet in Samaria. But she will not stop there."

"No, no, no," Obadyah murmured under his breath. The strength he had found inside of himself for a few moments was gone.

"My messenger arrived this morning," Naboth said.

Obadyah, trying to absorb the weight of his news, could not stop shaking his head. "The manner of Benjamin's death is something I do not wish to repeat," Naboth continued. "I beg you, spare me that pain."

"I have witnessed the method in which Jezebel takes a life," Obadyah said under his breath.

Naboth nodded.

Obadyah stood and moved to the edge of the terrace. "How can I tell her? What will I say?" Obadyah starred out into the valley. What had been gorgeous and grand, now just reminded him of how small he truly was.

"You will bear the weight of young Eliah's heart," Naboth said, coming to his feet. "And you will bear the responsibility of her care," he said, placing a hand on Obadyah's shoulder. "Yahweh will strengthen you when the time is right to tell her," Naboth pulled on Obadyah's shoulder forcing him to look him in the eye. "Yahweh asks nothing of you he has not prepared you for."

"I am a slave, a…" Obadyah's voice cracked as he felt himself fall further into weakness. "You don't understand. I am not capable of…" Obadyah paused. He could feel all the insecurities of his past creeping back in. "…of even being a man, much less a father."

"Yahweh disagrees."

"Yes," Obadyah replied, "He often does."

"Jezebel will demand our attention. But not today. The son of my dear friend has come into my home. How can I serve you, son of Theophanes?"

"I require workers," Obadyah replied, "craftsmen, builders, stonemasons. And accommodations for myself and Eliah."

"Consider your needs met. You will stay here with me until your task is complete."

Obadyah opened his mouth to object.

"Please," Naboth continued, "I will accept nothing less."

Obadyah immediately thought of old Tukulti. The kindness and respect he had shown Theophanes was now mirrored in the face of Naboth. However disgusting Theophanes's relationship with the kings, Obadyah could not help but feel something genuine had drawn these men to his father. The fierce loyalty he saw in Naboth's eyes left him at a loss for words.

"Will this space suffice?" Naboth asked motioning to the terrace on which they sat.

"It will indeed. Thank you, Lord Naboth."

Obadyah felt his world spinning once more. He could not seem to survive a day without a new weight pressing on him. And now, Benjamin is dead. He was not prepared to hear that, even less to accept it. And yet he could not ignore the task set before him by King Ahab. While his heart told him to run to Eliah, to sweep her up and go find a corner in which to hold her and cry, the business of his new role demanded his attention. Obadyah stretched his hand towards Naboth. The two men grabbed one another's forearms. A deal was struck.

"I will send for my foreman. He will be your servant while you complete your work. He has family in Nazareth who are suffering because of the drought. I will send for them as well. My servants will be your servants."

"I'm overwhelmed by your kindness," Obadyah said.

"I do not have enough hours left in my life to repay your father for the kindness he has shown me. Yahweh has been merciful by bringing you here."

The men extended their arms towards one another once more in mutual appreciation and in agreement of the terms put forth by Naboth.

"Now," he said, "I see no need to muster laborers at this hour of the day. Please, join us at my table."

While feasting was the last thing on Obadyah's mind, he and Eliah had not had a decent meal since they left Samaria. She would need strength in the days to come. Obadyah accepted his host's invitation.

Descending the ladder to the main floor of the house, Obadyah paused when he came to the stables. Eliah did not see him approach. Obadyah remained quiet and watched as she stroked the ears of her furry new friend. He leaned in to hear her humming the same song she had sung in the inn at Dothan. Obadyah's stomach turned with the reminder of the news he would eventually deliver. The agonizing task fell to him. He could not fathom it. Soon he would break Eliah's heart.

Naboth proceeded out of the front door of his home. He grabbed the ram's horn again and blew three long alerts. When all of the workers scurrying about the house gathered to Naboth, he made his announcement. "My friends," he began, "allow me to introduce, Obadyah and Eliah." Naboth reached over and put his hand on Obadyah's shoulder. "They are my friends. And now they are yours. Leave your work for tomorrow. Tonight," Naboth said, "let us feast!"

The men and women cheered with one voice and hurried to their tasks. Some went back towards the fields. Some headed towards town. Others entered Naboth's house. Everyone seemed to know their responsibility when feasting was at hand.

As bodies moved about, Eliah caught Obadyah's attention. Her eyes were locked on a woman who casually left the gathering and strolled towards the house. The woman was holding the hand of a little girl. Obadyah could not help but smile at the sight, the girl's arm reaching up with all its might, her two plump bowed legs struggling to keep pace with the woman's stride. Eliah's eyes followed them until the pair disappeared inside Naboth's home. Then, before they tore their gaze away, two tiny eyes peaked back out at them.

Unbeknownst to Obadyah, Naboth had been observing them. "That is Accoah," Naboth said. "We named her that because she was abandoned on the shore at Acco. It seems her parents had hoped she would be taken by the tide. My men were traveling back from a rendezvous with your father when they found her."

"May I speak to her?" Eliah asked.

"You can try. She is very shy." Naboth replied.

"I'm not shy," Eliah announced.

"Truer words have never been spoken," Obadyah added.

"Accoah would be very happy to have a nice young lady to spend time with," Naboth said.

Without a word, Eliah headed off to the house.

"May I show you my vineyard?" Naboth asked Obadyah.

"Please," Obadyah replied.

The men made their way to the trail which descended towards the Jezreel Valley.

"Have you been affected by the drought?" Obadyah inquired.

"It has increased the hours we must attend to our crops. But the fresh water spring at Jezreel has sustained us."

"Perhaps it is the spring which entices the queen. That and the soil of the valley."

Naboth nodded. "Strategically there is no better place to dwell. Jezreel overlooks a direct route to the Sea where the valley meets the Carmel Ridge. And to the east," Naboth pointed, "it connects to the Jordan River Valley. Any chariots or armies approaching can be identified from quite a distance."

"Jezebel is no fool for having chosen this site."

"With high places to Baal at Megiddo," Naboth said, "I sensed Jezebel encroaching. Still, it is a bit overwhelming to know that the King and Queen of Israel will be my neighbors."

The men turned a corner of the trail and stepped out on the landing of Naboth's wine press. A stone retaining wall surrounded the upper chamber of the press. A square pool chiseled out of the bedrock descended to a trough where crushed grapes ran to a circular vat below.

"You tread out your wine in the midst of your garden?" Obadyah asked.

"I have discovered that it is more productive to have a press which is convenient for my laborers."

"They serve you well."

"I am blessed. Many of them have come from your father."

"I thought my father did not deal in slaves."

"He does not. Nor do I. I hire laborers, I do not enslave."

Obadyah listened as Naboth explained the wine-making process from the treading floor to the series of vats which collected the juice from the pressed grapes. The contrasting colors and textures of the fruit and its vine soothed Obadyah. It was a stolen moment of peace amidst the turmoil of the last few days, and the days to come. Naboth broke off a twig containing a large cluster of grapes and handed it to Obadyah.

Naboth and Obadyah finished their tour of the vineyard and headed into town. Jezreel was a small village. A handful of vendors lined the streets and a few new homes were being constructed towards the valley floor. Certainly not a bustling metropolis. Still, Jezreel was growing steadily with each passing season. Having explored the higher lands, Obadyah selected a plot of ground above Naboth's allotment where he would construct a palace retreat for Ahab and Jezebel.

When dusk settled in the valley, the men made their way back to Naboth's home. Coming into sight of it, Obadyah could see Eliah in the distance dancing with little Accoah. Naboth's workers had taken up flutes and stringed instruments and were accompanying the girls as they spun around, the fringes of their dresses flying. Naboth began to clap his hands in time with the beating drums.

Obadyah couldn't help but smile. Joy for a moment displacing the sorrow eating him up on the inside. He had to tell her. He had to find the strength. Eliah reached for Obadyah's hand. Naboth was given a tambourine. Eliah spun Obadyah and Accoah around, keeping in step with Naboth's musicians.

"Again, again," Accoah said when the song came to an end. Accoah came alive with the music, her eyes as bright and round as a newborn calf. Her fine brown hair and long white dress bounced around her as she flopped about like a delicate baby bird.

"Let us feed our guests, little one," Naboth replied, "and then we shall dance again."

Obadyah moved out in the yard with the workers and assisted them. They stacked crates upon timbers, creating a long table that would accommodate everyone.

Taking his place at the head of the table, Naboth reached for Accoah's hand. Accoah then reached for Eliah's hand. When everyone seated around the table had joined hands, Naboth began:

> Bless Yahweh, O my soul.
> Bless His holy name.
> Bless Yahweh, O my soul
> Bless His mighty works.
> Bless Yahweh, O my soul
> With all that is within me
> Bless His holy name.

As eyes opened, hands dropped and the feasting began.

"Do you celebrate often in this manner?" Obadyah asked. Obadyah had only a faint memory of normal life experiences like these. That there were people whose lives did not revolve around a palace, a royalty dynasty, and the unrelenting struggle for power, had been something, for so many years, he was forced to try to imagine.

"Every Sabbath and, of course, when special visitors are among us," Naboth said, offering Eliah his warmest smile.

Obadyah looked around the table at the laborers who were nourished by Naboth's generosity. His heart soared amid the simple beauty of fellowship and sustenance. And then his heart sank with the reality of two imminent destructive forces: drought and Jezebel. "Should this drought continue," Obadyah said, "I will sustain you with the king's provisions."

"Should this drought continue," Naboth replied, "I will accept your kind offer."

CHAPTER 37

THE DROUGHT

Zoë soaked a piece of bread in the last bit of honey. Samara reached for Zoë's plate. Zoë did not let go but brought the plate up to her mouth and licked it clean. Samara laughed. The two women had become quite comfortable in their routine, Zoë finally allowing Samara to serve her.

"If you do not need me, I'd like to walk to the hilltop and await Nimshi's return," Zoë said.

Samara nodded and retired to her room for her afternoon rest.

Zoë made her way through the back portico and up the trail that ascended past the garden. She found a level place above the house, giving her a clear vantage point of the approach from the village. She sighed as she looked out over the land. Canaan began showing signs of having been forsaken, the ground seeing not a single shower nor even a drop of dew just as Elijah had predicted. Crops withered. Rivers were reduced to muddy streams in the absence of life sustaining rains.

Zoë reached for her heart, dry and brittle. Everything her eyes took in, she felt inside. As the land awaited Yahweh's mercy, she knew, she too would not know nourishment until she was in Obadyah's presence once more. Guilt swept in. She was cared for. Theophanes delivered fresh water from the spring at Khirokitia, a village on the island of Cyprus. With new pots arriving every forty days, they were able to ration their consumption, supporting themselves and their modest garden behind Samara's home. *How can I justify any longing? How can I wish for anything more?*

Zoë saw Palmsquat in the distance. She rushed to meet Nimshi.

"How does my aunt fare?" she asked.

"She struggles," Nimshi replied, "but she survives, as does her son."

Zoë's heart stirred at the mention of the baby her uncle Kalbu rescued from the fire during the Baal sacrifice ceremony. She longed to see the little boy, to look at the tiny face her blind uncle could not see but had heard, the boy's cries ringing out as his precious life was tossed into the flames.

Taking Palmsquat's lead, Zoë insisted Nimshi ride in the wagon for the final ascent to Samara's home. Zoë guided the wagon around the side of the house.

Samara, having risen from her rest, opened the gate. "How was your journey, Nimshi?"

"Satisfactory, My Lady."

"Satisfactory, in the midst of drought, is success."

"It is indeed, My Lady."

"Was Donatiya in need?"

"She mixes Kalbu's skin salves. She trades the healing ointment for oil and flour. She is sustained by word of Zoë's good health. And by the nourishment of Samson."

"Samson?" Samara replied.

"Samson?" Zoë added.

"Yes, Samson," Nimshi replied, "her son."

Zoë and Samara looked at one another with the joy only women understand at the mere mention of a baby's name.

"This is a Hebrew name?" Zoë asked.

Samara nodded. "I spoke of Samson on one of my visits to your aunt and uncle's home."

"Recite it to me, the story of Samson," Zoë pleaded, "just as you told it to my aunt and uncle?"

"Please, proceed inside," Nimshi said. "I will tend to our supplies and to Palmsquat."

Zoë had become sensitive to Nimshi's exhaustion. She thought she might argue with him. But she reminded herself that leaving Palmsquat's care to another, was a far greater discomfort to Nimshi than the pain of spending one more hour on his feet.

Hurrying inside, Zoë sat down on the edge of Samara's couch.

Samara ambled to the kitchen for a cup of tea, speaking loudly enough for Zoë to hear. "Samson judged Israel prior to the anointing of Israel's first king."

"I have heard of the judges," Zoë replied. "The tale of Deborah is quite inspiring."

Samara entered, handed a cup to Zoë, then sat down next to her. "Samson was a Nazir. He was consecrated, set apart."

"He was a priest?" Zoë asked.

Samara shook her head. "Priests are Levites, descendants of Aaron, Moses's brother. They were set apart by Yahweh to minister to Him at the tabernacle. A Nazarite vow is different. Any Hebrew, man or woman, can take a Nazarite vow and set themselves apart.

"Set themselves apart for what?"

"Well, in Samson's case, to deliver Israel from the hands of the Philistines."

"The sons of Ammon?"

Samara nodded. "Those residing in the five cities of Philistia: Ekron, Ashdod, Gath, Ashkelon…"

"And Gaza!" Zoë added. "Sidon embraces the gods of Aram, Moab, and Ammon."

"Sadly, Israel had embraced them as well. At the time of the judges it was written, 'The sons of Israel forgot Yahweh their God and served the Baals and the Asheroth.'"

"What is required to become a Nazir?" Zoë asked.

"There are three commitments a Hebrew must make to keep the Nazarite vow. First, a razor must not touch his or her hair. Second, no wine or fermented drink can touch their lips. And finally, a Nazir must never touch the dead."

"Yahweh saved Israel through Samson because he kept this vow?"

"Yahweh gifted Samson with unimaginable strength. As his hair grew, so did his conquests. It is said he killed a lion with his bare hands and that he slew over a thousand Philistines. So, as you can imagine, when the Philistines discovered him in Gaza, they gathered their men intent on killing him at dawn."

"But he escaped!"

"Samson arose under the cover of darkness. But, instead of stealing away in the night, he stole the gates of their city, tore them from the ground, posts and all, and carried them off. I have been told the gates of the city of Gaza still remain, preserved for more than two hundred years at the top of the mountain opposite Hebron."

"The Philistines would have thought Samson was a god!" Zoë said.

"I can assure you, he was a man. I know this because his downfall came at the hands of a woman."

"But…what he did, it is impossible…."

"Things that are impossible with man are possible with Yahweh."

"Why would Yahweh grant Samson miraculous strength, help him deliver His people, and then allow a woman to destroy him?"

"The woman who betrayed Samson was called Delilah. And while it is true that she gave away his secret, she was not the reason he lost his strength. And though Yahweh allowed the Philistines to shave Samson's hair, Yahweh did not abandon Samson either. What happened to Samson, he did to himself."

"We are often our own worst enemy," Zoë said.

"No one felt the sting of that truth, like Samson. Once his strength was gone, the Philistines gouged out his eyes, bound him in chains, and made him a grinder in the prison."

"I ache for Samson," Zoë said. "He was given so much, and he threw it away."

"Yes. But that is not the end of the story."

Zoë's head shot up.

"Samson made several poor decisions throughout his life. But it was that one night in the wrong bed, that one moment of weakness with the wrong woman, that cost him his strength, his eyes, his freedom, and his dignity. Remember, my dear, we are free to choose, but we have no say in the consequences we suffer as a result of those choices."

"But why, why would Yahweh allow…"

"Why would Yahweh allow it?" Samara interrupted. "Would you have a God who forced His will on you?"

"I suppose not, but…"

"But perhaps giving you the freedom to choose is a mistake?" Samara interrupted again.

Zoë shook her head, frustrated and confused.

"Allow me to tell you how the story ends," Samara said, reaching her hand over and resting it on Zoë's knee.

Zoë's eyes met Samara's, eager for understanding. And though she could not muster the courage to say the words, what she really wanted, what she always wanted, was simply a happy ending.

"One day, the Philistines gathered in celebration of the victory granted them by their god, Dagon. Samson was captured. Yahweh was defeated. The lords of the Philistines would bask in their glory by humiliating their adversary. 'Call for Samson that he might amuse us!' they said. No one seemed to notice, no one seemed to care, no one seemed to mention the fact that Samson's hair had started growing again. Samson stood before the house of the lords. He could hear the stomping of feet on the roof. The sound of voices speaking on top of one another filled his ears. The chaos of the crowd was deafening. There were thousands of Philistines gathered in one house. Unbeknownst to Samson, more than three thousand, in fact. While the Philistines raved, Samson prayed. While the Philistines mocked, Samson called on his God and begged Him, "strengthen me Yahweh, this one last time."

"And?" Zoë interrupted.

"And, what?"

"Samara!" Zoë scolded. "What happened?"

Samara smiled. "Samson asked the boy who had escorted him from the prison to lead him up the stairs. The boy obeyed leaving Samson between the two middle pillars on which the house rested. Samson braced himself against them, one with his right hand, the other with his left. Then Samson said, 'Let me die with the Philistines!' He bent with all his might so that the house fell on the lords and all the people. As it happened, the dead whom he killed at his death were more than he killed in his life."

"So it was when Samson was weakest that he was strongest."

Samara smiled. "Yahweh has a tendency to work that way."

"I have been angry with Yahweh for allowing my uncle to save little Samson. There is nothing weaker than having no sight. But now I know, he had to be weak, he had to be blind," Zoë choked on her words, "so that he could act with Yahweh's strength." Zoë swallowed her tears.

Samara spoke up. "It was just a few weeks before your uncle was burned that I told Donatiya and Kalbu the story of how Samson asked Yahweh to use him, even if that meant he would die. After I spoke, Kalbu turned to Donatiya and said, 'From now on, call me Samson!' To which your aunt replied, 'I'm not calling you Samson, you dusty old rug.' To which Kalbu answered, 'If you want me to respond you will!' 'Why,' your aunt had asked. 'Why must you insist I call you Samson?' 'Because,' Kalbu replied, 'I belong to Yahweh now.'"

Zoë put her face in her hands and freed her tears.

Samara rested her hand on Zoë's arm. Samara, usually lacking in affection, was never lacking a good story. "Can I tell you about another one of my visits with your aunt and uncle?" she asked.

When Zoë looked up at Samara there was a lightness in her face. Her eyes glowed with a delight Zoë had not yet witnessed. Samara's demeanor drifted like fresh morning dew across the couch and fell on Zoë. Heartened by Samara's cheerful tone, Zoë wiped the tears off her cheeks.

"When I arrived at your aunt and uncle's home," Samara began, "I found

Kalbu working on his pottery. We were enjoying a fairly sound conversation when Kalbu asked me to place his sea sponge into the receptacle against the back wall. I retrieved the honeycomb from his hand and proceeded past the assortment of dusty treasures to the location indicated by your uncle. I arrived to find not one, but three receptacles. The first was labeled 'clean.' The sign above the second read, 'crusty.' The third said, 'not too crusty.' I paused in long deliberation as to the condition of the object in my hand. It clearly was not clean. That left me with two remaining options. As I considered the state of the sponge, I considered the state of Kalbu who seemed to sense my struggle and yet made no effort to assist me. In the end I chose 'not too crusty.' However, I must admit, to this day I wonder if I made the right choice."

Zoë laughed. And without pause, her laughter turned once more to tears. After a few minutes she raised her head and made eye contact with Samara. "My aunt is too old to be a mother and too young to be a widow."

"Yahweh disagrees."

While that fact was clear, it was not at all comforting. Zoë had no sooner settled into a peaceful acceptance of Yahweh and her frustration with Him returned. Despite her determination to think Him different, she found herself wishing He were the type of God who could be won by acts of devotion which Zoë would happily perform in trade for His care of her aunt.

CHAPTER 38

THE PROPHET AND THE PROPHETS

"Lady Samara, My Lady, tis me, tis Jashar."

Zoë arose and propped herself on one arm to see what the commotion was outside her window. The sun had just broken free from the shadow of the earth, and she had to squint against its rays. When her eyes adjusted, she saw Jashar, the young boy Samara often petitioned to run errands for her. Zoë's heart stirred remembering the time she and Obadyah found Jashar fishing at the docks. It was he who ran to town announcing news of Jezebel's prophecy battle.

"My Lady, My..."

Nimshi appeared. "Quiet, Jashar! You will wake Zoë!"

"Nimshi, Sir, please, I must speak to..."

"Yes, yes, Jashar, I know!"

"But, I have news of Donatiya."

At that Nimshi motioned for the boy to follow. They proceeded from the front entrance to the garden behind Samara's home.

Zoë scrambled out of bed and rushed to dress herself.

"My Lady!" Nimshi called out.

Zoë ran to the door, eager to hear any news yet afraid the news was bad. Her heartbeat thudded in her ears. She rounded the corner of the house to the gardens just as Nimshi approached with Jashar.

Samara was breaking up the bits of dry soil around her withering plants. She stood and rubbed a low spot on her back. "Is that you, Jashar?" she said.

"Tis me, My Lady. I bring word of Donatiya!"

"Very well. But you will have tea first before you speak."

"But, My Lady…"

Nimshi, quick to tend to Samara's request, turned back to the house.

"Bring one for yourself as well," Samara added.

Nimshi bowed. "Yes, My Lady."

Zoë pleaded, "Let the boy speak, please, Samara."

"In good time," Samara said with a sharp glance. "A long and dusty walk produces a thirst that must be quenched."

Zoë conceded, hiding her impatience. "Yes, of course, my apologies Jashar."

They returned to the house where Nimshi was already exiting the kitchen with a tray supporting four cups of tea.

Samara gestured to the living area. "Let us sit together."

Each one obeyed, took a cup from the tray, and found a place to recline.

"You may begin," Samara stated.

"I was in the village yesterday," Jashar said, "I was trying to sell my mother's baskets. Well, trade them, I mean, for lentils or oil or grain. A man approached me. As he emerged from the crowd, I sensed he was a stranger to our village. The hood of his cape cast a shadow over his face. He reached out. My attention was drawn to his hand. I was eager to make a trade which would provide for my mother and my sister."

"What did his hand contain?"

"Beans, My Lady. Beautiful round beans! When my eyes beheld them I immediately turned so that I might fetch the best of my mother's baskets to offer him in trade. When I turned back towards him, he removed his hood. It was then that I recognized him, My Lady. It was Elijah!"

"Elijah? In Zarephath? Are you certain?"

"His presence before me was as sure as mine is before you now!"

"Did you speak with him?" Zoë asked.

"I opened my mouth to speak but what came forth was only silence. I handed the prophet the basket I had chosen. He handed me a pouch full of beans and then he walked away."

"Elijah in Phoenicia?" Nimshi said. "What does this mean?"

"I know not. But this I do know," Samara replied. "Yahweh's word which goes forth from his mouth will not return to him empty, without accomplishing what he desires, and without succeeding in the matter for which he sent it."

Zoë could hide her impatience no longer. "But what of Donatiya?"

"I know where Elijah went when he departed from my presence."

"You followed him?" Zoë asked.

"Yes, My Lady, and I speak to you this truth. The prophet proceeded from the village to the home of Donatiya."

Zoë, Samara, and Nimshi all sat in silence.

Jashar's eyes met each one to no reply.

"Did you hear me, My Lady?" Jashar asked, looking at Samara. "Elijah dwells with Donatiya!"

"We heard you, Jashar," she replied. "You are certain? It was the prophet of Yahweh."

"I watched this same man receive sustenance from heaven. When he dwelt at the brook of Cherith east of the Jordan. The ravens brought him bread and meat, My Lady, both in the morning and in the evening. It is Elijah!"

Silence continued as everyone appeared stunned by Jashar's revelation. When no one addressed him Jashar spoke once more.

"My Lady?"

"Yes, Jashar."

"May I speak further?"

"Yes, please," Samara replied.

"I witnessed the prophet from a distance. He entered your aunt's home," Jashar said looking at Zoë, "I waited until evening, My Lady, until Elijah departed."

"Where did he go?"

"I did not approach him as I was intent on speaking to the lady of the house."

"And did you find Donatiya?"

"Yes, My Lady, I told her I was in your employ and she received me joyfully. She gave me this to give to you."

Jashar swung around the pouch he had slung over his shoulder. He opened a woven sack attached to a rope and produced a golden brown loaf.

"Smell it, My Lady," Jashar said, cracking open the bread.

Samara drew in the aroma.

"Tis heavenly, is it not?"

Samara tore the bread in two and passed it to Zoë. She did not realize how much she missed the spoils of the palace, impervious to drought, until she filled her lungs with the savory scent. Zoë passed the bread to Nimshi who cradled it with both hands.

"Splendid, yes?" Jashar asked.

"Splendid indeed," Samara replied.

"I beg you, My Lady," Jashar continued, "imagine, just imagine the smell when the bread is first pulled from the oven. There is not a more fulfilling scent on this earth."

At that Nimshi rose and proceeded with the loaf to the kitchen.

"And how is it that you traveled to my home without consuming this? Surely your family's table is not overflowing these days."

"It was a struggle, I promise you," Jashar confessed, "to not run home to my mother and present her with this bread from heaven. Why I am here and not in my mother's kitchen is what I came to tell you. This bread…" Jashar paused. "It comes without end."

"Elijah brings more bread?" Zoë asked, holding out her half of the loaf.

"No, My Lady. Donatiya brings forth bread for the prophet."

"How can this be?" Samara asked. "For you yourself informed us of the little bit of oil and the handful of flour which remains."

"The prophet petitioned your aunt for bread. Donatiya informed Elijah that this would be the last loaf after which she and her son would surely die. Elijah said to her, 'Do not fear; make me a little bread cake first and bring it out to me, and afterward you may make one for yourself and for your son.'"

"Donatiya trusted the word of the prophet."

"Yes, My Lady. And since that moment her jar of oil and her bowl of flour remain full."

"The prophet replenishes her flour and oil?"

"No, no," Jashar responded. "The prophet does nothing. Tis Yahweh, My Lady. Yahweh provides for Donatiya and her son just as Elijah spoke to her saying, 'For thus says Yahweh, God of Israel. The bowl of flour shall not be exhausted, nor shall the jar of oil be empty, until the day that Yahweh sends rain on the face of the earth.'"

Zoë's shoulders fell as the tension which had consumed her with worry finally left. She drew in a deep breath. Donatiya and baby Samson would be nourished until the drought is over. The peace that filled her that day would forever find her at each baking of new bread.

"Thank you, Jashar," Zoë said, reaching for the boy.

"You will enjoy a warm slice of bread with us," Samara insisted, "before you return to the village."

"Yes, My Lady."

CHAPTER 39

THE NEXT PSALTER

Dawn had barely settled and the midday heat was chasing it away. Obadyah counted the provisions as they were being loaded. Wheat and barley that had been ground by Naboth's workers so that it could easily be made into a paste for stone baking. Figs, olives, and dates as well as pomegranates filled the small wagon that would provide for the prophets of Yahweh holed up in the caves at Gilboa. Obadyah slid the back gate into place just as Naboth arrived with a jug of goat's milk and some honey.

"Your generosity knows no bounds," Obadyah said.

Naboth waved him off and said, "There is no need for you to make the delivery. Allow me to send my men."

"Thank you my friend, but there is a baker from Dothan I must…"

"I want to go," Eliah interrupted, appearing in the doorway half awake.

Obadyah let his eyes linger on Eliah, the excruciating task ahead of him back in the forefront of his mind. Should he allow her to go along? Perhaps this was his window of opportunity. Perhaps it would be better if Amos was there to comfort Eliah. Obadyah looked away from Eliah when what he really wanted confronted him. Perhaps Amos would deliver the news of Benjamin's death. Shame overwhelmed him.

"That's not a good idea," Obadyah said.

"What do you mean?" Eliah replied, "It's a wonderful idea!"

"I have traveled with you before," Obadyah said, a smile creeping up onto his face, "I speak from experience."

"As do I. For perhaps you will die from boredom should you choose to travel without me. Besides, you know Buckets will not mind you if I am not there."

Obadyah leaned past the wagon to get a look at Buckets as though he was considering Eliah's argument. When it hit him that the beast was Eliah's only living tie to her father he conceded.

"I suppose you are correct. Go, prepare a sack."

Eliah smiled and ran back into Naboth's house.

As the last of the supplies were being loaded, Naboth approached Obadyah. "Where is Eliah? Is she not traveling with you to Gilboa?" he asked.

"She is," Obadyah sighed. "Waiting on a little girl," Obadyah cleared his throat, "I mean, a young lady, is like waiting for this drought to end."

The men had no sooner spoken and Eliah appeared. With disheveled hair, half-closed eyes, and her lamb in her arms she climbed into the back of the supply wagon and laid down.

Obadyah opened his mouth to object but no words could be found. He watched as Eliah wrapped her arm around the little newborn and pulled it into her chest. The lamb settled into the warm bed Eliah had made by curling her body around the baby animal. So much tenderness and innocence in one scene. In one precious life.

Naboth nudged him in the ribs. "Best to let her take the animal," he whispered. "And Obadyah," Naboth continued, "perhaps while you are away, you might find a time to speak to Eliah."

Obadyah nodded. He knew it was time to tell Eliah about Benjamin's death. But he still didn't know how, when, or even if he had the strength.

"You are her family now," Naboth said, resting his hand on Obadyah's shoulder.

Obadyah nodded once more, a silent pledge to his friend that what needed to be done would be done before they returned.

"The trail to the caves on the eastern ridge is about four hours from here. You should arrive mid-day."

Obadyah nodded a final time and set out towards the prophet's caves.

Obadyah, Eliah, and Buckets made their way east. The Gilboa mountain range could be seen in the distance as they proceeded through the valley. What the valley inhabitants called Ketif Shaul, Saul's shoulder, slowly came into view. The bald rock covered surface of the north face of the mountain, framed by pine trees, was easily identifiable.

With Eliah asleep in the wagon, Obadyah was free to think. As he considered all that had happened and what was ahead, fear gripped him. The responsibility of Eliah fell to him. Yahweh, it seemed, gave no consideration to what Obadyah thought he was capable of enduring. Remembering his time with Adonis, Obadyah recalled having begged her for the formula whereby his heart could find rest from its perpetual ache. Obadyah shook his head. He had thought then that the depth of his sorrow was the most intense it could be. He now knew that was only the beginning.

Yahweh wasn't simply teaching him how to live with pain, he was expanding his heart's ability to endure pain, to work in the midst of pain. It was not enough to carry the weight of his own sorrow. He must learn to carry others.

And still, Obadyah knew, he had only grazed the heartache his mother felt each day. He marveled at her ability, not just to survive, but to produce and serve. Though the sustaining love of her eldest child was gone, she loved. Though heartbroken by tragedy, she loved. How does she find the courage to open her eyes each morning? Another morning of loss, another surge of pain, another test of stamina. Obadyah had always longed for his mother's heart because of what it could give. He now realized he was given his mother's heart because of what it could take.

"Obadyah, look!" Eliah shouted.

"What is it?" Obadyah asked, bringing the wagon to a halt.

"Over there." Eliah scooped up her lamb and attempted to point towards a crop of boulders at the base of the ridge ahead of them.

"What? I don't see anything."

Eliah gently laid her lamb down on his straw bed and hurried to Obadyah's side. Obadyah picked her up.

She turned his head and placed his cheek next to hers. "Guide your eyes with mine," Eliah said. "See those rocks in the distance?"

Obadyah squinted, reaching with his eyes beyond Eliah's finger tip.

"A leopard?"

"An Arabian leopard! Do you see how his fur blends into the earth behind him?"

The blond base coat of the large cat matched the backdrop of stone perfectly making discerning its shape almost impossible. Obadyah's eyes found the cluster of black spots moving across the rocks giving away its location.

As Obadyah stared off into the distance, Eliah said, "Your lovingkindness,

O Yahweh, extends to the heavens, Your faithfulness reaches to the skies. Your righteousness is like the mighty mountains; Your judgments are like a great deep. It is you, O Lord, who preserve man and beast.'"

Obadyah's eyes swung to Eliah. He quickly set her down and then knelt next to her. "Eliah," he said, "where did you learn that?"

"From my father. They are the words of King David."

"Your father taught you those words?"

Eliah nodded. "He is a prophet, remember?"

"I remember, but…"

"My father is also a psalter," Eliah interrupted, "a guardian of scrolls." Eliah casually turned and made her way back towards the wagon. As she walked, with her back to Obadyah, she said, "My father protects the words of Yahweh given through David."

Obadyah stood silent. Benjamin, a keeper of the psalms. The precious scrolls of King David, destroyed just as Benjamin was.

"My father was training me to become a psalter, before…well, before Jezebel," Eliah said.

Obadyah's heart sank. He knew what he must do. He knew now was the time. He reached inside himself searching for courage.

"Obadyah!" Eliah shouted.

"Yes. What is it, Eliah?"

"Let's get going," Eliah said, and she began skipping down the road.

"Eliah" Obadyah said, as he hurried to catch up.

"Yes?" Eliah replied.

Obadyah was silent.

"Well, what is it, brother?" she asked, picking up a few rocks and tossing them aside.

Obadyah could not speak. He opened his mouth but he could not find a single word. *Maybe Naboth is wrong about Benjamin. Maybe the prophets were able to rescue him.* Obadyah was reaching, desperate for a hope he knew he would not find. *I am a coward!*

"Obadyah!" Eliah said once more.

"Yes?," Obadyah replied. *Yahweh, Help me! I cannot do this!*

"What's wrong with you?" Eliah asked.

"I…I was just wondering…do you know any other psalms of David?"

"Yes, of course," Eliah replied.

Obadyah stopped. He grabbed Eliah's shoulders and turned her towards him. "How many of David's psalms do you know?" he asked.

"Hundreds," Eliah replied.

Eliah jumped off of the back of the wagon and ran up the trail to the cave entrance.

"Eliah, wait!" Obadyah yelled.

Eliah did not slow down at Obadyah's urging but continued towards the prophet's hideout.

"Eliah! What about your lamb?" Obadyah said, hoping to get her attention. But Eliah was moving too quickly.

Obadyah had just caught up when Amos appeared.

"Did you find him?" Eliah asked. "Did you bring my father?" She said as she ran past Amos into the cave.

Obadyah's gaze found Amos who could not hide his sorrow.

"We found Benjamin," Amos said, "but…I'm sorry, Obadyah. Jezebel found him first."

Obadyah looked past Amos into the cave. His heart sank. Eliah, still, stood staring at the body of her father.

The two men entered the cave together, coming alongside her.

"We have washed him," Amos whispered. "He is ready for burial."

"Tend to my donkey, will you?" Obadyah asked.

Amos nodded and walked out.

Obadyah crouched beside Eliah.

"They found him," she said, her eyes locked onto her father's lifeless body.

"I know."

"He was not afraid to die," Eliah said.

"I know."

Eliah continued to stare at her father. "Obadyah?"

"Yes, Eliah."

"Do you know about 'the shadow of death?'"

"No."

"The shadow of death is the darkness that comes over you when you know you are about to die."

Obadyah remained silent, patient for all of Eliah's words.

"There is a secret though," she continued. "My father told it to me. He said, 'Even though I walk through the valley of the shadow of death, I fear no evil, for Yahweh is with me.'"

Eliah glanced at Obadyah out of the corner of her eyes. "The shadow of death, for those who belong to Yahweh, is not fearful darkness. It is the shadow of cherub wings."

"Your father was brave."

"My father is brave."

"He is," Obadyah replied.

Eliah turned to face Obadyah. She dropped her head, collapsing into his chest, sobbing.

Obadyah reached for her.

Tucking her head into his neck, he held her.

Eliah wept.

Eventually, her cries softened and she fell asleep in his arms. Obadyah felt Amos lay a hand on his shoulder. He motioned silently towards the back of the cave. Obadyah carried Eliah past her father, deeper into the cave where he found a bed and laid her down. He walked out and returned seconds later with Eliah's lamb. He gently tucked the animal in next to her.

Obadyah left the cave with Amos beside him. He turned his face to the sky and felt the heat of the sun. "We will bury Benjamin today," Obadyah said. "Prepare a ceremony for the departed prophet. He will have a psalter's burial."

Amos nodded and motioned for the other prophets to follow his lead.

It was critical that the funeral for the prophet be complete prior to the setting of the sun. The incense burning against the night sky would surely reveal their presence at the caves to those dwelling in the valley.

The prophets worked with diligence, collecting stones for Benjamin's burial. As the men brought the rocks, Amos meticulously placed them. The sarcophagus began taking shape. When the last stone was delivered, the prophets, more than fifty in number, stood in silence as Amos laid the final stone.

Six prophets of Yahweh carried Benjamin's body from the cave to the burial spot.

"I will retrieve the Frankincense," Amos announced.

Obadyah nodded and returned to the cave where Eliah slept. She was perfectly still, her lamb curled up beside her. Obadyah knelt down and rested his elbows on the blankets which covered Eliah.

"Help me, Yahweh, please," Obadyah said. "Give me wisdom and strength, I beg you, that I might have healing words for Eliah." Obadyah rested his hand on Eliah's shoulder and she stirred awake. She rolled over and looked at Obadyah. He remained silent, patient for Eliah to speak when she was ready.

"My father is dead," Eliah said.

"He is."

"Can I stay with you?"

"Yes, Eliah, you can stay with me. Always." He reached for Eliah and hugged her. Memories of the first time he hugged her came to him, complete with her reprimand. Obadyah was eager to get this one right. He held her tight and did not budge until she let him go.

"Will we bury my father today?"

"Yes. We are ready to return him to Yahweh."

"Can my lamb come with me?"

"Yes, of course. Are you ready?"

Eliah nodded. Lifting her tiny lamb, she settled him on her right hip. She wrapped her arm around him, supporting him as his feet dangled by her side. She reached for Obadyah. He took her hand and they made their way, together, to the cave opening.

As they descended the trail past the first turn, they came upon the assembled prophets. The Frankincense was burning. Its balsam fragrance filled the air. Eliah drew in the fresh citrus smell as a fine mist of resin fell.

The baker fanned the mist in the direction of Eliah and Obadyah. They made an earthly exchange for the flesh of their brother, their prophet–the sap of the Boswellia tree entrusting one of their own to the earth. They received the oil by wiping the balm into the skin of their arms. In unison the prophets spoke:

> Willingly we will sacrifice to You;
> We will give thanks to Your name,
> O Yahweh, for it is good.
> To You we shall offer a sacrifice of thanksgiving,
> And call upon the name of the Yahweh.
> Heed the sound of our cry for help,
> Our King and our God,
> For to You we pray.

When they finished their prayer, the prophets encircled Benjamin's body. Six of them lifted him up, securing their hands to his burial wrapping: one at his head, two on each side, one at his feet. As Benjamin was lowered into the sarcophagus, Eliah, Obadyah, and the prophets of Yahweh went to their knees.

They waited for Eliah to conclude the ceremony. No one moved, nor was a word spoken in respect of Eliah's suffering. When she was ready, she chose her psalm. Then, together with one voice they all said, "Blessed be Yahweh, the God of Israel, who alone works wonders."

CHAPTER 40

THE VICTORY AT KISHON

Obadyah stood outside the prophet's cave, his eyes fixed on the Jezreel Valley below. What had been an expansive and lush landscape was now tawny, beaten, and aged.

"We continue to locate prophets," Amos said. "We have had success transporting them under cover of darkness to Saul's mountain."

Obadyah nodded but did not break his stare.

"Lives are being saved even while death surrounds us," Amos continued. "And we found this," he said, dropping a bullae coin into Obadyah's hand.

Obadyah's eyes were drawn away from the valley to the small object resting in his palm.

"It is Jezebel's emblem," Amos said, pointing to the letters 'YZBL' carved into the top of the clay button. "She stamps her notice of condemnation with this seal."

"A tetramorph?" Obadyah said, raising the bullae closer to his eyes.

Amos nodded. "A chimera, is it not?"

Obadyah licked his thumb and rubbed it over the image.

"The head of a man, the body of a lion, and the tail of a serpent. But what about the fourth element? What does Jezebel mean by placing wings on this creature?"

"Perhaps it is in honor of the winged deity of the Assyrians. For I have heard Jezebel craves their power, sending messengers to return witness of the manner in which they conquer."

Obadyah winced. The images Tukulti had drawn of the slaughter of his family by the Assyrian ruler rushed before him. "The creature clutches an ankh between its claws."

"The sacred symbol of matriarchy." Amos said, taking a seat next to the opening of the cave.

Obadyah closed his hand around the clay seal and sat down beside him.

"Jezebel," Amos said, "you know her?"

"I do."

"Is she…as terrifying as I imagine her to be?"

"Her face is painted like fine pottery. Precious jewels dangle from her ears. Even the lids of her eyes shimmer with gold dust. But none of her adornments hide her fury. She is to be feared as one would fear the evil spirits which tormented King Saul. For she is empowered by their affection for hatred."

"But why? Why does she despise us so?"

"Because Yahweh has what she wants."

"Our love?"

"Our worship."

Obadyah threw a tarpaulin into the back of the empty wagon. "I will return in three weeks."

"We will be diligent in our rationing as we await your return," Amos replied. "And we will continue to retrieve prophets until we can house no more. The curse of Saul's death, as well as the drought, ensures our safety."

Obadyah nodded.

Amos continued. "Few venture far from home these days. With Jezebel on the prowl seeking the blood of prophets and our brothers and sisters seeking each day's sustenance, we will be secure here as long as your deliveries continue."

"Ahab has made Jezreel his priority. And my men are loyal. They know not where the extra supplies are going and they know not to ask as they too are desperate to provide for their families."

"Things are going according to plan."

Obadyah thought about those words and how few things in his life went according to his plan. There had been so much failure, so much pain, so much disappointment. Was there any reason to keep hoping for a different future, a peaceful future? The sound of bleating drew his eyes up. Eliah, a short distance away, was laying on her side stroking her baby lamb as it danced around her soaking up her attention. Obadyah's hope returned.

The castle at Jezreel began to take shape. Obadyah and Eliah dwelt at Naboth's home while Obadyah oversaw the construction of the royal residence. From sunup to mid afternoon, he was on the hillside, directing the men under his command. Faithful to his routine, he joined Eliah for tea each day and then ventured into Naboth's vineyard in the evening. They did what they could, but the vines continued to wither and die.

Days turned into weeks and weeks into months until the long-awaited time had come. Obadyah's appointment with his father. Obadyah mounted his horse early in the morning, the first day of the week he and his father had parted exactly one year before.

"Where are you going?" Eliah asked through a yawn.

"I have an appointment."

"With Ahab?"

"No."

"With Jezebel?"

"No."

"With Amos?"

"No."

"With…"

"With my father," Obadyah interrupted.

"The Captain?"

"Yes, my father, the captain. Now may I go?"

"Theophanes! Captain of the Phoenix!" Eliah spoke as if she were announcing him as the lead in a play. She then pulled her blanket up around her shoulders and turned back towards Naboth's house. Having received his small charge's permission to depart, Obadyah heeled his horse. He proceeded a short distance down the road when Eliah turned. "Obadyah," she yelled, "do you know what this means?"

"What does this mean, Eliah?" Obadyah replied, turning his horse back around.

"It means you are going to visit my father, too."

Obadyah smiled, happy that Eliah saw her future with him and his family, even if it meant Theophanes would play a part.

Obadyah pulled his horse to a stop within speaking distance of his father.

"Son." Theopanes said, nodding towards his men who obeyed their captain taking their leave.

"Captain." Obadyah dismounted the horse, letting the reins hang loose. The horse knew he was free and wandered a short distance away to search for a clump of grass.

"How have you been?" Theophanes asked.

"Well." Obadyah approached his father. The two men stood on the grassy bank that descended to the meandering Kishon which flowed peacefully past.

"Do you know what happened here?"

"Here? At the river?"

Theophanes nodded. "Ask your mother to tell you about The Mighty Kishon next time you see her."

"Or you could tell me."

Theophanes turned towards his son. "Oh, yes. Of course."

Theophanes sat down. Obadyah followed, taking a seat a comfortable distance from his father.

"Do you recall the rule of the judges?" Theophanes asked.

"The leaders of Israel before the kings?"

Theophanes nodded. "It was during that time a man named Jabin, King of Canaan, reigned in Hazor. The sons of Israel cried to Yahweh, because Jabin had nine hundred iron chariots and he oppressed the Hebrews severely for twenty years."

"Who was judging Israel under Jabin's oppression?"

"Deborah."

"Deborah versus Jabin. Intriguing."

"Your mother reminds me of Deborah."

"She certainly shares Deborah's wisdom, but I can't see her battling nine hundred iron chariots."

"You forget, son, your mother has conquered sorrow. Nine hundred chariots would be light work for her." Theophanes paused.

Obadyah gazed away from the river, his eyes finding his father. He appeared just as he had before, rugged, impenetrable. And yet there was a softness in his voice Obadyah did not remember.

"Deborah summoned Barak, the captain of Israel's army. She advised him to march his troops to Mt. Tabor, saying, 'I will draw out to you Sisera, the commander of Jabin's army, with his chariots and his troops to the river Kishon, and I will give him into your hand.' Barak, emboldened by Deborah's presence, replied, 'If you will go with me, then I will go; but if you will not go with me, I will not go.'"

"You have to wonder how such a man became a captain."

"We all have things we fear," Theophanes replied, "the best and the worst of us. But Deborah would not fight Barak's battle for him. What she did, however, was just as important. She fortified his heart." Obadyah listened, surprised by his father's insight as well as his interest in Hebrew history. "Women can use their strength in two very different ways. They can empower men or overpower them. Deborah was a fortifier for she said, 'I will surely go with you; nevertheless, the honor shall not be yours on the journey that you are about to take, for Yahweh will sell Sisera into the hands of a woman.'"

"A story with two heroines. Mother would be so pleased."

Theophanes smiled. "Barak sent his troops down into that valley from Mt. Tabor," Theophanes pointed. "As Deborah had instructed. The army of Israel met Sisera's men here at the Kishon river. As the battle wore on, Sisera sensed that Israel would prevail so he fled to the tent of a man named Heber, the Kenite. It seems there was peace between Jabin, King of Canaan and Heber the Kenite. Sisera entered Heber's home confident he would find a safe place to hide as Barak pursued what was left of the Canaanite army."

"Did Heber welcome him?"

"I do not doubt he would have, but Heber was not home. However, Jael, his wife, was."

Obadyah looked up and found his father's eyes.

"She invited him in. She covered him with a blanket. She even brought him fresh milk. Unbeknownst to Sisera, Jael did not share her husband's loyalties. Where Heber had aligned himself with the rulers of Canaan, Jael had made her peace with Yahweh."

"And?" Obadyah said.

"And when Sisera fell asleep, Jael crept in. With a hammer in one hand and a tent peg in the other, she swung. Theophanes slammed the palm of his hand atop his fist. "With one swift strike Jael secured Sisera's head to the ground."

"She must have been a decent tent builder." Obadyah grinned.

"Like I said. A woman will either empower a man or overpower a man. And it seems your Yahweh has a use for both."

Obadyah smiled, turning again to gaze to the Kishon. A westerly wind kicked up rippling the surface of the water. He filled his lungs with the crisp air, engaged with the story and the pleasant exchange with his father. Still, the question heavy on his heart stirred with an ache that would grant him no peace. Obadyah looked to his father and then looked away. He wanted to speak, wanted to know, but fear overtook him once more. Yahweh had given him a purposeful job to occupy his mind, and the responsibility of a little girl, a little sister—his reason to rise each day. Still, he felt as though his muscles had been clinched, locked tight for more than a year. Staring out at the water, preparing himself to receive a blow, he searched for the courage to ask his father about Zoë.

"She lives," son. Theophanes suddenly said. "She lives and is well."

Obadyah's head dropped, every muscle relaxing in response to the news his mind, no, his entire body had been waiting for. He drew in a long breath. His lungs filled with hope.

Theophanes smiled. "You have changed," he said. "You have learned patience since we last spoke."

"I have learned many things since we last spoke."

"So it seems."

"Do they suffer hardship, Mother and Zoë, because of the drought?"

"It is difficult…for everyone. But they fare better than most since the captain of the Phoenix will not let drought destroy those he loves."

"And it seems you have not changed since we last spoke."

"Indeed, I have not," Theophanes smiled. "Honestly, Son, what change was there to make? Is it possible that I might become more handsome and appealing?"

Obadyah smiled and shook his head. The personality of his father, for the first time, inspired laughter rather than contempt.

Theophanes stood up and cleared his throat. "How is Jezebel's residence coming along?"

"It progresses."

"Is Ahab pleased?"

"Yes, Sir."

"It seems you have inherited at least one of your father's traits."

"I take no pride in pleasing this king."

"Take no pride in it if you wish, but bringing pleasure to people of power is a valuable skill."

"I serve my king by necessity, not desire."

"Do I not serve with the same motive?" Theophanes replied.

Obadyah's eyes widened. His gaze locked on his father.

"Everything in life comes by barter, Son. From the boys at the docks who trade fish for milk, to allegiances with kings for the security of nations. My services, my homage, even my fawning and flattery, are my currency. And loyalty pays the highest returns."

Obadyah felt a tightening in his chest. How had he not seen it before now? His own motive now staring him in the face. No! He is different! He's a slave. He has no choice. And yet all his efforts to talk himself into what he wanted to believe only reinforced what he now knew. He was his father's son.

Theophanes was right, about his motives and about life. Most people functioned by trade. But then he thought of Naboth. What would be his return? He welcomed us with no expectation of reward nor promise of pay. He accepts us, provides for us, even while I work to bring his enemy to dwell at his doorstep!

And then there was his mother. What was her reward in acquiring Nimshi? A few silver coins? There was no benefit in gaining a mouth to feed. Unless. Unless she too was bartering for something when she agreed to house Nimshi. Obadyah had long suspected there was something more to the story of his mother's crippled servant. But what?

Obadyah's thoughts shifted suddenly back to his father. He had always wondered why Theophanes would not trust Yahweh. Now, for the first time, he could see it. Theophanes knows Yahweh won't barter with him!

Obadyah was reminded of the words of King David, what he said after he stole Bathsheba. To Yahweh David prayed, 'You are not pleased with burnt offerings. For You do not delight in sacrifice, otherwise I would give it!' David longed for Yahweh's forgiveness, wished there was something he could do to trade for it. How easily his problem could be resolved if only Yahweh would barter: a sacrifice in exchange for absolution. But David knew something about the character God that Theophanes did not. Forgiveness is not for sale. And Yahweh cannot be bought—by any human act, no matter how grand or sincere.

"When...when your brother..." Theophanes began and then quickly stopped.

Obadyah waited patiently to hear what his father had finally decided to speak to him about the day his brother died.

"When Micah died, I was faced with a choice. I chose to pay the price Ethbaal demanded. Your seed for your life. I understand you are angry with my decision, but know this—I also spared your mother the pain of multiplied sorrow. And son, by this trade, I also spared Nimshi."

Obadyah's head shot up. "Nimshi? Mother's cripled servant?" "But what does he have to do..."

"He killed your brother," Theophanes interrupted.

Obadyah felt his spine tighten, the muscles of his back pulling on his shoulders. That longing he thought he had conquered, the craving for distance between him and his father, returned.

"The oak planking I was delivering that day was being carted up from the bay. I had already proceeded to the courtyard when I heard a commotion behind me, panic in the voices of my men. I turned just as the wood began to sway. Nimshi was there. He struck your brother. He said Micah had spooked the horses, displacing the load. Michah fell. I ran back down the beach. I could see Micah in the distance laying in the sand, disoriented, attempting to crawl away from Nimshi. Before I could get there the load tumbled over, crushing both Micah and Nimshi. My men rushed in, we fought to remove the logs. But the only sound we heard was Nimshi screaming. Micah was silent.

"I wanted to kill Nimshi. Believe me, son, I did. But when I saw him, laying there on the sand, his legs bleeding, twisted, and broken, I could not find the strength to pull my sword. He was weeping, crying for my forgiveness."

"He was desperate! He begged you for mercy only when his fate confronted him!"

"He was desperate. But when he voiced his sorrow, I was left with only two options: mercy or revenge."

"You spared the man who killed Micah but would not spare me this fate? You speak of mercy? But what about justice?"

"Justice is the burden of gods and kings. I should be quite deceived should I think I can know which actions are just and which are not."

The truth, from his father's own lips, now burned inside of him. But Obadyah did not share his father's uncertainty. Nimshi's actions were indefensible.

"Perhaps, Son," Theophanes sighed, "one day you will understand."

"Understand? This is what I understand. You spared a murderer. You forced mother to care for a murder, one whose loyalties surely continue to rest with an evil dynasty. Did you even consider this? That each of Nimshi's trips to town were not to secure supplies but to report to Ethbaal?"

"You are angry. I don't blame you. And perhaps you will never forgive me. I don't blame you for that either. But I would not put your mother at risk. You may not trust me. You may not even believe me. But, neither your lack of faith or confidence in my motives has any impact on the truth, I know men. I know Nimshi. And son, whether you will admit it or not, I know you.

Obadyah was left once more at the mercy of his father. Though his frustration with Theophanes remained, so did his dependance on him.

CHAPTER 41

THE TROUBLER OF ISRAEL

"I have something for you." Theophanes said, loosening the cord of his saddlebag. He handed his son a clay jug.
"From mother?"
"From Zoë."
Obadyah's eyes brightened.
"It's just water." Theophanes said, his tone revealing the fact that he knew it was much more. "Please tell me you have a gift I can take to the girl. If not, I will be forced to pick up something at the market and tell her it is from you. I'll lie all day long before I'll show up at your mother's house empty handed."
Obadyah reached into his sack and pulled out a wreath of woven flowers.
"An aureole," Theophanes said. "From Naboth's vineyard?"
"The flowers were the last to bloom before the drought choked them out."
"I will include this with my next delivery."
Obadyah nodded.
"So," Theophanes continued, "same time, same place, next year?"
"How shall I notify you of my supply needs?"
"Send a messenger in six months time to Zarephath, to Jashar. He will find me."
"Father."
"Yes?"
"Thank you."

Eliah ran down the trail to meet Obadyah.

"How was the captain?"

"He was fine."

"Was he not glorious?"

"You tell me. As I suspect you will regardless…."

Eliah jumped into the wagon before Obadyah could finish his sentence.

"What are you doing?" he asked.

"I'm digging through your wagon to see what treasures you have received from the captain."

"Those are Jezebel's supplies not…"

"What's this?" Eliah interrupted.

"It's a jug of water."

"It's beautiful." Eliah ran her fingers across the eagle painted across the bottle's belly.

"My mother made it."

"Tell me about her."

"She is patient, kind, creative, and wise."

"Does she know how to bake sweet bread?"

"Of course she does, she…"

"What does this say?" Eliah interrupted once more.

"What does what say?" Obadyah replied.

"Here. Look. There is a message under the rope," Eliah slid the braided twine up and over the pot's spout.

Obadyah paused, surprised to see the inscription.

"It's Hebrew," Eliah continued, "it says, 'My tears have been my food day and night." Eliah turned the jug around and continued to read, "These things I remember and I pour out my soul within me." She read the signature silently. "Zoë has sent this to you!" Eliah exclaimed.

"Yes," Obadyah confessed.

"I cannot wait to see her, someday." Eliah said.

"Nor I."

With the final two wagons of supplies delivered by Theophanes, Obadyah commissioned furniture constructed from oak harvested from Mt. Tabor. The aroma of Arabian spices permeated the palace. Precious stones from Egypt and sandalwood oil from India enveloped the princess's bed chamber. Purple fabrics from Obadyah's home town in Phoenicia laced the regal lodge. The crowning accent? Two stone lions covered with gold which originally resided abreast Solomon's throne.

It had been three and a half years since Elijah announced the drought, and Obadyah was nearing completion of his work on Jezebel's retreat. As each month had passed, the royal residence had grown. There was a palpable excitement in the air. Naboth glowed with pride, his joy overflowing for Obadyah's accomplishment. Yet, in the midst of cheerful anticipation, there was a heaviness as the end of construction would mean the arrival of the queen.

With a knot in his stomach, Obadyah drafted the message to Jezebel. By the time it would arrive, the palace would be finished.

Though the capital of Israel remained at Samaria, Jezebel and her maidens moved into her new palace at Jezreel. Obadyah could see Jezebel's caravan rolling up the valley. A dozen carriages paraded down the street as locals gathered in awe of the royal spectacle. Jezebel did not acknowledge the peasants who waved and greeted her. Her eyes were locked straight ahead reaching for the first sight of her new residence.

Once Jezebel had settled into her new home, she called for Obadyah. As he approached the queen Obadyah took note of her maidens standing at her side. Adonis, Aphka, and the new Athena. Obadyah knelt before the princess in the throne room he had constructed for her. She did not say a word. He kept his head facing the floor and awaited her instructions. Jezebel continued to remain silent. Obadyah could feel her eyes boring into him. It was several unbearable moments before she finally spoke.

"What pleases you more," Jezebel finally said, "pleasing your queen or pleasing Adonis?"

Jezebel relished the first time Obadyah and Adonis had been in the same room since the day she attempted to force them into bed together. She would not miss an opportunity to remind Obadyah of the hardest day of his life.

"I serve at your pleasure alone, my Queen," Obadyah replied, sober and emotionless.

Obadyah did not lift his head. He was not the same boy who had spoken up so carelessly the night he and Zoë returned late to Ethbaal's palace. He no longer felt the rage that surged through him when he faced Jezebel on the beach after having thrown Zoë into the Mediterranean. Obadyah had paid every price his emotions had demanded of him. He would no longer be led about like a sheep. Not by his own impetuousness. And certainly not by Jezebel. Obadyah remained, unrattled by Jezebel's silence, and unmoved by her goading. Then he wondered. Am I calloused? Has evil hardened me, robbed me of my emotions, left me cold?

"Return to Samaria!" Jezebel suddenly barked. "I cannot endure the sight of you."

Without a word Obadyah rose. He bowed without lifting his head, turned, and walked out.

"Where are you going?" Eliah asked.

"I must return to Samaria," Obadyah replied as he continued to load supplies into the saddlebags of his horse.

"How long will you be gone?"

"I don't know."

Obadyah felt the weight of Eliah's stare. He stopped what he was doing and looked at her. It was not until that moment that it occurred to him, he might not be coming back. He belonged to Ahab. If Ahab remained in the Northern Kingdom capital, Obadyah would be forced to reside there as well.

Eliah's eyes fell, her face pale, her expression empty. Obadyah opened his mouth to reassure her. But he could not find the right words. He could not find any words.

"You are not coming back," Eliah said.

"Of course I am!" Obadyah replied. But he knew Eliah was too bright to be won over by forced enthusiasm. She had always seen right through him. Now would be no different.

They stared at one another, the truth a somber fog surrounding them. But Obadyah would not amend his statement. And Eliah, it seemed, would not let go of her hope.

"Do you promise?"

Obadyah looked into the eyes of the little girl who had laid on his stomach through the night sealing his wounds from the bear attack. The young lady who sang to him, taught him how to speak to a woman, and showed him the right way to give a hug…it needs to hurt a little. She had recited to him the precious psalms her father had entrusted to her. And, in the midst of her countless, frustrating, uncomfortable questions on their trip from Samaria to Jezreel, she had won his heart.

Obadyah could see her desperation. It was the same look she had had when she appeared under the tarp in his wagon and she asked him to be her friend. His mother had warned him against making such commitments. And he knew very well that Yahwah discouraged vows. But, after all Eliah had given him, he could not walk away from her without giving her this one thing she was asking of him.

"Yes, Eliah. I will come back. I promise."

Obadyah appeared before the king of Israel as instructed.

"Arise, Obadyah, for your work has pleased me."

"My heart sings with news of your satisfaction, My King."

"Your accomplishment at Jezreel has earned you my highest praise and, more importantly, my trust. It is with this assurance I bid you your next task."

Like a moth caught in a spider's web, Obadyah's next duty was upon him.

"Despite my pleasure," Ahab continued, "my mood is somber as we continue to suffer in the midst of this godless drought. Go, I command you, throughout the land of Israel to all the springs of water and to all the valleys. Perhaps we will find grass and keep the horses and mules alive and not have to kill more of the cattle."

Obadyah departed immediately to survey the land of Israel.

Obadyah kept moving. The cloud of drought scorched earth threw up dust with every step. He could not avoid wearing the dirt. It covered his body, creeping into every crack and crevice. He could only hope to try to keep the grit from finding his eyes and his mouth.

With every step came a sharp longing to run. But where? And to whom? To Zoë? To Eliah? To his mother? To abandon his post would only lure Jezebel to them. And he could not lead evil to those he loved. Why did he allow himself to dream? How could a eunuch from an idol town ever have some greater purpose in this world? His thoughts dried up, the drought mimicking every desolate emotion he could not escape.

Then his eyes drifted ahead. On the road, moving towards him, a lone traveler. Obadyah squinted attempting to make out the silhouette emerging in the fog. The manner of his gate, his hairy appearance under cloak, the leather girdle bound about his loins resembled what was said of the prophet of Yahweh. Soon the man was within speaking distance.

"Is it you, Elijah?" Obadyah inquired.

Without a word, Elijah's gaze locked on Obadyah. Obadyah fell to his knees.

"Arise," Elijah harkened. "Return to Ahab. Arrange a meeting for me with the king of Israel."

Obadyah rose, his hand reaching for the back of his neck. He began to pace before the prophet. "I am your servant," Obadyah began, "and I have revered Yahweh from my youth. But…" Obadyah could not suppress the memory of the prophet who met his fate at the end of Jezebel's arrows. Obadyah squeezed his eyes shut attempting to drive away the thought of his body constricting every time his flesh was pierced. "How can I honor this request?" Obadyah blurted out. "Have you forgotten the nature of this king? For should I obey, Ahab will surely destroy you!"

Elijah stood silent, patient for Obadyah's compliance.

Torn, Obadyah said, "Or perhaps the Spirit of Yahweh will carry you where I do not know; so when I come and tell Ahab and he cannot find you, he will kill me." Obadyah rattled on. "Has it not been told to my master what I did when Jezebel killed the prophets of Yahweh, that I hid Yahweh's prophets in caves?"

"I know you fear Yahweh," Elijah replied, "for Yahweh has sent you to me this day. It is Yahweh who has said, 'Go, show yourself to Ahab, and I shall send rain on the face of the earth.'"

The news of the end of the drought enlivened Obadyah, yet he remained hesitant.

Then, Elijah pledged, "As Yahweh lives, before whom I stand, I will surely show myself to Ahab today."

Obadyah felt a rush of confidence. The prophet who announced the coming drought was now giving Obadyah his solemn word. Obadyah departed and sought Ahab.

Obadyah and Ahab set out to meet Elijah.

When the prophet was within sight, Ahab rested his hand on his sword. The king's chariot slowed as it approached Elijah. Obadyah pulled on the reins. Ahab remained in his chariot and looked down on Elijah. The king and the prophet of Yahweh faced one another for the first time.

"Is it you, you troubler of Israel?" Ahab said.

"It is not I who have troubled Israel," Elijah countered, "but you and your father's house because you have forsaken Yahweh and followed Baal."

Obadyah's heart raced. Elijah's words were antagonistic, his tone disrespectful. Obadyah feared bloodshed was imminent.

Ahab opened his mouth to reply.

Elijah cut him off. "Send and gather all Israel at Mount Carmel, together with 450 prophets of Baal and 400 prophets of the Asherah, who eat at Jezebel's table."

"You dare command me?"

"I challenge you. Before all Israel. Surely Baal will prevail over one prophet of Yahweh."

Without a word and without drawing his sword, Ahab motioned for Obadyah to proceed. Obadyah obeyed. Coaxing their steed, they left Elijah in a cloud of dust.

"This duel will mean the end of the drought," Obadyah said, revealing to Naboth the encounter between Ahab and Elijah. "And," he continued, "perhaps the end of Baal worship in Israel!"

"Rightly do you place your confidence in the prophet," Naboth replied, "however I suspect Elijah's victory will only further enrage the queen. Faith, dear boy, is a commitment which holds us above our circumstances. Victory does not inspire it, nor does defeat overcome a heart devoted either to good or evil."

"But could not the people of Israel doubt their faith in Baal and return to Yahweh?"

"Is that not what Samuel promised the descendants of Abraham," Naboth replied. "Saying, 'If you return to Yahweh with all your heart, remove the foreign gods and the Asherah from among you and direct your hearts to Yahweh and serve Him alone; He will deliver you from the hand of the Philistines.' But the hearts of the people of Israel blow with the wind, their allegiance forever split between the God of their fathers and the gods of their land."

"Then perhaps their hearts will blow back to Yahweh."

"Perhaps," Naboth said, "and if so, Yahweh will strengthen them."

Obadyah had no sooner reached for a glimmer of hope and the truth returned. "Jezebel is not like the people of Israel," Obadyah remarked. "She does not share their weakness. Her heart does not sway, nor does it move with the changing seasons." What remained of the hope that had sparked inside him, was quickly extinguished. "Whether enlivened by victory or enraged by defeat," he said, "the outcome is the same for Jezebel and those she has set her face against."

The following morning, Obadyah rose early to pack his horse.

"Where are you going?" Eliah said, appearing suddenly behind him.

"Why are you awake so early?" he replied.

"I could tell you were trying to sneak away."

Obadyah shook his head and faced Eliah. "I left the terrace as I have every morning."

"No. You used to descend the latter with haste. This morning you paused and stared at me for a few minutes."

"You were sound asleep. How did you…? Nevermind," he said, knowing the explanation would not make sense to him anyway. And she was right, of course. This morning was different. He had not planned on pausing at the top of the ladder. He had not told himself to take one last glance at her. And yet there he stood, thanking Yahweh for the blessing of the little girl he had once thought a chore. And, to his own shame, had wanted to be free of. What was it about this journey that caused him to pause and take in the sight of Eliah one more time before he left?

"I must notify Jezebel's seers."

"About the duel with Elijah?"

Obadyah's surprised look faded quickly this time. "You overheard my conversation with Lord Naboth."

"Of course I did," Eliah replied.

Obadyah smiled, shaking his head once more.

"Can I go with you?"

"Eliah. This is an important task and…"

"And no one wants to be working with a little girl around."

"A young lady," Obadyah corrected.

Eliah smiled.

Word of the duel between Yahweh and Baal spread quickly throughout the northern kingdom. For two weeks the people of Israel and Phoenicia made their way to Mount Carmel eager to witness the confrontation. The western edge of the Jezreel Valley was saturated with tents, thousands having gathered to view what was sure to be a historic event.

Having completed his task, sending hundreds of Jezebel's prophets before them, Obadyah joined the king's caravan. As Mt. Carmel came into view, he imagined the possibility he might catch a glimpse of Zoë. Like a stream ignited by the midday sun, Obadyah could feel his blood warming.

Obadyah saw to the raising of the king's tents. By evening, with the royal court settled, he was free to wander down the makeshift streets. Children pulled carts to and fro as whispers floated through the crowds. Obadyah's eyes scanned his surroundings. He pushed his way past a few vendors who had set up shop hoping to capitalize on the large numbers gathered. As he did, he overheard a man say, "He was in Zarephath."

Obadyah's ears alerted to the name of Zoë's hometown. He stopped. "Who was in Zarephath?" he said, forcing his way into the stranger's presence. Before anyone could reply, Obadyah repeated his question. "Who was in Zarephath?" He said it with an urgency that surprised the men. He didn't care. He knew his authority was equal to his marking, and he would use it.

"Elijah, My Lord," one of them finally said.

Obadyah locked his eyes on the men, staring down each one to detect their honesty.

"It was just as I said, My Lord. Elijah has dwelt with a widow in the village of Zarephath these past three years."

"Do you know this widow's name?"

"Donatiya, My Lord. The common potter's wife."

Obadyah felt the sting of conflict. Joy at the mention of Donatiya's name, pain as the reminder of Kalbu's death pierced his heart.

"Please, forgive me for upsetting you, My Lord," the man replied.

Obadyah caught his breath and returned his attention to the conversation before him. "And what of the boy, the one belonging to the widow? Is he well?"

The men began to chatter under their breath.

"What?" Obadyah demanded, "what news do you keep from the king's overseer?"

"Word spread of his death, the boy having suffered the same fate as the potter."

Obadyah could not hide his despair.

"Do not be saddened, my Lord, for the child lives! His breath was returned to him by the prophet."

"Elijah healed the boy?"

"Elijah breathed life into the boy after his life had left him. Then, as suddenly as the prophet appeared in Zarephath, he was gone."

Obadyah spoke his appreciation to the men and walked away. He moved efficiently through the crowds taking note of who might pose a threat to the king. As he continued to survey the surroundings, his mind wandered. It had been more than three years since his eyes beheld her. Three years since he heard her voice. Three years since he abandoned Zoë in the middle of the Sea. What if he saw her? Would she recognize him? Would she seek him? Would she be willing even to cast her eyes upon him after what he had done?

Perhaps she has moved on, he thought, found a strong young Phoenician who could give her children. What reason could there possibly be for waiting all these years for a slave to find her, for a eunuch to love her? As quickly as his mind sought Zoë, he abandoned his memories, his present role choking out his hope. And yet his mother's words remained, "Solicit your heart's contentment before this life renders it forever hardened."

CHAPTER 42

THE CHALLENGE AT CARMEL

Obadyah surveyed the crowd. The people moved closer to the base of Mt. Carmel. When Elijah appeared on a plateau above, everyone stopped where they were and gave the prophet their attention.

"How long will you hesitate?" Elijah roared, pulling all ears in his direction, including Ahab's. Silence rippled through the multitude. Ahab set down his chalice and came to his feet. Obadyah moved closer to the king, motioning for his guards to tighten their perimeter.

The hesitation of which Elijah spoke was a Hebrew word normally used to describe the hitch in a lame man's walk. His criticism bore a tone of mockery.

"How long," Elijah continued, "will you stutter, trip, and stumble, O Israel?"

A rumble of whispers surfaced. Ahab grinned when the grumbling grew. Obadyah feared for the life of the prophet. He accused them, fearlessly. The behavior for which they were being charged left the sons of Jacob exposed, Elijah's rebuke finding the shoulders of those gathered.

Obadyah let his eyes wander. A few of those gathered appeared concerned. Some were angry. But most of the faces he observed were vacant, ignorant. *Do they not know that their wavering is their infidelity?* Israel had adopted not only the gods of foreign lands, but their ambivalence as well. Having placed Yahweh on the shelf with all other deities, was He now out of their reach?

Elijah continued, "If Yahweh is God, follow Him. But if Baal, follow him."

"It is Yahweh who allows his children to walk away and chase after

Baal," one man in the crowd yelled.

Obadyah bristled at the man's callousness. What was Yahweh to do with these stubborn people? Force them to stay? Yahweh could only do what any good Father would do, remind them of his love for them and appeal to them for their hearts. Love offered and love received, the exchange of a rose. Love demanded and stolen, a stem of thorns.

"Call on the name of your god," Elijah said, "and I will call on the name of Yahweh. The God who answers by fire is God."

The murmuring that rippled through the crowd prompted no outbursts. How could they possibly object? Elijah stood alone, a single prophet of Yahweh, before 450 prophets of Baal.

Elijah asked for two oxen to be brought before them. Obadyah looked to Ahab.

"My Lord?" Obadyah said.

Ahab nodded.

Obadyah motioned for Ahab's men to lead the oxen up to the plateau where Elijah was waiting.

Jezebel's prophets prepared their oxen and called on Baal, "O Baal, answer us."

There was no voice and no one answered.

The clerics of Baal began to leap about the altar they had made. They raved like drunken sailors, dancing in a chaotic mash of howling and sweat.

Ahab laughed.

Obadyah wondered at the king's reaction. Was the behavior of the priests out of character? Could Ahab finally see what was clear to Obadyah? Jezebel's religion was nothing more than a show, a performance for her benefit.

The people, initially entertained, eventually bored of the ranting priests of Baal. When the crowds began to dwindle, Elijah spoke up. "Perhaps Baal is relieving himself or is on a journey."

The people roared in laughter, their attention swinging back to Mt. Carmel.

Elijah did not let up. "Call out with a loud voice, O mighty prophets of Baal, for maybe he is asleep and needs to be awakened."

To Obadyah's surprise, Jezebel's prophets did as Elijah suggested. They yelled in great earnest and began cutting themselves with swords and lances, according to their custom. They continued to rave, babbling incoherently. But there was no response, no answer, no fire, even the people lost interest and gave Baal's prophets no attention.

When evening approached, Elijah appeared once again. "Come near to me," he beckoned.

The few people who were still attentive to the mountain mustered those around them and proceeded towards Elijah. The movement attracted the attention of others who had scattered. A crowd began to form at the base of Mt. Carmel.

Obadyah looked on as Elijah took twelve stones according to the number of the tribes of the sons of Jacob. He built an altar in the name of Yahweh. Then he dug a trench around the altar, as one might till a row, readying it for seed.

Having arranged the wood, Elijah grabbed the oxen's muzzle. He lowered the animal's head, as though leading him to graze. When the beast opened its mouth, Elijah slipped his sword under the bull's chin. He slid the blade across the animal's throat. Blood poured onto the ground. Elijah secured the reigns. As the bull thrashed, Elijah drew the animal's head into his body. He continued to hold the beast as he slowly fell to the earth.

Next, Elijah asked for pitchers of water to be brought to him. Grumbling flowed from the crowd. Obadyah marveled. There could be no more an audacious request than to demand water in the midst of a drought. What was their most precious commodity, Elijah called for without hesitation. A murmur began to stir. Some who'd gathered threw up their hands and stomped off. Elijah continued to wait patiently as though he knew they would eventually comply. Voices rose. Men spoke over one another. A few scuffles ensued. But eventually the multitude gathered at one tent. Obadyah watched from a distance as pitcher after pitcher of precious water emerged, each parting the sea of people like a newborn brought forth to a waiting father.

Men carried the water on their shoulders, handing it off to others when their muscles wearied. One by one the vessels were delivered to Elijah. There was a moment of hesitation when Elijah asked them to pour the water out over the altar. The man holding the first urn paused and looked at Elijah. He nodded. The man tipped the pot. Water flowed out to the gasps of the crowd. Even Obadyah found himself clenching his jaw as the priceless water filled the trough.

After soaking the altar, Elijah said, "Do it a second time."

To Obadyah's surprise they did it a second time.

Then Elijah said, "Do it a third time."

Obadyah expected the crowd to refuse. But no one voiced an objection. They returned with haste to the tent which had been supplying the water.

When the people's attention followed the final pitcher as it made its way towards Elijah, the tent became visible. And so did Zoë.

All eyes studied the prophet of Yahweh. All eyes but two. Obadyah caught his breath. The drought for him was finally over. Obadyah studied Zoë as he would appraise a jewel, precious and valuable. Her skin, just as he remembered it, smooth as sand. Wild strands of her hair blew in front of her face, muting the glow of her eyes, sapphires in the sun. A scurry of people surrounded her. Like a hummingbird, she was there and then she was gone. Was it her? Had he really seen her? His hand reached for his clenching stomach just as she appeared once more. Obadyah watched. She moved like the wind that chases acacia trees. Afraid of losing sight of her, Obadyah ducked behind the wall of a neighboring tent. How vast the distance between seeing and being seen.

Obadyah peered around the corner, and drew in his breath, filling his lungs with the air infused with her presence. The cautious strides of the girl he remembered, the girl under Jezebel's thumb, were now the confident steps of a woman, independant, free. He smiled, warmed by the peace of her demeanor. Then his stomach tensed. Would he ever feel worthy of her? Be worthy of her? Obadyah leaned out when she fell out of sight once more. Why does she delay? What task has stolen her from my eyes?

When she appeared again Nimshi was at her side. The muscles in Obadyah's chest clenched. The man who killed his brother, arm in arm with his beloved. He took a deep breath and told himself to relax. But his body would not obey him. Zoë led Nimshi to a flat stone facing the elevated plateau where Elijah stood. She held him tightly as he shuffled along. When he turned to sit he stumbled. Zoë reached for him, steadying him. Obadyah grit his teeth as she gently lowered Nimshi to a seated position. Zoë knelt beside Nimshi, rubbing his knees.

Three years had taken its toll on Nimshi. The affliction of his deformed legs and the pain of each step, reflected on his face, as it should, Obadyah scoffed. How can Zoë treat him with such tenderness? Obadyah clenched his fists. Perhaps his pain is a reminder to him of what he did.

Then, as quickly as he allowed himself the pleasure of Nimshi's suffering, he was overcome with despair. He felt sick, his stomach pushing the bitterness inside of him to the top of his throat. What kind of man finds solace in the suffering of another? I have feared the mark which my body bears, he thought, and all along it was not my flesh, but my heart which is not worthy of her.

Zoë laughed.

"What pleases you, My Lady?" Nimshi asked.

"It is Elijah. I cannot help but smile."

"How so, My Lady? For he frightens me."

As the crowd pushed their way closer to the base of Mt. Carmel, Zoë rubbed eucalyptus oil on Nimshi's knees. She gently wrapped them in plantain leaves securing them with bamboo strings.

"Yes, I suppose I am a bit frightened of him as well. Does it not amuse you, however, to think of Baal away on a journey, having forgotten to notify even one of his 450 prophets that he would be unavailable for the duration of his holiday? Or, as Elijah said, perhaps Baal is having some digestion issues today." Zoë laughed once more. "What are the chances Elijah's challenge would come forth on the very day that Baal just happens to be, you know, indisposed."

Nimshi smiled. "Yes, I suppose you are right. There is something amusing about the gods enduring our…our impositions."

"Are you able to walk?" Zoë asked.

"With your assistance, My Lady."

"Hold onto my shoulder. Lean on me."

Nimshi obeyed and Zoë led him towards the crowd.

"Over there, My Lady," Nimshi said, pointing to a boulder with a flat top. "I shall see the prophet of Yahweh well from that stone there."

Zoë complied, leading her friend to the rock he had chosen. Once Zoë had steadied Nimshi, she moved around in front of him. Grasping both of his hands, she lowered him down.

"Are you comfortable?"

"Yes, My Lady. Thank you."

"Will you be well here? I would like to ascend the mount a bit and get a closer look."

"I am fine," Nimshi replied. "Please, go."

Zoë smiled. She placed her hand on Nimshi's shoulder. Turning, she pushed her way into the crowd. The winding path which eased the assent was cluttered with people. Zoë had no option but to leave the trail. Placing her hands on the ground in front of her, she climbed up towards Elijah. She pushed her way through the people as her ascent met another path. Each time she took the direct and difficult route, climbing the loose rocks to a closer vantage point.

Zoë looked up to gauge her progress. In the distance she noticed someone else climbing just as she was. Watching him leap from one stone to another stirred up a memory. Something about the way he moved reminded her of the time she scaled the boulders at the hanging rocks. When the stranger lifted his head to plan his next step, she saw his face. Obadyah.

The scene before her could not compete with what captured her eyes. Obadyah paused. Zoë turned away. She was not prepared to see him, even less to be seen by him. Taking a seat on the stone closest to her, she rested her face in her hands.

Slowly, she lifted her head, hoping to catch just one more glimpse of him. But he was gone. A surge of panic rose in her chest. Scanning the sea of faces, she found him moving up the mountain once more. Zoë pushed her way through the flow of people, her eyes locked on Obadyah. He was just ahead of her now and above her. He continued to move swiftly towards the level place where Elijah stood.

He had changed. His hair was long, shoulders broad. His arms thick like that of a laborer, not a servant of the crown. He reached with one arm while at the same time looking down to secure his footing. It was then she saw it. His mark. Jezebel's symbol branded into his shoulder. A cross representing Asherah and her sovereign matriarchy. A loop, Asherah's open arms. It was a replica of the idol presented by the sorceress to Jezebel at the Sidonian fair. Zoë cringed. Obadyah belongs to Jezebel. He had endured her abuse and her humiliation of him. And now he wore her name on his body.

And yet, Obadyah seemed to have shed his insecurities. The weight of a eunuch was no longer visible in his body nor his expression. He moved with courage. *Is he content? Does he not carry the emptiness I feel?*

The water Elijah received from the people flowed around the altar and filled the trench. The prophet came near the sons of Jacob and said, "O Yahweh, the god of Abraham, Isaac and Jacob. Answer me, O Yahweh, that these people may know that you, O Yahweh, are God."

Zoë looked up. A strange sound filled the air. The rumble grew until she could feel it reaching into her chest. All eyes turned towards the heavens. Above them appeared something like a sphere of fire with a tail of flames that stretched across the sky. With the determination of an eagle diving towards its kill, the fireball raced towards the earth. Before she could react, before she could run, flames fell upon Elijah's altar. In a matter of seconds the sacrifice was consumed. The blaze did not wane, bringing the water in the mote to a boil. The sound of sizzling intensified until the blaze licked up every drop of water.

People began falling on their faces. From the midst of the crowd someone yelled out, "Yahweh, He is God!" Then another said, "Yahweh, He is God!" The chant rose. Every voice surrounding Zoë spoke in unison and with one conviction.

Then Elijah said, "Seize the prophets of Baal. Do not let one of them escape."

The people of Israel rushed the mountain top. They secured the feeble priests. Elijah led the multitude down the mountain to the brook of Kishon.

Zoë closed her eyes. Though Jezebel's prophets would pay for their crimes, Zoë could not bear to witness the bloodshed, the judgment violent and swift. A sentence of death. Justice for the countless lives taken by Jezebel in the name of Baal.

She thought of Kalbu and the precious love he had shown her. The fierce tenderness with which he cherished Donatiya. The sweet affection he displayed for Palmsquat. The conviction which thrust him into the flame set to consume a stranger's newborn. One life, she thought, worth more than a thousand prophets of Baal!

When Zoë opened her eyes, she caught sight of Obadyah. He moved away from the scene. Zoë followed him, conflicted. *Am I his vulnerability?* Her imagination led her like a helpless ewe to the place where uncertainty awaited.

Then, as suddenly as he started, Obadyah stopped. He directed his eyes to the western sky. Zoë, hiding, followed his gaze. A cloud, as small as a man's fist, hung over the sea. A cool breeze kicked up off the water blowing her hair back. She looked back to Obadyah. He was gone.

CHAPTER 43

THE BATTLE AND THE WAR

Obadyah pushed his way through the soldiers he had left to guard Ahab. "My King," he said, "we must depart, rain is coming!"

"So Elijah has said," Ahab replied.

"Listen to the word of Elijah, My Lord," Obadyah begged, panting. "For if Yahweh brings forth fire at his request, with what downpour will he answer His prophet?"

Ahab stared at his overseer. The rumbling in the distance grew.

"Prepare the chariot," Ahab said, and then turned back into his tent.

Obadyah grabbed a soldier and began giving instructions. In a matter of minutes the king's carriage arrived.

Obadyah burst into Ahab's tent. "My Lord, we must go!"

Obadyah led Ahab to the royal chariot. He climbed aboard. Obadyah followed and took hold of the reins. When he cracked a whip, the horses jumped. A plume of dust filled the air as they raced off leaving slaves and supplies behind.

Clouds mounted. Obadyah tensed. On a perfect day it was a three hour ride from Carmel to Jezreel. The sky grew black. Obadyah yelled, urging the stallions on. Then the winds came. A gust forced them to steady their stance. Ahab grabbed the side of the chariot with both hands. He had no sooner braced himself and the sky broke open. Water poured from the heavens. Obadyah looked up. For a second he welcomed the cool rain on his face. But the pleasant sound of droplets meeting the earth faded as water pooled in the bottom of the chariot. Relief that the drought had ended could not be celebrated. The fine dust blanketing the road quickly turned to clay. The horses slowed. Obadyah wiped his eyes with his forearm.

"We must hurry! I must deliver news of the day's events to the queen!" Ahab yelled.

Ahab's chariot continued to slow. Mud soaked trenches began to swallow the wheels. When they came to a halt, Ahab's eyes betrayed a fear Obadyah had never witnessed. Obadyah jumped out of the chariot, his feet sinking into the earth. He worked feverishly as Ahab barked orders. Obadyah retrieved stones and branches, laying them before the trapped wheels. He moved to the horse's lead and pulled with all his might. Ahab continued yelling commands, but Obadyah could not hear him over the pounding rain. Obadyah fought with the horses. They bucked and stomped, driving their hooves further into the siphoning clay. Obadyah panicked when he realized he could not dislodge his foot. He bent down to loosen the strap of his sandal just as a crack of thunder pierced the air. Obadyah pulled with all his might, the mud tightened its grip before finally yielding. He had to get the team off the road. When the carriage broke free Obadyah drug the stallions up the ridge. The higher elevation would lengthen their trip by hours, but they would escape the mud and hopefully escape with their lives.

Obadyah and Ahab burst into the queen's chambers soaked to the bone.

Jezebel leaped to her feet and ran to her husband. "The drought is over! We must celebrate!" she said, throwing her arms around Ahab.

Grabbing his wife's shoulders, Ahab pushed her back. He revealed to her all that Elijah had done and how the people had killed her priests.

Jezebel's eyes narrowed. She turned her attention to Obadyah. "I have a message for your prophet, eunuch," she said. "You are Elijah?' Well, I am Jezebel! May the gods do to me and even more, if I do not make your life as the life of Baal's servants by this time tomorrow!"

Jezebel stormed out, Ahab followed close behind.

Once the king and queen were out of sight, Obadyah left the castle and ran to Naboth's residence.

"Obadyah! It's raining!" Eliah said, rushing into his arms.

"I have to return to Carmel. I have an urgent message for Elijah," Obadyah replied, setting Eliah aside.

"He is in town at the carpenter's inn," Naboth said. "We received word he entered there an hour ago."

"What? How? Nevermind, I must go. I must warn him."

"Warn him of what?" Eliah asked.

"Jezebel."

"What of Jezebel?"

"Eliah, I must go!" Obadyah said, pushing past her.

The innkeeper, aware of Obadyah's standing before the king, directed him at once to Elijah's room.

"Elijah, servant of Yahweh." Obadyah said as he knocked. "Elijah, servant of Yahweh. I bring word from the queen."

When the door opened, Obadyah found the prophet's eyes. "Elijah, prophet of the most high God, Jezebel seeks your life."

Elijah offered no reply. "Please, servant of Yahweh, heed my warning!" When Elijah remained silent, Obadyah's voice rose. "Depart with haste! For Jezebel will not sleep until she has destroyed you!"

"What word do you bring of Elijah?" Jezebel demanded.

"I bring no word of Elijah," Obadyah replied, his eyes leaving the queen and finding Ahab. "My word concerns the King of Aram."

Ahab swallowed. "Ben-hadad?"

"He and his vassal kings have besieged Samaria."

Ahab and Jezebel continued to stare at Obadyah.

"These are the words delivered to me by his servant," Obadyah said. "'Your silver and your gold are mine; your most beautiful wives and children are also mine.' My Lord, Ben-hadad threatens the destruction of the city if you do not hand over all that is precious to the throne."

Obadyah, distraught for the residents of Samaria, was also relieved. Ahab now had more pressing issues than his wife's obsession with the prophet of Yahweh.

"Call the elders to advise me on this matter." Ahab demanded.

Obadyah bowed and departed. While locating the king's advisors, Obadyah found Amos, the baker of Dothan who had gathered the prophets to the caves of Beth Shan.

"Please," Obadyah begged, "seek the word of the Lord on behalf of Israel."

"Why?" Amos replied. "Surely you do not maintain hope for this king?"

"I am his servant. He is my king. I must hope. For perhaps with your word his heart will turn to Yahweh." At Obadyah's persistence, Amos followed him to Jezreel.

"Arise!" Ahab said. "How do you advise concerning Ben-hadad?"

"Do not consent to this demand, O King," the leader of the elders replied, "for it is within your power to retake Samaria."

"Do you agree?" Ahab asked Obadyah.

"Hear not my word, My King, but please, I beg you, hear the word of Yahweh for the God of Israel brings a message to you," Obadyah motioned towards Amos.

Ahab nodded.

"Thus says Yahweh," Amos began, "have you seen this great multitude? Behold, I will deliver them into your hand, and you shall know that I am Yahweh."

Ahab looked at Obadyah.

Obadyah steeled his eyes. His jaw locked. Silence filled the room. No one let a sound escape them, Ahab's breathing the only discernible noise. Then Obadyah silently cried out. Show mercy to your king, Yahweh.

"Gather the rulers of the provinces of Israel and 7,000 sons of Israel to accompany us to Samaria," Ahab commanded.

"Obadyah! Welcome home!" Naboth said.

Obadyah did not reply. Naboth approached, placing his hands on Obadyah's shoulders. "Come. Rest." Naboth followed Obadyah up the ladder to the upper roof chamber he and Eliah had shared for more than three years.

"Where is Eliah?"

"She and Accoah are down by the spring."

Obadyah sank into the couch, weary.

"What is it my friend? Was not the king successful in regaining Samaria?"

"He was," Obadyah said, "But we failed to capture Ben-hadad who escaped on his chariot."

"Surely Ben-hadad will muster troops and return."

Obadyah nodded but he couldn't find the strength to say what needed to be said.

"Speak, son, for whatever has you downcast, surely we can resolve."

"By Yahweh's word, Samaria was saved. Ahab was granted salvation from the destruction of the enemies of Israel. But rather than honor the word of the Yahweh, Ahab saw an opportunity. Looking to gain an ally as the threat of an Assyrian attack looms, the king has made peace with the enemy of Israel."

"Yahweh protected Ahab," Naboth replied, "and now Ahab will

disregard His word?"

Obadyah sighed. "Ahab is following his own heart."

Naboth shook his head. "Surely there is no one like Ahab, fully committed to doing evil in the sight of the Lord, urged on by his wife, Jezebel."

Having spent a month in Samaria securing the king's residence, his children, and his belongings, Obadyah returned to Jezreel and to the house of Naboth. He could think of nothing but seeing Eliah and surprising her with the new cloak he had purchased for her. Over the past weeks, he thought often of how he had dismissed her so quickly the last time they were together. He cringed at the memory of pushing her aside when he left in search of the prophet Elijah. Obadyah breathed a sigh of relief as the days of longing to apologize to Eliah were finally over.

When Naboth's vineyard came into view on the horizon, Obadyah smiled and heeled his horse. In the distance he could see people scurrying about. Everyone seemed busy with movement, but not as they were the first day Obadyah and Eliah arrived. That day they celebrated with a grand feast. This was different.

Still a hundred fathoms away, Obadyah stepped down from his horse. He grabbed the first man he saw.

"What is happening?"

"Ahab sought to purchase the vineyard."

"And"

"And Naboth refused."

Obadyah's head dropped. He knew exactly what that meant.

"And then Naboth refused Ahab a second time. That is when Jezebel summoned Naboth to the palace. She stated her intention to give him a seat at her table to honor him."

"Please tell me Naboth did not trust the word of the queen?"

"He shared your suspicions, My Lord, but he had no choice. He had to go."

"Why?"

"Jezebel had already summoned Eliah."

Obadyah made no reply. He turned and threw himself on his horse's back. His heels met the mare's belly in time with his beating heart. Adrenaline fed his muscles as he charged towards town. At full speed, he turned the corner into the heart of the city.

Ahead he could see a gathering of men. Obadyah jumped down off his horse and pushed his way through the crowd. The few slow to step aside Obadyah shoved out of his way. When he reached the center of the mob, Obadyah fell to his knees. He reached for the cloaked body laying facedown on the ground. He turned the man over. Naboth.

Obadyah cried out as he held his friend's head in his hands. He felt as though he was being burned by an invisible flame, being scorched from the inside out. "No, no, no!"

The group of men sneered but quickly quieted when one caught sight of Obadyah's mark. He could hear whispers behind him and the scuffling of feet as the crowd began to disperse. Obadyah held his eyes on his friend. Naboth's blood, still warm, ran from his skull and fell into the palm of his hand. Leaning over Naboth's beaten and broken body, Obadyah felt a weakness he had not known before.

Obadyah's vulnerability turned to anger and then quickly to fear. Eliah! He rose and grabbed the first man he could reach.

"There was a little girl here." Obadyah said.

"Yes, there was a girl, My Lord. She left the palace and came down to the street when the execution began."

"Jezebel's residence?"

"Yes, My Lord. It is for that reason she was spared."

"What do you mean she was spared?"

"She threw herself on the condemned man and…well, I'm afraid several stones struck her. We tried to pull her off. We held her away until the sentence was carried out."

"Where is she?"

"She went that way," the man said, pointing towards Naboth's property.

Obadyah shoved the man out of his way and ran back down the road. Crossing the threshold of Naboth's house he called out, "Eliah!"

There was no answer. He moved swiftly to the ladder which led to the upper chamber and yelled once more.

"Eliah!"

No answer. The vineyard. Obadyah left the house and raced towards the rows of vines. Then he stopped. He listened. There was only silence. The house, the outer yard, the threshing floor, the vineyard, it had all been abandoned. There was not a soul anywhere.

Chasing the vines Obadyah continued to call out, "Eliah, Eliah, are you here?" A slight sound rushed by his ears, as faint as a field mouse. Obadyah stopped. He held his breath and listened.

"Here," he heard a small voice cry out.

Obadyah dashed in the direction of the voice. When his steps found the sound, he threw himself to the ground. His heart sent a shock through his body as though he had been struck by lightning. He tried to speak but could only fight for his next breath.

"Jezebel watched," Eliah said. Her eyes reached for him as her tears welled up. The magnitude of Jezebel's wickedness, the heartache of Naboth's execution, the peace of Obadyah's presence, all the battling emotions that had fallen upon Eliah in the span of a single hour found Obadyah in a single glance. Obadyah reached down and drew Eliah into his arms.

"She..., she..., sat in her window and ...."

"Shh," Obadyah whispered, pulling Eliah up into his chest. "Do not give that evil woman one more second of your thoughts." Then Obadyah looked into Eliah's eyes. He could see her consciousness fading. He could feel the life draining from her. Yet he was careful to not let her see his fear. Smiling, he looked into Eliah's eyes. "Let's get you cleaned up." He carried Eliah to the stream at the outer perimeter of Naboth's land. He knelt down next to the brook. He took water into his hand and used it to clean the blood from her face. Obadyah carefully pushed the strands of blood soaked hair away from Eliah's eyes. He brought a handful of water up to her head. He poured it over her wounds. As soon as the water was gone, a fresh stream of red ran down her cheek. Obadyah put pressure on her wounds. The memory of waking to Eliah laying across his belly rushed back. She had stopped his bleeding. He could not stop hers. He closed his eyes, screaming inside his head.

"I was brave." Eliah said.

Obadyah opened his eyes and found Eliah with a casual smile. "You are brave," he said, "just like your father."

Eliah smiled. Then her body began to shake.

Obadyah pulled her heart tight against his.

"Obadyah," Eliah whispered in his ear.

"Yes, Eliah."

"Will you...sing...to me...before I go...to sleep?"

Obadyah did not pause for a second. He began to sing the song he refused to sing at the inn at Dothan. The song she sang for him the day he found Eliah flowed from his heart. He had never told her, but Eliah's Song had crept into his mind many times since that night. Now, the words poured out of his mouth. He gave them back to the little girl who had given so much to him. But not just him. This little psalm keeper had revealed the words of David she had preserved in her mind. Thus preserving for a nation the precious words of Yahweh.

It was midway through the song when Eliah stopped shaking. Obadyah kept singing. Eliah's body went still.

When he had finished Eliah's Song, Obadyah looked up. In the corner of his eye he saw something move. He couldn't make out what he was seeing, his sight clouded by tears. He rubbed his eyes and attempted to focus on the form resting a short distance away.

"Accoah?"

The little girl who had befriended Eliah the day of their arrival at Naboth's residence sat with her blanket pulled up tight against her face. The little girl who spent years following Eliah around the vineyard stared back at him. Though Obadyah always greeted Accoah when he returned home each evening, she would hide behind Eliah. Accoah grew accustomed to Obadyah's presence and eventually would peek around Eliah and give him a smile. But she had yet to allow him to touch her. In fact, the only man she let hold her was Naboth. Looking into her half hidden eyes, Obadyah felt the full weight of Accoah's fear. How she had been left by the vineyard workers who fled he could not fathom. But he understood completely why she did not leave Eliah.

Suddenly it occurred to Obadyah that it wasn't Eliah, but Accoah who called out to him from the vineyard. She had followed him to the stream and listened to him sing. And now her eyes peered desperately over the top of her clenched hands.

Obadyah shifted Eliah's body to his left side and with his right hand he reached out to Accoah. She stared at his outstretched arm. Obadyah, patient, continued to reach for her without saying a word. Accoah drew her arms into her chest. Obadyah waited, his tears running silently down his cheeks and dripping one-by-one onto Eliah's body. After a few minutes Accoah moved over next to Obadyah. He wrapped his arm around her. She laid her head down on Eliah's lap.

CHAPTER 44

THE TREASURE OF ELIAH

Eliah lived for two days after the stoning of Naboth, but she did not wake up once she closed her eyes at the stream. Obadyah held her the whole time. He spoke to her. He cried over her. He sang to her. He had never felt so powerless, so aimless, so worthless. When she took her last breath Obadyah remembered the words of King David that Eliah had shared with him. When David's baby boy died and David knew he could not bring him back, David said, "I will go to him but he will not return to me."

When Yahweh brought Eliah into his life, Obadyah knew she was the reason he would abandon the king. Eliah was what gave his life value, purpose. And now Yahweh has taken her. How could He do this to him? Why was He doing this to him? She was the keeper of the psalms! He, just a eunuch. What use am I without her?

Accoah followed Obadyah to a cracked boulder near the stream. He squeezed himself through the opening and gently laid Eliah's body down. He placed his hand on her cheek and closed his eyes. "A soul for whom the world is not worthy," he said. When he emerged back out into the light of day a tiny face looked up at him. Obadyah smiled at Accoah. He took hold of her hand, and his new purpose.

With Jezebel distracted by her recent acquisition of Naboth's vineyard, Obadyah took a chance and reached out to Adonis. His heart had sparked the day she arrived in Jezreel with the queen. He knew Jezebel brought Adonis to Samaria after their day together in the palace bedchamber. But he had only gotten glimpses of her when he made his reports to Ahab concerning his progress in Jezreel.

"We should not be meeting like this, Obadyah," Adonis said.

"Forgive me. I do not wish to endanger you. But, please, hear my request. Tomorrow you are free from your duties at the castle."

"Tomorrow I serve from outside the castle doors rather than from within. You of all people know, we are never free."

"Still," Obadyah replied, "I must ask this of you. Please, there is a little girl. Accoah. She was being cared for by Naboth."

"The man condemned by Jezebel?"

Obadyah nodded. "I have hidden her in the cracked boulder next to the spring."

"Does Jezebel know she lives?"

"It is assumed she fled with the rest of the vineyard workers."

"And what will you do with her?"

"I am taking her away from here."

"You're abandoning the king?"

"There is no hope for freedom, Adonis. There never was. Accoah needs me."

"And what do you need of me, Obadyah?"

"Go to her, please. Stay with her tomorrow so that I may complete one final task for Ahab."

"You put me at great risk."

"I know." Obadyah's head fell, "I'm sorry," Obadyah whispered.

"What if a eunuch is sent with me tomorrow?"

"Everyone will be at the vineyard."

"Should I be alone as you anticipate, you will have my help from sun up to sun down."

Obadyah took a deep breath and rested his hand on Adonis's shoulder.

"How will I recognize these rocks hiding the little girl?" Adonis asked.

"Go to the spring, follow the stream away from town. I will call out to you when you are within sight."

Adonis nodded.

"Thank you, my friend." Obadyah whispered and then departed in the direction of the king's quarters.

"Where have you been, Obadyah?" Ahab said when Obadyah entered the throne room of the Jezreel palace. "Have you not heard the joyous news?"

Obadyah had hoped his absence would be overlooked in light of the celebration of Naboth's death and acquisition of his vineyard. He decided to ignore the king's inquiry and instead mirrored his enthusiasm.

"I have, My King. Congratulations!" Obadyah felt his spine tighten the second the words left his mouth. It was not the lie that convicted him. Nor was it the conflict between his tone and the true state of his emotions. It was his fawning. All he could see in that moment was his father standing before Ethbaal winning him over with his flattery and false praise. Obadyah cringed when it occurred to him that he was no longer becoming his father. He was his father.

"Perhaps this does not bring the same pleasure afforded by victory in battle, but it is splendid, is it not?"

"Indeed, Lord King," Obadyah bowed. "Shall I inventory the estate for you?"

"Yes. We begin tomorrow. And find those Galileans who served Naboth. I will need workers to maintain my new garden."

"It will be done. Forgive my absence from your celebration tonight, My Lord, as I must set out at once if I am to recover Naboth's workers."

"Go. But meet me at the vineyard in the morning. And Obadyah, plan two hours past sunup for I anticipate our celebration will go long into the night."

Obadyah bowed once more and departed the palace. He hurried down to the stream and made his way to the cracked rocks. He pulled himself up, calling out for Accoah in a loud whisper. Reaching the crevasse, he peered over the edge. Curled up in a ball on the palm branches he had laid down for her was little Accoah.

Obadyah paused and looked in the direction of the rock where he had hidden Eliah. He wanted to go to her. He had to remind himself she was gone. Obadyah squeezed himself through the opening and jumped down next to Accoah. He placed his hand gently on her head and closed his eyes. Please Yahweh, I beg you. Strengthen me for this task. Give me wisdom as we flee. Go before us. Protect us from the hands of those who wish our destruction.

Adonis appeared the next morning just as she'd promised. Obadyah scanned the horizon for any feet which may have followed and eyes that would be quick to report the wandering of the queen's lady. When he felt it safe, he jumped down startling Adonis.

"Forgive me," he said, reaching for her. "Here, let me help you."

Obadyah lifted himself atop the boulder and then took Adonis's hands in his. He pulled her up and then lowered her into the tiny cave where he and Accoah had been hiding. Adonis looked at Accoah who sat silently against the wall with her blanket wrapped tightly around her.

"Accoah. This is Ares." Obadyah said.

Adonis's head swung in Obadyah's direction. "I have not heard my name since…since Ethbaal's palace."

"I have never forgotten your name. Or your kindness."

"It is you who showed me kindness by lying to Jezebel about our…our intimacy."

Adonis did not wait for Obadyah to reply. She sat down next to Accoah and looked into her eyes. "Are you hungry?" Adonis asked, reaching into her sack to retrieve some bread.

Accoah looked at Obadyah.

"Go ahead," Obadyah smiled, "Ares is our friend."

Accoah moved her blanket away from her face just enough to bring the bread up to her lips. "Ares is going to stay with you today."

Accoah pulled her arms into her chest. Her large brown eyes and long thick eye lashes peeked out over the top of her blanket and reached for Obadyah.

"Be still, little one. Do not worry," Obadyah said, taking her hands in his. "When I return we will leave this cave together and journey to the coast. And then you and I will splash in the ocean."

Accoah nodded.

Obadyah placed Accoah's hand in Adonis's hand. "Stay here with Ares, I will return tonight." Obadyah rose to leave. He squeezed himself through the crack above them and then paused to look back at the two girls. His heart shuddered, fearful of leaving them even for a few hours. But he knew, he had no choice. He took a deep breath and jumped down.

Racing towards town, Obadyah looked up at the sun. It was almost three hours past sunup. He began to sweat. As Naboth's vineyard came into view, so did the royal carriage which was stationed next to the house.

"My Lord and King." Obadyah said, bowing as he entered Naboth's home.

"What keeps you this morning, Obadyah?"

"I should not be kept by anything except the king's business, My Lord, as I know it will please you greatly to begin work on your new estate as soon as possible."

"You have retrieved the workers?"

"Indeed, My King, they arrive tomorrow," Obadyah said, lying to his master once more.

Ahab grinned and then quickly turned.

"There is nothing of value here," the king said. "Use the residence to house the slaves."

Obadyah bowed.

"Has My Lord visited the outbuildings?"

"Men are there now retrieving the wine."

Obadyah clenched, knowing very well that what was hidden amid the vats would soon be discovered. It was only a matter of time before someone announced the findings to the king. Obadyah had to get to the cellar before Ahab's men reported to him.

"My King," Obadyah said, "if I may, allow me to lead you down to the cellars."

"Why? Are there vases filled with gold?" Ahab smirked.

"Not gold, My King, but a valuable treasure. Spoils worthy of a king."

"And how is it that you have knowledge of a hidden treasure amid Naboth's possessions?"

"My eyes and ears are forever attentive to the prosperity of my king."

"Very well," Ahab replied, "take me to this treasure."

Obadyah led Ahab to a cool dark room at the back of Naboth's cellar.

"What is all of this?" Ahab asked.

Obadyah reached down and removed the lid from one of Kalbu's pots. He reached in and pulled out a scroll.

"My Lord," Obadyah said, "they are the words of your father, King David."

Ahab reached for the parchment, taking it from Obadyah's hand. He began to read. "Yahweh is my shepherd, I shall not want. He makes me lie down in green pastures. He leads me beside the quiet waters. He restores my soul. He guides me in the paths of righteousness for his name's sake. Even though I walk through the valley of the shadow of death, I fear no evil, for You are with me. Your rod and your staff, they comfort me. You prepare a table before me in the presence of my enemies. You have anointed my head with oil. My cup overflows. Surely goodness and lovingkindness will follow me all the days of my life. And I will dwell in the house of Yahweh forever."

Ahab tossed the scroll onto the pile of pottery. "What use is this to me, Obadyah?"

"Are not the words of the king worth preserving, My Lord?

Ahab stood silent.

Obadyah could see that Ahab was thinking but not convinced. "Perhaps, My King," he continued, "should you wish to barter with the king of Judah."

Ahab's demeanor changed at the thought of purchasing an ally in the Southern Kingdom. Obadyah, still desperate, longed for reassurance that the words of Yahweh would be protected.

"In the eyes of many in the Kingdom of Judah, these scrolls, your scrolls, My Lord, are as precious as jewels."

Obadyah looked for confidence in Ahab's expression, searching for any sign that the psalms would be saved. Time was running out so Obadyah took a chance.

"My Lord. There is more." Obadyah paused and waited for Ahab's eyes. "I implore you, My King," Obadyah whispered, "speak with your queen. For it was revealed in my hearing when I served at the feet of Ethbaal, that hidden within the scrolls is the location of Solomon's shields."

Ahab's eyes brightened. "The three hundred missing gold shields?"

"The very ones, My Lord!" Then Obadyah leaned in towards Ahab and whispered, "The lost treasure of Solomon, My King."

The greed in Ahab's expression was the confidence Obadyah needed to be able to walk away from the scrolls. He had done all he could to protect Yahweh's Word. What he and Eliah had spent years inscribing, every precious word of Yahweh he could pull from her mind, would be preserved. For how long he did not know. That would be for Yahweh to decide.

Obadyah had spent three years constructing Jezebel's palace. It was his work during the day. But at night, he recorded the words of David, as Eliah recited them to him, each psalm hidden in the storehouses of her memory. It was all he had left of her. And now it belonged to Ahab. But the scrolls would be saved, even if they would not be cherished. Perhaps, Obadyah hoped, one day they would find their way into the hands of the King of Judah and David's message would be shared with those who are faithful to Yahweh.

As important as the scrolls were, Obadyah knew he must walk away from them. His heart ached with disappointment, but not regret. He could not risk Accoah being destroyed as Naboth and Eliah had been by the evil of Jezreel—the evil of Jezebel.

Obadyah oversaw the relocation of the scrolls. Each of Kalbu's pots, glazed with his healing ointment, were carefully moved from Naboth's cellar to Jezebel's palace. What Obadyah and Eliah had carefully tended to was now resting in the hands of evil.

"Yahweh is sovereign." Obadyah reminded himself as he laid each scroll, unprotected, under the nose of Jezebel. What Obadyah had believed about Yahweh, that he would preserve His Word, he now had to trust. Before he left, Obadyah grabbed one random scroll and slid it under his belt.

Without a second glance Obadyah turned his back on the words he had inscribed and the palace he had built. His steps were swift, his back straight, his eyes fixed forward. He left the home and grave of Naboth, his dearest friend. And with more confidence than he had felt in years, Obadyah hurried to the hiding place where he had left Accoah with Adonis.

"Ares, I'm back," Obadyah said, his eyes cresting the edge of the cleft. There was no reply. "Ares, are you there?" Obadyah jumped through the opening down into the cave where he had last seen Adonis and Accoah. It was empty.

CHAPTER 45

THE GIFT OF ADONIS

"Ares!" Obadyah yelled, his head peeking out of the cleft like a mother bear leaving her den in spring. Were they discovered? Did Adonis panic? Has Jezebel found them? Obadyah jumped down out of the shelter and began to pace. Where do I even begin to look? I have failed once more to protect the ones I love. Faint, Obadyah leaned back against the rock he had just descended. His legs would no longer bear his weight and he slumped to the ground.

Obadyah's anxiety met his grief, and the truth of his brother's death returned. In a moment of panic the reality his mind had shielded from him rushed in. It was Obadyah who brought his younger brother to the beach that day. Once the memories started, they could not be stopped. They flooded back like the torrent of a wadi. His mother had told him his brother was too young to go. It was Obadyah who disobeyed her. It was Obadyah who snuck his little brother into a cart and brought him to the shore. Yes, Nimshi struck him, but it was Obadyah who had led him there. His brother died because of him.

Of all the things which had been done to Obadyah, none compared to what he had done to himself. He closed his eyes and beat his chest–anything to feel something other than the pain of who he knew he was.

"Obadyah! What is it? What's wrong?"

Obadyah jumped to his feet. Standing before him was Adonis and Accoah. Relief rushed through him, quieting his memories.

"Where have you been? I feared the worst."

"Accoah took me to Eliah," Adonis said. "We cleaned her and wrapped her in preparation for your trip."

Obadyah reached out and took Accoah's hand. "Where is your blanket, little one?" It was not until that moment that Obadyah realized he had never seen Accoah without it.

Accoah pointed in the direction where they had hidden Eliah's body.

Obadyah sighed. His heart broke for little Accoah. He picked her up knowing his touch would not take away her pain. But knowing as well, it was all she had. And she was all he had too.

"Thank you, Ares."

"I am happy to have earned the trust of Accoah and was pleased to help her honor Eliah."

"Come with us!" Obadyah suddenly said, surprising Adonis and himself. Adonis immediately began shaking her head. "Come with me and Accoah. Leave Canaan. Leave Jezebel!"

"I cannot."

"Why can you not?"

"I have known nothing but palace life, Obadyah."

"I understand. But…"

"I am not a young girl anymore," Adonis interrupted. "I do not yearn for adventure. I desire only my routine and the safety of my royal dwelling."

Obadyah nodded. He would press her no more. "Yahweh is pleased with your kindness to us today."

"And you?" Adonis inquired.

"I too am grateful, more than you ever will know."

"I will pray for you, Obadyah. I will petition Athena's god on your behalf."

"Petition Yahweh on your own behalf, Adonis. His eyes roam the earth in search of those whose hearts are His. Should you seek Him, He will find you. And show you a purpose far greater than your service to the queen."

"Speaking of…I must go." Adonis knelt down. She took Accoah's tiny cheeks into her hands. "You are beautiful and brave," she said. Then, finding Accoah's hands and wrapping them up in hers, Adonis said, "Now tell me, what are you?"

Accoah looked Adonis in the eyes and said, "I am beautiful."

"And?" Adonis said.

"I am brave."

Adonis reached for a chain hanging around her neck. She lifted it over her head. And slipped it over Accoah's head. The pear-shaped amethyst which had adorned Zoe's brow the last night Adonis saw her now came to rest on Accoah's chest.

Accoah looked down.

"Is that...?" Obadyah asked.

Adonis nodded.

Obadyah caught his breath as the night of Jezebel's prophecy game came back to his mind. Obadyah closed his eyes. He could see Zoë standing on the bench in the courtyard of Ethbaal's palace. He could see the amethyst pendant resting against her forehead. The image was as clear as if she were standing in front of him. Accoah reached for the jewel. She held it away from her chest, and gazed at it. She smiled, glowing with the radiance of a princess.

"When will you leave?" Adonis asked, standing to face Obadyah.

"At nightfall."

"And what of Eliah?"

"I cannot leave her, any part of her, in this place."

"You will carry her and Accoah?"

"Accoah is strong. She can walk by my side."

"Her strides cannot match yours, Obadyah. And she will tire quickly, especially if you travel at night."

"Then I will carry her as well."

"Obadyah, it's too much."

"What choice do I have?"

"Allow me to help you."

"You have helped me, Adonis. Now please return to the palace before Jezebel misses you."

"There is a farmer I know."

"I know a few farmers as well. They are all sustained by the queen."

"There is one who is not. We are...friends. We are...close."

Obadyah's eyes locked onto Adonis. She hesitated to return his gaze, but she could not hide her smile.

"His name is Gideon. I will speak to him on my way back to town. He has a horse and carriage."

"You bless us once more, Adonis. But know this, I cannot wait should Gideon's fear of the crown delay him. We cannot lose our cover of darkness."

"Gideon fears Yahweh," Adonis said.

"I dare say," Obadyah smiled, "I have not heard of a Phoenician with so many Hebrew friends."

Adonis returned his smile. "Goodbye, Obadyah." Adonis reached for Obadyah's hand. He took her hand in his.

"Goodbye, Ares."

Obadyah watched as Adonis walked away. He recalled the day they spent together, young, naked, and afraid. Jezebel had tried to force them into bed. Instead, she ignited a relationship that would lead to her own betrayal. What Obadyah could make no sense of at the time, now overflowed with meaning. The friendship he and Adonis had built in those few awkward hours gave him the confidence he needed to ask her for help with Accoah. Obadyah marveled at how Yahweh put the uncomfortable and unpredictable pieces of his life together into something that made sense, something with a meaning far greater than the circumstances of the immediate moment. And now Adonis would return to the life they both seemed destined for. As she walked away Obadyah wondered if she was the wise one. But then Accoah reached for his hand.

Obadyah lowered Accoah through the crack between the boulders. "Time to rest, little one." he said, helping her nestle in. He took her cloak and laid it on top of her, tucking in the edges.

Obadyah sang Eliah's song to Accoah until she fell asleep. He was about to settle himself in next to her when he noticed a satchel resting against the wall. Adonis must have left it for them. He reached for the pouch and tugged on the rope loosening the top. He peered over the brim. Dates, almonds, olives, and pistachios. It was both the physical and emotional sustenance he needed to take the difficult steps ahead of him. Obadyah leaned his head back, took a deep breath, and closed his eyes. Yahweh has provided once more.

CHAPTER 46

THE TIME TO GO

"Awaken, my love," Zoë heard a man say.

"Samara, please, you must arise," the voice said.

Zoë stirred as the male voice in their room grew louder.

"It's our son," the man said.

Zoë, now alert, saw Theophanes across the room shaking Samara.

"Samara," Theophanes said, "look at me."

Samara opened her eyes, the fear of the inevitable announcement now evident in her face.

"Obadyah has abandoned the King."

Samara let out a breath.

Zoë's head dropped. Obadyah was alive. Theophanes's news, though dire, was the best bad news she had ever received.

Samara reached for her husband.

"Samara," Theophanes continued, separating himself from his wife. "We must go. It won't be long before Jezebel uses you as a bargaining chip for Obadyah's return."

Samara swung her feet around to the floor and made her way across the room to Zoë's bed.

"Zoë! Quickly! We must depart!"

Zoë was already upright. She reached for her lantern, but Samara stayed her hand.

"We must leave in darkness. Gather your things, one bag only, and meet me at the portico."

Zoë arrived to the sound of Samara arguing with Nimshi.

"My Lady, hear my heart," Nimshi said, "I must stay."

"No, my friend," Samara corrected, "you must depart with us."

"I have caused you much sorrow, and you have shown me only grace. I know it has been…" Nimshi paused and looked down, "it has been terribly hard for you to dwell with the man who killed your son."

Zoë's mouth fell open. She knew Samara had a son who died, but she never could have imagined it was at Nimshi's hand. This whole time, Samara had never uttered a bitter word. Not once had her tone revealed anything but kindness to the man who took the life of her boy. It was clear now, they both were showing one another mercy. In not talking about it, neither one drew attention to what was, for both of them, heartbreaking.

"Just as it has been difficult for you, Nimshi," Samara replied. "But now is not the time to dwell on our emotions. We must go."

"My Lady," Nimshi said, putting his hand on her arm.

"Yes, Nimshi."

"I will remain here."

"But…"

"My Lady, please!" Nimshi interrupted. "It is time for us to part ways. It is time for you to go. It is time for me to stay."

Samara looked into Nimshi's eyes. Zoë could hear the determination in his voice. "Besides, you cannot take Palmsquat where you are going and I cannot leave her."

Samara smiled. Nimshi took Samara's hand in his. Lowering his head, he kissed the back of her hand and without a goodbye he turned and limped back towards the house.

"Are you ready?" Theophanes pressed. "We must get off shore before sunrise."

"Farewell Nimshi," Zoë said. Nimshi stopped, turned and gave Zoë a smile. He bowed his head. When he rose, a single tear fell off his cheek.

Zoë walked over to Palmsquat. She ran her hand over Palmsquat's floppy ears. When Palmsquat lifted her head Zoë lowered hers. She rested her forehead on the forehead of the animal that had brought her uncle such joy. Then, without a word, she quickly turned and hurried to catch up with Theophanes and Samara.

Zoë and Samara boarded the row boat waiting on the beach. Theophanes rowed them to the side of Phoenix. Climbing aboard, they found a place on deck to sit. Samara grabbed Zoë's hand. The two women pulled their belongings onto their laps.

"Where are we…"

"Shhh," Samara replied.

Zoë obeyed, closed her eyes. As the Phoenix pulled anchor, Zoë laid her head on Samara's shoulder.

Obadyah jostled Accoah awake.

"Get up little one, it's time to go."

Accoah rubbed her eyes and stretched her legs. When Obadyah helped her to her feet she began scurrying about. "Are you looking for your blanket?" Obadyah asked. Accoah nodded. "Your blanket is with Eliah. You gifted it to her, remember?"

Accoah calmed and grabbed her cloak.

Obadyah attempted to help her wrap it around her shoulders but Accoah shook him off. Wadding it up, she tucked it under her chin.

Gather our provisions," Obadyah said, pointing to the satchel.

Accoah obeyed, her small hands taking far more time to complete the simple task. But he needed her help. They had to hurry.

When they arrived at the cavern where Obadyah had laid Eliah he rigged a rope around her body. Gently, he swung her over his shoulder so that she rested against his back. "Come, we must go."

Accoah followed, dragging the satchel.

"I'll take that."

Accoah handed him the satchel.

It was not long before Accoah started falling behind. Adonis was right, her little legs were no match for this journey.

Obadyah scooped her up. With Accoah in his arms and Eliah on his back, Obadyah prayed for the arrival of Adonis's friend. It was an hour to the crossroads. He could feel Accoah slowly drift to sleep. Her arms and legs relaxed. Now bearing the full weight of two bodies, Obadyah straightened his back, took a deep breath, and forged ahead.

As his legs tired, Obadyah could only think about his rendezvous. There were two roads departing Jezreel. Gideon would have traveled the northeast road towards Shunem and Obadyah the northwest road towards Nazareth. If Adonis was right, when Gideon reached Shunem he would head west to intersect the northwest pass and eventually with Obadyah.

With each step Obadyah watched and listened. When the faint sound of turning gravel caught his attention, he picked up his pace. In the distance, the shadow of a cart appeared. Gideon.

"I am Obadyah, friend of Adonis."

"Yes I know," Gideon said. "A large Hebrew with a body on his back and a little girl in his arms is hard to miss even in the dead of night."

"I suppose it is." Obadyah paused expecting a moment of introduction or perhaps a bit of help but neither came. Gideon just stood there leaning against the side of his wagon.

"Well," Gideon said, gesturing to the back of the wagon, "what are you waiting for, an invitation?"

"Oh, yes, forgive me." Obadyah said, moving quickly to the wagon bed. Switching Accoah over to his left arm he twisted the latch on the gate until it opened.

Obadyah laid Accoah down on the hay bed. Accoah stirred, pulled her knees up to her chest, then fell back to sleep. Obadyah shifted Eliah's body around to his chest. He removed the ropes from his shoulders and placed her gently in the back of the wagon. He swung the gate up and reached for the latch.

"What are you doing?" Gideon asked.

"Latching the gate?" Obadyah replied, thoroughly confused.

"Lay down next to the little girl."

"Sir, please, allow me to lead your horse."

"You are Ahab's overseer, are you not?"

"You know that I am."

"I am prepared to risk my life for Adonis, but I have no desire to invite execution."

"I understand."

"Then let's get going!" Gideon demanded, pointing to the wagon.

There was no reason for Gideon to show Obadyah any respect, he was no longer Ahab's overseer. In fact, he was a criminal. Obadyah jumped over the back gate and laid down in between Eliah and Accoah.

Gideon covered his stowaways and then spread several buckets or rotten vegetables on top of them. Obadyah cringed, pulling his tunic up over his nose.

"When the sun comes up the smell from the wagon will keep people a safe distance away. This won't be a pleasant ride, but Adonis only said safe, she did not say enjoyable."

It was obvious, Gideon did not want to be there. But Obadyah had put his trust in Adonis. And he would not doubt that. "Thank you," Obadyah said from beneath the tarp.

"Just pray the stench of the vegetables hides the stench of that body."

Obadyah clenched his jaw. He could feel his anger simmer at the callousness of Gideon. Precious Eliah, so vibrant, so passionate. So full of life. Now, just a body? But, Obadyah would not let his emotions get away from him. He could not let his sadness consume him. He gathered himself and drew Accoah in tight against his chest. For Eliah's sake, Accoah's safety would be his only objective now.

With Accoah sleeping soundly beside him, Obadyah's mind took him back to another wagon ride. He could not help but smile at the memory of laying next to Zoë as Kalbu led Palmsquat to his mother's house. With the image of Zoë forever before him, Obadyah needed only to close his eyes and she was there. If only there was a world where longing for your love was your day's single task. Where reaching for your love was done with your arms not just your mind. Where the warmth of her presence was as pleasant and sure as the morning sun.

His emotions which had chased him his entire life, and the fears he could not seem to overcome, he could finally see the part they played in preparing him for this journey.

He had fought for so long. And it was those who loved him most he fought against the hardest. Anger with his mother for giving him her wisdom rather than her sympathy. Anger with his father for imposing his will, and anger with himself for his enduring weaknesses. But it was his frustrations with Yahweh for His unapologetic sovereignty over all of it that kept him from becoming the man he longed to be. As he lay in the back of a strangers wagon, he realized the power he had once had as Ahab's overseer was now gone. The pride he had once felt in the construction of Jezebel's retreat meant nothing. The body of the most precious person he had ever known was laying beside him. And he had failed to protect her. Defeated, Obadyah finally surrendered. He abandoned his insecurities and his fears. And in a moment of anguish and clarity, he let go of Zoë. He did not lie to himself. He knew he would never stop longing for her. She was part of him the way his flesh surrounded him. It was something only death could destroy. But he would choose a life without her if it meant Accoah would be safe. He would not just give his life for that purpose, he would find contentment each day in his love and care for the little girl whose life Yahweh had placed in his hands.

When the heat from the rising sun crept through the tarp Obadyah heard some commotion. Wheels turning. Carts creaking. Voices of people talking around them. They had entered a town. Obadyah's body lurched suddenly when a hole grabbed the wheel of the wagon. Gidoen's horse bucked and came to a quick halt.

Accoah stirred and tried to rise. She began to whine.

"Shh," Obadyah whispered in her ear, "stay still, little one."

"Allow me to help you," Obadyah heard a stranger say.

Their feet shuffled to the back of the wagon. Obadyah's heart raced. He put his hand over Accoah's mouth and whispered in her ear. "Shh. Stay quiet, Accoah. You are safe." Sweat ran off Obadyah's forehead dripping onto the back of Accoah's head. He held her tight, hoping it wasn't too tight, and kept whispering. "Stay still. Shh, you are safe."

"Thank you, sir," Gideon replied, moving quickly to the stranger's side.

"It's not often I see a transport of rotten goods," the stranger said with a chuckle.

"Yes, well…" Gideon began, then suddenly stopped. "What are Ahab's guards doing here?"

"Retrieving something of marginal importance I would assume." the stranger replied. "If they truly wanted to be useful they would stop and help us."

"My cargo is not worth their trouble," Gideon said.

The stranger chuckled and replied, "I will lean on the wheel while you prod your horse."

Obadyah could hear Gideon scurry to the front of the wagon. A few seconds later the wheel broke free. Accoah stirred with the sudden movement.

"Accoah, I am here, you are safe," Obadyah reminded her once more. Accoah quieted down but Obadyah wondered how much longer he could keep her calm.

The voices around them faded away. The thump of horses' hoofs subsided until the only creaking they heard was that of their own cart.

"We are stopping at my friend's farm," Gideon announced.

Obadyah breathed a sigh of relief. "Do you hear that?" Obadyah said to Accoah, "just a little longer and we will get up and stretch our legs."

"I will bring you water," Gideon said.

CHAPTER 47

THE WAY OF THE SEA

"Brother!"

"Gideon!"

"What brings you into my humble presence?"

"Good company and a good meal."

"Perhaps I can provide you with only one of those."

"Very well, I will take the meal."

The two men laughed as Gideon led his horse into his friend's stable.

"Shall I free the horse?"

"I cannot stay long. I would prefer to keep her tethered if you don't mind the stench of my load in your barn."

"The stalls have yet to be cleaned today, so I doubt your stench will surpass mine."

When the sound of footsteps disappeared, Obadyah pushed the rotten produce aside. Accoah popped up like a rock badger after a long winter's nap. Obadyah smiled as he stroked a few strands of her tousled hair.

"Thirsty," Accoah said.

"I am too, little one. We will have water very soon."

Moments later they heard the shuffling of footfalls.

Obadyah grabbed Accoah, tossing them both back to their hiding place.

"It is safe," Gideon said.

"Where are we?" Obadyah asked, sitting up once more.

"Aphek."

"You have made good time."

"The sooner we reach the shore, the sooner I can return home. Here is a bucket of water for you and my horse. I will do what I can to bring you food, but I cannot make any promises."

"Thank you, Gideon."

"Do not bother to thank me until we reach the sea. Ahab's soldiers are in town. Nothing is sure. I will take a meal with my friend and then we will continue onto Acco."

"How much further?"

"Three hours to the coast."

"Would it not be better to travel at night?"

"It would be better not to put my friend at risk."

Obadyah nodded and clinched his teeth. He wasn't thinking clearly. There were no more defined roles. He could not rely on his position or his discernment. His heart was driving him now.

"My apologies," Obadyah replied. "We leave when you are ready."

When Gideon secured the stable door, Obadyah jumped down and reached for Accoah. "Here," he said, drawing up a ladle of water to her lips.

She drank it all and reached for more. Obadyah dipped the ladle again and brought it up to Accoah's mouth. She took a sip and then moved the cup from her mouth to Obadyah's. When the rim met his lips Accoah tipped the ladle. Obadyah drank. Accoah kept her hands on the cup the whole time, the water pouring out of the sides of Obadyah's mouth.

"Shall we give the horse a drink, too?" Obadyah asked.

Accoah nodded. Obadyah lowered the bucket and the horse slurped up the water as enthusiastically as they had.

Accoah reached out to touch his velvety nose. She pulled away when her hand found the coarse whiskers.

Obadyah put her hand in his and they reached out together.

Accoah giggled.

Thinking of their remaining journey and hours Accoah would be forced to lay still, Obadyah said, "Let's stretch our legs."

Obadyah took Accoah's hand and the stranded pair circled the wagon. Obadyah widened his steps each time around, Accoah did her best to mimic his stride. She stopped suddenly when the beam of light reaching through the uneven slats of the thatch roof caught her directly in her eyes. She squinted and rubbed her eyes. Having hidden Accoah in the rocks and then buried her under debris in the back of the wagon, Obadyah realized she had not seen the sun in three days.

"It will take time to adjust to the light."

Accoah looked down at the lines the sun made on the ground. She put both of her feet together and hopped from one beam to the next. Obadyah followed. Soon Accoah was giggling each time Obadyah's large feet stirred up a plume of dust. Obadyah felt the tension in his muscles give way. He smiled, grateful for a few moments of freedom.

Accoah seemed as though she would never tire of their jumping game. Eager to keep her moving and laughing, Obadyah decided he would see how many lines he could jump. When he looked ahead, he noticed a darkness obscuring the last line. He turned his attention to the outer wall where the eyes peering in on them quickly disappeared. Had their jumping drawn someone to the barn? Obadyah cursed himself for his carelessness. The eyes were low, perhaps it was only a child who had wandered past. Still, Obadyah was concerned. Every life that came into contact with him was at risk.

It had been a little over an hour when Obadyah heard Gideon approaching. He tucked himself and Accoah away just before the barn door slid open. Obadyah listened as Gideon and his friend conversed.

"I wonder where my boy is," the man said, calling for his son.

Obadyah tensed, helpless to know where those eyes that had found them had fled.

"Do not bother the boy, I'm happy to cover the wagon if you would be so kind as to part with the contents of a dirty stall."

"Yes, of course. My dung is your dung," the man laughed.

"Thank you, brother," Gideon replied.

Obadyah had no idea what Gideon had told his friend, or if his friend could be trusted. But there was nothing he could do. When he abandoned his post, he became powerless. All he could do now is hide. Darkness returned for Obadyah and Accoah as pitchfork after pitchfork of manure was spread out covering the rotten produce in the wagon.

"Be strong, little one," Obadyah whispered in her ear, "just a few more hours."

Obadyah slid Accoah's back up against the outer wall of the wagon so that the bulk of the refuse rested on him. "Close your eyes. Do not be scared. I am here. I will always be beside you."

When they were a safe distance from the farm in Aphek, Gideon dropped a sack behind him where the tarp met the bench.

"Here," Gideon said, "a few walnuts and some dates."

When Obadyah's fingers found the pouch, he pulled it under their covering. He took a piece of fruit from the bag and touched it to Accoah's lips. He could feel her mouth reaching for him, a baby bird pleading for her mother's next morsel.

"The boy," Obadyah said, "your friend's son…he saw us in the barn."

"It is too late to worry about that. We will intersect the Way of the Sea in less than an hour." Gideon said. "We travel directly north from there to Acco. The road conditions will improve, but the congestion of travelers will increase as well. And the road is often patrolled. This last leg of our journey will be the most difficult."

Obadyah would work harder than he ever had in his life in his efforts to keep Accoah quiet and content. Songs and stories of their future together brought some amount of peace to her, and to Obadyah as well.

"This is the last road, Little One," whispered Obadyah. "Tonight we…"

"Halt!" a voice demanded.

"Yes, yes, just…just give me a minute," Gideon said, slurring his words.

Obadyah's hand reached over and covered Accoah's mouth.

Ahab's men.

"Where are you headed with this…this costly cargo?"

Another voice responded in laughter.

Obadyah strained his ears, listening to the horses' steps. There was a soft snort beside him, no more than a few inches from his position in the cart. One horse meant one soldier. Where was the second? He expected there to be two, but he needed to know their position if Gideon's deception did not succeed.

Ahab, when on the hunt, ordered his men out in pairs, two in every direction. The duo which did not return indicated the direction his army would take in pursuit of his enemy. The rumble of soldier's voices confirmed there were more than two. Obadyah felt a slight relief. It meant the soldiers only happened upon them.

"What is dung to one man is…is diamonds to another." Gideon said in an overly loud voice.

"The dung of a drunkard," another man said. "How precious."

Ahab's men laughed.

"Would you like to taste, I, I mean see, see the contents?" Gideon stammered.

"We've seen and smelled enough! Move along before my horse and I become sick."

Obadyah removed his hand from Accoah's mouth and breathed a sigh of relief. Gideon prodded his horse onward.

The world outside quieted. The busy road was finally behind them. They were headed west towards the coast. It would be less than an hour until they arrived. They had made it. They were safe. Obadyah could not help but feel a bit of confidence. He hummed soft lullabies to Accoah, encouraging her with news that their journey neared completion.

Accoah wove one hand tightly through Obadyah's fingers. With her other hand she played with the hairs on his arm, pulling them up and then flattening them down.

"The coastline is in sight," Gideon announced. He clicked his tongue urging his horse to pick up its pace.

Obadyah began praying. Thank you Yahweh…

He no sooner started to pray and the wagon came to an abrupt stop.

"What business brings you to Acco?"

The voice was stern, thick with authority.

"Pardon?" Gideon replied.

Obadyah sensed fear in Gideon's voice. As the horse drew closer to the wagon Obadyah recognized the sound of chiming pieces of metal. The military headdress of Ahab's infantry. The embellishments which adorned the soldier's saddle were unmistakable. Ahab's two sentry's were upon them.

"Your cargo? Do you truly mean to be delivering waste to a coastal town?"

"Indeed, for this load is a special mix of dung ordered by a farmer on the outskirts of Acco."

"Special dung, eh?" One of the soldiers repeated.

"What is his name?" the other soldier asked.

"His name?" Gideon replied.

Gideon was faltering. Obadyah could hear his heart pounding in his chest. He untangled his hand from Accoah's. Pressing his lips up to her ear he whispered, "Lay still, Little One. Be brave." He gently pushed Accoah away from him and waited.

"The farmer who ordered this dung?" the soldier repeated. "What is his name?"

"Well, you see, my master didn't…" Gideon paused.

Obadyah flung the tarp back. He jumped from the wagon onto the soldier closest to him. Obadyah locked his arm around the neck of Ahab's soldier. The stallion bucked. Both men fell to the ground. Before the soldier could react, Obadyah grabbed the knife from his belt and slit his throat. In a matter of seconds, the soldier was dead.

Obadyah jumped to his feet. Blood from the knife ran off his hand

and dripped onto the ground. He fixed his eyes on the second soldier who remained on his horse. He was smart to not sacrifice his mount to help his comrade. His elevated position gave him an advantage. As well as a means of escape should the fight not go in his favor. They stared at one another. The eyes of the soldier narrowed when recognized Obadyah as Ahab's overseer.

"Traitor!" he said.

"Then I must die," Obadyah replied.

Obadyah hoped his words would enkindle the soldier, goading him into challenging Obadyah where they stood. His only fear was leaving Accoah. Should the soldier flee, he would have no choice but to give chase.

The horse scuffed his feet, snorting. It was ready for battle.

Obadyah's breaths were loud and quick. Then, out of the corner of his eye, Obadyah saw the tarp move. Accoah's head popped up. The sight of her drew his eyes away. The soldier seized his opportunity and charged. Obadyah swung his eyes back towards the rushing horse just as the soldier swung his sword. Obadyah ducked. The blade grazed his head. He slid beneath the horse's belly and jumped up on the opposite side. He grabbed Ahab's sentry and pulled him to the ground with the full force of his weight.

Obadyah knew in a second this man was stronger and more skilled. If he had any chance of surviving, Obadyah would have to secure his sword. He locked his legs around the man's stomach and squeezed. He held him, his muscles clinched, until the soldier was fighting for air. Then Obadyah turned, forcing the soldier onto his back. He had him pinned. The soldier continued to thrash as Obadyah brought his knife to the man's throat. He turned at the last second and Obadyah's knife sliced through his cheek. Ahab's man tightened his grip on his sword. Obadyah drove his blade into the soldier's arm, forcing his hand to release the sword. Obadyah reached for the man's sword, but before he could secure it someone picked it up. Obadyah could not see who it was. But he knew a single outcome was imminent. One of the two of them was about to die. Before Obadyah could consider his next move the sword was thrust into the heart of Ahab's soldier. Obadyah, thinking perhaps Gideon had decided to join the fight, turned and fixed his eyes on the mystery assailant.

"Byblos?"

Theophanes's first mate stood above him with the blood soaked sword in his hand.

"Your father sent me to assist you," he said, "but if I am honest I had thought I would only be escorting you to the Phoenix. But this…" He swept his arm across the scene, "Well, this complicates things."

Obadyah pushed himself to his feet. He handed Byblos his knife and walked back to the wagon. He reached for Accoah. She leapt into his arms, threw her arms around him, and buried her face into his neck.

"It's okay, Little One."

Accoah pulled her head away and looked into Obadyah's eyes.

He smiled. They were together. They were safe. Accoah found the place where the soldier's sword glanced Obadyah's forehead. For the first time, he felt the blood trickling down his face onto his neck. Accoah wiped the blood away with her hand.

"It's all right, Little One. I am fine."

Obadyah caught sight of Gideon who stood at a distance staring at the bodies of Ahab's men. Obadyah turned to Byblos. "Load the bodies," he said, "and sink the wagon."

"Shall I dispose of the horses?" Byblos asked.

"Strip them and let them go. We will be gone before they find their way back to Samaria."

Byblos nodded and grabbed the arms of one of Ahab's soldiers. He began dragging the body towards the wagon.

"I am in need of a wagon on my farm," Gideon said.

"And you shall have one," Obadyah replied.

Obadyah shifted Accoah from one side to the other. Resting his hand on her back he turned towards Byblos. "Purchase a new wagon for my friend," Obadyah said. "Fill it with goods from the village."

"Consider it done, My Lord," Byblos nodded.

Obadyah looked at Gideon. He could read the confusion on his face. But there was no time to explain.

"When Byblos returns with your new wagon, you will be free to depart," Obadyah told Gideon.

"I am not waiting here where the blood of Ahab's soldiers was spilled!" Gideon replied.

Byblos stopped what he was doing, his eyes now locked on Gideon. Obadyah knew the man's tone had given Byblos pause. Byblos then looked to Obadyah, awaiting his next instructions.

"He is to be trusted," Obadyah declared, although he was not entirely sure that was true. Gideon had been gruff and unsettled from the moment he appeared. Obadyah did not know Gideon. And for that reason there was no reason to trust him. But he knew Adonis. And he could think of no reason to not trust her.

Byblos moved quickly and retrieved the second body, all the while keeping an eye on Gideon. When Byblos prepared to load Ahab's soldiers into the wagon, he pulled back the tarp. Eliah's small body, carefully wrapped, was laying in the bed.

"My Lord?" Byblos said.

Obadyah placed his hand on Eliah's body. He paused and drew in his breath. Thoughts of Eliah came rushing back to him. Her eyes, how they lit up when she discovered the water jug from Zoë. Her smile at every mention of sweet bread. Her voice when she sang the psalms. Not now, he thought. There's no time! Obadyah set Accoah down in the wagon next to Eliah.

"My Lord, we must move," Byblos said.

"Just one second," Obadyah said, meeting Accoah's weary eyes. He didn't realize he was crying until he felt Accoah wiping his tears away. Standing in the wagon, she could just reach his cheeks. Obadyah pulled Eliah's body from the wagon. Accoah reached for her, just as Obadyah had done. He watched as she mimicked his every move. Closing her eyes, as he had done, moving her lips in silent prayer just as he had. He never could have imagined he would be a big brother to Accoah. He had only longed to be a big brother to Eliah. When they had left the inn in Dothan, he committed himself to that, not knowing if she would ever be reunited with her father. He kept his promise to Eliah. He came back to her. But all along Yahweh had different plans. Obadyah placed the rope over his head, Eliah's body coming to rest on his back once again.

"I can take care of that for you, My Lord," Byblos said.

"Thank you, my friend. This is something I must take care of myself."

Byblos nodded and leaned in to speak privately in Obadyah's ear. "Follow the trail to the shore. Stay hidden until I return. At nightfall we board the Phoenix."

Obadyah reached for Accoah. She wrapped her arms around his neck.

Obadyah walked over to Gideon, Eliah on his back and Accoah's legs dangling on either side of him. "In the name of Yahweh, I thank you."

"It is only Adonis's gratitude I seek."

"I am confident you will have it."

The two men nodded at one another. Obadyah made his way to the trail that led to the shore. He did not look back.

CHAPTER 48

THE GREAT ESCAPE

Obadyah led Accoah for an hour on the seabound trail. When she slowed, he did not carry her. He urged her on, hoping to tire her enough that she might sleep when the time came to board the Phoenix. At the first sound of waves in the distance, Obadyah left the trail and began looking for a place to rest, somewhere they would be hidden and safe. He forced his way through a bed of coarse reeds, knowing there would be a stream on the other side. The flowing water cut its way through the brush and bramble on its way to the Mediterranean. Obadyah tucked Eliah's body inside a thicket of bamboo. He took Accoah's hand and guided her to a shallow place where the water trickled over the stones.

"Sit down, Little One."

Accoah tumbled to the ground. Obadyah knelt down next to her and removed her sandals. He dipped his hands in the stream and began washing her feet. He took her hands in his. Submerging them in the water, he scrubbed each tiny finger, washing away the blood, his blood that she had wiped off of his cheek. Obadyah inspected Accoah's arms and legs to see that she was clean. Then he looked at her face. Her green eyes glowed on the canvas of her dark brown skin. She smiled. A sense of peace overcame him. Every decision he had made for her felt strong, right. He stared at her, wondering what power could come from the simple glance of this gentle child. His hand reached for her head. He brushed her hair out of her face. She flinched when his fingers caught. It was only then he noticed her hair, tossed and matted from hours under a tarp. Reaching for her head he attempted to untangle the knots of hair.

"Forgive me," he said. He continued to work.

Accoah winced again.

"I'm sorry."

Accoah remained still and did not say a word.

"There," Obadyah said, when he was finished. "How do you feel?"

"How do you feel?" Accoah said back, mimicking him.

Obadyah laughed. "I am well, Little One, I am well."

Obadyah pulled out the leavened bread Byblos had given them. He broke off a piece for Accoah and then a bite for himself. They took turns eating until the bread was gone.

Darkness was moving in. Obadyah needed to get his eyes on the Phoenix. He took Accoah's hand and led her a few paces away from the stream. He found a small opening amid the reeds and spread out her cloak.

"You must rest now," he said. "We will have a grand adventure when you awake."

Obadyah wrapped the edges of Accoah's cloak around her shoulders and began singing to her. He was only a few words into Eliah's song when Accoah started singing with him.

Obadyah thought back to the night in Dothan when Eliah asked him to sing. "Just one song," she had begged. His heart sank. Why had he refused? What he could not do then, he did now. Eliah had shown him the power of songs, the power of psalms.

When Accoah's voice trailed off, he waited a few more minutes to ensure she was asleep. Then he crept away.

He made his way back to the stream and followed it to the place where it entered the sea. Scanning the beach from a protected position, he looked for Byblos. He was not there. But Ahab's soldier's were. A dozen or more milled about. A few stood around a fire. One by one the men shed their baldrics. The blades of their swords found the sand, the hilts poised at waist height for easy access. They passed a jug between them. Obadyah could hear rough laughter ringing out. They were drunk. He stayed in the shadows of darkness and crept closer, hoping to get a look at their faces. His eyes followed the bottle as it made its way around the circle. That's when he saw him. Theophanes.

Obadyah clenched his fists. The same fists that drew his father's blood aboard the Phoenix years ago. The same fists he thought he had conquered. But anger was still inside him. Bitterness still haunted him. Will it always be there, waiting beneath the surface, patient for just the right situation to appear and haunt him? He could not let his weakness distract him. Accoah needed him. He could not see her succumb to Eliah's fate. He would not.

"Help me, Yahweh!" Obadyah said under his breath.

When he looked back to the beach he found Byblos. He followed his eyes to the bay where several small boats were being rowed to shore. Torches lit up the bay revealing the Phoenix and next to it Ahab's vessel. Obadyah trembled. He had not seen the Lynx since he threw Zoë from its deck. Byblos was directing Theophanes's men as they came ashore. They carried trays of food and countless jugs of wine. They met Ahab's men with raucous revelry.

Obadyah waited and watched. From time to time he would see Byblos's eyes wander the beach and then return to the gathering of men. Theophanes moved about the crowd, slapping men's backs and filling their cups to the brim. As the night wore on, Ahab's soldiers began to stagger. Some had already passed out. Others were retching into the sea. The ruckus that had filled the bay began to subside as one-by-one Ahab's men were slumped over their cups, some falling face first into the sand. Obadyah watched as his father's men disarmed Ahab's soldiers. Theophanes's crew moved quickly and efficiently through Ahab's cohort. His father had prepared for this.

When Byblos left to relieve himself, Obadyah moved in his direction. Having finished his business, Obadyah tapped him on the shoulder. Byblos spun around.

"Greetings, My Lord," Byblos said.

"That was quite a celebration," Obadyah replied.

"It served its purpose. Are you ready to depart?"

Obadyah nodded. "Wait here." Obadyah hurried back to where he had laid Eliah. He strung her body across his back and moved quickly to where Accoah slept. He picked her up. She stirred but did not wake. He carried both girls to where Byblos was waiting.

"I will walk ahead of you," Byblos said. "Should someone awake and see you, I will put them down."

"No," Obadyah replied.

Byblos stopped. "My Lord, there will be bloodshed. We are prepared to…"

"I am not concerned with bloodshed. Accoah is my only concern. Take her." Obadyah said, handing Accoah to Byblos.

Accoah squirmed in Byblos's arms but remained asleep.

Byblos tried to hand her back, a look of panic on his face. "My Lord, I can't…I don't know…my captain says I must fight."

"You will fight. But tonight you will fight for something more important. You hold Yahweh's healer in your arms, Byblos."

Byblos looked down, his eyes wide. "She belongs to the gods?"

"No, my friend. She belongs to God."

Byblos swallowed and awaited his next instructions.

"I will follow you," Obadyah said. "Should Ahab's men rouse, I will deal with them. Get to the nearest boat. Alert the rowers. I assume they are waiting?"

"Indeed, My Lord."

"You have only one task tonight, Byblos. Get Accoah safely aboard the Phoenix."

"And what about you?"

"Don't wait for me."

"But the child, My Lord, she will call for you when she wakes."

"Do not wait for me!"

Byblos nodded. He shifted Accoah to his left arm. With his right hand he undid his belt. He handed Obadyah his sheathed knife and sword.

Obadyah took the weapons. Then he paused.

"What is it, My Lord?" Byblos asked.

Obadyah rested his hand on Accoah's back. Her warmth passed through her tunic and found his palm. He closed his eyes. "Protect her Yahweh, I beg You," he said. He opened his eyes, his gaze locked on Byblos. "You hold priceless cargo."

Byblos nodded. "And what of the body?" he asked, motioning with his head in the direction of Eliah. "Shall I take her as well?"

"She stays with me." Obadyah remembered his promise to Eliah. He would not leave her, even in death. Should he not make it off the beach, his body would come to rest with hers.

Byblos nodded, turned, and made his way to the beach.

Obayah walked behind them, using all of his training to be silent. Still hidden in the shadows, he laid Eliah's body down. He waited for Byblos to walk out onto the sand. Byblos moved swiftly around the snoring men. Each of Byblos's steps sent a rush of courage to Obadyah's heart. Accoah was closer to safety.

Byblos was half way down the beach when one of Ahab's men caught sight of him. The drunken soldier paused, rubbing his face. He appeared confused by what he was seeing, but he would realize it soon enough. Ahab's men were no fools. When Byblos ignored him and continued on, the soldier stumbled to his feet. Obadyah ran toward him, yelling in the direction of the soldier. The man turned just as Obadyah swung, landing a punch square to the soldier's jaw. He stumbled but held his ground. Well trained indeed, Obadyah thought.

Drunken soldiers scurried. One by one they attempted to find their balance, and their weapons. Theophanes's men attacked. A soldier threw himself at Obadyah who plunged his knife into the man's belly. When the soldier fell, Obadyah looked to the water's edge. He saw a rowboat and a man within it. Byblos was handing Accoah to the man. Obadyah blinked, straining to identify him in the darkness. Theophanes reached for Accoah. When she was in his arms, Obadyah knew she was safe. Despite his anger, his persistent frustration, and his enduring bitterness, Obadyah realized in that moment he trusted his father.

Another one of Ahab's men rushed him. Obadyah swept him aside and drove his blade into the soldier's ribs, shoving him to the ground. Obadyah looked back towards the bay. Byblos and one of his mates pushed the boat out until their feet could no longer touch. The two men swung their legs over and grabbed the oars. They rowed furiously. Obadyah caught a glimpse of Accoah in his father's arms just as another soldier grasped him from behind. He brought Obadyah to the ground. They rolled and thrashed, sand flying as they tossed one another back and forth. Obadayh connected on several blows but Ahab's man freed himself from Obadyah's grip and ran. When his feet gave way in the sand Obadyah jumped onto his back. He wrapped his legs around the soldier's torso and squeezed. The crook of Obadyah's elbow found the man's neck. The soldier went limp in a matter of seconds. Obadyah threw him aside and came to his feet. He gathered himself and tried to control his breathing. He scanned the beach. His father's men were tearing through the drunken soldiers. Knives swung. Swords plunged. Blood poured out onto the sand. Obadyah closed his eyes, longing to drown out the sights and sounds of violence and death. When he opened his eyes he saw several of Ahab's men rushing towards the row boats.

"No one reaches the Lynx!" Obadyah yelled. Theophanes's men left their battles and pursued the escaping men. Theophanes's sailors overtook Ahab's soldiers as they raced towards the shoreline.

Obadyah surveyed the scene. Out of the corner of his eye he caught sight of a boat that was being pushed off shore. Obadyah raced into the Mediterranean. He was chest deep in water when he reached Ahab's soldier. Leaping onto him from behind, they sank beneath the surface. Water churned as they brawled. Both men came up for air and then became entangled and submerged once more.

Obadyah fought for every breath. His lungs started to burn. His muscles began to ache. Every struggle he faced when his father hung over the side of the Phoenix returned. Then he thought of Eliah. He saw her breaking through the crowd of Jezebel's executioners. He saw her throwing herself onto Naboth as they stoned him to death. He could see her using her small body to protect him, to do what was impossible to do, save him. Obadyah felt Eliah's heart pounding in his chest. Strength returned to his limbs. He threw Ahab's man aside and rose up out of the water. He filled his lungs. It was time to finish this. He grabbed the soldier and threw him under the water. The man writhed. Obadyah held him down. He could feel the man's strength wane. Sensing him fading, Obadyah's grip tightened. Then, he heard a voice in his head. It was soft. It was faint. But it was clear.

"Mercy," the voice said.

Obadyah loosened his grip.

"Mercy," Obadyah heard Eliah say. Suddenly, Obadyah was back at the well in Dothan, standing next to Eliah as she recited the tale of Joseph. His brother's wanted him dead but Judah showed Joseph mercy casting him into a well.

Obadyah let go of Ahab's soldier. His head flew out of the water. He jumped up coughing and gagging. When he gathered himself he looked at Obadyah. It was only then Obadyah recognized him.

"You?" Obadyah said.

The man who had fired the fatal shots into the chest of Yahweh's prophet while Jezebel sipped her afternoon wine stared back at him. Obadyah's pulse quickened. "Do you remember me?" Obadyah said.

The man nodded but did not utter a word.

It was then Obadyah realized he was in the exact place his father had been. He was standing in his father's shoes. The mercy Theophanes had shown Nimshi, the mercy that Obadyah resented now stared him in the face. The same choice lay before him: forgiveness, unbidden and undeserved. Would he walk in the steps of his father and spare the life of a stranger, a murderer, an enemy?

"What is your name?" Obadyah asked.

Still panting like a dog, the man met Obadyah's gaze. He did not answer. He seemed confused by the question.

"What is your name?" Obadyah repeated.

Jezebel's executioner looked around. Theophanes's men lined the shore waiting for Obadyah's word. He was the last of Ahab's soldiers alive and he was surrounded. He had no choice but to comply.

"Adino," the man said. The two men continued to stare at one another as Adino attempted to steady his breathing. Then he said, "Why did you spare me?"

"The God of the prophet you destroyed told me to."

Adino looked confused. Obadyah waited.

"What now?" Adino said.

"Now you choose. Theophanes or Jezebel."

"I choose mercy," Adino said.

"Yahweh is gracious and merciful, slow to anger, abounding in lovingkindness." The psalm Eliah had recited to him so many times, flowed from his lips. Obadyah looked into the man's eyes. Was he seeing what Theophanes saw when his father had looked into Nimshi's eyes that fateful day? How could he, a follower of Yahweh, not show mercy when his father who claims no faithfulness to Yahweh, had?

"Mercy you shall have," Obadyah said.

Theophanes's newest sailor rowed out to the Lynx. Adino yelled for his captain as his boat approached the ship. The men aboard the Lynx raced to the side and looked over.

"It was an ambush!" Adino said. "They are dead!" Catching his breath, he repeated, "They're all dead!"

"Who attacked you?" the captain of the Lynx asked, leaning over the side of his vessel.

"I did," Obadyah replied.

The captain spun around. Standing before him was Obadyah and Theophanes's men.

The sailors aboard the Lynx rushed them. Obadyah stepped aside and let Theophanes's men finish the job.

"Well done," Obadyah said, looking over the side of the Lynx.

Adino nodded.

Obadyah dropped him a line. Adino slowly and carefully wrapped the rope around Eliah's body. Obadyah had demonstrated his mercy to Adino by trusting him with the task of holding his captain's attention while Obadyah snuck aboard the Lynx. But it wasn't until he placed Eliah's body in the bow of Adino's row boat that Obadyah could feel the fullness of the mercy he had given. He was finally able to set down his anger and see the world through Eliah's eyes, see his world with Yahweh's eyes.

Obadyah reached for Eliah's body. When the last of Theophanes's men tumbled over the ship's rail, they pulled anchor.

CHAPTER 49

THE JEWELS OF THE ISLE

The Lynx met up with the Phoenix in the open sea. Obadyah thanked his father's men. He picked up Eliah's body and laid the rope over his shoulder. Once she was securely resting on his back he boarded the Phoenix. As he climbed over the ship's rail his eyes searched the deck for Accoah. Byblos approached him.

"She is there, my Lord." Byblos said, motioning in the direction of Accoah. Obadyah removed Eliah's body and handed her to Byblos. He hurried to Accoah's side. She was sleeping soundly.

"Did she awaken?" Obadyah asked Byblos.

Byblos shook his head.

"Accoah," Obadyah whispered. "Wake up."

Accoah stirred. "I am here, Little One." Obadyah picked up Accoah. She squinted, rubbed her eyes, and smiled.

As the sun rose behind them Cyprus came into view. Though Obadyah had longed to bring Zoë to the island, he was grateful to be bringing Accoah. He was at peace with Yahweh's will. Obadyah closed his eyes. He had not permitted himself to think of his beloved. Though images of Zoë were always there, he had learned to redirect his thoughts. Still, he knew he would never be free of his longing for her. Should his eyes never meet hers again. Should she wed another and give her love away. Should Yahweh's purpose for her life be fulfilled without him, his heart would forever seek hers.

Obadyah knew he had no grounds for longing for her. He had already been given what he asked for. Zoë lived. She survived her execution.

Obadyah thought back on that moment she stood before him. What Jezebel anticipated would be heartache for them both was Obadyah's deepest desire, to be at his beloved's side in her most vulnerable moment. It was then that Obadyah knew, evil would never triumph.

As the crew saw to the mooring of his vessel, Theophanes invited his son to disembark. Obadyah, Accoah, and Theophanes waited just beyond the dock as Eliah's body was brought ashore.

Theophanes had acquired sea salts in Acco which his men applied to Eliah's body. They wrapped her in fresh linens. Two wagons awaited them. Theophanes took the first, Eliah's body resting in the bed behind him. Accoah and Obadyah mounted the second and followed Theophanes as he made his way through town.

Obadyah watched the people as he rode by, each one silently offering their condolences. Just before the last section of town, Theophanes halted his horse. He walked over to one of the street vendors. When he returned he handed Accoah a parasol. He showed her how to hold it and then gave Obadyah a wink before returning to his wagon. Obadyah shook his head but managed a smile.

There could not be a more lovely sight than the rock outcropping which marked their arrival to Theophanes's island home. Obadyah took a deep breath and lowered his head.

"Thank-you Yahweh," he said.

"Accoah. I have a surprise for you," Obadyah said, lifting her up.

When he reached the top of the highest boulder, the stone carved home of Theophanes came into view. Obadyah yelled, eager to greet his young friend who was not so young anymore. "Ashur!" Obadyah said. He descended the steps which led them down to the circular patio.

"He is not here," came a soft voice from the trail behind him. Obadyah spun around. "He is swimming in Aphrodite's tears," Zoë said.

Obadyah lowered Accoah to the ground. He was frozen where he stood. Zoë kept walking towards him. Before Obadyah could grasp what he was seeing, Zoë was within his reach. "I saw you at Mt. Carmel when Elijah confronted the prophets of Baal."

"I saw you as well," Obadyah replied.

"It pleases me to see you here."

"Yahweh blesses me beyond my comprehension."

Obadyah looked down when he felt a tug on his legs. "Zoë, allow me to introduce you," Obadyah said, "this is my friend, Accoah."

"Sister," Theophanes interrupted.

Obadyah's head turned in Theophanes's direction.

"Accoah is your sister. Sorry, son, I thought it best not to tell you. Of course Naboth disagreed. But I needed you to focus on your work for Ahab."

"Did mother…?" Obadyah said, looking down at Accoah as if he were seeing her for the first time.

"I could not tell your mother where I'd taken her. I knew she would surely search for her. I simply told her Accoah was well and loved and that I would bring her home as soon as it was safe."

Obadyah had no idea his parents had had another child after his appointment to Ethbaal's court.

"After the king demanded I give you over in payment for the king's merchandise having overturned on the beach, when Accoah came along, I worried for her safety," Theophanes said. "Of course I wanted to bring Samara and Accoah here years ago, but your mother would not leave Israel when you could not."

Obadyah felt a lump form in his throat. His mother had stayed. For him. She had endured sorrow, fear, even drought. But she did not leave her son.

"Is mother…? Is she…?"

"Samara," Theophanes yelled, his voice carrying into each chamber of the house. "Samara," Theophanes yelled again, "Obadyah and Accoah are here."

Samara girded her cloak and slowly descended the stairs to the patio. She walked towards her son and her little girl.

"Son," she said, making eye contact with Obadyah.

Obadyah could not utter a word. He reached for his mother. He pulled her into an embrace. When he released her, he watched a tear roll down her cheek. His strong, stoic, wise mother was crying.

Then Samara looked down. Her daughter. Samara knelt. Accoah wrapped her arms around Obadyah's legs. Samara leaned over where Accoah's eyes were peeking out. Accoah hid her face.

"Accoah," Obadyah said, "Don't be afraid. This is my mother."

Accoah looked up at Obadyah and then looked over at Samara.

"And this is your mother too," he said. Obadyah wasn't sure how to explain everything that had happened and was happening to little Accoah. Naboth and Eliah, the only family she had known, were gone. Obadyah was all she had left. And yet a whole new family stood before her. Her family. Her father, Theophanes had kept his word to Samara. He brought their daughter safely back to the arms of her mother. Having left Accoah with his most trusted friend, there could have been no safer place for his precious daughter. There wasn't a place more loving than the home of Naboth. And then Yahweh brought Obadyah to her. While evil dynasties reigned. While Jezebel conquered and schemed, Yahweh's eyes and his sovereign protection fell on a little girl who was gifted the psalms by a prophet's daughter. A young lady named Eliah.

Obadyah leaned over and tried to pull Accoah off of his legs. She grabbed a hold of him. But when Obadyah continued to tug on her, Accoah loosened her grip and allowed Samara to hold her. The tears from Samara's eyes ran onto Accoah's back as she pulled her daughter into her chest.

"I have something for you," Samara said.

When Samara turned, Tukulti was standing there. He held the blanket Samara had knit for her little girl. Then Accoah pushed herself off of Samara and grabbed Obadyah's hand.

"What is it, Little One?" Obadyah asked. Accoah, without a word, pulled Obadyah back up the stairs and over the rocks to the chariot. When they returned to Samara's side, Accoah handed her mother the parasol Theophanes had purchased for her. Then she reached for her new blanket.

It was Ashur who chose the burial plot for Eliah. Obadyah recognized the moss pad where he and Ashur had jumped on his first visit to Cyprus. Were Eliah fully grown, the grave site would not have suited. But it was the perfect sized plot for a young lady.

Theophanes, Samara, Ashur, Zoë, Accoah, and Tukulti followed Obadyah who carried Eliah's body. They walked together in silent procession down the path towards the shore. Before they took a meal, before they conversed, before the sun set in the sky that day, they buried Eliah. As they stood beside her grave, Obadyah pulled from his belt the Psalm of David he had taken from amid the hundreds he and Eliah had recorded at Naboth's vineyard.

"For the choir director. A Psalm of David," Obadyah read, "I waited patiently for the Yahweh. He turned toward me and heard my cry for help. He brought me up out of the pit of destruction, out of the miry clay, and he set my feet upon a rock making my footsteps firm…" Then suddenly Accoah reached for Obadyah's hand. Obadyah stopped reading. When he did Accoah said, "He put a new song in my mouth." Obadyah pulled Accoah up into his arms. He turned her towards him and smiled. She smiled back. When the tears fell from his eyes she rested her hand on his cheek. Looking into his eyes, she continued, "A song of praise to our God; May many see what Yahweh has done, and trust in him! How blessed is the one who trusts in Yahweh. There is none to compare with you."

The tears Obadyah had saved for Eliah fell freely. He stared at little Accoah who rarely spoke more than a few words. Eliah had given her the Psalms! The psalm keeper had passed on the words of David to Yahweh's little healer. God's Word would endure.

Obadyah reached into his tunic and pulled out a rock. A special rock unlike any other rocks in Israel. He placed his thumb in the indentation and then brought the rock to his lips. He kissed it and returned the stone to his pouch.

Lord Naboth once told me, "your father will find a way to make it safe." He was right. He found a way, through my brother Obadyah who found me in the vineyard the day my friend, my sister Eliah lay dying at my side. He protected me as we ran from Ahab and Jezebel. He let me go on the beach at Acco so he could stay and fight. He pursued me in the Lynx meeting up with the Phoenix in the middle of the Mediterranean. He brought me back to my mother's arms.

My father, the captain of the Phoenix, was not suited for land dwelling, nor to a life of peace and solitude. It was only a week after we arrived at Cyprus that he announced he was leaving. Though we were all sad to see him go, we knew he was protecting us, the only way he knew–buying loyalty, spoiling young rulers, making peace in high places all for the safety of those he loved.

On the day of his departure, Theophanes removed Obadyah's branding. My father would deliver the patch of skin which contained Jezebel's mark, evidence of my brother's death, to Ahab. My mother made no objection to Theophanes leaving. I doubt there was ever a thought in her mind he would stay. Still, we knew that in her heart, she wished him with her, with us all.

Zoë fretted over her aunt. And while Donatiya longed for her niece as well, she was content dwelling in the home she had shared for so many years with her beloved Kalbu. Her son, Samson, who had been rescued by her husband and healed by the prophet Elijah, brought her much joy. My father reassured us, each season, when he passed through Phoenicia that Donatiya was not in need. He also mentioned Nimshi's and Palmsquat's frequent visits to the village of Zarephath.

More than six years had passed since Obadyah and Zoë first knew their hearts were knit together. And it was less than six days before they committed themselves forever to one another. Taking vows of faithfulness at the arched rock, Theophanes pronounced Obadyah and Zoë wed. They celebrated their union by leaping into the Great Sea.

EPILOGUE

Everything that has a beginning has an end...even evil.

Not long after my brother Obadyah brought me safely to Cyprus, Ahab went to war with the Arameans. He attempted to disguise himself by removing his royal attire. But as it happened, a stray arrow, shot at random, found its way through a joint in Ahab's armor. His driver turned away from the battle as Ahab's blood ran onto the floor of his chariot. By the time they reached the capital of Israel, Ahab was dead. His men washed his chariot by the pool of Samaria and the dogs licked up his blood in the place where the harlots bathed, according to the word spoken by Elijah the prophet.

From Saul and his bloody house, to the conquering Assyrians, to the kings of the Northern Kingdom, the gruesome violence and bloodshed associated with the rulers living in that time in history, in my time in history, cannot be overstated. But of all the blood-thirsty monarchs there had never been anyone like Ahab, firmly committed to doing evil in the sight of Yahweh, urged on by his wife Jezebel.

Life on Cyprus could not have been more peaceful. The joy of family was felt every day until the day we buried Tukulti. The old Assyrian who had rescued his grandson, who built the home we lived in, who faithfully served Theophanes, became a precious grandfather to me. Zoë had told me of her sorrow at the loss of her uncle Kalbu. It was a heartache I could not fathom until the day Tukulti took his last breath.

It was the year of Tukulti's death, fifteen years after Ahab was buried, the queen of Israel met her fate. Jezebel's end came at the very place her wickedness began, her dressing table. The year was 841 BC. The widowed matriarch of Israel sat before her maidens who adorned her with makeup and jewels. She glanced out her window as plumes of dust appeared on the horizon. The commander of the army of Israel, a formidable warrior named Jehu, approached. Word of Elijah's anointing of Jehu had made its way to Jezreel. And from there to the ears of Theophanes.

Jezebel's servants continued in preparation of their queen. Every attendant, that is, but one. Adonis, the queen's oldest among her maidens, stood by noting the single bead of sweat which ran down Jezebel's temple. Adonis quickly wiped away the evidence of the queen's fear. Elijah had prophesied concerning the destruction of the house of Ahab. Yahweh, at long last, would avenge the blood of the saints who died at the hand of Jezebel.

Jezebel, eyes painted, head adorned, leaned out of her palace window high above the street. When Jehu entered the gates of the city, Jezebel yelled down, cursing his rebellion. Ignoring the queen, Jehu found the eyes of those attending her and called out to them.

"Jezebel or Yahweh?"

Adonis did not hesitate. She pushed Jezebel over the rail of her balcony. When she landed on the stone road beneath the window, Jehu commanded his chariot driver to trample her.

Later that evening when Jehu sent his men to retrieve Jezebel's body they found nothing more of her than her skull, her feet, and the palms of her hands. This was according to the word of Yahweh's servant Elijah. In Jezreel the dogs shall eat the flesh of Jezebel; and the corpse of Jezebel will be as dung, so they cannot say: This is Jezebel.

Obadyah and Zoë asked Theophanes to search for Adonis. For several years he returned to Cyprus with no word. She was not taken by Jehu, nor was she serving in the house of Ahab. Though they pressed him at each one of his visits to the island, Theophanes's report was always the same. "It seems she has disappeared." I clung to the necklace Adonis had first placed on Zoë's forehead and later, around my neck. I did not take it off even once until the day my father mentioned a farmer and his wife encountered by Byblos, his most trusted sailor, at the port of Acco. It seems the Hebrew farmer had recognized Byblos. When Byblos offered his greeting the farmer's wife enquired about a little girl she had known for a precious few hours. Without a word, I immediately removed the necklace and placed it in my father's hands. He knew what I was asking him to do.

AFTERWARD

The most malevolent rulers Israel had ever known were dead. But their evil did not die with them. For sin, like the color of our eyes, somehow finds its way from one generation to the next. Reaching out of the grave, fuller, stronger, more potent—a child conceived with tainted blood, inspired to carry on her parents wicked ways.

Though Ahab had fathered 70 sons over the course of his life, it was Athaliah, his daughter by his wife Jezebel, who would bring the blood lust of her parents from the Northern Kingdom of Israel to the Southern Kingdom of Judah. The legacy of the evil couple would continue. But Yahweh would not forget His people, raising up a new hero to contend with the offspring of Jezebel, a young woman named Jehoshabeath. But that is another story…

ABOUT THE AUTHOR

Born in Dallas, Texas, Rebecca's family eventually settled in the heart of West Michigan. Long before she discovered her love of writing, Rebecca found a home on the soccer field, leading her to Michigan State University where she earned her BA in Business.

After graduating, she returned to Dallas to pursue a Masters of Biblical Studies from the renowned Dallas Theological Seminary. This decision marked the beginning of two profound decades as a Bible teacher in Grand Rapids, Michigan. She now dovetails her experience, insight, and passion into leading Bible studies and crafting Christian fiction.

When she isn't writing, she works as a soccer coach in West Michigan, passing on her knowledge and love of the game to today's youth.

Rebecca's anchor is her family. Married to Chuck May for 25 years, she's the mother of two children, Emily Elizabeth and Jacob Wesley. They are her inspiration and joy. And let's not forget her delightful brood of ducks—Donna, Blue, Olive, and the ever-philosophical Socrates—who provide comic relief as well as a reminder to slow down, waddle, and enjoy the little things in life.

INDEX OF NAMES

Abraham. Father of nation of Israel
Accoah. Girl cared for by Naboth
Adonis. Lotus of love. One of three servants of Jezebel
Ahab. King of Northern Kingdom of Israel. Married to Jezebel
Amos. Baker from Dothan
Aphka. Delight of the earth. One of three servants of Jezebel
Aphrodite. Goddess of Olympia
Ares. Adonis's birth name
Ark of Yahweh. Ark of the Covenant
Asa. King of Southern Kingdom of Judah
Asherah. Fertility goddess. Consort of Baal
Ashur. Tukulti's grandson
Ashurnasirpal. King of Assyria
Astarte. Warrior goddess of Canaan
Athena. Goddess of wisdom. One of three servants of Jezebel

Baal. Canaanite fertility god. Premier god of Phoenicia
Barak. Captain of army of Israel at time of Deborah
Bathsheba. Woman with whom David committed adultery
Ben-hadad. King of Aram
Benjamin. Eliah's father. Keeper of palace stables in Samaria
Byblos. First mate of Theophanes aboard the Phoenix
Buckets. Benjamin's donkey

Dagon. God of the Philistines

David. Second king of the United Kingdom of Israel
Deborah. Judged Israel prior to the time of the kings
Donatiya. Zoë's aunt, Kalbu's wife

Eliah. Daughter of Benjamin
Elijah. Hebrew prophet at the time of Jezebel
Ethbaal. King of Sidon

Gideon. Judged Israel, friend of Adonis
Goliath. Philistine giant who challenged David

Heber. Husband of Jael
Hebrew. Descendant of Jacob
Hiel. Rebuilt the city of Jericho
Hiram. Famed Phoenician sailor

Ishtar. Mesopotamian fertility goddess

Jabin. King of Canaan
Jael. Slew Sisera with a tent peg
Jashar. Young boy. Friend of Obadyah and Samara
Jeroboam. First king of the Northern Kingdom of Israel
Jezebel. Daughter of Ethbaal. Wife of Ahab. Queen of Northern Kingdom of Israel
Joash. Gideon's father
Jochebed. Moses's mother

Kalbu. Zoë's uncle. Husband of Donatiya

Levite. Descendants of Levi. Tribe of Israelite priesthood
Lynx. Ahab's ship

Mattan. Priest of Baal
Micah. Obadyah's brother
Mighty One. Yahweh. God of Abraham, Isaac, and Jacob
Miriam. Moses's sister
Moses. Hebrew raised by Pharaoh's daughter. Leader of Exodus

Naboth. Vineyard owner. Resident of Jezreel. Friend of Theophanes

Nazir. Person who keeps Nazarite vow
Nimshi. Samara's servant

Obadyah. Eunuch slave in the court of Ethbaal
Omri. King of Northern Kingdom of Israel. Father of Ahab

Palmsquat. Kalbu's donkey
Pharaoh. King of Egypt
Philistines. Inhabitants of the southern coast of Canaan
Phoenix. Theophanes's ship

Queen of Sheba. Visited King Solomon

Rachel. Athena's informant

Samara. Obadyah's mother
Samson. Nazir. Judged Israel. Boy rescued from Baal
Samuel. Prophet of Yahweh during united kingdom of Israel
Saul. First king of the united kingdom of Israel
Sisera. Canaanite captain of Jabin's army
Solomon. David's son. Third king of the united kingdom of Israel

Theophanes. Captain of the Phoenix
Thutmose. Pharaoh at time of Exodus
Tibni. Challenged Omri's rise to the throne
Tukulti. Assyrian, built Thophanes's home
Tukulti-Ninurta. Father of Ashurnasirpal King of Assyria

Yahweh. The Living God

Zimri. Reigned seven days in Israel. Died in palace fire
Zoë. Niece of Donatiya and Kalbu, Athena in Jezebel's court

BIBLE REFERENCES

EXODUS
2:3	146
28:1-43	208
34:6	18

NUMBERS
6:2	208

DEUTERONOMY
10:16	18

JOSHUA
1:9	35
6:26	121

JUDGES
3:7	211
4:7-9	226
6:13, 25	107
6:29-31	108
10:14	109
16:3	210
16:21, 25	209
16:28, 30	210

1 SAMUEL

7:3	246
12:23	255

1 KINGS

10:9	59
10:11,17	55
17:1	125
17:13-14	216
18:5	238
18:13	244
18:15; 18-19	240
18:21	245
18:24, 27	246
18:37, 40	251
19:2	253
20:3	254
20:13, 15	255
21:25	256

2 KINGS

9:37	299

2 CHRONICLES

16:9	107, 268

PSALMS

5:2	229
8:1, 3-4	174
23	223, 264
25:5	87
36:5-6	225
39:12	78
40:1-2	295
42:3	236
50:14, 23	225
50:15	41
51:16	233
54:6,	225

103:1	207
119:165	54
136:4	225

PROVERBS

18:2	89
18:7	91

ISAIAH

55:11	216

MICAH

6:8	57

MATTHEW

23:6	125

LUKE

18:27	208

ROMANS

5:5	136

1 PETER

5:8	156